B L

Duets™

**Two brand-new stories in every volume...
twice a month!**

Duets Vol. #81

Popular author Carol Finch takes us to Hoot's Roost,
Oklahoma, where there are quite a few single
cowboys who don't give a hoot about marryin'.
But when two sexy city girls show up in town, that
changes everything. Enjoy Carol's funny, romantic
Double Duets stories about The Bachelors of Hoot's
Roost—where love comes sweeping down the plain!

Duets Vol. #82

Delightful Tina Wainscott is back with another
quirky Duets novel where the hero is driven to
distraction by the gorgeous free-spirited heroine
living next door! Tina tells "a charming story
full of love and laughter," says *Rendezvous*. Joining
her in the volume is talented Candy Halliday with a
story about a pilot hero who's always winging it
when it comes to relationships. It takes a special
woman to bring this guy down to earth!

Be sure to pick up both Duets volumes today!

W9-CGM-188

Lonesome Ryder?

"The last thing I wanted was to be laid up and have a woman under my roof!"

Laura regarded Wade through her narrowed gaze. "So, you're saying that you're afraid of women."

"I'm saying nothing of the kind," he said, highly affronted. "You're all of five foot nothing and I'm six-three in my stocking feet. Whaddya gonna do? Break my other leg?"

"I'm not referring to physical fight," she clarified. "I'm talking about emotional terror. You figured you couldn't make a woman happy so why try, right? It's easier to give up, to quit." She turned toward him then, all fierce determination. "Well, *I'm* not a quitter, Mr. Ryder. Now, go take a load off while I whip up supper," she ordered, shooing him on his way.

Wade was so surprised by the unexpected turn of events that he was halfway across the room before he realized he'd allowed her to boss him around. *Hell!*

He didn't want to share his personal space with a female, especially one as tempting as Laura. He wanted her to vamoose—pronto. He'd push and prod until she lost her temper and spit out the four-letter *Q* word. Then he'd have her exactly where he wanted her...besides naked in his bed....

For more, turn to page 9

A lean, sexy cowboy filled the entrance of the restaurant.

Stephanie was instantly reminded of a scene from a Western movie—the macho hero swaggering throught the swinging doors of a saloon with the sun at his back.

A jolt of sensual awareness shot through her. She was instantly reminded of the teenage crush she'd had on him, yet Quint had barely known she existed.

No way was she going to let him charm her out of her panty hose.

"Stephanie Lawson, it's been a long time," he drawled. "Wow, honey, you look terrific."

"Quint Ryder," she said, "you just tracked mud on my expensive carpet. The cleaning bill will be in the mail."

His charming smile faltered momentarily, then he tossed her one of those aw-shucks glances. "Sorry, sugar. I was expecting the tiled floor of the diner, not fancy carpet."

"We aren't open for business yet, so kindly take your muddy boots and make yourself scarce."

Quint reared back, clearly shocked. He probably expected to score when he turned on that country charm. Well, Stephanie wasn't about to add her name to the women on his to-*do* list!

For more, turn to page 197

HARLEQUIN DUETS

ISBN 0-373-44147-9

Copyright in the collection:
Copyright © 2002 by Harlequin Books S.A.

The publisher acknowledges the copyright holder
of the individual works as follows:

LONESOME RYDER?
Copyright © 2002 by Connie Feddersen

RESTAURANT ROMEO
Copyright © 2002 by Connie Feddersen

This edition published by arrangement with Harlequin Books S.A.

® and TM are trademarks of the publisher. Trademarks indicated with
® are registered in the United States Patent and Trademark Office, the
Canadian Trade Marks Office and in other countries.

Visit us at www.eHarlequin.com

Printed in U.S.A.

Lonesome Ryder?

Carol Finch

TORONTO • NEW YORK • LONDON
AMSTERDAM • PARIS • SYDNEY • HAMBURG
STOCKHOLM • ATHENS • TOKYO • MILAN • MADRID
PRAGUE • WARSAW • BUDAPEST • AUCKLAND

Dear Reader,

Welcome to Hoot's Roost, Oklahoma, where Wade Ryder has no intention of letting the love bug take a bite out of him ever again. He lives in a female-free domain of cattle and horses—until he's laid up by a ranching accident. Suddenly he's saddled with a temporary housekeeper and that's when the trouble starts. Laura Seymour is irresistible, but Wade has a broken leg already, and the last thing he needs is a broken heart. He's about to discover that the love of one very special woman can cure just about everything.

In the second story, cousin Quint Ryder, the ladies' man, meets his match in a sassy redheaded restaurateur who's immune to his flattery. His legendary reputation with women is on the line when the locals appoint him to charm Stephanie Lawson into converting her fancy-schmancey restaurant back into a blue-collar café so everyone can enjoy the former menu of meat 'n taters. Can Quint wrap her around his little finger? Or will Steph wrap Quint in a French crepe and serve him up as the Special of the Day? Or will they discover that love'll getcha if you don't watch out!

Enjoy!

Carol Finch

Books by Carol Finch

HARLEQUIN DUETS
36—FIT TO BE TIED
45—A REGULAR JOE
62—MR. PREDICTABLE
72—THE FAMILY FEUD

HARLEQUIN HISTORICALS
592—CALL OF THE WHITE WOLF

SILHOUETTE SPECIAL EDITION
1242—NOT JUST ANOTHER COWBOY
1320—SOUL MATES

This book is dedicated to my husband, Ed,
and our children—Christie, Jill, Kurt, Jeff and Jon.
And to our grandchildren—
Brooklynn, Kennedy, Blake and Livia.
Hugs and kisses!

THE MOMENT SHE WALKED through his front door, Wade Ryder knew this situation had disaster written all over it in screaming neon letters. Even worse, his first cousins, Tweedle Dee and Tweedle Dumb, were waggling their eyebrows and grinning like the idiots they were as they swaggered behind the blond-haired, blue-eyed knockout who was to become Wade's temporary cook and housekeeper at the ranch.

The goddess in designer jeans and a trim-fitting pink knit blouse smiled politely. When her baby blues twinkled down on Wade everything inside him tightened like a saddle cinch and alarm bells clanged in his head. He swore under his breath at the immediate effect the woman had on him. She was the picture-perfect image of style, class and refined elegance. She was one hundred percent woman—all tantalizing curves and generously proportioned swells. In a word—dangerous.

From unpleasant experience Wade knew that the more attractive the woman the more perks and privileges she demanded—expected—from a man. Yup, this female was pure venom in denim and she was going to be trouble, no doubt about it!

Anger and resentment roiled through Wade while he sat in his recliner, beaten down by life's unexpected pitfalls. He looked crumpled and wrinkled, while the gorgeous female appeared fresh, wholesome and so spiffy

that he wanted to muss her up, just so he'd feel better
about himself. And that made him feel worse about himself so he directed his frustration to her. It was a vicious
cycle, to be sure.

Wade felt as bad as he looked. A plaster cast encased
his left leg from below his kneecap to his toes. A sling
and splint held his sprained left wrist and throbbing arm
against his tender ribs. His hair was ruffled from raking
his one good hand through the thick black mass that
begged for a long-overdue haircut. His left eye was a
putrid shade of purple. He felt trampled and battered—
which he had been, literally. He also felt as if all his
frailties, insecurities and vulnerabilities were exposed to
the world, and especially to this woman who'd invaded
his private male sanctuary.

Wade's gaze swung from the smiling goddess to his
traitorous, mischievous cousins. "Leave everything to us,
cuz," they'd said. Wade had gone along with their bright
idea, only because he'd been in so much pain and misery
that he barely knew who or where he was. Big mistake.

His cousins, Vance and Quint Ryder, knew he'd sworn
off women—and with excellent reason—six years ago.
So naturally, the ornery rascals thought it'd be great fun
to kick him while he was down. Damn their hides. They
were standing behind the goddess who was every man's
fantasy come true, making no attempt whatsoever to
swallow their stupid grins or display the slightest bit of
sympathy for his mangled condition. Well, as soon as
Wade was up and around again, he was going to kick his
cousins' butts and make them like it!

Quint Ryder, the legendary ladies' man of the family,
cast one last gawking glance at the goddess's shapely
derriere then stepped forward to make the introductions.
"Laura Seymour, this is our cousin, Wade Ryder." He

grinned outrageously for Wade's benefit. "Vance and I found the perfect temporary cook and housekeeper while you're recuperating. She's the answer to your prayers."

Quint's grin was as wide as the Oklahoma panhandle and Wade itched to punch that expression off his cousin's face. This woman wasn't the answer to Wade's prayers; she was his worst nightmare. He preferred a miraculous recovery, not a tempting female underfoot.

When Wade reluctantly agreed to temp help he'd sort of envisioned the modern version of Alice from *The Brady Bunch*. Instead he got Miss June from *Playboy* magazine. Hell! He just couldn't catch a break.

Wade ground his teeth—which had practically been jarred out of his head during the ranching accident that left him virtually helpless. It wasn't a feeling he was comfortable with. Having *her* in his home, emphasized those feelings of frustrated uselessness and helplessness—in spades. Wade prided himself in being capable, independent and self-reliant. Now, everything he was, and strove to be, had a discolored bruise on it and he had to rely on a crutch to ensure his balance.

Damn that Black Angus bull that had run right over the top of him then tried to make mincemeat of him. That beast was hamburger!

The bombshell with the peaches-and-cream complexion—and not one bruise or flaw to mar her bewitching face—stepped forward and extended her hand. "I'm sorry to hear about your accident. It's nice to meet you, Mr. Ryder."

"Is it? What's so nice about it?" Wade stared at her well-manicured hand, as if she were trying to foist off a three-day-old dead fish. He wasn't going to permit physical contact because he had no intention of keeping her. He didn't want to touch her or see her again—ever.

Her hand just sort of hung there in midair before she realized there wouldn't be any shaking going on. Wade acquainted her with his fiercest glare and stared her down until her smile faltered and she backed away self-consciously. His conscience tried to beat him black and blue because of his rude behavior, but what was one more bruise on his battered body, he asked himself.

Vance Ryder, the playful practical joker of the family, stepped front and center to smooth over the awkward situation, but Wade had no intention of making it easy on his cousin.

"As you can tell, Laura, our cuz isn't in a happy place right now. His severe pain is making him surly. Don't pay Wade any mind. He'll be more sociable when he's feeling better."

"No, I won't," Wade contradicted grouchily. "This is as good as I ever get." For effect, he flashed Ms. Forbidden Temptation another lethal glare. Her smile evaporated and she stared warily at him. A little timid, was she? Good. He could scare her off with very little effort. He had her at a disadvantage because she was in his home with a room full of strangers and she was trying her best to be polite.

Vance's fake laugh filled the silence then he said, "Wade's just kidding around." His narrowed, warning gaze locked on Wade. "Aren't you, cuz?"

"Yeah," Wade growled, teeth bared. "This is how I look and act when I'm kidding around. You don't wanna be around here when I'm in a really bad mood. Now, why don't you take a hike, lady, so I can have a private chat with my cousins."

Laura's head snapped up and her eyes flashed. She opened her mouth then must have thought better of lighting into him because she clamped her lips together and held her tongue. Obviously offended, she strode quickly out the door.

Wade instantly understood why Vance and Quint had trailed behind Laura. Her designer jeans clung to the curve of her tush as if they'd been tailor-made to fit her hourglass physique. The mesmerizing sway of those denim-clad hips drew Wade's gaze and held it fast. He had to give himself a mental slap before he could drag his attention to his cousins.

"Did we do good or what?" Quint murmured as his all-consuming gaze followed Laura until she disappeared from sight. He sighed dramatically. "That's one fine-looking, USDA prime-choice female, Wade. Almost makes me wish I'd been the one run over by a bull so Laura could take care of me."

"I want her out of here, pronto," Wade snapped. "You know I've sworn off women and I don't her want underfoot."

"Aw, c'mon, cuz," Vance cajoled. "Laura is perfect for this temporary position. She's going to take a new job teaching math and computer science at the high school in Hoot's Roost this fall, so she has the summer free for this short-term employment. As a bonus she can update your computer programs for your livestock and expense accounts. Plus, she hasn't found a place to live, so she can give you round-the-clock attention. She'll be doing you a service and you'll be helping her out by providing room and board."

"What!" Wade howled in disbelief. "You expect me to have that woman at my ranch 24/7? No freakin' way!"

"Simmer down," Quint spoke up. "You have enough injuries without sending your blood pressure into the red zone."

"I should've had my head examined when I agreed to

send a notorious ladies' man and a world-class practical joker to locate a temporary housekeeper. I didn't much like the idea to begin with and I like it even less now. That woman is not staying at my ranch. Discussion over!''

Quint's perpetual smile turned upside down as he loomed over Wade. ''She's staying here,'' he said in no uncertain terms. ''Your accident happened at *my* ranch and it was *Vance's* cantankerous bull that stomped all over you, so *we* feel responsible. Furthermore, you stepped in front of us like a shield when that cursed bull came after us when we separated him from his harem of cows. You received extra points for heroism for that maneuver and you took the brunt of abuse that bull dealt out.''

''Therefore,'' Vance put in as he came to loom beside Quint, ''*we* are paying Laura's salary because that's only fair. We made a pact years back to trade off our work and share our ranch chores so we could cut down on the expenses of hiring extra help during cattle drives, branding, inoculation, hauling livestock to market and planting crops. That was the deal. When one of us needs help the other two assist. We share our tractors, machinery, corrals and breeding stock.''

Yeah, they did, Wade silently agreed. The arrangement had worked splendidly and saved time and expenses—until he'd ended up in the emergency room at Hoot's Roost Hospital and was informed by the doctor on duty that he'd be taking a forced vacation for the next six to eight weeks.

''You can growl, snarl and fuss at us all you want,'' Quint invited, ''but Laura Seymour isn't leaving until *we* say so. *You* can't fire her because *we* hired her. I suppose you could put her up in your hired man's bunkhouse, but that'd make you look more ungrateful and unappreciative than you do now.''

If Quint thought the remark would jump-start Wade's conscience he could forget it. Wade's conscience had disowned him about fifteen minutes earlier. ''Fine, put my new housekeeper's luggage in Duff's cabin. She can cook in his cracker-box kitchen and tote my meals up to the house.''

Vance rolled his eyes in disgust. ''C'mon, Wade. Duff doesn't even have a dishwasher. The appliance he refers to as a stove only has one functioning burner and the temperature regulator on the oven doesn't work.''

''Plus,'' Quint added, ''Duff's washing machine is almost an antique. Hell, it doesn't agitate as easily as you do. You can't make Laura haul laundry and meals from the bunkhouse to here. That'd be cruel and unusual punishment.''

Wade sighed audibly. Okay. So he was overreacting— a little. Maybe. But he still didn't want that woman underfoot. Hell, he could still smell the lingering scent of her perfume. If he dared to shut his eyes he predicted he'd see Laura's alluring vision standing in the sunlight that streamed through the east window, making her blond hair glitter like spun gold. She looked too dainty and refined to fit into life on a working ranch. She also appeared too petite to haul around heavy loads of laundry and move furniture to dust and vacuum. No, she looked like the kind of woman who needed—expected—to be waited on hand and foot by a man.

''Now, you be nice to Laura,'' Quint ordered, wagging his index finger in Wade's face. ''Vance and I are doing you a favor by giving you time to recuperate. We've got cattle—yours as well as ours—to brand and inoculate. We don't have time to keep house, feed you and do your laundry. I don't have to tell you that this is one of our busiest times of the year."

No, he didn't, Wade thought sourly. He was going to be sitting here, feeling as if he'd let his cousins down while they busted their fannies working cattle, swathing and baling hay to provide winter forage. Wade was used to working hard, right alongside his cousins. Inactivity was going to drive him nuts. Having Laura *Seymour*— and he preferred to *See Less* of her—would drive him straight down the road to Nutsville.

"We're not budging on this," Vance said. His customary good-natured smile was suddenly nonexistent and he stared somberly at Wade. "Laura is here to stay so you better get used to the idea. We'll be around to check on you, same as you'd do if one of us was laid up, because family's family and we stick together through thin and thick."

"Damn straight," Quint chimed in. "We're doing this for your own good." True to form, Quint couldn't remain serious overly long and his famous lady-killer grin returned full force. "Besides, cuz, that new high school teacher is hot and there hasn't been a woman in your house, aside from your mother and our mothers, for six years."

"Exactly right and I'd planned to keep it that way until you two bozos decided to have a little fun at my expense," Wade grumbled bitterly. "Just remember that payback's a bitch and I'll *definitely* be repaying you for this stunt."

His cousins shrugged, undaunted, and Quint said, "Bring it on, cuz. Just don't forget that when we rodeoed together we were every bit as tough as you, so you better bring along your lunch, 'cause it'll take you all day to pound us both flat."

Wade was aware that pounding his cousins into the ground would require considerable time and effort. When he and his cousins followed the rodeo's suicide circuit nobody messed with the Ryder cousins who'd been all for one and one for all—still were. Same went for Cousin Gage who'd traveled the circuit with them. When one of them got banged up or broke a bone while riding broncs or bulldogging the other three covered as best they could. They pooled their winnings, shared expenses and helped each other through hard times.

Right now, Wade should be feeling grateful for the loyalty and support, but the prospect of having a woman in his home after all these years was setting as well as an indigestible meal on a queasy stomach.

A thought suddenly occurred to Wade that made him feel a smidgen better. Maybe he couldn't fire the goddess who'd been hired to keep house while he recuperated, but he could antagonize her until she quit. It wouldn't take much, he predicted confidently. He'd leveled one mutinous glare on her earlier and she'd backed off.

Like most women, she'd be outta here when the going got tough—and he'd make sure it did. If Little Miss Schoolmarm thought she'd taken a cushy job and latched onto a prosperous rancher as an added bonus then she better think again. He already had one ex-wife's memory to remind him that women weren't worth the trouble. He'd also had enough rodeo groupies hovering around him to know females were only interested in what a cowboy had in his wallet—and his blue jeans.

Yes indeedy, Laura Seymour would be as good as gone after Wade made things difficult for her. He'd give her two days. Three days tops. She'd pack her bags and hightail it into Hoot's Roost to rent an apartment.

"Okay, fine," Wade agreed begrudgingly. "She can stay…for a while."

"Great!" Vance and Quint chorused.

Quint spun on his boot heels and headed for the front door. "I'll bring in Laura's luggage."

"And I'll help," Vance insisted then shot Wade a mischievous grin. "We'll put her stuff in the bedroom next door to yours so you can call for help…if you need some in the middle of the night."

Need some in the middle of the night? Wade clenched his one good hand into a fist as his cousins swaggered off, cackling like a couple of hens. "Ornery cusses," he muttered at his cousins' departing backs. He was in the middle of a full-blown crisis and they were busting a gut laughing—at his expense. They didn't have a clue how he'd felt when Bobbie Lynn betrayed him, rejected him, deceived him and ran off with her new lover. If that wasn't enough to sour a man on women then Wade didn't know what was.

These days, Wade rebelled and withdrew the instant he felt a serious attraction to a woman. And he'd damn sure felt the hum and sizzle of physical awareness the instant Laura Seymour entered the room and stood there in the shaft of sunlight that spotlighted every appealing feature of her face and emphasized the voluptuous curves on her body.

Ms. Temptation had definitely arrived on the scene and Wade wanted her gone—ASAP. He'd built a six-strand barbed wire fence around his heart after Bobbie Lynn hurt and mortified him. Wade wasn't going through that again—ever. He mistrusted the female gender, lost all respect for women and he wanted nothing to do with them, aside from the occasional gratification of sexual needs. And since he was in no condition to satisfy basic lust he didn't want to share his space with Laura Seymour, goddess extraordinaire.

He'd manage to take care of himself—somehow. He didn't want Laura laundering, handling his underwear and attacking his pet dust bunnies that hid under his furniture. What he wanted was to get her out of his house—pronto.

LAURA SEYMOUR DRAPED her arms over the top rail of the pipe-and-cable corral and battled her irritation with Wade Ryder while she stared at the cattle grazing on the rolling Oklahoma hills. This ranch was so peaceful and serene that she momentarily forgot about her less than pleasant introduction to Wade. If not for that rude, unsociable cowboy-in-a-cast, this temp job would've been absolutely perfect for her.

She muttered under her breath, remembering the menacing expression on Wade's handsome face the moment she walked through his front door. The look he directed at her implied that he'd like to book her on a one-way express flight to a place where the hottest of climates prevailed.

She tried to tell herself that the hostility and resentment radiating from Wade Ryder wasn't a personal affront. His pain and frustration, caused by incapacity and injury, must've given rise to his black mood, she diagnosed. She'd never caused such an adverse reaction to anyone—that she could recall, leastwise.

When he'd dismissed her so rudely she'd been tempted to lash out at him, but she'd been trying to make a good first impression. Apparently she hadn't. Wade had looked and behaved as if he disliked her on sight. Ironically he'd had the opposite effect on her. In addition, she'd been distracted by the astonishing family resemblance between the three men who looked more like brothers than first cousins.

According to Quint Ryder there was another first cousin named Gage who was out of the country on business and rented his ranch to them during his absence. She wondered if Gage was as ruggedly handsome as his other cousins. Probably.

Laura had never been in a room with so many strikingly attractive men—excluding her four older brothers. While her brothers were the collective picture of suave sophistication and refined good looks, the Ryder cousins were the personification of tall, dark and devilishly handsome. Yet, it was Wade Ryder, looking rumpled, surly and vulnerable, who'd drawn her curiosity and interest. She couldn't recall feeling such an immediate attraction to a man before. Something about him simply called out to her on a basic level.

Not that her attraction to him mattered, Laura reminded herself sensibly. Attracted or not, she was here to fill a temporary position that would enable her to make a down payment on the quaint little farmhouse she'd seen for sale when she drove into Hoot Owl's Roost—or Hoot's Roost as the locals referred to the rural community. She'd fallen in love with the house immediately and she intended to accumulate the money to make the farm her own—by her own means, without the unwanted assistance of her overprotective brothers who'd probably find all sorts of fault with the house.

Moving to Oklahoma was a declaration of independence from her well-meaning but smothering brothers. Laura wanted to prove to herself, and to her brothers, that she could manage her life and make sensible decisions without her brothers' constant input. That was another reason why this summer job and this situation with

Wade was so important to Laura. She could reassure her brothers that she could handle herself around a man without falling head over heels for the first one she met—one who hadn't been screened and checked out by her brothers.

"Laura?"

She glanced over her shoulder to see Quint and Vance sauntering downhill, looking more devastatingly handsome than any two men had a right to, smiling the kind of smiles that made females from eight to eighty sigh in appreciation. All that glossy raven hair and those swarthy physiques wrapped in chambray, denim and leather were impossible to ignore. But in Laura's opinion, Wade Ryder was the biggest, baddest, most dangerous heartthrob of all. And why? Because she detected a hint of vulnerability and defensiveness about him that she identified with. Because he was far from perfect and she'd spent too much time around her all-too-perfect brothers who put Mary Poppins to shame.

"The job's yours," Quint announced. "We put your luggage in a spare bedroom. We'll be around at the end of the week to check on Wade and see how you're managing with him."

Laura smiled gratefully. "I'm sure he'll appreciate your company. I'll see that his household runs smoothly while he recuperates."

Vance grinned slyly. "You might offer Wade a massage every now and then," he suggested. "He's sore and achy after my bull steamrollered over him."

"Plus, Wade's home could use a cheery touch," Quint inserted with a smile. "You know, a few bouquets of wildflowers, all the windows flung open wide to allow plenty of light and fresh air, that sort of thing."

"And change things around a bit," Vance added.

"The place has looked the same way for years. New furniture arrangements might perk him up a little."

Laura frowned when the Ryder cousins exchanged amused glances. "Sure. No problem. I can handle that."

"Well, then, we'll get to work and leave you and Wade to get acquainted." Quint touched the brim of his hat and nodded politely. "See ya in a few days. We'll be back to inoculate Wade's cattle for him."

"Bye, Laura," Vance said with a wave and a grin.

When the men climbed into the fire-engine red pickup and roared off in a cloud of dust, Laura squared her shoulders, stiffened her resolve and headed for the house to unpack her belongings. She was going to be helpful and cheerful and prove to Wade that she wasn't an unwanted inconvenience in his home. He'd find no fault with her, she vowed. She'd take her job seriously and put in a hard day's work for a hard day's pay.

This would be no different than the first week of a new school year, she mused as she strode toward the sprawling ranch-style brick home on the hill. It always took her and her students several days to get acquainted and for them to adjust to her way of conducting class. It took a week for her to evaluate the various personalities of her students and determine the best way to deal with them. The same held true for Wade Ryder. In a week she'd know how to handle him and her duties. Things at the ranch would run like a well-oiled machine, she convinced herself.

Mentally prepared, Laura pasted on a smile and ventured inside the house. Wade was still ensconced in the massive leather recliner in his very masculine, no-frills living room. The ranch décor, with landscape paintings of rolling hills, rustic barns and grazing livestock, fit this rugged rancher, Laura decided. The room lacked a woman's touch and the heavy drapes were drawn—save the one window near the front door. She'd take Vance and Quint's suggestion to give this dark room an open, visitor-friendly appearance.

"What the hell do you have in those three coffins my cousins dragged in here? Dead bodies?" Wade asked abruptly.

The snide questions and the harsh tone in which they were delivered caused Laura's smile to wither on her lips. She halted in midstep. "Coffins?" she repeated, bemused.

"Yeah, those coffin-size suitcases," he said, grimacing as he leaned sideways to retrieve the glass of ice water on the end table. "In case you haven't noticed, this is a ranch, not a resort hotel that requires scads of fancy clothes to attend scheduled activities. A couple of pairs of faded jeans and T-shirts are all you need."

Laura reflexively flinched at his catty insinuation that her country-club attire, packed in those coffin-size suitcases—as he referred to them—was inappropriate for her new job. If Wade was trying to aggravate her, he'd succeeded. While it was true that she came from a privileged background she never flaunted wealth and she certainly didn't consider herself better than anyone else. But one look in Wade's direction indicated that *he* thought that *she* thought she was just a step below royalty and hadn't put in a day's work in her life. That was nowhere near accurate. She and her brothers prided themselves in being hard workers. Wade had no right whatsoever to presume anything about her when they'd only just met.

Man, this guy was a real piece of work! He might be as handsome as sin but he acted like the very devil!

"I'll go unpack," she said between her teeth as she made a beeline across the spacious room.

"That'll probably take you the rest of the day," he said, then smirked. "I guess I can forget about your squeezing in time to scrounge up something for my supper."

The smart-ass comment brought her up short. She glanced back at those glittering green eyes that shouted disapproval and animosity. "My job description is to cook, clean and ensure you take care of yourself during your recuperation, *Mr.* Ryder," she said in a tone she usually reserved for ill-mannered students. "Supper will definitely be served. What time do you usually eat?"

He scoffed, as if she'd asked a stupid question. "This is a ranch, Seymour. You've obviously never been within shouting distance of one before, or else you'd know that supper is scheduled around chores that always come first."

She smiled in mock sweetness. "And obviously you won't be attending your usual chores for a while." Her rejoinder caused his brows to bunch up on his scratched forehead, which gave her a small degree of satisfaction. "Therefore, we can establish a schedule for eating and you can depend on my having food on the table at dinnertime. Now, I'll ask again, Mr. Ryder, what time would you like to eat this evening?"

"Six forty-five," he grunted, then wet his whistle with ice water.

Laura was pretty sure the same said liquid flowed through the man's veins. What a foul-tempered bear he was! He might have rugged sex appeal oozing from his pores and a body like nobody's business, but he had the disposition of a wounded grizzly and he was making no effort to make her feel wanted or welcome.

"Fine, six forty-five it is," she said.

"Good. I'll eat in here...in my recliner...by *myself.*"

He made it crystal clear that he didn't want or need her company. Not that she cared, of course. She'd rather eat in a cafeteria with a bunch of teenage students during a food fight than dine with him anyway.

When she walked off he jacked up the volume of the TV where an old Western, starring John Wayne, was playing. If he was trying to annoy her, he was doomed to disappointment this time. She was a John Wayne fan from way back and *The Man Who Shot Liberty Valance* was one of her favorites.

Liberty Valance had nothing on Wade Ryder, she decided on her way down the hall. Both men leaned toward mean and nasty and deserved a good shooting.

2

LAURA NEATLY STACKED HER underwear and socks in the empty dresser and hung her clothes in the walk-in closet. Pensively she contemplated ways to give the living area a more welcoming appearance. For sure, she'd let plenty of light into that dark room, place scented candles and potpourri on the end tables and fill the area with vases of wildflowers. Then she'd rearrange the furniture to give the room better balance.

Laura stashed her suitcases in the corner of the closet then hiked off to appraise the kitchen and check to see what kind of food was on hand for supper. She was pleased to find an ultramodern kitchen at her disposal, but the reckless arrangement of food in the cabinets offended her sense of order. She set about organizing the boxes, cans and jars in alphabetical order so she wouldn't waste valuable time rummaging to locate items while cooking.

She was halfway through the process when Wade hobbled into the kitchen on his crutch and braced his battered body against the doorjamb. "What the hell do you think you're doing?" he all but roared at her.

Refusing to let him rile her, Laura pivoted and tossed him a high-voltage smile. "I'm reorganizing the kitchen."

"It was the fine the way it was," he grouched. "I'll never find a damn thing now."

"You won't have to because I'm in charge of KP duty for the next six to eight weeks," she reminded him, striving for a noncombative tone—which wasn't easy since he was glaring thunderclouds on her sunny smile.

"You're working here, not taking over the place," he growled. "Put that stuff back where it was...now."

Even bruised and mauled, the man could still come off looking ominous and intimidating. Laura forced herself not to shrink away from him the way she'd done when they first met. Learning to hold her own was good practice, she realized. Her fairy godbrothers were no longer waving their magic wands, paving the way for her and running interference. She'd landed her new teaching position by herself and she was taking absolute control of her life for the first time in twenty-five years. Wade was a test of her character and gumption and she had no intention of failing the test.

"When my employment is terminated I'll arrange your kitchen the way you had it." She gestured carelessly toward the cabinets. "I'll cram stuff on the shelves so you'll have to waste time locating ingredients. Happy now, Mr. Ryder?"

"No," he mumbled, shooting her a disgruntled glance.

Admirably she shrugged off his hostility and resumed the task of arranging items that began with *N*. Silence reigned for several moments while she progressed through *O* and *P* and skipped over *Q* to place a box of rice on the shelf.

"Where're you from, Seymour? You don't speak Oklahoman."

"Colorado." She plunked down the spaghetti sauce next to the rice.

"What happened? Did the school administration fire

you and you had to leave the state to outrun your reputation?''

Laura gnashed her teeth as she swiveled around to meet Wade's insolent smirk. The man didn't know how close he'd come to having a jar of spaghetti sauce smack him right between his moss-green eyes. ''No, as a matter of fact I come highly recommended by my principal.''

She had no idea why she was defending herself to him. She certainly didn't owe him an explanation and he didn't deserve one. She'd never had acceptance issues with her associates, either. Most people gravitated toward her friendly, nonconfrontational nature. All except His Grouchiness. He seemed to derive wicked pleasure from provoking her.

''No doubt, you came with all sorts of recommendations,'' he said in a tone that implied scandalous activities. ''Did the principal's wife resent the competition? Did you move on before she stamped a scarlet letter on your forehead?''

Laura quivered with outrage. The horrible man had the audacity to stand there, assassinating her character, judging her by his lowlife standards and condemning her in one felled swoop. ''I was *not* having an affair with my principal,'' she defended hotly. ''For your information my principal was a *she!*''

''Gad, that's even worse,'' he said distastefully.

The man was insufferable! ''I came here to be on my own and work in the same school system with my college roommate, not that it's any of your business,'' she all but shouted.

Wade shook his tousled raven head. ''I've got a news flash for you, Seymour, the PTA isn't going to approve of striking up your old affair with your college roommate, either.''

Laura didn't know what possessed her to react so violently to his goading. Her ability to apply restraint and self-control, after years of dealing with challenging students, failed her completely. Before she realized what she'd done, the container of salt that she had clenched in her fist was sailing across the room and smacked Wade squarely in the chest. With a horrified gasp, she watched him stare at the container that plopped on the tiled floor. He turned his death-ray glare on her and Laura's face flushed with mortification. Damn it, she'd let him get to her.

With extreme effort, Wade doubled over to retrieve the salt container then tossed it back to her. "I guess you don't think I'm injured in enough places already, huh?"

Regretful and embarrassed, Laura emitted an inarticulate sound and refused to meet his mocking gaze.

He smiled wickedly, then added, "I'll bet your résumé failed to mention that you're prone to violence when provoked. How many students have you clobbered when they've managed to tick you off, Seymour?"

Laura was so frustrated and angry that she was shaking. Her heart jackhammered in her chest, spurred by an overdose of adrenaline. She wanted to grab this infuriating rascal by the throat and strangle him for making her lose her temper. She almost never lost her temper. But Wade Ryder, the devil incarnate, had witnessed her complete loss of control.

"You aren't going to let loose with the waterworks, too, are you?" he taunted. "If you're going to cloud up and rain every day, I'll make sure I have flood insurance."

"I wouldn't give you the satisfaction of seeing me cry," she snapped at him. "Just go away."

"Nope, this is *my* house and *my* kitchen."

"Fine then, I qu—" Laura shut her mouth so fast she nearly cropped off the tip of her tongue. No matter what the man said to her, no matter how often he goaded and insulted her, she wasn't going to quit. She *wanted* this job. She *needed* this job for a dozen good reasons.

He arched a dark, challenging brow, daring her to complete that sentence. "Yes, Seymour? You were saying?"

Laura might not have been the modern-day version of Einstein, but she was smart enough to deduce that A: Wade Ryder didn't like her. And B: He didn't want her crowding his private space. And C: He was trying to provoke her into quitting her new job before she had twenty-four hours under her belt. She didn't understand *why* he wanted her gone because she didn't know him well enough to determine what made him tick. But, for pure contrariness alone, she wasn't giving this cantankerous rancher the satisfaction of hearing her say she quit. She wasn't a quitter and she'd dealt with troublesome students during her four years of teaching at the elite private school in Colorado—a job her brothers had pulled a few strings to secure for her....

The thought served to bolster her firm resolve. She was going to tough it out on her own, no matter how snide and sarcastic Wade Ryder proved to be. She wasn't a wuss, even though most of her former students weren't in the juvenile delinquent category of kids who tested her temper and challenged her authority on a daily basis— not like Mr. I'm-Gonna-Give-You-Hell-Just-To-See-If-You-Can-Take-It Ryder. No matter how mad he made her—and he'd made her plenty mad already—she wouldn't quit. She'd stay, if only to aggravate *him*.

"I'm *not* quitting," she told him as she squared her shoulders and tilted her chin to a determined angle. The fact that she was trembling with frustration probably de-

tracted from her defiant stance, but she'd get better at
dealing with this rascal. Now that she knew he was deliberately trying to get rid of her, she'd refuse to take him
seriously, wouldn't allow him to annoy her. In fact, she
could be as disagreeable as he was if she really tried.

"If you aren't quitting then you better toughen up,"
he goaded her. "I have no intention of letting up on
you."

"Why? Because it goes against your sour, surly nature
to be nice to people?" she flung back.

Wade didn't so much as flinch when she flashed him
a smirk. With jerky, agitated motions, she resumed stocking the kitchen cabinets in alphabetical order. He felt like
a first-class ass for provoking Laura. His conscience—
which he was trying to ignore—was screaming some
pretty raunchy curses at him for behaving so badly.

Silently he marveled at her organizational abilities that
the White House would envy. Hell, the woman could
probably run a small country all by herself and still take
a couple of days' vacation each week. But if he was to
succeed in his campaign to rout Ms. Temptation from his
house then he couldn't pay her compliments or cut her
any slack.

An apology flocked to his tongue, but he refused to
voice it because being nice to her would defeat his purpose. And damn it, he was uncomfortably aware of Laura
Seymour in her trim-fitting, perfectly creased jeans and
her pink knit blouse that displayed the full rounded swells
of her breasts. Her perfume kept trying to lure him across
the kitchen to get a stronger whiff and his good hand
itched—and so did the injured one—to map the alluring
contours of her goddesslike body.

Sheesh! Of all the women in all the world why did she
have to be the one hired as his temporary housecleaner,

cook and bottle washer…? *Bottle,* that's what he needed,
he decided instantly. After a few drinks he'd be numb to
the goddess in designer jeans.

Wade hobbled across the room and reached up to the
top shelf to retrieve a bottle of hooch. He accidentally
bumped into Laura when she grabbed the box of tea bags
to align them beside the spaghetti sauce. Her breasts
brushed the side of his left arm and Wade snatched a
quick breath—only to be assailed by that citrusy scent
that had been driving him crazy from the far side of the
room.

When he glanced down his gaze collided with those
enormous powder-blue eyes, surrounded by a hedge of
long, thick lashes. Then his attention dropped to the teasing hint of cleavage displayed by her V-necked blouse.
Feeling like a kid who'd been caught with his hands in
the cookie jar—or wherever—because *he* knew that *she*
knew what had momentarily distracted his attention, his
gaze bounced guiltily back to her face. Her full, tempting
lips were only a scant few inches from his. Wade didn't
dare draw breath, for fear of breathing in her essence so
deeply that he'd succumb to the reckless urge to kiss her
and find out if she tasted as delicious as she looked.
Gawd, he'd known she'd be pure trouble!

"What are you doing?" she asked, a hitch in her voice,
a flush of color on her face.

*Checking you out, though that's the last thing I'd
planned to do,* the voice of honesty replied. But Wade
decided to play dumb. He could do dumb if he had to.
"Whaddya mean, what am I doing?"

Blushing profusely, her gaze focused on his mouth,
Laura gestured toward the top shelf where his hand had
stalled in midair. "If you're reaching for that whiskey

bottle, that isn't a wise idea. Pain medication doesn't mix with liquor. Your doctor wouldn't approve, Mr. Ryder.''

"First off, I decided to forego that pain medication because it makes me woozy.'' He ignored her when she muttered something about preferring woozy to downright cranky.

"Secondly, you can drop that *mister* stuff, professor,'' he instructed, then backed away from temptation personified.

"I'm not a college professor,'' she clarified. "I'm a secondary school instructor.''

"Yeah, whatever. Fact is that my doctor is Jack Daniel's and he makes house calls.'' He snatched the bottle off the shelf and set it on the counter with a decisive thump. "Hand me two glasses.''

"I don't want a drink,'' she informed him.

"I'd hope not. You're on the clock. *I* want two glasses, one for each hand.''

She stared pointedly at his left wrist that was draped in the sling. "You only have one good hand,'' she reminded him.

"So what? Just hand me the damn glasses.''

She didn't move, just stared him down as if he was one of her belligerent students.

"Fine then, I'll get it myself, which only goes to prove that I don't need you.''

Before Wade could reach around her to grab the glasses she plucked them off the shelf and set them down with a clank.

"Thanks, professor,'' he said, and not very politely.

"You're welcome, Ryder. But you should know that you don't get extra credit for doing things for yourself when you're supposed to be resting all those body parts you injured while bull wrestling.''

"I wasn't bull wrestling," he corrected.

"Yeah, whatever."

When she tossed his caustic words back in his face he gnashed his teeth, then realized his jaw was as sore as the rest of his abused body.

"According to your cousins' version of the incident that required immediate medical attention," she went on, "you valiantly distracted the big bad bull before he flattened Vance and Quint. But I suspect that you were just trying to clamber out of the way so that thousand-pound brute could vent his frustration on your cousins."

Wade's chest swelled with indignation—which served to remind him that his ribs were exceptionally tender. "I didn't turn tail and run," he huffed and puffed and blew her theory down. "My cousins may be ornery cusses, but I didn't see any sense of all three of us getting trampled so none of us could handle the ranch chores."

"Oh, I see," she said in pretended thoughtfulness. "You just wanted an excuse to take some time off and let your cousins handle the hard work."

The comment cut like a Weed Eater. "Hell no! Are you nuts, lady?" he roared. "The last thing I wanted was to be laid up and have a woman under my roof!"

Wade slammed his mouth shut and cursed himself soundly. It was never wise to let the enemy know your battle plan. If Laura hadn't figured out that he was trying to get rid of her any way he could, she surely suspected it now.

She regarded him through her narrowed gaze then went back to alphabetically stocking the shelves. "So, you're saying that you're afraid of women and that fear defines who you are."

"I'm saying nothing of the kind," he said, highly affronted. He twisted the cap off the whiskey with a vicious jerk and purposely slopped the amber liquid on the counter as he filled his glasses. "You think I'm afraid of you? Not hardly. You're all of five foot nothing and I'm six-three in my stocking feet. Whaddya gonna do? Break my other leg? I don't think so!"

"I'm not referring to physical fright," she clarified. "I'm talking about emotional terror."

"That's ridiculous," he protested.

She reached over to grab a dish towel to mop up his mess then tossed him a sly glance. "Then you're saying that you don't appreciate women in the same capacity that most men do."

"If you're asking if I like sex, which is none of your business, by the way, the answer is: Yes, I like sex as much as the next heterosexual guy. I just want sex on my terms. No strings attached, no commitment."

"So basically you're saying you just don't like women, but you don't mind using them to scratch the occasional itch," she paraphrased.

Hoo-kay, so that sounded cold and insensitive. But yeah, she'd pretty much hit the nail on its proverbial head. Thanks to Bobbie Lynn he'd never let a woman close enough for prolonged periods of time to form an emotional attachment. "Right," he replied. "Sex is impersonal. You get some when you need some. Like filling an empty fuel tank."

She paused momentarily from her chore to glance sideways at him. He could tell she was offended, which was fine by him. He didn't want to like her and he didn't care if she liked him, either. The less she liked him the sooner she'd realize working here was a mistake and she'd take a hike.

"This is fascinating," she said, staring at him with those luminous baby blues that had the power to make him weak in the knees. "Explain to me how sex can be impersonal when the act itself involves baring pretty much everything you *are* to someone else in the most intimate manner possible?"

Wade grabbed some ice cubes from the fridge, plunked them in his glasses and then tossed back a shot of booze. It gave him time to formulate his reply. "Well, ya see, professor, this is where we get into the differences between men and women," he lectured authoritatively. "Women think you're supposed to attach meaningful emotion to sex, but men just like to get laid because it makes 'em feel good all over." He noticed her face had become splotchy with color, so he pressed the issue. "A man's psyche isn't so difficult to understand, despite all that mumbo-jumbo those psychological experts like to spout. We just want two things from life. One—" he waved the glass of Jack Daniel's in her face "—is a swig of booze, and the other is getting naked with a woman when the mood strikes."

She was highly offended or extremely embarrassed— he wasn't sure which. Her peaches-and-cream complexion turned candy-apple red. Her eyes were shooting sparks, too, he noted.

"You want to know what I think?" she asked in a tone that reminded him of a hissing cat.

"No, not particularly." He downed another slug of booze. "But you're probably planning to tell me anyway, right?"

Apparently that really ticked her off because she glared at him and said, "I think you're a throwback to the caveman era and your Neanderthal mentality sucks!"

Unfazed, he took another drink. "You're entitled to your opinion, professor, but don't come crying to me when you think you've landed Mr. Right and he doesn't meet all your fairy-tale expectations of love and romance.''

He winced when her fuming glance zeroed in on his right hand that held his sweating glass of booze. He knew what she was going to ask before the words were out of her mouth.

"Is that a wedding band? It certainly looks like one. Why are you wearing it on the wrong hand?" she quizzed him like any self-respecting schoolmarm.

"Because I married the wrong woman. It's a reminder never to make that disastrous mistake again, so long as I live.''

"Ah," she said pensively. "No wonder you have so many hang-ups. That explains a lot.''

He stiffened and glowered down from his advantageous height, annoyed by that smug little smile on her rosebud mouth. "That doesn't explain squat. I don't have hang-ups.''

"Sure you do." She returned to her task of stocking the cabinets. "You probably got your itsy-bitsy heart broken and you're holding all women responsible for the traitorous act of one femme fatale. What did she do? Cheat on you?''

"None of your damn business," he said through his teeth.

"That's why this house shows no signs of a woman's touch. You've become a card-carrying woman-hater, haven't you?''

She thought she was so damn smart, did she? Well, she was right, but he didn't cotton to how easily she'd read him.

"You tried to erase all evidence that there was a woman in your house who got under your skin." She stacked three cans of tuna then reached over to grab three cans of turkey. "You figured you couldn't make a woman happy so why try, right? It's easier to give up, to quit."

She turned toward him then, all fierce determination. "Well, you need to know that *I'm* not a quitter, Mr. Ryder, no matter how hard you try to drive me away. I intend to do my job exceptionally well. One look at you testifies to the obvious fact that you need my assistance to keep this place shipshape while you recuperate. Now, go take a load off your broken leg while I whip up supper. Go on, scram," she ordered, shooing him on his way. "You're slowing me down."

Wade was so frustrated by the unexpected turn of events that he was halfway across the room before he realized he'd allowed her to boss him around. Hell! He'd let that woman have the last word. That would never do.

"Just stay out of my way, professor, and I'll stay out of yours," he felt to compelled to say.

"Fine."

"Good!"

Muttering at his live-in housekeeper, he limped off on his crutch. He cursed his devilish cousins with every uneven step and returned to the living room with his glasses of whiskey. As he lowered himself gingerly into his recliner he watched John Wayne's character drop Liberty Valance in his tracks. If only he could dispose of Laura Seymour that easily! She might have thought she had him all figured out so she could deal effectively with him, but she was way wrong about that.

Now, more than ever, Wade wanted her gone. When a woman started picking around in a man's brain, he was in heap big trouble. And this particular woman was too blasted smart if she could analyze him in the course of one afternoon. He'd have to work harder at driving her away so he could reclaim his private, female-free domain. Besides, he'd kept his emotions in cold storage for years and he didn't want Laura to defrost them. Keeping them frozen solid worked best.

As for his traitorous cousins, he wasn't going to kick their butts, as soon as he was able. He'd decided to murder them for foisting this particular woman off on him. He suspected Vance and Quint were trying to do a little matchmaking—kill a couple of birds with one stone, as it were. Well, they'd wasted their time with this prank. Laura Seymour wasn't the kind of woman he wanted in his life—not that he wanted any kind of female in his life, mind you, because he didn't. He especially didn't want to share his personal space with a female as tempting and intelligent as Seymour. She stirred up his hormones and put his conscience under duress.

True, he'd been raised better than to be unspeakably rude and disrespectful to women—his mother would've killed him if she'd overheard that exchange in the kitchen. Of course, his mother didn't fall into the Women category. She was, after all, his mother. And okay, so maybe all women weren't as treacherous as Bobbie Lynn. But Wade's track record indicated that he was a lousy judge of the female of the species and he naturally attracted women who were all wrong for him. That said, the best course of action was to avoid close association with all varieties of females.

Furthermore, he mused as he sipped his hooch, he wasn't about to let his younger cousins pick women for him. They enjoyed all varieties of women. The more women the better, so they claimed. What did they know about finding the elusive Ms. Right? Nothing, that's what. Otherwise those two clowns would be wedlocked by now.

Wade knew that when it came to women Vance and
Quint had stumbled and fallen a couple of times themselves. They chose to handle their humiliation in different
ways. Quint preferred to shield his emotions by flirting
outrageously with everything in skirts and he was swift
enough of foot to dodge wedding nooses that flew his
way. Vance relied on teasing humor to sidestep emotional
land mines. As for Wade, he chose avoidance and
barbed-wire barriers to protect his heart.

Whatever worked, he supposed. But the fact remained
that the Ryder cousins—even the absentee Gage—were
considered highly prized bachelors in Hoot's Roost.
Come to think of it, his maternal cousins were in great
demand as well. The whole passel of male cousins were
decent looking—if that mattered—and they were successful—and that *did* matter to females who power-
shopped for low-maintenance husbands who could provide for their wives in the wealthy manner to which they
aspired.

Well, gold diggers need not apply at the Ryder
ranches, Wade mused. As for Laura Seymour, he wanted
her to vamoose—pronto. Now that he knew he had the
ability to make her mad he'd push and prod until she lost
her temper and spit out the four-letter *Q* word. Then he'd
have her exactly where he wanted her…besides naked in
his bed….

Wade jerked upright, shocked by that whimsical
thought. He didn't want to visualize how Laura would
look naked because that would lead to more trouble than
he had already. Wade squelched the testosterone-induced
fantasy that leaped to mind and concentrated on the
movie. He wasn't going to give his new housekeeper another thought—except to conjure up ways to get rid of

her, while he listened to her rummage around in his kitchen, as if she owned the place.

SWIFTLY AND EFFICIENTLY, Laura bustled around the kitchen, preparing the evening meal that she felt certain Wade couldn't fault. She'd covered the basic food groups to provide a well-rounded, nutritious supper. Immensely pleased with herself, she sauntered into the living room, toying with the devilish urge to dump the food on Wade's head rather than politely placing the tray on his lap. To her disappointment he stared distastefully at his plate.

"What the hell is this?" he asked incredulously.

"Well, duh, it's supper. What does it look like?" Laura mentally patted herself on the back for her sassy rejoinder. Already, she'd learned to counter Wade's intimidation with lightning-quick sarcasm. After a few weeks of dealing with him she was positively certain she could hold her own with any man. She might have been a little timid and unsure of herself in the past, since her brothers tried to map out her life and speak in her behalf, but she was learning fast.

Wade glanced up from the tray and said, "Do you have the slightest idea where you are, Seymour?"

Puzzled, she replied, "On an Oklahoma ranch?"

"Well, if you figured that out all by yourself, did you also notice this is cattle country?"

She had no idea where he was going with this line of questioning. "Yes, I do believe I saw a herd of cattle grazing the pastures."

"Good, it's a relief to know you're not blind, just dense."

She could feel her temper simmering, but she valiantly suppressed her mounting irritation. "And your point, provided there is one, would be?"

He made a stabbing gesture toward the stuffed poultry and dressing, smothered in gravy, on his plate. "I raise cattle, therefore I support the beef industry, *not* poultry. You don't feed a cattleman a damn chicken. Jeez, Seymour, are they giving away teaching certificates to the highest bidder these days?"

"Jeez, Ryder, if you don't eat chicken, then what are all those frozen breasts doing in your freezing unit?"

A wave of heat flooded through her when his gaze focused deliberately on her bosom. He delighted in rattling her—that conversation they'd shared in the kitchen about the depersonalization of sex indicated as much. She should be highly offended by his telling glance. Indeed if another man stared so blatantly, unblinkingly, at her chest she would have been outraged and insulted.

For some unexplainable reason the red-hot, seductive glimmer in Wade's green eyes sent her senses reeling and heightened her awareness of him. Which she didn't need, thank you so much. She was aware of him—to the extreme. His deep, smoky voice sent hot chills down her spine. His muscular physique kept drawing her unwilling attention and feminine speculation. He was distractingly handsome with that thatch of raven hair, those hypnotic eyes, those deeply tanned and chiseled features, those broad shoulders and horseman's thighs. He looked solid and unyielding and he exuded some mystical aura that fascinated her on an elemental level.

She tried to tell herself that she was intrigued because she wasn't accustomed to hanging out with cowboys. Teachers, yes. Businessmen, you bet. But not rugged, macho hunks like Wade Ryder.

"Hello? Anyone home?" Wade taunted.

Color splashed across her cheeks in such a rush that Laura feared the sudden pressure would blow off the top of her head. He'd caught her ogling him. Worse, she was probably drooling. Enough of this nonsense! She wasn't going to let herself become the least bit interested in this woman-hating cowboy and his hang-ups. He was a waste of time and effort.

"Earth to Seymour," he prompted again.

"What?" she mumbled.

"I said…" he drawled very deliberately, "I like plump, juicy breasts occasionally, but not on a regular basis. Beef is my mainstay, so don't forget it when you're puttering around the kitchen, throwing together some slop to feed me."

Puttering? Throwing together slop? She'd slaved over this meal, damn it. She glared at him, then noticed he was trying to get a reaction from her. He was waiting for her to pop her cork so he could toss out another insult that would infuriate her to the point of quitting. Well, it wasn't happening, she vowed fiercely. She would not be provoked!

Before she could respond he thrust both empty glasses at her. "Make yourself useful and fill 'em up, will ya?"

She snatched up the glasses, careful to avoid contact with his long, lean fingers. "With poison? Gladly. I'll be back in a flash with a deadly dose."

Wade watched her stalk off, her hips swishing like an angry cat's tail, and he sighed gratefully. Thank you, God! He needed a quick time-out. Staring at her well-proportioned chest and watching her blush got his male body all riled up. That he didn't need—not in his condition. When she'd given him that thorough once-over he'd been positively certain that not *all* his body parts were nonfunctional. If not for the supper tray on his lap, Laura would've noticed his aroused condition and likely razzed him unmercifully about it.

Damn it, he didn't like the way Laura made him feel, the way he reacted to her, the way his thoughts detoured down lusty avenues when she got within five feet of him.

On the spur of the moment he decided that he wasn't going to repay his cousins by killing them swiftly and mercifully for dumping Laura on his doorstep. No, he'd roast them over an open fire...or drag them behind a galloping horse around the perimeters of the ranch...or stake them over a den of fire ants, that sort of thing.

Wade pretended a fascinated interest in the television when he heard Laura stamping back into the room. When she slammed down the glasses of whiskey on his tray, he said, "Took you long enough."

"I had to scrounge around the cabinets to locate the hemlock and arsenic," she muttered spitefully. "Here, pick your poison. Anything else, Your Grumpiness?"

He flicked his wrist, dismissing her. "That'll do it."

"It'd better." She performed a quick about-face toward the kitchen. "Otherwise I'll have to restock the poisons because we're fresh out. Just my luck that I got stuck with a man who's just too darn mean to roll over and die after a couple of lethal doses."

3

WHEN LAURA STORMED OFF, Wade broke into a reluctant smile. Who would have thought the timid schoolmarm he'd met only a few hours ago possessed quicksilver sass and lively spirit. Of course, it made getting rid of her more difficult, but it was an entertaining challenge.

Wade recalled that if he dared to use that snotty tone on Bobbie Lynn, she simpered and mewled until her thick mascara bled like hot tar down her makeup-coated cheeks. However, Laura Seymour didn't bleed mascara because she didn't coat her face with war paint. She had the kind of natural beauty and flawless skin that Bobbie Lynn tried to acquire artificially.

Gawd, why he'd married that woman he couldn't recall. She'd whined incessantly about the isolation of ranch life. She'd demanded favors for passion and dangled sex in front of him like a carrot before a mule. Fool that he'd been, he'd tried to make her happy, had given into her to make their marriage work because Ryders were supposed to wed forever. At least his parents had. Same went for Vance's parents, Quint's parents and Gage's parents. The four older-generation Ryder brothers had discovered everlasting love and produced four Ryder cousins who'd never found their soul mates.

Maybe love skipped a generation, Wade mused. He was the only one of the Ryder cousins who'd waded into the wedding pool. He'd failed big time. He'd been such

a blind idiot that he'd been the last one to know Bobbie
Lynn was fooling around on him and took him to the
cleaners when she trotted merrily off to Dallas, leaving
him to deal with the humiliation and small-town gossip
that spread faster than a plague of locusts.

Wade had worked double shifts after the financial disaster left in ex-wife's wake. He'd learned his lesson
well. Women would screw you over if you gave them
half a chance.

The reminder of his ex reaffirmed his belief that he
never wanted to put himself in a position to be betrayed
or rejected again. He was better off without a woman in
his life. Yup, he'd just keep hammering away at Laura
until she threw up her hands and stalked out—for good.
He had enough trouble trying to recuperate from the painful accident. He didn't want to play the fateful hand
women dealt out to men.

Wade had learned—the hard way—that women always
played with loaded dice and they stacked the deck. Yet,
even knowing that, Wade couldn't keep his mind off
Laura while he prepared for bed that night. She was in
the room next to his, probably peeling off her clothes.
All that soft, silky skin bared—

He inwardly cursed the wayward direction of his
thoughts, struggled from his jeans then plopped on the
bed. When he noticed a moving shadow in the hall he
hurriedly snatched the bedspread over his lap to cover
himself.

He glared at Laura when she stepped uninvited into
his bedroom. "Next time try knocking first," he muttered.

"Sorry." Her gaze bounced from his bare chest and
bare legs to his face. She blushed, but she moved bravely
toward him. "I thought a massage might help you relax."

Wade nearly came unglued when she placed her hands on the tense muscles of his neck. "Don't touch me!" he yelped.

She snatched her hands away as if she'd been scorched. "I'm only trying to do the job I was hired to do," she explained as her gaze dipped once again to his chest.

"Go do it somewhere else." He clung desperately to the bedspread that concealed his hips. "I don't want a massage."

"You look pretty tensed up to me," she observed.

"Maybe it's because you're invading my private space when I'm not dressed," he grumbled, his male pride prodding him. He didn't want Laura to see his battered and bruised body when, in comparison, she was the picture of health and beauty. This was *not* helping him feel better about himself.

She studied him for a pensive moment then smiled down at his scowl. "Know what, Ryder?"

"No, what, Seymour?" he asked, feeling himself caving beneath her beguiling smile.

"I still think you're afraid of me," she teased playfully. "And you know what else?"

"I give up. What else?" he questioned, wishing she'd hotfoot it from the room and leave him in peace.

"I'm going to kill you with kindness while I'm working here. No matter how mean you are to me, you aren't going to have a single complaint with my work."

"Probably not since I'll be dead," he countered.

He hadn't intended to amuse her with the comment, but apparently he had because she chuckled. "Well, good night then. If you need anything just give a holler. I'll have your breakfast ready when you get up in the morning."

After she exited Wade raked his fingers through his hair and sighed. He wasn't sure he could keep up this pretense that he disliked Laura when everything in him responded to her disarming smile and her enjoyable companionship.

Well, he reminded himself as he stretched out gingerly on his bed, he'd just have to try harder to remain remote and distant. He tried to concentrate on ways to alienate Laura, but he was just too exhausted. Sprawled on his back, he fell asleep with forbidden fantasies swirling around his head.

BY THE TIME WADE HOBBLED into the kitchen the next morning on the crutch he used for balance, Laura had one load of clothes washed and stuffed in the dryer and the rest of the laundry sorted. She also had bacon and pancakes staying warm in the oven.

"Morning," she greeted cheerfully.

Wade mumbled unintelligibly then motioned toward the living room. She presumed he wanted to eat in his recliner so she fixed his plate. Surprisingly he didn't poke fun at her cooking, just wolfed down the food and asked for more. Although he'd previously announced that he didn't need her company during meals, Laura grabbed the dust cloth and spiffed up the living room.

"I really like your ranch," she said conversationally.

"It's mine and you can't have it," he replied, flashing her a dark look from beneath lowered brows.

"Well, shoot, and here I was, ready to write you a check for the place," she said breezily.

"Could I have a little more orange juice, ple—" He clamped his mouth shut and glared at her.

"Sure." She breezed over to pluck up the empty glass. It amused her that Wade had to force himself *not* to be polite. She sensed that he wasn't as mean as he wanted her to think. She'd have to remember that when he purposely goaded her.

"I thought I'd take a look at your computer programs this afternoon," she said as she handed him the glass of juice.

"Fine, whatever," he mumbled then took a sip.

"More coffee?" she offered.

"Yeah, tha—" He closed his mouth and thrust out the cup.

"If you don't mind, I'd like to hike around the ranch in my spare time. I haven't had the chance to go on nature walks or ride horseback since I was a kid at summer camp."

"Just don't scare the cattle. I'm in no condition to stop a stampede."

Well, at least he hadn't forbidden her from looking around the place, she mused. Of course, that was because he wanted her out from underfoot occasionally.

When she reentered the living room, she noticed Wade had set aside the empty tray and was looking hopelessly lost. She imagined an active man like Wade was having trouble with his sedentary existence. Laura wheeled toward her bedroom to gather a few books that she'd brought with her.

"Here, these will occupy your time." She handed him two suspense thrillers for his reading pleasure.

Wade stared at the books then glanced up at her. "I'm too old for book reports, professor," he said flippantly.

"Would you prefer something else to read?"

"Yeah, *Playboy*. They're in my bottom dresser drawer."

If he was trying to aggravate her, she'd prove that it was a waste of his time. "Sure thing. Coming right up."

He frowned, apparently disappointed that she hadn't objected. Laura swallowed a smug grin and strode down the hall. She'd never actually had her hands on the men's magazine before so she thumbed through it on her way back to the living room. She couldn't help but wonder if the busty and bare bunnies were the types Wade preferred when he was in the mood for female companionship.

"Find something interesting in there, Seymour?" he asked when he caught her staring at the centerfold.

"No, *Playgirl* is more my style," she insisted saucily. "I plan to pin up a few beefcake posters in my bedroom, as soon as I have time. You don't mind, do you?"

"Fine by me. Then maybe you won't be barging into my room to sneak peeks at me," he razzed her.

Her mouth dropped open. "That was not what I was doing last night!" she objected, affronted.

"Could've fooled me," he said, and grinned wickedly. "I may be crippled up, but I'm not blind. You looked your fill."

Her face flooded with color because he was right and they both knew it. She'd definitely looked him over when she saw him sitting on the edge of his bed—arms, legs and chest bare. Having lived with four brothers, she'd seen men in various states of undress. But Wade's power-packed, muscled body had had more of an arousing effect than she wanted to admit.

"Well?"

She jerked her gaze to his face when she realized she was staring at him, remembering how he looked without his shirt and jeans. "Well, what?"

"Are you going to deny it, Seymour?" he challenged.

Laura knew he was trying to get her goat again, but she refused to let him. "No, I'm not," she replied. "You're a stud muffin, Ryder, and I suspect you know it. If I had your picture I'd pin it on the wall beside the other beefcakes.''

When his mouth dropped open and he was left speechless, Laura smiled in triumph and went back to dusting the furniture. She wasn't sure but she thought she might've won that round. Wade didn't make another peep for an hour.

Although she knew Wade was trying hard to make himself difficult to live with she suspected that he wasn't normally a grouch. He was being deliberately cantankerous for her benefit. She'd have to remember that the next time he tried to annoy her in his ongoing attempt to make her quit her job.

WADE WAS GREATLY RELIEVED when his cousins showed up at the end of the week. Leaning heavily on a single crutch, Wade slowly progressed down the hill to reach the barn where Quint and Vance were unloading their saddled horses from the stock trailer. He battled the feeling of uselessness as he watched his cousins tighten cinches and bridle their cow ponies.

"So, how goes it with the housekeeper, cuz?" Quint asked, tossing Wade a smile.

Although it was going better than he preferred, because Laura had been amazingly efficient the past few days, Wade said, "I don't know how much you're paying Seymour, but it's too damn much for what little she does."

Vance's dark brows jackknifed. "You don't say."

"I do say."

"What's wrong *exactly?*" Quint asked.

"Where do I start? The woman tried to burn off my tongue with her thirty-weight-motor-oil coffee that's as hot as molten lava, and her cooking skills are barely existent." Wade made a face and cringed—although the truth was that her coffee was just the way he liked it, and she was such an excellent cook that he gobbled every bite of her meals.

Quint and Vance exchanged glances then stared toward the graveled driveway, noting that Laura's low-slung sports car was gone. Wade used it as another strike against her.

"I haven't gotten a full day's work out of her yet," he went on. "This afternoon she took off to visit her friend."

"Well, I'm sure that once she gets settled into a routine things will run smoothly," Quint defended her.

"Yeah well, it's your money," Wade said with a lackadaisical shrug. "But I'm tellin' ya, she's as useless as a headache. I have to wake her up every morning by nine to fix my breakfast. She barely has time to prepare lunch while she's watching all those soap operas."

Wade was laying it on thick and his conscience was snarling at him for voicing lies, in hopes of convincing Quint and Vance to can her. Truth was, the woman was so energetic and efficient that it wore him out watching her buzz merrily from one chore to the next.

Like a whirling dervish, she'd attacked the mountain of laundry that had piled up before Wade was injured, as well as the mound that had built up after he'd come home in a cast and sling. The kitchen and bathrooms were spotless, and the house had been vacuumed and dusted within an inch of its life. Laura had also booted up his computer to look at his ranching programs. Like a physician conducting an examination, she'd decided what sort of updates he needed then called in her order. And presto, the software arrived by overnight express. Wade had seen her in his office loading the new software and transferring information like the pro she was.

However, if he gave her a ringing endorsement he'd never get Seymour out of his hair—and off his mind.

Sure 'nuff, having her underfoot 24/7 was driving him up the wall. He was starting to like her. When he deliberately provoked and tormented her, in hopes of driving her away, she sassed him playfully. When he tried to communicate through insults—to annoy her—she responded by insisting that he was suffering from a persecution complex brought on by the hang-ups left in the wake of his ex-wife's betrayal and that he needed to get over himself. And worse, Wade was actually enjoying their conversations, their verbal sparring and her saucy sense of humor. That was not good.

It had been a long time since he'd experienced such an intense and profound physical attraction to a woman. He wanted her—of course, that went without saying, because she was extremely desirable and tempting. But what scared the bejeezus out of him was that he liked being with her, liked sharing his long hours of his inactivity. That was very bad!

Wade was getting so desperate that he was stooping to concocting outrageous fibs. He was tattling to his cousins, trying to convince them to dismiss Laura. He wasn't very proud of himself, but this was about self-preservation!

Vance appraised Wade's freshly laundered, wrinkle-free chambray shirt and jeans then smiled wryly. "You don't look the worse for wear," he observed.

"That's because I hand wash my own clothes," Wade said.

"Uh-huh, sure you do." Quint smirked. "I hope you realize we aren't buying this crock of malarkey you're shoveling out."

Damn, he was afraid of that. "Fine, turn a blind eye

while she blows off her duties," Wade muttered. "Throw your money down the toilet. What do I care?"

Quint chuckled as he effortlessly mounted his buckskin gelding. "I don't know why you just don't admit you like Laura and get it out in the open."

"I most certainly don't like her!" Wade objected— loudly. Another outright lie. He did like her. That was the problem and it wasn't getting better.

"Right." Vance scoffed. "Ask me, you're protesting a little too much, which is a dead giveaway in my book."

Wade swore ripely. This was his cry for help and his ornery cousins weren't listening. A man couldn't even count on his family to save him from disaster.

"Mind if we borrow Frank?" Vance asked as he reined his sorrel toward the corral.

"Sure, take my cow dog, too. You've already stuck me with Seymour. What's one more traitorous act between cousins?"

"Gawd, cuz, you're breakin' my heart," Quint drawled.

"I think I'm gonna break down and cry." Vance, grinning playfully, wiped imaginary tears from his eyes and sniffled.

"Fine, you guys can sit there cracking wise, but I'm telling you that Seymour shirks her duties and you're paying her for doing diddly-squat."

Wade whistled. Frank, his loyal blue heeler, bounded from the barn, wagging his stub of a tail. Frank lived to round up and cut cattle from the herd. He was as efficient as two men on horseback and worth his weight in dog chow.

When Frank stared devotedly up at him, Wade patted the dog's head then gestured toward the pasture. "Bring 'em in, Frank," he ordered. When Frank spun on his haunches and sprang into action, Wade cut his cousins a quick glance. "Just stay out of Frank's way. He can do everything except open and shut the gates."

Quint leaned away from his horse to unlatch the gate. "Did you teach Frank to inoculate and brand, too?"

"If he could handle something like that I'd have him in the house, cooking and cleaning, because he could run circles around my temp housekeeper," Wade flung back.

Duff—the bowlegged cowboy, who'd worked at the ranch since Wade was a toddler, and now, recently retired, helped out part-time—appeared at the barn door. "Need some help with roundup, boys?" he asked as he dusted blades of straw from his shirtsleeves.

"Naw," Vance replied. "Frank's gonna do all the work. Quint and I will just sit back and twiddle our thumbs until the cattle are penned up."

Duff grinned, displaying his missing front tooth, and then he gestured toward the barn. "Laura brought down a stack of sandwiches, chips, colas and fresh-baked apple pie and stashed them in the fridge so you boys'd have some lunch. She went to town to restock groceries and pick up supplies. That little gal is something when it comes to working around here. She even helped me muck out the barn and feed the horses before she drove off."

Wade winced when his cousins' narrowed gazes branded him the liar he was. Damn Duff and his flapping jaws!

"Not getting our money's worth?" Quint smirked.

"Lazy?" Vance scoffed.

Duff's whiskered jaw dropped open and his sunken chest swelled with irritation. "Wade said that about her?" he hooted. "Hell, the little gal even came by last night to bring me supper and spiffed up my place while I ate. I forgot a house could look *that* clean and smell *that* good. She even brought me a vase of wildflowers to brighten up the place."

Great, Wade's strategy to convince his cousins that Seymour wasn't pulling her salaried weight was blowing up in his face. How was he to know Duff was going to shout her praises to high heaven?

Duff didn't shut up, either. He just kept yammering on and on about how "that gal" was the "best thang" that had happened around here in a decade and how she was the "pertiest thang" he'd every laid eyes on in all his sixty-six years.

"I'm feeling nauseous." Wade turned an awkward one-eighty and limped toward the house. "I better go lie down."

"First you better stop, drop and roll, right where you are," Quint called after him, "Your pants are on fire, *liar.*"

"Does his nose look like it's growing longer to you?" Vance asked Quint in mock concern.

"Yup, ol' Pinocchio is in big trouble," Quint teased.

"Darn tootin' he is," Duff chimed in. "His mama and daddy raised him better than to pull a stunt like that!"

Serenaded by teasing laughter Wade returned to the house. He'd gotten no help whatsoever from that quarter. He'd have to run Seymour off the ranch on a rail—all by himself.

LAURA BEAMED IN DELIGHT when she saw Annie Nelson jogging across the street to meet her for lunch. Annie didn't look much different than she had in college. She was still an attractive bundle of energy and quick with a friendly smile.

"I'm so glad you had time to meet me in town today,"

Annie enthused as she gave Laura an affectionate hug. "Sitting and gabbing is going to be just like old times."

When Annie led the way into Hoagie's Diner, Laura set aside her frustration of trying to gain Wade's respect and his ongoing attempts to convince her to find another job. Dining with Annie was the distraction she needed.

Laura studied her surroundings as she plunked down at the corner booth of the busy café. The place was filled to capacity during the lunch hour and two harried-looking waitresses were darting from one booth to the next, taking and delivering orders. The mom-and-pop diner was doing a driving business and the smell of hamburgers and fries caused Laura's stomach to growl in eager anticipation.

"You'll love the food here," Annie assured her. "Best hamburgers, chicken fried steak and cream gravy in three counties. And you're going to love Hoot's Roost, too."

"It's definitely a change from Denver," Laura commented as she perused the fifties, malt-shop style café then glanced down at the laminated menu. "But I love the wide-open spaces here and I'm enjoying this new feeling of independence."

Annie raked her shiny mahogany-colored hair away from her face and grinned. "I'll bet your brothers have been calling every other day to check on you."

Laura nodded her thanks to the waitress who set two glasses of ice water on the Formica tabletop. "Actually my brothers have been away on a business trip so I've had several days of reprieve. I sent them postcards to inform them that I've moved. But I fully expect them to call to grill me about my summer job when they return to Denver."

Annie sipped her water and her hazel eyes glinted with curiosity. "So...how's it going with Wade?"

She shrugged evasively. "It's a job."

"Yeah, right. Like you didn't notice the man's so good-looking that he could jump-start a woman in a coma. He's a babe magnet, same as his cousins. I should be so lucky to be surrounded by the gorgeous Ryder cousins. Sounds like tough work if you can get it."

Annie sighed dreamily. "Even when the Ryder cousins were in high school they were gorgeous, athletic and in great demand. Even though I was just in grade school at the time, I loved to watch them play basketball, baseball and rodeo. They were something to see in action, lemme tell ya."

"Well, Wade might've been a sports dynamo back then but now he's two-hundred-plus pounds of bad attitude," Laura confided to her good friend. "He doesn't want me in his house and I can supply you with a ten-minute list of his offenses if you're interested. Even worse, when he goads me I sass him right back, without showing an ounce of my former restraint. The man is turning me into the worst version of myself."

Annie shrugged, unconcerned. "It's probably good practice for you. I always thought you were too restrained when your brothers were breathing down your neck, trying to run your life. You just caved in and let them intimidate you. As far as Wade's concerned, it's understandable that he doesn't want a woman in his house after he made the mistake of marrying the original bitch goddess of Hoot's Roost. Bobbie Lynn didn't make life easy for him, and it left a bitter taste in his mouth about women in general. I heard recently that she's already ditched her second hubby and moved on to number three."

"Bobbie Lynn, huh?" Laura mused aloud.

Annie grinned wryly. "You know the type. Prom

Queen, Homecoming Queen and voted most popular girl on campus. All the guys in high school went gaga over her. When Wade returned from college she made herself instantly available by dropping her current fiancé like a hot potato. Not long after Wade and Bobbie Lynn married, while he and his cousins were traveling the rodeo circuit, she started sneaking around on him."

"No wonder Wade swore off women," Laura mused aloud. "Bobbie Lynn obviously has fidelity issues."

"You can say that again! You'd think Bobbie Lynn would've recognized the good deal she had going, but she was never known for her commodity of brains, only her eye-catching looks and seductive wiles. I think she even tried to hit on Wade's cousins, but they have a hard-and-fast rule about remaining loyal to one another," Annie informed her. "Even Quint drew the line and wouldn't budge when Bobbie Lynn practically threw herself at him. No matter what the gossip circulating about Quint being a ladies' man, he does have scruples, so don't let anyone around here tell you differently."

Laura grinned in amusement. "Is there anyone in this town whose background you *don't* know?"

"Nope," Annie replied breezily. "I've lived here all my life. I know who's related to whom and which branch of which family tree juts out from what direction. It helps to understand the dynamics of this podunk town when you're teaching school here. It prevents you from shooting off your mouth and offending someone's shirttail cousins."

Laura must have looked a bit shell-shocked because Annie leaned over to pat her hand consolingly. "Not to worry. I'll be there at school to debrief you when your students troop into your classroom. Of course, my music room is at the opposite end of the hall from the math and computer rooms.'' She grinned playfully. ''We wouldn't want to break your students' concentration while they're calculating square roots, ya know. All that screeching and howling in my classroom would be a distraction. But I can be at your end of the hall in just over a minute if you need me.''

Laura slumped against the back of the vintage vinyl booth. ''Sometimes I still can't believe I actually packed up, moved away from my brothers and have a life of my own now. The next order of business is to convince the superintendent and school board that I can transform all my students into Nobel prize-winning mathematicians... What if I can't?''

Annie chuckled. ''You'll do fine here. What happened to your self-confidence, girlfriend?''

''Wade has been trouncing all over it,'' she muttered.

''Well, he's an idiot if he doesn't know what a great deal he's got in you,'' Annie said loyally.

''Maybe you should tell him that. I don't think he's figured it out by himself.'' Laura shut her mouth when the waitress reappeared to take their order.

When Mildred—according to the plastic name tag pinned on her Pepto-Bismol-pink blouse—scuttled off, Annie leaned forward, all eyes, all ears and profound concentration. ''Okay, what's up with Wade?''

Laura hadn't meant to unload on her friend, but she felt the urge to vent her frustration. ''Well, for starters, he's determined to dislike me. He nearly came unglued when I offered to give him a massage to help him relax. Sheesh, the way he carried on you'd think I possessed the touch of death. He rarely eats in the same room with me and you wouldn't think it'd kill him to say thanks for dinner or for laundering his clothes or cleaning his house every once in a while. In fact, he bites backs the words *please* and *thank you* when they occasionally start to slip out.''

Annie slouched in the booth, nodded her head and said sagely, ''Ah-ha.''

''Ah-ha, what? What's that mean, Ms. I'm-Privy-To-Background-Information-On-Every-Resident-of-Podunk City?'' Laura blew out a frustrated breath. ''See there? What'd I tell you? Wade's bad habit of being flippant and sarcastic is rubbing off on me.''

Annie grinned wryly. ''Jeez, Laura, surely a smart woman like you can figure out what's going on with you and Wade.''

''Well, color me stupid, but I don't get it. All I know is that Bobbie Lynn disillusioned him. He mistrusts those of us of the female persuasion and I have this ridiculous obsession to prove to him that I'm not a blasted thing like her.''

''I'm no psychiatrist, but I'd say he finds you extremely attractive and that worries him so he's trying to build walls to keep you at arm's length.''

''Phfft!'' Laura erupted. ''Your analysis is way off base. He just doesn't want me around, no matter what I try to do to earn his trust and friendship.''

Annie arched a delicate brow. ''And you're trying hard to win his trust and friendship because…?''

Laura squirmed uneasily and sent a prayer of thanks winging heavenward when Mildred returned with their burgers and fries, buying Laura time to collect her thoughts and her composure.

''Because?'' Annie prompted.

She should've known Annie wouldn't drop the subject. The woman, after all, had the tenacity of a pit bull.

When Laura pretended an interest in her basket of

French fries, Annie snapped her fingers, demanding attention. *"Because...?"*

"You're a real pest," Laura grumbled.

"No, I'm not," Annie replied. "I'm your best friend. I care about you and I feel responsible for convincing you to move here to teach. I also feel responsible because I'm the one who lined you up with this summer job when Quint and Vance were asking around town about a temp housekeeper. And if I were having man problems, I'd spill my guts to you so you could make me feel better. But since my boyfriend and I are getting along dandy fine, I don't need a sounding board like you do. So, admit it. You're sort of interested in Wade, aren't you?"

"That's ridiculous." The lie rang false the instant it popped off her tongue. "Besides, I just moved here."

"Uh-huh," Annie said.

Then Laura said, "I'm starting a new job in the school system."

And Annie said, *"Uh*-huh."

Laura said, "I'm not looking to start a relationship."

Then Annie said, "Uh-*huh.*"

"And most certainly not with Count Grouchiness."

"No, of course not," Annie patronized, lips twitching.

"Clam up and eat, Annie," Laura muttered darkly.

Annie threw up her hands, as if held at gunpoint. "Fine, but you need to brush up on your geography so you'll realize this is the state of Oklahoma, not the state of Denial."

"Cute."

"Thanks. I like to think so," she said, fluffing her hair and batting her lashes.

Laura couldn't stay aggravated with Annie. Reluctantly she smiled and Annie smiled back and all was right with the world again. Even if Wade Ryder wanted to drive her away and her awareness of him just kept mush-rooming from one day to the next. She couldn't help thinking that beyond that six-feet-three-inches high and five-feet thick wall Wade had erected around his emotions there was a man she'd really like if he'd open up and share a small part of himself with her.

After their tasty meal, Annie offered to give Laura a tour of the town. She pointed out the tag agency so Laura could get her new driver's license. She introduced her to the pharmacist at the drugstore, the owner of the hardware store, the furniture store and every other business owner in town.

Laura and Annie ended up in the town square where a concrete hoot owl in perpetual flight rose above the gurgling circular fountain. They treated themselves to snow cones from the sidewalk vender and sat down to rest after their hike. Annie's boyfriend stopped by on his way into the courthouse and chatted a few minutes before tending his errands.

The afternoon spent with Annie was exactly what Laura needed to revive her spirits and regroup before purchasing groceries and supplies and heading back to engage in another verbal battle with Wade. Of course, there was the off chance that she'd get lucky and return home to discover that Wade had died of rabies during her absence, she mused with a wicked grin.

4

TIME HAD GOTTEN COMPLETELY away from Laura while gabbing with Annie. With a heavy foot on the accelerator Laura zoomed back to the ranch, knowing she'd probably catch hell from Wade for getting a late start on supper. The man didn't need another excuse to criticize her.

According to Annie, Laura should continue swapping saucy retorts with Wade, just to let him know he couldn't drive her away. Fine, she could do that. It sharpened her wits, after all, but she'd rather call a truce and be herself rather than being *en guarde,* lunging and parrying in verbal swordplay.

Arms laden with groceries, supplies and the potted plants she'd picked up on impulse, Laura struggled through the front door to see Wade lounging on his leather throne, surfing the TV channels. She ignored him, glancing instead at the closed drapes. She'd flung them open wide before leaving the ranch that morning. Now they were shut tightly, enshrouding the room in gloom and doom.

"What happened, Seymour? Did you get lost?" Wade asked. "I knew I should've given you a compass and drawn you a map."

"Oh, sorry, I didn't see you looming there in the shadows," she tossed back flippantly as she juggled the paper sacks and plastic bags in both arms. Four more sacks dangled from her fingertips.

"I distinctly remember asking you not to yank open all the drapes and allow the glaring sunlight in here."

"Right, Count Drac, I forgot that blood-sucking vampires prefer cryptlike darkness," she countered as she headed for the kitchen without glancing in Wade's direction. "Now where'd I put that stake I intended to drive through your heart? It's never around when I need it."

He ignored her taunt. "Why'd you change the furniture in here? I nearly broke my other leg when I rounded the corner, expecting the furniture to be exactly where I set it."

"Well," she said, halting in the middle of the room. "According to feng shui—"

"Who the hell is he? And what does he know about rearranging my ranch house!" he blustered.

"Feng shui is the Chinese philosophy of interior design," she explained.

He let loose with a disgusted snort. Surprise, surprise.

"It's based on the theory that if you change your environment, you can change aspects of your life."

"I liked my life just fine until you got here," he grumped.

"Well, feng shui will make you feel better," she insisted, "because now this room is well balanced and well lighted—or it would be if you'd open the drapes. This room creates and promotes the flow of positive energy to counter your negativity."

His response was another disgruntled snort.

"So, how'd the roundup and branding go today?" she asked.

"Fine. Quint got kicked in the shin while inoculating one of my calves," he reported.

"I'm sure that made your day."

"Damn, Seymour, whaddya do? Have your tongue sharpened while you were in town?" he called after her.

"Ah, you noticed. Glad to know I didn't waste my money."

"Are we eating tonight? Or am I supposed to chew on my fingernails to stave off the hunger pangs?" he asked.

Laura dumped the sacks on the kitchen counter and grinned to herself. She wasn't sure, but the bite in his words didn't seem as sharp as it once was. Now his tone leaned more toward teasing humor. Could it be that Wade actually missed having her around to torment and was actually glad to have her back? Naw, must be her imagination and Annie's ridiculous notion that beneath all that razzing and taunting Wade liked her and was determined not to let it show.

"Supper will be ready at the usual time, Your Majesty," she called to him. "Oh, and before I forget to tell you, I took the liberty of inviting Duff up to the house to dine with me tomorrow night."

"Liberties aren't included in your job description," Wade threw back.

"Too bad. He's going to teach me to play poker, guzzle beer and smoke cigars. He also promised to teach me how to two-step later in the week so Annie and I can go honky-tonkin' Saturday night. She's gonna set me up with a hot date."

"You don't have to shout," Wade muttered as he propped himself against the kitchen wall.

"Sorry, I thought you were still in the living room."

"I wouldn't advise accepting any date Annie Nelson arranges for you. She has lousy taste in men."

Laura paused from sorting and arranging the cold food in the fridge and flung him an annoyed glance. "There was nothing wrong with her taste in men during college.

I met her boyfriend, Mark Childress, this afternoon. I'd give him an eight on a scale of ten.''

"A five would be pushing it," he remarked.

Laura let her appreciative gaze wander over Wade's muscular physique, admiring the way he filled out his shirt and jeans. Annie was right. Wade Ryder oozed sex appeal. He was definitely beefcake material and she'd like to sneak another peek at all the rippling muscle and sinewy flesh concealed beneath his clothes.

"Depends on who you're comparing him to," she said belatedly. Compared to Wade, Mark wouldn't register a three.

Whoa, don't even *start comparing other men to Wade,* she cautioned herself. That implied Wade was the standard measure of excellence.

"What are you looking at, Seymour?" he questioned as he glanced curiously down his torso. "Did I button my shirt improperly?"

Laura snapped her attention back to the interior of the fridge and placed the food on the glass shelves. "Not to worry. You're properly buttoned up, except for your lip and it would require surgery to keep that shut."

"I'm trying to make friendly conversation." He scowled at her and his thick brows flattened menacingly over his eyes.

Friendly? That'd be the day. "Don't strain yourself, Ryder. You have enough injuries already," she snapped.

He held his tongue so long that Laura glanced up to determine the problem. Her breath lodged in her throat when those laserlike green eyes zeroed in on her. His penetrating gaze made a thorough sweep of her knit blouse, denim shorts and the exposed length of her legs. She felt her body burn each place his riveting gaze touched. Was something going on here that she'd missed while she had her head stuck in the fridge? How could they possibly have gone from snappy repartee to this sizzling sensual awareness that leaped back and forth between them like two-twenty volts of electrical current?

One smoldering look from Wade and desire contracted inside her like a coil of fire. She'd never experienced anything remotely like this before.

Laura felt as if time had ground to a halt, as if the looks passing between them were trying to define themselves. Yet, she wasn't sure she could correctly decode the message he was sending because she constantly received mixed signals from him. Nevertheless, she was helpless to restrain the feminine vibes her body bleeped at him. Just what the heck was going on between them? She wished she knew for certain.

Was it hot in here? Suddenly the heat seemed stifling and breathing was a real chore. Her gaze dropped to the sensuous curve of his mouth and Laura was struck by the tormenting realization that she was starving to death for a taste of him. She wondered what it would be like to exchange kisses rather than saucy retorts, wondered how it would feel to be pressed familiarly against that rock-solid body, despite his encumbering cast and sling.

Call her reckless and crazy but she'd really, *really* like to know how it felt to be kissed and held by him. For the sake of curiosity, if nothing else. Oh right, who was she kidding? Her curiosity wasn't the only thing that was dying to find out how well he kissed.

Laura's heart stalled in her chest when Wade pushed away from the wall and took one, then two hobbling steps toward her. Then he halted in his tracks, muttered something to himself and stood there, looking at her as if he was waging some tormenting internal battle. Her heart plummeted to the tiled floor and she felt like whaling him upside the head for refusing to approach her. He just kept staring at her with that exasperating mixture of hungry need and wary caution.

Hoo-kay, if *he* didn't have the gumption to just kiss her and get it over with then she'd have to take the initiative. After all, she'd come to Oklahoma to break old habits, explore her newfound freedom and make her own decisions without her brothers' constant censorship.

Mustering her courage, Laura closed the small distance between them, pushed up on tiptoe and kissed him squarely on the mouth—and felt a blast of heat sweeping through every fiber of her being. Instinctively she pressed closer, craving something more. But Wade didn't hook his right arm around her waist and pull her snugly against him. He didn't even kiss her back—which was a huge disappointment. It didn't do a thing for her self-confidence, either. He just stared at her with those glowing green eyes, as if he wanted to kiss her back but refused to let himself do it. Now she *really* wanted to whale him upside the head!

Determined to blunder through the awkward silence, Laura dropped down on her heels and plastered on a breezy smile to conceal her embarrassment—and there was plenty of that pulsating in her face, she was sure.

"Why'd you do that?" His voice crackled like static and his massive chest expanded with ragged breaths.

"Why didn't *you* do it so I wouldn't have to?" she countered shakily.

Seconds ticked by while she tried to draw a breath that wasn't thick with the tantalizing scent of him. Hoo-boy, how was a woman supposed to extricate herself from such an awkward encounter? She had no idea! Why didn't he say something, damn it? Snippy insults were better than this maddening silence that stretched between them like a rubber band about to snap.

"Well, that answers that," she said lamely.

He didn't so much as blink. His gaze just bored into her. "What was the question?"

Thoroughly exasperated, she swatted him on the chest with the back of her hand. "You're impossible!"

"Then quit," he suggested. His face was such an unreadable mask that she wanted to grab him by his shirt collar and shake the stuffing out of him.

"Not on your life, buster," she erupted. "You can't fire me and I refuse to leave. You're stuck with me!"

"Not necessarily," he begged to differ. "A cleverly arranged murder is still an option."

She smirked at him. "You'd never get away with it. And you know what else?"

"I'm afraid to guess because I'm probably being graded on this, professor. You'll deduct the number of wrong answers from the right ones and I'll end up with a score of zero."

Laura cocked her head and studied him pensively. Was he teasing her with that dry wit that could stir up a cloud of dust? She was pretty sure he *was*. Wow! A real breakthrough!

In a moment of what was surely impulsive insanity, Laura looped her arms around his neck, surged upward and kissed him again. His mouth softened ever so slightly, but she didn't stick around to embarrass herself again, just in case he refused to kiss her back a second time. With a loud smack for her grand finale she broke the kiss, wheeled around and wobbled over to the sink, hoping he'd take his cue and leave so she could splash water on her face and cool off.

While Laura ran the faucets full blast and stared out

the kitchen window Wade pivoted around and hobbled into the living room on one crutch, one broken leg and two unsteady knees that threatened to fold up like lawn chairs. He couldn't breathe normally and sensual awareness echoed through him like feedback to a microphone. He made it to the recliner—barely—before he collapsed.

"Aw, damn," Wade whispered roughly. And that was putting it mildly! He'd watched Laura bend over and poke her head in the fridge and his gaze and attention had been immediately drawn to the swell of her breasts and the alluring curve of her fanny. Desire had shot through him like a lightning bolt.

He'd taken two impulsive steps toward Laura then grabbed onto his self-control with both fists, telling himself that touching her would be a huge mistake because he was afraid to trust the hot, wild sensations she aroused in him and the ravenous hunger he felt for her. He'd been wrong to trust his feelings and desires before and he'd paid dearly, thanks to his ex. But Laura had had the courage to walk right up to him and finish what he'd foolishly started.

Now he wished he didn't know that she tasted like raindrops during a spring shower. He wished he didn't know that the slightest brush of her lush body could make him hard and aching in the time it took to hiccup. He wished he didn't know that he'd never be satisfied *not* tasting her again, *not* touching, *not* being as close to her as two people could get because he was so intensely attracted to her that it was downright unnerving!

"Aw…damn…" he repeated. Another wave of tormenting desire crashed over him and threatened to drown him in forbidden wanting. What the hell was he going to do with that woman when he couldn't fire her, she wouldn't quit and he was starting to like her way too much?

THE NEXT DAY, WADE was still searching for the answer to that question while he lounged in his recliner. He glanced up from the TV when he heard the front door swing open. He inwardly groaned when Laura strolled inside, wearing a wet T-shirt and shorts that clung to her curvaceous body like a coat of paint. Traitorous desire delivered a quick knockout punch as his gaze roamed helplessly over her. Damn it! He'd been sitting here, listing all the reasons he needed to keep his distance from Laura and here she came again, tormenting him to no end. Wanting her, and refusing to do anything about it was wearing him out.

He frowned disapprovingly when he managed to drag his eyes off Laura's shapely body and noticed Frank was at her heels. "What's he doing in the house? He's a cow dog."

Laura reached down to pat Frank's damp head. "I thought you might enjoy having Frank around for company, so Duff and I bathed him and applied some flea and tick medication."

"I don't want him in the house," Wade insisted.

"Sure you do," she contradicted as she crossed the room.

Her wet clothes demanded his attention again and he gritted his teeth against the insane urge to reach out and map the exquisite terrain of her feminine body. Well hell, so much for trying to stifle the desire that looking at her engendered. Arousal was becoming the conditioned response to seeing her. Damnation, he was turning into a basket case!

"Frank, you stay here and visit with Wade while I start

supper," she ordered, then headed for the kitchen. "Duff should be here soon."

"*Ooofff.*" Wade grunted when Frank bounded onto his lap and sat there staring happily at him. Wade sighed in defeat and scratched behind Frank's ear.

The woman was definitely taking over his home and his life, he realized. She dominated his thoughts, too. And lately, most of those thoughts originated below his belt buckle.

When Frank used Wade's crotch as a springboard to bound from the chair, he grimaced uncomfortably. He muttered a salty curse when Frank trotted to the kitchen to rejoin Laura. Damn dog had turned traitor and was getting attached to Laura.

Wade sat there in his chair, wondering how much longer he could hold out against this woman's devastating charms. She'd rearranged his life, left her memory all around his house and she had him wanting her to the extreme. He honestly wondered if the self-control he'd taken for granted for years could fortify him until she was out from underfoot. Wade had the uneasy feeling that one of these days he'd buckle to this inevitable attraction and wind up getting hurt all over again.

Would Laura be as hard on his heart as Bobbie Lynn had been? Wade liked to think not, but he still wasn't sure he wanted to take the risk of caring and finding out for sure.

"NO, NO, NO, YA DON'T CLAMP a cigar between your teeth like that," Duff instructed. "Hold that bad boy like this."

Laura watched her mentor of newly acquired vices bite down on his stogie and then she imitated his technique.

"That's better," Duff said. "Now squint your eyes a

bit and look down at the cards in your hand. Don't
change expression, either. That's a dead giveaway that
you're holding something good.''

Laura conjured up the somber expression that was
Wade's trademark then studied her poker hand. She
glanced at the paper Duff had filled out so she'd know
if a flush beat a straight and where a full house fit in the
winning sequences.

"Now, casually take a sip of beer," Duff told her.
"And slouch in your chair a bit. You look as if you're
ready to pounce. Nonchalance is the name of the game
here.''

Laura draped herself negligently in her chair and took
another sip of beer. It wasn't her beverage of choice, but
in Duff's book of etiquette, poker and beer went together
like peanut butter and jelly.

"Gimme two," Duff requested as he puffed his stogie
and squinted at his hand of cards.

"You bet, slick. The dealer takes one."

While Laura dealt the cards, Wade lingered by the
kitchen door, feeling like an outsider in his own home.
Earlier, while he was eating alone in the living room,
he'd heard Duff and Laura jabbering and laughing and
he'd turned an unbecoming shade of envy green because
he wasn't in there enjoying her company when he really
wanted to be.

Duff, he noticed, had gotten all gussied up to join
Laura at the table for dinner. You'd have thought the old
coot was on a date, considering he'd shaved the stubble
off his face and ironed his striped Western shirt and jeans.

Wade smiled in amusement as he watched Laura em-
ulate Duff's gestures and puff on the cigar she had
clenched between her teeth. Well hell, he just couldn't
take this feeling of isolation another minute. He was go-

ing to limp in there and invite himself into the game. With Duff as a buffer he could share an enjoyable evening with Laura without doing something stupid—like kissing her senseless the way he wanted to.

Laura glanced up when Wade rounded the corner. He barked a laugh when she gave him an one-eyed squint, her poker face intact, her stogie tilted at a jaunty angle. "Better have your ATM card handy if you want to join in this game, ace," she drawled playfully. "This is high stakes, y'know."

Wade's gaze dropped to the stack of pennies on the table then he hobbled over to retrieve what was left of the whiskey he'd poured down his gullet the first night Laura arrived.

"Duff says beer suits poker better," Laura informed him.

"I'm sticking with Daniel's." Wade filled two glasses. "What's up with this need to learn to play poker, Seymour?"

She shrugged casually. "I've led a sheltered life up to this point, so I've decided to broaden my horizons and Duff is helping me. Are you in on this hand, Ryder? Or do you want to sit there and nurse your whiskey?"

"I'm in. What's the game?" Wade awkwardly parked himself in a chair while Duff dealt the hand.

"Seven card stud, stud," Laura replied, grinning playfully around the stogie clamped in her teeth. "Duff's teaching me a variety of games tonight."

"She's beaten me at half of 'em, too," Duff said. "Even for a beginner, this little gal is dang lucky at cards."

Wade took a quick peek at the two cards in the hole, then watched Duff deal four cards face up. He darted a glance at Laura's exposed hand and he nearly choked on his booze. Three aces stared back at him. His accusing gaze swung to Duff who wore a wry grin. The old rascal was cheating. He had to be. He was letting Laura win to ensure she had a good time.

Sure enough, Laura breezed through the first two hands and collected all the pennies. After fifteen minutes of one incredible hand after another, no matter which game Duff suggested, Laura raked in the winnings.

"Go ahead and play without me," she insisted as she snuffed out her stogie. "I left a load of laundry in the dryer and I better remove it before everything wrinkles."

She leaned over to give Duff an affectionate peck on the cheek before she strode off. When Laura kissed Duff, Wade swore the old man died, right there in his chair, and went straight to heaven. Wade glanced over his shoulder, noting the sly smile on Laura's lips—and he realized the woman was far cleverer than he'd given her credit. He'd bet his last penny that she'd purposely invited Duff to the house to treat him to a home-cooked meal and harmless female companionship, before luring in Wade so he could enjoy their company. Since Wade had made it clear he wanted to keep his distance from Laura, she'd ensured that he didn't spend all his evenings alone. Frank, who was sprawled on the living-room floor, catching a few Zs, was another example of her wily strategy.

"That's some woman," Duff murmured as he dealt a hand of seven-card stud. "I can't figure out why you wanted Quint and Vance to think she wasn't doing her job...unless..."

Wade squirmed beneath Duff's gimlet-eyed squint. "Unless what?"

"Unless you're afraid of getting too attached to her," he said perceptively.

"Are we going to play poker or gab?" Wade asked.

"I can do both at once." Duff picked up his cards and gave them a quick look-see. "If I was thirty years younger you wouldn't see me trying to drive that perty little gal away."

"Well, you're not, so act your age and ante up."

Duff chuckled as he flipped a penny toward the center of the table. "Gonna play your hand close to your vest, are you, boy? Okay, fine. You do that. But you need to know that Frank and I are perty attached to that little gal."

No kidding. Wade would've sworn his loyal cow dog would never defect to the enemy camp. They'd worked cattle together for years and Frank often rode shotgun in the pickup when Wade made trips into town. They were best buddies. But it was evident that Frank was allowing a woman to come between them.

"You should see Frank follow at that gal's heels when she ventures outside," Duff went on. "She always takes time to give him a pat on the head or scratch behind his ears. She must've picked up some dog treats in town because I saw her slip one to Frank while she was running water in the cattle tank for me after supper."

Swell, thought Wade. His dog was suffering a bout of puppy love and so was Duff. Quint and Vance thought Laura was the perfect temp help who could do no wrong. The whole world was ganging up on him.

Despite how hard Wade tried not to get emotionally attached, he liked having Laura around. Worse, he'd actually missed her when she'd gone to town and he'd sat there in his chair, ears pricked, listening for the sound of her car zooming down the graveled road.

"You gonna bet or sit there staring into space, boy?" Duff prompted.

"Depends on whether you're going to cheat the way you did while Laura was in the game," Wade flung back.

Duff grinned unrepentantly. "I just wanted to show her a good time during her first experience at poker. So shoot me."

"Don't tempt me." Wade tossed a penny on the table.

Duff snickered as he called the bet. "Maybe you oughta just shoot yourself and put yourself out of your misery. Knowing you, it'd be easier than admitting you actually *like* having that little gal around. And just so you know, I may be old, but I ain't blind. I've seen the way you look at her when you don't think anyone notices, so don't bother denying it."

Wade scowled sourly when Duff laid his winning hand on the table. "Damn, sometimes you just can't win for losing."

Duff gathered up the beer cans and tossed them in the trash. "You've got a win-win situation going here. Don't screw it up, son. Give yourself a chance at happiness."

With that parting advice Duff walked out the back door to return to his cabin. Wade's shoulders slumped. He reached for his whiskey and took a sip, wishing the taste of liquor could curb the thirst that had been tormenting him. He wanted to feel Laura's lush mouth beneath his again, to feel her shapely body brushing against him. But he was afraid he wouldn't be able to stop with a few kisses.

Afraid. There was that word again. The more he thought about it, the more he thought Laura might be right. He *was* afraid. Not of women in general, but afraid of *her*. Afraid his self-control would slip and his suppressed feelings for her would come pouring out. Afraid of this ever-growing attraction. Afraid of the pleasure he derived from being *with* her—and not just in bed. He could've accepted and acknowledged the sexual attraction. It was a given. It was these deeper feelings that really had him worried.

Wade knocked back another drink, shuffled the cards and played solitaire until he was tired enough to hit the sack. But when he retired for the night, he kept picturing Laura smoking a cigar, squinting up at him with a cocky grin, sipping a longneck—in attempt to broaden her horizons.

Wade fell asleep with a grin on his lips.

SATURDAY NIGHT, BORED nearly to death, Wade sat in his recliner, surfing the TV channels and finding not one decent program to watch. When an unexpected knock rattled the front door, Wade glanced sideways. "It's open!"

His curious gaze transformed into a sour scowl when Kevin Shelton, the history teacher, walked inside. Brown hair neatly clipped and styled, Kevin stood there on two good legs, his hands tucked in the pockets of his khaki slacks. His trendy clothes and good looks caused Wade to mutter under his breath. In comparison to Mr. Teacher of the Year, Wade felt like a beat-up old geezer.

"Hi, Wade," Kevin said. "Is Laura ready?"

"Probably not," Wade grumbled. "She's a woman, after all. Isn't it indigenous of the gender to always be late?"

"Hi, Kevin," Laura called out—proving Wade wrong about her punctuality. She emerged from the hall, looking all too seductive in a tight-fitting miniskirt that emphasized the length and feminine curve of her legs and thighs.

"Well, isn't this cute?" Wade said under his breath.

"Here's Ken and Barbie, decked out for a night on the town."

He stifled the feelings of possessiveness that roiled through him. He didn't want Laura to go out with Kevin, but he had no right whatsoever to object. "You better have her home early," Wade demanded before he could stop himself.

Laura's sculpted brows elevated in surprise as she glanced over her shoulder to stare curiously at Wade.

"Sure thing," Kevin said, smiling awkwardly.

"She punches the clock at seven sharp in the morning. I don't want her dragging butt when there's work to do." God, he sounded like a grumpy idiot. Jealousy was gnawing at his male pride and there wasn't a damn thing he could do about it.

"Not to worry, boss." Laura slung the strap of her purse over her shoulder, causing the clingy fabric of her knit top to strain against her breasts. Wade glowered when he noticed Kevin's attention had dipped to her bosom. "My duties won't suffer, you can count on it," she assured him.

Wade crooked his finger at her, summoning her to him. When Laura walked toward him, his male hormones started bouncing around like a pinball. He willfully ignored the drastic effect she had on him.

"What do you know about this guy?" Wade asked quietly.

"Not much, but Annie likes him," Laura reported.

"Then maybe Annie should date him," Wade muttered. "For all we know he might be the modern version of the Boston Strangler and Jack the Ripper rolled into one."

Laura snickered. "That should make you happy. If he murders me and dumps me in the nearest river you'll be rid of me without dirtying your hands with the dastardly deed.''

''Hadn't thought of it that way,'' he said, just so she wouldn't get the idea that he cared what happened to her.

''Anything else, boss?'' she asked when she noticed Kevin had shifted impatiently from one well-shod foot to the other.

''Yeah, if he drinks, *you* drive home,'' he instructed. ''He's probably a lush in hiding.'' He shot Kevin a black look. ''And if he gets fresh, let me know and I'll send my cousins over to kick his preppy butt.''

She grinned outrageously. ''Maybe I want him to get fresh. Maybe I'm looking for a little action. Ever think of that? It's my life, you know, and I'm broadening all my horizons.''

Wade went into a slow burn. Envy and jealousy ate at him like battery acid. ''If you aren't home by midnight I'm coming to find you, broken leg or not. Got it?'' He flashed Kevin another thunderous glare for good measure. If Mr. Teacher of the Year wasn't on his best behavior, Wade wanted it understood that there'd be hell to pay. When Kevin squirmed beneath the piercing stare, Wade was pretty sure he'd gotten his silent message across.

''Just stay on guard, Seymour,'' Wade cautioned. ''You've broadened your horizons enough for the week.''

''Your concern is touching,'' she said, grinning. ''That's really sweet of you, Ryder.''

''I'm anything but sweet and you know it,'' he grumbled before she sauntered over to join her handsome date.

When the door closed behind them Wade swore ripely. He knew Kevin Shelton was closer to Laura's age and more her type, but that didn't stop him from wishing that blond knockout was on *his* arm tonight.

Frustrated, Wade switched to the Discovery channel to watch the next exciting installment on baboons that got liquored up on fermented fruit in the jungles and awoke with hellish hangovers.

5

WADE HOBBLED DOWN THE HALL to complain about the fact that it had been two days and Laura still hadn't moved the furniture back to its normal arrangement. Also, she'd flung the drapes open wide—again—after Duff had driven him into town for a doctor's appointment and a haircut. Even with the new walking cast the physician had wrapped around his leg and the lack of the sling on his arm, Wade had nearly tripped and fallen as he rounded the corner to the kitchen—again. He'd conked his head on that blasted hanging plant Laura had placed near the front door on the porch. She'd spaded up the unattended garden that encircled the front porch, planted scads of colorful flowers that attracted butterflies and humming birds. You couldn't walk outside without getting slapped in the face with sweet scents or winged insects.

Damn it, she was turning his house into a jungle and decorating the place in a girlie manner. There were baskets of potpourri and scented candles taking up space on the end tables and coffee table. The house smelled…well, sissified. It offended his masculinity. If this kept up he wouldn't recognize the place. The woman had definitely gone too far! He had to put a stop to it.

Already, he barely recognized Frank! Now that Laura had allowed the cow dog in the house—against his orders, he might add!—the canine rubbed up against his leg, shoved his snout under Wade's hand and demanded to be petted. The dog was getting soft, lounging around the house instead of chasing rabbits, possums and raccoons that tried to overrun the place. Frank had been perfectly satisfied with his lot in life as a cow dog until Laura started fawning and fussing over him, feeding him doggie treats and taking him with her on long evening walks and horseback rides. Another month of this and Frank wouldn't be worth shooting!

As for Duff, he was so besotted with "that little gal" that he'd yakkety-yakked all the way to Hoot's Roost and back. He'd reported that Laura had been showing up on his doorstep with covered plates of roast beef, fried chicken and gravy, and stayed to polish her poker skills or practice the two-step. Wade, however, sat alone on his leather recliner, watching the boob tube and listing the reasons he should keep his distance from that woman.

Then, of course, there were Quint and Vance whose recent prank involved leaving cutout hearts made of red construction paper on the pickup seat. Earlier in the week Vance had disguised his voice and phoned to tell Wade that he'd won an all-expense-paid honeymoon vacation to the Bahamas. Wade scowled. His life was out of control and it was Laura's fault.

Wade pulled up short in the hall when he heard Laura's cell phone ring while she was putting away his laundry.

"Hello, handsome," she said cheerily. "How've you been?"

Handsome? Who the hell was she talking to this time? He'd heard Laura answer her phone the previous day with: "Hi, gorgeous? How are you, Jerret?" How many men did this bombshell keep on a string at one time?

"My job is going fine. I figured you'd call as soon as you got my postcard from my new residence in

Oklahoma,'' she said, then paused when the man—obviously—on the other end of the line inserted a comment. ''Who? Wade Ryder? The old rancher I'm working for? Are you kidding?''

Old? Wade winced. She thought he was *old?* The eight years separating them wasn't so much, was it? To hear her talk, Wade was fast approaching his golden years.

''No, he isn't much trouble,'' Laura insisted. ''I stir up oatmeal so he can gum it for breakfast. For lunch I open a can of soup, mash it up and serve it to him. I put a bib around his neck so he doesn't dribble all over his clothes.''

Gum it? Wear a bib? Hell! Wade smoldered in offended dignity. Obviously she didn't want her boyfriend to fret about male competition.

''Don't be absurd, Davie. The man has a broken leg, a sprained wrist and bruised ribs. He can't chase me around the kitchen and he certainly couldn't catch me. I'm perfectly safe. Stop stewing… So how are things in Denver?''

No doubt Laura had left more than one lover behind in Colorado. Then, of course, there was that ''hot date'' Laura had accepted with Kevin Shelton and met up with Annie Nelson and her twerp boyfriend on Saturday night. Wade was thankful he hadn't allowed himself to succumb to the need to kiss Laura back. It sounded as if she delighted in playing the field and keeping all her options open…just like Bobbie Lynn.

The thought caused Wade's brow to pucker in annoyance. His instincts were right on target. He'd known this situation with Laura had Waterloo written all over it from the beginning. It was a damn good thing he'd kept his distance, even if his physical attraction to her was driving him nuts.

"Of course, I'll come back to Denver before I start teaching in the fall," Laura assured the caller, then paused to listen a moment. "I already told you I'm not falling for this old fogy rancher. He's a grouch, among other things, so stop worrying about me, will you?"

Wade grimaced. If Laura thought he was an old coot and big grump, why had she kissed him that day in the kitchen? He'd thought there'd been some kind of connection between them. Something like, oh, say, mutual attraction. Apparently she'd just been toying with him.

Wade was still standing in the hall, simmering in irritation when Laura said, "I love you, too, Davie," then disconnected. Before Wade could regain his composure and step around the corner her phone rang again. Man, she had men lined up like jets on a runway, didn't she?

"Hi, Everett. I've been expecting your call. How was your trip?... Yes, Mr. Ryder is doing better." She sighed audibly in response to whatever lover boy Everett had to say. "Will you stop freaking out? Nothing is going on here. Mr. Ryder doesn't even like me so you can quit thinking I'm being mauled on a regular basis."

Obviously Everett asked for a description of Wade because Laura said, "Oh, he's a shriveled-looking old guy with ill-fitting dentures and a cast on one leg. He went to the doctor for a checkup, so he no longer has the sling on his arm, just a bandage on his sprained wrist. He wears faded overalls, has a patch over one eye from cataract surgery and his steel-wool-gray hair stands out every which way from his head. Are you satisfied now that nothing is going on between us?"

Wade gnashed his teeth until he nearly ground off the enamel. Laura was painting quite an unattractive picture of him so her boyfriend wouldn't be jealous. Of course, Dear Everett probably had no idea that he was her third caller in two days and that she'd painted the town red with the high school history teacher.

"I love you, too, Everett," she murmured then hung up.

Wade gathered a full head of steam, prepared to light into Laura for the furniture arrangement, candles, pot-pourri and frothy green plants that littered the house and the front and back porches. And he couldn't forget those uncomplimentary descriptions of him. He didn't even make it into the room before that blasted cell phone rang again. Hell, he was going to have to make an appointment to bite her head off.

"Hi, Michael. I've been expecting your call," she enthused. "I miss you, too.... Oh, God, you didn't!"

Wade waited expectantly, wondering what Dear Michael had done that provoked her disapproval.

"I can't believe you did that!" she huffed. "Of course, Wade Ryder doesn't have a criminal record. He's a rancher not a bank robber."

Wade's eyes popped. This boyfriend was so paranoid that he had Wade checked out? Man, talk about thorough, suspicious and excessively jealous!

"Well, that must've been a typo," Laura said into the phone. "He's not thirty-three. He's eighty-three. He wears hearing aids and I have to yell so he can understand what I'm saying to him. He has no hair, wears eyeglasses as thick as ice cubes and has very few teeth. His favorite friend in the whole world is his dog. Now, do you really think I'm going to have romantic notions about the man?... I'm perfectly safe here and I'll be back in Colorado for a week before the fall session of school starts. In the meantime, you need to get a grip, Michael. I'm not falling in love with Wade Ryder so you can calm down and relax."

Wade didn't wait for Laura to disconnect because he figured he'd have to barge in before another incoming call demanded her attention. The moment Laura realized he'd been standing in the hall, eavesdropping on her conversations, her face turned a fascinating shade of guilty-as-hell red. His condemning gaze locked on her and he didn't let her off the hook when she flashed him a blinding smile.

"Bald? Toothless? Gums his food?" Wade gritted out.

Her chin came up and she stared defiantly at him. "You have no room to complain, Ryder. Duff said that you told Vance and Quint that I can't cook, don't clean and that I sleep until nine, at which time you wake me up to fix your meal."

"Well, that's different," he muttered.

"How are your white lies different from mine?" she asked, arching a challenging brow.

"I'm trying to get rid of you since you won't quit."

"And I'm trying to reassure Michael, David, Everett and Jerret that nothing is going on between us so they'll stop worrying about me."

"Just how many lovers do you usually keep on a fishing stringer at a time?" he asked brusquely.

"None," she replied just as brusquely.

"Oh, really? Then what was that 'Hi, handsome' and 'Hello, gorgeous' all about?" he challenged.

Laura spun around to stuff Wade's clean briefs in the dresser drawer. "I have four overprotective brothers who happen to be every bit as handsome as you are—"

Laura slammed her mouth shut and darted him an embarrassed glance. She hadn't intended to let her tongue loose without first engaging her brain. Wade stared at her, flashing a rare smile, undoubtedly gloating over her unintentional compliment. As if he didn't already know he was drop-dead handsome, the jerk.

"You think I'm handsome?" he asked. "Without hair or teeth? Wearing overalls and listening to you yell at me because I'm hard of hearing? I gotta tell ya, Seymour, with you it's hard to separate the lies from the truth. So what *is* the truth? Were those your boyfriends or your brothers?"

Laura shoved the dresser drawer shut with her hip and stamped over to the walk-in closet to hang up his chambray shirts. "They are my older brothers. My mom died when I was six and I lost Dad when I was twelve. My brothers taught me to work, but when it comes to friendships and relationships they watch over me like mother hens, because my dad made them promise to take care of me. I can't even turn around without one of my brothers looking over my shoulder, checking on me, telling me what to do and how to do it."

"So you packed up and moved to Hoot's Roost and you're bustin' loose in Oklahoma with your newfound liberation," he presumed. "You're trying your hand at poker, beer and cigars because your brothers aren't around to advise you against it?"

"Precisely." Laura strode from the closet to pluck up two pairs of jeans that had the left leg whacked off at the knee to accommodate Wade's cast. "My brothers are afraid I'll fall for some jerk who doesn't deserve me while they aren't around to screen my dates and do background checks. My mistake was actually giving them your name. I should've lied about that, too, so Michael couldn't run your criminal record." She glanced at him sweetly. "But it's nice to know you aren't a convicted rapist or murderer."

"Just a grouch," he remarked, smiling grudgingly.

"Right, Mr. McGrump, so what do you want for lunch?"

"Fried crow, maybe," he said. "I guess you aren't some floozy who toys with men."

Laura nearly fell over when Wade smiled at her again. This was a genuine, good-natured, peace-treaty smile and it made her weak in the knees. Her heart somersaulted around her chest, making it difficult to breathe normally.

Gone was that harsh expression Wade usually tossed at her when he tried to push her away—emotionally speaking. He didn't look as defensive as usual, either. She could feel the same wave of internal heat coursing through her that assailed her that day during The Kiss In The Kitchen Incident.

She wasn't going to do *that* again, she promised herself. There wouldn't be another one-sided kiss with Wade Ryder. She'd embarrassed herself plenty that day.

He just stared at her, the way he had that day in the kitchen and Laura had learned better than to let electrified silence stretch between them because her feminine imagination ran wild. "Did you want something else, besides grilling me about those phone calls?"

"Yeah, I need to do something I forgot to do the other day," he said as he limped deliberately toward her.

Laura hovered by the closet door, unsure of his intentions, unsure if she was going to survive her erratic heartbeat that was pounding against her ribs like a nail gun. "What did you forget to do?" she chirped.

"This."

And then he bent forward and kissed her, *really* kissed her. His mouth was like liquid heat on hers. A soundless purr rolled through her body and she went up in flames. His right arm curled around her waist, towing her gently against that incredibly lean, muscled body. When her lips parted involuntarily to grab a quick breath, he deepened the kiss, plunging his tongue into her mouth to devour her.

After that, Laura couldn't remember why breathing was necessary. She was surviving quite nicely on the heady sensations that spun through her body.

The musky scent of his cologne infiltrated her senses. His splayed hand pressed against the small of her back, guiding her forward until she could feel his arousal. Indescribable pleasure ricocheted through her. Her senses were so saturated with the feel, the scent and the taste of him that she responded by kissing him with all she had in her.

Man, oh man! When Wade Ryder dropped that grouchy attitude and got down to the serious business of kissing a woman he did it up right. Oh sure, Laura had been kissed before, but never so expertly, so hungrily. He taught her things she'd never known about kissing. And, never in her experiences with the men that her brother's screened and approved for her dates had she heard bells clanging in her head and seen stars explode behind her closed eyelids.

Somehow or another her arms became anchored around his neck and she was straining closer, arching against him, aching for more—and he provided. He curled his arm around her shoulders and angled her sideways, providing him with better access to her mouth. His free hand glided over her waist and drifted higher to cover the swell of her breast.

A multitude of cravings blossomed inside her. Laura moaned in pleasure as he brushed his thumb over the fabric that covered her taut nipple. The sensations he aroused in her exploded and burned a searing path to the core of her body. She clung to him like a drowning swim-

mer as the whirlpool of swirling passion towed her under.
She was swallowed alive by the overwhelming need to
taste him, to feel him, to mold herself shamelessly against
him until she couldn't tell where her pulsing body ended
and his began....

"Well, well, what do we have here?"

The sound of Vance Ryder's amused voice caused
Laura to lurch back hastily. She stumbled over Wade's
cast. Wade, who was trying to untangle himself just as
quickly, tripped over her feet. They both teetered off balance. Wade tried to brace himself against the closet
door—which banged against the wall—while simultaneously reaching out to offer Laura support.

She saw his hand groping for her in midair as he stumbled forward in futile attempt to catch her before she fell.
Helplessly she nosedived downward. With a shriek of
alarm, she thrust out her arms and barely caught herself
before she slammed her head on the floor. All that saved
her from being crushed by the two-hundred-plus pounds
of Wade's powerful body was Vance's and Quint's agile
lunge to upright him.

"What are you two doing here?" Wade growled as his
cousins propped him against the wall. "Don't you ever
knock, damn it?"

"We did knock," Quint replied, grinning devilishly.
"I guess you were just too busy to hear us." He reached
down to hoist Laura to her feet. "You okay, honey?"

"Her name isn't honey," Wade snapped.

Blushing profusely, Laura glanced at Wade who reminded her of a Doberman in attack mode. She was more
than a little startled that he'd leaped so quickly to her
defense against Quint's careless endearment. Wade's
ruddy-colored face indicated that he was as embarrassed

as she was. Quint and Vance, however, appeared to be enjoying themselves immensely.

"We stopped by to see how you two were getting along and to hear what the doctor had to say," Vance said, making no attempt to contain his snickers.

"Obviously Laura hasn't been neglecting you." Quint teased, then hurried on when Wade bared his teeth and snarled. "The house is clean, I noticed. The kitchen is spotless and I just *love* what you've done with the furniture arrangement in the living room."

Wade flashed Quint a menacing glare. "Since when are you into interior decorating?"

"Me? I'm into all things domestic, cuz," he said with an effeminate flick of his wrist. "I'm thinking of hiring my own housekeeper so I can get some…of those scented candles and that dried whatever-you-call-it."

"Potpourri," Wade informed him, then scowled.

"Right. Potpourri." Quint's broad shoulders shook in attempt to restrain howls of laughter. "What scent is that stuff? Hot-to-trot spiced apple?"

Wade's fist curled as he shook loose from Vance's supportive grasp. "You guys are dead meat, as soon as I can throw punches at you without reinjuring myself."

"So, what's the good word from the doctor?" Vance questioned, undaunted by the threat. He glanced pointedly at the walking cast and noted the missing arm sling. "He must've lifted a few restrictions and given permission for you to add a few more physical activities to your day, huh?"

Wade's temper hit the end of its tether. "Get out!"

His booming voice had no effect on his evil cousins, he noted. They just cackled in amusement. Most definitely death by torture, he decided spitefully. He'd rip out his cousins' vital organs, dip their bodies in boiling oil, string them upside down in Death Valley and leave them to the buzzards.

It was bad enough that Vance and Quint were razzing him, but Wade refused to allow Laura to suffer another nanosecond of embarrassment. As it was, a blush was all over her like a bad rash. He hitched his thumb toward the door, giving her an out, and realized belatedly that it'd been a long time since he'd wanted to protect a woman from anything.

"Could you get us some cool ones, please, Seymour? My cousins and I need to have a private powwow here."

She made tracks, leaving Wade to face his cousins alone. "What do you morons want, besides to harass me unmercifully?"

Quint, amber eyes twinkling, tried to bite back another grin—and failed miserably. "What I *want* is what you were getting when we interrupted, but we just came by to tell you that cattle prices are up and we're going to haul a semi load of livestock to the stockyards tomorrow. We've already separated your calves so it won't be any big deal to swing by here and take a load to town if you're ready to sell."

"Fine, thanks," Wade mumbled.

For several minutes Quint and Vance managed to talk business and discuss arrangements to swath hay in one of Wade's alfalfa meadows. When Laura returned with three chilled beers, Quint and Vance managed to show a little respect and didn't torment her—much. For that Wade was grateful.

Every protective instinct he possessed, ones he hadn't bothered to employ in years, had gone to point the moment his cousins walked in to see Wade practically giving Laura a tonsillectomy. It was bad enough for his cousins to see him hot and bothered, when he'd only intended to give Laura a hasty kiss—and why he'd impulsively decided to do that didn't bear thinking about! Whatever it was that was going on between Laura and him—and kept them lip-locked for several incredibly intense moments—Wade didn't want his cousins meddling in it.

Maybe he'd kissed her because he'd overheard her tell her brothers that he disliked her and he wanted to prove to her that wasn't quite true. Maybe he'd just been simmering like a Crock-Pot since that Kiss in the Kitchen and he wanted to vent the bottled needs that were bubbling through him. And maybe he was hooked on Laura and simply couldn't control the need any longer. Worst case scenario, Wade mused.

Wade walked his cousins to the front door then closed it behind them to ensure privacy. He turned to the two men. "Okay, here's the rules," Wade said in a no-nonsense tone. "You juveniles can give me hell like you always do, but lay off Laura. Got it?"

"Damn, cuz, you're sure sensitive and protective all of a sudden," Vance observed. "Wonder what that means?"

"It means Laura is too classy to put up with your devilish taunts," Wade said bluntly. "I just found out that she has four overprotective brothers who check up on her like parole officers. If you torment Laura I'll sic her brothers on you, then work you over myself when I feel better."

"Sheesh, it's getting to where a guy can't have a bit of fun around you anymore," Quint joked. "You need to lighten up before Vance and I get to thinking you're in love and it's making you hard to live with."

"I am not in love," Wade denied vehemently.

"Okay, in lust then," Vance clarified, a devilish glint

in his dark eyes. "Maybe I should call Gage's emergency paging service to let him know. I'm sure he'll want to make arrangements to come to the States for your wedding."

"There isn't going to be a wedding," Wade said with a savage snarl. "You can write that down in stone."

"You and Laura are just going to live in sin?" Quint asked in feigned shock. "You and the schoolmarm? That can't be good for her reputation."

Wade's good arm shot toward the pickup and he flashed his cousins his best bad-ass expression. "Beat it, you yahoos."

Quint held up his hands in mock supplication. "Sure, Wade, just simmer down. Call us if you need us to pick up supplies. You know, like...oh, say...a lifetime supply of condoms...or whip cream to slather—"

Growling, Wade gave Quint a shove. Quint collided with Vance who grabbed the supporting post on the porch before he cartwheeled down the steps. "I'm going to get the shotgun so you better be gone when I get back," Wade threatened gruffly.

His evil cousins, sharing guffaws at Wade's expense, sauntered away. Wade lurched around—and banged his head on the hanging pot of geraniums. The basket swung crazily then whacked him on the skull a second time.

"Damn it, Seymour!" he bellowed as he stalked into the house. "Move that cursed pot of flowers before it gives me a concussion!"

SINCE WADE HAD BEEN DISTANT and remote the past couple of days—after they'd been caught kissing in the bedroom—Laura was anxious to be out of the house. Wade was determined to ignore the incident and Laura didn't dare bring it up. What could she say? He obviously regretted his impulsiveness and chose to pretend it never happened—though she'd replayed those steamy, mind-jarring kisses and caresses about a gazillion times.

Since Wade hadn't wanted to come within ten feet of her lately, she'd given him a wide berth and looked up Duff and Frank when she felt the need for companionship. Annie had called to see if she wanted to come by her house to watch a rented movie, but Laura had declined. She knew Annie had her hands full caring for her invalid father, and probably needed female company as a change of pace. Laura had promised to drop by later in the week. But tonight she needed to take a horseback ride and be alone with her thoughts.

"Saddled and ready," Duff announced when Laura entered the barn. "Sure you don't want company, hon?"

Laura smiled warmly at Duff, but shook her head. "After the evening riding lessons you've given me I should be able to manage on my own." She took the reins and led the good-natured mare outside. "I'd appreciate it if you'd stop in to check on Wade. He's been a little cranky the past few days."

"A *little* cranky?" Duff snorted. "If I wasn't so thick skinned I would've quit a week ago. I oughta call his parents, uncles and aunts and tell 'em to come straighten him out."

His parents? Wade hadn't mentioned them, although Laura had seen a few family pictures in his bedroom. Since he hadn't volunteered information she hadn't asked. Of course, he'd only been communicating with her in monosyllables lately and he hadn't bothered with details like parents.

"Where are Wade's parents?" she asked, curious about Wade's background.

"All the Ryder brothers decided to retire from ranching about the same time,'' Duff explained as he wandered over to refill the water tank for the livestock. ''The whole bunch of them were making good money off the oil wells drilled on the ranches so they put their heads together and came up with the idea to deed their ranches to their sons. They all moved to south Texas to one of those fancy retirement villages.''

''They must be a close-knit family,'' she mused aloud.

''Yup,'' Duff replied. ''I'm a carryover from their ranching heydays and I got to know all of them real well. Since they get along grandly they took up golf and tennis and go off on sightseeing tours together. But they return to Hoot's Roost for extended holidays. I guess they wanted their only sons to have the chance to live their own lives without outside interference from the older generation ranchers.''

Laura smiled, wondering what that would be like to have an understanding family that recognized the need for individual independence. She doubted her brothers would ever realize she'd grown up and that she wanted to make her own way in the world. She suspected that in their minds, at least, she'd always be a vulnerable teenager in need of guidance.

''So, Wade is the only cousin who's ever been married?'' she asked as she stuffed her boot into the stirrup and pulled herself onto the saddle.

''Yup, the other three don't seem to be in any hurry to fall into the same snake pit Wade stumbled into.'' Duff scowled distastefully. ''His ex-wife was something else—and then some.''

So Laura had heard from Annie. No wonder Wade wasn't interested in getting serious about a woman. He'd been soured on marriage—for life.

''Now, me, I married two good women,'' Duff commented. "Lost 'em both." He smiled fondly, momentarily lost in memories, then glanced up and winked at Laura. "But now that I've got you around, I don't feel so lonely anymore."

"Thanks, Duff. You are just the sweetest man." Laura leaned down to plant a quick kiss on his cheek and accidentally knocked his Resistol hat off his head.

"Go on now, gal." Duff swooped down to grab his hat. "Be back before dark and take Frank with you. Don't worry about Wade. I'll visit with him until he tells me to skedaddle."

Serenaded by hoot owls, cicadas and quail, Laura trotted off with Frank on her heels. She dug a dog biscuit from the pocket of her jeans and tossed it to Frank then watched him gobble it up in two bites.

Ah, she could get used to this way of life, she mused contentedly. For the first time—ever—she was free to ride off into the sunset without her brothers double-checking her estimated time of arrival. She loved being away from the hustle and bustle of the city. She liked galloping over the rolling hills and being alone with her private thoughts. Country life suited her perfectly. If not for her undeniable attraction to Wade, who tried to avoid her more often than not, she'd have the world by the tail—

Laura's thoughts scattered like buckshot when the mare abruptly reared up and Frank started to bark his head off. Laura barely had time to register the sight of the coiled snake that Frank pounced at before the mare took off like a cannonball. Heart pounding, Laura roped her arms around the horse's neck and held on for dear life. Her riding skills, thanks to Duff, were passable, but she had grave concerns about her ability to stay in the saddle when the mare plunged through the underbrush, gathered her hindquarters and took a flying leap over the creek. A low hanging tree limb scraped off Laura in mid-leap. She landed with a squawk and a *kersplat.*

Well, so much for a pleasure ride, Laura mused as she floundered to gain her feet in the waist-deep water. Suddenly she had a respectful appreciation for the Ryder cousins who'd probably made a few crash landings during their rodeo heydays.

Laura sloshed ashore. The thunder of hooves indicated the mare had circled back to the barn, leaving Laura afoot. She inwardly groaned as she approached the house. Just her luck that Wade was lounging on the front porch in a lawn chair. Even at a distance she could see the teasing grin that crinkled his face. Here was his big chance to razz her. She knew he couldn't pass it up.

"Most folks go horseback riding *then* shower," Wade remarked as she strode toward him, her boots squishing. "Figured a city slicker like you would get it ass-backward."

When she was all set to snap at him for tormenting her, he looked her up and down and said, "Are you okay, Seymour?"

The hint of concern in his voice got to her. He might not want her underfoot, but he did care about her—in his own way.

"Yeah, I'm okay." She plucked at the T-shirt and jeans that clung to her body. "Bruised my pride, is all."

His eyes darkened and he looked the other way. "Shed those boots so you don't leave tracks on the carpet," he said gruffly. "My housekeeper's a clean freak, ya know."

"I better unsaddle the mare first," she said, pivoting on her muddy boot heels.

"I'll take care of the horse," he volunteered as he rose to his feet. "Go inside and shower."

"No, I'll do it," she insisted. "You have a broken leg and I saw Duff walking back into his cabin when I came through the underbrush by the creek."

When she started down the steps he grabbed her arm. She noticed his gaze had dropped to her clingy shirt, but he quickly jerked his eyes back to her face. "Duff already talked my good leg off so I sent him home. I'll take care of the horse. I've ridden and handled livestock with broken bones and sprains lots of times before. Now go."

She stared up at his chiseled mouth, impulsively wanting to kiss him for his kindness and his concern. To her surprise, he bent down and kissed her squarely on the mouth.

"You look too damned good all wet," he muttered as he stepped back. "Now get out of my face and hit the showers."

When he turned and limped away, Laura smiled to herself. For all his bluster and teasing she had the inescapable feeling that Wade liked her and that he, like she, couldn't resist the occasional kiss. The only difference was that *she* didn't put up resistance to the attraction. But *he* did.

Laura decided, on her way to the shower, that falling off a horse and landing in the creek was worth it if the evening ended with one of Wade's sensuous kisses.

6

AFTER SEEING LAURA in those soggy clothes that displayed her curvaceous figure, and that impulsive kiss he'd given her, Wade spent a long frustrating night of dodging one erotic fantasy sequence after another. He suffered through a nearly intolerable cold bath to get his raging hormones under control then kerplopped in his recliner. It was barely seven o'clock in the morning and already he could use a nap.

He could control his unruly needs until Laura left, he told himself resolutely. He could hold out until his leg healed. He could deal with the flower vases that filled the room with tantalizing scents, the candles that triggered titillating images of making love by the light of flickering flames. He could endure the furniture arrangements that signified she'd touched his home, his life. But having Laura so tormentingly close on a daily basis left him frustrated by desire. He was about ready to pull out his hair by the roots.

After the doctor had removed the splint, his left wrist had healed to the point that he could move the injured joint without yowling in pain. If not for this cast that still made bathing and walking an adventure he'd feel about half normal.

Wade's thoughts trailed off when an unidentified thump prompted him to twist sideways in his chair. He frowned in concern when he saw Laura weave unsteadily from one side of the hall to the other and heard her whimpering moan. Her blouse was inside out and her shorts were twisted sideways. Her face was as white as salt and the blond hair she usually corralled at her nape with some sort of elastic thingamabob was in a tangle around her shoulders and tumbled down her back. If he didn't know better he'd swear she was suffering the hangover from hell. But he knew she hadn't rendezvoused with Duff last night to practice the intricacies of smoking stogies, guzzling beer and learning to cheat at poker.

Wade levered himself from the recliner to follow Laura as she staggered along the living room wall, bracing her arm for support. "What's wrong with you?" he asked, concerned.

"Nothing." She squinted at him through bloodshot eyes.

She wobbled into the kitchen to drag a skillet from the lower cabinet. She groaned when the stainless-steel skillet clanked against another pot. "Oh, God..." she gasped, then grabbed the side of her head as if it was about to explode.

"Gimme that skillet, Seymour," he ordered, then lowered his voice when he saw her wince as if he'd yelled directly in her ear. "I'll fix my own breakfast. Go back to bed."

"No." Partially doubled over, Laura braced her trembling body with a stiff arm against the edge of the stove. Grimly she set the skillet on the burner. "I'm going to fix your breakfast, same as I do every morning. You aren't going to have one complaint that I'm not taking proper care of you."

"I hate to break the news to you, darlin', but you don't look like you can take care of *yourself*," he pointed out.

"Doesn't matter," she whimpered. "I won't let you down."

Wade's brows furrowed worriedly when he noticed her lips had turned a pale shade of blue and beads of perspiration formed a watery mustache on her upper lip. "Wha'd you drink last night before you went to bed? The poison meant for me?"

"Iced tea," she whimpered then caught herself when she swayed dizzily. "Please close the blinds. The sunlight is boring holes in my skull."

Obviously she was extremely sensitive to light and sound, he noted. The poor woman could barely keep her feet beneath her and her peaked skin was turning an alarming shade of green. "Hey, Seymour, all teasing and tormenting aside, you better go lie down before you fall down."

"No, I can do this." Determinedly she shuffled over to the fridge to grab a slab of bacon and three eggs. She pivoted clumsily and bumped her hand on the edge of the counter. Egg yolks plopped to the floor. "Oh, God," she groaned then staggered. "Go 'way, I think I'm gonna be sick—"

When she gagged and her knees buckled beneath her, Wade really got alarmed. He lunged forward to steady her and she swayed against him. He wrapped his arm around her and pressed her clammy body against his to maintain her balance—and his.

"I have to clean up the mess," she chirped.

"Leave the mess. We better call the doctor," Wade said.

"I'm okay," she tried to assure him while shiny tears streamed down her bloodless cheeks and her body trembled like tremors of an earthquake.

"Damn it, woman, if this is what you look like when

you're okay, I'd hate to see you when you're really sick. You're officially off the clock. I'm putting you in bed and you're going to stay there," he commanded.

Her breath came out in uneven hitches, as if she were fighting to keep from hurling all over them both. "Bathroom," she wheezed sickly.

Wade took off as fast as he could move on his bum leg. He banged his tender wrist against the wall when he turned a short corner. Laura stumbled into him, then just sort of wilted at his feet before he could prop her up. When her eyes rolled back in her head Wade jerked her up and held on tight.

"Hey, stay with me, Seymour. One invalid around here is enough."

With effort, Wade managed to maneuver Laura into the bathroom. She dropped to her knees and bowed humbly to the porcelain god. Feeling utterly helpless, and overcome with sympathy, Wade listened to her retch, swear and retch some more.

"Please go 'way," she panted as she crawled on all fours toward the bathtub. "Don' wan' you t' see me li' this."

"I'm not leaving," he insisted. "What can I do to make you feel better? Tell me and I'll do it."

Sluggishly Laura draped herself over the edge of the tub to pound the drain stopper into place. Then she turned on both faucets full blast. "Crackers." She raked her disheveled hair from her waxen face then propped herself heavily against the wall to stare vacantly at him. "7UP."

Wade cast her a worried glance, afraid to leave her alone for fear she'd keel over into the tub, take on as much water as the *Titanic* and drown while he wasn't here to save her. The tears that slid down her pale cheeks like twin rivers were really getting to him. She looked so

utterly miserable and nauseous that he felt the urge to
gather her in his arms and offer comfort and compassion.

"Don't get in the tub until I get back," he ordered as
he wheeled toward the door.

"'Kay," she mumbled then propped her head against
the tiled wall.

Wade moved as fast as he could down the hall, bracing
both arms on the walls to ensure he didn't stumble. Hurriedly he grabbed the crackers off the shelf and accidentally knocked the other items from the cabinet. Boxes and
jars avalanched alphabetically onto the counter then
plopped on the floor. He left the mess where it was and
scrounged in the pantry for the can of 7UP that he kept
on hand for medicinal purposes to counter queasy stomachs.

In a flash he was half skipping, half hopping down the
hall to reach the bathroom posthaste. "Here's—"

His voice dried up when he veered around the corner
to see Laura peeling off her blouse. She was braless—of
course, he'd figured that out the instant he saw her staggering down the hall, looking like death walking. His
helpless gaze roamed over the swells of her breasts and
the trim indentation of her waist. Damn, she was more
perfect in the flesh than in his arousing dreams and he
was about to go into cardiac arrest!

When she reached down to squirm out of her shorts
and panties, leaving the garments in a tangled pile beside
her, Wade forgot to breathe—couldn't breathe. Air evaporated in his collapsing lungs and he opened his mouth
to warn Laura that he was in the room, but he couldn't
speak to save his life. His entire body went into sensory
overload and he was pretty sure the sight of her exquisite
body was going to be imprinted on his eyeballs throughout eternity.

Dazed, he watched her creamy breasts rise and fall with each panted breath. He saw her eyes glaze over and her bloodless cheeks turn another shade of pale. The poor woman was functioning on automatic pilot. She was so disoriented that she barely knew where she was and what she was doing.

Damn, just his luck that his forbidden fantasy came true right smack dab in the middle of a nightmare. He was seeing Laura in all her shapely splendor and glory— a visual feast for the male appetite—and she was so oblivious that she had no idea she'd stripped naked in front of him.

Wade jerked to attention when he noticed the tub was dangerously close to spilling over. He lurched across the room to switch off the faucets then glanced down at Laura who'd curled up in a naked ball, her forehead resting on her bent knees, her wild tangle of hair tumbling over her bare skin like a golden waterfall.

She glanced up, eyes completely out of focus, when he accidentally clanked his elbow against the sliding glass door. She looked pale, frail, vulnerable—and breathtakingly naked, he couldn't forget that! The barbed-wire fence Wade had strung around his heart rusted and broke, right there on the spot.

"My purse," she wheezed. "Bedroom. Medication." Her head flopped against her knees and he heard her labored breathing as he maneuvered around her to retrieve the medication.

Sweet mercy! What was wrong with her, Wade wondered frantically. Did she have some life-threatening condition she failed to mention? No, she wouldn't have dared mention any ailments for fear he'd use it against her in his ongoing attempt to see her dismissed from employment.

Wade cursed himself viciously for making life intolerable for her since her arrival at his ranch. Well, he'd make it up to her, take care of *her* for a change, even if he had to steel himself against seeing her gloriously naked and couldn't do a damn thing about fulfilling his wildest fantasies.

Resolved, Wade snatched up her purse from the dresser and rummaged for the plastic bottle of medication. He whirled around and headed for the bathroom, lickety-split. Laura was exactly where he'd left her—curled up by the tub, whimpering softly. Wade grabbed some soda crackers and the can of 7UP.

"Here, eat some crackers and chase it with 7UP before you take the medication," he instructed, forcing himself to look her in the eye rather than allowing his gaze to wander appreciatively over her. Hell! Not looking at her was tormenting him to no end.

"Close the blinds," she whispered. "Too much light."

While she munched on crackers and sipped the drink, Wade limped over to shut the window, plunging the room into shadows. It didn't prevent him from seeing all of Laura's satiny flesh and rounded curves, however. It seemed to be his comeuppance to suffer all the torments of the damned.

"How many capsules?" he asked as he twisted open the lid of the medication.

"Two." Laura held out a trembling hand so he could drop the capsules in her palm. Arms shaking, she brought the medication to her quivering lips and swallowed convulsively.

When she'd washed down the medicine with the drink, Wade set aside the can and sack of crackers. Before he could stop her she draped herself over the edge of the tub.

"Bathing in your condition might not be a good idea," he said worriedly.

"Part of the treatment," she mumbled groggily. "It's what eases the pain until the medication takes effect."

He hooked his arm around her waist to help her maneuver into the tub. He inwardly groaned when the peaks of her breasts skimmed his good arm. He gritted his teeth as he placed his hand on her bare hip to situate her in the steaming bath water.

Wade was paying penance for every taunting criticism he'd tossed at Laura. He himself had said that paybacks were a bitch, hadn't he? Well, sure 'nuff. Watching Laura battle this mysterious ailment and seeing her stark naked, *touching* her while she was stark naked was heaven and hell in one.

"Towels and inflated bath pillow," she murmured as she braced herself against the back of the tub.

Wade reached over to retrieve two towels and the bath pillow that was suction-cupped to the tiled wall. He tucked them behind her head to keep her face elevated from the water. Obviously she was accustomed to taking precautions while she dealt with this mysterious ailment.

Inappropriately, desire slammed through Wade as his betraying gaze glided over her perfectly formed body. Definitely a goddess, he mused. One very sick, very oblivious goddess, judging by the dazed look in her eyes and the lack of color in her face.

Wade awkwardly slid to the floor beside the tub and stretched out his fractured leg. He sat there, watching Laura dribble warm water over her head and whimper like a dying coyote. Instinctively he reached out to trail his hand over her silky arm, as if his tender caress could heal her pain.

She sighed heavily and groaned. Tears of pain mingled

with the trickling water that streamed over her face. Wade decided, right then and there, that he preferred to be run down by a ton of Black Angus beef-on-the-hoof than to watch Laura suffer. The woman was tearing out his heart by the taproot and she wasn't even trying to. She was just lying there in a tub of water, shivering and grimacing and moaning. She was killing him inch by inch, second by agonizing second.

"What's causing this?" Wade continued to stroke her arm. "Is this some sort of female problem or something?"

"Partially. Migraine," she mumbled.

"That bad?" he asked with a wince.

"Twenty on a scale of ten. The queen mother of migraines. Cursed, debilitating headache..."

Her voice trailed off as she breathed a ragged sigh. Eyes squeezed shut, teeth clenched against the pain, her head sagged against the inflated pillow. He suspected her survival instincts were on automatic pilot because no matter which way she shifted or squirmed she always kept her chin up and her face averted from the water. She never actually dozed off, just lay there, battling the pain as best she could.

Wade turned on a slow trickle of water from the faucet to reheat the water. He sat with her for twenty minutes, stroking her arm, the streamlined curve of her hip and elegant contour of her thigh. Meanwhile, he cursed the hungry need pounding at him and this killer headache that made this lively, spirited woman helplessly nonfunctional.

He was a pathetic bastard, he chastised himself. Here he sat with his body thoroughly aroused, gawking at pure feminine perfection, committing every silky inch of Laura's shapely physique to memory and wishing the one time he'd found her naked that it could've been in his bed where he was naked, too. Yup, he was the most pathetic bastard in the western hemisphere. Maybe even on the entire planet. He was a walking hormone with the scruples and decency of a slug. He knew all these things; he just couldn't make himself feel ashamed enough to look away from her gorgeous body. Hell, he'd have to stitch his eyelids closed *not* to ogle her.

Boy, if the brothers Seymour had the slightest idea that Wade was not age eighty-three, sans teeth, sans hair, sans twenty-twenty vision that was totally focused on their baby sister, they'd be all over him like sharks in a feeding frenzy. They wouldn't appreciate knowing their precious sister was sprawled naked in his bathtub while he sat here, pinpointing the location of every mole, not to mention that teardrop-shaped birthmark four inches—no, make that five inches—above the inside of her left knee.

They wouldn't like knowing that her pink toenail polish was the same color of her nipples that had brushed against his arm earlier. The brothers Seymour would most especially not appreciate knowing that he'd had his greedy hands all over Laura and that the vivid image of her perfection was indelibly and eternally etched on his mind.

Oh, yeah, if he had a sister that he'd felt responsible for and watched over for years, he'd definitely kill the weirdo who sat beside the tub, rubbing her all over under the pathetic pretense of making *her* feel better.

"Wade! Where are you?"

Wade jerked his hand off Laura's bare hip and struggled hastily to his feet. Damn, Duff was in the house! If he found Wade in here with Laura the old goat's paternal instincts would explode like a nuclear warhead.

Casting one cautious glance at Laura to ensure her

head remained above water and she wasn't in danger, Wade hurried down the hall. He found Duff in the kitchen, surveying the mess on the floor and cabinets.

"What happened? Did a tornado blow through here?"

Wade grabbed a paper towel to mop up the shattered eggs. "No, Laura tried to fix breakfast while she was in the grips of a migraine."

Duff's stubbled jaw dropped to his expanding chest. "You made that little gal cook while she had a murderous headache! Are you nuts!"

"No, of course I didn't," Wade muttered. "I made her lie down." He didn't mention that she was lying naked in the tub. Duff would undoubtedly be as outraged as the brothers Seymour had he known. The secret would die with him, Wade vowed.

"I just came to tell you that Vance and Quint are here to borrow your tractor and baler. They're going to get the hay put up before the rain. The weatherman says we're in for a toad-strangler tonight. That alfalfa will mold and rot if it's left in windrows in the meadow."

Wade dug into his pocket for his keys. "Why don't you drive into town and stop by Hoagie's Diner to pick up sandwiches for lunch. Since Vance and Quint will want to work through the noon hour to save time, we need plenty of food to take to the field. While you're in town, stop by the market and pick up a six-pack of 7UP for Laura. I have a feeling she won't be able to keep much of anything else down for a while."

"Sure thing," Duff said. "You take good care of that little gal and I'll keep up with your cousins."

Wade smiled gratefully. "Have I told you lately that I'm glad to have you around? I'm sorry I've been so cranky and ill tempered. It's just—"

Duff flung up his hand like a traffic cop. "It's okay,

boy. I know that broken leg is making you crazy. Having that perty little gal around, getting you all stirred up, can't be easy, either. You know I'll be here for you, as long as you don't mess up the good deal you've got by having that gal here. And while I'm in the process of lecturing, which I don't do too often, you can stop comparing her to your ex because they're nothing alike.''

Wade rolled his eyes. "Are you finished, Dear Abby?''

"No, I'm not and you need to pay attention when I give you the benefit of my advice and opinion,'' Duff went on determinedly. "If you have a half a brain in that thick head of yours you'll marry that little gal before somebody else snatches her up.''

"I swore off marriage after the first one went sour,'' Wade said darkly.

"Well, you can swear back on it as easily as you swore off,'' Duff insisted. "If you cut that little gal loose and declare open season on her, even your cousins will be hovering around her. Just how would you feel about that, huh?''

Wade scowled and Duff nodded. "That's what I thought. Now, that's all I've got to say about that.'' He thrust out a gnarled hand. "Gimme those keys. I'm outta here.''

Wade tossed the keys to Duff and swallowed a grin as the bandy-legged old cowboy hurried off to tend his errands. Quickly Wade set the kitchen to rights. He hobbled to the bathroom again to ensure Laura hadn't gone under, while Duff was lecturing him about treating her with the consideration, courtesy and respect Duff thought she deserved and insisting that Wade shove a wedding ring on her finger before the prowling tomcats around Hoot's Roost—his cousins included—latched onto her.

When Wade tiptoed—or some fact simile with his broken leg—into the bathroom, he tested the water temperature with his fingertip. Definitely cold. The same temperature he used for the bath he took to cool his heels—and other parts of his masculine anatomy that needed to chill out. Before Laura's hands and feet shriveled up like prunes he decided to remove her from the tub. He reached down to drain the water then grabbed a dry towel. Laura roused while the water gurgled and belched its way down the drain and she struggled to clamber from the tub. Wade leaned over to graze his hand over her colorless forehead and swore ripely. Damn it, she felt like a block of ice!

Going down on his good knee, he gently curled his arm around Laura's waist and pulled her toward him. She just sort of lay there on his shoulder like a waterlogged caterpillar, semiconscious. Wade wasn't sure how he was going to hoist her up when he only had one good arm and leg on his battered body. His ribs were still tender and he'd felt the strain when he'd helped Laura into the tub.

Well, didn't matter if he ripped ligaments and tendons loose in his attempt to haul her from the bathroom. He was going to get her into bed—somehow or other.

His mouth set in a grim line, Wade contorted his body to drag Laura's limp body forward. Her head dropped against his belly and her hands dangled on his crotch. Wade repositioned her hands. With her motionless body draped over his right shoulder and her face pressed against his chest he gritted his teeth and carefully rose to his feet. He was reminded of his rodeo days when he'd ridden broncs while injured and in pain. He'd simply "cowboyed-up," same as he was doing now.

If one of his evil cousins swung by while he was carrying Laura to the bedroom the man was dead meat, family or not. Thankfully, however, Wade made it to his bedroom without causing himself excessive pain—and without an uninvited intruder bursting in on him.

Balancing Laura on his shoulder, he leaned over to jerk down the bedspread and sheet. The muscles of his rib cage protested as he twisted sideways to lay her gently on his bed. Like a rag doll, her head and arms flopped, but she only opened her eyes for a moment before they fluttered shut. Boy, that medication must've kicked in, he mused. She could be in orbit around the planet Pluto and never know it. Although she was still shivering, her teeth chattering, she didn't open her eyes as he covered her up.

Wade walked over to shut the drapes on both windows. His hand stalled, wondering why he'd automatically flung the drapes in his room wide-open when he awakened this morning. Damn, she had *him* doing it, even when he fussed about keeping the house dark.

He glanced back at Laura who looked as helpless and vulnerable as a woman could get. It dawned on him that, although he hated seeing her in this condition, he was glad to know that, for once, *she* needed *him*. Until now, she'd been efficiency at its finest and he'd felt useless, inadequate and frustrated by his lack of agility and ability.

Mulling over all the changes Laura had made in his home, and in him, Wade exited the room to fix himself something to eat. He needed to keep up his strength if he was going to play nursemaid to his patient. He had no idea how long these painful bouts with migraines lasted. Hours? Days? Well, it didn't matter. He was going to take care of Laura until she was back on her feet. He owed her that much for taking care of him, for putting up with his taunts and his criticism. It was payback time, he told himself on the way down the hall.

LAURA GROANED GROGGILY and opened heavily lidded eyes to the darkness. The loud drumroll of thunder, roaring wind and pounding rain had awakened her. She had no idea where she was. All she knew was that the blinding, nauseating pain in her skull had subsided into a throbbing ache.

She was all too familiar with the various stages of her symptoms, having dealt with these hellish headaches for the past several years. The new medication her doctor prescribed shortened the agonizing phases of pain. For that she was grateful. In a few more hours she'd be able to function with a tolerable headache—as long as there were no loud noises, no glaring lights and no unpleasant scents that retriggered those Godzilla-size pains in her skull.

Another vicious clap of thunder exploded like a cannon, rattling the windowpanes. The storm churned and rain came down in torrents. Laura heaved a weary sigh and squirmed onto her side to cover her ultrasensitive head with a pillow.

"Are you awake?" came the low familiar voice from the shadows.

"Yes." She lifted her throbbing head and glanced toward the disembodied voice. "Wade?" Befuddled, she surveyed the dark surroundings. "Is this your room?"

"Yeah, I thought you'd be more comfortable in my king-size bed so you could thrash and sprawl every which way."

Laura levered onto one shaky elbow when she found herself wondering if she'd fixed him something to eat for breakfast. She had no idea what time it was, but the last thing she remembered was thinking she had to make her way to the kitchen—or catch hell for shirking her duties. The thought had her clambering to gain her feet.

"Whoa, stay where you are." Wade sank down on the edge of the bed and gently urged her head against the pillow.

Laura rolled toward him when the mattress dipped beneath his weight. Her cheek slammed into his cast. "Ouch."

"Sorry." He stroked her hair from her face and then placed his palm on her forehead to check for fever. "Annie said you needed toast and tea. Do you feel like eating now?"

"Annie?" she croaked. "You called Annie?"

"I figured she'd dealt with these bad spells during college and she'd know how to make you more comfortable."

Why was he being so nice to her? This wasn't how she expected this scene to play out. There had to be a catch somewhere. She might be loopy from the headache and medication, but she knew Wade didn't like her and would use this against her the first chance he got.

"Here, take a drink of this," he instructed as he leaned away to retrieve the tea, then pressed it to her lips.

"Thanks." She took a cautious sip.

"Now the toast," he ordered.

Laura pillowed her head against his thigh to munch her toast when holding her head up got to be too much of a chore. She reached out, requesting another sip of tea, then let her hand drop against his leg. She smiled droopily when he curled his arm comfortingly around her shoulder.

"Annie said these spells usually last twelve to twenty-four hours. Sometimes longer," he murmured.

"Uh-huh," she mumbled sluggishly.

She rubbed her cheek against his thigh and cuddled closer to his warmth and strength. She closed her eyes to savor the feel of his hand brushing lightly over the sheet that covered her back. Suddenly it dawned on her that she was naked. There was nothing between her chilled skin and the sheet!

Her eyes shot open and jumbled memories tangled with the cobwebs in her brain. How'd she get in his bed...naked? The vague recollection of holding a handful of raw eggs that shattered in her fingertips drifted through her thoughts. She remembered a bout of nausea and that wild frantic realization that her headache was reaching alarming proportions.

Laura swallowed uneasily. "How'd I get in your bed?"

"I carried you."

"With a sprained wrist and broken leg?" she croaked.

"I didn't think dragging you down the hall by your heels would be a good idea," he teased gently.

"You should've left me where I was...where was I?"

There was a noticeable pause before he said, "In the bathtub. I didn't think I should leave you there indefinitely. I was worried about your safety."

"Hot water and steam soothes the headache. I've followed that procedure for six years..." A sick feeling suddenly settled in the pit of her stomach. If she'd been in the tub—which she always was when she realized a King Kong-size headache was setting in—then she must've peeled off her clothes. She usually remained in the tub until she felt drowsy then she stumbled off to bed.

"Oh...my...God!" she bleated.

"Just relax," Wade soothed her. "Everything's okay. Go back to sleep. If you need anything I'll be right here."

Laura inched away from him, humiliated, mortified by the prospect of what might have happened while she was in the grips of this murderous headache. Had she stripped naked in front of him? She couldn't remember. Or had he undressed her and helped her into the tub? Either way she could never look him in the eye again. It would be beyond embarrassing.

"I'm sorry," she choked out. "I didn't mean to—"

"Shh-shh," he interrupted. "All that matters is that you're feeling a little better and you've eaten." He tucked the sheet around her. "You're also coherent. That's an improvement."

Laura squeezed her eyes shut and cursed whatever she'd done while she was in pain. Now Wade had the perfect excuse to boot her off his ranch. *He* was caring for *her*, for heaven sake. *She'd* have to pay *him* for playing nursemaid.

Well, she couldn't worry about that now, not when those little demons with jackhammers, dynamite and pickaxes were still digging a tunnel through her skull. She and Miss Scarlett would just have to worry about that tomorrow.

On that procrastinating thought she surrendered to the steady thump in her head and went back to sleep.

Laura inched away from him, humiliated, mortified by the prospect of what might have happened while she was in the grip of this horrendous headache. Had she enjoyed whatever flood of intimacies she couldn't remember? Had he aroused her and before? No, the first, latter way she could never look him in the eye again. It would be beyond embarrassing.

"I'm sorry . . ." she choked out. "I don't even know . . ."

7

WHEN LAURA ROUSED AGAIN she felt a warm, comforting strength enveloping her, soothing the cold shivers that had overtaken her body. She knew this drill—the progression from blinding pain and acute sensitivity to a steady throb in her skull and finally to the icy chills that gave way to exhaustion. But what she didn't recall in her previous experiences was this sensation of being held. Wow, these migraines were taking on new dimensions. Sighing tiredly, she snuggled closer to the compelling warmth and dozed off.

Later, when she reached a higher level of awareness she realized she wasn't alone in bed. Laura's head popped off the pillow and she stared apprehensively at the shadowy form beside her. With each passing second the fog in her brain parted and it dawned on her that her bare flesh was pressed familiarly against a naked male chest.

When she tried to inch away, a brawny arm clamped around her. "Go back to sleep."

Laura's heart very nearly beat her to death while she lay there, still as stone. She wasn't sure she could cope with the aftereffects of this particular headache because it came with the knowledge that she was in bed with Wade Ryder. Good gad! What had she done while she was suffering a lapse of sanity?

"Your teeth were chattering. You were shivering and

thrashing," Wade whispered. "I was trying to warm you up."

Well, it had worked, she thought. The sensations spilling through her were rising to a boil. She wasn't sure she trusted herself to lie beside him when she was fully awake and her imagination was conjuring up all sorts of intimate scenarios.

Clamping the sheet around her bare breasts Laura wiggled and wormed until there was a foot of dead air space between them. There, that was better. She glanced at the digital clock. It was 7:00 a.m. She'd lost an entire day. Damn!

When Wade rolled sideways and propped his head on his hand to stare at her, every ounce of nerve and gumption she'd mustered in her previous dealings with Wade abandoned her like an infantry of army deserters. She scooted off the bed, taking the sheet with her.

She gasped when she noticed Wade was wearing nothing but those white briefs she'd washed and put away several times during her employment. Seeing his magnificent body—an artwork of powerful muscles and masculine contours—sprawled in bed, sent her face up in flames.

"I'm really sorry about this," she yammered nervously. "I'll fix breakfast after I shower. And about what happened—"

"Seymour—" he interrupted.

"This doesn't happen often," she cut in quickly. "I'm only plagued by these migraines four or five times a year." She gulped for air and battled for composure. "So you don't have to worry that I can't perform my job—"

"Seymour—"

"And if I said or did anything to embarrass you—or embarrass myself that I can't remember doing—I'm sorry about that, too,'' she rattled on. "I never remember much about these lapses and...well...I'm just really, *really* sorry if I inconvenienced you.''

Clutching the sheet in a death grip, Laura scurried from the room with more speed than dignity. She'd never been so humiliated in her life! Furthermore, she knew she'd handed Wade a loaded gun to turn on her. Now he'd have an excellent excuse to see to it that she was fired.

Castigating herself thoroughly, she dashed into the bathroom to shower and face the upcoming day that she anticipated to be pure, demoralizing hell.

WADE BIT BACK A GRIN as he watched Laura hightail it from the room. She wasn't clear on what had happened? That was good. He'd just as soon she didn't remember that he'd hovered beside the bathtub, ogling her like a pervert.

Fully aroused from the pleasure of holding her luscious body, while she shivered and mumbled throughout the night, Wade limped off to take another cold bath. When he exited his private bathroom, the smell of bacon lured him down the hall.

As predicted, Laura had prepared a hearty breakfast—no doubt, her way of apologizing for the inconvenience and embarrassment she might've caused him.

Wade still couldn't get over that. He couldn't remember a woman ever apologizing for inconveniencing *him* and not upholding *her* end of a bargain. His ex-wife's methods involved twisting the situation and blaming *him* for whatever happened.

A wry smile pursed Wade's lips when Laura turned away the moment she saw him approach. He knew this was his golden opportunity to torment her, but he didn't have the heart to do it, not after seeing her so helpless and vulnerable. Besides, he'd vowed to compensate for treating her badly.

"Mmm, smells good. I'm famished," he said as he awkwardly lowered himself into a chair at the table.

Laura gave him a startled look, but she didn't make a peep, just busied herself by washing the skillet.

"We received a much-needed rain last night," he went on conversationally. "Even better, my cousins baled the hay before the storm hit. They can look forward to a well-deserved day off while the ground and the other alfalfa meadows dry out enough to swath more hay."

She cut him a suspicious glance. Clearly she was uncertain what to make of his suddenly sociable attitude. "Did you tell your cousins what happened?"

"Nope."

"But you're going to use it as leverage against me, in hopes of getting me fired, right?"

"Nope."

She stared warily at him. "You're being exceptionally nice to me, same as you were last night. Why?"

"Why not?" he questioned, smiling affably.

She shrank away, as if he'd taken a bite out of her rather than smiled at her. There was a near-desperate look on her face when she said, "You've changed the rules and messed everything up. I don't know how to deal with it."

"You don't?" He took a bite of bacon. "Why not?"

"Why not?" she repeated, flustered.

He shrugged and grinned. "Sure, why not?"

"Stop saying why not! And stop smiling at me like that. It makes me I—oh, never mind." She wheeled toward the back door. "I'm going to feed Frank and check on Duff."

Wade chuckled in amusement. Laura was accustomed

to the routine of being teased and tormented and she'd learned to toss snappy rejoinders at him. Now she wasn't sure how to react to him. Nothing like keeping a woman off balance, he mused as he gobbled up his tasty meal.

AN AMUSED GRIN PURSED Wade's lips as he lounged on the front porch, watching Laura trot off on her evening horseback ride. It amazed him that she'd taken to country life so quickly, so naturally. Her enthusiasm for the ranch pleased him, reminded him that he'd taken a lifestyle most folks envied. Through Laura's eyes Wade had gained a fresh appreciation of his blessings.

Although Laura hadn't spoken more than ten words to him the past few days, he'd remained on his very best behavior. Suddenly everything was turned around backward. Now *she* was going out of her way to avoid him. That should've made him happy. It didn't. He wanted to share the closeness he'd felt the night Laura lay sleeping in his arms. Something vital had shifted inside him that night. He'd seen *her* frailties exposed, rather than *his,* for a change.

He'd lost count of the times he'd wanted to walk up to Laura, pull her into his arms and let whatever might happen, happen. Somewhere along the way he'd gotten tired of fighting these betraying feelings he felt for her. He was quickly losing interest in abiding by the vows he'd made when Bobbie Lynn walked out. Maybe he should just go with these feelings and see where they led, see how Laura felt about them.

His thoughts trailed off when he heard a pickup whizzing up the driveway. His cousins piled out and ambled toward the porch. Wade reflexively braced himself for another round of teasing that he'd come to expect from his devilish cousins.

"Gee, is it time for another razzing already?" he asked.

"Nope." Vance said as he ascended the steps. "Laura called this morning and said she thought you needed a change of scenery. She asked if we'd show you a good time."

Wade glanced into the distance to see Laura, with Frank on her heels, disappearing into a canopy of cottonwood trees. "She did?"

"Yeah," Quint confirmed. "We've been instructed to accompany you to Hoot's Tavern so you can socialize with the local yokels." Quint waggled his dark brows. "It's Saturday night and there's no cover charge for the ladies. There should be at least three women to every man at ye ole watering hole."

Laura was sending him out to fraternize with available females? True, Wade was ready to fly this coop, but lately he'd had only one woman on his mind. But maybe this was Laura's way of telling him that she wasn't interested.

"C'mon, cuz, let's go shake a leg while the live band plays our favorite country songs," Vance said, breaking into Wade's troubled thoughts. "Oh, sorry. I forgot. You won't be too agile on the dance floor."

"But not to worry." Quint hauled Wade to his feet. "You can hold court at the table and charm your local fan club."

Wade didn't want to hold court, didn't want a passel of women hovering around him. He just wanted Laura… Oh, hell, he was getting in too deep. Couldn't have that!

"Sure, why not? I'm ready for a night on the town."

WADE SAT AT HOOT'S TAVERN, holding a longneck in his hand, listening to the band belt out a fast-tempoed country song. A previous intimate acquaintance was perched on his lap. She brushed her size D, artificially enhanced bosom against his shoulder, just so he wouldn't forget she was there.

This was exactly what he needed. Something simple. Something uncomplicated. So why did he feel like a turncoat?

Sandi Parker, the well-rounded female perched on his lap, leaned close to whisper in his ear. "It's too crowded and noisy in here. Let's go over to my place so we can have some privacy…I've missed being with you."

Wade knew he must be crazy not to take Sandi up on the offer, but he also knew he'd been kidding himself for the past two hours. Sandi was only a substitute for the woman he really wanted. "Sorry, Sandi, but I'm not up to that yet," he declined. "Better go find someone else."

Sandi flashed him an offended glance. "Your loss, hotshot. I could've made you forget your troubles and put a satisfied smile on your face."

When she sauntered off to find herself another Mr.-Right-For-The-Night, Wade glanced across the barroom to see his cousins cuddled cheek to cheek with their respective dance partners. He surged from his chair and zigzagged between the couples to tap Quint on the shoulder. "Gimme your keys. I'm going home."

Quint gaped incredulously at him. "We can't leave yet."

"*I* can," Wade insisted, then glanced at the woman who was rubbing provocatively against his cousin. "I'm sure you and Vance won't have trouble finding a ride home."

Quint placed his keys in Wade's outstretched hand and smiled wryly. "Are you sure you know what you're doing?"

"No, but I do know I can't stay here when I..." His voice trailed off before he said something Quint could use to harass him. "Thanks for the night on the town, but I've already had all the fun I can stand so I'm leaving." He limped away, knowing that going home was probably the last place he should be now, considering the turbulent emotions sloshing around inside him.

Wade maneuvered his left leg into the truck and shifted sideways on the bench seat to make himself more comfortable. Awkward but manageable, he mused as he cruised down the graveled road at twenty miles an hour. He'd suffered broken body parts while on the suicide circuit and he'd never let it slow him down while riding, driving or doing chores. He wasn't about to start now, either.

Maybe he shouldn't go home, but it was the only place he wanted to be—with the only the woman he wanted to be with.

DRESSED IN HER NIGHTGOWN, Laura lounged in Wade's oversize recliner, watching the evening news and feeling strangely dissatisfied and restless. Probably because Wade's tormenting scent clung to the chair, reminding her of the night he'd held and comforted her while she fought the Battle of the Migraine. That night had become a milestone in Wade's attitude toward her. But she'd been afraid to trust his friendly conversations and disarming smiles. Consequently she was suspicious, waiting for the other shoe to drop.

She'd asked his cousins to get him out of the house for the night. He needed a change of scenery and she needed time to...well, to talk herself out of the mushrooming feelings Wade inspired in her.

Every time he cast one of those devastating, knock-you-to-your-knees-and-keep-you-there grins in her direction, something warm and fuzzy enveloped her. Sure, she'd known she was physically attracted to Wade. Who wouldn't be? Heavens, she'd have to be dead and buried a couple of weeks not to react to a swarthy, muscular babe magnet like Wade Ryder. Even battered and limping around on his walking cast he exuded an aura that she was hard pressed to ignore.

Laura could understand the intense physical attraction, but it was the emotions he drew from her that concerned her. She was too sensitive to him. Too affected by his frustration with his injury and inactivity. Too responsive to his dry sense of humor that he'd been directing at her quite a lot lately. And she couldn't forget how she'd reacted every time he'd kissed her. She'd reached the point that she found excuses to be with him—so naturally she took steps to avoid him because all these unfamiliar sensations alarmed and confused her.

She had the unshakable feeling that she was falling in love with Wade, the woman-hater. That wasn't part of the plan, damn it. One of the reasons she'd taken this job was to prove to her overprotective brothers that she could deal with an attractive man without falling for the first one who came along that hadn't been screened and approved. And wham! Here she was, wishing for a commitment, aching for a definite sign that Wade shared these disturbing feelings that assailed her.

"You're an idiot," she muttered at herself. Wade had made it vividly clear from the onset that he didn't want commitment or another marriage because his ex had run his heart through the wringer and he wasn't interested in putting himself in a position to be rejected or humiliated again. Even knowing that, she'd spent the past couple of days battling the tormenting urge to fling her arms around his neck and communicate all these baffling feelings he inspired in her.

The humbling truth was that she was ready for a reckless fling, if Wade wasn't interested in a long-standing commitment. No, that wasn't exactly right, she corrected as she sprawled negligently in the chair. If she really wanted a fling, for the simple sake of *flinging,* she had no doubt she could find a man to accommodate her. What she wanted was for *Wade Ryder* to be the man who taught her what her overprotective brothers prevented her from experiencing—all out, just-do-it-because-it-makes-you-feel-good passion. The kind Wade had mentioned the first night she met him.

So here she sat with all this bottled need and frustrated curiosity—and no outlet. A pensive frown clouded her brow when a puzzling thought occurred to her. Could it be that all those taunting insults that she and Wade had volleyed back and forth were a sign of two sexually frustrated people who didn't have a handle on what they were feeling for each other and didn't know what they wanted to do about it—if anything?

Laura had certainly discovered the meaning of spontaneous combustion when Wade kissed her and caressed her. True, she didn't have a wide frame of reference because of her limited experience—thanks to the brothers Seymour—but to her, Wade's kisses had been off-the-charts and nuclear explosive.

Maybe Annie was right after all. Maybe Wade behaved as if he didn't like her and didn't want her underfoot because he *did* like her, *did* share this frustrating attraction and was trying to dodge emotional landmines. Humm. So if A + B wildly supercharged C, should she—being the newly liberated female who was testing her independent wings—act on her attraction to prove this mathematical equation?

The voice of caution asked, *Hey, Einstein, are you sure you haven't miscalculated? If you come on to Wade and you've misjudged the reasons for his behavior you're going to be thoroughly humiliated.* Newfound liberation, it seemed, came with responsibilities attached. She'd have to accept the consequences. No more blaming her brothers for stifling and protecting her. She'd have no one to blame but herself.

Laura was in middebate with the voices of reason and temptation when the front door swung open. Lo and behold, there he was—the topic of intense discussion, looking ruggedly handsome and overwhelmingly desirable. When his gaze zeroed in on the hiked hem of her flimsy nightgown, Laura's first impulse was to jerk it down to decency—but she didn't. She had the unmistakable feeling he'd seen far more of her when she was battling her ferocious headache.

"You're home early, dear," she said, striving for a light, breezy tone. "I wasn't expecting you for hours. Did you have a good time with your cousins?"

"Not particularly," Wade muttered, his gaze glued to the exposed length of her legs.

The epiphany came to her while she watched Wade appraise her with those beguiling eyes that were turning a darker shade of green with each passing second. His guard was down. She'd received enough interested glances from men to recognize masculine curiosity when she saw it. If she intended to test the waters with Wade, this was the time, she decided. The question was: Did she have the courage to face embarrassment if he wasn't interested in…well…letting things heat up between them and seeing how it turned out?

Why shouldn't she go for it, she asked herself. She liked the man—a lot. She liked his looks, his offbeat sense of humor, his attempt to comfort and care for her when she'd suffered from the debilitating headache. She knew he was hardworking, successful and that he'd thrust himself in front of an enraged bull to protect his cousins, even if he did curse them for teasing him. That indicated that he was loyal and self-sacrificing to those he cared about. He possessed scads of qualities she admired, come to think of it.

"What are you doing in my chair, Goldilocks?"

"—Papa bear said gruffly," Laura finished for him. "I'm here because it's not too hard. It's not too soft, but it's *juusstt* right. Yup, I'm sitting in your chair, so what are you gonna do about it, Ryder?" She struck what she hoped was a seductive Cleopatra pose and smiled impishly at him.

It was most definitely a seductive pose and the effects were shooting through Wade's body at supersonic speed. Damn! He'd spent the entire drive home from town trying to tell himself that just because he wanted Laura like hell blazing didn't mean he could—or should—have her. But here she was in her practically transparent nightie, her golden hair flowing over her shoulders like a glittering sequined cape, looking impossibly tempting. He really couldn't catch a break when it came to this woman, could he?

Although Sandi Parker hadn't gotten a rise out of him, Laura left him hard and aching in the time it took to blink. He didn't like it much, but he'd come to the realization during the drive home that Laura Seymour had gotten completely under his skin. He'd seen her gloriously naked. He'd held her all through the night. He'd kissed her, touched her and had erotic dreams that left him waking up in a cold sweat. He loved her sassy spirit, her determination, her courage to stand up to him and not to let him drive her away.

Now, what was he going to do about all these feelings, needs and desires that were thrumming through him? Take a cold bath or take the risk of getting in over his head and having his carefully guarded emotions turned loose like Pandora's opened box?

Wade shut the door, buying a little more time to make his decision. His head told him to tramp off to bed—alone. His heart told him to explore this…thing…between them.

He must've lingered in indecision too long, because Laura's teasing smiled faded and she self-consciously tugged at the hiked hem of her nightie. She slid gracefully from his chair and tossed the remote control to him.

"Here you go, Your Highness. The chair and the tube are all yours." She smacked herself lightly on the forehead. "What am I saying? Everything around here is yours, isn't it?"

"Except *you,*" he heard himself say in a husky voice that he barely recognized as his own. He'd committed the ultimate no-no—he'd just admitted aloud to himself, and to her, that he wanted her. He'd have to sit himself down and figure out why later. But not now. Definitely not now.

Laura broke stride halfway across the living room. The backwash of lamplight glowed through her sheer gown, clearly defining her feminine assets. Wade bit back a groan. He needed no more reminders of how she looked naked. Been there, seen that, even if she didn't remember every tantalizing moment the way he did.

"I beg your pardon?" she said, eyeing him uncertainly.

"No, I beg *your* pardon," he said as he moved instinctively toward her, tired of battling his attraction for her. "And if you don't want to be kissed, you better say so now because I'm starving to death for another taste of you."

He halted in front of her, staring down into her upturned face—a face that haunted his days and his nights. He waited—nobly, and that damn near killed him!—for her to make her decision. If the thought of a kiss—and whatever else might follow—didn't appeal to her then he wasn't going to push. He wanted her so much that it made his teeth ache, but he'd never in his life forced himself on a woman—and he sure as hell wasn't going to start now. Especially not with this woman because, damn it, what she thought of him mattered greatly to him—though he valiantly tried not to let her know it.

"Do you realize what you might be letting yourself in for?" she asked, staring somberly at him.

"Probably not. I told you that men's brains are located below their belt buckles." If she'd dared to glance down she'd have known that for a fact because his body was reacting to their close proximity. Hell, who was he kidding? He'd been aroused just staring at her from the far side of the room.

"So if I said I wanted a one-night stand so I could experience one of those real-good-feel-good times that you told me about, then you'd be game? Because that's all you're looking for these days, right? Because you don't want to clutter up sex with emotions, right?"

That's all *she* wanted? Or was that all she expected from *him?* Wade wasn't exactly sure what she implied, but he wasn't about to step out on an emotional limb and hand her a chain saw. "Right," he said eventually.

"At least you're honest. I can't fault you for that."

She draped her arms around his neck. "So kiss me and make it good, because I'm dying for another taste of you, too."

She didn't have to ask him twice. Wade hooked his good arm around her waist and hoisted her off the floor to press her tightly against him. His mouth touched down on her dewy lips and a floodgate of pleasure raced through him. He devoured her, even while telling himself to slow down. Just because he'd been without a woman for months was no excuse to hit on Laura like gangbusters. Wade forced himself to surface for a breath of air, to determine if he'd come on so strong that Laura was having serious reservations. To his surprise, she looked as dazed and desperate and needy as he felt.

"Mmm," she murmured as she moved evocatively against him. "You kiss even better than you torment and insult. Kiss me some more, will you?"

Far be it from him to disappoint her—or himself. "My pleasure, darlin'." Then he kissed her again and lost himself to the wild, throbbing sensations that tumbled over him.

Wade felt her pulse matching his accelerated heartbeat, felt his hands gliding over the curve of her bottom. When she curled her legs around his waist and settled familiarly against him, he staggered for balance. Damn his bum leg and walking cast. He didn't need to be encumbered and inhibited when he felt these uncontrollable, *un*inhibited feelings blasting away at him like howitzers. He wanted Laura—here, now. He didn't want to end up looking like a clumsy oaf while trying to make it to the private darkness of his bedroom.

Panting for breath Wade pushed her slender legs away from his hips. When she arched a questioning brow, Wade gestured his head toward the carpet and grinned rakishly at her. "Ever done it on the front room floor?" he asked as he made short shrift of her flimsy nightie, leaving her wearing nothing but those sexy bikini panties.

"Absolutely never," she wheezed, covering herself modestly while her face blossomed with color.

"Good." Smiling, he traced the elegant line of her jaw, her cheekbones. "Then I'll be your first."

She opened her mouth to reply, but when his hand skimmed over the rapid pulsations of her throat and drifted downward to encircle her taut nipple with his index finger, her voice evaporated—which was fine by him because he was about finished with the chitchat. He pressed his lips to all that smooth silky flesh and savored the pleasure coiling inside him.

Her response to his touch flattered and inspired him to drag more of those breathless little gasps, those erotic shivers from her. When he drew her down beside him on the carpet and bent to brush his lips over the dusky peaks of her breasts, her hand clenched in his hair, holding him to her, silently asking for more. He gladly accommodated because pleasuring her brought him immense satisfaction.

His hand swirled over the velvet plane of her belly to peel off her panties then he stroked her inner thigh. He realized immediately that this wasn't a purely selfish sexual encounter. He wanted her to be with him every step of the way, wanted to know that he wasn't disappointing or rushing her. Taking without giving to Laura wasn't an option, though he wasn't sure he wanted to analyze why that was so important.

When he cupped her in the palm of his hand, felt the damp heat of her arousal, he groaned with the impatient need to be inside her, to feel her surrounding him, holding him in the most intimate way imaginable. When he stroked her with thumb and fingertip she cried out his name, arched toward him and burst into hot liquid flame, burning his fingertips with the heat of her desire for him.

She was panting for breath, begging him to satisfy the burning ache he'd aroused in her and Wade couldn't shed his breeches fast enough to suit himself. Damn this cast anyway, he thought as he wrestled with his jeans and briefs and simultaneously fumbled to grab protection from his wallet.

"Wade?"

He glanced down into her passion-drugged baby blues and fell all the way to the bottom of his heart. No women had ever looked at him the way she did, as if he held all the answers to the universe, as if he were the great and wonderful wizard who could wave his magic wand and make each and every one of her fantasies come true. That marveling expression on her face prompted him to lean down and kiss her tenderly, then glide his tongue between her lips as the same moment that he slid between her thighs, using the leverage of his right leg to press into her and join his body intimately with his. Despite his hampering cast he plunged deeply into the hot, velvet warmth of her body, and then went perfectly still when he realized she was tight and tense and—uh-oh...

He reared up on his forearms to stare down at her in incredulous disbelief. Was what just happened exactly what he thought just happened? He might not have had any experience with this sort of thing, but he wasn't totally clueless.

"You should've told me," he accused, but his voice wasn't harsh, only rough with barely restrained need.

"Don't get all emotional on me, Ryder," she murmured as she lifted her hand to smooth away his concerned frown. "We're playing by your rules, after all.

And if you dare stop now, you might as well know I'm probably going to kill you.''

Her teasing reassurance and her willing smile sent him sliding past the edge of honorable restraint. When she shifted beneath him, accepting his masculine invasion, he rolled to his back and felt her body hot and tight and welcoming.

Then it was all over but the shouting. His body was moving on its own accord, driving upward, marveling at the pleasure streaming through him. He felt her trying to match his cadence, to do her fair share. But her fair share sent Wade tumbling over another lofty cliff and he tried to clutch at his self-control—and found himself holding only a fistful of air. Sensation upon indefinable sensation hammered at him like hailstones.

He clung desperately to Laura, whispering words in her ear that probably shocked her speechless. He was desperate to have her with him in that wild, frantic moment when ecstasy swamped and buffeted him. If he messed this up for her, he'd get a gun and shoot himself when it was done. He'd never been so afraid of disappointing anyone before, never cared so much that a woman came completely undone at the exact same moment he did. But it mattered. It mattered a lot with Laura.

"Wade!"

He felt the wild convulsions of rapture clamoring through her and echoing into him. Her body contracted around him as he shuddered in helpless release. He collapsed on the floor, gasping for breath, then cursed himself when he remembered they weren't lying on a bed but rather the living room floor.

Wade inwardly groaned when reality hit him right between the eyes. This was not the way he'd wanted to initiate Laura into passion—on a floor with him so frantic

to have her that he hadn't even taken time to doff his
shirt and barely managed to peel off his jeans. It hadn't
been tender and sweet. It had been an eruption of reckless
desire and turbulent emotion. Criminey, talk about in-
considerate and insensitive... Now where'd he keep his
pistol?

"Wade?"

Laura studied the tormented look that settled on his
rugged features. She wasn't about to allow his obvious
guilt to spoil the most incredible, remarkable moment of
her entire life. He'd touched her from outer body to inner
soul and she had no regrets about what passed between
them. It felt too right, too inevitable. She had every right
to decide who was to be her first lover and she'd chosen
well. That he cared enough to feel guilty only made her
love him all the more.

"I'm sorry. We shouldn't be here on the floor. I
shouldn't be here with you like this—period," he muttered as he tried to withdraw from her.

She clamped her hands on his hips and narrowed her
gaze on him. "If you move, damn you, you're a dead
man."

He smiled wryly, not quite meeting her gaze. "I was
just on my way to load the gun."

She framed his face with her hands, forcing him to
look directly at her. "I'm not sorry. Men!" she said with
teasing amusement. "Always trying to attach emotional
strings to sex. All we women want are two things. One:
a cool one to wet our whistles. And two: real-good-feel-
good recreational sex. You know, like filling up an empty
fuel tank."

His face turned ruddy red and he muttered, "I'm definitely going for the gun."

"Good, then I can hold you at gunpoint and make you

make love to me again because if you think for one minute that I've waited this long and that I only plan to do
this once, you are mistaken.'' She lowered her head, her
lips hovering inches from his. ''Show me more, Mr. Ryder, show me more...''

When her sweet, sassy mouth melted against his lips
like warm honey, Wade's brain short-circuited and his
body hardened, as if it had been hours, not minutes, since
he'd made love to Laura. Frankly, he was amazed at his
resilience and stamina. Considering this past month of
limited activity, he would've expected to be exhausted.
However, desire, like Phoenix rising from the ashes, left
him hard and aching and moving rhythmically against
her.

Laura's adventurous hands slid over the flexed muscles
of his chest then to his hips, stroking him, encouraging
him. And this time *she* whispered all sorts of explicit
instructions in *his* ear, causing unbelievable passion to
erupt between them all over again.

When she gasped and chanted his name, Wade drove
into her harder, faster, deeper. When she nearly squeezed
him in two, as if she wanted to get closer to him than
she already was—and how was that possible?—he drove
into her one last time and heard her name tumbling from
his lips in a full-throttled groan.

He chastised himself for behaving like a passion-
starved adolescent getting it on on the seat of his pickup.
This was madness! He had no business doing what he'd
been doing twice in the same night with a woman who
hadn't known diddly about sex—except what she'd read
in books or watched on the silver screen. He had no scruples and his conscience was throwing a conniption, but
Wade tuned it out and nestled his head against the curve
of Laura's shoulder in the aftermath of fantastic passion.

He'd never felt so close to a woman before, during or after sex…until now. It rattled him, but truth was, he was exactly where he wanted to be—and here he'd stay, until she dozed off and he gathered the strength to move away.

8

LAURA AWOKE TO THE WARBLING of birds and shafts of sunlight streaming through the living room windows. She rolled sideways and realized there was a pillow beneath her head and a quilt draped over her nude body. She smiled at the thought of Wade being considerate enough to ensure she was as comfortable as she could be—given where she'd spent the night.

She had no recriminations about what transpired between them. She'd made her decision the previous night and she'd been prepared to live with it. Wade, she suspected, was waging an internal battle of regret and guilt. For all his bluster he was an old-fashioned kind of man. The look on his face, when he'd realized he was her first time on the floor—or anywhere else for that matter—spoke volumes.

He, of course, was going to shoulder all the blame for what happened, she predicted. He'd work up a full-blown case of guilt. She'd also lay good odds that he'd take a wide berth until he figured out how he should behave now that his live-in housekeeper held an intimate position in his household.

Laura grinned as she tucked the quilt around her and headed for the shower. This should be interesting. She was in love with a card-carrying woman-hater who'd probably dream up excuses why they shouldn't be together—temporarily or permanently. Oh certainly, she was realistic enough to know that Wade didn't want permanence. He might never come to trust a woman with his heart after he'd been burned—badly.

She'd have to find a way to reassure him that she wasn't like Bobbie Lynn or any other woman who perceived him as a prize catch because he was handsome and successful. She didn't care about his money. She cared about the man himself, what he stood for and against.

Her love, he'd soon learn, was unconditional and didn't come with stipulations or time frames. She was, after all, a newly liberated woman. She wasn't the one with emotional baggage and hang-ups left over from a broken marriage. She'd just be herself and enjoy the time she spent with Wade. If she got her heart broken then she'd cross that bridge when she got there. For now, she was happier than she'd ever been, reveling in her love for Wade and her newfound sense of freedom.

WADE HAD BEEN BERATING himself since the moment he awakened that morning. He hadn't been able to face Laura so he'd inched away from her, bathed, dressed and limped from the house. Hobbling at a hasty, uneven gait, he'd gone in search of his cousins, hoping he could help with a few chores that he could manage on the walking cast. He needed something to occupy his mind and his time.

He found his cousins at Quint's ranch—at the scene of Wade's debilitating accident. The men were trying to load Vance's cantankerous bull that had trampled Wade.

Vance frowned curiously when Wade pulled his pickup to a stop beside the loading chute. "Whaddya do? Decide to come back for more?" he teased.

Wade glared at the snorting bull as he piled from the truck. "No, I have cabin fever. I need to work."

Quint strode over to hand Wade a whip. "Stay behind the bull, on the *outside* of the chute. See if you can persuade that blockheaded beast to load up in the stock trailer. Vance and I will get in front of him, on the *inside*. Maybe when he gets mad enough to chase us he'll end up in the trailer before he realizes it."

"Don't let him run over you," Wade advised as he limped toward the reinforced steel chute. "I guaran-damn-tee you won't like hobbling around with a cast."

"I hear ya, cuz," Vance said as he swung agilely over the top railing of the chute. "If anyone else gets injured, this maniac is definitely hamburger. I don't care what he's worth for breeding purposes."

Wade popped the ton of beef-on-the-hoof on the rump, urging him forward. The bull swung his broad head and snorted, knowing full well that he was king of the barnyard. The snapping whip affected him about as much as a pesky fly landing on his rump.

Vance, daring fool that he was, stripped from his shirt and slapped the bull on the nose to antagonize him. "Come on, you old bastard, come 'n get me. I dare you."

Snorting, the bull pawed the dirt, lowered his head and charged down the lane. Quint and Vance leaped onto the opposite sides of the chute at the last possible second. The bull clattered into the stock trailer then whipped around to make his escape in the same direction he'd come. But Quint dropped the metal gate in place, imprisoning the bull.

"Gotcha," Quint said triumphantly. He glanced over at Wade. "You think you can drive this rig over to Vance's place and unload this rascal without straining yourself?"

"Consider it done," Wade confirmed. He'd already proven he could angle his body beneath the steering wheel to reach the brake and accelerator so he could drive. It wasn't easy, but it was certainly doable.

"Thanks, that'll save us some time." Quint bounded to the ground and jerked off his work gloves. "Vance wants to move his cows and calves to the north pasture, and then we need to check the cattle and fences over at Gage's place."

"I'll stop in town and grab some hamburgers for lunch," Wade offered. "I'll be back here in a couple of hours."

Quint frowned curiously. "Won't Laura be expecting you for lunch?"

"Just because I have a temp cook and housekeeper doesn't mean I have to check in at noon," Wade said defensively. "I can come and go as I please, ya know."

Vance grinned slyly. "Who are you trying to convince?"

"No one. I'm just stating fact. I don't have bed check or posted lunch hours. I'm my own man. Just because we—" Wade shut his trap—fast. He wasn't about to tell these two hooligans that just because he'd *made* love to Laura didn't mean he was *in* love with her.

"Just because?" Quint prompted. "Something happen when you got home last night that we should know about?"

Wade pivoted on his good foot and hobbled toward the waiting pickup and trailer. "I'll be back with lunch."

He scowled when he saw his cousins trading grins. He vowed, there and then, that if either of them ever got tangled up with a woman, the way he'd gotten tangled up with Laura, he'd never let them hear the end of it.

"WOW, THIS PLACE IS REALLY something," Annie Nelson commented as she entered the tidy living room that was adorned with plants, candles and baskets of potpourri. "I didn't know Wade was into all this stuff."

"He's not." Laura gestured for her friend to take a seat. "I bought all this stuff to perk up the place. I figured I'd use it in my new home."

Annie lounged casually on the sofa and darted Laura a curious glance. "Still have your heart set on buying the old Draper homestead?"

"Absolutely, although I suspect my brothers will think the place isn't modernized enough for me to live in."

Annie snorted. "Sounds like them. But, ask me, that place has plenty of potential. I'd be interested in it myself if I didn't need to stick close to Dad. If things happen to get serious between Mark and me, his home is just around the corner from our place so I'd be close at hand."

Laura sipped her iced tea. "Is it going to get serious?"

Annie shrugged. "I'm twenty-five and my biological clock is ticking. I'd like to have a family before I collect Social Security." She regarded Laura inquisitively. "So, how are things progressing with Wade? I was surprised when he called, all concerned about how to deal with your migraines. The way you carried on about how much he disliked you, I would've thought he'd just leave you lying wherever your killer headache struck and step over you on his way out the door."

"He does have his compassionate moments," Laura murmured evasively. And his *passionate* moments—though he'd avoided her as if she'd contracted leprosy since they'd made love two nights ago. He'd busied himself with as many outdoor activities as he could manage after their intimate encounter. He'd called to leave stilted messages, saying he wouldn't be home for lunch or supper. She didn't know what Wade was doing with his time, but he wasn't spending it here, with her. Which couldn't be good for his mending leg and sprained wrist.

"Kevin Shelton called last night to see if you might be interested in driving into town and joining us at Hoot's Tavern Saturday night," Annie reported, smiling impishly. "The poor man must've been intimidated by Wade because he wanted me to be his go-between to ask for dates. Guess he was afraid to come out here and meet up with Wade again."

"Sure, sounds fine," Laura decided on the spur of the moment. She wasn't going to hang around here, waiting for Wade to return from his journey on the Guilt-Trip Express. He didn't want permanence, after all. Heavens, he didn't seem to want temporary, either. But she'd hoped that he'd felt the same incredible connection she'd experienced that night....

"Something wrong?" Annie questioned perceptively.

Laura forced a smile. "Not a thing. Why don't we go into town tonight, grab some supper and rent a chick flick?"

"What about Wade's supper?"

Laura shrugged nonchalantly. "I'll fix him something that he can nuke in the microwave. It's not like we always share meals. He usually prefers to dine alone."

"Still? He really is determined to resist your countless charms, huh? Idiotic man."

Laura smiled past the feeling of rejection that settled around her heart when she let her guard down. Optimistic though she tried to be, she wondered if loving Wade was a lost cause. But what had she expected? He had told her from the get-go that he didn't want commitment. Fool

that she was, she'd thought that loving him had the power
to change him.

Halfheartedly Laura wandered alongside Annie who
suggested a leisurely walk around the pastures to enjoy
the fresh air and open spaces. She kept telling herself to
get her act together, to look forward to the future of her
new teaching assignment and the acquisition of her down
payment for the farm home on the outskirts of town.

She had her freedom and a new life ahead of her,
didn't she? What did she need with a gun-shy bachelor?
Hadn't she convinced herself to adapt Wade's casual attitude toward sex? Hadn't she told herself, repeatedly,
that rejection—if it came her way, which it had—was
one of the consequences she'd have to handle now that
she was her own woman?

So, the sensible course of action was to get on with
her new life, full steam ahead. Just because she wasn't
woman enough to hold Wade's interest didn't mean other
men didn't find her attractive. As Annie said, it would
be nice to start a family before her golden years. There
were plenty of men around Hoot's Roost and one of them
might appreciate her. She might find someone who could
make her happy. She certainly wouldn't find Mr. Right,
sitting around Ryder Ranch, mooning over Wade.

LAURA WIGGLED AND WORMED her way into the sexiest
dress she owned and then pinned her hair atop her head,
letting a few wispy strands dangle around her face. She'd
applied a light coat of makeup then studied her reflection
in the mirror. She didn't look half-bad, she decided.
She'd acquired a tan after hours of riding horseback and
tending outdoor chores. Of course, the pricey dress did
its part to complement her figure. Sure should've, considering its high-dollar price tag.

Annie, Mark and Kevin were meeting Laura at Hoot's Tavern where a popular country band was doing a gig. And, after the past few days of watching Wade dodge her like flying bullets, she needed a night on the town, needed the reassurance that she hadn't contracted a plague that repelled all men.

Of course, what she really should do was make another play for Wade, to prove to him that she could be utterly casual about sex. He didn't have to know her heart was in it, not just her body. She could just behave as if it wasn't. She could secretly savor another magical night in his arms and keep her feelings to herself. He was a man, after all, she reminded herself. Why would he decline recreational sex when he claimed that was the only kind that interested him?

"Oh, right, that guilt-issue thing," she reminded herself. He'd obviously decided she was off-limits. Well, phooey on him. She was going out to enjoy herself at the tavern. He could stay here and rot for all she cared.

Determined of purpose, Laura spun away from the bathroom mirror and strode down the hall. She stopped short when she saw Wade and his cousins lounging in the living room, a cool one in hand and a pro baseball game playing on the tube.

"Whoa, mama!" Quint choked as Laura sauntered past him. "Where are you headed, gorgeous?"

"Hoot's Tavern." She tossed him a saucy smile and a wink.

"Save me a dance," Quint requested. "I'll be there in a couple of hours."

"Same goes for me," Vance said. "You look terrific."

"Thanks," Laura paused, hand on the doorknob. Her gaze automatically leaped to Wade who looked as if he were chewing on a lemon. So what else was new?

Quint's attention bounced to Wade then resettled on Laura. "Um...are you seeing anyone seriously, sweet-heart?"

Wade, she noticed, looked as disinterested in the question as any man could get—which served to annoy her. She'd given herself far too much credit to think for even one second that their night had meant anything special to him. "Nope," she said to Quint. "Nobody special."

Laura recalled what Annie had said about the Ryder cousins being careful not to encroach on each other's territory when it came to the women they dated. When Quint and Vance's gazed curiously at Wade, as if silently asking *his* permission to ask *her* out, she gnashed her teeth. Her temper hit full boil when Wade took a sip of his brew then shrugged lackadaisically.

Damn him! She refused to let him sit there like some all-powerful dictator who had the right to decree whom she could see socially. She'd dealt with that nonsense with her brothers, but she'd be damned if Wade got away with that!

"Don't look at him," Laura snapped. "He's not my father or one of my brothers and he has no say in the matter. After all, *I'm* only using *him* for sex and I can go out with whomever I like, whenever I like." On that parting shot, Laura sailed out the door.

WADE CHOKED ON A SWIG of beer and sputtered for breath. While he sat there wheezing, his cousins gaped at him. Curse that woman! He'd been careful not to let these two yahoos know about that fateful night, right here on the living-room floor with the drapes flung wide-open. Hell's bells, he couldn't even walk through the room without the memories bleeping across his mind, getting his body all riled up.

"She's using you for sex?" Quint croaked, frog-eyed.

Wade wiped the dribbles of beer from his shirt, sent a few choice expletives flying in Laura's wake and said, "She's kidding. She also has a smart mouth."

"So, you really don't care if Quint or I ask her out?" Vance questioned. "You know we'd never try to beat one another's time with a woman. So if you'd rather we didn't—"

"Why would I care?" Wade interrupted.

"You're sure?" Quint grilled him, watching him astutely.

"Do you want it in writing?" Wade asked sarcastically. "She's only my housekeeper. I don't have any claim on her." But he *was* going to strangle her for dropping that live grenade in his lap before she sashayed off in that body-hugging blue dress that advertised every luscious curve and swell of her sensational body, and that light coat of makeup that emphasized the stunning blue of her eyes, those thick lashes and that kiss-me-mindless lipstick that defined the sensuous curve of her mouth.

He was sitting here, stewing in jealous-green juice, wishing he'd be the one holding her close on the dance floor at the bar, letting all the men in attendance eat their hearts out and wishing they could exchange places with him. The thought sent a hot wave of desire sizzling through him. Damn it, that woman was turning him into a nut case!

He'd been trying to keep his distance from her and that was driving him crazy. He'd never treated her with the courtesy and respect she deserved from the moment she'd arrived and that hounded him to no end. And he sure as hell hadn't spent the time she deserved when they'd made love, ensuring the encounter was as special for her as it should've been. No, he'd been desperate and impatient and he could kick himself all the way into next week for behaving like a randy teenager who couldn't get enough of her quickly enough to satisfy himself. Sheesh! Every time he thought about how passion had turned him into a wild and uncontrolled sex fiend his guilty conscience flayed him alive.

She claimed she'd been satisfied but what did she know about sex? he asked himself. It wasn't like she had scads of experience to draw upon. With Laura, he'd practically turned into a minuteman. So desperate and needy that he couldn't summon enough self-restraint to make it last. Wham, bam, thank you ma'am. Now he was sending her out into the world with her distorted perception of what sex was like and she'd probably find someone who'd take more time with her and she'd realize he hadn't done justice to making love with her.

Hell and damn! He'd screwed up. And anyway, where was he supposed to find the words to make her stay, to make her understand that what he felt for her scared him spitless, that all that baloney he'd spouted about having sex on his terms—no strings attached—no longer applied? He wanted something deeper with her because she'd stirred something deep inside him that night and he'd been running scared ever since. He'd made love with her as if there was no tomorrow and then he'd gotten cold feet when he realized how much she meant to him. That woman had him so rattled that he didn't know straight up from siccum!

"Wade? Yoo-hoo?" Quint prompted, smiling wryly.

Resurfacing from his deep thoughts, he scowled. "What?"

"You really don't care if Laura dates one of us?" Quint questioned, his probing gaze locked on Wade.

"C'mon, cuz, I want the truth, the whole truth and nothing but."

"Yes, I care, damn it," he blurted out, knowing he'd get razzed but was just damn tired of holding all these tormenting feelings Laura aroused inside another moment. Possessiveness? You betcha. Jealous? That, too. A need to be with her that surpassed everything he'd ever experienced? Yup, definitely. But Bobbie Lynn had shredded his self-confidence and self-esteem and she'd taught him to be less trusting and more cautious before he laid his heart on the line again.

Vance and Quint exchanged meaningful glances, then Vance said, "So that's why you've been avoiding her all week and have been hanging out with us, even when you should've stayed off that mending leg. You've been afraid you'll get hurt again. Might as well face it, she's got your number and you're already halfway over the moon for that woman. There's nothing left to do but admit it to her and to yourself."

"And lemme tell ya, cuz," Quint said, adding his two cents' worth. "Laura ain't no Bobbie Lynn. If you've got half a brain you'll make double damn certain that woman doesn't slip through your fingers and land in another man's hands."

"Great," Wade said, then snorted. "Now I'm listening to advice for the lovelorn from a practical joker and a ladies' man. I really do need my head examined!"

"Did my ears deceive me? Did he say *love*lorn?" Vance taunted. "Did he just say that four-letter word aloud?"

Wade muttered under his breath when his cousins reverted to their teasing deviltry. "Just you wait," he warned. "There'll be women in your future who'll cut your legs out from under you and turn you wrong side out. Then we'll see who has the last laugh.''

''Ah, now he's a fortune-teller and soothsayer,'' Quint mocked playfully as he glanced around the room. ''Where's your crystal ball? Did you have to put it in storage to make room for all your sissified candles and potpourri?''

Wade flicked off the TV and hitched his thumb toward the door. ''Thanks for dropping by. Don't let the door hit you in the butt on your way out.''

''Hey, the game!''

''Go watch it on your own TVs,'' Wade interrupted. ''I'm going to Hoot's Tavern.''

''To keep surveillance?'' Vance asked, grinning wryly. ''Fine, we'll come with you.''

LAURA REALIZED THAT SHE'D drawn considerable notice when she walked into the bar with Kevin who placed his hand on the small of her back in some sort of male territorial ritual. She didn't pay a lot of attention to it because her thoughts centered around the parting shot she'd delivered to Wade on her way out the door. She couldn't believe she'd said that in front of his cousins, knowing how mischievous they were. Or maybe that's why she'd said it, so they'd give Wade hell.

Although two attractive cowboys approached to ask her to dance while Annie's boyfriend and Kevin were at the counter ordering a pitcher of beer, Laura politely declined. Furthermore, she shouldn't even be here with Kevin when her heart was back at Ryder Ranch.

Damn, she was an imbecile, she realized. She'd lost her temper with Wade and her pride had dictated her actions. She'd committed a tactical error. If she wanted to prove to him that she was loyal and true blue, reassure him that she was nothing like his faithless ex-wife she should've stayed home. *Not* invited him to a showing of Bobbie Lynn Revisited!

Laura sighed in frustration. She needed a how-to-manual so she'd know the appropriate approach to take with Wade because, Fact Number One: She was in love with the man and there was no denying it. Fact Number Two: She wanted him to know that she was dependable and reliable.

After what she'd been through the previous week, while her self-esteem took several direct hits, she could only begin to imagine Wade's humiliation during the split-up. Bobbie Lynn had destroyed his pride and trust and had dragged him through a divorce that was all the gossip of the small town.

How would *she* feel if she were in his position? Probably wary and cautious and reluctant to trust her emotions. The realization that she'd handled Wade all wrong put Laura on her feet in one second flat.

"Where are you going?" Annie questioned when Laura snatched up her purse.

"I can't do this," Laura told her. "I agreed to meet you and Kevin here at the tavern for all the wrong reasons."

"Yep, that's what I figured," Annie said astutely. "You've got a bad case of the hots for Wade and distraction just won't cut it."

Laura glared at her self-satisfied friend. "Don't you ever get tired of being right?"

"Nope, but I'm glad you've faced your feelings and have decided to confront Wade with them." Her gaze narrowed. "You *are* going to confront him with them, aren't you?"

Laura fidgeted uneasily. "I don't know. I—"

''Oh my, three heartthrobs all in a row. Be still my beating heart.''

Laura wheeled around to determine who had captured Annie's rapt attention. When she noticed the Ryder cousins had arrived on the scene and that they did, indeed, look devastatingly handsome, her knees nearly folded up beneath her. If she hadn't lost her heart to Wade already she wasn't sure she could decide who was the most handsome cousin among them.

She frowned curiously. Why was Wade here? What did that mean? Was he out to show her that he could lure any woman he wanted with one come-hither glance and that patented Ryder smile? Did he intend to play one-up to retaliate against her outrageous comments? Well, *she* was finished playing spiteful, juvenile games, even if Wade wasn't. Furthermore, Kevin Shelton deserved better than to be strung along. She needed to talk to him before she left.

Laura lurched around to intercept Kevin as he strode toward the table. She set aside the pitcher of beer then grabbed his hand to draw him out of earshot. ''I'm sorry, Kevin,'' she said gently and sincerely. ''I shouldn't have accepted this date because I'm interested in someone else.''

His smile faltered when he glanced toward the Ryder cousins. ''I figured I had competition. Judging by the glare Wade is flashing at me, I'd say he wants me out of your life.''

Laura glanced back to note Wade's narrowed gaze boring down on them. She, however, suspected that mutinous frown was directed at *her*. She mustered a smile and turned her attention back to Kevin. ''I value our friendship and I want us to have a good working relationship at school.''

"That won't be a problem," he assured her. "But would you mind telling Wade that we don't have anything going so he won't box my ears?"

Laura relaxed when Kevin grinned and graciously accepted her apology. "I guess I'll be seeing you at school."

"Sure thing, as long as Wade isn't trailing behind you," He chuckled when Wade shot him another pointed glance. "Ask me, the man has it bad for you, Laura."

More like Wade had it *in* for her. Well, too bad. She wasn't hanging around here. She was going home to curl up with a good book. If Wade wanted to reaffirm his masculinity by flirting with every female in attendance, then fine. More power to him... But *she* didn't have to watch.

Wade frowned curiously when Laura nodded abruptly as she strode toward the door. "Where are you going?"

"Home," she said.

"I thought you had a date." He glanced sharply at Kevin who'd taken a seat beside Annie.

Laura shook her head. "It wasn't an official pick-you-up-at-your-door and bring-you-home date. I told Kevin I'd only see him in a professional capacity when school starts."

His gaze locked on her. "Any particular reason why?"

She noticed Quint and Vance leaned in closer, clearly hanging on her every word. She would've loved to be a fly on the wall, eavesdropping on the conversation that had taken place after she dropped her bomb and left the ranch. Judging from the expression on Quint and Vance's faces they were dying to know what was going on. Well, maybe they needed to be reassured that she wasn't like Bobbie Lynn, too.

"The reason I'm not seeing Kevin socially again is

that I'm already using you for sex and it's probably too complicated to keep more than one man on a string at a time.'' She glanced from Wade to Quint and grinned elfishly. "How *do* you juggle all your women without hurting someone's feelings?''

Wade's lips quirked in a smile that made Laura's heart hopscotch around her chest. Vance snickered and Quint flashed her one of his notoriously scampish grins that was guaranteed to melt a woman's heart—just not *her* heart because she was hopelessly stuck on Wade.

Quint shrugged his broad shoulders and said, "Sorry, that's a trade secret, darlin'.''

"Since you're leaving, Wade can hitch a ride home with you," Vance insisted. "It'll save us a trip back to his place. Besides, he only came along to keep surveillance on you.''

Laura glanced up, startled.

"Clam up, Vance," Wade muttered darkly.

Laura regarded him warily. "My brothers didn't happen to contact you three guys and ask you to keep an eye on me, did they?''

"No, Wade thought of it all by himself," Quint supplied helpfully.

Her chin shot up. "That wasn't necessary. I'm old enough to know what I want and I can take care of myself.''

"Good for you, sweetheart. Glad to hear it," Quint said as he nudged Wade forward. "Now take your sex slave off our hands so we can kick up our heels and have some fun.''

"Don't mind if I do." Laura clasped Wade's hand and towed him toward the door. "I'll stop by the Hoot 'n

Holler convenience store and pick up some chocolate syrup and whip cream for tonight's experiments.''

Quint and Vance snickered in amusement and gave her the thumbs-up as Laura led Wade out the door.

9

"YOU MIGHT AS WELL POST a notice announcing that we're an official item on the local billboard," Wade told Laura as they strode across the parking lot. "When you arm my cousins with that kind of juicy gossip they'll blow this town sky-high."

"Well, I'll just have to deal with it then." Marshaling her courage, she headed for her car. "The fact is that I like you and I think you like me—to some extent, at least—even if you're too afraid of women to admit it." Since he didn't correct her assumption she took it as a good sign. "I think it's time we stopped all this ridiculous posturing and maneuvering and pretending, don't you? At least, *I'm* going to behave like a mature, sensible adult. I'm through playing games and it's time we reached an understanding of some sort." Her arm shot toward her low-slung sports car. "Now get in and sit down," she said in her best schoolmarm voice.

"Yes, ma'am," he said very obediently. "Did I mention that you look incredibly hot in that blue dress?"

"No, you didn't. It's nice to know you noticed."

"I'd have to be blind in both eyes not to notice or react to you. And that's a fact." Wade tried to wedge his broken leg into the compact car, but there wasn't room. Muttering, he finally gave up trying, leaned sideways and stuck his broken leg through the open window.

"That's good to know. And may I say that when the

Ryder cousins walked into the bar every feminine head turned in synchronized rhythm to scope you out. That was a very impressive grand entrance.''

"Was it? I didn't notice. I was too busy watching Kevin and the other male patrons drool and slobber all over themselves while they were gawking at *you*.''

Laura twisted in her bucket seat to meet his gaze directly. It was difficult to maintain a serious expression while he sat there with his leg draped over the window, but she managed. "Wade, I want to ask a favor.''

"If it involves whips and chains, in addition to the cream and syrup, the answer is no. I've suffered enough pain the past month, but thanks all the same.''

The teasing smile on his lips put her at ease. "I'll keep that in mind, but I'd like for you to stop avoiding me, because you need to stay off your leg and let it heal. And just because I don't want to see anyone else I don't want you to panic and think I'm trying to make demands on you, other than my own physical demands for sex," she stipulated, grinning elfishly. "You'll be my love slave and I won't put any long-term expectations on you because you'd probably freak out and we can't have that. But I want us to be square on this.''

There, she'd said it. She'd established the ground rules for this official affair she wanted to have with Wade.

Wade made himself as comfortable as possible in the cramped confines of her car. "So, you plan to use me for sexual experimentation and I'm not to worry that you have aspirations of taking the keys to my truck, stealing my horse, bowling over my dog, charming my hired man, booting me off my own ranch and claiming it as your own. That about sum it up?''

She nodded and her heart contracted when he flashed her a teasing grin. "In addition, you don't need to worry that I'm after your money because I can guarantee that I'm not.''

His lips pursed in pretended contemplation. ''Right. Got it. You're just after my body, battered though it is.''

Laura put the car in Reverse and backed from the parking space. ''Exactly right. You turn me on, Ryder, and I've become a disgustingly shallow person who's only interested in using you to satisfy erotic and sinful pursuits of the flesh.''

''Fine, then let's go home and I'll show you a few things that I was too needy to take time to show you the first time.''

Laura pushed on the brake and stopped the car in the middle of the parking lot. ''Oh for heaven sake, is that why you've been avoiding me?''

He glanced away and gave a jerky nod. She wanted to reach over and hug him for being so sweet. He was far more caring, conscientious and gentlemanly than he liked to admit if he'd been worrying about whether he'd thoroughly satisfied her. And things were definitely looking up, she mused. He'd implied that he planned to show her what seduction was all about. The prospect made her go hot all over.

''Just one more question, Ryder.''

''Okay, hit me with it.''

''I had my heart set on making enough money for a down payment on the old Draper place. So, when you've completed your instructions for Sexual Fantasies 101 and my employment is terminated, I'm not going to owe *you* money, am I?''

Wade chuckled and the warm, rich sound of his laughter crumbled the last corner of her heart. Hearing him laugh and seeing him smile did wonders for her attitude. She and Wade had reached an understanding—now that she'd assured him that she wasn't asking for more than he was prepared to give. Having him, one day at a time, was better than not being with him at all. She wasn't going to look too far into the future, just live in every pleasurable moment with Wade. Loving him as she did, she intended to make the most of her time with him.

WADE SENT LAURA OFF TO THE kitchen to grab a bottle of wine and some glasses. Hurriedly he picked up the scented candles and potpourri from the living room and hobbled down the hall. Tonight he was going to compensate for rushing through that first night.

Tonight would be different, he promised himself. He'd teach Laura the intricacies of slow, deliberate seduction. Maybe he didn't have Quint's legendary finesse or Vance's playful charm that attracted women in droves, but Laura meant something special to him. She was honest and brave enough to admit she had feelings for him, too.

He wasn't going to fight his feelings for her, just take a chance with his heart again. No more teasing insults. No more avoidance. He'd let his guard down and be himself when he was with her.

"Oh, my…"

Wade lit the last candle and turned to see Laura, still wearing that devilishly sexy blue rubber-band-of-a-dress, standing at his bedroom door. The wine bottle was clamped in her right hand and two stemmed goblets dangled from the fingertips of her left hand. The flickering candlelight and shifting shadows glided over her shapely figure and hauntingly lovely face like a lover's caress. Wade could fully appreciate the Seymour brothers' dedication to protecting the crown jewel of their family from the wiles of men. She was, by anyone's standards, an absolute knockout. She was bright, witty and spirited. The entire feminine package could bring a man to his knees and leave him begging for scraps of her affection.

And you could write this down in stone. If Wade ever had daughters he wasn't going to let any hormone-driven, sex-starved males within a mile of them. Children... A vision of little girls with golden hair and China-blue eyes tugged at his heartstrings. But before Wade got all mushy and sentimental he turned his attention to the beguiling woman at his bedroom door. He had his hands full at the moment—wanted his hands full of her sultry flesh. He wanted to give her such pleasure that she'd never turn away from him, that she wouldn't want to leave him when her employment ended and the fall school session began.

"I thought you objected to scented candles and such," Laura murmured as she studied the dainty lights Wade had distributed around the room.

"I've changed my mind about a lot of things," he murmured as he limped toward her.

"For instance?"

He took the bottle, uncorked it and filled their glasses. "Things like open drapes, miniblinds, women...et cetera."

"Interesting," she murmured, then sipped her wine. "You've got quite the seduction scene playing here. Does it always work well for you?"

"Dunno, you're the first woman who's been in my bedroom in six years. You tell me. Is it working?" His lips grazed hers in the slightest whisper of a kiss and he felt her melt on his mouth like intoxicating wine.

"I don't know," she whispered as she set her glass, and his glass, on the dresser. "You had me the first time I walked through your front door."

"Yeah?" He grinned rakishly as his hands glided down her hips to draw her body familiarly against his.

"Yeah." Smiling provocatively, she looped her arms around his neck. "You were too busy breathing fire at me to notice."

Hoo-boy, taking it slow and easy was probably going to kill him because his male juices were already at full boil. Didn't matter though. He was her designated sex slave. Fulfilling her fantasies was his duty—his greatest pleasure. If necessary, he'd die trying to show her the best time she'd ever had. Tough job, but someone had to do it.

"Mmm, you kept grinning at me like that and your legendary ladies' man of a cousin will have some dangerous competition." Laura raked her fingers through his hair. "Do I dare ask what you're thinking that provoked such a devilish smile?"

"You might not want to know what sexual fantasy I've planned for you," he growled huskily. "Might scare you off and you'd drop the class. But, be warned, I've got plenty of hands-on experiments planned this evening."

When Laura glided brazenly against the hard evidence of his arousal Wade groaned then wondered *who* was instructing *whom*. The woman was a natural-born seductress. She'd be downright dangerous with a little tutoring and practice. He, of course, would be more than happy to accommodate.

"Lesson number one," he murmured as he mapped the curve of her derriere. "Allow a man to undress you because the visual unveiling at his own hands is like an aphrodisiac."

"Point noted," she whispered as she rubbed up against him again and left him with the nearly overwhelming urge to throw back his head and howl.

Hands trembling, he slid the thin straps of her dress off her shoulders. He couldn't resist pressing a kiss to her scented skin. The fragrance of her perfume was driving him crazy. It filled his senses until he felt lightheaded. But determinedly, he focused on drawing the clingy fabric down her breasts until he could feast his hungry eyes on the creamy swells encased in a matching blue bra.

"My, my," he wheezed, heart pounding like a jackhammer. "You're definitely color coordinated, aren't you?"

"I like to think that I have exquisite taste," she teased, her voice noticeably husky.

"Let's check that out." He dipped his head to flick his tongue across the slope of her breasts. "Absolutely exquisite taste." He drew the stretchy fabric to her waist, then to her knees, exposing a scrap of lacy blue, barely there bikini panties. "Mmm," he murmured, "very nice. The only thing better would be if you weren't wearing any underwear at all."

"I'll make a note of that," she said unsteadily. "But aren't you a little overdressed here?"

"We'll get to that in due time." Wade discarded her dress, pulled the pins from her hair and led her to his bed—where she should've been that first night. Every time he remembered taking her on the floor he wanted to kick himself.

He scooped her up in his arms and gently laid her on his bed. Her blond hair spilled across his pillow as she arched leisurely then drew up one knee. Desire spiraled through him in rapid succession. Wade swallowed another tormented groan. *Slow and easy,* he chanted silently as he unbuttoned his shirt.

"Shouldn't I be doing that?" she asked. "Doesn't the same theory apply?"

Wade flicked open the last button then tossed aside his shirt. His hands dropped to the snap of his jeans and he saw her eyes widen as the hiss of the zipper filled the electrified silence. "You decide which technique works best for you," he suggested as he pushed his jeans down then heeled-and-toed out of the boot on his right foot.

Her admiring gaze roved over him. "I've never seen male strippers in person, but I doubt they've got anything on you."

Her appreciative stare intensified his desire. Watching her watch him, while he was drinking in the seductive sight of her lying on his bed, sent another wave of need crashing over him. Wade shoved his briefs over his hips and heard her gasp. He remembered there hadn't been much time for looking, only touching that first time. But Laura was definitely looking her fill now, and she apparently approved because she was all eyes and gaping mouth.

Grinning, Wade reached down to close her jaw then kissed her. Her hand stroked his chest, leaving fires burning in the wake of her touch. He could become addicted to having her hands all over him. She seemed eager to explore the textures and planes of his body. He was eager to teach her to pleasure him. But not now. He'd dedicated this evening to discovering every inch of her body by touch, by memory, by heart.

She curled willingly against him as he eased down beside her. For a moment Wade simply held her in his arms, marveling at how perfectly they fit together, at how much pleasure he derived from being with her.

Gad, he was starting to sound sappy. If he dared to confide these remarkable feelings to his cousins they'd have a field day. But there you had it. Laura stirred something intense and profound inside him. He wanted to probe the heights and depths of every conceivable pleasure, prolong every sensation—only with *her*. The realization gave him the patience needed to savor rather than devour, to linger in each kiss and caress. This was going to be a night to cherish, a night of intimate discovery, he promised himself.

Laura felt herself melt the instant Wade's gentle hands glided over her body. He deftly disposed of her bra and bent his head to whisper his warm breath over her ultrasensitive flesh. He flicked his tongue against her left nipple and she felt sizzling pleasure sear the very core of her being. He cupped his hand over her right breast, kneading her gently, and then plucked at the beaded crown with his fingertips. Laura instinctively arched upward and moaned as white-hot desire coiled inside her. Incredible sensations pulsed through her. The world spun away as she gave herself up willingly to him.

Laura swore she'd gone into nuclear meltdown when his hand drifted from the peak of her breast, across the plane of her belly to her inner thigh. She moaned aloud when he traced her heated flesh through her bikini panties. The feel of his skillful hand trailing along the elastic leg band aroused her, tormented her until she was half crazy with the need to have him inside her.

And all the while that his fingertips were gliding intimately over her his tongue encircled her nipple, holding her spellbound in incredible pleasure. She forgot to breathe when his fingertips glided beneath her panties to skim her moist flesh. When he dipped his finger inside her, spreading her, stroking her, Laura's breath sighed out of her body and she swore need itself replaced the air in her lungs. Sweet mercy, she was a quivering mass of unfulfilled hunger and he was making her ache with frenzied desperation!

"Come here," she pleaded, clutching impatiently at him.

Wade shifted beside her and smiled seductively. "The lesson isn't over yet. It's just begun so don't get timid and mistrusting on me because I'm not going to hurt you. I'd never hurt you. I'm going to show you that there's more to passion than what we shared the first time."

"What are you talking about? I wasn't complaining. I want you now—ah…" Her voice dried up when he moved down her body, trailing hot, greedy kisses over her belly and her hip, then peeled away her panties.

The world spun into oblivion when he dipped his head and his mouth glided over her secret flesh. She all but melted into the mattress when he nudged her legs apart, opening her to his erotic kisses and caresses. She shivered in helpless spasms when he tugged at her, aroused her with his lips, his tongue and his fingertips. She cried out his name when blazing pleasure exploded through her.

Need and desperation, so intense that her entire body shook with it, claimed her. Convulsions rocked her with each stab of his tongue, each stroke of his fingertip. She'd never imagined such intimacy, and certainly never experienced anything like this. Yet, the pleasure, incredible though it was, seemed empty without having him buried deep inside her.

"If you don't come here, right now, I swear I'll kill you," she gasped. "Please…Wade…now!"

While she shuddered in pleasure and swore impatiently at him, Wade donned protection, and then levered himself over her. This time he'd given her the sun, one beam at a time, taught her how hot passion could burn, and she'd responded to him in sweet, total abandon.

He angled his head to skim his lips over her mouth, hot with the sultry scent of her passion. He let her taste her own response on his lips and let her embrace the intimate knowledge that he'd touched her, tasted her completely. She was his in every way imaginable.

Arms shaking with barely restrained need Wade held himself above her as she writhed desperately beneath him. He surged forward gently—though it took what little self-control he had left not to bury himself to the hilt. Each time he slowly withdrew, Laura cursed him for driving her crazy. But he smiled wickedly at her, watching the candlelight flicker over her face, witnessing the hungry desperation of need he'd summoned from her.

He was still marveling at the power he held over her and the fact that this woman was honest enough to let him know how much pleasure he gave her when she knotted her fists in his hair and dragged his face to hers. She kissed him as if she was dying and he was her only hope of rescue. The last of his willpower skyrocketed out the window and scattered in a hundred different directions. He drove into her with the same wild, frantic need that he'd experienced that first night he'd made love with her. His body moved rhythmically against hers, plunging and retreating in frenzied cadence.

Wade was afraid he'd squeezed her in two when the ineffable sensations pelting him caused him to clutch her against him. But he couldn't make himself let go, couldn't stop. She did this to him. She turned all things sexual into all things emotional and spiritual. Sometime between the day she'd walked into his life and this incredible moment of intimacy she'd stolen his heart and soul.

He knew at that precise moment that he was a goner, despite his fierce vows, despite everything. The inescapable knowledge that this woman possessed him, consumed him, occurred to him at the same instant that the wild, whirling sensations of pleasure converged on him like the intense ray of a laser beam. Shudder after helpless shudder racked his body. Wade was sure his stampeding heart was going to beat him to death as he gasped for breath and saw a kaleidoscope of brilliant colors exploding behind his eyelids.

To say that Laura rocked his world was the understatement of the millenium.

Sometime later, after Wade swore he'd passed out from an overdose of passion and finally came to, he mustered the energy to lift his tousled head. Laura smiled in what he assumed to be pure feminine satisfaction. And that made him feel good all over. He'd compensated for that first night when she'd gotten him so hot and bothered that he'd barely managed to exert any control whatsoever over his runaway desires.

"That was certainly an intense session, Dr. Love," she purred throatily. "But next time I swear I'm dying, and you *let* me die a couple of times, I'll drop out of your class."

"No, you won't," he teased confidently, loving the fact that the passion between them was tempered with playful humor—something he'd never before experienced until Laura came along. "You're an inquisitive scholar by nature, professor. You're too curious to know what else you have to learn."

Her smile faded as she reached up to trace his eyebrows, his cheekbones, and the curve of his lips. "Wade, I—" She clamped her mouth shut, refusing to complete the comment.

He kissed her tenderly. "What is it, sweetheart?"

She shook her head and her tangled blond hair shimmered in the shifting light. "Never mind about that. Could we call an official truce? As much as I like exchanging teasing insults with you, because it keeps my wits sharpened, I like being with you like *this* so much better."

He grinned roguishly. "You like *this* better than tossing zingers? So do I, darlin', so do I."

When she smiled again, she nearly blinded him. "Yeah, that's kind of what I had in mind," she said. "I'll get plenty of opportunities to remain mentally alert with my new students who'll test my mettle, just to see how far they can push me. But I can only get *this* from you."

"And that's enough to satisfy you?" Wade cursed himself soundly when the insecurity left in Bobbie Lynn's wake flew from his lips.

Laura framed his face in her hands. All amusement left her elegant features. "Your ex was a dozen kinds of fool, Wade. I'm sorry you married a woman who didn't deserve you. I don't want the past to mess up what we have here and now. Deal?"

"Deal," he confirmed. "No more hang-ups, darlin'. I'll just be your devoted plaything."

Wade didn't want her to leave him—ever. But he kept telling himself that Laura was caught up in newly discovered passion and newfound liberation. She couldn't sort out how she honestly felt about making this relationship permanent yet. Wade had been spouting off for years that he'd never marry again, but the concept of *not* being with Laura, *not* having exclusive rights to her, made him oddly dissatisfied and restless.

One day at a time…and let's not forget about the incredible nights, he told himself as he cuddled up against her and drifted off into erotic dreams.

10

MICHAEL SEYMOUR PRESSED the button to roll down the tinted glass window. He stared at the two dark-haired cowboys who were filling the gas tank to the fire-engine-red pickup. "Excuse me, I wonder if you could give us directions."

The cowboys turned on their boot heels to toss him a cordial smile, but Michael just stared grimly at them. He and his brothers were not in sociable moods. Since the moment they'd discovered their sister had fed them conflicting information about her new employer they'd been silently fuming. Hurriedly they'd rearranged their business schedules to make this hasty trip to Nowhere, Oklahoma. Another thorough background check indicated that Wade Ryder was indeed thirty-three, not eighty-three. He'd been divorced and they suspected he was taking advantage of Laura.

For years Michael and his brothers had tag-teamed duties to ensure their baby sister didn't get mixed up with conniving men. They'd kept her well chaperoned from the day she'd been left in their care. They'd sent her to an exclusive girls' school and arranged for her to attend college in Denver so they could keep close tabs on her.

Naturally they'd done background checks on her roommate, Annie Nelson, when Laura insisted that she be allowed to live on campus the last two years of college. They'd let Laura and Annie know their activities were being closely monitored and they'd arranged for their sister to teach at an elite private school in town after her graduation.

Until now, until Laura had applied for this teaching position in this podunk town, hundreds of miles from their watchful eyes—without consulting or informing them—the Seymour brothers had been in control of the situation. They'd kept their promise to their father to shield and protect Laura from disappointment and harm.

If Wade Ryder, the pervert, thought he could take advantage of Laura Seymour—by forcing her to feed her brothers false information and holding her captive in the middle of nowhere—then he was in for a rude awakening. There were four reasons—and they were presently seated in this black Cadillac—why he wouldn't get away with it. He'd receive his just deserts.

The very idea of *not* upholding the solemn promise the Seymour brothers had made to their dying father outraged Michael. Oh, yes, Mr. Ryder would pay dearly, Michael vowed.

The cowboys sauntered over, draped their arms on the top of the Caddy then peered down at Michael and his younger brothers. "Whoya lookin' for, fellas?" one cowboy drawled.

Jerret leaned forward from the back seat and snarled, "We're told Laura Seymour is presently…um…working for Wade Ryder. Any idea where we can find them?"

Michael noted the cowboys' dark brows shot up like exclamation marks, then they grinned. "Sure, but Laura is already taken. Wade staked his claim and won't let anyone near her, so you can forget any interest in her."

Murderous fury roiled through Michael's body and he clamped a death grip on the steering wheel. "She's our sister," he all but spat.

"Laura's your sister, huh? Well, how 'bout that. Nice wheels, by the way. We don't see all that many Cadillacs tooling around in cattle country. You boys must be from the big city, right?" the second cowboy questioned.

Michael was in no mood to chitchat with the modern-day versions of Gene Autry and Roy Rogers. "You were about to give us directions to Ryder Ranch," he said, teeth clenched.

"Oh, yeah, we were, weren't we?" Grinning for no reason Michael could account for, the first cowboy gestured toward the two-lane highway. "Just mosey down this road to Hoot's Tavern. Then go two more miles to the old farmhouse."

"That'd be the Draper place," the second cowboy put in. "There's a rusted sign out front that says: Tractor Repair. But nobody lives there. The place is for sale."

Damn, thought Michael, they'd definitely arrived in Hicksville and encountered the village idiots.

Everett leaned over from his rigid position on the passenger side of the front seat and said impatiently, "Then what are we supposed to do? Send up smoke signals?"

The cowboys chuckled good-naturedly. Of course, *they* weren't sitting in the car, envisioning the worst scenarios that could've befallen their little sister after she hired on with that lecherous rancher who probably held her captive and kept her isolated for his fiendish purposes.

"Naw, no need for smoke signals. Hang a left onto the graveled road. Don't speed off in a cloud of dust 'cause that road's rougher than a corncob. You'll rattle your teeth plumb outta yer heads," the second cowboy drawled.

Michael bit down on a catty comment that would've hurried along these slow-talking yahoos, who kept grinning for no apparent reason—except that they were extremely dense and the Seymour brothers had the misfortune of stumbling onto them.

"Go four miles on that graveled road," the first cowboy instructed. "You'll see Ryder Ranch on your right. Don't pay any mind to the cow dog that guards the place. He'll only light into one of you, so three of you should make it to the front door in one piece."

"And old Duff? The hired hand? Don't fret when he shows up with a loaded shotgun," the second cowboy added. "He's blind in one eye and he can't shoot straight. Yeah, you should be relatively safe until you tangle with Wade Ryder himself."

Michael slammed his hand down on the button to automatically raise the window. Seething, he shoved the Caddy into gear and took off down the highway.

"I get the first crack at that Ryder character," David growled as he smacked his right fist into his left hand.

"We should've checked out this situation sooner," Jerret muttered angrily. "That bastard probably stole Laura's cell phone and cut his phone line so she couldn't call for help."

"I don't care if she did sign a teaching contract out here in the boondocks, she's coming home with us after we clean Ryder's clock," Everett fumed.

Michael didn't utter another word. He was too busy picturing the pleasurably vindictive task of taking Wade Ryder apart with his bare hands, then letting his spiteful brothers have their turn. The man was definitely going to be worse than roadkill when they were through with him!

QUINT PILED INTO HIS RED truck, switched on the ignition and glanced at Vance. "You don't think we laid it on too thick with the Seymour brothers, do you?"

Vance propped his arm over the open window and

chuckled gleefully. "Are you kidding? Those four stuffed
suits deserved exactly what we gave them."

"Amen to that," Quint agreed. "Snobs one and all.
It's a wonder Laura turned out so well if she had to put
up with those highbrows."

"Since we probably lined Wade up to be murdered on
the spot, I suppose we should cruise out to his ranch to
watch the fireworks," Vance said as Quint drove off.

"Wade can be murdered or he can marry Laura. His
choice," Quint said, snickering. "This should force a
showdown. Ask me, those two might as well take the
next step and make this a permanent commitment. The
only way to separate them these days is with a bucket of
cold water."

Vance chuckled as they tailed the black Caddy past
Hoot's Tavern. "Yeah, that nonsense about *no wedding*
being written in stone didn't throw me off track. I left a
message on Gage's pager, asking him to come home for
the ceremony. It'll be nice to have the entire family together again."

"For Wade's funeral or his wedding, whichever comes
first," Quint said, snickering. "I guess we'll have to get
gussied up in monkey suits one way or the other."

LAURA DISMOUNTED FROM THE mare and waited for
Wade to swing down from the gelding and balance on
his good leg. She sighed appreciatively at the sight of
him, remembering the pleasure they'd shared the past two
weeks. Since Wade was scheduled to have his cast removed the following day, he no longer needed her help.
She'd have no excuse to remain at his ranch. Even the
anticipation of beginning her new teaching assignment
couldn't overshadow the knowledge that she was going

to miss being with Wade like crazy when they were no longer sharing the same house.

They'd become inseparable—tending chores, horseback riding and making love. She couldn't imagine what her life was going to be like without him in it constantly. She ached to voice the words that whispered through her heart, but she'd held them back, for fear of spoiling the magic between them. She preferred to remain suspended here in paradise until Wade indicated that it was time for her to leave.

She smiled ruefully when Wade stepped up behind her and looped his sinewy arms around her waist. "Hey, sweetheart, why the sad face?"

She nuzzled her cheek against the solid, muscular wall of his chest, then tilted her face up to silently request his kiss. When he complied, the sense of loss that was gnawing at her multiplied tenfold. "Thanks, I needed that."

"No kidding. The most insatiable female I've ever met," he teased, green eyes twinkling. "Not that I'm complaining. In fact, I'm all for skipping lunch and going right to dessert."

Laura turned in the circle of his arms and pushed onto tiptoe to kiss him soundly, hungrily—putting everything she had into it. "Ever done it out behind the barn?"

"Nope," he growled roughly as he skimmed the palm of his hand over the cotton fabric that covered her taut nipples. "But we've about exhausted all the places there *are* to do it. The floor, the table, up against the wall, on the sofa. In broad daylight with Duff puttering around the barn might not be such a hot idea."

She rubbed against the evidence of his arousal and smiled seductively. "Okay, killjoy, but you might want to know that I'm not wearing a stitch of underwear."

"Hot damn, this I gotta see..." His voice trailed off

when the crunch of gravel and the slamming of car doors indicated visitors had arrived. Wade grabbed the reins to both horses and limped around the corner of the barn.

Laura trailed behind him then silently cursed when she recognized the unexpected guests. She wanted Wade all to herself, wanted to savor every moment alone with him. But from all indication, her private interlude with Wade had come to a screeching halt. Laura inwardly groaned as she watched the four impeccably dressed men stalk toward the front door of the house, totally ignoring Frank who'd bounded from the barn and began barking up a storm.

"Damnation," Laura muttered, staring into the distance.

Wade glanced down at her in concern. "What's wrong?"

"Pretty much everything. Those are my brothers."

Wade's wide-eyed gaze swung back to the identically dressed men whose grim expressions spelled trouble. Well, hell, this should be fun.

"Over here!" Wade called, waving his free arm.

"Shh-shh!" Laura grabbed his hand and jerked it down. "We can be mounted up and long gone before they catch us."

Wade appraised the alarmed expression on her face. He wasn't sure why she was upset. Was it because she didn't want her brothers to know she and Wade were a couple? Was she ashamed for her family to find out how it was between them?

That thought caused Wade to grit his teeth. What the hell was this? A summer fling that was about to come to a skidding halt because the brothers Seymour had arrived and Laura didn't want them to know she'd been fooling around with a country bumpkin while she was testing her independent wings?

The four men wheeled with the precision of soldiers on parade and glowered at Wade. Not that he was intimidated. He'd been in enough barroom brawls during his rodeo heydays to know he could take a punch as well as he could throw one. Despite the unfavorable odds, he'd be damned if he'd bound onto the saddle and hightail it through the pasture like a coward.

"Wade Ryder, I presume," Michael Seymour sneered.

"Wade, let's go," Laura implored. "This could get ugly."

He stared at her for a long moment. "Are you ashamed of me and what we have going?"

"No, but I want you in *one* piece." She shot her brothers an apprehensive glance. "They want you *in* pieces."

Wade watched the four men—whose eyes were various shades of blue and whose hair was various shades of blond—loosen their ties, peel off their expensive coats and toss them on the hood of the Caddy. Like grim-faced warriors headed into battle, they advanced forward with their fists knotted and their jaws clenched tightly. Their stormy gazes locked on Wade. He was pretty sure they had murder on their minds.

"Hi, guys." Laura forced a cheery smile. "What are you doing here?"

"It's okay, honey, you don't have to pretend anymore," Everett growled, his formidable glare boring into Wade like a worm into an apple. "He can't hurt you anymore."

"Hurt me?" Laura stepped directly in front of Wade like a human shield. "The only one who's hurt around here is Wade." She gestured toward the cast on his leg.

"Right," David growled. "He'll be lucky if all he

ends up with is another broken leg and a couple of mangled arms.'' He turned his ferocious snarl on Wade. ''You bastard! You're going to pay for this!''

Wade glanced up when he heard the roar of an approaching truck. It appeared that his rescue brigade had arrived. Good, three against four odds were acceptable. Of course, he'd be happier if Gage was here to make them perfectly even because the brothers Seymour looked mad enough to spit nails—and big enough to make every punch count. Damn, considering how dainty and petite Laura was he'd sort of envisioned her brothers as medium height and build. Wrong. These four men could've been the starting line for a pro football team.

''Hey, fellas!'' Quint called as he bounded from the truck, waving his arms in expansive gestures. ''Remember us?''

''What do you want?'' Jerret snapped rudely.

''Well, ya see,'' Vance drawled as he moseyed down the hill. ''We forgot to tell y'all somethin'.''

''What's that?'' David demanded impatiently.

''Our names happen to be Ryder, too.'' Quint's good-natured grin evaporated and he got that dangerous glint in his eyes that you didn't see too often, but you never wanted to ignore it when you saw it. ''We're real partial to Cousin Wade, so don't even think about beating him to a pulp.''

Wade smiled to himself. Although his cousins delighted in tormenting him until hell wouldn't have it, they were prepared to provide backup when trouble arose. And Wade was definitely in trouble because the brothers Seymour didn't look the least bit intimidated by the arrival of reinforcements. They still looked madder than four wet roosters that were crowing about exacting revenge against Wade in their sister's behalf.

"What's going on out here?" Duff asked as he emerged from the barn. "Who are these guys?"

"Back off, Duff, we mean you no harm," Michael growled.

Wade's surprised gaze shot to Quint who flashed him an I'll-explain-later glance.

Duff squinted at the Seymour brothers. "Okay, fine. I'll get the shotgun and don't think I won't use it if you boys start trouble," he said, then stalked back into the barn.

And then the brothers Seymour broke into a dead run, charging directly at Wade with teeth bared and fists cocked.

"Stop it!" Laura threw herself directly in the path of her oncoming brothers. "Don't you dare touch him!"

Everett pulled up short and reached out to steady Laura before he accidentally plowed over her. Laura wrenched her hand free and flung out both arms like a human roadblock. "That's enough! I am sick to death of you riding to my rescue, as if I don't have enough brains in my head to lead my own life and make my own decisions!"

That got the brothers Seymour's attention. They stared at Laura as if they'd never seen her before. How was it possible? Wade had never been able to see past her, think past her.

"That's right," Laura ranted on, hands fisted on her shapely hips, head tilted upward and glossy blond hair ruffling in the breeze. "Now pay attention here, bros. This is *my* life. I appreciate your care and concern, but you never let me breathe or fully experience life. I never learned to stand up for myself until Wade taught me."

The four men focused their menacing gazes on him. He just stared them down and let Laura have her well-deserved say, even though his protective instincts urged him to let loose on her overprotective brothers with both barrels blazing.

Like a teacher calling her class to order, she snapped her fingers in her brothers' faces. "Look at me and pay attention here. Nothing has been going on that I didn't want to go on," she told them bluntly. "For your information, and you better listen when I say this, damn it, I love this man and you are *not* going to beat him up."

She loved him? Wade's jaw dropped to his chest and he staggered slightly, stunned that she had the courage to admit her feelings in front of God, his cousins, her brothers and Duff who was hovering beside the barn door. *She loved him?* After he'd given her hell for a month, then avoided her when the feelings she stirred inside him had him running scared for fear of getting his heart trounced on again?

"Love?" David snorted. "You wouldn't know love if it walked up and bit you, shortcake. How could you? We never let you date a man for more than a month."

"*After* said date had been thoroughly checked out and met our approval," Jerret added.

Michael flashed her a surreptitious glance. "You know why that was necessary, so don't pretend you don't."

Wade had no idea what that meant. But apparently Laura did because she said, "Yes, I know why it was important, but I was careful, just as you insisted. I bailed out of every relationship at the first indication of ulterior motive."

Wade was totally lost here. He hadn't a clue what they were discussing.

"And what about him?" Everett's arm shot toward Wade like a speeding bullet. "Does he know?"

"What the hell are you talking about?" Wade asked worriedly. "Her migraines? Are they symptoms of a life-threatening illness?'' His alarmed gaze swung to Laura. "Damn it, why didn't you tell me?'' Cold fear knotted in his belly and his heart plummeted to the soles of his feet. Oh, God, she was suffering from an incurable ailment that was going to take her way from him forever! *Oh, God!*

Laura waved him off. "No, no, no, forget the migraines. We have greater issues to discuss here than that." She lurched around to confront her brothers. "It wouldn't have mattered if Wade was the first man or the twentieth man I met when I claimed my independence from you."

She bore down on one of her brothers who stood second from the left. "I love Wade and I sorely resent that remark about not knowing love if it walked up and bit me, Davie. Wade makes me happy and I want to be with him. I love the way he looks and who he is deep inside. So you better get used to the idea that I'm staying in Hoot's Roost. Furthermore, Wade doesn't treat me like a helpless female who requires constant guidance and supervision. He lets me be me. He has excellent reason not to trust women because he was betrayed once, but he trusts me and respects me for who I am."

Four narrowed gazes zeroed in on Wade. So there, he thought, proud as punch of Laura for asserting herself toward her domineering brothers. That she was willing to stand up to them, *on his behalf,* made his self-esteem swell to near bursting. She loved him and she wasn't afraid to admit it. Damn, this was one helluva woman.

"In addition," she went on determinedly, "Wade has every right to decide how he feels about me—without your interference. If he doesn't love me back, if he doesn't want me in his life permanently then it's his place to say. You aren't going to twist his arm a dozen different ways and bully him into making a commitment. You got that?''

Four Seymour gazes bounded from Laura to take Wade's measure. He'd held his tongue long enough. He'd allowed Laura to have her say, but now it was his turn. ''I do have a choice and I choose Laura, whether you bozos like it or not.'' He limped boldly forward to wrap his arm around Laura's waist. ''I'm crazy about your sister. I intend to be there to nurse her through the next migraine, although it drives me nuts to see her in such pain. But I'll be there every time she needs me, just like she's been here for me.''

''You tell 'em,'' Duff put in. ''We're keeping this gal.''

''I love her like crazy, but I refuse to stifle her and smother her because she's enjoying her newfound independence. I admire her intelligence, her optimism, her work ethic and I adore her sense of humor—which, by the way, it appears she's needed to put up with the likes of you. And you might as well know, here and now, that I'm not ever letting her go. I'll provide for her, keep her safe and make her happy as best I can. So…'' Wade rolled up his shirtsleeves, prepared to take them all on if they objected to the roundabout proposal he'd offered Laura. ''Who's first? Everett? Michael? Davie? Jerret? I want to marry her if she'll have me. Any of you have a problem with that?''

''Marry me?'' Laura tweeted, her gaze swinging to Wade.

''Thanks for asking, professor. Don't mind if I do,'' he said playfully.

Wade noticed the brothers Seymour were grinning at him. So were Quint and Vance. He supposed there was cause for amusement because he'd just broken a long-standing vow—one he swore was etched in stone. Well, things changed. Laura had changed him. He wanted to marry her, if she agreed to it. He wanted to spend the rest of his life trying to please her, even if he had to listen to his evil cousins razz him for being a lovesick hypocrite.

"He really doesn't know, does he?" Michael asked, chuckling. "He is totally clueless, isn't he?"

"He's not clueless," Laura defended as she roped her arms around his waist and snuggled closer. "But no, I didn't tell him and I'm not sure I want to, either."

"Tell me what?" Wade questioned. "Whatever it is, it doesn't matter. We'll work through it together."

Davie chuckled. "Ever heard of the Glori Computer Software Corporation?"

"Sure. Who hasn't?" Wade replied, befuddled. "I'm not a computer whiz, but I know the international company is worth megabucks and most businesses use their programs. In fact, I think your sister updated my programs with Glori Software."

Jerret said, "Our dad named the company after Mom."

"Oh, hell…" Wade glanced accusingly at Laura. "You're disgustingly rich, is that it? Your brothers have protected you from money-hungry boyfriends with dollar signs in their eyes? Well, I can't blame them for that. I'd probably react the same way."

While Quint and Vance stood there, their lips forming silent *wows,* Wade stared at the brothers Seymour. "Okay, fine. You want me to sign a prenuptial agreement? No problem. I have no objection. All I want is Laura as my wife."

Wade watched the four men put their heads together for a private conference then Michael said, "We've decided to sign Laura's trust over to her and drop our guardianship. Obviously you're not after her money.''

''Damn straight he's not.'' Vance grinned wickedly.

Wade inwardly winced. He knew that look and it was pure deviltry—the practical joker at his best.

Vance flicked Wade one of those just-try-to-shut-me-up looks and added, ''I think my cousins and I need to kick *your* citified butts for raising a sister who uses men for her own shallow purposes. *Your* precious baby sister has turned *our* poor, battered cousin into her sex slave. If I were you, I'd be concerned about getting these two married, PDQ.''

''We don't want to see Wade's reputation ruined more than she's already ruined it.'' Quint smiled mischievously. ''It puts a black mark on the Ryder family name, ya know. And it isn't doing a thing for the Seymour name, either.''

Wade decided he was still going to have to kill his cousins for embarrassing Laura to the extreme. Her face gushed with color, from her neck to her hairline. Her brothers cast condemning glances at her, making her squirm self-consciously.

''You're in big trouble,'' Michael muttered ominously.

''We raised you better than that,'' Jerret said gruffly.

''You're definitely marrying this cowboy,'' David declared.

''The sooner the better,'' Everett insisted. ''And you *will* be staying with us until the ceremony.''

Wade put his one good foot down on that one. ''No, she won't. I want her here. That is, if this is where she wants to be.'' He glanced down at Laura. ''Your choice, sweetheart.''

Laura flung her arms around his neck, threw back her

head and graced him with a smile that rivaled the brilliance of the sun. "I love you, Wade."

"I love you, too, darlin'. Marry me?"

"I'd love to. Looks like I won't be buying the Draper homestead after all." She kissed him squarely on the mouth, then flung herself into her brothers' arms for a family hug.

Wade watched the oversize men melt beneath Laura's beaming smile and joyous laughter. Well, maybe those goons weren't so bad after all. Obviously they loved their sister dearly, devotedly. He certainly had *that* in common with them.

When Laura offered to give her brothers a tour of the ranch house, Wade remained behind. He crossed his arms over his chest and narrowed his gaze on his mischievous cousins. "Who gave the brothers Seymour directions to my ranch without any advance warning?"

"We did," Quint said unrepentantly. "But this modern version of the gunfight at OK Corral turned out all right."

"Turned out perfect," Vance added. "We'll get you hitched before school starts." He gestured toward the brothers Seymour. "They'll insist on it, too. Can't have the new schoolmarm in Hoot's Roost living out here in sin. It's bad for our reputation. Don't want you ruining our good name."

"That'll be the day," Wade said, then scoffed. "Between Quint's legendary black book and his long string of admiring women and your notorious practical jokes and your female fan club I've barely been able to hold up my head in town. I wouldn't be surprised if that's why Gage took the job that keeps him out of the country indefinitely. He's probably too embarrassed to settle down on his ranch and face the humiliating gossip you've caused.''

"Aw shucks, cuz, we aren't that bad," Quint drawled.

"No, you're worse and I'll laugh myself silly when I hear wedding bells ringing over your heads," he threatened.

"Ain't happenin'," Quint said confidently. "Staying single is my motto."

"Ditto," Vance said with all the arrogant confidence that had become Wade's own downfall.

"We'll see." Wade pivoted toward the house. "Will you unsaddle the horses for me? I'm going to the house to get acquainted with my future brothers-in-law. Who knows? I might end up liking them more than my own evil cousins."

"Naw, they're too uptight and stuffy," Quint insisted. "Better stick with us. We're the ones who showed up to guard your back when those city slickers decided to dismantle you. Where are ya gonna find loyalty like that, huh?"

"Thanks for that, at least," Wade murmured. "Come up to the house for a cool one and bring Duff with you. But you better warn him not to entertain visions of giving Laura away at the wedding in her father's stead. I predict the brothers Seymour will claim that privilege."

Wade limped to his house, glad to have his future with Laura resolved. He should thank her brothers for bringing the situation to a head. He'd been reluctant to stick his neck out and ask Laura if she wanted to make things permanent between them. Because of her brothers and his cousins' interference there was nothing left to settle except the wedding date.

Wade hoped Laura's brothers didn't have visions of camping out on his ranch to ensure there was no more hanky-panky until after the wedding. If he were saddled with overnight guests who refused to leave until after the nuptials, he doubted Laura would complain about sneaking out behind the barn. After all, it was *her* idea.

Epilogue

"DAMN, I THOUGHT THEY'D never leave," Wade muttered as he watched the guests vacate the driveway.

Laura smiled in amusement as the last of her family, and his enormous family drove away. It had been a hectic week of hasty wedding arrangements and phone-call invitations. Laura knew Wade was exceptionally pleased that Cousin Gage had arrived minutes before the ceremony—although the long-lost cousin could only spare a few hours to visit with his relatives before he flew off as quickly and mysteriously as he'd come. No one offered details about Gage's present occupation, but the moment he walked through the door of the church that had been filled to capacity she knew her prediction that all four Ryder cousins were drop-dead handsome was right on the mark. The groom and his three best men were definitely a sight to behold.

Wade expelled an audible sigh of relief. "I haven't had you all to myself for a week. We couldn't even sneak off without a damn chaperone tailing us. How'd you tolerate growing up with constant surveillance?"

Laura shrugged then smiled wryly at her new husband. "I thought you might have appreciated the time you spent without me while my brothers were underfoot. There was a time when you couldn't run fast enough or far enough to avoid me."

"But now that I have that blasted cast off, I'll be doing

considerable chasing.'' He waggled his brows suggestively. "We'll see who's running scared now."

"You don't frighten me, you big phony," she said. "Despite all that growling I tolerated when I first arrived I've discovered that you're just a marshmallow on the inside."

Wade drew her gently into his arms and smiled down at her with so much love and affection that Laura could scarcely breathe. She still couldn't believe that he belonged to her and she belonged to him forever and ever.

They'd both changed considerably since they'd first met. She'd learned to take control of her own life, to stand up for herself. Wade had learned to trust, to believe in the power and magic of this love that had blossomed between them.

"Where do you want to go on our honeymoon?" he murmured as his lips skimmed that sensitive point beneath her ear. "Name the place, sweetheart. I'll make the arrangements."

Laura looped her arms around his neck and nestled familiarly against him. "I'm already in paradise. There's nowhere else I'd rather be as long as I'm with you."

"Yeah?"

"Oh, yeah, definitely. We can take a honeymoon during Christmas break. But right now I just want to take my final exam in my Sexual Fantasies 101 class that had to be postponed when my brothers showed up to breathe down my neck."

Wade scooped her up in his arms and headed down the hall, thankful that hampering cast was gone. He intended to take up where they'd left off—before the inconvenient intrusion.

When he laid Laura on their bed, she came to her knees to help him doff his shirt and slacks. Then she proved to him that she could be an exceptionally inventive seductress. The brazen touch of her hands and lips left him drifting in erotic oblivion. She whispered her love for him on every inch of his body and then he returned the favor enthusiastically.

In the dim light the diamond ring he'd placed on her finger winked at him with a promise of a long and happy future. Wade smiled as he came to her, giving her all that he was—the best of what he could be—because her love for him made it easy to believe in forever.

And when they were one, united in body, mind and spirit, Wade knew beyond all doubt that'd he'd gotten it right the second time around.

Laura Ryder was his wife, his life and his footloose and fancy-free cousins didn't have a clue what they were missing. *He* was the one who'd had the last laugh and he was looking forward to a lifetime of Laura's love.

Restaurant Romeo

Carol Finch

HARLEQUIN®

TORONTO • NEW YORK • LONDON
AMSTERDAM • PARIS • SYDNEY • HAMBURG
STOCKHOLM • ATHENS • TOKYO • MILAN • MADRID
PRAGUE • WARSAW • BUDAPEST • AUCKLAND

1

QUINT RYDER SIGHED wearily as he cruised his red 4x4 pickup through town. Although it was only noon he was already exhausted. The previous night's storm had wrought havoc at his ranch, as well as his cousins' ranches. Earthshaking explosions of thunder, sizzling lightning bolts and howling winds had sent livestock into a full-blown panic. Since the crack of dawn, Quint had been on horseback, alongside Cousin Vance, wallowing in mud and tracking down stampeding cattle. He was tired and hungry and he had to pick up rolls of barbwire to replace the half-mile of fence the cattle had taken out during their midnight escape after which they scattered all over creation.

Still dressed in mud-splattered jeans, boots, shirt and chaps, Quint pulled into the only available parking space at Martin's Feed and Farm Supply. He frowned curiously as he tramped inside to nod a greeting to his country neighbors. The place looked like a farmer/stockman convention.

It wasn't unusual for farmers and ranchers to congregate in the feed store, especially after storms that kept them out of the field. It was the best time to restock supplies and chitchat with neighbors. Ordinarily there was plenty of laughter, playful teasing and lighthearted conversation. However, that wasn't the case today. Quint's neighbors were grim-faced and solemn.

Quint braced himself, anticipating the news that someone in the community had been involved in a serious accident or died. "What happened?" he asked the store at large.

The place erupted. Everyone started talking at once and Quint flung up his hand to halt the garbled explanation. "Whoa, fellas. Who died?"

Wes Martin, the store proprietor, appointed himself spokesman of the disgruntled crowd. "Hoagie's."

Quint's eyes popped and his jaw dropped. "Hoagie Lawson died?"

"Naw, he's alive and kicking, but Hoagie's Diner is dead and gone," one of the ranchers grumbled.

Quint still didn't get it. True, he'd been out of town— out of state actually—for a week. His cousins had volunteered him to haul the stock trailer to Austin, Texas, to pick up the high powered Black Angus bull they'd purchased to replace the cantankerous beast that had broken Cousin Wade's leg and tore out fences like they were going out of style.

Quint had been out of the gossip loop for a while so he didn't have a clue why or when Hoagie's Diner had passed from existence.

The mainstay for lunch and supper in Hoot's Roost, Hoagie's Diner had been a landmark for decades. The Fifties' style malt shop was the place—in addition to the feed store—where cattlemen and ranchers gathered to exchange ideas, farming techniques and other useful information.

"Hoagie Lawson is closing down the café?" Quint questioned incredulously. "Why'd he do that?"

"Because his hoity-toity daughter has come back to town to take over. Hoagie and Wanda have decided to retire and tour the U.S. of A.," one of the farmers muttered sourly.

Quint still didn't see cause for concern. Maybe he was just too damn tired to assimilate facts. "So, what's the problem?"

"What's the problem?" Wes Martin hooted, his thick chest swelling up like a bagpipe. "Stephanie Lawson, fresh from one of Dallas's five-star, la-di-da hotels and restaurants, has decided to remodel the place. There's been a string of semitrucks unloading boxes of stuff all week. Carpenters, electricians and plumbers have been filing in and out there like you wouldn't believe."

"Rumor is that there'll be no more burgers 'n fries for lunch. No more meat 'n taters for supper. This sure as hell ain't Big D, but that woman's trying to pretend it is," Randel Bentley put in sourly. "We've got to do something about it!"

Another uproar erupted. Everyone yammered at once. Quint picked up the name Stephanie Lawson and something about wearing coats and ties and eating foreign cuisine. Objections and complaints about the change in management flew around the feed store like whizzing bullets. It finally sank into Quint's tired mind that the new owner of Hoagie's Diner wasn't planning to cater to the rural crowd and that's why everyone was up in arms.

The vision of a tall, scrawny redhead with eyeglasses the size of goggles and a mouthful of metal braces leaped to mind. Oh, yeah, Quint remembered Stephanie from his high school days. She'd been about four years younger—a clumsy, geeky bookworm who'd reminded him of a giraffe.

She'd taken over the café and wanted to turn it into an upscale restaurant in the boondocks of Hoot's Roost? Hell, that was just plain crazy.

This was the heart of cattle country, for Pete's sake. The majority of residents of the community were from the blue-collar crowd, not businessmen in power suits who attended power lunches and conventions. What the hell was that woman thinking?

Obviously she wasn't thinking, Quint decided. During high school her IQ tests had bordered on genius, but apparently she'd failed Common Sense 101 in college. Anybody with half a brain knew farmers and cattleman just wanted a place to grab a burger before heading back to their waiting tractors or bounding onto a horse to work livestock. They got dirty and greasy and sweaty and they sure as hell didn't have the time or inclination to shower and change into a tux before heading off to wolf down some grub!

Sheesh! No wonder the locals were in an uproar. Life as they knew it was changing. Furthermore, the Ryder cousins had a long-standing verbal agreement to sell beef to Hoagie. Had Stephanie decided the contract was null and void now that she'd taken over?

"Now we've got no dining option except Hoot 'n Holler convenience store," Clem Spaulding complained.

Quint grimaced. From the sound of things his growling stomach was in for a huge disappointment. He wouldn't be picking up burgers and fries to go. He'd be choking down one of those dried out, cellophane-wrapped sandwiches, a sack of potato chips and canned pop for lunch. Damn, his taste buds had been all set for a juicy cheeseburger and the best French fries in three counties.

Frowning, Quint stared through the plate-glass window and glanced across the town square toward what once had been Hoagie's Diner. The new sign read: Stephanie's Palace. A white-and-gold banner flapped in the breeze, informing the townsfolk that the café was closed for remodeling. Quint squinted to read the smaller print.

"Does that sign say only open from 5:00 p.m. until 10:00 p.m.?" he croaked in astonishment.

"Yup, that's what it says," Clem assured him. "If you could read the other fine print from here you'd know it also says coats and ties only. That girl's plumb lost her mind! Who the hell does she think she is? The Queen of Sheba or something?"

Everyone started yakety-yakking again. Then Wes Martin waved his beefy arms in expansive gestures, demanding attention. "I've got it!" he hollered over the roar of the grumbling crowd.

Everyone shut up fast. All eyes turned to Wes whose pudgy face displayed a smile that made his full jowls wrinkle like an accordion.

"What have you got?" Clem demanded anxiously.

"The solution to the problem with this fancyschmancy restaurant that we don't want. We need a spokesman to approach the new owner and convince her to cater to local clientele." His smile widened as he stared directly at Quint. "Someone who's known for his trademark charm and his way with women. Someone whose legendary reputation qualifies him to handle this type of situation."

Quint cringed when he became the focus of profound attention. Speculative gazes and wry smiles bore down on him. "Just hold your horses, fellas. I know what you're thinking, but—"

"It's perfect!" Wes enthused, quickly cutting off Quint's objection. "You've got a knack with the ladies. They all seem to love you."

The crowd nodded agreeably and converged on Quint. He snatched a quick breath before his friends and neighbors suffocated him in the ever-tightening circle that prevented him from making a run for it.

Sure, it was true that he enjoyed women, appreciated their alluring scent and their shapely physiques. Also true, he did seem to have a knack of attracting women, but he didn't have time for the crusade of sweet talking Stephanie Lawson into reverting to the previous menu and observing the same hours her parents kept.

"Look, fellas, I'd like to help you out, but I've been running myself ragged for a month with this new herd of flighty cattle. Plus, we've been shorthanded since Cousin Wade and his new bride took off on a mini honeymoon trip while Laura is on fall break from teaching school."

Quint could tell right off that no one was buying his excuse. His friends and neighbors were staring at him as if he was the perfect solution to their problems and they had no intention of taking *no* for an answer.

"You've gotta do it, Quint," Randel Bentley insisted. "If anybody can charm Stephanie into seeing the error of her ways it's you."

Quint panned the store, noting that some of his maternal cousins were in attendance. There were several of them who had a way with the ladies, he reflected. Unfortunately exaggerated rumors had labeled *him* the king of charm when it came to luring women. That's what small-town gossip would do for you, he reminded himself. Once you acquired a reputation—earned or not—you were stuck with it.

"All you've gotta do is swagger over to the café, flash one of your knock-'em-dead smiles, flirt with her until her eyes glaze over and her heart goes pitty-pat and presto! She'll be ready to listen to our complaints," Clem Spaulding said confidently. "For you, this'll be a cakewalk and we'll have the old lunch and supper menu reinstated. Life in Hoot's Roost will return to normal and you'll be the local hero. Hell, I'll even buy your lunch for an entire week if you pull this off!"

A round of "here, here" echoed through the feed store. Quint sighed in frustration. "Damn it, guys, I just came into town to pick up a few rolls of barbwire. We've got cattle running loose and we have fence to fix."

Wes Martin braced his stocky arms on the counter. Eyes narrowed, he focused his steely gaze on Quint. "Well, pal, you aren't getting barbwire from me unless you turn all your charm on Stephanie Lawson."

Quint jerked upright. "That's blackmail! You can't do that."

"'Course I can. I can refuse service to whomever I want 'cause I own this store and what I say goes. And don't think you can pull a fast one by sending in your cousins to pick up barbwire. I won't sell it to them, either, not until you get this mess straightened out."

"And you can't borrow wire from the rest of us, either," Randel Bentley spoke up. Dozens of heads bobbed, seconding Randel's decree.

Quint swore under his breath and his stomach grumbled, reminding him that he'd skipped breakfast and didn't have much to look forward to for lunch. "Okay, fine," he muttered resentfully. "I'll give it a shot, but I need that barbwire, as soon as I get back. Vance is waiting for me to return with the supplies so we can build fence."

"Deal," Wes said. "But if Stephanie doesn't come around after this short visit you aren't off the hook. And if you have to hunt around town to track her down then do it. Nobody has actually *seen* her yet. Apparently she parks behind the café and enters the back door. Probably afraid to show her face for fear we'll lynch her for leaving us high and dry at meal time."

Quint spun on his boot heels and stalked off, serenaded by vocal encouragement from his fellowman. Evidently Stephanie Lawson had returned to her hometown with grandiose visions that conflicted with local needs and expectations. The male members of the community were spitting mad. The woman hadn't figured out that the best way to a man's heart was through his stomach. Well, if she wanted to make a success of her café she'd have to compromise all those visions of grandeur.

Quint cut across the town square and circled the gurgling fountain where a concrete owl glided in eternal flight. He made a beeline for Hoagie's Diner—or rather, Stephanie's Palace. He tried to overlook the fact that he was tired, hungry and a mite out of sorts because of the blackmail tactics. He had to put himself in the right frame of mind to deal with a woman who'd made more enemies than she could shake a stick at.

Man, the pressure was on. Until now, charming and

flirting with women had come naturally. But now he'd been sent on a mission to wrap this particular female around his little finger and he was getting all tensed up. Must be the fatigue and gnawing hunger, he told himself. Either that or the remembered image of the skinny kid from high school was niggling him.

The thought of swaggering in the café to confront that frizzy-haired beanpole high school freshman left an unpleasant taste in his mouth. But, he reminded himself as he strode across the street, there were times when a man just had to do what a man had to do. He'd just have to pour on the charm and hope like hell that Steph responded to it.

STEPHANIE LAWSON CHECKED off another item on her to-do list after the carpet layers handed her the bill and filed outside. Admiringly she surveyed the plush red carpet and interior decor that had transformed her parents' hometown diner into an elegant restaurant that was reminiscent of a Roman palace.

Miniature statues formed a columnlike wall that separated the lounge from three intimate dining areas. Pedestal tables and carved chairs filled the space to capacity. Gold-fringed drapes, golden urns, gilded molding and ornamental furnishings added touches of grandeur to her business establishment.

This restaurant was destined for greatness and notoriety, Stephanie assured herself as she scanned her surroundings, paying close attention to every sumptuous detail. She was going to prove to her former boss—the creep—that he'd made a critical mistake in dealing with her. After he'd given the promotion to her male counterpart and hit on her, as if *she* owed *him* personal fringe benefits, Stephanie had resigned on the spot. In addition, she was still fuming over the fact that her weasely boss had stolen her ideas and had taken them as his own to impress his superiors.

"Backstabbing male chauvinist," she muttered bitterly.

She'd given that man four years of her inventive and creative expertise and he'd betrayed her. Well, she'd learned her lesson from that charismatic playboy. Last she'd heard from her friends on the hotel and restaurant management staff, business had slacked off and things weren't running as efficiently as they had been before Stephanie left town. Good, it served the jackass right for taking her for granted and trying to charm her into becoming his sex toy.

Once she'd turned Hoot's Roost into the cuisine capital of Oklahoma she'd be in great demand and offers from metropolitan hotels would be arriving left and right. If there was justice in this world her former boss would be demoted and someday *he'd* be working for *her*—but not for long!

The sound of laughter jostled Stephanie from her vindictive musings. Her new employees had gathered around the beverage counter, chatting among themselves. She'd hired a few high school students and stay-at-home moms to work the evening shifts. They were an assertive and personable group of individuals who could provide efficient service for her clientele.

Stephanie inhaled a deep breath and mentally prepared herself for her orientation session with her staff. She wanted to ensure a good working relationship and instill a sense of pride in the new restaurant. In short, she wanted her staff to feel the same desire to succeed that she did.

She'd only taken one step toward the beverage counter when the front door suddenly swung open. Glaring sunlight streamed into the dimly lit interior. The breath Stephanie had drawn in gushed from her chest like a deflating balloon when she saw the tall, muscularly built man, wearing a Resistol hat, leather chaps—that showcased the fly of his jeans—and boots. The bright backwash of sunlight silhouetted his broad shoulders and masculine physique that filled the entrance of the restaurant. Stephanie was instantly reminded of a scene from a Western movie—the macho hero swaggering through the swinging doors of a saloon with the sun at his back.

Although the cowboy looked completely out of place in her elegant restaurant he'd certainly made a grand entrance and captured everyone's attention.

The waitresses turned in synchronized rhythm to stare at the intruder. Stephanie squinted into the bright light, sensing something familiar about the man but unable to identify him because the slanting shards of sunlight and shadows beneath the brim of his hat concealed his facial features.

Stephanie inwardly groaned when she realized the cowboy was wearing muddy boots that were undoubtedly leaving tracks on her newly laid carpet. Damn it, she hadn't even paid the bill and already her carpet needed cleaning.

Irritably she watched her female staff swarm toward the unexpected arrival. What the blazes was going on here? In the time it took to blink the group of women had surrounded the cowboy and they were chattering and giggling at whatever he'd said to amuse him.

His charming smile intact, the towering cowboy glanced over the women's heads to stare directly at her. Now that her eyes had adjusted to the light, she recognized that powerful build and handsome face, even if she hadn't seen the man in more than a dozen years. A jolt of sensual awareness shot through Stephanie, causing her to sway on her feet. Quint Ryder, legendary ladies' man of Hoot's Roost, had arrived on the scene in his mud-caked boots and all-too-sexy leather chaps.

Although Quint Ryder had been one of the standout heartthrobs in high school, age and maturity had enhanced and accentuated his rugged good looks. Stephanie was instantly reminded of the hopeless crush she'd had on Quint during those days when she'd been an awkward, self-conscious teenager whom boys ignored while they fawned over the cheerleaders and homecoming queens.

Quint had barely known she existed. He'd been dating her best friend and next door neighbor, Melinda Pendleton. Naturally Stephanie had kept her infatuation to herself and never told another living soul that Quint Ryder inspired her secret fantasies. She'd known that Melinda Pendleton was older, more attractive, more experienced in dealing with boys and far more deserving of Quint's masculine attention. But that hadn't stopped Stephanie from eating her heart out over Quint Ryder—her unattainable dreamboat.

Stephanie remembered seeing Quint and Melinda cuddled up on the front porch swing, necking like crazy one summer night. She'd watched them through the blinds of her bedroom window and it'd nearly broken her heart to know she'd never have the chance to snuggle up to one of the local superstar athletes who was so well built and handsome that the mere sight of him gave Stephanie hot flashes and heart flutters.

However, Stephanie had come to despise Quint when he'd dumped Melinda and left for college. Melinda had been crushed and Stephanie had consoled her distraught friend for months. Even way back then, Quint had earned a reputation of a love 'em and leave 'em kind of guy. No doubt, he was still the type who fell in love every other week and didn't have a faithful bone in his wildly attractive body. To this day he probably still cracked open his little black book and perused his female roster to select his date du noir.

Stephanie suspected that dozens of women had caught his attention through the years, but she doubted anyone had stolen his fickle heart. Most likely, he'd left a string of broken hearts trailing behind him, no matter where he went. But even knowing he was bad news, women couldn't seem to resist his sensual charm and flirtation—which was evident in the fact that he hadn't been in the restaurant for all of two minutes and already he'd collected a harem.

Quint sidestepped his female admirers and moseyed toward her, looking like God's gift to women dressed in full western regalia. Her pulse involuntarily quickened, but she battled for dignified composure. No way was she going to let Quint charm her out of her panty hose—just as her former boss, the creep, had tried to do. And failed. She was immune, on guard and determined to resist Quint Ryder's legendary charm.

Quint halted so closely in front of her that he crowded

her personal space with his dominating male presence. When he flashed her one of those patented Ryder grins, Stephanie stiffened defensively. Her chin rose a notch and she glared at him. She'd be damned if *she* melted at his feet!

"Stephanie Lawson, it's been a long time," he drawled in a deep, ultrasexy voice that sent a skein of excitement flying down her spine. "Wow, honey, you look terrific."

Those tawny eyes, surrounded by a hedge of thick black lashes, roamed boldly over her body in an invisible caress. Damn, he was good. Even better than her former boss—and he'd been more suave and masterful than most. Quint could jump-start a feminine heart with one of those killer smiles and intimate glances that suggested he had X-ray vision and could see exactly what she was wearing beneath her professional business suit.

Quint Ryder—no matter how much seductive charm oozed from his pores—wasn't getting the better of Stephanie Lawson. She'd gone from awkward adolescent to fully developed woman and she remembered, with vivid clarity, that she hadn't attracted male attention until she'd acquired feminine assets. Her drastic transformation had allowed her a hard look into the male psyche. Although she was the same person on the inside men hadn't wanted anything to do with her until she'd metamorphosed from caterpillar to butterfly.

Men, she'd discovered, were superficial creatures that focused on skin-deep beauty, but they weren't all that interested in the personality and character housed in an appealing exterior. Stephanie hadn't forgotten how she'd been ignored, how her self-confidence and sense of self had suffered from one crushing emotional blow after another during adolescence. Therefore, she'd never permitted her outward appearance to go to her head and she'd been mistrusting and cynical about the male attention she'd attracted the past few years.

Her boss, as well as numerous businessmen—married and single alike—at all those conventions she'd helped organize at the Dallas hotel had hit on her constantly. She'd heard all the flirtatious come-ons and had been the recipient of scads of all-consuming glances. She'd been offered one-night stands and casual affairs at first meeting and she'd learned to handle herself in situations such as this.

"Quint Ryder," she said with the slightest inclination of her head. "You just tracked mud on my expensive carpet. The cleaning bill will be in the mail."

His charming smile faltered momentarily then he tossed her one of those aw-shucks glances that lit a fire under her temper. "Sorry, sugar, I was expecting the tiled floor of the diner, not fancy carpet."

Stephanie gnashed her teeth. When businessmen on the make called her sugar, honey and sweetheart it always got her dander up. The fastest way to earn her animosity was to attempt to reduce her to a sex object. That was Numero Uno on her list of pet peeves.

"We aren't open for business yet so kindly take your muddy boots and make yourself scarce," she demanded brusquely.

Quint reared back as if she'd slapped him. Clearly he was accustomed to a woman swooning at his feet, not lashing out at him. He probably expected to score when he turned on that country charm and allowed a woman to feast on his rugged masculine beauty. Well, Stephanie wasn't about to add her name to the women on his to-*do* list!

"Gee, darlin', I was only trying to be neighborly," he murmured, using that deep resonate voice as a weapon to disarm her. He flashed her another hundred-watt smile. "I just stopped by to welcome you back to Hoot's Roost."

"Fine, I've been properly welcomed." She pivoted on her heels, dismissing him as if he was no more important than a head of cabbage. "If you'll excuse me, I have a training session planned for my staff—" Her voice dried up when his lean fingers clamped around her elbow, halting her forward motion and sending heightened awareness sizzling through her.

"In a minute, honey. This is important," he murmured so close to her ear that she nearly leaped out of her skin. "I need a private word with you in your office. I presume it's still in the back of the café."

"I'm not interested in anything you have to say," she told him sharply.

"Tough. You're going to hear me out, nonetheless." He glanced over his shoulder to smile charmingly at her staff as he propelled her toward the office.

Twice Stephanie set her feet, but he uprooted her. While she silently fumed he shoveled her into the private niche then closed the door with a decisive snap. She swore, there and then, that no matter how charming he tried to be that she wouldn't let her adolescent crush on him affect her in the least.

2

STEPHANIE JERKED HER ARM from his grasp and glared pitchforks at him. "How dare you waltz in here, interrupt and manhandle me!"

Quint deflected her annoyed glare with a beaming smile. "I wasn't manhandling you. I was gallantly lending my support."

"You think I'm as clumsy as I was in high school?" she challenged.

He opened and shut his mouth, clearly caught off guard by her question.

"So you *do* think I was clumsy in high school," she fired at him while she had him off balance.

He recovered, flung up his hands and tossed her another of those potent grins. "Look, I'm sorry about the carpet and the interruption, but I have a request from the local citizens. They asked me to convey their disappointment over the change in menu and café hours. They'd like you to revert to the former business hours."

"So you're Hoot's spokesman, are you?" she asked, scrambling to grasp the reins of her temper.

Another heart-stopping smile flew in her direction. She forcefully ignored it and clung to her indignation.

"Yeah, I am. The thing is, this rural community has certain dining needs that your folks catered to and the locals have come to expect," he continued diplomatically.

"So the local yokels sent you over here to sweet talk me into reverting to the blue plate specials, I presume."

He nodded and grinned charmingly. "A compromise might be good for your new business. Surely it wouldn't hurt to open for lunch so you can cater to your hometown neighbors. Besides, your folks have a contract with Ryder ranches to buy beef and we've done business with your mom and dad for years. I want to make sure you and I have a good working relationship."

"So, you're worried that you'll lose money because I won't need the same supplies of beef?" she asked as she stationed herself behind her desk, hoping the maneuver would remind him of her position of authority.

"That, too, Steph." He flashed her another killer grin.

She winced at the use of the shortened name she'd picked up in school. A dozen years ago she'd been abbreviated and overlooked. She'd never been invited out on a single date and she'd attended her senior prom with two other wallflowers. The man didn't realize he'd stepped on one raw nerve after another since he'd swaggered into her restaurant, but he kept supplying her with justifiable reasons to erect a defensive barrier against all that high-voltage sex appeal he was directing at her.

Maybe her female staff couldn't resist that cowboy charisma, but she *could*. And she *would*.

Stephanie braced her hands on the desk, narrowed her gaze, stared into those whiskey-colored eyes that could intoxicate you if you let them and said, "Look, Romeo, you're wasting your charm on me. This is my restaurant now and I intend to run it the way I see fit. You with me so far?''

His sensuous lips twitched and his amber eyes gleamed with sexual promise as he nodded and drawled, ''I've always been able to stay with a woman, step for step.''

Stephanie gnashed her teeth at the suggestive comment, cursed his turbocharged sex drive and then continued. ''It's my intention to bring some class and sophistication to our hometown and to draw clientele from the surrounding areas. I want the Palace to be a dining experience, not the place a bunch of greasy farmers and dusty cowboys congregate for coffee breaks and to chow down on *grub*. This isn't a chuck wagon...it's a five-star restaurant and you're way out of line.''

Quint's disarming smile vanished as he braced *his* hands on the front of her desk as well and hunkered down to stare her squarely in the eye. She was astonished at how intimidating he could be when he lost all his charm.

''I'll admit I'm tired and cranky so forgive me for being blunt, Steph, but it seems to me that you've gotten a little uppity after your stint in Big D. This is your hometown and we're your friends and neighbors. Anybody with a brain in her head would realize that catering to the locals makes good business sense. If *they* ain't happy *you* won't have a business to run for very long. Furthermore, nobody gets gussied up in coats and ties around here, except for church, weddings and funerals. And it's going to be *your* funeral if you don't listen to the voices of the blue-collar masses.''

''Did you ever stop to think that the female population of Owl County might appreciate a little class and style?'' she challenged, going head to head with him and enjoying every moment of it. "Apparently you've been selected by the male crowd because of your reputation. You've been sent to charm me into catering to your gender in the community. But what about the women? Did you take a poll or survey of the female citizens before you sauntered over here to tell me how to run my business?"

"No, but—"

"I thought not," she interrupted. "You're only the mouthpiece for the farmer/stockman crowd, aren't you? Well, let me tell you something, Mr. Thrill-A-Minute Ryder. Femininity is alive and well, even in the outback of Owl County. I don't expect you to believe this, being the male chauvinist and womanizer you obviously are, but the other half of the local population applauds my decision to remodel this restaurant so women can be escorted out on the town by their menfolk. Women want to sample French, German, Oriental and Italian cuisine. They want *out* of the kitchen and *into* a classy restaurant that provides ambience and atmosphere. They want the opportunity to dress up and dine out with a man who didn't just tramp from the barnyard with cow patties stuck on his boots."

When he snorted in contradiction, Stephanie lifted her chin. "You men seem to think you run the world, but I've got a news flash for you, *sugar*, women are in control and we have been for quite some time. We just haven't let you bozos know it yet because you haven't evolved far enough, intellectually and emotionally, to grasp the concept. So we've just strung you along for years. But a playboy like you probably needs advance warning because it will probably hit you the hardest."

Quint glared at her. Not to be outdone, she glared right back.

"Fine, sweetheart, we'll see how successful you are when the doors open. Mark my words, your staff will be standing around, twiddling their thumbs because you won't have any patrons to serve in your personal version of Caesar's Palace," he said and scoffed at her. "You must've gotten too big for your breeches while you were rubbing shoulders with all those citified snobs you served on the chow line down in Dallas."

"I did not *serve* the clientele," she said through gritted teeth. "I *managed* the restaurant."

"Bully for you, babe," he said sarcastically.

Stephanie snatched up her clipboard, wishing she could crack it over his handsome head. "You are dismissed." She thrust several copies of the new menu at him. "I have a training session to conduct and you're causing a delay."

Head held high, she strode off, but Quint followed in her wake. "This discussion is far from over," he said, breathing down her neck.

"Oh, yes, it is," she threw over her shoulder. "When you come to dine with us, make sure you scrape the mud off your boots."

"I wouldn't be caught dead in this place," he muttered at her.

"Good," she flung back. "Having to step over your dead body might kill my customers' appetites. Can't have that."

She heard his muted growl behind her, but she didn't look back, just plastered on a cheery smile as she sailed toward her waiting staff members.

When Stephanie heard the heel of Quint's hand thud against the door as he stormed out she swallowed a triumphant smile. The male population had sent their resident Casanova to charm her and he'd failed miserably. That should teach Quint and all the other men in this town a lesson.

Her motto was going to be: Don't mess with the new and improved Steph.

She'd become independent and savvy and she couldn't be pushed around these days. She might've been overlooked and quickly disregarded as a teenager, but she'd come into her own during adulthood.

If the inflexible men in this town wanted to dine out they'd have to come around to her way of thinking. And if they wanted to engage in the Battle of the Sexes they wouldn't win. These days, women were a force to be reckoned with, even out here in the boondocks. The outdated male mentality of Hoot's Roost was about to be challenged. This was, after all, the new millenium and things were about to change—with or without male approval!

QUINT STALKED ACROSS the town square at a fast clip. He was annoyed to the extreme and stunned to the soles of his muddy boots. Both emotions were battling for supremacy inside him, making him uncertain whether he was angrier or more shocked by the confrontation.

Man oh man, Stephanie Lawson was so incredibly beautiful that she'd taken his breath away. All that glorious hair blazing like a burning bush! That flawless porcelain skin, that voluptuous figure, those eyes that were such a pale shade of blue that they reminded him of glittering mercury. She was the combination of Helen of Troy's legendary beauty and Cleopatra's mythical sensuality. He'd been mesmerized—until she opened that sassy mouth and lambasted him with both barrels.

There he'd stood in her Roman palace of a restaurant, expecting to encounter the older version of a skinny redheaded teenager with unfashionable glasses and a mouth full of orthodontic metal, and wham! That image had shattered in a zillion pieces when he'd glanced over the waitresses' heads to see Steph, spotlighted by sunlight, looking like a vision from his wildest fantasy.

Damn, she was beyond *hot!* And generously endowed—man, he'd found himself alternately staring at her breasts and butt. It was shameful but true. And feisty—he doubted she'd back down from the devil himself. And prickly—like thorns protecting a delicate rose. And mouthy—ah, those lush, inviting lips begged to be kissed expertly, and often.

Quint sighed audibly. He still couldn't believe she was the same uncoordinated kid with the Olive Oyl physique that he'd known in high school. In the old days she'd been so clumsy she tripped over her own feet and the textbooks she kept clutched to her flat chest went skidding down the hall like bowling pins.

Nowadays, she moved with poise, confidence, grace and the kind of sensuality that made his male radar bleep. Gone was that patch she used to wear to correct some faulty muscle in her eyeball. Nowadays, he stared into those silvery eyes, surrounded by a fringe of long, sooty lashes, and he became mesmerized. He'd felt dowdy and grungy and dirty in comparison to her sleek, stylish appearance.

Damn, talk about the radical transformation from female frog into princess! Steph Lawson had filled out in all the right places and he'd itched to run his fingers through that flaming red hair that tumbled over her shoulders like a fiery cape.

And those legs! Quint sighed in male appreciation. Even in her conservative silk business suit her legs had gone on forever. He'd stood there wondering what it'd be like to have those long, gorgeous legs wrapped around him while they were making love. The mere speculation was enough to make him hard and needy in two-seconds flat.

Unfortunately Steph was five feet seven inches of sassy feminist attitude and he'd run headlong into a brick wall when he turned on the charm. Either he was losing his touch or the woman disliked men on general principle—and *him* in particular. What had he ever done to stir such animosity in her? Hell, they'd only been nodding acquaintances a dozen years ago.

Quint wondered if she'd gotten her heart stomped on the same way Cousin Wade had before he fell head over heels for his new wife. Wade had made the attitude adjustment from woman-hater to devoted husband, so surely Steph Lawson wasn't a hopeless cause. It was simply going to take considerable effort to lure her under his spell and convince her to become attuned to the dining needs of the community.

Quint hadn't wanted this assignment—had been blackmailed into it, he thought with a scowl. But now he saw Steph as a personal challenge, a test of his ability to handle women. He'd never had a problem, or met with so much resistance, until he clashed with that copperheaded queen of cuisine. Although Quint wasn't easily discouraged, he did admit that it was going to require dedicated effort just to get Steph to be *civil* to him.

His pride was still smarting when he entered the feed store to see the crowd of men staring expectantly at him. It was galling to admit that he'd been shot down, crashed and burned during his mission. But there you had it. He'd failed—big time.

"Well?" Wes Martin demanded impatiently. "How'd it go? Do we have our noon hour and lunch specials back yet?"

Dozens of male eyes bore down on him. Feeling conspicuous, Quint shifted from one muddy boot to the other. He swallowed his pride and said, "Uh, no."

A collective groan wafted across the store.

"You mean she wouldn't even listen to reason?" Clem Spaulding asked.

Quint passed out the sample menus Steph had thrust at him before she kicked him out of her café. "According to Ms. Lawson, Hoot's Roost is in need of style and sophistication and she plans to provide it," he reported. "You aren't going to believe the drastic changes in the decor. Ever been to Caesar's Palace in Las Vegas?"

More than half of the baseball caps and cowboy hats in the store bobbed like buoys on the sea.

"Well, that's what we've got, minus the slot machines and roulette tables. It's classy and ritzy, I'll give her that. According to Steph our wives and girlfriends want a place to be wined and dined," Quint explained. "If we're not careful, battle lines will be drawn over this new restaurant and this is going to become a conflict of philosophies, not a dining dispute."

"What the hell is this? A feminist movement under the guise of a new café?" Randel Bentley questioned in alarm.

Quint nodded grimly. "I advise you to watch your backs, guys. If Steph does get the women around here all riled up and rallying around her, life as we know it is bound to change."

"Then you've got to stop her," Wes said frantically. "The wife and I have been battling over who wears the pants in the family for decades. As it is, I only get to wear them half the time, and only when I have her permission."

"Same goes at my house," one of the older ranchers spoke up. "Men have been giving ground for years. Quint, if you don't put some of your legendary moves on that woman we're all roadkill! You don't know what it's like, son. First they run you down and cut you off, then you're fixing your own meals and doing your own laundry."

"Then they get that cold-shoulder routine going and it's frostbite city and you gotta apologize, whether you're wrong or not," Elmer Campbell added grimly. "You're our only hope for survival. If you don't get to Steph before she brainwashes our womenfolk we'll all be slaves to the fairer sex."

Quint stared in disbelief at the men who'd gathered around him. They were dead serious, he realized. Hell, they were afraid for their lives!

Well, if this was any indication of what wedlock or steady dating was like it was a damn good thing he hadn't stumbled into the snake pit and been bitten—repeatedly—by a female viper. Well, except for that one time while he was on the rodeo circuit, he reminded himself. He'd been young and he'd fallen hard for a high-spirited cowgirl. Before he knew what hit him, she'd taken him on the ride of his life.

That blond-haired rodeo queen from Montana had mystified him for six months and then trampled him in the dirt. The day she'd told him she was pregnant and it wasn't his child Quint hadn't wanted to believe it because he'd thought he was in love for the first time in his life. Turned out she'd been two-timing him with a sophisticated suit. She'd trapped the man she'd set her sights on and used Quint as the jealousy factor. She'd dangled Quint by his heartstrings—which only went to show you that it was one thing to admire and appreciate women, but taking them seriously was a disaster waiting to happen.

Good gad! Maybe he and Cousin Vance had screwed up royally when they matched up Cousin Wade with his new wife. No, he reassured himself quickly. That match was entirely different. It was a perfect match. Laura was as devoted to Wade as he was to her. That was an exception to the rule and Wade was happier than Quint had ever seen him. In fact, Wade was so blasted happy and cheerful and lovesick that it was nauseating.

"You've got to do something," Wes demanded, jostling Quint from his wandering thoughts. He looked Quint up and down then frowned in disapproval. "First off, you need to spruce up before you confront Stephanie again. Come to think of it, you look like you've been wallowing in a pigsty. No wonder she didn't take an instant shine to you."

"Yeah, that's probably it," Randel inserted. "You

didn't have your best foot forward today. When you swing by her place tonight you better bathe in cologne and put on your best duds. You know, make a better impression.''

"Tonight?" Quint echoed. He had visions of crashing on the couch after supper to catch up on needed rest.

"Hell yes, tonight," one of the older cowboys persisted. "Take her out to Hoot's Tavern and two-step her around the dance floor. Whisper sweet nothings in her ear. It's worked for you before, hasn't it?"

"Well—" Quint didn't have the chance to finish his comment before Wes leaped back into the conversation.

"Of course, it's worked for him. He's always had more female admirers than anyone else around town—even more than his own cousins who never seem to be without women when they want them."

Quint wanted to point out that his *supposedly* legendary reputation had been overblown and embellished by gossips for years. He wasn't quite the lover boy these local yahoos liked to think he was. True, he had no problem attracting women. Never had. But he did have scruples and standards and his conquests did not number in the hundreds, despite the wild rumors circulating about him.

"So it's settled," Randel said resolutely. "You take out Stephanie tonight, show her a good time and butter her up. Once you've won her over you can influence her thinking."

Quint wasn't sure any man could influence that strong-willed, hell-on-wheels redhead, but pride clamped down on his tongue, preventing him from admitting that in public.

Hoo-kay, he'd give it another shot, he decided. The males of the community were counting on him and he didn't want to lose the lunch specials or the beef contract. Once he had Steph eating out of his hand—if that was possible without getting a few fingers bit off, and he'd hate to lay odds on it—he'd persuade her to cater to the cowboy crowd and the menfolk would be back in hog heaven.

"I'll see what I can do," Quint announced. When the round of cheers that resounded around the feed store died down, Quint stared directly at Wes. "But I really do have to have barbwire, fence clips and steel posts to pin up the cattle or I'll be on horseback long past dark and I won't have time to take out Steph."

Wes eyed him warily. "How do we know you won't take the wire and bail out on us?"

"I said I'd do it, didn't I?" Quint said, affronted.

"Yeah, but I want your word of honor," Wes demanded.

Quint sighed audibly. "Fine, my word of honor. I'll do my manly best to change Steph's mind about the café."

The crowd smiled collectively in satisfaction.

"I've got a five spot that says Quint can charm Stephanie out of her new menu," Randel called out. "Anybody wanna call that bet?"

"Nope," the crowd chorused as they pulled their wallets from their hip pockets and slapped dozens of Lincolns on the counter.

"We're behind you one hundred percent and nobody's betting against you, Quint," Clem said. "The money pot is yours, as soon as you convince Stephanie to revert to the old menu.''

Oh, great, now they were going to *pay* him to soften her up and bring her around to the male way of thinking. Blackmail *and* bribery? This situation was getting worse by the minute!

''I don't even know where Steph is staying,'' Quint mumbled.

''I heard she's staying in that garage apartment that Idabelle Witham rents out to make extra money.'' Wes lurched around and lumbered toward the warehouse door. ''Bring your pickup around back. I'll have one of the boys load your barbwire and you'll be good to go.''

Quint made his way down the aisle and became the recipient of dozens of encouraging slaps on the back. He had a bad feeling about this situation, but his growling stomach was a grim reminder of what and where he'd be eating lunch in the future if he failed this mission for the good of *man*kind.

''WHERE THE HELL HAVE YOU been so long?'' Vance grumbled as Quint piled from his pickup. ''Did you have to make that wire yourself?''

Quint strode to the bed of the truck to unload the wire, clips and steel fence posts. ''No, there was a crisis in town and I got sucked into the middle of it,'' he muttered.

''Yeah? What crisis is that?'' Vance snorted skeptically.

Quint carried barbwire to the clunker truck they used to haul fencing supplies over the rough terrain of the pastures. ''Hoagie's Diner shut down for good.''

"What?" Vance hooted. "Why? When did this happen? Why wasn't I told?"

"Probably because you've been stuck out here all week, handling all the ranch chores while I transported the new bull home and Wade's off on his mini honeymoon. So don't bother swinging by Hoagie's for to-go orders at lunch. You'll have to pick up stale sandwiches at Hoot 'n Holler," he said, and made an awful face. "And I can guaran-damn-tee that eating straw is tastier than those dried-out sandwiches. I'll have to be starving to death before I waste money on that meal again."

"What happened to Hoagie?" Vance asked, stunned.

"He sold out to his daughter, Stephanie."

"Stephanie?" Vance halted in midstep, rolls of barbwire dangling from his gloved hands. "Giraffe girl? Frizz-head red? Scarecrow Steph? The kid with the eye patch and goggle-size glasses? *That* Stephanie? Whoa, I don't *even* want to think what the older version of that teenager looks like!"

Obviously Vance had the same trouble getting past the remembered image of Stephanie in high school. Like Quint, Vance would have to see her in the flesh to believe the incredible metamorphosis she'd undergone. "That's her all right, except she's turned into one hot tamale. She's as beautiful as her tongue is sharp. Plus, she's got a chip on her shoulder the exact size of the polar ice cap. Plus, I'd have to marinate her in syrup for a week to sweeten her up. She is *not* your everyday average female."

"You are kidding," Vance said and snorted.

"Nope, I'm as serious as a heart attack, cuz. She's super-duper-deluxe gorgeous. However, she plans to open her new restaurant only in the evenings." Quint plucked the sample menu from his shirt pocket and handed it to Vance.

"Open from five till ten?" Vance croaked like a water-logged bullfrog.

"Yup." Quint stacked the steel posts in the bucket-of-rust truck.

"Coat and tie?" Vance howled in dismay.

"Yup and yup," Quint confirmed.

"Is she nuts?"

Quint thought about that for a few moments and said, "Yup."

"Well, no wonder all the men in town are upset. Where are we going to eat a decent meal and congregate to chitchat?"

"Town square," Quint replied. "That's where I choked down my packaged bologna sandwich before I drove back to the ranch."

Vance stared incredulously at the menu. "Canapés? What the hell's that? Crepe? Is that the French word for crappie fish?"

"Beats me. I have no idea what any of that stuff is. I can't even pronounce most of it."

"No beer on tap?" Vance howled as he gaped at the menu.

"Nope, just wine that's aged longer than we have. Plus, our verbal agreement for our beef contract has been drastically reduced," he reported grimly. "Whatever Steph is serving only requires a third of the beef we previously provided for Hoagie."

"Well, hell," Vance grumbled. "We've got to do something about this. We need to come up with a plan."

Quint scowled. "All the men who gathered at the feed store already came up with one this morning. I was shanghaied into sweet-talking Steph into changing her mind about the new hours and the fancy menu."

"So, how'd that go?" Vance questioned as he strode around to the driver's side of the rusty truck. "Good, I hope."

"Nope." Quint climbed in and grimaced when a metal spring poked through the threadbare seat cover and pricked him in the butt—he was instantly reminded of his confrontation with Steph. "She filleted me with her rapier tongue, told me to mind my own business and to keep my beak out of her business. But the local yokels refused to let me off the hook after I struck out with her. They even took up a collection pot as incentive to have another go at Steph."

Vance chuckled as he switched on the ignition. The truck sputtered then growled to life. "They are *paying* you to seduce a woman? You know what that makes you, don't you?"

Quint swore foully. "Clam up and drive, cuz. And by the way, you're going into town with me tonight. I've been ordered to take Steph to Hoot's Tavern and show her a good time—if that's possible."

"Oh, no, you aren't dragging me into this. You're the charmer in this family. I'm only good for a laugh—" Vance slammed his mouth shut in a hurry and glanced apprehensively at Quint. Vance was smart enough to know he'd just stuck his foot in his mouth.

"Gotcha." Quint grinned wryly. "You're going to keep her laughing with your corny jokes while I compliment her stunning good looks. Maybe between the two of us we can melt down that ice cap and get her to listen to reason.''

"I don't know about this," Vance said warily.

"You wanna eat your own cooking for the rest of your life?" Quint challenged. "No more burgers 'n fries to-go while we're doing fieldwork on tractors and rounding up cattle on horseback. You wanna dress up *every* single time you eat out?"

Vance grimaced as he steered the clunker truck around a grove of pecan trees. "No."

"Then you're going to help me out. I think I've just met more woman than I can handle," he admitted begrudgingly.

The humbling admission caused Vance's jaw to drop to his chest while he stared, agog, at his cousin.

"Close your mouth," Quint muttered. "You look like a damn fish."

"I can't believe you said that," Vance said then threw back his dark head and howled in laughter. "Met your match, huh? *This* I gotta see to believe."

"You'll see all right. After you've reacquainted yourself with Steph you can correct me if I'm wrong. This is some kind of woman we're dealing with and you're going to be amazed at how much she's changed since high school."

Flashing Quint a dubious glance, Vance drove across the rolling pasture to repair the broken fence. Quint braced himself as they bounced over the rough terrain. He had the unshakable feeling that all the smooth lines of flattery he'd casually tossed at other women through the years weren't going to faze Stephanie Lawson. He'd have to come up with something new and inventive to dismantle her stubborn defenses.

Yup, he definitely had his work cut out for him, he decided. He'd gotten the impression that Stephanie Lawson just plain didn't like him and had no intention of getting to know him better. Which was a damn shame because that feisty, incredibly shapely, long-legged redhead had certainly nabbed his attention and he hadn't been able to get her off his mind.

have to come up with something new and inventive to override her stubborn nature.

Fortunately, he'd had a work ail out for him. He decided the easiest, the quickest, solution that encouraged Stephanie plans the . . . . and he wanted to Beluga. know what he had . . . . was a safe of big about . . . . that had the instincts, ... less and curiosity fueled the attention . . . be long

---

3

AFTER STEPHANIE'S confrontation with Quint, she decided she wasn't going to sit around and wait for the men in town to gather a strong force against her. She was taking the offensive approach—immediately—and doing some preliminary damage control. Her first order of business was to place ads, announcing her grand opening, in every newspaper in the three surrounding counties. All the newspaper reporters she'd contacted asked to do an interview and she'd quickly agreed. The extra promotion would ensure her business got off to a good start.

She'd sent off her staff with piles of sample menus to distribute to local businesses—especially ones owned and frequented by women. If the men in town were going to attempt to control and manipulate her, she'd call upon superior firepower—women.

The next phase of her siege involved rolling up her sleeves, marching into the kitchen and preparing a sample entrée to distribute to various female pillars of the community. She delivered food to the owners of all three local beauty shops, two clothing stores and a travel agency—to name a few.

She also took a sample of coq au vin to Leta Martin who kept books for her husband's feed store. Leta had been away from the office, but Stephanie left a note that said: "Compliments of Stephanie's Palace" on top of the foam box. Sabotage at its finest, she thought with a wicked grin.

She made a note to deliver a sampler plate to Wade Ryder's new wife when she returned from her honeymoon.

Stephanie placed land mines of entrées all over the county and gave a personal invitation and sales pitch to every woman she encountered. She hoped that by doing so, the complaints from the males of the species would blow up in their faces.

Her last delivery was to her landlady, Idabelle Witham, who always had her finger on the pulse of Hoot's Roost. A former postal employee, Idabelle knew practically everyone in town and who was related to whom. Idabelle could help put Stephanie in touch with other women who could throw their weight around this town and ensure the restaurant met with success.

When Stephanie rapped on the front door, Idabelle appeared almost immediately. "Hi, hon, how's the remodeling going?" she said as she motioned her renter inside.

"Almost completed," Stephanie reported as she presented the wiry, energetic older woman with a styrofoam box. "I'd like you to sample one of our entrées and give me your honest opinion."

Idabelle led the way to the dining-room table. "What's with this free sample delivery service, hon?" she asked as she set aside the box and strode over to fix two glasses of iced tea.

Stephanie watched the trim, gray-haired woman—who'd become her substitute parent after her folks took off to tour the country—buzz around the kitchen then take her seat. She smiled, wondering if she'd have that much vim and vigor when she reached retirement age.

"I decided to launch an assertive promotional campaign for the restaurant after I received a visit from the appointed spokesman for the men of the community. They're conspiring against me and objecting to the change in menu and dining hours," she explained. "I've been warned that if I don't serve meat 'n taters and burgers 'n fries I'll be driven out of business."

Idabelle sniffed in annoyance. "That sounds like some of the old coots who try to run the show around here." She took a bite of the entrée, sat back in her chair and sighed in culinary delight. "Mmm, this is fabulous. Where'd you learn to cook this fancy stuff? It wasn't at your family diner because I know for a fact that you served up burgers and chicken fried steaks, right alongside your folks."

"I attended cooking school during the summers when I was in college," she informed Idabelle. "I've always enjoyed cooking as much as restaurant management. Unfortunately the hidebound men in town aren't going to give me a chance. In fact, they sent Quint Ryder over to charm me into following their dictates."

Idabelle's eyes twinkled in amusement. "I'll bet you shut him down, didn't you?" When Stephanie nodded, Idabelle grinned and said, "Well, good for you, hon. Quint needs a wake-up call. That handsome rascal has always had an easy time of it when it comes to luring women. Now don't get me wrong, he's a fine, hardworking man, just like his cousins. But Quint has had women fawning over him and throwing themselves at him for years. You're exactly what he needs. You're strong-willed, challenging and bright.''

''But I don't *need* him hounding me while I'm trying to launch my business,'' Stephanie muttered. ''I practically tossed him out of the restaurant this afternoon, but he more or less told me that he'd be back.''

Idabelle gobbled up the succulent meal then lounged in her chair, studying Stephanie speculatively. ''You know, hon, you might want to rethink your strategy of butting heads with Quint.''

Bemused, Stephanie watched a mischievous smile purse the older woman's lips. ''What are you suggesting?''

''It seems to me that with your good looks and sharp mind you could outfox that handsome playboy and beat him at his own game.''

''Charm him before he charms me?'' she questioned dubiously.

Idabelle nodded her head and grinned. ''Ever tried that with any of the skirt-chasers I suspect you've had trailing after you lately?''

''No, I haven't. I've pretty much told my shallow-minded admirers where they could go and what they could do with their sexual innuendoes when they got there.''

''Well, maybe you should change tact with Quint.''

''I'm not sure I'd be good at it. I've spent the past few years learning to repel male attention and zero time trying to attract it.''

''Time to learn a new strategy,'' Idabelle insisted. ''Think about it. The men in town decided to send their Goliath to bring you down. If you turn your charm on him he might defect to *your* camp. It'd teach the old fogies and young bucks around here a good lesson.''

''Interesting concept,'' Stephanie mused aloud.

''Yep. Your cooking is already out of this world so that's a point in your favor. In fact,'' she said, struck by a sudden inspiration, ''we can use your cooking skills as part of your promotional plan.''

When Stephanie stared at her, befuddled, Idabelle hurried on. ''For the past six years we've had a fall festival called 'A Taste of Country' in the town square. We set up food booths and folks from all over the area purchase tickets to sample all varieties of food. Then we donate the profit to the volunteer fire department for protective gear or to the city parks for playground equipment. Whatever our community needs.''

Stephanie smiled conspiratorially. ''And you want me to set up a booth to sell samples from my restaurant. Great idea, Idabelle. I'll do it.''

''Good. The next thing we have to do is launch a counterattack on Quint, the male mouthpiece in town. You're attractive so all you have to do is dress to emphasize your feminine assets—and you've got plenty of 'em, hon. And last of all, you've got brains and you've already figured out what Quint's up to. The man won't stand a chance with you.''

Stephanie smiled in amusement. ''If nothing else, you're good for my ego, Idabelle. But maybe I should practice my wiles on a playboy of lesser caliber before I take on Quint Ryder.''

''Nonsense!'' she contradicted. ''Where's your sense of challenge and adventure?''

''Opening this restaurant is adventure enough. I

thought my subtle plan to sway the women of the community to my side was a sensible strategy."

"Nothing wrong with that," Idabelle agreed. "But if you want to win a battle you strike on more than one front." She gestured toward Stephanie's no-nonsense business suit. "Change wardrobe when Quint comes around. I guarantee he and the rest of the men will be too distracted to realize what hit them until it's too late. If you use your body and your brains this battle against the men will be a slam dunk."

"Well, I suppose I could give it a try," Stephanie said uncertainly.

"Tell you what, hon, after I finish watering my garden I'll drop by your apartment and we'll have a look at your wardrobe. I can hold my own as a seamstress. I could make some alterations to your clothes if you don't have anything suitable for Operation Quint. Ruining his reputation should be highly entertaining."

Stephanie still wasn't sure this was such a hot idea, but Idabelle shooed her off, promising to drop by later.

Halfheartedly, Stephanie tramped off to her garage apartment. She banded her hair into pigtails, peeled off her silk suit and headed for the shower, still wondering if following Idabelle's advice about Quint was the right strategy.

She certainly didn't perceive herself as a sex siren. Pushing men away was a reflex she'd definitely have to overcome. Never in her life had she purposely tried to lure a man. How could she possibly be good at it? Cooking and restaurant management were her forte. Behaving like a diva was *not!*

If she could pull this off—and that was a gigantic *if*—

she'd dedicate this scheme to Melinda Pendleton, and all the nameless women who'd fallen for Quint Ryder's devastating charm, cried their eyes out over him and had become nothing more than footnotes in his life.

The thought of seduction in the name of revenge inspired her. If she dressed and acted the part of a sex siren, maybe this scheme would work. But in Stephanie's opinion, Idabelle's plan amounted to lowering herself to Quint's level.

After a quick shower Stephanie rummaged through her closet and dresser drawers to locate a pair of cutoff denim shorts and a contour-hugging, strappy, cream-colored knit camisole that she only wore beneath a conservative jacket. Stephanie donned the skimpy outfit, stared into the mirror and barked a laugh. Suddenly she resembled the one thing she'd sworn she never wanted to be—a sex object. Without a bra, the knit camisole hugged her breasts like a coat of paint. The cutoffs were so short that her bare legs looked about ten feet long. The pigtails that spurted from the sides of her head like twin fountains of damp curls made her look all of fifteen.

Hurriedly, Stephanie slapped on a fresh coat of makeup—a little thicker than usual—and applied red lipstick. A second glance in the mirror convinced her that she looked like a second-rate prostitute. Well, maybe this would convince Idabelle to discard her plan and conjure up another one—like going head to head with Quint like a staunch feminist.

When the doorbell chimed Stephanie padded barefoot across her apartment. This outrageous new look was likely to shock Idabelle out of her support hose, she predicted.

Stephanie whipped open the door, struck what she hoped to be the queen mother of provocative poses—chest thrust out, one hand resting on a cocked hip—and said, "So, whaddya think—?"

Her voice dried up and she inwardly groaned when she realized it wasn't her landlady who'd come to call. Lo and behold, there stood Quint Ryder and his cousin Vance. Their jaws scraped their broad chests and their unblinking gazes locked on her breasts then slid down the length of her bare legs.

Well damn, thought Stephanie as she battled down a self-conscious blush. Now she'd have to let the Ryder cousins look their fill because she'd flat-out asked for it. There was nothing to do but stand here, paste on a saucy smile and blunder her way through her vamp routine...and hope like hell that she could pull it off.

FLABBERGASTED, QUINT GAPED at Stephanie. Suddenly the practiced flirtations that usually tumbled easily from his tongue were stuck in his throat. Beside him, he heard Vance's sharp intake of breath and knew his cousin was having as much difficulty breathing and forming coherent thought as Quint was.

Damn! Quint had speculated that Steph had a body like nobody's business concealed beneath her professional business suit, but jeez! Even in his wildest imaginations he'd never expected her to be *this* stacked. Oh man, her killer body was incredibly well defined in those short shorts and that flimsy top that showcased the fullness of her breasts to their best advantage and accentuated the trim indentation of her waist.

Her legs were about a mile long and Quint's attention

kept bouncing from her bare legs to her well-endowed chest like a pinball. All that glorious hair was swept up in pigtails that exposed the slender column of her neck and emphasized the oval shape of her face. And those glossy red lips of hers were driving him downright crazy!

Dazed, speechless—and his tongue hanging out, no doubt— Quint wondered what the hell had happened to the feisty feminist who'd chewed him up and spit him out during his lunch hour. He was beginning to wonder who the real Steph Lawson was. The shy, self-conscious teenager of days gone by, the no-nonsense business-woman or this saucy siren who held him and his cousin spellbound? It sure would be a lot easier if the real Steph Lawson would stand up and identify herself.

"To what do I owe this pleasure?" Steph asked as she stepped aside to let Quint and Vance enter her apartment. "You two stud muffins definitely give new meaning to *double* dating."

Quint, his jaw locked in wide-open position, started to sweat. His chest clenched as if he were suffering muscle spasms. Paralyzed, he stood on the threshold until Vance nudged him through the doorway. Quint was still trying to think of something clever and witty to say when Steph motioned them toward the small table in the compact kitchen area.

"Have you eaten supper? Or have you already ap-peased that particular appetite?" she asked outrageously.

Quint swallowed his tongue, blinked a couple of times and tried to match this unexpected facet of Steph's per-sonality to the female barracuda he'd encountered earlier. Who *was* this woman? And why was she tossing out all those brazen comments that were usually *his* style? The woman had him so far off balance that he couldn't think straight.

His thoughts derailed—again—as he watched her saunter across her apartment. His gaze dropped to the shapely curve of her fanny. Hypnotized, he watched her pull three cartons from the fridge and pop them into the microwave. Even when the timer *dinged* Quint couldn't jerk himself from his trance.

Goggle-eyed, he appraised the seductive goddess who set the meals and silverware on the table. When she gestured for him and Vance to park themselves in the chairs, they automatically sat. A moment later she joined them at the table and set glasses of iced tea in front of them.

"So," she said as she opened her steaming entrée. "Do you boys usually work in pairs?"

"Uh...no," Vance wheezed.

Great, thought Quint. When you were counting on Vance's clever wit to defuse tension he failed you completely.

Quint picked up his fork, yanked his gaze off Steph's full bosom and took a bite of chicken that was coated in some sort of mysterious sauce. At first bite his taste buds went into full-scale riot. Damn, this stuff was good. After the tasteless sandwich he'd choked down at lunch and the skimpy TV dinner he'd nuked for supper this was a feast fit for a king.

"Mmm, this is great," Vance said between ravenous bites. "What is it?"

"Coq au vin." She smiled at Vance—she'd never smiled at *Quint* like that. "Do you like it?"

"I love it." Vance flashed her a patented Ryder grin and said, "I love *you*. Marry me."

Quint sputtered when the bite of chicken clogged his windpipe. He gave his cousin a look that said: *That's supposed to be* my *line*. Vance's answering stare said: *Yeah, so why didn't you say it? Cat got your tongue?* But what really got to Quint was Steph's response of lighthearted laughter. The sound went all through him, touching all those places he'd protected for years—like his heart and his soul.

She had bewitched him completely, he realized in dismay. The sexy sight of her knocked him for a loop. Her sassy comments surprised the hell out of him. Her radiant smile and laughter left him with a warm, fuzzy feeling. That wasn't good because he'd decided long ago to appreciate a woman without getting emotionally involved. He remembered what it was like to get his heart trampled and he'd vowed not to let it happen again. In fact, his motto had become: Single forever.

"By the way, Steph, you look fantastic," Vance complimented, finally stepping up to the plate to carry the conversation.

"Thanks, Vance, you look pretty fantastic yourself. So how's the world been treating you?"

"Can't complain." Vance tossed her one of his playful grins and Quint gnashed his teeth, marveling at the bite of jealously gnawing at him. He should be pleased that Vance was making headway with Steph because it would let Quint off the hook in this crusade to win her over and convince her to change her menu. But to his deep dismay, Quint realized he was envious of Vance's ability to conduct a conversation while he sat there, unable to think of one single solitary thing to say. Gawd, what had happened to him?

Before he knew it Vance was questioning Steph about her parent's sightseeing trip—asking where they'd been, what they'd seen and where they were going next. She responded easily to Vance and their dialogue continued during the meal.

Feeling left out, Quint sullenly polished off the best food he'd tasted in years then panned the small living quarters to note the expensive artwork and tasteful furnishings that seemed more suited to a spacious condo. Obviously she'd turned citified since she went off to college and then entered the metropolitan work force. He couldn't shake the feeling that this business venture in her hometown was just a stepping stone to bigger and better things in her career.

"We thought you might like to join us at Hoot's Tavern for a beer," Vance said as he pushed away from the table. "You know, sort of a get-reacquainted-with-the-folks-in-town kind of evening. Isn't that right, Quint?"

Gee, he was surprised that his cousin and Steph noticed he was still here. They'd been yammering nonstop and he hadn't contributed diddly-squat to the conversation.

"Uh...right," Quint said stupidly.

"Actually, my landlady is going to drop by for a visit this evening," Steph said then glanced expectantly toward the door. "She should be here any minute."

Vance glanced at Quint, silently urging him to leap into the conversation. Quint didn't. He just sat there like a bump on a log. Damn it, what was the matter with him? He'd never had trouble relating to women or contributing to conversations. Suddenly he felt like the world's biggest dud. He'd mentally prepared himself to encounter the fiery female he'd met this afternoon and he couldn't seem to shift mental gears.

"Maybe I can make it some other time," Steph said, tossing Vance a blinding smile.

"Sure, I'll give you a call. Thanks for supper. It was delicious," Vance said as he followed Steph toward the door.

Still in a befuddled daze Quint stumbled clumsily from his chair, his attention focused on where Steph had been—in those form-fitting barely there cutoff shorts—instead of where he was going. It was a wonder he didn't crash into the wall.

The instant the door clicked shut Vance rounded on Quint. "What the hell's wrong with you? You barely said two words to Steph."

"Did you *see* her?" Quint questioned.

"Of course, I saw her. And you're right. She's drop-dead gorgeous. But you dropped the ball, cuz. I got the chitchat going and you just sat there like a tongue-tied doofus. What's the matter with you?"

"Did you see those legs? Those eyes? They're the most fascinating shade of silver-blue—"

Vance grabbed Quint's arm and gave him an abrupt shake. "Snap out of it, man."

Quint shook his head and tried to collect his thoughts. "I've lost my touch. I can't handle Steph."

Exasperated, Vance stared at him. "Of course, you can. March yourself back to her door and say *something*. You were appointed for this mission, remember? Now, go."

Quint stumbled when Vance shoved him harder than necessary toward the door. *Say something.* Vance's terse command rang in his ears, but for the life of him Quint couldn't think of a single opening line, not one solitary come-on that'd worked like a charm for years.

He sucked in a deep breath and wrapped his knuckles on the front door, hoping that something witty and flirtatious would tumble off his lips the way it usually did when he encountered an attractive woman.

STEPHANIE HALF COLLAPSED against the door when the Ryder cousins exited. Jeez, she wasn't cut out to play these saucy sex siren routines. Being breezy and flippant felt unnatural to her. This was definitely going to take practice, she decided. She'd made it her objective to fling outrageous comments and beat Quint to the punch, but it was hard work that took conscious effort.

Gabbing with Vance hadn't been too difficult. She could handle him, no sweat. But Quint? That was another matter entirely. She was intensely aware of him, even when she tried her best to ignore him.

Stephanie was still sagging against the door for support when another rap resounded. Thank goodness Idabelle had arrived to take her mind off her frustrating attraction to Quint.

When she opened the door, there stood Quint, wearing a megawatt smile. Stephanie inwardly groaned. Damn, she was going to have to play the siren again and try to keep him off balance.

"That was fast," she said. "But I guess you're the type who usually works fast. You came back to see if I wanted to go out to the tavern *after* my landlady's visit, right?"

"Uh...yeah," he mumbled.

Stephanie turned away to saunter across the apartment. She knew she'd caught Quint off guard by second-guessing the reason for his return visit. When she pivoted to glance back at him he was still hovering in the doorway. She suspected he'd been checking her out while she sashayed across the room because it took him a moment to raise his gaze to her face.

In amusement she watched Quint close the door. He opened and shut his mouth like a trap a couple of times then appeared to gather his wits.

Knowing she'd flustered him gave Stephanie the needed confidence to play her role. "Sorry, handsome, I'm really not in the mood for loud music at the tavern tonight. It's been a long day and I plan to hit the sack early."

"I'm the early to bed type myself. Need company?" he asked, eyes twinkling like pyrite.

Rats, he'd recovered his powers of speech and his ability to toss come-ons. That wouldn't do, she decided. She had handled Quint satisfactorily when *she* controlled the conversation.

She steeled herself against all that masculine sex appeal that radiated from him like a potbellied stove as he swaggered toward her. "Some other time maybe. Actually it's my practice to take test drives, just to get a feel for what I can expect from a man before I invite him to my bed for wild, sweaty sex."

When his dark brows jackknifed and his jaw sagged Stephanie decided to keep striking hard and fast before he could react. "So, let's see how you rate on a scale of lukewarm to red-hot."

She looped her arms around his neck, brushed provocatively against him and kissed him as if she were starving to death for him. She wasn't sure why she did it. Maybe to keep him off balance. Or maybe because she'd secretly wanted to be the one sitting on that porch swing all those years ago, smooching with her dreamboat.

Whatever the case, she kissed Quint for all she was worth and rubbed against him like a cat. When she raked her fingers through his shiny raven hair, his Resistol hat tumbled to the floor and hit the carpet with a soft *thunk*.

If she had her way, her kiss would pack enough wallop to knock him out of his boots and leave his head spinning like a windmill. But since she was short on practice and experience in the romance department she doubted she could send this sex god reeling. He was rumored to have oodles of experience and expertise. But that didn't stop her from giving her all, especially since kissing Quint caused an unexpected explosion of her senses and set her body to humming like a tuning fork.

Wow! When he melted against her the same way she'd melted against him and his brawny arms fastened around her, as if he couldn't pull her close enough to satisfy himself, Stephanie forgot to breathe, couldn't think. Hot, blazing sensations boiled through her as he deepened the kiss and dropped his splayed hands to her bottom to press her into the cradle of his thighs.

He was definitely aroused, she realized. She'd done that to him? *Her?* Her newfound power over him filled her with heady satisfaction, especially when she heard his quiet moan—or was that *her* voice? She wasn't sure because she was so lost in the scent, feel and taste of him that her brain and body were going into nuclear melt-down.

Her hands must have developed a mind of their own for they'd gone from stroking his thick hair to measuring the broad expanse of his shoulders. She hadn't realized she'd snapped open his Western shirt until her fingers were gliding greedily over the hair-roughened muscles of his chest.

Good grief! What was happening to her? She was transforming into a sex fiend after one steamy kiss. Well, three, actually, she recounted. She'd kissed him and he'd kissed her back then she kissed him again. Her tongue mated with his in some kind of frantic ritual that stole her breath and left her body on sensual overload.

The man was a walking minefield of repetitive explosions—and she felt as if she was coming apart in his arms. His hands were all over her and her hands were all over him. That wasn't good because she was totally out of control—and no longer cared. All that mattered was kissing him, touching him, absorbing his appealing scent and savoring every delicious moment for as long as it lasted.

All these years she'd wondered what she'd missed while she'd harbored those secret fantasies about Quint. Now she knew that he could awaken a woman's wildest desires, demolish her inhibitions and leave her aching for more. With that knowledge came the shocking realization that she had an extreme case of the hots for the kind of man she tried to avoid.

Of course, she'd be back to disapproving of him again—as soon as she marshaled the willpower to stop kissing him, stop touching him and stepped back into her own space to gather her scattered wits.

The sudden rap on the door jerked Stephanie to her

senses and sent her lurching backward. The back of her knees hit the arm of the sofa and she kerplopped on the cushions with all the grace of an elephant. Even worse, her hands were still tangled in Quint's shirt and she accidentally pulled him down on top of her.

They sprawled on the sofa, his hips wedged intimately between her legs, the hard evidence of his arousal pressing against her feminine heat. When he reared up on his forearms they stared at each other in startled amazement. More impatient raps hammered against the door while she and Quint tried to bring their hot and heavy breathing under control.

"Well, that was fun, but Idabelle must be here," she croaked, cursing her distorted voice. She shoved Quint aside, sending him cartwheeling to the floor in her haste to regain her feet and assemble her shattered composure.

Stephanie readjusted her camisole that'd somehow gotten twisted sideways, then she dragged in a shuddering breath. Well, that was an experiment gone bad, she decided. She'd discovered she couldn't trust herself with Quint Ryder. He had more male magnetism than any woman could handle—even a woman who knew he was perpetually on the make. She'd gotten in over her head and she was smart enough to know it. This harebrained scheme that Idabelle dreamed up was *not* going to work!

She sucked in another cathartic breath and demanded her pounding pulse to return to normal. On her way to the door, she glanced sideways to note Quint had rolled agilely to his feet, raked his fingers through his hair—that *she'd* left standing on end—and hurriedly snapped his shirt. When he plucked his hat off the floor he cut her a quick glance. She suspected his stunned look identically matched the one on her face. She quickly schooled her expression and opened the door.

Stephanie motioned her landlady inside and glanced toward the curb to note Vance was leaning negligently against the side of a pickup.

"Well, hello there, Quint. Good to see you," Idabelle greeted cheerfully.

"You, too, ma'am." Quint, she noticed, recovered in time to flash the older woman a charming grin as he swaggered out the door.

Stephanie resisted the urge to fan herself as she closed the door on the worst temptation she'd ever encountered. Grateful for the interruption, she turned her attention to her landlady and tried to ignore the erotic sensations that were sizzling through her.

QUINT HEADED FOR THE PICKUP, wondering what the hell had just hit him. For sure, he hadn't expected Steph's kiss or the jarring impact it left on his body. Damn, that woman had blown him away when he least expected it. She'd been doing that since their first confrontation and he'd been knocked off kilter ever since.

"Well?" Vance asked impatiently. "Did you make headway?"

"I dunno," Quint mumbled as he eased beneath the steering wheel.

"Whaddya mean you dunno?" Vance grilled him. "Are you taking Steph out?"

Quint smirked. "Believe me, cuz o' mine, nobody *takes* Steph Lawson anywhere. If we were dancing, I suspect she'd be leading."

Vance cocked his head and studied Quint astutely. "You've got me confused here."

Quint aimed the pickup toward the tavern. "That makes two of us. I need a cool one and I need it fast."

"I don't know what your problem is, but you better get your act together," Vance lectured. "If you don't win over Steph the men in town are going to string her up for dispensing with the lunch hour menu. Wes Martin drove by while I was standing on the curb. He told me a bunch of guys are planning to form a picket line at the grand opening and boycott the restaurant until Steph agrees to cater to their demands."

Quint groaned aloud. He didn't need this. The pressure of trying to sweet talk Steph was bearing down on him. Hell! After that mind-jolting, knock-you-on-your-butt kiss she'd delivered he didn't want to talk about cafés and menus. He just wanted to get naked with her, grab hold of her gorgeous body and lose himself in the fiery contradiction that went by the name of Steph Lawson.

What was *wrong* with him? He couldn't seem to maintain his perspective when he was with her. He just got all hot and bothered. Worse, she kept him mentally off stride and the methods he customarily used on women absolutely did not apply to this particular woman.

Quint cursed himself soundly when he damn near missed the turn. He cut a sharp left turn that caused Vance's head to slam into the side window. Quint stopped in the parking lot at Hoot's Tavern and drew a steadying breath. Damn it, the tantalizing memory of kissing and caressing Steph was affecting his ability to function. Vance was right. If he didn't get a grip, he was headed straight for disaster!

4

STEPHANIE WAS AMAZED at the turnout for 'A Taste of Country' festival in town square. Portable smokers, grills, folding tables and chairs surrounded the gurgling fountain. Dozens of people in town had brought their specialty dishes to serve to the huge crowd. While Stephanie lugged aluminum trays of German cuisine to her food booth she noticed Quint and his cousin Vance were cooking steaks on their oversize grill. To her left, several women—Idabelle Witham included—were dishing out cole slaw, potato salad and homemade hot rolls. To her right was a dessert table heaping with goodies.

For two hours Stephanie and one of her waitresses dished up food and chatted with the festivalgoers. While the police force blocked off the side street with their cruisers, a local band tuned up their instruments then burst into one of Garth Brooks' fast-tempoed songs. The diners tossed their disposable plates in the trash bins and headed to the street to two-step and line dance the night away.

Stephanie was well pleased with the way the day had gone. She'd received hundreds of compliments about her cuisine and promises to show up at her new restaurant. She was relieved to know she'd have customers, even if the local men's committee threatened to boycott.

Gathering up the aluminum pans, she tossed them into the recycling bin then zigzagged through the dancers to lock up her restaurant. She decided to hang around the festival for another hour then head home. It had been another tiring day and she was beat. Tomorrow promised to be a carbon copy. She definitely needed to catch up on her sleep.

"THERE SHE GOES," Wes Martin murmured as he loomed behind Quint. "Now's your chance. Go over there and ask Steph to dance."

"I'll tell the band to play a slow song," Clem Spaulding volunteered.

Quint scowled when Wes and company practically shoved him toward the street. He glanced over his shoulder, hoping Vance would discourage this mob from shanghaiing him into another conversation with Steph. Hell, he wasn't sure he was ready for that just yet, seeing how he still hadn't recovered from those lip-sizzling kisses they'd shared a few nights earlier.

"Do your duty, Cousin Q." Vance grinned and winked. "You're the man for this mission."

Muttering, Quint strode off. He didn't like being a specimen under a microscope while putting moves on Steph. He could barely function around her as it was. Having that determined group of men spying on him and breathing down his neck wasn't going to make it easier.

Quint inhaled a fortifying breath and homed in on Steph as she locked the restaurant door. Before she could turn around to face him he grabbed her elbow. "Let's dance."

Startled, she glanced up at him. "Thanks, but it's been a long day."

"That's okay. It'll be a short dance," Quint countered, forcing himself not to look directly into those mesmerizing eyes, for fear he'd get tongue-tied and go brain dead again. When he was with Steph it was usually touch and go, he reminded himself.

"Have you given some thought to reopening for lunch?" he asked as he led her to the street.

"None whatsoever," she replied.

The band broke into one of Elvis Presley's oldies but goodies, "Can't Help Falling in Love." Quint nearly groaned out loud as he slipped his arm around Steph's trim waist and drew her up close and personal. That's all it took for the memory of their mind-boggling kiss to snap into place and send erotic sensations zinging through his body. The feel of her moving rhythmically against him made his throat close up, his chest tighten and his male body clench.

Oh, man, this was going to be one long tormenting dance. He needed to say something romantic or toss out a compliment about how great she looked in that form-fitting blouse and those jeans that clung to her arresting curves. Unfortunately his brain short-circuited, leaving his unruly body on autopilot.

Quint tightened his hold on Steph, drawing her ever closer. He caught a whiff of her shampoo as he nuzzled his chin against the top of her head. He felt her breasts pressing against his chest, her hips gliding against his aroused body and he moaned in sweet torment. Her hand curled around his neck as she tucked her head against his shoulder and all but melted against him. Her response made him squeeze his eyes shut and fight like the devil for self-control.

While the band played, the world went out of focus. Quint couldn't see the couples swaying around him, couldn't see the streetlights or the full moon that hung in the vault of night sky like a neon beach ball. All he could see was provocative images of him and Steph rolling around on his king-size bed, ripping clothes off each other and taking this dance to a horizontal level. The vivid thought sent pure testosterone pulsing through his veins.

Damn, he was on fire here! Call out the volunteer fire department! Four alarm and getting hotter by the second!

His hold on Steph got even tighter as he buried his face in the silken flames of her hair and absorbed the scent of her perfume.

Man on a mission, man on a mission, he chanted silently. But it didn't do any good. The dead-last thing on his mind was a lunch menu. Help! His body was enduring sensual torture because he ached to glide his hands all over her, the way he'd done that night at her apartment when he'd suffered one of the worst lust attacks of his life. He wanted to tip her face up to his and kiss her to death. Oh, man, he wanted that—badly!

Unfortunately they were in public and jumping her bones, right here beside the town square, would get him arrested. But that didn't mean he couldn't enjoy the fantasy while they danced. It was that or nothing. So he just held her a little closer than propriety allowed and suffered the sweet torment of wanting what he obviously wasn't going to get.

When the song ended, Quint forced himself to step

back into his own space. He'd intended to turn and walk away so he could find a private place to sink to his knees and howl in frustration, but his gaze dropped to her mouth—and stuck there.

She licked those luscious lips and swallowed, as if her mouth was as dry as his felt. He inwardly flinched as hungry need jackhammered through him.

"Thanks for the dance," she said, her voice wobbly.

"My pleasure," he managed to get out, just barely.

"Well, g'night."

When she turned and walked away Quint stood there, watching the graceful sway of her hips, watching the street lights gleam down on that long hair that reminded him of shimmering flames. When she disappeared around the corner into the shadows like a vanishing dream, Quint forced himself to blink and draw breath. Damn, what the sweet loving hell was the matter with him? If he believed in witches—which he didn't—he'd swear that woman had cast a spell on him. She had him tied in so many knots that the Great Houdini couldn't get him loose.

Quint didn't have time to gather his wits before Wes and company arrived to stare inquisitively at him.

"Well?" Randel Bentley demanded. "Any luck?"

Annoyed, Quint glared at the crowd of curious men. "We just danced, for Pete's sake."

"Yeah, but you were dancing pretty close," Clem observed.

"There wasn't enough room between you for a mosquito to breathe," Wes noted. "Surely that means something. I'd say you're getting somewhere with her."

"Yep, progress," Randel declared. "Maybe you

should follow her home. You know, take up where you left off.''

''Not tonight,'' Quint said as he elbowed his way through the clump of men. ''We're rounding up and working cattle this week. I'm going home to bed.''

The men muttered in disappointment as Quint aimed himself toward the Ryder food booth to pack up the truck. Maybe he should leave town until these yahoos forgot about this ridiculous seduction scheme. He didn't want to be a part of it because the sensations Steph aroused in him were getting entirely too complicated.

Hurriedly Quint packed up and drove away. He needed to find a place to cool off after slow dancing with Steph.

Like maybe Antarctica.

STEPHANIE, WITH CLIPBOARD in hand, double-checked kitchen supplies in the restaurant. For the past two days she'd tried to keep her mind on business, but erotic thoughts of Quint kept cropping up every time she turned around. The fact that he'd called twice didn't help, either, she mused as she and her chef—who was also her best friend—inventoried the kitchen.

Quint had urged Stephanie to consider the needs of the locals and she kept insisting the citizens give the restaurant a chance and stop resisting change. Although their conversations had been brief and focused on the restaurant, the mere sound of his voice triggered forbidden longings and memories of the white-hot sparks that had sizzled between them when they'd kissed, when they'd danced. That dance of seduction had nearly done her in. She'd been so totally immersed in him that it was a wonder she'd been able to walk away under her own power.

She'd been so shaken and achy from the sensations he aroused in her that she'd barely gotten a wink of sleep that night.

The appalling fact was that Stephanie was wildly attracted to that raven-haired hunk of cowboy. Bottom line, she'd softened up toward him, which probably wasn't good because he was a heartbreaker deluxe.

"Stephanie, where are you? Yoo-hoo!" Idabelle called abruptly.

Stephanie handed the clipboard to her friend whom she'd met in chef school—a friend who'd needed to leave her old life and ex-husband behind to begin again. Dawn Peters had leaped at the chance to take this job and Stephanie was delighted to have her on board.

"My landlady is here," Stephanie told the attractive brunette. "If there's anything you need that I've overlooked, jot it down and I'll take care of it."

Dawn smiled warmly. "Don't know what it would be. Looks like you have everything under control, as usual. I always said you were efficiency at its finest."

Leaving Dawn to the last minute inspection, Stephanie strode off to see Idabelle perusing the restaurant.

"Wow, this is spectacular," Idabelle exclaimed then dropped her gaze to the shortened hemline of Stephanie's skirt. "Much better. I'm glad you took my advice about the clothing and made yourself more visible around town. Your food booth at the festival was a big hit, by the way."

Stephanie smiled. "Thanks for the suggestion. I made contact with several potential customers that evening. And thank you for altering my skirts and offering fashion advice."

"Don't mention it, hon."

Idabelle's smile faltered. Stephanie tensed. Her land-lady wasn't her usual perky self. "What's wrong?" she asked warily.

Idabelle plopped down in a nearby chair. "I just talked to Leta Martin at the feed store. She told me she was doing bookwork in the office while the menfolk were having their first conspiracy meeting last week."

Apprehensively, Stephanie took a seat across the table from Idabelle. "And?"

"And all men are imbeciles," Idabelle muttered. "Except for my Clarence, God rest his soul. According to Leta, folks are making bets on the outcome of this feud. The men in town definitely blackmailed Quint into charming you. Wes refused to sell supplies to Quint until he buttered you up."

The news hit Stephanie like a blow to the solar plexus. Although she knew Quint was trying to court her under false pretenses, it still hurt to discover that he'd had his arm twisted a dozen different ways to seek her out, to dance with her, to call her on the phone.

"I guess I shouldn't be surprised," Stephanie murmured.

"There's more, hon," Idabelle said grimly. "The moronic men in town took up a collection to pay Quint, as soon as he convinces you to revert to your parents' practices with the café."

Stunned, Stephanie lurched back in her chair as if she'd been slapped. "They *hired* him to try to seduce me? He's doing it for money?" she crowed in astonishment.

Idabelle's gunmetal-gray head bobbed in confirmation.

"Yep. I've been passing the word to all the women in town. They're clamoring to your side of this issue like you wouldn't believe. You won't have to worry about packing the house during your grand opening because the females in the area will be out in full force to show their support."

Idabelle withdrew a folded paper from her purse that was the approximate size of a mail carrier's pouch. "Here's the list of women requesting reservations for Friday, Saturday and Sunday nights. I also called my friends from neighboring towns and explained the situation. They'll be here, too, hon."

While Idabelle yammered on about filling the Palace to capacity, feelings of hurt and rejection lambasted Stephanie. Quint had buckled to *blackmail* and *bribery?* Damn him!

Silently fuming, Stephanie bounded from her chair. She'd take him apart like a jigsaw puzzle. She'd chew him up one side and down the other, then she'd never speak to him as long as she lived—or he lived, whichever came first.

"Idabelle, I need a favor."

"Anything, hon," the older woman said magnanimously.

"Will you help Dawn Peters check over the supplies while I take care of some unfinished business?"

"Sure thing. Where are you going?"

"To see Quint," Stephanie said between clenched teeth.

Idabelle's graying brows nearly rocketed off her forehead. "You're back to butting heads with him again? But what about our scheme?"

"Phooey on that," she muttered. "I'm going to teach him a lesson he won't soon forget."

Stephanie wheeled toward the door and stalked outside. Angry, she piled into her car and made a beeline toward her apartment to change clothes.

The men in this podunk town *paid* Quint to be nice to her? *Paid* him? Her temper boiled over as she veered into the driveway. Quint Ryder was damn well going to pay for hurting her, using her. And these wasted feelings of physical attraction were going to end, here and now, she vowed resolutely. She was going to enjoy a little revenge then she wasn't going to spare him another thought—ever!

QUINT LIMPED ACROSS the corral, bearing down on the contrary cow that had split from the herd and had given him a swift kick on her way by.

"Watch yourself, cuz," Wade Ryder cautioned from his lofty position on the top rail of the corral. "That animal is loco, just like the bull that plowed over me last summer."

"Bring her around to the holding pen," Vance called out needlessly.

Well, duh, thought Quint as he advanced on the flighty, thousand-pound cow that had come unglued when they separated her from her calf. To hear his cousins shouting instructions over the bawling herd that was pinned in the lot you'd think he was a greenhorn on his own ranch.

Okay, so maybe he'd been a teensy-weensy bit distracted the past few days, but that didn't mean he couldn't handle his cattle operation. He'd done this drill a few hundred times, after all. It sure as hell wasn't the first time he and his cousins had separated cows from their calves for branding and inoculation. And it certainly wasn't his fault that this particular cow had suffered a bad case of separation anxiety and claustrophobia. She'd bailed over the top of the corral, leaving broken rails and fence posts in her wake.

When the nervous animal tried to bolt and run the wrong direction, Quint snapped the whip in the dirt, sending up a puff of dust. The wild-eyed cow kicked up her heels and charged off in the direction that Quint wanted her to go. Once Vance let her through the gate to the pasture and watched her head north at a dead run Quint breathed a sigh of relief. Now that the sorting phase was completed he and his cousins could get down to the business of doctoring and castrating the weaning calves and moving them to Cousin Gage's lush pastures that had been standing empty the past month.

Quint practically snarled when he saw Wade glance at his watch for the fortieth time in two hours. "Easy, big guy, it's not lunchtime yet. Surely you can pry yourself away from your new bride for another hour."

Wade grinned as he bounded agilely to the ground. "What can I say? We just returned from our mini honeymoon. I'm used to being with Laura 24/7. I like it. A lot."

"*We know,*" Vance and Quint said simultaneously.

"That's all you've talked about, ad nauseam, all morning," Quint grumbled as he tossed aside the whip and scooped up the box of syringes, medication and wound protector.

"Hey, gimme a break. I'm happy."

"Fine, be happy, but don't rub it in our faces," Quint said, and scowled.

Wade glanced curiously at Vance. "What's with him?"

Vance snickered. "Woman trouble."

Wade cocked a thick black brow. "Anybody I know?"

"Steph Lawson. Remember her from high school?" Vance prompted as he urged two calves down the narrow metal lane toward the squeeze chute.

"Steph?" Wade croaked. "The shy redhead with the eye patch? *She's* Quint's latest conquest?"

"Not exactly," Vance said, chuckling. While Vance updated Wade on the change of management at the café, Quint positioned himself beside the squeeze chute then tested the branding iron. It was red-hot, just like the redhead Cousin W and V were presently discussing.

"No lunch hour!" Wade howled. "Where am I supposed to take Laura for lunch?"

"Hoot 'n Holler," Vance suggested. "According to Quint the packaged sandwiches are awful."

"Well, hell," Wade grumbled.

"My sentiments exactly," Vance agreed. "Same goes for the other farmers and ranchers in the area. Quint has been appointed to change Steph's mind, but he can't handle her."

Wade jerked upright and stared incredulously at Quint. "Can't handle a woman? When did this happen? I wasn't away from home that long!"

"Cute, cuz," Quint muttered sourly. "Can we cut the yammering and get to work here?"

Wade chortled playfully. "Can't handle Steph? This I gotta see."

"That's what *I* said," Vance said. "Sure 'nuff, Quint can't handle her. He gets tongue-tied when he gets within ten feet of her. Can barely even remember his own name."

When Wade cast him a speculative glance Quint ignored him. There was work to do and he was in no mood to discuss his failures with Steph.

Quint was grateful when his cousins stopped razzing him and focused their concentration on moving the calves down the lane to the squeeze chute and locking them in the headgate for branding and inoculation. They were halfway through the process of working the herd of young calves when a cloud of dust appeared on the graveled road.

"Company's coming," Vance noted. "Wonder who that is?"

"Dunno. Don't care," Quint mumbled as he gave another injection. "I just wanna finish up here ASAP and get this young herd transported to Gage's pasture before their mamas decide to break through the gate to reclaim their calves."

One of the basic rules of ranching was to quickly remove weaned calves to distant pastures. Otherwise, you could expect broken fences and mingled cattle. No way was Quint going to risk having to drive to the feed store for more barbwire. No telling what blackmail technique Wes Martin and his cronies would use on him next.

"Holy kamoley," Wade wheezed while he worked the headgate to free the calf Quint had inoculated and branded. "Who is *that?*"

Quint, who was still hunkered down on his haunches, refilling the syringe, glanced over his shoulder to see the object of his tormented dreams sauntering down the hill, wearing trim-fitting blue jeans and a knit top that hugged her gorgeous body like a glove.

"Aw, damn," he muttered.

"That's Steph," Vance informed Wade, then grinned devilishly.

"Get outta town," Wade mumbled, goggle-eyed.

"Yup, none other. Changed considerably, hasn't she?" Vance questioned as he flashed Quint an ornery smile. "Now you know why lover boy's had trouble handling her."

Quint winced. Steph wore the identical look of hostility that he'd encountered during their first confrontation. He didn't have a clue why she was here, but if the glare she was directing at him was any indication, she'd like to see him pushing up daisies in the north forty.

"Take over for me, Vance," Quint requested as he dusted off his chaps and handed over the syringe.

"Sure, tiger. Want me to jot down some opening lines for you, too, since you never can think of anything to say to her?"

Quint scowled at his mischievous cousin and cringed when he heard Wade snickering behind him. He and his cousins were notorious for ragging each other unmercifully. It had been more fun, however, when Vance and Quint had ganged up to torment Wade when he got in over his head with Laura. Now the boot was on the other foot and Quint was feeling the pinch of frustration.

As Quint strode toward Steph she swung a long shapely leg over the top rail of the corral and perched above him. Her glorious red hair caught fire in the sunlight and streamed over her shoulders like lava. Quint itched to grab a handful of that fiery mane, pull her head down to his and kiss her senseless. Unfortunately she didn't look the least bit receptive. She looked mad as a hornet and he had no idea why.

"Something wrong, Red?" he asked cautiously.

She stared across the corral to watch Wade and Vance work the calves. "Yes, as a matter of fact. I have a problem with searing brands on cattle. It looks painful. I think you should find another method to ID."

Quint did a double take. He wasn't sure what he expected her to say but that wasn't even on the list. "Say *what?*"

The calf bawled and flinched when Vance set the heated iron against its hip. "That," Steph insisted. "It's cruel and barbaric. I want you to stop that practice immediately."

Quint squinted up at her. "What do you expect me to do? Spray paint a *QR* brand on the hides every other week?"

"Sounds good to me. Much less painful."

"Sorry, but that's unreliable. It'd be too easy to alter brands and that promotes cattle rustling. Plus, it's too damn much work to do it every few days."

"Are you sure those needles you're poking into those calves are sterile?" she asked as she watched Wade vaccinate another calf. "Doesn't look all that sanitary to me. I think I'll call the animal protection association and see what they have to say about it."

Quint's eyes narrowed and he really hated that he had to look up to where she sat on her lofty perch. He'd felt he'd been at a constant disadvantage since he'd met her and this wasn't helping. "Look, Steph, I don't mean to sound rude, but this is my cattle operation and I've done it long enough to know what works best."

She arched a delicate brow and looked down her nose at him. "Is that a fact? Well, you certainly didn't blink twice before you showed up at my restaurant to tell me how to run my business. Why shouldn't *I* have some input into *your* methods of operation?"

Uh-oh, he'd walked into that and never saw it coming.

"And furthermore, Don Juan, you can forget trying to cozy up to me to change my mind about reverting to the old menu and previous business hours," she said through a sneer. "I know you were blackmailed and paid to be nice to me, you gigolo! I'm just thankful I wasn't foolish enough to let myself fall for all that premeditated charm. And don't you ever come near me again, damn you!"

Her voice had risen to a shout, drawing Vance's and Wade's rapt attention. All activity at the squeeze chute came to a screeching halt.

Well, hell! Quint swore under his breath as Steph swung her leg over the rail—nearly taking his head off with her boot heel—and hopped to the ground. She stalked toward her car, her long-legged strides eating up the freshly mowed lawn with incredible speed.

Quint bounded over the fence and jogged to catch up with her. "Wait a sec, Steph. I can explain."

"You can go to hell with my blessing!" she spewed furiously.

"Damn it, woman, I've been talking to your departing back since that first day." He snagged her arm and propelled her toward his house—away from his eavesdropping cousins.

"Let me go!" she shrieked so loudly that she nearly blasted a hole in his eardrum.

"Not until I've had my say," he growled back at her.

"I do not want to talk to you—ever," she sassed.

"Fine, then I'll do all the talking and you can do all the listening." Quint strode swiftly up the steps, across the porch and into the house. He slammed the door and positioned himself in front of the escape route.

"First off, I didn't want to get involved in this mess."

"Of course not," she spat angrily. "But since you're the biggest flirt in town you were voted the man of the hour and you took the job because you were *paid* to do it! How much am I worth on the market? Or rather, how much was it worth for you to butter me up until we ended up in bed together for fifteen *forgettable* minutes of your time?"

He ignored the snide insult. "I did *not* take pay. Those yahoos at the feed store took up a collection as incentive, but I sure as hell didn't ask for it and I didn't accept it."

"No, because, according to the report I heard," she went on hurriedly, "you had to earn your pay before the men forked over the dough to you. Even worse, I discovered there's a bet in town that you can seduce me *out* of my clothes and *into* handling my business the way you and the other men see fit!"

Damn, he really wished she hadn't discovered anything about that ridiculous fiasco. This whole situation had swelled out of proportion and Quint was standing right smack dab in the middle of a minefield.

"What was between us that night at your apartment and during the street dance is separate and far removed from that stupid bet," he told her.

"Right. And cows fly," she muttered bitterly. "All I wanted to do was return to my hometown to start my own business, to provide a classy restaurant. A place folks could gather for wedding rehearsal dinners, birthday celebrations, holidays and family reunions. A place with elegance and ambience and succulent meals. But no, you men dug in your boot heels and resisted change. It's your way or the highway, right? No variation allowed—"

Her voice broke and her luminous eyes filled with tears. She wiped them away, obviously appalled that she'd broken down in front of him—the man she considered her worst enemy.

When he impulsively reached out to draw her into his arms to comfort her, she stiffened her spine, jerked up her trembling chin and stepped back a pace.

"No way, lover boy," she said on a seesaw breath. "All you care about is bagging your limit of females. I refuse to be your catch of the day, your flavor of the week. I don't want your touch or your pseudocompassion." She glanced over her shoulder to stare down the hall that led to his bedroom. "Are there revolving doors to prevent traffic jams?" Her disdainful glare bore into him. "Knowing the way you like to play the field, you could be a one-man baseball team who scores repeatedly. But I'm not playing your games and I want nothing to do with you!"

Her insulting sarcasm succeeded in igniting his temper. "Fine then, I don't want anything to do with you, either, Red. I don't know why you're all-fired intent on proving yourself to the men of the world. All I know is that you don't give a flying fig about the needs of hardworking men in this town. All you care about is putting a five-star restaurant on the map and on your almighty résumé so you can move on to fry bigger fish in some cosmopolitan hotel. You don't care what this town needs, only what you want. And just so you know, sugarplum, those kisses we shared—and let me remind you that *you* kissed *me* first—had nothing whatsoever to do with this battle over restaurant menus."

"Right," she said, and smirked.

Quint bore down on her, using his towering height to his advantage. "Exactly right, Red Riding Hood. You turn me on, that's a fact. You're beautiful. You're feisty as hell and you're smart. I'm attracted to you. That's also a fact."

"You're attracted to anything in a skirt because, for you, lust is a state of being. Woman-chasing is your favorite sport," she flung back. "Furthermore, I prefer my snakes in the grass to hiss and rattle, not flash pretend smiles and toss premeditated compliments."

Quint scowled. He felt like the boy who'd cried wolf one time too many. His credibility had been shot to hell because of his exaggerated reputation with women. The one time in his life that he wanted to be believed, needed to be believed, Steph scoffed at him. He knew what casual flirtation felt like and this *wasn't* it. Not with *her*.

"You think it's always like this for me? Well, let me tell you something, Red. I've never had trouble flirting with women, except with you. I've never been struck speechless, except with you. I don't like it that you're different, that none of my former rules apply to you. But that's the way it is. When I kiss you I go up in flames and lose the ability to reason."

Quint didn't know what words to use to convince her

that kissing her triggered emotions and sensations he wasn't accustomed to dealing with. He just grabbed hold of her before she could react. He wrapped her in his arms and kissed the breath clean out of her, trying to prove that this was serious and separate from the crusade he'd been roped into.

And suddenly his overheated temper—and hers—erupted into something wild and desperate and all-consuming. In the space of a heartbeat, the feel of her lush lips beneath his, the feel of her voluptuous body crushed to his torso demanded his undivided attention. Vaguely he was aware that Steph had clamped her arms around his neck for support and that he'd clutched her hips against his because he felt so hot and needy that *not* holding her tightly against him was the worst brand of torment imaginable.

And speaking of brands, he thought dazedly, she was searing him with fire, leaving him burning each place their bodies touched. As before, he couldn't get enough of the taste of her, wanted to absorb her enticing scent, wanted full-body contact with her to go on forever.

Sure, he'd kissed his share of women, but it had *never* affected him quite like this. Kissing Steph was physical heaven and hell in one. It was also emotional suicide. He connected with her on some intangible level that blew his mind and tortured every square inch of his hypersensitive body.

Now, like the first time they'd kissed, his hands roved all over her and hers glided all over him, matching touch for frantic touch, making him want her in the worst possible way. He didn't realize he'd backed her up against the wall and hooked her long legs around his hips until he was pressing intimately against her, while simultaneously ravishing her mouth. She returned his explosive passion, kiss for desperate kiss, making him hotter and wilder by the second.

When the door flew open unexpectedly and the brass knob gouged him in the spine Quint found himself smashed even closer to Steph. They both froze, panting for breath, staring incredulously at each other as Vance and Wade invited themselves inside the house.

5

"YO, CUZ!" WADE CALLED OUT. "We came in to make sure you haven't killed each other yet."

"Maybe they're getting it on in the bedroom," Vance ventured.

Quint slammed his elbow against the door and enjoyed a smidgen of satisfaction at hearing Vance yelp when the knob hit him. Wade poked his head around the door and raised his eyebrows as he appraised Quint and Steph who were still wrapped around each other like tangled vines.

"Nope, not in the bedroom," Wade said teasingly to Vance. "They're right here. Appears they couldn't make it that far." He extended his arm to shake hands with Steph, whose fingers were clamped in Quint's tousled hair. "Wade Ryder." He flashed her a grin. "It's been a long time, Steph."

Quint gave Steph high marks for quickly recovering her composure as she unhooked her legs from his waist. "Nice to see you again, Wade." Her voice was nowhere near steady, but that didn't stop her from trying to maintain her dignity. "I hear congratulations are in order since you've married recently. A high school teacher, right?"

"Yup. Smartest thing I ever did," he proclaimed. "I had to get permission from her four overprotective brothers who gave serious thought to killing me." His smile turned upside down momentarily. "They still call twice a week to ensure I'm treating Laura right." He glanced at his watch. "I gotta run. I'm meeting Laura at the school cafeteria."

Vance poked his grinning face around the door. "I'm on break, too. Are you going to feed me, Quint, or do you intend to be otherwise occupied during the noon hour?"

When he waggled his brows suggestively, Steph shot around the Ryder cousins and headed outside without another word or second glance.

Wade and Vance bore down on Quint, making him squirm in his skin.

"I could've sworn you two were arguing before you came in here," Wade said wryly. "It must've been a pretty heated discussion." He glanced pointedly at the two snaps on Quint's shirt that had come undone. "Were you trying to rip each other's clothes off to give each other artificial resuscitation? No wait, that's not a prelim for that life-saving technique, *is it?*"

Quint puffed up like a disturbed toad and his face turned an embarrassed shade of red. "Stop giving me a hard time. I thought you were in a rush to leave. So scram!"

Wade threw up his hands in supplication and backed off. "Calm down, cuz. No need to bite my head off. You already kissed Steph's lips off...and who knows what else you were doing behind the door."

When Quint opened his mouth to tell Wade where he could go—and to take Vance with him—both men burst out laughing. It did nothing for Quint's surly disposition.

Wade ambled off, promising to return in an hour.

Vance strode toward the kitchen to fix himself a sandwich. Quint inhaled a bolstering breath and mentally prepared himself for another round of tormented teasing during lunch.

Sure 'nuff, Vance never let up on him while he choked down three peanut butter and jelly sandwiches and devoured half a bag of potato chips.

STEPHANIE TOLD HERSELF she was entirely too busy to give her embarrassing surrender to Quint a single thought during the following few days of last-minute preparations for the grand opening. Reporters had interviewed her. She'd double- and triple-checked supplies and appliances. She'd also conducted a test run of dinner with her staff's families as guests.

She and Dawn Peters worked side by side in the kitchen and Stephanie was grateful to have her hands and mind occupied constantly. She felt comfortable in the restaurant routine. It was what she'd trained for, what she did with her life.

She did *not* get seriously involved with men, she reminded herself repeatedly. They were more trouble than they were worth. If the humiliating incidents with Quint Ryder weren't prime examples of that then Stephanie didn't know what were! She fumed each time she remembered he'd been paid to seduce her. That really stung her pride and she couldn't get past it.

"Hey, pay attention," Dawn yelped, jerking Stephanie from her resentful reverie. "I'm not an exceptionally temperamental chef, but if you pour salad dressing on my Coquilles St. Jacques I'm gonna be ticked off."

"Sorry." Stephanie moved away from the gourmet

scallop entrées before she smothered them in salad dressing.

"What's up with you anyway?" Dawn demanded as she focused on creating another culinary delight.

"Man trouble," Stephanie admitted reluctantly.

"Ah, the Ryder character that your landlady mentioned, right? Well, take it from a woman who knows, you're better off without a main squeeze. Sex for the sake of sex is one thing, but getting emotionally involved isn't worth the effort. Been there, tried that. Didn't work."

Stephanie decided her cynical friend was exactly the person she needed to talk her down from the emotional cliff she found herself teetering on. Dawn had been through the divorce wars and had her deadbeat, two-timing husband legally removed from her life. These days Dawn was megaindependent and was looking for nothing but an occasional good time.

"I don't want Quint Ryder complicating my life, especially not right now." All she had to do was convince herself of that.

"At least you've admitted he's a potential problem," Dawn said as she dished up the steaming entrée and garnished the plate. Quickly she pivoted to hand the plate to the waitress for delivery. "Now get on with your life and let's make this restaurant a smashing success. Deal?"

"Deal," Stephanie affirmed.

"When you need a pep talk then come see me," the dark-haired chef insisted. "If you want me to give Quint a piece of my mind I'll be glad to do that, too."

"Not necessary. I'm sure by now he's moved on to his next conquest or rekindled a few old flames to keep him warm at night."

"Sounds like a man," Dawn muttered darkly. "Of course, my ex didn't see anything wrong with having a few flings *during* our marriage. It was perfect for him. I busted my fanny cooking on late shifts and he tore up the sheets with his best friend's girlfriend."

"That bites," Stephanie said, wincing.

"Big time," Dawn agreed. "Once a cheater always a cheater, I always say. Your playboy is definitely bad news."

Stephanie couldn't agree more. She was going to avoid Quint, refuse to speak to him. Never mind that when she lay in bed at night her body tingled with remembered passion and unfulfilled desire. But that was just physical. She *didn't* miss the appealing sight of him, the tantalizing feel of his power-packed body nestled familiarly against hers. *Didn't* miss his masculine scent, his skillful touch—or so she tried to convince herself. And what she really didn't miss was his lack of scruples and integrity. He ranked right down there with the bottom feeders in the cesspool of life. Right alongside her former boss. He was devious, manipulative and untrustworthy.

"Hey, boss. Can you and Dawn come in here for a minute?"

Stephanie nodded at the waitress then washed off her hands. She and Dawn entered the dining area to be greeted by applause. The glowing compliments from the patrons reminded her that this is what she did best. If she had any sense she'd stick with what worked and the devil take Quint Ryder.

"I'd say we're a hit," Dawn murmured as they reentered the kitchen. "When word-of-mouth spreads you might have to buy out the hardware store next door to add seating space. According to Idabelle, this place is going to be jam-packed tomorrow night for the official grand opening.''

Stephanie hoped Idabelle's predictions came true. She'd sunk her entire savings into this venture and barely had enough left to cover three months' rent. If business went well during the next two years she might be able to cut down to serving meals Thursday through Sunday evenings. She knew of several successful restaurateurs who made enough profit four nights a week to support themselves comfortably.

She winced, remembering what Quint had said about this endeavor being no more than a gold star on her résumé—or something to that effect. Okay, so maybe she'd been looking farther down the road. But what was wrong with planning ahead? She was a career woman who'd decided a few years back that she'd probably never have a husband and family. For certain, Dawn Peters's dream of combining a career and family had shattered in a gazillion pieces. The moral of that story was that most men of her generation were unreliable and the only thing a woman could count on was her career.

And that, Stephanie reminded herself as she served up one of Dawn's mouthwatering desserts, would continue to be her focus. She'd wasted her last thought on Quint Ryder. He could charm and seduce every eligible female in three counties and she wouldn't care. He didn't do in *love* and he was a heartache waiting to happen. She had better things to do with her life than get mixed up with that incurable flirt.

WADE RYDER CAME THROUGH Quint's front door without bothering to knock. His green eyes smoldered beneath his jutting brows as he stalked up to Quint who was lounging on the sofa, sipping a cool one.

"Thank you *sooo* much!" Wade snarled down at him.

Startled, Quint stared at his cousin. "What'd I do?"

"Thanks to you and your mishandling of this male versus female feud that's erupted over the new restaurant, my wife and I had our first argument!"

Quint flinched when Wade's booming voice bounced off the walls. "You argued over *what?*"

"She insisted on attending the grand opening at Stephanie's Palace and I said I was sort of caught in the middle because of your position as spokesman for the male population. And she said, 'Fine, be an idiot. I'll go with Annie Nelson and the other women teachers. You can cook your own supper.'"

"Now wait a minute," Quint protested. "I refuse to take the blame for your domestic quarrels. I don't even want to be involved in this fiasco."

"Well, you are." Wade grabbed Quint's arm and hoisted him from the couch. "According to Vance, the male picket line is going to pace the sidewalk tonight and I don't want Laura hassled, so we're going to be there for crowd control."

Despite Quint's objections—and he had several— Wade frog-marched him outside where Cousin Vance waited in his idling pickup. Quint found himself wedged in the front seat between his cousins' broad shoulders.

"Hoot's Roost is not going to become a battleground," Wade insisted. "You started this mess when you agreed to speak for the men and you're going to see it through."

Quint would've thrown up his hands in frustration, but there wasn't room while he was sandwiched in the middle like a slice of Spam. "What the hell am I supposed to do? I've called Steph and left messages. She refuses to call back. That pretty much indicates she's sticking to her guns when it comes to never speaking to me as long as she lives. As for Wes Martin and company, they're too radical to listen to reason. They want their burgers 'n fries and meat 'n taters. No compromise allowed."

Wade blew out an exasperated breath. "All I know is that Steph delivered a sampler plate to Laura at school yesterday. She and the other teachers raved over the gourmet meal and they promised to attend the grand opening. Since my name's Ryder—which has become synonymous with *mud*—I'm not particularly welcome at the restaurant because word spread like wildfire through the female population that you took money to charm Steph."

"I did not take money!" Quint yelled. "I had nothing to do with that damn bet, either. And I sure as hell didn't ask to be blackmailed!"

"Can it, cuz," Wade growled. "All I have to say is that I don't want your sex life to screw up my love life."

"I don't have a sex life," Quint muttered.

"Yeah, right," Vance said, and smirked. "Wade and I saw you and Steph clinging together behind the front door. Looked pretty hot and heavy to us."

"Nothing happened." Quint said through gritted teeth.

"Not for lack of trying on your part, Romeo," Wade said sarcastically.

Quint clamped his mouth shut and stared through the windshield while Vance made fast tracks to town. No one would believe he was an innocent victim caught squarely between a mob of hidebound men and a strong-willed woman who was making him so crazy he woke up in a sweat at night. The fantasies just kept getting hotter and wilder and Steph had the starring role in every one of his erotic dreams.

Quint groaned in dismay when he saw the picket line of his male neighbors and friends marching back and forth in front of the Palace. Cars and trucks lined the streets and scads of elegantly dressed females were pushing their way through the picket line to enter the restaurant. Quint rolled his eyes and swore when one of the women whacked Wes Martin upside the head with her purse when he tried to prevent her from reaching the door. Several other women joined the fracas by pounding nearly every male skull to display their objection to the boycott.

"Get moving, Quint," Wade demanded the instant Vance parked the pickup. "Go talk some sense into Wes and his picket-line brigade before all hell breaks loose."

Quint clambered from the truck and headed for the picket line. His cousins were hot on his heels. Before Quint could utter a word someone stuffed a sign in his hands and forced him into the march. He glanced over his shoulder to see that Vance and Wade had received similar treatment. When Quint tried to break ranks his neighbors closed in around him. Same went for Wade and Vance.

"We gotta stick together since you failed with Steph," Clem Spaulding said behind him. "My wife is in there with Randel and Wes's wife, chowing down on that gourmet food. We gotta make a stand or those females will be walking all over us from now till Doomsday."

Although Quint halted to allow Idabelle and her gray-haired friends to pass, the men around him shot him a look that branded him a traitor. Idabelle flung her nose in the air and stalked past him. Great. He'd become an enemy to men and women alike.

He'd planned to lay low tonight, to kick back and watch a flick on the tube. Instead here he was, walking the line with the men of Hoot's Roost while the women dined on Steph's delicious feasts. Plus, Wade was royally ticked off and blamed Quint for causing marital problems with his new bride. Vance, of course, found the situation amusing and was cracking dumb jokes right and left. Problem was, no one was laughing. As Quint predicted, the battle lines had been drawn. The skirmish between the sexes was in full swing.

As for Quint, all he wanted was the chance to take up where he and Steph had left off behind his front door. Fat chance of that ever happening again.

STEPHANIE GLANCED OUT the window then silently cursed when saw Quint and his cousins pacing the sidewalk. She'd hoped Quint wouldn't participate in the boycott. She would've taken it as a positive sign that he'd meant what he said about the sexual sparks between them having nothing whatsoever to do with this local protest. The fact that he was present and accounted for assured Stephanie that he'd fed her another line and that kissing her senseless and making her body burn with unappeased desire were part of his scheme to manipulate her.

Damn that man! Despite her better judgment, she'd wanted to believe that this…thing—whatever it was between them—was separate from the feud. Obviously she was the Queen of Wishful Thinking and that suave, seductive cowboy had mesmerized her with those gorgeous amber eyes and world-class smile.

Fuming, Stephanie lurched around, pasted on a cheerful smile and mingled with the female patrons. When Laura Seymour-Ryder motioned her to the corner table, Stephanie approached warily. She'd taken an instant liking to the attractive blue-eyed blonde, but she kept in mind that Laura was still a Ryder and Stephanie wasn't particularly fond of the name at the moment.

"I just wanted to tell you how much my friends and I are enjoying our night out," Laura imparted with a smile. "We're behind you one hundred percent. I love my husband and my cousins-in-law dearly, but we're siding with you and we're here to offer moral support."

Stephanie's shoulders sagged with relief. "I can't tell you how much I appreciate your help and encouragement. This conflict with the men has gotten completely out of hand. I'm not trying to alienate anyone. Truly. I'm only trying to get my business off the ground."

"And those darn-fool men are determined to dictate what you can serve and when you can serve it," Annie Nelson said. "You go, girl. Don't give them the upper hand."

Stephanie forced herself to concentrate on the positive aspects of her business. She glanced around the dining areas, noting only two empty tables. This evening was a success and she should be satisfied with that. She didn't need this illogical, unproductive infatuation for Quint niggling her. Heavens, she'd spent years harboring fanciful dreams about him during adolescence. Wasn't that enough?

Knowing Quint was insincere and that he was using her as a pawn in this skirmish of men against women should've cured any romantic notions of him for life.

Clinging fiercely to that thought, Stephanie ambled off to visit with the occupants of each table before entering the kitchen to give Dawn Peters a helping hand.

QUINT MOUNTED HIS BUCKSKIN gelding and watched Wade's cow dog, Frank, bound toward the grazing herd. Frank was eager, as always, to round up cattle and herd them into the corrals. Quint and his cousins were in the process of sorting steers and heifers to haul to the stockyards for sale.

These days, working with Cousin Wade was no picnic because he held Quint personally responsible for the ongoing debate with Laura over the Palace.

"Have you talked to her yet?" Wade questioned abruptly.

Quint glanced sideways as he trotted his buckskin gelding over the rolling terrain. "Nope. She still won't return my calls."

Wade muttered several expletives. "You could go see her, ya know. There are other means of communication."

"I'm going to have to agree with Wade on this one," Vance put in. "It's been two weeks and Steph's business is going great guns. She's got customers galore driving to Hoot's Roost from surrounding communities. Her restaurant keeps filling to capacity so she isn't going to reconsider opening for lunch unless you keep reminding her that the men around here are starving to death for burgers 'n fries at high noon. I, for one, am getting real sick of my own cooking."

Ditto for Quint. He missed Hoagie's noon specials like crazy, but he seriously doubted Steph would allow him within speaking distance. He'd seen her on the street in town the previous week and she'd looked right through him as if he were invisible. He, however, had been completely aware of her and her new high-rise hemline that displayed her long shapely legs to their best advantage and those scoop-necked blouses that offered a teasing hint of cleavage beneath the jacket of her suit.

Of course, he hadn't been able to get anywhere near her because the men in town had recently adhered to the policy of walking on the south and west streets that surrounded town square. The women had segregated to the east and north streets. It was the dumbest thing he'd ever seen. He'd speculated this battle over the restaurant would divide the sexes, but never in his worst nightmare had he imagined it would become taboo for men and women to use the same blessed sidewalk!

There was even an unwritten law that men didn't enter the grocery store, filling station or other businesses during the hours frequented by women. Damn, the townsfolk had turned into nutcases!

Although Quint was catching flack from his cousins he personally blamed Wes Martin and the older coots who'd pushed this protest to the limits.

"So," Wade said, jolting Quint from his troubled thoughts, "what are you going to do about this festering problem?"

Quint watched Frank circle the herd of cows and yearlings on the hillside then put them into to motion. "Nothing. I'm out of the loop," he announced.

"No, you're not," Wade contradicted. "You're dead

center on this. If you don't go see Steph on your own accord I'll haul you to town myself.''

"And I'll be riding shotgun with a *loaded* shotgun," Vance insisted, his customary lighthearted grin nowhere to be seen. The man was dead serious for a change.

Quint expelled a breath. "Okay, fine. I'll go see her tonight, but I can tell you that it won't change anything. That's one headstrong woman and she doesn't like me.''

Wade and Vance gaped at him as if he had grapevines sprouting from his ears.

"*Not* like you?" Wade crowed. "Hello? Remember, we saw you two up against the wall, giving each other tonsillectomies. Obviously there's *something* about you that woman likes.''

"That's separate from this feud," Quint clarified. "And anyway, that was only a one-time thing. Well, two, actually.''

Wade and Vance's dark brows shot up like exclamation marks. "Separate?" they echoed incredulously.

Quint squirmed uneasily in the saddle and felt the unfamiliar heat of embarrassment sting his cheeks. "Uh…yeah.''

He knew for sure that he should've kept his trap shut when his sadistic cousins commenced to laughing like hyenas. "Zip it. You'll scare the cattle," Quint muttered at them.

"You're getting serious about Steph and she won't give you the time of day." Wade cackled in amusement. "Oh, that is rich. So the mighty ladies' man has fallen, has he?''

"I never said that," Quint shot back, glaring bullets.

"Didn't have to," Vance said, snickering. "Now that

I think about it, this is beginning to make sense. The first time we went to Steph's apartment your tongue got stuck to the roof of your mouth and you couldn't think of even one of your usual lines of flattery.''

"Because she's *un*usual? Aside and apart from the nameless women from your past? This from the incurable flirt who's already filled his lifetime quota of women? The playboy who's had more women in his lap than napkins?'' Wade snickered. "Well, don't expect sympathy from us, cuz. If you want sympathy, go look for it in the dictionary because that's the only place you'll find it.''

"Golly gee,'' Vance cooed teasingly. "You must have it bad for Steph. You know, the *L* word. Bet you haven't even realized that yet, have you?''

"I do not have it bad for her!'' Quint exploded then cursed when his thundering voice sent the herd of cattle into a fast trot.

"Well, hell,'' Wade muttered when his experienced mount bounded after the scattering cattle, forcing him to hang on for dear life. "Spread out! Frank can't handle this herd if they decide to stampede!''

Quint was thankful for the distraction, even if it meant containing a startled herd. At least this served to get his tormentors off his back. It disturbed him that he couldn't take their ornery teasing as well as usual. Furthermore, he didn't appreciate the fact that Red Riding Hood was such a sensitive subject with him. That definitely wasn't a good sign.

He *wasn't* serious about her, he tried to assure himself. She was a challenge, was all. He was wildly attracted to her. That went without saying. And so what if he kinda liked the fact that he had to work at building a relationship with her, that she wasn't swayed by his smiles and that he had to make an effort to gain her respect and trust.

Not that he'd gained either one. He hadn't, Quint mused as he raced northwest to cut off the herd before it headed back in the direction it had come. Steph considered that blackmail and bribery business to be conclusive evidence against him. How in the hell was he going to convince her that he wasn't as devious as she believed when she'd already tried and convicted him of being a big bad wolf with hidden agendas?

Quint tapped his heels against the buckskin's flanks to increase speed. He decided he'd have to worry about Steph later. Right now he and his cousins had their hands full of stampeding cattle. And, of course, he was getting blamed for that, too.

STEPHANIE FLOPPED BACK on her sofa like a landed fish. Lord, she was tired. The tension in town was getting to her, hard as she tried not to let it show. Being snubbed and avoided by the male store owners wasn't a feeling she was comfortable with. Plus, keeping the hectic pace at the restaurant was wearing her out.

Worse, she found herself searching for Quint's handsome face in every crowd of men on the street. Was she insane? She'd wanted him to make himself scarce and he had. So why wasn't she pleased about it?

Because she missed their verbal sparring, missed those scorching kisses that assured her she was still a woman, not a career robot.

She was definitely going insane, she decided. She was suffering a carry-over fascination from adolescence that wouldn't leave her be. Quint was the man she'd wanted and never had. Somehow he'd become the ideal dreamboat, even though she was now mature and sensible enough to know he wasn't good relationship material.

Whoa, back up the truck, she thought to herself. Who said anything about wanting a relationship? She didn't have the time or inclination. She didn't do affairs and Quint Ryder had the reputation of preferring casual flings. Their basic perspectives were so far removed from each other that you could've placed the Pacific Ocean between them and still had room to spare.

What, exactly, did she want from Quint? she asked herself pensively. To have Quint fall in love with her, just so she could say she'd beaten him at his own game? Was spite subconsciously dictating to her?

Stephanie sighed audibly. Truth be told, she didn't know what she wanted these days. Seeing Quint again resurrected feelings from her tormented adolescence and stirred up old disappointments, disillusionment and insecurities. She was so confused and frustrated that she wasn't sure she recognized herself these days.

When a steady thump rattled the front door, Stephanie glanced at the grandfather clock in the corner. It was ten-thirty. Who'd come calling at this time of night? She glanced down at her ragged denim shorts and threadbare T-shirt that was about a hundred years old—and looked it—then shrugged. She might as well look as frazzled as she felt. Plus, her defenses were down around her knees. If Wes Martin and his lynch mob had decided to make her the honored guest at a necktie party she wouldn't be able to put up much resistance tonight.

And boy, would her mom and dad be upset when they returned tomorrow from their lengthy sightseeing tour to find their only daughter swinging from the tallest tree in Hoot's Roost.

6

STEPHANIE HEAVED HERSELF off the sofa and padded barefoot to the door. She flinched when she saw her late-night guest step from the shadows. She didn't know which was worse, finding Quint on the porch or Wes Martin's modern-day vigilantes.

"Long time no see, Red Riding Hood," Quint said as he walked, uninvited, into her cracker-box apartment.

"Do come in," she said after the fact. Damn, he looked good—all clean and fresh from a shower. He smelled incredible, too. She didn't recognize the brand of cologne, but it tempted her close enough to inhale another tangy whiff.

Quint smiled wryly as he surveyed her cramped apartment, focusing his amused gaze on several articles of clothing that she'd draped over the furniture like afghans. "Too busy at the restaurant for menial housecleaning, huh?"

Self-consciously she walked over to scoop up her lacy black bra she'd cast off the minute she returned home. "Sorry, Romeo, if you're thinking of wearing this around your neck like a trophy of victory you can't have it." She shoved the skimpy garment into her hip pocket. "This is the closest thing I have to clean underwear right now. I haven't had time to do laundry."

He gave her one of those slow, penetrating stares and the devil's own smile that could give a woman—especially one whose defenses were practically nonexistent—hot flashes. "Going commando, are you, Red? Want me to take a load of clothes home to wash for you?"

"No." She turned her back on that killer smile. "You'd probably wash it and wear it, just so you could tell every male in town that you'd been in my lacy panties."

She heard his amused chuckle behind her. "That's a clever tactic," he said. "Wonder why I never thought of it before?"

"Probably because you usually get what you want and can brag about it without having to resort to half-truths...wine?" she offered in the same breath.

"I'd rather have...beer." His low, suggestive voice sent warm tingles ricocheting down her spine.

"Sorry. Wine or water. I'm having wine."

"Fine, bring on the wine."

Steph padded toward the corner that served as her kitchen/dining area then grabbed a chilled bottle and two glasses. Drinking while she was so exhausted probably wasn't a good idea, but with Quint underfoot, she needed something to take the edge off her all-too-sensitive female radar.

Hurriedly Stephanie filled both glasses, gulped down three quick swallows then topped hers off. She pivoted, only to find Quint crowding her space. He practically eclipsed the lamplight beside the couch with his towering height and broad width. Shadows angled across his clean-shaven jaw, leaving a dark contrast to thick-lashed eyes that glittered like golden nuggets. Stephanie took another hasty sip, hoping to numb herself to his potent effect.

"Thanks, Red," he said as she shoved the glass at his chest. "Maybe I do need a taste of something sweet tonight."

Stephanie veered around him to plop on the couch. "Bad day? Surely the cows and heifers weren't giving you grief. After all, females of all species adore you, don't they?"

Quint sank down beside her then cut her an annoyed glance. "I'm trying to be nice."

"Better stick with what you know," she sassed before gulping more wine.

She was amazed how quickly her body reacted to the wine, until she remembered she'd nibbled on a salad at lunch and neglected dinner entirely. The wine hit her empty stomach with the same impact that Quint had on her feminine body. She was feeling giddy—from the wine, of course, not because of him.

"I know you're aware of the broadening division between the males and females in town," he said as he stretched his long jean-clad legs out in front of him. "I'm catching all sorts of flack from my cousins and other men about the no-lunch plan."

"What? Men can't assemble their own sandwiches for lunch?" she asked in mock shock. "And it's my fault that men are inept in the kitchen?"

When Quint draped an arm over the back of the sofa, Stephanie eyed him cautiously. If he put any moves on her tonight she was very much afraid she'd melt in his lap. Between the wine and exhaustion she'd probably be a pushover.

When Stephanie inched away to maintain a respectable space between them, Quint frowned. "No matter what you think, I'm not the Big Bad Wolf," he grumbled. "I only came to talk, not gobble you up."

"Really?" She batted her eyelashes at him. "But I thought that's what playboys like you did best?"

Apparently she'd ticked him off—which pleased her immensely—because he jerked off his hat and slammed it down on the arm of the sofa. "Damn it, Red, the men in town might simmer down if you'd compromise and revert to your parents' lunch menu. Once they set foot inside the Palace at lunch, chances are they'll be more agreeable about accompanying their wives and girlfriends to dinner. Serve a causal lunch to appease them and maybe this town will get back to normal."

"No," Stephanie said stubbornly. "I'm making enough profit at night that I don't need to do lunch, especially after the way the men in town have been treating me."

"This goes way beyond profit/loss issues," Quint argued. "I'll be honest, I miss taking a break from ranch chores and cruising into town for lunch to socialize for an hour with my neighbors. My cousins and I are isolated together most of the time and we enjoy the midday break. Shop owners appreciate the same break from their routines, too. We need you to cater to a few of our needs."

"I'm not going to burden myself with more work," she said tiredly. "I've been so busy the past six weeks that I've met myself coming and going." She took another sip of wine, laid her head against the back of the sofa and sighed. "Why can't people just take what I have to offer without making more demands than I can handle right now?''

Quint noted the dark circles beneath those incredible silver-blue eyes. She did look tired and mussed up. Her clothes looked like ragbag rejects and her hair cascaded around her like tangled flames. Damn, even when she wasn't at her best she was still breathtakingly beautiful to him.

He hadn't wanted to admit how much he missed feasting his hungry eyes on her until she'd opened the front door. Maybe he *was* the Big Bad Wolf—when it came to her, at least. For sure, every time he looked at her he wanted to howl in sexual frustration then do something about it.

"You'll be pleased to know," she continued, "that Idabelle informed me the highway department just began construction on a four-lane road south of town. I could tell the difference tonight at the restaurant. We didn't have a full house. That should make you happy."

Quint was having one helluva time concentrating on the conversation when his gaze dropped to the sensuous curve of her mouth.

As usual, when he got within a few feet of Steph, his male body conjured up all sorts of interesting activities other than conversation. Even as the betraying thought skittered across his mind, his fingers speared gently into that silky mass of flame-colored hair that continually intrigued him. He knew she'd think he was coming on to her, in hopes of convincing her to add a lunch menu, but nonetheless, he leaned in close, staring at her ripe lips in rapt fascination. He wanted that sassy mouth beneath his—now. He wanted to taste the wine on her lips and drink deeply until he was intoxicated with her.

Then suddenly he was kissing her and she wasn't pitching a fit about it. She just sort of slumped against him and opened her mouth in invitation. This time wasn't anything like the last two times they'd been overcome by combustible lust. This was different from anything Quint remembered experiencing.

And yes, he was sorry to report that he *was* experienced with women. Not to the extent of the wild rumors, but experienced all the same. But there was a unique gentleness, a sense of giving and taking between Steph and him that was unfamiliar and incredibly satisfying to him. To say that he was stunned by the strange sensations spilling over him was the understatement of the decade, but he liked the inexpressible feelings—way too much.

"Mmm," she murmured when he finally allowed her to come up for air. "What were we debating? I forget."

"So do I," he whispered shakily as he stared into her silver-blue eyes and got lost in their shimmering depths. "I can't think past you."

When her arms glided across his chest and settled on his shoulders he slid his hands around her waist then walked his fingers beneath the hiked hem of her T-shirt. He figured he'd get slapped silly when he cupped the full mound of her breast and brushed his thumb over the beaded nipple. Instead she arched against him and moaned deep in her throat.

Fascinated by the sound that reminded him of a purring cat he caressed her tenderly, repeatedly. When she didn't object he lowered his head to skim his lips over the thin fabric that covered her nipple. She all but melted as he drew her onto his lap and suckled her again.

Desire slammed through him as he crumpled her shirt in his fist and drew the fabric away to feast on her creamy flesh. Damn, she was some kind of built—definitely more than a handful. Enthralled, he dipped his head again to touch his lips to her nipples and flick the dusky crests with his tongue.

Another soft moan wobbled in her throat as he treated himself to another taste of her satiny flesh. His hand strayed on its own accord, dipping beneath the hem of her shorts, feeling her quivering heat beneath his exploring caresses.

Quint forced himself to withdraw his wandering hand and focus on kissing those lush lips. He knew if things got out of hand—or in hand, as this case happened to be—Steph would think he was trying to manipulate her in the name of the male crusade. Much as he wanted her—and damn but he wanted her badly!—he wasn't going to let her think the worst about him.

"You could've had me," she murmured against his lips. "Between the wine and—"

"I know," he interrupted then kissed her with more gentleness than he realized he possessed. He simply held her to him for the longest time, his arousal pressing against her hip, her head tucked in the crook of his arm.

Vaguely he became aware of her methodic breathing and he glanced down at her face. Her thick lashes, like silky paintbrushes, lay against her porcelain cheeks. Her lips were turned up in a hint of a smile. He'd like to think he was responsible for that expression.

Well, damn, she'd gone to sleep in his lap. That hadn't

happened before. So much for those exaggerated rumors about him being a dynamo lover boy, he mused, and smirked. The woman he wanted to seduce the most had conked out in his arms. Man, wouldn't his cousins have a field day with that!

Quint gently eased Steph off his lap and watched her scrunch up on the sofa. Her hair tumbled over the cushions like a river of fire. The wine had obviously worked like a sedative. Damn, *he* was still hard as stone and *she* was soft in repose. Yup, he did have a way with women, didn't he?

Quint rose to his feet, tugged at the too-tight fit of his jeans and strode off to locate a quilt to cover Steph. When he returned he noticed the scrap of black lace peeking from her hip pocket. Temptation and golden opportunity were just too great to resist.

Grinning devilishly he tugged the bra free and stashed it in his shirt pocket. He hadn't taken what he really wanted from Little Red Riding Hood, but he'd swiped a memento. He wondered if she'd recognize the significance of the *almost* night they'd spent together. Probably not. Steph was usually too busy looking for the worst in him to see the best in him.

Casting one last glance at temptation in its purest, sweetest form, Quint walked out into the night. He nearly stumbled over his own boots when it dawned on him that something had shifted and resettled inside him. When he was with Steph he never got that niggling feeling that assured him that it was time to move on. His survival instincts should be kicking in right now. Those restless feelings should be hounding him as they had in the past.

But they weren't. Go figure.

Could it be that he'd adjusted to dealing with a strong, iron-willed woman who didn't fawn and flatter him and chase after him like most women did? Damn if he didn't respect and admire that about her.

Go figure that, too.

STEPHANIE AWOKE WITH a groan and tried to move her left arm, which cradled her head. Her arm was asleep and she could barely feel her fingers. Gracious, she'd slept like the dead.

Too much continuous tension and activity, she diagnosed. Definitely too much wine.

Disoriented, she levered onto her elbow and glanced sideways. She realized she'd crashed on the couch, with a quilt tucked around her. When had she retrieved a quilt? For that matter, when had she fallen asleep?

The tantalizing memory of Quint's kisses and caresses washed over her. Hurriedly she glanced down, expecting to find herself naked and quite possibly ravished by Hoot's Roost's version of the Big Bad Wolf.

She remembered thinking that his kisses and caresses felt so good she wanted them to go on forever so she could savor those incredible sensations that hummed through her body. But he had stopped—obviously. Otherwise she'd be stark naked right now.

Stephanie frowned, bemused. So why hadn't he taken advantage of the fact that she'd partaken too much wine on an empty stomach and drowned all her defenses? Because he was honorable? Or because she just didn't appeal to him, just as she hadn't in high school? He'd backed away, even though he'd been paid to seduce her? Or had he been trying to prove to her that this thing between them—and she wouldn't go so far as to label it a relationship!—was indeed separate from the ongoing conflict over her restaurant?

Stephanie struggled to her feet and staggered to the shower. She wished she knew Quint's motive for *not* making her another notch on his bedpost. Considering how dopey and drowsy she'd felt last night she doubted she'd have put up any resistance whatsoever, especially when his masterful touch had turned her body to liquid fire. So why *had* he stopped? Integrity or lack of interest?

Feelings of inadequacy pulsated through her in rhythm with the shower spray. She must be a basket case, she decided as she doused her head to wash her hair. She didn't want to become one of Quint's nameless conquests and yet she was secretly disappointed that nothing actually happened between them. Sheesh, talk about your drastic contradictions!

"Get a grip," Stephanie muttered at herself. She needed to dress and restock supplies at the restaurant. The suppliers from Dallas had promised early delivery this morning and she needed to get moving.

Grabbing a towel, Stephanie dried off hurriedly then reached for the underwear in the hip pocket of her denim shorts. *Gone.* Hair dripping in puddles on the linoleum floor, she checked the other pocket. She swore she'd tucked her bra in her shorts so she could wash it by hand and toss it in the dryer while she applied makeup and styled her hair this morning.

Quint…Stephanie jerked upright. That ornery rascal must have swiped her bra. Well, she had news for him. He'd never be able to fasten the thing around his broad chest. If he showed up in town with the damn thing draped around his neck, boasting to the Neanderthals that he'd brought her to her knees—and to her back—with his irresistible charm, she'd kill him.

The prospect of being humiliated in public worried her while she rummaged through the dirty clothes hamper to hand-wash her undies then thrust them in the dryer. Just when she softened up toward Quint and let herself believe he wasn't as bad as she wanted to think he was, he'd pulled some infuriating stunt—like taking pay for trying to seduce her, like joining the picket line and stealing her undies.

Her body sizzling with apprehension, Stephanie dressed and scurried off to work. To her vast relief she didn't see Quint walking the streets, waving her undies like a banner. She was greeted by the menfolk with nothing more than the customary snub and frigid glances that branded her as the town's turncoat.

When Stephanie saw the delivery truck swing around the corner toward the back door she quickened her step. She had to unload the supplies herself before thawing out the meat for the evening's Italian gourmet specialties.

"QUINT! GET A MOVE ON!" Vance called from the living room. "I left the truck running. We're burning daylight!"

Quint quickly fastened his work shirt and stuffed his feet in his scuffed boots. He'd overslept—once he'd finally gotten to sleep sometime after 3:00 a.m. Vivid dreams, interspersed with some serious tossing and turning, had plagued him all night. Nothing new there. He'd had the same problem every night since he'd left Steph asleep on her sofa.

"Yo, Wade's here. Impatient as ever," Vance hollered. "Let's go!"

"I'm coming," Quint yelled back. "Keep your pants on!"

"Wasn't planning to take them off," Vance threw back.

With wheat planting in full swing, Quint and his cousins had been auguring grain by the truckloads and driving their tractors around in circles to get the majority of the fall drilling completed before the forecasted rains. Wade wanted the fieldwork finished by the weekend so he could devote full-time to his wife. Even after several months of marriage Wade went flying like a homing pigeon to be with Laura. Damn, the man still had it bad.

Quint hurried down the hall then stopped dead in his tracks when he saw Vance, grinning like an idiot, dangling the lacy black bra from his index finger. Quint inwardly groaned when his cousins stared wickedly at him.

"Souvenir, boyo? Or have you become a cross-dresser who favors feminine paraphernalia?" Wade taunted.

Well, hell. Quint had laundered the skimpy garment with his dress clothes and laid it over the back of his recliner, intending to swing by Steph's the first chance he got.

"Belong to anyone we know?" Vance teased, eyes twinkling like polished obsidian.

"Gimme that," Quint demanded. When he shot out his arm to retrieve the garment Vance jerked it out of his reach.

"Not so fast, lover boy. Answer the question first."

Quint glared at Vance. "I thought you were in an all-fired rush to fuel the tractors and get to work."

"Yeah, but first things first," Wade insisted as he took the scrap of black lace from Vance and twirled it on his forefinger. "I'm surprised you remember how to unhook these contraptions. To my knowledge you haven't had an official date in almost two months."

"So, what's up with that?" Vance questioned. "If you don't watch it, cuz, you'll lose your Don Juan status."

"Quit clowning around and gimme that," Quint ordered gruffly. When he lunged toward Wade the garment went flying across the room—and into Vance's hand. Swearing, Quint found himself in the middle of a game of keep-away. "That's enough, you juveniles."

"Whose is it?" Wade asked. "Where's the matching lace panties? Are you wearing them?"

Quint muttered several more expletives at his demon cousins. "Yeah, as a matter of fact I am. I get my kicks from wearing women's thong bikini panties. Got a problem with that?"

"No, whatever makes you happy, girlie-boy," Vance teased. "I—" His voice dried up as he glanced over Quint's shoulder. "Uh-oh."

Quint lurched around to see what had nabbed Wade's and Vance's attention. He could've kicked himself all the way to Christmas when he saw Steph standing outside the glass storm door. The look of hurt, embarrassment and humiliation that claimed her beguiling features was like a sucker punch in the gut. He knew what she was thinking. Hell! He could practically *hear* her thinking the absolute worst about him.

Her humiliation transformed to anger in the blink of an eye. She whipped open the door and stalked inside to jerk her bra from Vance's fingertips. She pivoted to glare at Quint. She couldn't have made her contempt more obvious if she'd pulled a gun and shot him. "If you're finished with show-and-tell, I'll take this back." She crammed the undergarment in her purse then stared down Wade and Vance. "By the way, he isn't nearly as good in bed as rumors claim he is," she declared. "I've had lots more fun all by myself."

With that, Steph spun on her navy-blue pumps that matched her business suit and stormed out. Quint was surprised the glass didn't shatter when she slammed the storm door to punctuate the fact that she was spitting mad.

"Wait a minute!" Quint called as he raced outside. "That wasn't what you think."

She opened the car door and flounced on the seat. "No? I'm not supposed to believe my eyes?"

"Not in this instance," he insisted as he stared down into her fuming face. "I just washed your bra with my clothes and had every intention of dropping it off at your place when time permitted. I've been busy lately."

Her smirk indicated she wasn't buying into his explanation. "Kindly remove your hand from the door or you'll get your fingers smashed and you'll find yourself dragged all the way to town."

Quint jerked his hands from the car the instant before she slammed the door. "Steph, I—"

She shoved the car into Reverse and threw gravel as she backed away. Quint wanted to hop in his pickup and chase her down, but mad as she was, he figured he'd be wasting his time and his breath.

Exasperated, he lurched around and headed toward his demonic cousins who were standing on the porch.

Wade winced. "Well, I guess that answers the question of ownership."

"Yeah, but that last part was more than I wanted to know," Vance said, lips twitching.

"Ditto for me. So...we better get to work," Wade said as he stared at the road. "Whoa, she took off like a bat out of hell. That dust cloud behind her is worse than a jet's vapor trail."

"Yup," Vance agreed. "Bet ol' Quint just got cut off indefinitely."

"Nothing happened!" he roared in frustration.

"That's what you said the last time we asked," Wade recalled as he strode toward the wheat truck. "Now I don't know what to believe."

"I do," Vance said helpfully as he headed for the bucket-of-rust pickup that was laden with tools and a barrel of tractor fuel. "I believe the former ladies' man of the Ryder clan can scratch Little Red Riding Hood's name from his black book."

"I do *not* have a black book," Quint muttered in annoyance. The thought of killing his evil cousins was starting to have tremendous appeal.

"Donated it to the Smithsonian, did you?" Wade asked. "Or was it *Ripley's Believe It or Not?*"

"I wish Cousin Gage were here," Quint muttered.

"Oh? Why's that?" asked Vance.

"So he could attend your funerals. You keep this up and neither of you will live to see sunset," he growled, teeth bared menacingly.

Wade squinted at the sun. "In that case, I'd say we've got twelve more hours to give you hell."

"Yup." Vance slid beneath the steering wheel of the

clunker truck. "Sure wish I could live long enough to watch Quint belly-crawl to Steph's apartment to beg forgiveness though. That'd really be something to see."

"Definitely going to require some serious groveling," Wade concurred as he piled into the wheat truck. "Who you riding with, Romeo? Me or the joker?"

Quint decided to drive his own truck to the field. He needed a few minutes of silence to recover from seeing the pained look on Steph's face. Damn, he'd really stepped in it this time. Of course, everything he'd done had made him look like a world-class jackass in Steph's eyes. In addition to knowing that she now despised him and believed the worst, he'd spend the day listening to his satanic cousins heckle him to no end.

As predicted, they did. By dusk Quint was so sick of Vance's corny jokes and Wade's tormenting taunts he was ready to go home, dead bolt the doors and curse a couple of blue streaks to his cousins' names.

STEPHANIE STARED GLUMLY at the sparse smattering of customers at her restaurant. Business had been dropping steadily since construction began on the new highway. The delays, detours and rough patches of road had discouraged traffic from venturing to Hoot's Roost for gourmet dining.

Tonight, only the loyal local females, such as Idabelle and her friends, had arrived to sample the German cuisine. At this rate the profit Stephanie had accumulated would be eaten up in overhead expenses and salaries. Creditors would be beating down her door and her visions of this being a stairstep to culinary success would scatter like ashes in a hurricane. Damn.

"Now don't you fret, hon," Idabelle said, patting Stephanie's hand. "Road construction won't last forever. The out-of-town customers will be back." She glanced at her friends. "Won't they, girls?"

The "girls"—whose hair colors were various shades of silver and gray—nodded in agreement.

Stephanie wasn't so sure. She knew the approaching winter months would discourage out-of-towners from making the drive. She'd anticipated that and she'd hoped the locals would reserve tables for upcoming holiday celebrations.

Because of the reduced number of customers, Stephanie and Dawn had carted leftover food to the Senior Citizen Center, the nursing home and to the schools as special treats for the elderly and the teachers. But free food, while a nice gesture that she enjoyed, didn't pay the bills.

She'd even humbled herself to taking serving portions to Wes Martin at the feed store, as well as the male owners of the hardware store and filling station. The men who formed the core of resistance had turned her away, announcing they weren't touching her fancy-schmancey gourmet dishes until she reopened for lunch and served burgers and fries.

Even her parents, who'd been the soul of encouragement and support in this endeavor, were casting her pitying glances and suggesting that she consider opening for lunch.

If the events of the past week weren't depressing enough, Stephanie had been mortified to the extreme when she'd driven to Quint's ranch to find the Ryder cousins tossing around her lacy bra. She'd gone there, believing Quint had only taken the undergarment as a playful prank. She'd left, steaming like a clam, certain he'd been boasting of his prowess in her bed and flashing a souvenir of her surrender.

Obviously he was guilty as charged since he hadn't phoned or come by to see her. Just when she'd gained a smidgen of faith in the man he'd disappointed her, had hurt her—badly.

The most humbling part of all was that she was going to have to reopen for lunch and cater to those Neanderthals. At least until the four-lane highway was completed. Then she'd have to begin her promotional campaign all over again to lure back out-of-town patrons.

Stephanie knew *she'd* be manning the stove and flipping burgers because Dawn Peters didn't want to log in more hours at the restaurant. Not only was Dawn a fantastic chef but she was a talented studio artist who painted her mornings away before reporting to work. In fact, several of Dawn's creations graced the walls of the Palace and added a touch of beauty to Stephanie's cramped apartment.

Thunder boomed overhead, rattling the windows and making Stephanie flinch. She glanced ceilingward. It was no surprise that the sky was about to open and rain on her parade. Business was bad. She'd become a social pariah to the male citizens in her hometown, and her ill-fated attraction to a man who saw her as no more than a challenge and threat to his legendary reputation was driving her batty.

How could she still want Quint? she asked herself incredulously. Why did she miss his company? Because she was a glutton for punishment, she decided. He hadn't been there to share the joy of her brief success or console her during her disappointments. In fact, *he* was responsible for her most crushing disappointments. Apparently she was one of those women whose curse it was in life to fall for a man who was absolutely no good for her.

Rain came down in torrents and the scant few patrons made mad dashes to their cars. The place emptied faster than a fire drill. Stephanie sent the waitresses home early, removed her silk jacket and bussed the tables herself.

When she strode into the kitchen with a pile of dirty dishes Dawn smiled apologetically. ''I've been cutting down the number of servings every night, but I still have leftovers.''

Stephanie wanted to bawl her head off when she saw the extra food stored in the fridge. That did it. She'd have to reopen at lunch and extend personal invitations to the local businessmen, ranchers and farmers who'd been complaining since she opened for business.

By the time Stephanie cleaned the kitchen and locked up for the night, the curbs were standing full of rainwater. Her leather shoes squished around her soaked feet as she darted to her car. She sat there for five minutes, eyes dripping tears, telling herself she was a failure and that fate and the local males had defeated her.

Jeez, could anything else go wrong with her life?

Scowling and crying simultaneously, Stephanie switched on the ignition. Nothing. Great. Her battery had obviously rolled over and died. Either that or Wes Martin's vigilantes had sabotaged her car so she'd have to scurry home on foot.

Stephanie clambered from her car—the traitorous pile of bolts and metal—and stalked down the deserted street.

She supposed she could use her cell phone to ask her parents to give her a lift, but she just couldn't bear another minute of parental pity. She'd just hike to her apartment in the rain then treat herself to a hot shower and a couple of glasses of wine. Surely the world would look a few shades brighter in the morning.

When lightning flickered across the sky and thunder rolled, Stephanie instinctively ducked away—and accidentally tripped over the uneven sidewalk. With a squawk of surprise she skidded in the grass and came to rest in an awkward sprawl. Muttering, she struggled back to her feet.

This wasn't the smartest thing she'd ever done, she mused as she stared at the gaping holes in her panty hose. If she didn't trip and break her neck, lightning could fry her and she'd drown in rain puddles. Of course, the men in town would be overjoyed. Nice to know she'd make somebody happy in this lifetime.

The sound of an approaching vehicle brought Stephanie's soggy head around. She inwardly groaned when she recognized Quint's red 4X4 extended cab pickup coming toward her.

The tinted window rolled down and Quint stuck out his head and yelled, "Damn it, woman, are you out of your mind?"

"Of course, I am," she shot back. "You don't see sane people playing chicken with lightning bolts, do you?"

"Damn it, get your damn butt in the damn truck. Now!" he shouted over another rumble of thunder.

Wow, three damns in the same sentence. Why was he ticked off? *She* was the failure who was soaked clean through and ducking Mother Nature's fireworks, not him.

As she scuttled toward the inviting warmth of the truck she heard Quint mutter, "Lord, give me patience to deal with this woman and hurry it up."

"Deal with *me?*" she grumbled as she piled into the truck then slammed the door. "Might I remind you that *I'm* the one who has issues with *you.*"

Quint glared at her. "Don't change the subject. Where's your car and why are you slopping around in this thunderstorm?"

"Dead battery," she reported as she stared at the wipers that slapped methodically against the windshield. "Or sabotage. Was that your doing?"

"Hell, no," he muttered.

She stared curiously at him, certain she'd heard a hint of indignation in his voice. When he opened his mouth again—probably to rake her over hot coals—she flung up her hand to deter him. "You can spare me the lectures on my stupidity. Just drop me off and get on with your hot date."

"I don't have a date, hot or otherwise," he informed her crisply. "I was on my way to see you."

"To apologize for swiping my underwear so you could flash it in front of your cousins and boast about something that never happened?" she flung at him.

Quint slammed the truck into gear. Tires squealed as he mashed on the accelerator. Clearly he was annoyed. Good. That made two of them.

"I've been planting wheat fast and furiously all week, trying to beat the rain," he muttered in explanation. "Since you constantly refuse to take my calls, I didn't waste time with that." He cut her a sharp glance. "And for your information, Little *Drowned* Riding Hood, I didn't flash your undies or brag.''

"Yeah, right," she said and sniffed. "Why don't I believe that? I bet it's because you've already stooped to blackmail and bribery. What's a little theft and boasting among enemies?''

Quint exhaled a loud sigh. "Why do I bother with you?''

"For money and the preservation of your reputation with women," she supplied as he veered into her driveway. "Thanks for the lift. It's your one saving grace.''

When she slid off the seat to make a hasty departure, Quint killed the engine and followed her.

"Go away," she grumbled as she fished her keys from her purse. "I'm not in the mood to deal with you right now.''

"Tough luck, toots. You're stuck with me so get used to the idea," he said, breathing down her wet neck.

Stephanie stabbed the key in the lock then shoved a sodden shoulder against the door. This, she decided, was the perfect way to top off a miserable evening. She'd have it out with Quint, once and for all. Tomorrow she'd regroup, reassess her business situation, swallow her pride, expand the dining hours and get on with her life. All this she'd do *alone,* she assured herself, because Quint Ryder was making her crazy, making her want things she knew she'd never have with him and she knew she'd be a billion times better off if she severed all ties with him—forever.

This was about self-preservation, she told herself. She couldn't let him hurt her more than he already had. She had to evict him from her life—permanently.

QUINT WATCHED STEPH SLING aside her wet purse and muddy jacket. He inwardly groaned when he noticed the way her beige blouse clung to her breasts like wet paint. Why couldn't he ignore her ample physical attributes and focus, instead, on her witchy disposition? And why did he feel the least bit sympathetic toward her when she'd been snapping and growling at him like a rabid Chihuahua?

Because she looked so alone and defeated, even while she was clinging fiercely to her pride. Ask him, she looked as if she was on the verge of tears, but she refused to break down in front of him. She didn't seem to want to let him know that she was vulnerable. Human, even. In her book, that was the Numero Uno No-No.

"What's wrong, Red?" he asked softly.

She wheeled around, her arms flailing wildly around her. Her eyes glistened with unshed tears and her hair clung to her peaked face like the strands of a mop. She couldn't have looked worse if she tried and yet everything about this woman tugged fiercely at his heartstrings. He decided one or the other of them was crazy. He just couldn't figure out which. *She* for tramping off during a thunderstorm or *he* for being unable to keep his distance from her. It wasn't as if he couldn't get female attention if he wanted it. Hell, women constantly chased him, called him. Yet, he was stuck on the one woman who ran the other way when she saw him coming.

"Everything's wrong with my life!" she blurted out on a hitched breath. "My business is going down the toilet because of the local male boycott and the road construction. Worse, you're here to witness my humiliating defeat!"

"Life is, indeed, a bitch." His lips twitched in amusement when she kept flapping her arms like a duck trying to go airborne.

"You can say that again." Her breath gushed from her lips like a deflating balloon. Defeatedly she plunked on the sofa. Her shoulders slumped as her head dropped to her hands and she stared down at her waterlogged shoes. "If I don't cave in and open for lunch I'm sunk. That will make you happy and the other men will be jumping for joy."

Quint sank down beside and draped his arm comfortingly around her shoulders. "Reopening for lunch isn't a bad thing," he murmured. "You'll appease the locals and stay afloat until the construction is completed. Things will be okay, Steph."

"No, they won't. The vigilante committee will think they've won this feud and brought me under their collective thumb. There'll be so much gloating going on that it'll make me nauseous."

Quint pulled her against him when he heard her voice crack, heard the quiet sob she was trying so hard not to let him hear.

"Swallowing your pride is never easy," he murmured against the top of her wet head. "My cousins and I have had to do the same thing. We've had to combine labor and share equipment to reduce expenses because the grain and cattle markets constantly fluctuate. You do whatcha gotta do and you learn to live with it.''

She sighed heavily. ''I guess you're right. I'll just do what I have to do to stay in business. I'll flip burgers and make the best of it.'' When she tilted her head to glance up at him, he fell into the depths of those hypnotic silver-blue eyes. ''Will you supply more beef to me?''

''Consider it done.'' He really wanted to kiss her, right there and then, but she looked so blasted vulnerable that it was getting to him—and he didn't even want to figure out why *not* taking advantage of her was so important to him. He pushed to his feet and hoisted her up with him. ''Now go take a shower and change into dry clothes. Have you eaten?''

''No,'' she murmured as he directed her toward the bathroom.

''Lord,'' Quint said, rolling his eyes. ''The woman owns a restaurant and she hasn't eaten. What's wrong with this picture?''

''Not hungry,'' she mumbled. ''Already consumed too many helpings of humble pie.''

''Well, you're going to eat tonight,'' he said in no uncertain terms. ''I may not be a renowned chef, but I'll whip up something while you're showering.''

''Thanks for the offer, Quint,'' she murmured. ''But it'd be better if you just left. For good.''

He dropped a quick kiss to her cold lips. ''Not gonna do it, Red. I'm staying here and cooking, so deal with it.''

She stared at him for a pensive moment. "Are you trying to confuse me on purpose?"

He arched a brow and grinned. "I'm confusing you?"

"Absolutely, positively. Just when I think you're the biggest, most insensitive jerk to walk the face of the earth you go and do something nice. I just can't for the life of me figure you out."

He flashed her another grin, took her by the shoulders and turned her toward the bathroom door. "Maybe you could try giving me the benefit of the doubt for once instead of applying all your cynical philosophies to me. Remember, I'm the one who's here when you need a friend. That counts for something in my book."

"I wish—" She clamped her mouth shut abruptly, shook her soggy head and strode off.

Quint wanted to drag her back and ask her what she wished for but she closed the door. Spinning around, he strode to her cubbyhole of a kitchen to rummage through the fridge. He could do breakfast with a reasonable amount of proficiency. He grabbed a dozen eggs, found some sausage patties in the freezer and tracked down half a loaf of bread. Damn, he thought. For a restaurateur extraordinaire, she didn't have much in the way of food in her apartment.

Nonetheless, Quint gathered up the ingredients and sighed contentedly. He'd been like a man on a mission for days on end, anxious to get the wheat planted so he could concentrate his efforts on getting back into Steph's good graces. Tonight was his big chance.

Why it mattered so much he didn't want to think about. It just did and that was a fact. He was exactly where he wanted to be, with the woman who'd taken up permanent residence in his mind and tormented his dreams. If nothing else, he wanted to walk out of here with the assurance that she considered him a friend, not her worst enemy.

In a matter of minutes Quint had bread in the toaster and eggs and sausage sizzling in a skillet. He knew Steph enjoyed wine so he poured her a glass. By the time she emerged from the shower, wearing a fuzzy blue robe that covered her from neck to feet, he had the meal on the table.

The grateful smile she tossed at him as she sank into the chair nearly did him in. "I can't remember the last time someone cooked for me. Must've been Mom when I was in high school. Since then I've been on the other end of cooking utensils. Looks good, Ryder."

"So do you, Red," he murmured huskily.

She chuckled as she stabbed her fork into the eggs. "Right. No makeup, no 'do, not much enthusiasm. Just the older version of the kid in school who never ran with the in-crowd. Good thing I'm not competing in a popularity contest in Hoot's Roost. I'd come in dead last."

"Don't be so hard on yourself," he chided gently.

"Why not? Everyone else is," she grumbled between bites. She took a long sip of wine then sighed tiredly. "I'm supposed to follow in Mom and Dad's footsteps, not chase my own dreams. Don't rock the boat. Keep the burgers 'n taters coming. Don't initiate change. Don't bring a touch of metropolitan life to small town America."

"Whoa, Steph, you're scaring me," he said, trying to tease her out of her blue mood. "Where's that feisty, sassy redhead who's been going toe to toe with me for weeks on end? Hell, I live for our confrontations."

She blinked, startled. "You do? Why's that?"

He shrugged and took a bite of sausage. "Maybe because I like a woman with fire and spunk. Not to mention enough sass to fill a semitruck."

"Hmm. I would've thought pushovers would've been more your style."

He reached across the narrow table to cup her chin in his hand, forcing her to meet his steady gaze. "I like you, Red. Is that so hard to believe?"

"Yes." Her gaze flitted away. "Yes, it is."

It dawned on him that beneath all that poise, assertive confidence and ramrod-stiff pride Steph suffered a few inadequacy issues. She projected a tough, savvy, worldly facade, but he had the unmistakable feeling that Steph hid behind a lot of protective barriers. She wasn't as comfortable with her sexuality and self-esteem as she wanted everyone to believe.

That sudden insight made Quint realize there were dozens of intriguing layers to Steph Lawson. Funny, he'd never taken the time to delve deeply into the female psyche before. With Steph he wanted to know what made her tick—even if it was equivalent to tampering with a time bomb.

"I like you, too, Ryder, and *that* scares *me*," she admitted while she stared at her plate, not at him.

"Well, there you go. I like you and you like me." Sheesh, he sounded like a fourth-grader fumbling through his first romantic discourse with a girl in pigtails who'd caught his eye. "So what are we gonna do about it?"

Steph took another sip of wine. When he noticed she'd drained the glass, he quickly refilled it. "We're going to do nothing about it. That's for the best," she murmured.

Quint shook his head and stared straight into her eyes. "Wrong answer. Maybe you have the willpower to back off, but I don't." He inhaled a deep breath and said, "I want you."

She stared at him for a long time, as if she were wrestling with a monumental dilemma. Then her expression changed and he sensed she'd reached a decision of some sort. He thought maybe they'd gotten past all that ritualistic posturing that had plagued males and females since time immemorial. His defenses were down. So were hers. All bets were off.

Quint shifted on his chair when she nailed him with such a penetrating stare that he couldn't look away from her. "You want the truth?" she asked.

He nodded and swallowed. He had the inescapable feeling this was the moment of reckoning.

"I want you, too, but if you're keeping score I don't want to be another statistic."

Her admission knocked him off balance. Of course, she'd been doing that since he'd met her. "You're not a statistic." He cleared his throat. "You mean you wanna...? You and me?" He hitched his thumb toward the miniscule bedroom. "In there?"

Despite the blush that crept across her cheeks she smiled and nodded. "And I'm sorry about that snide crack I made to your cousins about...um...your prowess and techniques. I wanted to embarrass you because I was embarrassed and royally ticked off."

He grinned. "Gee, I barely noticed."

She chortled at his teasing remark then climbed to her feet to amble to her bedroom. Quint followed her, his male body shouting hallelujahs. He'd had hot dreams about this possibility, but he'd figured the chances of getting naked with Steph were about one in a million—and that was being optimistic.

Her bedroom was as dark as a cave and so silent that he could hear her robe gliding down her body like a whisper of wind. Desire hit him so hard, so fast that he wobbled unsteadily on his boot heels. He didn't need any visual incentives with Steph. He could see her image shimmering like a specter from his fantasies. She'd been his lover for weeks, if only in his dreams.

"Truth," she murmured quietly. "I'm a lot better at cooking."

He almost laughed at her humble admission because he seriously doubted that. He peeled off his shirt and tossed it carelessly aside as he heeled-and-toed out of his boots. He was out of his jeans and briefs in nothing flat, feeling his way toward the bed—and stumbled over her discarded robe.

"*Ooof!*" Quint's knees hit the edge of the bed, causing him to pitch forward. He thrust out an arm to brace his fall and felt the full mound of her breast beneath his hand. He jerked away immediately. "Sorry."

Damn, he was fumbling like a rookie, but he told himself he'd be on top of his game when he stretched out in bed.

"Let's see what you've got, Ryder," she whispered as she looped her arms over his shoulders and turned him toward her.

The comment struck him as amusing, and he chuckled as he clamped his hands on her waist and dodged her oncoming kiss. "Slow down, Red Riding Hood. I barely know where I am in here."

"Just so you know *who* you're presently with is all I care."

He squirmed sideways to prop himself on his forearm and stared down into her shadowed face. "Believe me, Steph, I've never been more aware of who I'm with. True, I've spent more nights than I care to count wondering how it'd be between us. So don't rush me."

His hand skimmed her breast and he felt her flinch. She seemed tense and apprehensive. Steph? Naw, couldn't be...could it? "We don't have to do this if you don't—"

"Yes, we do." She hauled off and kissed him so desperately that he forgot what he was going to say. His noble intention of taking it slow and savoring every erotic moment—until he brought her to climax and buried himself deep inside her—flitted off in the wind. He'd wanted to spend the entire night learning her body by touch, by taste, but he was suddenly attacked by a fit of lust.

Desire exploded inside him as she seized his mouth in a lip-blistering wallop of a kiss and glided her silky body over his. He fleetingly remembered telling Cousin Vance that no one *took* Steph anywhere to do anything. She was a leader not a follower. But in this, it seemed to him that she was trying a little too hard to be assertive and assume control.

Of course, *thinking* that, and doing something about allowing her to call all the shots, were two different things. And furthermore, she had him so hot and aching from just kissing the breath out of him and squirming above him that he wanted her now. Just as he'd wanted her right there on her sofa that first night, right smack dab in the middle of that street dance and up against the wall that day at his ranch.

Where the hell had his self-control gotten off to? he wondered as he kissed her feverishly and pressed her hips against his throbbing arousal. She was making him crazy. She always made him crazy.

"Slow down," he gasped as he arched helplessly toward her. "This isn't a race to see who crosses the finish line first. If we keep up this pace it's gonna be me and I'd prefer a photo finish." He rolled over, pinning her beneath him. He felt her breasts heaving against his laboring chest, as if she, like he, was struggling to draw air into her starved lungs. "Hold still a minute."

"Why?" she asked, panting for breath.

He stared down into her shadowy face, mesmerized by the glimmer in those mercury-colored eyes. "Because...oh hell, I dunno."

And then he plundered her mouth and sank onto her lush body, feeling the fierce impact of desire hammer him again and again. His pulse was off the charts, his breathing ragged, his hands kneading and swirling over every supple inch of her that he could touch.

A strange kind of desperation assailed him as he guided her legs apart with his knees. Sanity momentarily returned and he remembered he'd left the necessary protection in the pocket of his jeans. Who knew where they'd gotten off to!

"Minute," he mumbled shakily. Man, where was his finesse? He'd been off stride since Steph kissed him senseless. Clumsily he rolled away to crouch on his hands and knees. With fiendish haste he groped for his jeans.

He fumbled with the foil packet, dropped it, cursed, and then retrieved it.

"What are you doing down there?" Steph questioned.

He didn't answer, just donned protection and returned to her. His fingertips glided over her moist heat, assured that she was as ready as he was. He eased into her welcoming softness, telling himself he'd be better the second time around—because there'd definitely have to be a second time, considering how awkward he was making this first time.

Teeth clenched against the frantic demands of his body, Quint drove into her. She was so hot and tight and—

"Oh, hell!" Quint growled between his teeth when he felt her flinch and heard the gasp she tried to swallow—and couldn't quite. Everything inside him stilled when the startling realization of what just happened hit him like a steamroller.

"Quint? What's wrong?" she asked, as her nails dug like spikes into his taut forearms and she held herself rigid beneath him.

"You should have told me you'd never done this before so I wouldn't hurt you," he muttered in self-disgust.

He eased away, so frustrated he wanted to yell and curse and slam his fist through the nearest wall. She'd been too proud and defiant to inform him that she wasn't in his league, sexually speaking. Probably because she thought he'd taunt her because of it. Well, she was *way* wrong about that. But simple honesty would've saved her from discomfort and him from stunned amazement.

He should've known. Should've recognized the subtle signs. He just hadn't realized what he was seeing until now. The defensiveness, the wary cynicism, the refusal to let a man too close—physically and emotionally. Then there was her strong-willed determination to finish whatever she started.

It was so like her, he realized. She was too proud, or embarrassed—he didn't know which—to admit this was her first time. He still couldn't quite wrap his dazed mind around that concept. It floored him that she'd up and decided tonight was the night. Why with *him?* What was he, her consolation prize for a business failure?

"Quint?" Her voice sounded small, uncertain. It cut through him like a serrated steak knife.

"What?" He sucked in an exasperated breath, got to his feet and paced the dark room. He stumbled over the discarded clothes, swore ripely, and then kicked the garments out of his way.

"If you think I'm using you for experimental purposes, because of your reputation with women, you're wrong," she told him. "True, I had the worst crush on you in high school while you were dating Melinda. I watched you make out with her on the porch swing and wished it could be me. But I knew it would never be because you barely knew I was alive. I certainly looked nothing like the girls you took out."

Quint stopped in his tracks and stared toward the bed. This was incredible! "So this is about an unfulfilled adolescent fantasy? Not a consolation prize after a really bad day? I don't know which scenario offends me more!"

"I just wanted tonight to be special, even though I know I'm just another available female body and sex is probably just another contact sport to you. But it's not to me," she told him. "I was too embarrassed to admit that I didn't know exactly what I was doing. I'm sorry if I didn't satisfy you. I just—"

Every ounce of roiling frustration and anger gushed out of him when he heard her voice shatter and she burst into tears. Now he'd really done it. He'd shot her fragile feminine pride all to hell. And why? Because he hadn't been very good—just like she'd spitefully told his cousins *before* the fact.

But what really bothered him was that, in light of what he'd just discovered, the one time he would've wanted the moment to be extraordinarily spectacular he'd bungled it. He'd never been with a woman who didn't know the score. Hell, Stephanie barely knew how to play the game!

Hard as it was for him to admit—because he wasn't very proud of himself—he'd just been fooling around in the past, appeasing physical needs then backing off when women started thinking in terms of permanent relationships. Now, when it really mattered, when he *wanted* it to matter, he felt like a heel and he'd made Steph feel that way, too.

Sheesh! He'd taken her where she'd never been and it hadn't been all that extraordinary for her. The local gossip mill considered him to be exceptionally proficient at this sort of thing, but he'd failed miserably. Failed *her.*

The thought of disappointing Steph drove him to his knees beside the bed. He reached out to caress Steph's quaking shoulder while she did her best to cry silently— and failed. And suddenly he could see through the haze of emotions churning around him and arrived at the one undeniable truth that stared him in the face. Where Steph was concerned this wasn't just about sex. Sure, he had the skills and experience to touch her and make it better. But what he felt for her wasn't the least bit superficial— it was something that went deeper, something rare and more profound. It wasn't something that could be appeased in the heat of the moment. It was something that involved the heart and stirred the soul.

Even if they didn't make love tonight it didn't matter. Well, it did, he acknowledged with a self-deprecating smile. He still wanted her like hell burning and he'd pretty much been in a permanent state of arousal since he encountered her. But now that she belonged to him and he belonged to her, on this amazing and abstract level, he could wait until another day. *If* he had to. If he didn't die of sexual depravation first.

"Hey, Red Riding Hood, don't cry," he whispered as he stroked her shoulder.

"Why not?" Sob, hiccup. "It feels damn good to vent all my frustration."

"There's a better way," he assured her as he eased up beside her. "Come here and let me hold you."

On a shuddering sob she cuddled up against him so trustingly that his heart rolled over in his chest like a trick poodle. He nuzzled his chin against the top of her head and wrapped her possessively in his arms. Nothing had ever felt so right. Correction. *No one* had ever felt so right, so necessary to his sense of peace and well being.

Deeply moved by that realization, he crooked his index finger beneath her chin and lifted her face to his tender kiss. "That was just a poorly executed dress rehearsal for the real thing, Steph," he whispered against her lips.

"My fault. If you have no objection, we'll try this again. I'm going to lead this time, okay? You can have your way with me, any way you want me, *next* time. Deal?"

He felt her smile against his lips. "So, we're going to do it until I finally get it right?"

"Until *we* get it right," he clarified.

Now that she wasn't trying so hard to convince him that she knew what she was doing and he was back on solid footing—because he knew where his heart fit into this—his male body was raring to go. He was intensely aware of her bare flesh nestled to his. His hand slid leisurely over the flare of her hip, coasted over her bent knee then back again.

"Now here's how this works. I touch you and you let yourself relax and enjoy it because I'll certainly be enjoying it." His fingertips traced a featherlight path over her belly to swirl around her nipple. "Can you do that? Relax, I mean?"

"Mmm, I guess so," she said. "Is it getting hot in here?"

"Extremely. But then I'm always hot and bothered when I'm with you."

He dipped his head to flick his tongue over the peaks of her breasts and felt her shiver against him, felt her give into the pleasure of his caress. He was so attuned to her that he shared each quivering response, each ragged sigh, as if it were his own.

His hands ebbed and flowed over her. Touching her was like touching exquisite silk. Her body was a study of lush planes, curves and contours created to fit perfectly against him. She was his to explore and he yearned to discover how and where she liked to be touched.

Each gasp and moan he drew from her delighted him beyond words. He was fascinated by the way she arched into his hands, the way she responded instinctively to him.

His fingertips and lips drifted lower, feeling her tremble in response to his brazen touch. The sheer wonderment of the magic flaring between them blew him away. His fingertips grazed her heated flesh and he felt her burning his hand like liquid flames, felt her quivering with the desperate need he'd aroused in her.

Maybe he shouldn't be taking intimate liberties so soon with a novice, but he'd never felt such an intense need to know a woman the way he wanted to know Steph. He wanted to taste her, absorb her, and teach her all the erotic pleasures of her body.

"Quint! Come here right now!" she demanded breathlessly.

"Ah, such a demanding woman," he murmured as his warm breath skimmed over her inner thigh.

"Qui—" Her breath broke when he offered her a lover's most intimate kiss.

Desire nearly blindsided him when he felt her body quiver beneath the onslaught of his intimate seduction. Need clenched inside him when she contracted around his fingertips and lips. Her voice shattered in a hoarse cry as pleasure rippled through her body. When he brought her to another shuddering climax, she pleaded with him to make the wild ache go away and let her hold him inside her.

Quint twisted sideways to ease between her legs then lifted her to him. And this time when he came to her, aching for her as much as he'd made her ache for him, they got it exactly right. He buried himself inside her and felt her burning hot and tight around him.

Desire blowtorched through him, burgeoning, searing them until it was as if they were sharing the same body, the same shuddering breath and the same soul. They were like a bird taking its first flight—gliding, spiraling, two wings beating in perfect rhythm—as they soared through ecstasy.

Mindlessly he drove into her and she matched him thrust for thrust. Together they discovered the heights and depths of frenzied passion. She held nothing back, and neither did he. He gave all of himself to her, realizing it could be no other way with Steph.

Intense, uncontrollable passion exploded around them, raining down like the thunderstorm that cleansed away all that had been before, leaving a purifying calm in its wake.

That was incredible. Perfect, Quint thought dazedly, as he collapsed above Steph and struggled to catch his breath. Nothing had ever felt so right, so clearly defined in his life. Quint was a man who'd been around the track enough to know that what he and Steph had shared was, in actuality, the first time he'd made love with all that he was and all he'd ever wanted to be. If that made any sense. Unfortunately it made perfect sense—and that scared the hell out of him.

Whoa! He was waxing poetic and harboring insightful thoughts all of a sudden. Was he the same man he'd been when he'd left home tonight? Nope. Definitely not. He'd just found himself. Plus, he'd just discovered why Cousin Wade seemed to glow when Laura crossed his line of vision, why that big brawny cowboy melted into mush when his wife smiled up at him. Pure magic. Quint had touched it tonight. He'd basked in the mystical mist and experienced an epiphany.

"Quint?" she murmured against his shoulder.

"Yeah, Stephanie?" he whispered back to her.

"I love you."

Her words spread across his spent flesh and sank into the deepest depths of his soul. He'd heard those words before, many times in fact. He'd said them a few times himself in the heat of passion. But the words had never carried any depth of meaning or caused such a fierce impact on him until Steph murmured them.

"Show me how much," he requested as he rolled onto his back.

"I'm not sure I know how to make it good for you," she admitted inadequately.

He smiled rakishly in the darkness as he placed his hand over hers. "Not to worry, I'll teach—"

His voice dried up when her fingers curled around him, stroking him, exploring him, making him ache for her with every fiber of his being.

She was, he discovered, a quick study. Before the night was out she had him begging for mercy—and he loved every moment of it.

8

STEPHANIE CAME SLOWLY awake, feeling the satisfying pressure of Quint's arms holding her spoon fashion against his hair-roughened chest. She smiled, remembering how she'd had her hands all over his magnificent body and discovered she had the power to devastate him as quickly—and repeatedly—as he devastated her with passion.

She glanced across the tangled sheet to count the astounding number of torn foil packets that littered the nightstand and floor. She grinned, remembering that Quint had made a fast dash to the convenience store to replenish his supply shortly before midnight. Hot, wild sex had taken on true meaning after last night. She hadn't gotten much sleep—not that she was complaining. Quint had fulfilled every erotic fantasy she'd ever had, plus a few she hadn't believed possible.

Mmm, the man definitely knew his way around a woman's anatomy. He'd taken her on several provocative journeys of self-discovery and taught her how he liked to be loved in return. The man was exceptionally thorough. And to think she'd considered sending him on his way and never seeing him again. No way would she have missed the magic she'd discovered last night in his arms.

Stephanie knew she'd probably made a tactical error

by impulsively confessing her feelings for him. But the words had come tumbling out, even when she hadn't wanted to admit them to herself, much less to a ladies' man like Quint. She'd done the unthinkable. She'd broken her own rules and disregarded Dawn Peters's sensible warnings.

She loved Quint Ryder, had always had a soft spot in her heart for him. She wasn't sure that was a good thing, though. She'd armed him with the knowledge that she was vulnerable to him. It hurt to know that dozens of women had undoubtedly said the same thing to him, dozens of times. She'd just joined the ranks of the foolish females who couldn't resist this amber-eyed cowboy with the skillful hands, seductive lips and spellbinding smiles.

She hadn't expected Quint to return her heartfelt confession, but she had to admit she was disappointed he hadn't said he loved her, if even in the heat of the moment. The thought prompted her to move away an inch at a time. She eased a bare leg over the edge of the bed then pulled herself sideways to stand up.

Quint stirred in sleep and flung his arm across the vacant pillow. His raven hair was in a matted tangle that gave him a boyish appearance. But Stephanie could plainly see in the dim light that filtered through the drapes that he was all man. It was her first glimpse of all that finely honed muscled flesh that she'd kissed and caressed during the night.

It was a wonder his skin wasn't chapped, as much time as she'd spent... Well, enough about that, she thought as heat suffused her face and erotic tingles simmered through her body.

She tiptoed from the room and headed for the shower.

She stuck her head under the mist then shrieked in surprise when she found herself hauled up against Quint's sinewy body.

"It's just me," he said as he roped his arms around her water-slickened body. "Expecting someone else?"

"Er...no." She felt awkward and self-conscious when the blaring light in the room revealed all secrets and emphasized the vivid differences between their naked bodies.

"Hey, you okay?" he murmured against the side of her neck.

"Just peachy. You?"

He turned her around to face him. His gaze flooded over her as he flashed her a wolfish smile. The intense heat in his eyes made her breath catch. Her heart thumped wildly against her ribs. Her gaze dropped, noting he was fully aroused. On a quick intake of breath she jerked her flustered gaze to his face.

He arched a brow and flashed white teeth. "First time for dual showers, too, I take it."

"Um...yes," she admitted, face flaming.

"Then what say we do it up right?"

She stared at him questioningly. "Do it *upright?*"

He chuckled as he cupped her face in his hands. "Yeah, that, too." He kissed her until she didn't care where she was, as long as she was with him and he was sending her senses reeling all over again. "I've got a few fantasies of my own to fulfill," he murmured as his hands began to work their seductive magic. "Up against the wall, Red Riding Hood. You and me..."

When he hooked her legs around his hips and pressed her back against the tiles, Stephanie's inhibitions swirled down the drain. She looped her arms over his shoulders and arched toward him. "My, you big bad wolf types sure do have voracious appetites."

"This one is very finicky about his feasts. He only likes red-hot redheads with big—" he grinned naughtily "—eyes. Kiss me, woman, or I'll gobble you alive."

She did—and he did anyway. His hands and lips skimmed over her breasts. Desire coiled in the very core of her being and she arched eagerly against him, aching to have him inside her, yearning to feel that indescribable pleasure shimmering through her like a neon kaleido-scope.

Stephanie marveled at this insatiable need he summoned from her. She'd gone from feeling self-conscious at being naked with him in broad daylight to staring straight into those mystifying golden eyes while he plunged and retreated until they were gasping for breath, clinging desperately to each other—and flying apart in each other's arms.

In the aftermath of quicksilver passion, Quint grabbed the soap and took his sweet time about washing her. Then he handed the bar to her, silently requesting the same titillating treatment. By the time they climbed from the shower the water was cold and Stephanie was still steaming from the explosive passion that surpassed nuclear fusion. Yep, the man was definitely radioactive, she decided.

"If you'll rustle up breakfast, I'll put the bedroom to rights," Quint bargained, giving her a playful swat on the derriere.

"Deal." Stephanie wrapped herself in a towel and strode off to grab jeans and a blouse. Her gaze strayed to Quint when he ambled, stark naked, into her bedroom. She decided she could be content just making a daylong study of his masculine physique. In short, the man was positively awesome and she wanted to feast her eyes and lips on him.

"Don't look at me like that," he warned, a teasing grin quirking his lips. "You'll be flat on your back before you can blink."

She tossed his a saucy grin. "Don't tempt me."

He barked a laugh as his arm shot toward the door. "Skedaddle, woman. If I'm not home in less than an hour I'll have to face my demon cousins and their taunting questions. You saw for yourself what they're like when they're in tormenting mode. We're supposed to pick up Cousin Gage at the airport for the Thanksgiving holidays and I don't want to be late."

When it dawned on her that Idabelle—and anyone else who happened down the street—might see Quint's red pickup parked in her driveway, she sped off to whip up French toast and bacon. If those pesky vigilantes got wind of her surrender it would make it even more difficult to show her face on the streets of Hoot's Roost. She had to send Quint on his way—fast.

QUINT BROKE STRIDE WHEN HE noticed the tense lines that bracketed Steph's mouth, noticed the way she dodged his intimate glances. What happened to the playful siren who'd worn him out most of the night?

When he tried to conduct conversation over breakfast she offered one-word responses. Maybe she was just trying to hurry him on his way after he mentioned his cousins. Quint decided he'd better give her some space. After all, she was new at this morning-after routine. But then, so was he. She probably wouldn't believe it, but it was the truth. He'd never slept over until he found himself wanting—needing—to wake up in the morning with Steph in his arms.

Quint dropped a kiss to her lips, thanked her kindly for breakfast and headed for the door. The casual comments he usually made when he'd walked away sounded inappropriate as they whirled around in his head. *That was fun. Let's do it again sometime really soon.* No way was he going to say that to Steph, even if it'd been the most fun he'd ever had and he wanted to do it again, and again, and again.

He pivoted on his heels, his hand resting on the doorknob. "This isn't goodbye," he told her. "You know that, don't you?"

Well, hell, that sounded almost as lame as his customary comments. He grimaced when she winced.

"I want us to go out on an official date. Oh, and I love you, too." The words just sort of fell out of his mouth.

He inwardly cursed at the casual tone of his voice and noted how her spine stiffened and her chin tilted up a notch in reaction.

Muttering at himself, Quint walked outside, knowing his timing couldn't have been worse. She hadn't believed him. He could see it in those expressive eyes that shimmered like mercury.

And speaking of bad timing! Quint swore colorfully when Wes Martin and his sidekick, Randel Bentley, stopped the two-tone brown pickup beside the curb. Both men were grinning like idiots.

Scowling, Quint stalked toward them. "If either one of you—"

"'Bout time we got some results. Took you long enough," Wes interrupted.

The older man leaned out the window to stuff a roll of bills in Quint's shirt pocket. When his gaze drifted over Quint's shoulder he felt impending doom descend on him. Quint followed Wes's gaze toward the apartment. His breath lodged in his throat and his heart hung in his chest like a shriveled prune when he saw Steph standing in the open doorway, staring at him with a look of such devastation and disappointment that he groaned aloud. Hell's bells! Another damning moment to spoil their relationship. With her, he was always screwing up in reverse.

"It's not what you think," he called frantically.

"Gee, where have I heard that before? Oh, I remember now. From you!" she shouted before she slammed the door with such force that the garage apartment rattled on its foundation.

"Beat it," Quint snarled at Wes and Randel. He wheeled about and jogged back to Steph's apartment to pound both fists on the door. "Open up!"

"Go to hell!" she railed at him.

"Where do you think I am now!" he shouted in frustration.

"In braggart's paradise? Collecting bets? You called them on the phone from my bedroom, didn't you? You wanted them here as witnesses."

"No," he denied categorically.

"I don't believe you! If you ever come near me again,

Quint Ryder, I'll get a restraining order. Go away and never come back—''

Her voice broke and she burst into tears. The sound was like a knife twisting in his heart. He wanted to hold her, to reassure her, but a locked door stood between them.

It might as well have been the Great Wall of China.

Swearing foully, Quint lurched around and stormed off. Why was it, he wondered, that everything pertaining to Steph backfired in his face? He was in love—*really* in love for the first time in his life—and the woman who held his heart hated him with a passion as intense as the passion they'd shared the previous night. Well, maybe this was what he deserved, but he'd be damned if he allowed Wes Martin and company to humiliate Steph.

Quint bounded into his pickup and whizzed toward home, hoping the local cops weren't on his tail when he broke land speed records. The very last thing he needed right now was to find his wicked cousins waiting on his doorstep, eager to torment him.

Sure 'nuff, Quint wheeled into his driveway to see Wade and Vance staring at him with teasing grins. ''I'm not in the mood, so don't start,'' he growled as he stamped toward the house.

''Whoa, got up on the wrong side of someone's bed, did you? I wonder whose?'' Vance taunted. ''Lack of sleep, huh?''

''This is a first,'' Wade noted, chuckling. ''An over-nighter?''

''I said...don't start!'' Quint all but shouted.

When Quint practically bit off Wade's head, Vance backed away. ''Down, boy.'' His gaze dropped to the rolled bills in Quint's shirt pocket. "You're moonlighting on the side...or on top? Which is it?"

Quint's temper detonated. He whirled on his grinning cousins with lips curled and teeth bared. "One more crack like that and I'll deck you both. Got it? And I've changed my mind about riding along while you pick up Gage at the airport. I think I'll just stay here and shoot myself a couple of times."

Wade and Vance gaped at him, and Wade said, "What the hell is the matter with you?"

His breath gushed from his lips like the downdraft of a thunderstorm. "I walked out Steph's front door this morning, just as Wes and Randel drove by. They crammed money into my pocket and Steph saw them do it."

Wade and Vance groaned in unison.

"Hoo-boy," Vance mumbled. "Hit the fan, did it?"

"Yup, big time. Now I've got to do some damage control because Steph has to open for lunch—"

"That's good," Wade interrupted.

"No, that's bad," Quint contradicted. "Wes and friends will think I talked her into it after we...well..." Quint shifted awkwardly beneath his cousins' probing stares. "Hell!"

"We get the picture. You're going to look like the local hero and she'll look the conquered prize," Vance presumed. "Go on."

"Steph had already decided to open for lunch because the road construction has cut into her profits and she's having trouble making ends meet. But that's not the way the men in town will see it, not after Wes and company spread the word that my pickup was in her driveway immediately before she announces that she's opening for noon business.''

The gravity of the situation soaked in. Vance and Wade stared grimly at him. "So now Steph hates your guts because she thinks you set her up. That about sum it up?" Wade asked.

"Pretty much."

"And you're so upset that you can barely stand still because...?" Vance prompted.

"Because I'm in love with her and I tried to tell her so." Quint grabbed a quick breath and noted his cousins were staring at him as if he were an alien from another galaxy.

"What happened to that business about staying single forever?" Wade asked.

"Same thing that happened to your claim never to remarry," Quint retaliated. "Things change, damn it. You said so yourself not so long ago. She's everything I never expected I wanted and now I don't think I can live without her. But Steph doesn't believe me because this overblown reputation is hanging over my head like a curse. I've got a pocketful of Lincolns that make me look as guilty as hell. As we speak, Wes and Randel are probably cruising around town, spreading the word that I charmed Steph into catering to the men's demands."

Wade grinned, damn him ornery hide. "Toldja love'd getcha if you didn't watch out."

"Are you gonna rub it in my face or help me?" Quint stormed at him. "I've got serious problems here!"

"Boy, I'll say you do," Wade said with cousinly candor.

"Damn it! What am I going to do!" Quint howled in

desperation. "It was her first—" He slammed his mouth shut so fast that he nearly clipped off his tongue.

Wade chuckled, nodded in complete understanding and rocked back on his heels. "Um...kinda gives you a new perspective on things, doesn't it?"

Quint had suspected Laura didn't have much experience, considering she had four overprotective brothers monitoring her every move. Wade's comment pretty much confirmed what Quint presumed to be true. Unfortunately things didn't look to be turning out quite so well for Quint.

"I've got to do something—fast—but I have no idea what!" Quint muttered, exasperated.

"Simmer down before you give yourself a coronary," Vance said. "We'll go pick up Gage while you talk to Wes. We'll drop Gage at his place to unpack then provide all the back up you need."

Quint raked his hand through his hair and realized he must've left his hat at Steph's place. She'd probably take a butcher knife to it before he could retrieve it. "Okay, thanks. I guess I better go back to town to do some damage control."

He watched his cousins stride away then he cursed a couple of times for good measure. Damn, he'd been in and out of so much hot water with Steph that he resembled a dishwasher. He'd be lucky if he could hold her still long enough to explain the situation. Even *he* thought he looked guilty as hell and he *knew* he was innocent.

Scowling, Quint burst into the house, grabbed an envelope and stuffed the cursed money in it. Spinning about, he tore off to town. He used his cell phone to call Steph, but she didn't answer so he tried the restaurant.

One of the waitresses informed him that she'd heard the tale that Wes and Randel were telling and she thought Quint was a total jerk. Plus, Steph wasn't taking his calls—ever—so he could crawl back under his rock. When the irate woman hung up on him, Quint muttered a few more choice expletives.

He was the first to admit that he'd had things going his way most of his life. But he'd discovered at the ripe age of thirty-two that life could get complicated and messy. He was scrambling like crazy because he was about to lose the best thing that had ever happened to him. Steph wasn't what he'd expected, but she'd turned out to be everything he needed. He'd recently discovered that his life wasn't complete and it wouldn't be until Steph loved him the same way he'd come to love her.

Like a man possessed, Quint barreled into the feed store. As usual, the place was packed after the recent rain. Damn, wasn't this how the trouble started?

When applause burst through the store Quint waved his arms, demanding silence. "Knock it off. You need to know that I had nothing whatsoever to do with the fact that Steph plans to reopen for lunch."

The farmer/stockman crowd smirked in contradiction.

Wes braced his brawny arms on the counter. "Even if she's opening for business, we aren't going to give her our business for a few days," he announced. "We'll make sure she's learned her lesson and we'll make her sweat a little."

Everyone nodded in agreement.

"No, you're not," Quint contradicted as he addressed the crowd of men. "You're going to support her the way you should have when she opened for business. Would you have pulled this stunt if the hardware storeowner decided to change the store hours? The service station owner? No, because the proprietors are men and the whole bunch of us, myself included, have been behaving like male chauvinists.''

"I still say we should wait a few days before giving Steph our business," Wes grumbled.

"We got our way and we're going to be good sports about it. No gloating, only a show of support," Quint demanded. He glanced over Wes's bulky shoulder. "Leta, you in there hearing this?"

Leta Martin, the exact opposite size of her burly husband, stepped around the door where she'd been eavesdropping. "I'm hearing," she said. She walked over to latch onto Wes's ear, giving it a twist. The man winced and blushed when all eyes focused on him. "Wes will be there with bells on when Steph opens for lunch." Her gaze bore down on the men who filled the store. "Same goes for the rest of you because I'm calling your wives immediately. Anybody who resists or complains will lose the right to credit his account. It'll be pay on delivery and what I say goes because I'm the bookkeeper." She gave Wes's ear another twist. "Aren't I, sweetheart?"

Quint bit back a grin when Wes nodded—carefully. Even though Leta Martin was flirting with fifty, she was still full of spit and vinegar. Just as Steph would be, Quint predicted. And Wes, for all his bluster, didn't want to lose the good deal he had going. Quint could tell by the way Wes's weathered face softened when he stared down at his wife of thirty years that he was still very much in love and devoted to her. The look in his eyes gave him away.

Quint wondered why he hadn't noticed before. Probably because he didn't know what it looked like or how it felt to be so head over heels for a woman that he was willing to do anything within his power to preserve the feelings that pulsed in rhythm with his heart.

He couldn't—wouldn't—lose Steph, he promised himself resolutely. His future happiness was at stake. "I've got places to go and things to do," he said, wheeling toward the door. "This ridiculous feud that never should've started in the first place is officially over. If Steph doesn't have a packed house when she opens for lunch, my cousins and I will be personally escorting all of you to the restaurant."

"We'll all be there," Leta affirmed, smiling triumphantly. "You can bank on it, Quint."

She pushed up on tiptoe to kiss Wes's pudgy cheek then flung her arms around him for a quick hug. Quint smiled as he strode out the door. He had the unshakable feeling that the reason this crowd of men had wanted him to wrap Steph around his little finger was that they held the hope that one man in Hoot's Roost could do what they hadn't been able to do in their own homes.

It was just one of those guy things, he supposed. But Quint's rocky relationship with Steph assured him that he didn't want to wear the pants constantly. He wanted to share his life, his future and his decisions with her. Equal partners handling designated duties and loving and supporting each other every step of the way.

Now, if he could find a way to convince Steph to love him again, to put faith in his love for her, things would work out dandy fine. But persuading her to believe that he hadn't betrayed her and that he cared enough to make a lifelong commitment to her was going to take some doing.

Next stop the flower shop, Quint decided as he ambled across town square. He glanced up at the concrete owl in perpetual flight, hoping the bird wouldn't make a symbolic deposit on his head but, instead, would smile kindly down on him. For sure, Quint needed all the help he could get to reassure the copperheaded queen of cuisine that he was sincere and devoted.

His wanderlust days were over. He wanted what Cousin Wade had found. He wanted what Wes and dozens of other men in town had discovered—but had too much male pride to admit. Well, Quint wasn't going to make that mistake, believe you him.

By the time he finished making arrangements there would be no place for Steph to run—except to him. When dealing with a strong, assertive woman like Steph, a man simply couldn't afford to miscalculate.

After Quint ordered a dozen red roses for love, a dozen yellow roses for friendship and a dozen pink roses—he didn't know what they symbolized but he purchased them nonetheless—he had them delivered to the restaurant. He made a beeline for Idabelle Witham's home and found her in the backyard, tending her riotous bed of chrysanthemums.

"Idabelle, could I have a moment of your time?" he asked politely.

Idabelle brushed off her jeans, removed her gardening gloves and gave him a hard stare. "You, young man, are in big trouble."

"I know, that's why I came to you for help." He

flashed her a high-wattage smile but it boomeranged back in his face because she frowned disapprovingly at him.

"I saw what happened this morning when you left," she snapped. "I also saw Steph's devastated expression when she hiked off to work. You oughta be shot. I'd do it myself, but I figure Steph deserves the honors."

"I want to marry her," Quint blurted out. "But she won't let me explain."

"You want to marry her?" Idabelle crowed.

Quint nodded and smiled. "Yup. Wedding and commitment. The whole ball of wax. But if you don't help me by evicting her so she'll have nowhere to go but to me I'll never convince her that we belong together."

"Evict her?" Idabelle bubbled with laughter. "Quint, you rascal. You're almost too clever for your own good. But since you've appealed to the hopeless romantic in me, I'll do it. Of course, you'll have to conspire with Hoagie and Wanda Lawson so Steph can't move home."

"Soon as I replace the dead battery in Steph's car, I'm heading over to the Lawsons'. I want to invite them to the wedding and rehearsal dinner I plan to book at the Palace."

The older woman clapped her hands together in delight. "We haven't had this much excitement in town since that woman-hating cousin of yours tied the knot. I hope Gage can make it home for the ceremony."

"He's on his way," Quint reported. "The whole family will be home for Thanksgiving so all I need is a willing bride."

Idabelle's smile sagged at the corners of her mouth. "You've got your work cut out for you."

"I know. Wish me luck," he requested as he turned to leave.

"You'll need more than that. If the look on Steph's face is any indication, you hurt her. Badly."

Quint gulped as he walked away. He tried to tell himself that he couldn't have hurt Steph if she didn't care deeply about him—way down inside, beneath the wounded pride and smarting indignation. Furthermore, he didn't believe she would have made love with him if she didn't feel something profound for him. He had to keep the hope alive that what she now perceived as betrayal hadn't killed her feelings for him and completely destroyed her long-ago fantasies from adolescence.

She just needed to be thoroughly convinced to take a chance on him. The thought gave Quint an inspiration and another glimmer of hope. He bounded into his truck, anxious to put all his plans in motion.

"HEY, BOSS, THESE JUST CAME for you."

Stephanie glanced up from the pile of bills that cluttered her desk to see Dawn Peters holding three dozen roses.

"They're from Benedict Arnold Ryder," Dawn reported as she thrust three cards at Steph.

Compensation, she mused bitterly. Whatever passed as Quint's conscience was obviously niggling him. No doubt, he thought he could return to her good graces by sending her flowers. Well, he thought wrong. Men were so clueless!

"Told you that men are the scum of the earth, didn't I? You mess with them and you get burned. That's a given."

Steph took the cards and stared at the message Quint had written and signed himself. *I love you. Quint.* Did he think that writing it down three times would work like a charm? Probably. After all, he relied heavily on charm when dealing with women. The jerk!

Tears welled up in her eyes, blurring her vision, blurring the meaningless words he'd jotted on the cards. He'd undoubtedly said those words so often to women that it was as reflexive to him as breathing.

How could she have been such a shameless idiot? With each passing day and each encounter she'd found herself losing another piece of her heart to that ladies' man. She'd known better. She'd even seen it coming a mile away. But despite all her self-preservation tactics and proud denials, she'd fallen in love, and he'd *betrayed* her, *conspired* against her, *used* her affection and her desire for him. She'd given her heart and soul to him and he'd cut her to shreds.

They hadn't made love, she reminded herself sourly. They'd had sex. She'd become another casualty of Quint's practiced seduction and she'd asked for it. That's what infuriated her most. She'd gotten lost in those pyrite eyes—fool's gold, for sure. She'd been bedeviled by his potent aura of male magnetism. But his only interest had been conquest. She'd become his catch of the day—literally—and now she wanted his heart—fried in boiling oil and served on a platter.

The spiteful thought prompted Steph to yank open the desk drawer and snatch up a pair of scissors. While Dawn held the expensive bouquets Steph viciously snipped off the delicate blossoms. Dawn chuckled in wicked amusement when Steph grabbed the dustpan, scooped up the decapitated rosebuds and dumped them in a plastic bag.

"Good for you, boss," Dawn said approvingly. "I'll deliver these for you. Shall I also tell Quint what he can do with his stems and his fresh sack of potpourri?"

"Yes, definitely tell him to stash 'em where the sun don't shine."

"You're spiteful and vicious, boss. I like that," Dawn said as she turned on her heels and exited the office.

9

QUINT FROWNED CURIOUSLY when he saw the vehicle hurtling down the graveled road.

"Is that the reluctant bride-to-be?" Cousin Gage asked as he turned away from the corral filled with bawling young calves.

"Nope, that's not Steph's car," Vance noted.

The Ryder cousins watched the car skid to a halt. Quint winced when he recognized the energetic brunette who bounded to her feet.

"Uh-oh," Wade murmured when he noticed the decapitated bouquets.

Dawn strode forward, nodded a curt greeting to the Ryder cousins then stared murderously at Quint. "Special delivery, ladies' man." She thrust the headless stems at his chest and the plastic bag into his hand. "Do I need to tell you where the boss suggests you stash this stuff or are you smart enough to figure it out all by yourself?"

Quint grimaced when his cousins snickered. "Thanks, but I get the big picture."

"Good, don't want you harboring any false delusions about the boss's sentiments after what you did."

"I didn't do it!" Quint burst out in self-defense.

"Innocent as a lamb, the way I heard it," Gage supplied helpfully.

Dawn shot him a black look. "Well, you heard wrong, pal. The boss wants all men dead, starting with lover boy here."

"I love her," Quint felt compelled to say.

"Gee, you sure have a weird way of showing it, Romeo," she said, and sniffed disdainfully.

"He does, though," Wade, Vance and Gage chorused in unison. "Believe it or not."

"I choose *not.*"

Quint got right in the shapely brunette's face, ignoring the glare she flashed at him. "Truth," he said. "Here's the whole truth and nothing but. I want to marry Steph and I need your help to convince her I'm in for the long haul."

Dawn stared at him so long and hard that he was tempted to squirm beneath her critical appraisal. "If you're lying to me, you're dead meat. Stephanie is my best friend. You better not screw this up, hotshot."

"He has Idabelle's approval and cooperation," Wade put in.

"He has Hoagie and Wanda's permission, too," Vance added, flashing a good-natured smile to lessen the tension.

"He also has our blessing, though I've yet to be reintroduced to my future cousin-in-law," Gage said, adding his charming smile to the mix. "So, are you going to help or hinder?"

Dawn studied Quint and his cousins for another long moment then nodded. "Fine, but the threat still stands. Now what do you want me to do?"

EVICTED? STEPHANIE COULDN'T believe it. Idabelle had given her two days' notice to remove her belongings from the garage apartment that she'd called home for two months. Idabelle had given the lame excuse that her family would be arriving for the holidays and staying until after Christmas and that she needed the extra space.

"So sorry, hon," she'd said, "but family comes first."

Stunned, Stephanie had gone to her parents to deliver the humbling news that she had to open for lunch to keep the business afloat. She'd asked if she could have her old room back until she could locate suitable living space.

To her dismay her parents—the two people in the world she'd sworn she could count on, being blood kin and all—turned her down. They claimed they'd made arrangements to remodel her old bedroom into a sunroom by knocking holes in the outside walls and installing floor-to-ceiling windows.

"What about the spare bedroom?" Stephanie had asked.

Her mother had explained that the spare room would become a storage room during the remodeling project.

The only bright spot in an otherwise devastating morning was that Hoagie and Wanda had volunteered to help with the cooking duties during the noon hour. They claimed they needed to be away from the house while the carpenters attacked the project. For that, Stephanie was grateful. She dearly hoped her parents would act as a buffer against the gloating males who showed up for burgers and fries.

By the time Stephanie returned home from the restaurant—after another depressing evening of serving no more patrons than she could count on both hands—she was mentally and emotionally exhausted. All she wanted was to soak in the tub, drown her misery in a glass of wine and wallow in self-pity before crawling into bed and pulling the covers over her head.

Stephanie howled in disbelief when she opened her apartment door and discovered the place had been cleaned out. She'd been robbed! Her furniture and belongings had been removed and there was nothing left but a few changes of clothing and a note pinned to the wall.

Outraged, she stamped over to read the note.

Your stuff is at my place. If you want it back, come and get it. Love,
Quint.

Muttering, she wadded up the note and hurled it against the bare wall. That arrogant rascal! How dare he! Is this how he'd repaid her for butchering his long-stem roses? Well, she'd call the cops on him. She'd file a complaint of grand theft and have him arrested and locked in the slammer. But first she'd storm out to his place and—

Stephanie jerked her thoughts to a screeching halt. No, she was not going near that man. That's exactly what he wanted her to do so he could work his devilish charm on her and ply her with meaningless phrases of love. His inflated ego was dictating to him, that was all, she mused. Quint Ryder, ladies' man extraordinaire, was accustomed to all women adoring him. Naturally it would bother him that one woman in town despised him to the extreme. Maybe he didn't want hard feelings between them when all was said and done. But he wasn't the one who'd had his heart ripped out by the taproot and had his pride mutilated. He was the one who'd had his way with her—all the livelong night.

The thought sent betraying tingles fanning through her body. Stephanie squelched the erotic sensations and vivid images. She swore she'd never speak to Quint again and, by damned, she wouldn't. She'd sleep in her office and bathe in the fountain in town square before she swallowed her pride and went to Quint to get her belongings back. She wasn't even going to thank him for replacing the dead battery in her car, either. Considering what he'd done *to* her, that was the very least he could do *for* her.

On that determined—well, okay, extremely *stubborn*—thought, Stephanie stalked back to her car and returned to her office. She didn't need a quilt to keep her warm tonight. She had a thick blanket of indignation to keep her toasty.

QUINT PACED THE FLOORBOARDS then switched direction to pace some more. He'd predicted—and his cousins had agreed—that moving Steph's furniture into his home would send her storming to his ranch for a confrontation. Obviously he'd underestimated the extent of her fury. That fiery redhead was so angry, willful and stubborn that she'd endure inconvenience to avoid seeing him again.

He'd sent more flowers to her and they'd been returned, decapitated, by one of her waitresses. He'd called the restaurant—repeatedly—and she'd slammed down the phone in his ear when she recognized his voice. He'd gone to see her three times in two days and she'd told him—through the locked door that separated them—to go to hell.

Time was running out, Quint realized. His parents, aunts and uncles would be arriving soon for the annual Thanksgiving feast. It was Cousin Gage's turn to host the get-together—which was why he'd flown home from abroad a few days early.

Quint had hoped to convince Steph to marry him and combine the ceremony with the holiday festivities. From the look of things, he'd be attending the wedding that he and his cousins had organized without his bride-to-be.

Maybe this was what a man who'd dodged serious commitment for years had coming to him, but Quint wasn't a man who gave up easily. During his rodeo days with his cousins he'd gotten his butt dumped in the dirt more times than he'd cared to count, but he'd pulled himself up by the bootstraps, climbed on the next raunchy bronc and tried again.

"Well, cuz? Are you ready to concede that it's time to activate Plan B?" Wade asked, grinning playfully. "You have a houseful of stolen furniture, decorative paintings and no bride-to-be."

"Somehow I don't think all that pacing is going to accomplish diddly-squat," Vance commented.

"In my line of work, there are ways to acquire necessary cooperation," Gage said, lips twitching. "Shall I apply a few of those techniques?"

"No." Quint halted in the middle of his crowded living room, beside the expensive sofa he'd swiped from Steph. The new additions to the room were a constant reminder that she belonged here with him. They *belonged* to each other. "Agreed, it's time for drastic measures, but this is her grand opening for the lunch hour. I plan to see to it that every table is filled to capacity by the locals. Maybe that'll improve her mood.''

"Cuz, nothing is going to improve that redhead's fiery mood until you go one on one with her,'' Wade insisted. "You have to force the situation to a head, the same way Laura's brothers did with me.''

"I well remember that incident, but this situation is different,'' Quint said as he went back to pacing around the extra furniture.

"Better set a time limit here,'' Gage recommended. "If she still refuses to speak to you by tomorrow evening, we need to act. Our families will be here soon and I've got turkeys to cook. *Your goose,* too, if it comes to that.''

Quint sighed heavily. "Fine, Plan B goes into effect tonight, unless she'll listen to reason over lunch.''

"Doubt it,'' Wade predicted. "But I'm looking forward to burgers 'n fries. It's been a while.'' He grinned wryly. "Luckily that's the only thing I've been doing without lately. Too bad you can't say the same, Don Juan.''

Quint scowled when his wicked cousins snickered. He grabbed the hat he'd retrieved from Steph's apartment when he'd heisted her furniture, then headed for the door. Maybe he couldn't persuade Steph that he'd meant what he'd said about loving her, but he could give her the business—and she'd have plenty of it today when she opened her doors at 11:00 a.m.

STEPHANIE STARED AROUND the kitchen door, watching her restaurant fill to capacity. According to her dad, there was a waiting line outside that spilled across the street to the park benches in town square. To her surprise, ever

Wes Martin tossed her a wave and peace-treaty smile when he came through the door.

"This is Quint's doing," Leta Martin said as she exited the rest room and halted beside Stephanie. "He plans to see that you recoup your losses." She winked before ambling to the table to rejoin her husband. "Give Quint a second chance. This wasn't all his fault."

Stephanie stiffened her resolve, despite Leta's comments. She held her head high as Randel Bentley and his wife strolled over to voice a similar comment. Mr. Charm might've buttered up the entire town and got her business back, but an influx of cash wasn't everything, she reminded herself. When a woman was hurting all the way down to the bottom of her soul and was desperately afraid that if she caved in she'd get burned again, no amount of money could cure the pain.

If she tried hard, she might be able to convince herself that she didn't really love him, didn't want him and need him in her life. She just needed to compare Quint to a severe case of the flu. She'd had him. She'd burned with fever because of him and now she was over him. Recovered. Immune.

The door swung open. Quint, surrounded by his three, handsome, raven-haired cousins—all of whom towered over six feet and looked positively devastating—formed a muscled wall of rugged but gorgeous cowboys. Stephanie knew she was in serious trouble when she stared appreciatively at the four men—and only had eyes for one.

Damn it, her heart muscles couldn't take another vigorous workout. She turned away quickly and headed for her office before she broke down and cried her eyes out.

After she'd locked the door, she plunked into her chair. She *wasn't* over him, she realized. She'd never be over him. He'd been a part of her dreams and thoughts since adolescence and he'd stolen her heart when she should've been smart enough and mature enough to know better. But she still wasn't going to speak to him, wasn't going to risk buckling beneath that pretentious charm and that lethal smile again.

Maybe he was dreadfully sorry this town feud had mushroomed into the battle of the sexes and he and she had been caught in the middle. Maybe he wanted to sign a truce and part as friends. But tossing out words of love that he didn't really mean wasn't going to cut it. She couldn't let herself take him seriously. Furthermore, she wasn't going to talk to him, for fear she'd blubber and wail and humiliate herself again.

"Steph!"

She jumped, startled, when Quint's baritone voice rumbled across her office like thunder. "What?"

"Open this door or I'll huff and puff and blow it down," he called out.

"Wrong fairy tale," she shouted. "Go tell it to the three pigs!"

After a moment of silence he said softly, "Steph, I need to talk to you, face-to-face. I love you."

The words caused her heart to squeeze painfully in her chest and made tears swim in her eyes. "No, you don't!"

"Do!"

"Not!"

"You're the only woman I want."

"Really?" She smirked. "How many women did you go through before you came to that conclusion?"

"Damn it, what's it going to take to convince you that I *do* love you?" he yelled.

"Try diving headfirst off a cliff. That should do it!" she yelled back.

"Open...the...door," he growled at her.

"No...way...in...hell," she growled back.

"I'm warning you, Steph, this is your last chance!" he threatened.

"Lucky me. You've already had *your* last chance so go away! To another planet preferably."

She waited tensely, then sagged in relief when nothing but silence filled her office. On one hand, she was glad to have him gone. On the other hand, she was disappointed he'd given up, because despite her good judgment she'd wanted him to do something drastic—like kick down the door and carry her off in his arms—to convince her that he *was* sincere, that he *did* care, that he *did* love her.

"You are so pathetic," Stephanie grumbled at herself.

The man made her so frustrated that she didn't know what she wanted from him. Well, she *did* know what she wanted, she admitted honestly. She wanted him to love her forever and ever because she wanted what her parents had. They were devoted to each other, had worked side by side in the café for years—just as they were doing right now. Because they enjoyed being together, no matter what the endeavor. They'd shared their lives through thick and thin and still had enough love left over to include her.

The vision of raven-haired toddlers with amber eyes and beguiling smiles hit her so hard she almost wept. Phooey on devoting her life to her career and ascending the corporate ladder to five-star success. That was just a substitute dream, a consolation prize for what she secretly wanted from life. She wanted a home and family with Quint, and a restaurant in her hometown that supplied everyone's dining needs.

Only problem was that she was too *afraid* of getting hurt again to let herself believe Quint was sincere. *Afraid* she wasn't woman enough to hold his interest longer than the other females who'd caught his attention temporarily. With his track record and her lack of experience, why should she believe their relationship would last more than a few weeks?

Stephanie sighed. If only he'd broken down the door, maybe she could've believed in him. But he'd given up on her without much of a fight. And that, Stephanie told herself, said it all.

When she was sure the Ryder cousins had had time to finish lunch and exit, she ventured from her office. To her amazement, the Ryder cousins were bussing tables because the waitresses couldn't keep up with the constant flow of diners. The moment the Ryders left, Stephanie returned to the kitchen to lend a hand.

She watched her parents chitchat as they went through their long-practiced routine of cooking side by side. Her heart bled with envy. She'd never have that, she realized. She and Dawn Peters were destined to be married to the job.

For hours Stephanie went through the paces of cooking, cleaning up and then preparing for the evening crowd of diners. She was heartened by the fact that the Palace was busy that evening. Even Wes Martin, Randel Bentley and Clem Spaulding and their wives showed up to sample the Oriental cuisine.

Stephanie made it a point to serve them herself—her way of burying the hatchet and mending fences. Now that the feud had ended, she realized the older generation of men weren't such a bad lot and Quint was right. This town did need a diner that opened for lunch. Early on, Stephanie might have been more agreeable to the request if she hadn't felt *forced* into it, if the men would've sent someone besides Quint—the only man she was acutely sensitive to.

She smiled inwardly when she noticed the older men were devoted to the women in their lives. Watching them together restored her faith in men. With the exception of one, of course. The jury was still out on Quint. He hadn't returned. If he really had given up that easily then she was just another fling to him.

When the door closed for the night, Stephanie and Dawn spiffied up the kitchen. Dawn dried her hands and glanced questioningly at her. "Wanna stay at my place?"

Stephanie smiled gratefully. "Yes, thanks for asking."

"You're going to have to collect your belongings sooner or later," Dawn reminded her as she scooped up her purse.

"I know. I just need a little time to—" Her voice became a startled shriek of surprise when the back door burst open and three men dressed in black pounced on her.

"You, Red Riding Hood, have a date with fate," Gage declared as he hooked his arm around her waist.

Stephanie gaped at Quint's cousins then shot an alarmed glance at Dawn. "Call the cops!"

Dawn smiled in amusement, while Stephanie squirmed for release. "Sorry, no can do. You need to collect what belongs to you. Sooner, not later, my friend."

Stephanie dug in her heels, but the kidnapping brigade dragged her through the back door. *"Et tu, Brute?"* she muttered at the woman she considered a kindred spirit and her best friend in the whole wide world.

"Hey, even I hold the hope that not all men are as treacherous as I think they are right now," Dawn countered. "Don't worry about opening up in the morning. I've got it covered." She shooed the Ryder cousins on their way then frowned darkly. "The threat still stands, you know."

"We haven't forgotten," Vance assured her, flashing her a wink and a smile.

Stephanie found herself hauled to an extended cab pickup and belted in place. Apparently Quint had sent Gage, Vance and Wade to do his dirty work for him. Why, she wondered, hadn't he come himself?

"You realize there are laws against this sort of thing, don't you?" she said as they whisked her out of town.

"Really? Hadn't heard that," Gage said, grinning.

"Well, if you weren't so stubborn we wouldn't have to resort to abduction," Wade inserted. "So I guess you'd have to say you asked for it."

Stephanie glared at him. "I'm going to tell your wife on you."

He shrugged, unconcerned, as he hung a left and cruised down the graveled road. "She knows where I am. She also approves."

"Most everybody does," Vance added. "You're the only hold out."

Stephanie stared through the windshield to see a porch light beaming in the distance. She tensed when the truck rolled to a stop and she saw Quint, spotlighted in the headlights, looking better than any man had a right to look. His arms were crossed over his broad chest, his feet askance. There was a determined expression on his handsome face, she noted.

"This is the part where we throw you to the wolves, Red," Gage announced in a gritty voice that startled Stephanie into casting him a cautious sidelong glance. "Don't try to make a break for it because we've been ordered to run you to ground."

"What *do* you do for a living?" she asked Gage curiously.

His white teeth flashed in the dim dashboard lights. "You don't have the security clearance for that kind of information, Red. Now scram. I've got turkeys to roast for Thanksgiving dinner." He gave her the evil eye. "Don't make me have to include you on the list of things to roast during the holidays."

When Stephanie made no move to climb down from the truck, Vance grumbled something about stiff-necked stubbornness, total defiance and inevitability. He unbuckled her seat belt, hooked his arm around her waist and set her abruptly to her feet. "Go get this over with so the rest of us can get on with our lives. *Please!*"

The truck circled around her then whizzed off. Stephanie stared at the looming figure that was suddenly swallowed in shadows. When she glanced past Quint she realized a porch swing had been installed and a bouquet of roses sat upon it. The implication that he had gone to a lot of trouble to ensure she talked to him sent her doubts and concerns flitting off in the wind.

Maybe he really did care about her. Maybe this just wasn't about clearing his conscience and making amends for hurting her in ways no man had ever done before.

"What's with the new porch swing?" She thought she already knew, but she needed to hear him say it.

"I intend to fulfill a long-held fantasy," he told her. "We're going to do some serious necking out here after we get things squared away. The porch light has been on to welcome you home for several days, but you never showed. You are one infuriatingly stubborn woman, Red Riding Hood."

"You have to be when you walk among the wolves," she said, standing her ground.

Quint waited, hoping she'd come flying into his arms, but then he realized that had been part of her hopeless lure. Women had chased him for years, but the ones who fell at his feet had no lasting appeal. This woman, whose hair burned in the porch light like a flame, drew him like the proverbial moth. Her electrifying silver-blue eyes bore straight into his soul. Her radiant smiles were beacons in the darkness. She'd become all things that were important and vital to him. He wasn't backing away—ever. He'd *out*stubborn her, he promised himself resolutely.

His future was on the line and he didn't want to mess this up. He'd spent the past several hours rehearsing what he intended to say, but now that the pivotal moment was upon him, he discovered he was having the same difficulty expressing himself as he'd had the first few times he'd confronted Steph.

Well, hell, he'd just go for broke and get this over with. All those smooth lines and casual flirtations that had been his trademark for years had never worked with Steph. He'd speak from the heart because she was the only one who'd ever inspired such deep-felt honesty.

Quint inhaled a fortifying breath and hoped like hell that she could recognize the truth and depth of his affection when it was staring her right in the face.

10

"I'M IN LOVE WITH YOU, STEPH," he said softly, sincerely, earnestly.

"You expect me to believe that you know what love is?"

"Of course, I know what it is. I've spent years researching what love is *not*. I've been cursing this fiasco that's made me look bad in your eyes and I didn't appreciate being blackmailed. I sure as hell wanted nothing to do with stupid bets and bribes. Furthermore, I don't want to spend the whole blessed night debating issues with you."

He took one step toward her, relieved that she didn't counter by taking one step away from him. "I'm sorry as hell that we got caught up in that feud, but it doesn't change how I feel about you. I want a life with you, Steph. That's why I brought all your stuff here, to prove to you that your expensive furniture compliments my ranch and that *you* complete *me*."

Steph took a tentative step toward him. "You think Red Riding Hood and the Big Bad Wolf really have a chance together? You do remember how that story ends, don't you?"

Quint winced. "Uh...yeah. I was sort of hoping we

could write our own ending. You know, happily ever after and all that. You'll say, 'I do,' and I'll say, 'Absolutely, positively.'"

"And then we'll have a passel of kids underfoot and we'll help each other run the restaurant and the ranch?" she asked hopefully.

Quint smiled when Steph took another step toward him. He advanced one step toward her. "Yeah, that's exactly what I have in mind."

"And there'll be plenty of wild, passionate sex in between?" she asked outrageously. "Gotta have the sex. I was really starting to like that part—a lot."

Quint chuckled as his heart filled with the hope that she'd forgiven him and was placing her faith in him. "With you, Steph, I'm really fond of that part myself." He took another step toward her, bridging the gap of distrust and misconceptions that had catapulted them apart just when things between them had really started getting good.

"I won't tolerate score cards or black books or phone calls from your wanna-be harem," she negotiated, then moved a step closer.

He was close enough to reach out and grab her to him and devour her, but he didn't because he suddenly understood this was the *only* woman he wanted to come willingly into his arms. "This is the truth," he murmured sincerely. "I don't want anyone but you. Haven't since the day I laid eyes on you again." He took a deep breath and said, "You're the one that I love."

His heart stopped beating when she stared up at him for a long, silent moment, trying to gauge the depth of his sincerity and commitment. Another defining moment, he realized. She was trying to decide if she could trust him to remain faithful to her, despite his previous, glorified reputation with women. Quint held his breath, hoping she could see the look in his eyes and the expression on his face. He'd never been more serious, so desperate to be believed than at this moment.

"You're the one, Steph. Cross my heart," he whispered.

Suddenly she flung herself into his arms and devoured his lips the same way he'd wanted to devour her but didn't, for fear of scaring her off. He held her to him, as if he'd just captured his missing half.

"You better mean it with all your heart," she murmured against his lips. "Don't forget I'm the one around here who can wield a meat cleaver. You don't want to know how many pieces I can carve you into if you're lying to me."

He chuckled as he nuzzled his forehead against hers. "And don't you forget that I'm the one who can rope and throw a calf in eight seconds flat. You try to make a run for it and I'll have you head-and-heeled and hogtied. Marry me, Steph. I need you like crazy. If we get the blood tests tomorrow we can be married after Thanksgiving."

She reared back in his arms, her eyes as wide as silver saucers. "After Thanksgiving? But there's guests to invite."

"Already invited," he confirmed.

"But I don't have anything to wear."

He grinned rakishly. "I've always liked it best when you're wearing nothing but me."

She swatted his shoulder and blushed. "Seriously."

"I'm not kidding around. That'd be my cousin Vance's forte."

"I'm still not going naked to my own wedding. Then there's the rehearsal dinner to organize."

"Dawn's got the meal planned and you surely have more sense than to argue with the head chef at the Palace."

"Flowers?" she asked, bewildered.

Quint smiled. "I ordered them while I was buying all those roses you viciously decapitated. Vance volunteered to cover that detail."

"Well, gee, I guess that doesn't leave much for me to do, does it?"

"Actually there's only one thing that's very necessary for you to do," he contended before he helped himself to another steamy kiss.

"What's that?" she wheezed when she came up for air.

"Tell me that you still love me," he murmured as he stared deeply into her eyes. He'd never wanted to hear a woman say those words more than he wanted to hear them from Steph, for this was the one time that really counted.

"You've heard that line for years, I'm sure," she replied impishly. "What can I possibly give a ladies' man that he hasn't had before... Hey!" Stephanie yelped when Quint abruptly scooped her off the ground, tossed her over his shoulder in a fireman's carry and stalked toward the house.

"Wicked woman! You're worse than all my cousins combined. Now you've done it. You've forced me to resort to another round of drastic measures," he said as he carried her up the steps and into the house.

"What are you going to do?" she asked as he toted her through the spacious living room that contained her furniture, as well as his. The room was crowded, she noted. Some of these things would definitely have to go. She hoped she wasn't one of them—ever.

"I'm going to torture you until you say the words," he told her on his way down the hall.

"So, you really *don't* have revolving doors to your room?" she noticed as he carried her across the threshold.

"Nope, never did. You should know better than to believe those wild rumors." He tossed her in the middle of the massive king-size bed that was covered with rose petals. "This is your bed of roses, Red. You snipped them off yourself and I'm not letting you out of here until you say the words I need to hear."

"You realize you're making me break every rule I have when it comes to men like you, don't you?"

He leaned down, bracing his sinewy arms on the edge of the bed. Offended, he peered at her from beneath jutting black brows. *"Men like me?"* he repeated ominously.

She nodded as she reached out to smooth away his frown. "You know, the wolf types who are only inter-

ested in a warm body, not the feelings and emotions attached to it.''

"Red," he said, "if you haven't figured out by now
that I need the whole package then I've done a lousy job
of getting my point across to you."

"Truth," she demanded, staring him squarely in the
eye. "What did you do with the cash you were paid to
seduce me?"

"I used it for the first installment on your engagement
ring because that seemed appropriate and fitting to me,"
he answered.

"And where is this supposed engagement ring now?"

"Burning a hole in my pocket," he informed her.

She studied his ruggedly handsome face, then asked,
"If we marry and I bubble up like a beached whale while
carrying our babies are you going to stray?"

"Nope, not a chance," he replied. "Next question."

"When I wake up in a lousy mood because of stress
or PMS are you going to walk? Take the path of least
resistance?"

"Nope," he said without hesitation. "Next question."

"Are you going to be here to help me raise our babies,
not saunter off to do your own thing and leave me holding a handful of dirty diapers?"

"Damn straight I'll be here," he confirmed earnestly.

"What if I don't want to get married at the post-
Thanksgiving ceremony you planned without my approval?" she challenged.

He had the decency to flinch, which assured her that
it had been desperation, not highhandedness that provoked him to back her into a corner. It suddenly dawned

on her that she should be immensely flattered that a former Casanova would voluntarily plan his own wedding, rather than being dragged, kicking and screaming, to it. He was proving to her that he was absolutely serious about making a commitment to her.

"Okay, we'll cancel it, if that's what you want," he said. "You name the time and place and I'm there. With a ring through my nose and bells on my toes, if that's what you want."

Stephanie pushed up to her knees and looped her arms around his neck. "Good, then I choose after T-day, too."

He flashed her a killer smile as he tumbled onto the bed with her wrapped in his arms. "Now then, Red, I want you out of your riding hood, PDQ. I want to get naked with you and practice making all those babies with silvery eyes and blazing hair."

"Amber eyes and jet-black hair," she contradicted as she tugged impatiently at his shirt.

"We'll compromise." He peeled off her blouse with swift efficiency. "A couple of each. How's that suit you?"

She tossed aside his shirt then kissed him for all she was worth. "Perfect...I love you like crazy, you know."

He suddenly went very still. His unblinking gaze bored into her like laser beams. "Do you mean that, Steph? For real? Not just because I whirlwinded you into this? Not just because you got caught up in the sex part and discovered you liked it?"

Stephanie's heart melted when it hit her like a bolt from the blue that Quint had a few insecurities she hadn't realized he possessed. She'd been too busy protecting her own insecurities to notice. He'd garnered a reputation as a playboy, and women wanted him because he was an incredible hunk of masculinity. But deep down inside where it counted he also wanted to be wanted and needed, just for *himself*. Not because he had a great bod, a terrific smile and a successful ranching business. Just because of the sum composite of heart, soul and conscience that made him who he was.

A sense of right and hopeful promise spilled through her as she stared at his expectant expression. She trusted this man with her heart. He gave her life and made her breathe. He made her feel whole, important and alive.

She looked into his soul and saw all the qualities she could admire for an eternity. He was as assertive and determined as she was. He was devoted and close to his family, just as she was. He anticipated the prospect of having a family of his own. He cared about his hometown and his neighbors, and he'd united the town to ensure her business didn't go under.

There was nothing superficial about Quint Ryder, even if he lived beneath the cloud of his reputation with women. And anyway, she'd heard it said that reformed playboys made exemplary hubbies—or something to that effect.

"Sure is taking you a long time to answer that question," he said uneasily. "Is this *for real* for you or not?"

Stephanie smiled at him and cuddled closer. "I was mentally listing all the reasons I love you. It's taking a while."

He arched a thick brow. "Yeah? You think I have redeeming qualities?"

"You mean...besides the hot, incredibly satisfying sex? Oh, most definitely," she assured him, eyes twinkling, lips twitching.

He slipped the engagement ring on her finger. When his head came steadily toward hers, Stephanie leaned toward him...but an unidentified thump and clatter from the front of the house sent them scrambling to their feet.

"What the hell?" Quint scowled as he made a grab for his discarded shirt.

"Quint, we're home! What's all this furniture doing here?"

"Damn, it's my folks! They weren't due until tomorrow." He snatched up Steph's blouse and tossed it to her. "I didn't plan this to embarrass you and force you into a shotgun wedding. *I swear,*" he said hurriedly.

She smiled as she buttoned herself into her blouse. The look on his face begged her to believe him and she wouldn't have disappointed him for the world.

"I believe you. Well, so much for a night of grand passion," she murmured as she placed her hand in his. "Let's go meet the folks, then maybe we can find time to do some necking on the new porch swing."

Quint hugged her close as he propelled her down the hall. "Thanks for being understanding. And there will definitely be some serious making out going on after we tuck my folks in bed for the night," he promised before he pasted on a smile and strode off to introduce Steph to his parents.

THE THANKSGIVING festivities and the wedding went off without a hitch. Steph got married in a dress that Idabelle had altered for the occasion. She didn't really mind because she didn't have a fetish for elaborate weddings and extravagant gowns that were worn only once. All she really wanted was a few minutes alone with Quint, but the reception hall at the church was still packed with guests who were gobbling up cake and punch as fast as Dawn could place it on the table.

Stephanie glanced curiously at Gage who cut through the reception line and leaned close. "Back door. Truck's waiting," he said in his best James Bond voice. "We booked you in a room under assumed names. Your luggage is waiting." He tucked a card in Quint's hand, as if discreetly exchanging some clandestine piece of information. "Now go."

Hand in hand, they ducked out the nearest exit. Quint chuckled when he bounded into the truck and looked at the address printed on the card. "My cousins must've assumed we didn't have the patience for a long drive."

Stephanie leaned over to stare at the card, then bubbled with laughter. "Gee, was I that obvious about wanting to get you all to myself so I could strip you down to your skin and have my way with you?"

"I figure they took their cue from me." Quint put the truck in gear and laid rubber. "In case you haven't noticed, I've been drooling over you all day, Mrs. Ryder."

When he veered into the driveway of Stephanie's former garage apartment, the place was lit up like a Christmas tree. Strings of colored lights dangled from the eaves. A neon sign that read *Do Not Disturb* blared in the front window.

"I'm going to have to kill that practical joker," Quint muttered. "Vance went too far this time."

"Kill him tomorrow. Tonight you're all mine," she declared as she hastily climbed down from the truck.

Quint opened the door to see his king-size bed—and nothing else—filling the living space. There was no waiting luggage, only a how-to sex manual resting on a red satin pillow. "I promise more respectable accommodations when we have time for an official honeymoon," Quint said as he closed the door. "And this—" he picked up the manual and pitched it over his shoulder "—we definitely don't need because we've already figured out how to do it right."

Stephanie strode over to the fridge to see that it had been filled with wine, a few beers and various foods reported to work as aphrodisiacs. Like she needed help in that department! Not hardly. But the practical joker and his mischievous cohorts had struck again.

Quint crossed his arms over his chest and braced himself against the wall. "I'll understand if you want to quit this place and go somewhere else. We can drive to Oklahoma City and be there in a couple of hours."

Stephanie sauntered over to unfasten his shirt, leaving his loosened tie draped around his neck. "This place is perfect for what I want to do with you," she murmured provocatively. "Last time you were here you made a hasty departure. You aren't getting off that easily tonight."

He arched a thick brow as she unfastened his pants and pushed them down his hips. His brow climbed even

higher when she divested him of his briefs. ''Is this another of those secret fantasies I didn't know about?''

''Nope, one in the making.'' She grabbed his tie and
led him back to the bed.

''Lose the dress, Steph. You aren't going to need it for
a couple of days,'' he growled, his golden eyes raking
her with hungry intent and crumbling patience.

Very slowly, very provocatively, she peeled off one
article of clothing at a time—until she was wearing nothing but an impish smile and the wedding and engagement
ring Quint had placed on her finger.

''Now, come here and let me love you for the rest of
our lives,'' he whispered, his heart in his eyes and a
promise of a bright future in his seductive smile.

Stephanie went to him eagerly. ''You know that adage
about being careful what you wish for because you just
might get it?''

''Mmm,'' he murmured, distracted.

''I don't think I'm going to have a problem with that,''
she said as her hands swept over his muscled flesh.

He chuckled naughtily and waggled his eyebrows.
''That's good because I gotta tell ya, Red Riding Hood,
I'm not going to have a problem with getting it, either.
So…are you about through talking?''

Stephanie roped her arms around his neck, nestled familiarly against him and smiled into his handsome face.
''All finished. Now, kiss me.''

''I thought you'd never ask.''

His mouth came down on her hers and he burned in
the fire and flames that Steph ignited in his soul.

Cousin Vance could play his practical jokes and

Cousin Gage could play his cloak-and-dagger games, if that's what they wanted. But Quint wanted nothing more than to join the ranks of the happily married and hopelessly devoted. Now the Ryder cousins were split in half—two married and two single. He wondered when Vance and Gage would cross to the other side and discover how much more fulfilling life was over here.

This, Quint decided, as love and passion sent him spiraling, was as good as it could get.

*   *   *   *   *

Watch for Vance and Gage's stories
in the next installment of

THE BACHELORS OF HOOT'S ROOST.

Coming soon only from
Carol Finch and Harlequin Duets.

COOPER'S CORNER

The newest continuity from Harlequin
Books continues in September 2002 with

AFTER DARKE
by *USA Today* bestselling author
Heather MacAllister

Check-in: A blind date goes from bad to worse for
small-town plumber Bonnie Cooper and city-bred columnist
Jaron Darke. When they witness a mob hit outside a
restaurant, they are forced to hide out at Twin Oaks.
Their cover: they're engaged!

Checkout: While forced to live together in close
quarters, these two opposites soon find one thing
in common: *passion!*

HARLEQUIN®
Makes any time special ®

Visit us at www.cooperscorner.com   CC-CNM2R

THE LIVING RECORD
OF A MAGNIFICENT EXPERIMENT

"The writers gathered here, without exception, write powerfully and meaningfully. There is development represented in the progression of these stories, exactly as there has been growth and change in the American society about which—and out of which—all of them were written.

"Each writer has been allowed only a single story: the aim has been not to portray the career of any writer, but the collective career of the pre-World War Two American story itself—its achievements, its history, and its constantly changing but always compelling face."

—from the Introduction by Burton Raffel

ABOUT THE EDITOR

BURTON RAFFEL is Professor of English at the University of Denver and an eminent poet and translator. The author of the recently published *How to Read a Poem*, he is now at work on *The Signet Classic Book of Contemporary American Short Stories*, a post-World War Two sequel to the present volume.

The
Signet Classic
Book of
American Short Stories

EDITED AND WITH AN
INTRODUCTION BY
Burton Raffel

A SIGNET CLASSIC

NEW AMERICAN LIBRARY

NEW YORK AND SCARBOROUGH, ONTARIO

Cover painting (detail), ''Babson and Ellery Houses, Gloucester,'' 1863 by Fitz Hugh Lane (1804–1865). Courtesy of the Cape Ann Historical Association, Gloucester, Mass.

Sherwood Anderson, ''Queer,'' from *Winesburg, Ohio* by Sherwood Anderson. Copyright © 1919 by B.W. Huebsch. Copyright renewed © 1947 by Eleanor Copenhaver Anderson. Reprinted by permission of Viking Penguin Inc.

Stephen Vincent Benet, ''The King of the Cats,'' copyright © 1929, copyright renewed © 1957 by Rosemary Carr Benet. Reprinted by permission of Brandt & Brandt Literary Agents, Inc.

Willa Cather, ''Neighbour Rosicky.'' Copyright © 1932 by Willa Cather and renewed © 1960 by the Executors of the Estate of Willa Cather. Reprinted from *Obscure Destinies*, by Willa Cather, by permission of Alfred A. Knopf.

John Dos Passos, ''Great Lady on a White Horse,'' from *Manhattan Transfer* by John Dos Passos. Copyright © 1925, copyright renewed © 1953 by John Dos Passos. Reprinted by permission of Elizabeth Dos Passos.

William Faulkner, ''Turnabout.'' Copyright © 1932 and renewed © 1960 by Curtis Publishing Co. Reprinted from *Collected Stories of William Faulkner* by permission of Random House, Inc.

F. Scott Fitzgerald, ''The Long Way Out,'' copyright © 1937 Esquire-Coronet, Inc; copyright renewed © 1965 Frances Scott Fitzgerald Lanahan. From *The Stories of F. Scott Fitzgerald*, Malcolm Cowley, Editor. Reprinted with the permission of Charles Scribner's Sons.

Ernest Hemingway, ''Up in Michigan,'' from *The Short Stories of Ernest Hemingway*. Copyright © 1938 by Ernest Hemingway; copyright renewed © 1966 Mary Hemingway. Reprinted with the permission of Charles Scribner's Sons.

James Thurber, ''The Evening's at Seven,'' copyright © 1935 by James Thurber, copyright © 1963 by Helen W. Thurber and Rosemary T. Sauers. From *The Middle-Aged Man on the Flying Trapeze*, published by Harper & Row.

SIGNET, SIGNET CLASSIC, MENTOR, PLUME, MERIDIAN AND NAL BOOKS are published *in the United States* by New American Library, 1633 Broadway, New York, New York 10019, *in Canada* by The New American Library of Canada Limited, 81 Mack Avenue, Scarborough, Ontario M1L 1M8

First Printing, February, 1985

4   5   6   7   8   9

PRINTED IN THE UNITED STATES OF AMERICA

CONTENTS

INTRODUCTION

Story-telling is surely one of the oldest of arts. "There never was a land in which stories did not exist," wrote Robert K. Douglas in 1892, explaining in the introduction to a collection of Chinese stories just why it was safe to assume that, in that land as in all others, "stories have been current from all time." Literally everyone tells stories, and probably always has. It is a plain and an undeniable truism that "story-telling is a broadly popular art," as the Italian novelist and critic P.M. Pasinetti noted in 1959, introducing yet another collection of tales out of yet another nation's narrative heritage.

But stories as a literary form and stories as oral narrative are at best distant cousins. And the reasonably distinct literary form—indeed, essentially a literary genre by now—which we call the "short story" is still more distantly connected to its popular origins. The "short story" as we now know it is at most two hundred years old. It is a completely literate form, a written form, and a prose form—and, as all historians of culture know, prose forms do not develop first, or even early, in any human civilization. Poetry is universal, and without exception takes chronological precedence. Prose is not at all universal, and, when it develops, comes only relatively late in a culture's history.

The "short story," furthermore, is even more narrowly defined. It portrays a character or characters of some degree of definiteness, involved in a narrative sequence (a plot) that, in the nineteenth century, was required to be reasonably clear; in the twentieth century such clarity is frequently blurred almost to the disappearing point. In short stories of well-defined plot, too, there is usually (though not necessarily) some resolution of plot complexities; this resolution is usually tied, and quite plainly tied, to the development of individual characters, and in particular to the problems of those characters. It is not quite so true of the short story as it is of the novel that, in the customary formula, character gives rise to plot, but it is often very nearly as true.

But perhaps the most notable characteristic of the short story as a form, though at first blush it hardly seems even significant, let alone controlling, is that a short story must be the sort of prose work which readers of magazines that regularly print "short stories" can expect to find in the pages of those magazines. This may seem an impossibly vague standard; in fact it is neither abstract nor, in practice, at all vague. For almost two hundred years magazine readers—and by now many literary critics as well—have spoken of short stories in terms of classifications that depend, and exclusively depend, on the name of the magazine in which those stories appeared. We commonly speak of "New Yorker" stories, and without further definition know exactly what we mean. So, too, we speak of "Redbook" stories, and once spoke of "Harper's" stories; we also speak of "little magazine" stories, and "pulp" stories, and "slick" stories, and so on. The common denominator, obviously, is the nature of the magazine. But the underlying common denominator affecting all these variously labeled varieties is the central fact of magazine publication. The short story as we know it, in truth, is a creature of modern printing, modern literacy, relatively inexpensive paper manufacture, modern distribution techniques, the large population concentrations of modern nations, and—for most of the form's existence—the absence of such overwhelmingly competitive entertainment sources as radio, movies, and television.

The Signet Classic Book of American Short Stories deals with the short story (which from this point on I shall call simply the story) as it has grown and flourished in the United States, from early in the nineteenth century to the outbreak of World War Two. (A second volume is entitled *The Signet Classic Book of Contemporary Short Stories*.) Almost alone among American art forms, in literature or elsewhere, the story was neither hopelessly derivative nor essentially a non-native creation. The modern story as it developed in other countries, England and France especially, came into being at more or less the same time as the American story, and for essentially the same reasons. There were influences back and forth, to be sure, as there always are; in time, the great story writers of each and every country came to have their natural and even inevitable effect on writers in other countries. But it was uniquely an even start—a race in which Americans began at much the same point as did the writers of other countries. Indeed, they even began with certain advantages, advantages which resulted in American story writers actually having important formative influences on European and British story writers, instead of the more usual situation in which we were borrowers, fifty years or so behind and struggling to catch up. In music, in all the visual and plastic arts, we were followers, not leaders. Our painters and our sculptors studied in Europe, and in England, until and even well into the twentieth century. So too did our musicians: not until after World War Two did American music stand fully on its own feet. We were, from the beginning, a growing nation, and until quite recently a very rapidly growing nation. But, for at least the first century of our growth, we were leaders in very little, and followers in almost everything—except, in the arts, as the writers of powerful, pioneering, deeply influential stories, read and imitated wherever printed literature was known and valued.

First of all, there were the American magazines, and their early analogues and predecessors, the "annuals." As early as the second decade of the nineteenth century, records Fred Lewis Pattee in *The Development of the American Short Story*, writers "published what in reality were little magazines of the modern type, pamphlet miscellanies issued at irregular periods . . . [and] continued as long as material held out or . . . the work succeeded." One form of such early little magazine, the "annual," was a bound volume, structurally a book but in purpose and nature much more a periodical. This form of printing and distribution for collections of short, magazine-style literature had originated in Europe and been quickly taken over here in the United States. Coming some twenty or thirty years before the establishment of the truly national magazines, the annuals proved eminently successful, making money for both their publishers and their contributors. (Christmas annuals, sometimes very elaborately gotten up, were especially remunerative.) These annuals "came at a critical moment," notes Pattee, "and their coming more than any other single influence determined the direction American literature was to go. . . . Almost every writer of the period from [N.P.] Willis to Edward Everett Hale [author of "The Man Without a Country"] at one time or another in his career was the editor of at least one of these [annuals]." Not simply a contributor, let me emphasize, but an editor: writers were not at all passive in the development and spread of the annual, any more than, later in the nineteenth century, they were merely passive contributors to magazines run by and for others. William Dean Howells, to mention an outstanding example, was as well known as an editor

as he was as a writer; William Cullen Bryant was perhaps better
known as an editor, Walt Whitman was an editor long before he
was even thought of as a poet, Ralph Waldo Emerson was the
principal founder of *The Dial*, and many others, some now
forgotten, some still read, served as reporters and editors and
even as publishers.

The economics of the rapidly changing, rapidly expanding
magazine field were of course crucial. Amateur writers may
work for an abstract love of literature; some of them may do
first-rate things in that cause. But professionals work for financial reward, trying when they can to live by as well as for their
pens. Samuel Johnson, that quintessential professional, said pithily
that "No man but a blockhead ever wrote except for money."
And it is professionals, not amateurs, who create the dominant
literary environment. The annuals not only paid handsomely, but
they demanded native themes, and they preferred to have those
themes handled by native authors. That is, not only did the
flourishing American annuals make it possible for professionals
to be professional, and in part to subsist as professionals, but
they had a clear enough sense of their market to provide readers
with American rather than with warmed-over foreign material.
As a training ground for writers, accordingly, as well as a
forerunner of the national magazines, the annuals were of critical
importance. They were perhaps equally important, too, as trainers
of their audiences, demonstrating in the most positive and encouraging way that there were American writers who could address
the needs and concerns of readers.

This is not the place for a history of American magazines. It is
important to note, however, that by 1833, the *Knickerbocker*,
published in New York City, had established itself as the first
truly popular monthly magazine. (It endured until 1865.) It
published the best of New York's writers, of course, but as
Frank Luther Mott notes in his *A History of American Magazines*
it published many Boston writers, too, and writers from the
South and even from the West. By 1841, Philadelphia had given
birth to *Graham's Magazine*, the literary editor of which from
1841–1842 was Edgar Allan Poe. *Graham's* gave the *Knickerbocker*
a good run for its money, publishing such writers as Longfellow,
Bryant, Lowell, and Cooper. By the second year of its existence,
Graham's had acquired a circulation of 40,000; not surprisingly,
it paid its contributors well. So too did *Godey's Lady's Book*,
founded in Philadelphia in 1830. By the late 1850s it set a record for
nineteenth-century women's magazines, reaching a monthly circula-

tion of 150,000. *Godey's Lady's Book* featured stories and poems by a great many well known American writers of the time.

Mott lists and describes a good many other magazines, including "the most famous southern magazine of these years," the *Southern Literary Messenger* (1834–64), edited by Poe in 1835–1837. And he concludes, most importantly for our purposes, with a reference to *Harper's Monthly*, "which introduced a new and highly successful formula into the business of magazine publishing." This formula was based largely on the pirating of popular English work; "after a few years many American contributors were introduced, [though] the serials [that is, the long tales which ran for many issues, sometimes for longer than a calendar year] were chiefly English for many years." The magazine had "a circulation of 200,000 before the Civil War, placing it far ahead of any other monthly magazine in the world." Again, let me underline the centrally important facts: the huge circulation was attained even before the Civil War, and it was huge not simply for the United States but for the entire world. In the early 1850s, *Harper's* itself announced with obvious pride that "Literature has gone in pursuit of the million, penetrated highways and hedges, pressed its way into cottages, factories, omnibuses, and railroad cars, and become the most cosmopolitan thing of the century." By 1873, *The Atlantic* was able to offer the sensational new writer, Bret Harte, a flat fee of $10,000—a large sum even today, but in those years truly immense—for a dozen contributions of any sort and of any length.

There is, of, course another side to this account of expansion and economic opportunity. He who pays the piper also calls the tune. William Charvat notes, in *The Profession of Authorship in America, 1800–1870*, how naïve it is to criticize such writers as Henry James and William Dean Howells without taking the trouble to understand that much of their work appeared serially. Episodes had to be designed for the space made available, month by month, in particular magazines. And the tastes of the readers of those magazines, and the editors too, had to be taken into account. Charvat has examined a good deal of the correspondence between writers and editors in these years, correspondence which has, as yet, not been published. He reports that it is often quarrelsome, often bitter. Speaking of Nathaniel Hawthorne, whose stories often seem to modern critics to over-explain themselves, Charvat emphasizes that magazine and annual readers demanded such heavy-handed, verbose passages: Hawthorne had little choice but to supply what was required. The work paid well; writers could earn respect in our money-conscious society by the increasingly respectable sums they could earn by their pens. It was useful not to be condescended to, not to be seen as superfluous, silly, "useless" (because non-profitable)—mere artists. But there was a price to be paid, and that price is still reflected, often, in what American writers wrote.

The economic and social context in which American writers lived and worked needs to be at least briefly detailed. James D. Hart's *The Popular Book: A History of America's Literary Taste*, provides some useful social contexts.

> Financial and cultural extremes [in the 1850s] were tremendous but they tended to melt at either end into the large, fluid body called the middle class. . . . It was also the ruling class. Aware of its social responsibilities, it extended the principle of public education so that, at least in the North, free education through high school began to be fairly common.

By 1870 there were 16,000 who successfully graduated from high school (56% being women); the percentage of literacy in that year was roughly 80%. By 1880 there were 24,000 high school graduates, and by 1890 and 1900 there were, respectively, 44,000 and 95,000 (fully 60% of this latter figure being women). Hart continues:

> The middle class established or supported libraries to which mechanics of the working class might turn for edification. It trebled the number of subscription libraries between 1825 and 1850. It sponsored lyceums, which by the 'forties numbered into the thousands, bringing men and women face to face with the speakers and writers who represented the great cultural guides of the middle class itself. Its inventive genius and money-making interest created machine-made paper and printing presses that turned out thousands and thousands of impressions an hour.

A Southern critic observed, at the time, that "The almost universal ability to read and the consequent love of reading have developed in this nation especially an immense middle class of ordinary readers of average intelligence," four-fifths of them, significantly, women.

II

The quality of American stories naturally varied: this was equally true elsewhere. Much that was written, and much that found its way into print, is eminently forgettable and has quite properly been forgotten. Turning the pages of nineteenth-century magazines is usually at best an amusing, at worst a depressing affair. (The prose is at least readable: much of the poetry is awful almost beyond belief and has to be experienced to be truly appreciated.) From a historical perspective, the sentimental, didactic, cloyingly proper and patriotic effusions of many then popular writers are invaluable: they point straight and true at the very heart of then prevalent attitudes. Better writers are harder to decipher, for they embody both more and also more original thought, fresher feeling, a freer imagination and, usually, prose that is considerably more expressive in its own right. However, "only the cynic and the heedless can disregard popular literature," observes Mott in *Golden Multitudes: The Story of Best Sellers in the United States*. "Here the sociologist finds material for his inquiries into the mores, the social historian sees the sign-posts of the development of a people, and students of government observe popular movements at work."

But much that has been forgotten does not deserve oblivion; some that has been forgotten is arguably as good and, in a few cases, perhaps even better than what has survived, what has endured as part of the received canon of American literature, still read, still taken seriously, still discussed by critics and other literary observers. This is, as I indicated a moment ago, truer by far of prose fiction (novels too, though they form no part of this book's scope) than it is of poetry. Nineteenth-century Americans wrote extremely well, on the whole; remarkably few published writers display what might be called genuinely bad style, and surprisingly many write with an ease, a concision, and a practiced exactness that twentieth-century America has to some extent lost (including, alas, some twentieth-century American writers). But the merits of such writers as Bayard Taylor, Rose Terry Cooke, Grace Elizabeth King, and F. Hopkinson Smith are in no sense merely stylistic or narrowly formal. Their literary standards are not precisely ours—but then, do we fully share Hawthorne's, or Poe's, or even Mark Twain's literary standards? Social values, too, are often different from what ours have become over the years. But these are powerful writers, working honestly with material that was important to their time and to which we, in this very different time, can still largely respond. We can learn from their stories too, how they felt and thought and even talked.

Famous and unfamous alike, American writers of stories worked diligently and often brilliantly at their trade. They were part of a larger authorial fraternity, active especially but not exclusively in England and in France, who in a very few years created the story form as we know it. Stories were casual matters, for the most part, before the nineteenth century, offshoots of a writer's momentarily diverted pen—splinters, as it were, from a workshop devoted to more important things. (I suspect that an interesting argument might be made that before the nineteenth century the story was much closer to the essay than it was to the novel. Consider the essays of Addison and of Steele, those of Samuel Johnson and, a bit later on, those of Charles Lamb.) Nor was the story of any large economic importance. There were few places where a writer could publish stories, few readers to write them for. But just as the invention of the fortepiano revolutionized the writing of keyboard music, and the invention of the commercially reproducible lithograph revolutionized the art of illustration, so, too, the rise of a mass audience of magazine readers necessarily revolutionized writers' approaches to and attitudes toward stories.

It would be hard to take the form more seriously than Poe did. Poetry was to him "the Faculty of Ideality—which is the sentiment of Poesy. This sentiment is the sense of the beautiful, of the sublime, and of the mystical. . . . Poesy is the sentiment of Intellectual Happiness here, and the Hope of a higher Intellectual Happiness hereafter." And yet, valuing poetry as he did, Poe could still declare in a review of Hawthorne's *Twice-Told Tales* that "We have always regarded the *Tale* . . . as affording the best prose opportunity for display of the highest talent." Indeed, he goes a good deal farther: the tale, he asserts, "has peculiar advantages which the novel does not admit. It is, of course, a far finer field than the essay. *It has even points of superiority over the poem*" [italics added]. Greater praise would be hard to imagine, from so star-struck an addict of "poesy." But what Poe principally brought to the story form in America had precious little to do with Ideality or Intellectual Happiness, or even with the subject matter of his romantic and frequently grotesque fictions. Poe was above all a craftsman, and significantly more expert in his prose than in his poetry; his standards were high and readily apprehendable:

Pen should never touch paper, until at least a well-digested *general* purpose be established. In fiction the denouement . . . should be definitely considered and arranged, before writing the first word; and *no* word should be then written which does not tend, or form a part of a sentence which tends to the development of the *denouement* or to the strengthening of the effect.

The standard was so very high, so tautly craftsmanlike in its entire vision, that Poe could declare that if "the very first sentence tend not to the outbringing of this [preconceived] effect, then [the writer] has failed in his first step." Final judgment of a story, in Poe's terms, has little or nothing to do with subject or even with treatment; it is all an issue of craft. "The true critic will but demand that the design intended be accomplished, to the fullest extent, by the means most advantageously applicable." So utterly rational and objective a standard is, to be sure, exaggerated—but not nearly so exaggerated as when applied by Poe to his or to others' poetry. Prose fiction is in truth more rational, more fully conscious and more deliberate than is poetry. What Poe demanded, therefore, could actually be realized; it was plainly possible for stories to have something like the tight, carefully planned structure he required. Novels were "objectionable," because of their length. "As [a novel] cannot be read at one sitting, it deprives itself, of course, of the immense force derivable from *totality*." But a story places "the soul of the reader . . . at the writer's control," if, that is, the writer knows what he is doing. "There are," Poe insisted, "no external or extrinsic influences—[whether] resulting from weariness or interruption."

So committed and clear a standard, joined to so deft and powerful an application of that standard in his own stories, could not but be influential. Hawthorne, for example, who labeled Poe one of "the obnoxious class of critics," and told him in a letter that "I admire you rather as a writer of tales than as a critic upon them," also responded to a third-party request for publishable material, being gathered by Poe for a projected magazine, by noting that "If I am to send anything to Mr. Poe, I should wish it to be worth his reception." (One of Hawthorne's recent biographers, James R. Mellow, notes that "Poe was among the keenest and most widely read critics of his time.") Hawthorne was not satisfied with the bulk of his own stories: "they have," he wrote, "the pale tint of flowers that blossomed

in too retired a shade.'' But his standards, too, though a great
deal more modestly expressed than Poe's, were extremely high.
''The author,'' he wrote laconically in his preface to *The Marble
Faun*, ''proposed to himself merely to write a fanciful story,
evolving a thoughtful moral . . .'' Writing to a friend, however,
who contemplated the production of some travel writing, he
shows distinctly Poe-like, detailed, passionate devotion to his
craft.

> If you meet with any distinguished characters, give
> personal sketches of them. Begin to write always before the
> impression of novelty has worn off your mind; else you will
> begin to think that the peculiarities which at first attracted
> you, are not worth recording.

And he insists: ''Think nothing too trifling to write down, so it
be in the smallest degree characteristic.'' The American critic
Paul Elmer More was sure that ''If Hawthorne and Poe, as we
think, possess an element of force and realism . . . it is because
they write from the depths of [the] profound moral experience of
their people.'' Whether we trace that ''force'' to the underlying
standards according to the light of which Hawthorne and Poe
wrote their stories, or to the sheer power and appeal of the
stories themselves, or to some combination thereof, it remains
clear that American story-writing had, at its effective start, two
immensely important exemplars, inventive, imaginative, and above
all sharply aware that the untethered, uncontrolled, unmastered
pen simply could not accomplish what needed doing. ''In very
great degree,'' Poe noted, truth is ''the aim of the tale.'' But no
less a commentator than the great French poet, Charles Baudelaire
(whose volume of translations from Poe, *Histoires Extraordinaires*,
did a great deal to spread the American's reputation far beyond
his native shores), saw the essentially craftsmanlike center of
Poe's work:

> Above all, he [Poe] was sensitive to the degree of
> perfection in the structure, and to formal correction. He
> would take literary works to pieces like a defective mecha-
> nism (defective, that is, in relation to its avowed aims),
> noting carefully the faults in manufacture; and, when he
> came to examine a work in detail, in its plastic form or, in a
> word, its style, he would, without omitting anything, sift
> the errors . . . , the grammatical mistakes, and all that

mass of surface scum which, in writers who are not artists, spoils the best intentions and distorts the most noble conceptions.

Washington Irving is a graceful and an important writer; his worldwide fame made many things possible for those who came after him. But Poe and Hawthorne are the true beginning of the American short story; it bears their mark, individually and jointly, for a great many years, and in nothing less than in the striving of other writers to match the intensity, the impact, which these early masters achieved. "Hawthorne had presented tales of intense moral situations," writes Pattee, "and had added a symbolism all his own; and Poe had added impressionism and 'unity and totality of effect.' " But the story form had barely begun to explore its possibilities. From their younger contemporary, Herman Melville, through a large number of nineteenth-century writers, the story form continued to grow, to expand. In the hundred years from Melville's "Bartleby the Scrivener," in 1853, to the stories of James Thurber and William Saroyan, the form became the complex, richly varied, sophisticated and wonderfully adaptable genre we know today.

And it is a vast distance to have traveled in so relatively short a time. (The novel did not grow to maturity so rapidly.) It was pressured growth, often so rapid and tumbling that the sense of what was happening seemed at least partially lost. There was economic pressure, especially in the golden years preceding World War Two, when large sums could be and often were made by a great many practitioners of the form. There was pressure from abroad, too, as masters of the form arose not only in England and France, but also in Germany, in Italy, in Spain, and then in Russia and in Scandinavia and eventually in the Far East, and Africa, and everywhere one looked. The challenge was great; the possibilities were multiple and ever-changing; and throughout this whirlwind period, lasting roughly from the Civil War to World War Two, American writers of stories were continuously in the forefront.

The story was (and still is) more of an international form than the novel, and easily as international a form as the drama. We cannot allow ourselves to forget that American story writers were part of a worldwide nexus of writers, a nexus active, prolific, and mercurial, out of which innovations and experiments continue to this day to pour into print. Today the story no longer occupies as central a literary position as it once did. But rumors

of its demise are totally unfounded: it is alive and well all over
the world, and in America not least of all.

American story writers enjoyed one as yet unstated but enormously important advantage through most of the years up to,
including, and, for a period, even after World War Two. The
form was in constant but on the whole healthy turmoil: it was
growing, changing, evolving. So too, taken all in all, was the
United States; no country in the world was experiencing such
rates of growth, in virtually all aspects of national life. The land
area of the United States in 1800 was 865,000 square miles; by
1860, it was just under 3,000,000 square miles. The population
in 1800 was just over 5,000,000; by 1860 it was over 31,000,000
and by 1900 it was 76,000,000. The Gross National Product for
1869, the first year of available statistics, is roughly one-third of
what the G.N.P. had risen to by 1900. Forty miles of railroad
track were laid down in 1830; in 1900 there were just under
5,000 miles of railroad track built. Fifty-six thousand postage
stamps had been sold in 1853 in the entire country; by 1900, that
had risen to a whisker under 4,000,000. We exported 107 million dollars of goods and services in 1800; by 1860, the figure
was 438 million dollars, and by 1900, it was a billion six
hundred and eighty-six million. We produced just over half a
billion short-tons of steel in 1876; by 1900, the total was well
over eleven billion short-tons. These statistical comparisons document only one part of the vast, brawling growth being experienced by the United States. Just as important for the arts, was
the sense which pervaded the American psyche in these same
years, the conviction that virtually anything was possible, the
belief that America's destiny was greater and more shining (and
rather more virtuous to boot) than the destiny of any nation ever
known on the face of the earth. What other country could have
produced, late in the nineteenth century, that ebullient bundle of
energy and high-powered moral rhetoric, Theodore Roosevelt?
There were dissenting voices, and more and more of them as the
Victorian era moved rapidly towards its brutal close in World
War One. But the country as a whole, and many (if not most) of
the writers, remained in the grip of an ever-expanding, ever-
improving, ever-victorious and triumphantly moral mind-set.
"America the Beautiful" was not simply a song; "God's Country"
had been created, and had prospered, and in ways religious,
political, and economic was serving as an example—God's own
example—to those of lesser nations or older nations or nations
that were inferior morally if not in more blatant ways.

How could American writers not be affected by these massive currents of thought and feeling, sustained as these currents were, in their turn, by even more massive and momentous developments in business and industry and government? And writers of stories, in particular, working in a form that because of its immediacy was peculiarly open to shifting social patterns, could not but be swept along and buoyed by what the nation as a whole was experiencing. In other literary forms, like drama and verse, this was not a time of progress, nor a time of experimentation. Drama was still hopelessly imitative of older European models. Poetry had reached the bland heights of Longfellow, Holmes, Whittier, and Lowell, and was soon to descend into the petty banality of the "Genteel" school that followed these early masters. The magnificent experiments of Walt Whitman and of Emily Dickinson were, in the one case, very little known and, in the other, almost totally unknown; Whitman and Dickinson were as yet basically esoteric developments, neither important nor in any serious way influential. There were important developments in the novel, to be sure, but that genre was still more attuned to foreign than it was to domestic forces. Cooper had begun the emancipation of the American novel, a cause in which Hawthorne and Melville too had enlisted. But it was only with Mark Twain that emancipation of the American novel began to solidify, and even by the time of Henry James's death, in 1916, the process was arguably not quite complete. The generation of Ernest Hemingway and F. Scott Fitzgerald still looked in some degree to Europe for their validation, despite the native advances staked out by Theodore Dreiser and Sinclair Lewis and Sherwood Anderson. We have been fully independent, in the novel, for perhaps fifty or sixty years at most. In the story form, however, we have been independent for something more like a hundred and fifty years.

If we attempt to classify the stories in this volume, some startlingly clear trends emerge. Four chief categories suggest themselves; they are not quite the categories used in the bulk of the critical literature, nor are they categories that would be viable for the analysis of other forms, for the novel, the drama, or for poetry. The largest and most obvious polarity is between what might be called Realist and what might be called Romantic. By "realist" I mean no more than a primary concern with reflecting things as in the opinion of the writer they seem to be. By "romantic" I mean no more than a primary concern with things as in some idealized conception they ought to be. There are realistic elements in even the most romantic of stories, just as there are romantic elements in many realistic stories; some writers, indeed, like Mark Twain, seem to fit comfortably in neither category. The third and fourth of my classifications are in no sense polarities: in fact, all of the stories I find myself listing either under "Satiric" or under "Polemic" are also, perforce, listed under other categories as well (most often as Realist).

I do not take these classifications terribly seriously, neither as to the categories employed nor as to the rubrics under which particular stories seem to me to fit. But the broad parameters do seem to be representative. Roughly two-thirds of the stories here printed (the stories rather than their authors, let me emphasize) fall into the loose category of Realist. Roughly one-third fall into the loose category of Romantic. Barely six per cent are labeled Satiric, just over fifteen per cent are labeled Polemic, but no story falls into either of these latter categories without also being listed under one of the two chief classifications. Again, the precise details are much less important than the broad picture that emerges, namely, a short story literature heavily realistic, but polarized by an almost equally strong romantic tradition. Neither satire nor polemics, though clearly present and reasonably well accounted for, would appear to represent dominant traditions. Other categories would make for differing results, even with this same group of stories, but not I think seriously differing ones. By and large, this is indeed what the tradition of the American story looks like, in its broad outlines.

And this was precisely how late nineteenth-century combatants, writers and critics alike, drew the battle lines. William Dean Howells, perhaps the closest thing to a literary "czar" of Samuel Johnson-like proportions this country has ever known, referred mockingly to "the foolish old superstition that literature and art are anything but the expression of life, and are to be judged by any other test than that of their fidelity to it." Howells was convinced that:

> in the whole range of fiction we know of no true picture of life—that is, of human nature—which is not also a masterpiece of literature, full of divine and natural beauty. . . . It is the conception of literature as something apart from life, superfinely aloof, which makes it really unimportant to the great mass of mankind, without a message or a meaning for them; and it is the notion that a novel may be false in its portrayal of causes and effects that makes literary

art contemptible even to those whom it amuses, that forbids them to regard the novelist as a serious or right-minded person.

Indeed, Howells argues that for his time realism was making exactly the same fight against decadence and frivolity that,

> at the beginning of the [nineteenth] century, . . . romance was making . . . against effete classicism . . . The romantic of that day and the real[ist] of this are in a certain degree the same. Romanticism then sought, as realism seeks now, to widen the bounds of sympathy, to level every barrier against aesthetic freedom, to escape from the paralysis of tradition. [Romanticism] exhausted itself in this impulse; and . . . when realism becomes false to itself, when it heaps up facts merely, and maps life instead of picturing it, realism will perish too.

It was hardly a new quarrel in American letters. "When a writer calls his work a Romance," Hawthorne wrote in the preface to *The House of the Seven Gables* (1851), a book he carefully subtitled "a Romance,"

> it need hardly be observed that he wishes to claim a certain latitude, both as to fashion and material, which he would not have felt himself entitled to assume had he professed to be writing a Novel. The latter form of composition is presumed to aim at a very minute fidelity, not merely to the possible, but to the probable and ordinary course of man's experience. . . . [And this writer] would be glad . . . if . . . the book may be read strictly as a Romance, having a great deal more to do with the clouds overhead than with any portion of the actual soil of the County of Essex.

In his preface to *The Blithedale Romance* (1852), similarly, Hawthorne speaks of wanting "merely to establish a theatre . . . where the creatures of [my] brain may play their phantasmagorical antics, without exposing them to too close a comparison with the actual events of real lives.

The romantic-realist controversy no longer seems to us controversial. For one thing, we have thoroughly settled the issue, in our own time, by totally amalgamating the two sides: the novel is neither fiercely realistic nor fiercely romantic, but any imaginable combination of both approaches—with an admixture, furthermore, of fantasy, surrealism, or minimalism. But it was a controversy of great importance in the era of Henry James and Howells and Frank Norris, just as it was of vital importance to Hawthorne and Melville. "In this world of lies," Melville exclaimed, "Truth is forced to fly like a scared white doe in the woodlands; and only by cunning glimpses will she reveal herself, as in Shakespeare and other masters of the great Art of Telling the Truth,—even though it be covertly and by snatches." The periphrastic coloring is typical of Melville, who believed that "an author can never—under no conceivable circumstances—be at all frank with his readers" (an opinion which he ventured to express, equally typically, in a private letter rather than in public print). That wildest of novels, *Moby Dick*, is exactly such a fevered blend of stark realism and sheer fantasy, of straightforward psychological verity and hothouse imaginings. And though he could not and indeed did not want to resolve the implicit dichotomies of this marvelous, brilliant, and deeply flawed book, Melville was sharply aware of his predicament, balanced forever uneasily between two extremes, and simultaneously indulging himself in both. "It will be a strange sort of a book," he predicted even before he had finished writing *Moby Dick*. "Blubber is blubber you know; tho' you may get oil out of it, the poetry runs as hard as sap from a frozen maple tree;—& to cook the thing up, one must needs throw in a little fancy, which from the nature of the thing, must be ungainly as the gambols of the whales themselves. Yet I mean to give the truth of the thing, spite of this."

It is easy to see how "Telling the Truth," in Melville's words, applies in the local-color realism of Harriet Beecher Stowe. In "Miss Asphyxia," published in 1869, she describes domestic activity in such clear and plainly accurate detail that a latterday sociologist might safely rely on its verisimilitude.

> Miss Asphyxia raked open the fire in the great kitchen chimney, and built it up with a liberal supply of wood; then she rattled into the back room, and a sound was heard of a bucket descending into a well with such frantic haste as only an oaken bucket under Miss Asphyxia's hands could be frightened into. Back she came with a stout black iron tea-kettle, which she hung over the fire; and then, flopping down a ham on the table, she cut off slices with a martial and determined air, as if she would like to see the ham try

to help itself; and, before the child could fairly see what she was doing, the slices of ham were in the frying-pan over the coals, the ham hung up in its place, the knife wiped and put out of sight, and the table drawn out into the middle of the floor, and invested with a cloth for dinner.

Twenty years later, Hamlin Garland's "The Return of a Private" has passages of the same sort:

> The station was deserted, chill, and dark, as they came into it at exactly a quarter to two in the morning. Lit by the oil lamps that flared a dull red light over dingy benches, the waiting room was not an inviting place. . . . Smith was attended to tenderly by the other men, who spread their blankets on the bench for him, and, by robbing themselves, made quite a comfortable bed, though the narrowness of the bench made his sleeping precarious.

Yet there are equally plainly elements of romanticism in both stories, and even in the passages just quoted. Both the bucket and the ham are personified and almost mythicized, in the Stowe tale. The child's wonder, too, is invested with a fairy-tale-like quality, as Miss Asphyxia herself is made to seem, at least in part, like some witch out of "Hansel and Gretel." Garland is more consciously and determinedly a realist, but even he adds touches like the "tender" way in which Smith is cared for, or the fact that the other men in caring for Smith have "robbed" themselves—touches that show, as the rest of the story shows still more clearly, that Garland is by no means so dedicated and absolute a realist as either he or some of his critics have fancied.

Indeed, the blending of realism and romanticism never stopped, no matter whose fiction we look at. Many of the most romantic writers have deeply realistic aspects; many of the most implacable realists are brushed with large streaks of romanticism. And there were writers who understood that neither side of the controversy could or should have undisputed sway over the other. Henry James, though a close friend of Howells and so devoted an admirer of Hawthorne that he wrote a critical book about him, was no controversialist when it came to romantic-realist dichotomies. He did say of Hawthorne's *The Scarlet Letter* that "The faults of the book are, to my sense, a want of reality and an abuse of the fanciful element—of a certain superficial symbolism." But this is hardly polemical, and James means these comments to serve as a way of highlighting what he calls "the passionless quality of Hawthorne's novel, its element of cold and ingenious fantasy, . . . the absence of a certain something warm and straightforward . . ." James may lean toward the realist side, but his is far too catholic, far too balanced an approach to set out formulae, as Howells does, the violation of which will produce fiction of an unacceptable sort. As James puts it:

> It goes without saying that you will not write a good novel [or story] unless you possess the sense of reality; but it will be difficult to give you a recipe for calling that sense into being. Humanity is immense, and reality has a myriad forms; the most one can affirm is that some of the flowers of fiction have the odor of it, and others have not; as for telling you in advance how your nosegay should be composed, that is another affair. . . . The only obligation to which in advance we may hold a novel [or story], without incurring the accusation of being arbitrary, is that it be interesting. That general responsibility rests upon it, but it is the only one I can think of.

Indeed, the dichotomy James is willing to make, and the only dichotomy, is that "between a good novel [or story] and a bad one." For the rest, fiction "is in its broadest definition a personal, a direct impression of life: that, to begin with, constitutes its value, which is greater or less according to the intensity of the impression." The advice James is willing to give writers, accordingly, is broad-ranging and of necessity general: "Try to be one of the people on whom nothing is lost!" Bluntly, he declares, "I can think of no obligation to which the 'romancer' would not be held equally with the novelist; the standard of execution is equally high for each." James recognizes that there are two different approaches; what he always returns to, however, is the insistent claim that "it is of execution [rather than theory] that we are talking." That, he emphasizes, is "the only point . . . open to contention." In short, "the deepest quality of a work of art will always be the quality of the mind of the producer. In proportion as that intelligence is fine will the novel, [the story], the picture, the statue partake of the substance of beauty and truth. To be constituted of such elements is, to my vision, to have purpose enough."

Such magnificent impartiality is of course beyond most writers and most men, even such first-rate men of good will as

Howells—or his determined opponent, Frank Norris. By a strange twist of historical truth, Norris is usually labeled, today, a "Naturalist," by which is meant, for the most part, that he is a descendant from but also a variant upon the approach called realism. Debts to such French writers as Zola are subsumed under the Naturalist label; so too are such definitional assertions as the following, drawn from *The Oxford Companion to American Literature*, where Naturalism is said to be "the method of literary composition that aims at a detached, scientific objectivity in the treatment of natural man." But what Norris actually called for was the triumph of romanticism, which he carefully distinguished (in part agreeing with James that execution is all that matters) from sentimentalism. "Romance, I take it," he roared— Norris' writing rarely uses the quiet tones of more decorous spirits—"is the kind of fiction that takes cognizance of variations from the type of normal life. Realism," on the other hand, "is the kind of fiction that confines itself to the type of normal life"—and in so doing "stultifies itself. [Realism] notes only the surface of things. . . . Realism is minute; it is the drama of a broken teacup, the tragedy of a walk down the block, the excitement of an afternoon call, the adventure of an invitation to dinner. . . . But to Romance belongs the wide world for range, and the unplumbed depths of the human heart, and the mystery of sex, and the problems of life, and the black, unsearched penetralia of the soul of man."

The writers represented in this anthology not only recognized but, in their work, practiced both these basic approaches, realism and romanticism—sometimes one, sometimes the other, sometimes both. However, Howells won the critical war, and more: critics have for years portrayed his side of the controversy as more than merely victorious. Howells represents, for most of those who have written about American fiction, all things Good and True and Right. It is not that there is no other side for these commentators, but quite simply that, for them, the other side deserved to lose, and therefore lost inevitably and totally and eternally. Even the names of some of those who fought on the wrong side, in this view of history, have been expunged from the record of American literature. Francis Marion Crawford, a novelist at his best the clear superior of Howells and easily the equal of much of James, has been essentially turned into a literary nonperson. So too has it gone with the once equally famous and widely read Winston Churchill (not the British politician), and the brilliant psychiatrist-turned-writer, Silas Weir Mitchell, and the powerful storyteller, F. Hopkinson Smith, and the sturdy penetrator into the feminine mind of the time, Margaret Deland, and many, many more. A few of these writers are represented in this collection, for to omit them is both to falsify literary history and also to deprive today's readers of important material, strong and revealing and affecting. Most cannot be properly represented here, either because, like Crawford, they wrote only a very few stories and most of those in a specialized genre (in his case, the supernatural tale), or because, like Deland or Mitchell, their talents are truly shown only in their longer work.

But of the thirty-three writers here represented, very few of those whose stories date from before World War One did not enlist themselves, to one degree or another, in this story or that, under the banners of realism, of romanticism, or of their own personal mixture of the two. Realism and romanticism were in plain truth the dominant and hopelessly intertwined literary ideologies through much of America's literary history, so that Howells' "victory" is more illusory than real, more a thing of after-the-fact critical judgment than of functional reality. Whether they were local colorists, writing about regional themes and characters, or whether they were satirists or polemicists, American writers not only knew only these two basic approaches, but when, in the end, they put by their sputtering, sometimes inarticulate quarrel over the respective merits of one or the other approach, it was not in order to raise the banner of realism and bury that of romanticism. Rather, it was—in the best Hegelian sense—to effect a new synthesis which inevitably embraced elements of both the warring sides, and in addition added other approaches, formulating no ironclad formula, but opening fiction to a host of new possibilities. In this sense the remarkable thing about twentieth-century American fiction from about the time of World War One, fiction both short and long, is how varied in approach it has become, virtually as a matter of principle, and how free it is of previously straitjacketing assumptions—like, for example, the controversial opposition of realism and romanticism.

It was a transformation, to be sure, which had been long in the making. Kate Chopin, records her biographer, Per Seyersted, "wanted her writing to be a spontaneous thing. . . . [In her stories] her emphasis was generally on character rather than on plot, on atmosphere rather than action." Much of "Madame Célestin's Divorce" is conversation between the only two characters, the lady and Paxton the lawyer. Even the physical descriptions are organized according to characterological revelation rather than mere scene-setting:

Madame Celestin always wore a neat and snugly fitting calico wrapper when she went out in the morning to sweep her small gallery. Lawyer Paxton thought she looked very pretty in the gray one that was made with a graceful Watteau fold at the back: and with which she invariably wore a bow of pink ribbon at the throat. She was always sweeping her gallery when lawyer Paxton passed by in the morning on his way to his office . . .

That is, Chopin's emphasis was a far more organic matter than could be accomplished by heavy reliance on either formulaic realism or formulaic romanticism: her best work, like the story here reproduced or her superb short novel, *The Awakening*, quite simply transcends both those operating principles in favor of a higher and more all-embracing synthesis. "Mrs. Pontellier's eyes were quick and bright; they were a yellowish brown, about the color of her hair. She had a way of turning them swiftly upon an object and holding them there as if lost in some inward maze of contemplation or thought." Edna Pontellier's suicide, toward which *The Awakening* has been beautifully pointed, organically embodies and combines landscape depiction and psychological realism in a blend that defies easy or over-exact labeling: "The water was chill, but she walked on. The water was deep, but she lifted her white body and reached out with a long, sweeping stroke. The touch of the sea is sensuous, enfolding the body in its soft, close embrace." *The Awakening* was published in 1899, but it reads very much like a comparatively recent twentieth-century novel.

Hoyt C. Franchere and Thomas F. O'Donnell, in their study, *Harold Frederic*, nicely say that "it would be something of an oversimplification to fit [Frederic] snugly into a school of realists and fail to recognize those other aspects of his career and of his multifaceted personality that formed Harold Frederic, the artist." Near the end of his most famous novel, *The Damnation of Theron Ware*, Frederic describes his main character with a stylistic touch, and also a clearly overriding moral purpose, that would not have been out of place in the novels of the 1920s:

Perhaps the face was older and graver; it was hard to tell. The long winter's illness, with its recurring crises and sustained confinement, had bleached his skin and reduced his figure to gauntness, but there was none the less an air of restored and secure good health about him. Only in the eyes themselves, as they rested briefly upon the prospect, did a substantial change suggest itself. . . . They did not soften and glow . . . at the thought of how wholly one felt sure of God's goodness in these wonderful new mornings of spring.''

Similarly, Ann J. Lane points out that Charlotte Perkins Gilman ''utilized history, sociology, philosophy, psychology, and ethics . . . [; many critics] consider [her fiction] too ideological, too didactic . . . [but] Gilman's fictional work, when viewed as a whole, erases the distinction between realistic fiction, which mediates struggles, and fantasies, which eliminate them. . . . Gilman used the variously common fictional forms to propagandize for her humanistic vision.'' The story here included, ''The Yellow Wallpaper,'' first published in 1892, opens like something we might expect to see in, say, the next issue of *The New Yorker*: ''It is very seldom that mere ordinary people like John and myself secure ancestral halls for the summer.'' Nor does the rest of the story convey a different impression: ''I lie here on this great immovable bed—it is nailed down, I believe—and follow that [wallpaper] pattern about by the hour. It is as good as gymnastics, I assure you.''

Observations of the same tenor can be brought forward for many and perhaps most of the writers here included. One more will have to do. Josephine Donovan's study, *Sarah Orne Jewett*, notes that ''to some extent Jewett shared in Howells' neoclassical spirit . . . Yet [her] ultimate vision was elegaic. . . . Her ideas are sometimes classical, sometimes Romantic; sometimes they even approach the poetical doctrine of the Symbolists.''

Exactly. And what is true for transitional writers like Chopin and Gilman, Frederic and Jewett, becomes still truer for the writers of our own century. ''There really is, to me anyway,'' Ernest Hemingway wrote to his editor, Maxwell Perkins, in 1926, ''very great glamour in life—and places and all sorts of things and I would like sometime to get it into the stuff. . . . [Writers] don't have subjects—Louis Bromfield [a very popular novelist] has subjects—but just write them and if God is good to you they come out well.'' It would be hard to be less programmatic, less involved in any sort of theoretical approach to the writing of fiction.

''I don't care much for facts,'' William Faulkner observed, in a 1946 letter to Malcolm Cowley, ''am not much interested in them, you can't stand a fact up, you've got to prop it up, and when you move to one side a little and look at it from that angle, it's not thick enough to cast a shadow in that direction. . . . I can't write an introduction," he concludes. Six years earlier, in response to a letter of inquiry from an academic critic, he had observed that "As yet I have found no happy balance between method and material. I doubt that it exists for me. . . . I decided what seems to me now a long time ago that something worth saying knew better than I did how it needed to be said . . ."

F. Scott Fitzgerald, indeed, employs a wholly new set of categories when he discusses fiction: "The dramatic novel," he wrote to John Peale Bishop in 1934, "has canons quite different from the philosophical, now called psychological, novel. One is a kind of *tour de force* and the other a confession of faith. It would be like comparing a sonnet sequence with an epic." The next year he notes, to the same correspondent, that "many good enough books are in the same key . . . Life is not so smooth that it can't go over suddenly into melodrama." How utterly different this is from William Dean Howells, proclaiming earnestly that "I can hardly conceive of a literary self-respect in these days [1891] compatible with the old trade of make-believe . . . If a novel flatters the passions, and exalts them above the principles, it is poisonous . . ." Again, it is flatly untrue that Howells' brand of realism, or any brand of realism, prevailed over romanticism. Thirty years after Howells wrote the words just quoted, the very frame of reference from which he operated had ceased to exist. Neither side, the realists nor the romantics, prevailed; neither side lost; both have endured, and, in their differing ways, both have prospered. Today we have "realists" like Philip Roth, and "romantics" like Bernard Malamud—but the categories are no longer meaningful, and perhaps do more harm than good. That, it will be remembered, was Henry James's point: there is in the end only good and bad, and what matters—*all* that matters—is how well one writes, not in what style or mode.

The writers in *American Stories* write well, without exception, write powerfully and meaningfully. There is development represented in the progression of these stories, there are approaches and points of view coming to life and then fading away in these pages, exactly as there has been growth and change in the American society about which, and out of the life of which, all of these stories have been written. It is a remarkably vital recording of experience, a remarkably rich and rewarding record to follow, from Irving, Hawthorne and Poe to William Saroyan. Each writer has been allowed only a single story: the aim has been not to portray the career of any writer, but the collective career of the pre-World War Two American story itself. No story is or possibly could be fully representative; every writer here included could have been exhibited in a different light by a different choice. I have tried to misrepresent no one, and above all I have tried as hard as I am able not to misrepresent the classic American story as I understand its achievements, its history, and its constantly changing but always compelling face.

—BURTON RAFFEL

Washington Irving
(1783–1859)

A New York merchant's son, Irving was trained as a lawyer, being admitted to the bar in 1806. Neither law nor business deeply interested him: even while studying law he had begun to write, publishing his first satirical sketches while still in his teens. A stylist from the first, his models were primarily 18th-century British essayists (though European writers too were significant influences: Irving was well read in a number of languages). His interest in history and his satirical bent combined, in 1809, to produce a History of New York, *supposedly written by an imaginary Dutch-American scholar, Diedrich Knickerbocker. Thereafter he drifted into politics, worked in the family business (which failed in 1818), and in 1818–19 turned decisively to literature, writing* The Sketch Book, *still his most famous work and the volume from which "The Specter Bridegroom" is taken. It was followed in 1822 by* Bracebridge Hall, *in 1828 by his* History of the Life and Voyages of Christopher Columbus, *and thereafter by volumes of Spanish and Western American history. In the 1840s he served as minister to Spain; his last years were spent at Sunnyside, a Hudson River estate.*

THE SPECTER BRIDEGROOM

A TRAVELER'S TALE*

He that supper for is dight,
He lyes full cold, I trow, this night!
Yestreen to chamber I him led.
This night Gray-Steel has made his bed.

SIR EGER, SIR GRAHAME,
AND SIR GRAY-STEEL

On the summit of one of the heights of the Odenwald, a wild and romantic tract of Upper Germany that lies not far from the confluence of the Main and the Rhine, there stood, many, many years since, the Castle of the Baron Von Landshort. It is now quite fallen to decay and almost buried among beech trees and dark firs, above which, however, its old watchtower may still be seen, struggling, like the former possessor I have mentioned, to carry a high head and look down upon the neighboring country.

The baron was a dry branch of the great family of Katzenellenbogen,† and inherited the relics of the property and all the pride of his ancestors. Though the warlike disposition of his predecessors had much impaired the family possessions, yet the baron still endeavored to keep up some show of former state. The times were peaceable, and the German nobles, in general, had abandoned their inconvenient old castles, perched like eagles' nests among the mountains, and had built more convenient residences in the valleys; still the baron remained proudly drawn up in his little fortress, cherishing, with hereditary inveteracy, all the old family feuds, so that he was on ill terms with some of his nearest neighbors on account of disputes that had happened between their great-great-grandfathers.

---

*The erudite reader, well versed in good-for-nothing lore, will perceive that the above Tale must have been suggested to the old Swiss by a little French anecdote, a circumstance said to have taken place at Paris.

†*I.e.*, Cat's-Elbow. The name of a family of those parts very powerful in former times. The appellation, we are told, was given in compliment to a peerless dame of the family, celebrated for her fine arm.

The baron had but one child, a daughter; but nature, when she grants but one child, always compensates by making it a prodigy, and so it was with the daughter of the baron. All the nurses, gossips, and country cousins assured her father that she had not her equal for beauty in all Germany; and who should know better than they? She had, moreover, been brought up with great care under the superintendence of two maiden aunts, who had spent some years of their early life at one of the little German courts and were skilled in all the branches of knowledge necessary to the education of a fine lady. Under their instructions she became a miracle of accomplishments. By the time she was eighteen she could embroider to admiration and had worked whole histories of the saints in tapestry with such strength of expression in their countenances that they looked like so many souls in purgatory. She could read without great difficulty, and had spelled her way through several church legends and almost all the chivalric wonders of the Heldenbuch. She had even made considerable proficiency in writing, could sign her own name without missing a letter, and so legibly that her aunts could read it without spectacles. She excelled in making little elegant good-for-nothing ladylike knickknacks of all kinds; was versed in the most abstruse dancing of the day; played a number of airs on the harp and guitar; and knew all the tender ballads of the Minnelieders by heart.

Her aunts, too, having been great flirts and coquettes in their younger days, were admirably calculated to be vigilant guardians and strict censors of the conduct of their niece, for there is no duenna so rigidly prudent and inexorably decorous as a superannuated coquette. She was rarely suffered out of their sight; never went beyond the domains of the castle, unless well attended, or rather well watched; had continual lectures read to her about strict decorum and implicit obedience; and, as to the men—pah! —she was taught to hold them at such a distance, and in such absolute distrust, that, unless properly authorized, she would not have cast a glance upon the handsomest cavalier in the world—no, not if he were even dying at her feet.

The good effects of this system were wonderfully apparent. The young lady was a pattern of docility and correctness. While others were wasting their sweetness in the glare of the world and liable to be plucked and thrown aside by every hand, she was coyly blooming into fresh and lovely womanhood under the protection of those immaculate spinsters, like a rosebud blushing forth among guardian thorns. Her aunts looked upon her with pride and exultation, and vaunted that though all the other young ladies in the world might go astray, yet, thank Heaven, nothing of the kind could happen to the heiress of Katzenellenbogen.

But, however scantily the Baron Von Landshort might be provided with children, his household was by no means a small one, for Providence had enriched him with abundance of poor relations. They, one and all, possessed the affectionate disposition common to humble relatives, were wonderfully attached to the baron, and took every possible occasion to come in swarms and enliven the castle. All family festivals were commemorated by these good people at the baron's expense; and when they were filled with good cheer they would declare that there was nothing on earth so delightful as these family meetings, these jubilees of the heart.

The baron, though a small man, had a large soul, and it swelled with satisfaction at the consciousness of being the greatest man in the little world about him. He loved to tell long stories about the dark old warriors whose portraits looked grimly down from the walls around, and he found no listeners equal to those that fed at his expense. He was much given to the marvelous, and a firm believer in all those supernatural tales with which every mountain and valley in Germany abounds. The faith of his guests exceeded even his own; they listened to every tale of wonder with open eyes and mouth, and never failed to be astonished, even though repeated for the hundredth time. Thus lived the Baron Von Landshort, the oracle of his table, the absolute monarch of his little territory, and happy, above all things, in the persuasion that he was the wisest man of his age.

At the time of which my story treats there was a great family gathering at the castle, on an affair of the utmost importance; it was to receive the destined bridegroom of the baron's daughter. A negotiation had been carried on between the father and an old nobleman of Bavaria to unite the dignity of their houses by the marriage of their children. The preliminaries had been conducted with proper punctilio. The young people were betrothed without seeing each other, and the time was appointed for the marriage ceremony. The young Count Von Altenburg had been recalled from the army for the purpose, and was actually on his way to the baron's to receive his bride. Missives had even been received from him, from Würzburg, where he was accidentally detained, mentioning the day and hour when he might be expected to arrive.

The castle was in a tumult of preparation to give him a suitable welcome. The fair bride had been decked out with uncommon care. The two aunts had superintended her toilet and quarreled the whole morning about every article of her dress. The young lady had taken advantage of their contest to follow the bent of her own taste, and fortunately it was a good one. She looked as lovely as youthful bridegroom could desire, and the flutter of expectation heightened the luster of her charms.

The suffusions that mantled her face and neck, the gentle heaving of the bosom, the eye now and then lost in reverie, all betrayed the soft tumult that was going on in her little heart. The aunts were continually hovering around her, for maiden aunts are apt to take great interest in affairs of this nature. They were giving her a world of staid counsel how to deport herself, what to say, and in what manner to receive the expected lover.

The baron was no less busied in preparations. He had, in truth, nothing exactly to do, but he was naturally a fuming bustling little man, and could not remain passive when all the world was in a hurry. He worried from top to bottom of the castle with an air of infinite anxiety; he continually called the servants from their work to exhort them to be diligent; and buzzed about every hall and chamber, as idly restless and importunate as a bluebottle fly on a warm summer's day.

In the meantime the fatted calf had been killed; the forests had rung with the clamor of the huntsmen; the kitchen was crowded with good cheer; the cellars had yielded up whole oceans of *Rhein-wein* and *Ferne-wein;* and even the great Heidelberg tun had been laid under contribution. Everything was ready to receive the distinguished guest with *Saus und Braus* in the true spirit of German hospitality—but the guest delayed to make his appearance. Hour rolled after hour. The sun that had poured his downward rays upon the rich forest of the Odenwald now just gleamed along the summits of the mountains. The baron mounted the highest tower, and strained his eyes in hope of catching a distant sight of the count and his attendants. Once he thought he beheld them; the sound of horns came floating from the valley, prolonged by the mountain echoes. A number of horsemen were seen far below, slowly advancing along the road; but when they had nearly reached the foot of the mountain they suddenly struck off in a different direction. The last ray of sunshine departed— the bats began to flit by in the twilight—the road grew dimmer and dimmer to the view; and nothing appeared stirring in it but now and then a peasant lagging homeward from his labor.

While the old castle of Landshort was in this state of perplexity a very interesting scene was transacting in a different part of the Odenwald.

The young Count Von Altenburg was tranquilly pursuing his

route in that sober jog-trot way, in which a man travels toward matrimony when his friends have taken all the trouble and uncertainty of courtship off his hands, and a bride is waiting for him as certainly as a dinner at the end of his journey. He had encountered at Würzburg a youthful companion in arms with whom he had seen some service on the frontiers, Herman Von Starkenfaust, one of the stoutest hands and worthiest hearts of German chivalry, who was now returning from the army. His father's castle was not far distant from the old fortress of Landshort, although an hereditary feud rendered the families hostile and strangers to each other.

In the warmhearted moment of recognition the young friends related all their past adventures and fortunes, and the count gave the whole history of his intended nuptials with a young lady whom he had never seen but of whose charms he had received the most enrapturing descriptions.

As the route of the friends lay in the same direction, they agreed to perform the rest of their journey together; and, that they might do it the more leisurely, set off from Würzburg at an early hour, the count having given directions for his retinue to follow and overtake him.

They beguiled their wayfaring with recollections of their military scenes and adventures; but the count was apt to be a little tedious, now and then, about the reputed charms of his bride, and the felicity that awaited him.

In this way they had entered among the mountains of the Odenwald, and were traversing one of its most lonely and thickly wooded passes. It is well known that the forests of Germany have always been as much infested by robbers as its castles by specters; and at this time the former were particularly numerous, from the hordes of disbanded soldiers wandering about the country. It will not appear extraordinary, therefore, that the cavaliers were attacked by a gang of these stragglers in the midst of the forest. They defended themselves with bravery, but were nearly overpowered, when the count's retinue arrived to their assistance. At sight of them the robbers fled, but not until the count had received a mortal wound. He was slowly and carefully conveyed back to the city of Würzburg, and a friar summoned from a neighboring convent, who was famous for his skill in administering to both soul and body; but half of his skill was superfluous; the moments of the unfortunate count were numbered.

With his dying breath he entreated his friend to repair instantly to the castle of Landshort and explain the fatal cause of his not keeping his appointment with his bride. Though not the most

ardent of lovers, he was one of the most punctilious of men, and
appeared earnestly solicitous that his mission should be speedily
and courteously executed. "Unless this is done," said he, "I
shall not sleep quietly in my grave!" He repeated these last
words with peculiar solemnity. A request, at a moment so
impressive, admitted no hesitation. Starkenfaust endeavored to
soothe him to calmness, promised faithfully to execute his wish,
and gave him his hand in solemn pledge. The dying man pressed
it in acknowledgment, but soon lapsed into delirium—raved
about his bride—his engagements—his plighted word; ordered
his horse that he might ride to the castle of Landshort; and
expired in the fancied act of vaulting into the saddle.

Starkenfaust bestowed a sigh and a soldier's tear on the untimely fate of his comrade, and then pondered on the awkward
mission he had undertaken. His heart was heavy and his head
perplexed, for he was to present himself an unbidden guest
among hostile people, and to damp their festivity with tidings
fatal to their hopes. Still there were certain whisperings of
curiosity in his bosom to see this far-famed beauty of Katzenellenbogen, so cautiously shut up from the world, for he was a
passionate admirer of the sex, and there was a dash of eccentric-
ity and enterprise in his character that made him fond of all
singular adventure.

Previous to his departure he made all due arrangements with
the holy fraternity of the convent for the funeral solemnities of
his friend, who was to be buried in the cathedral of Würzburg,
near some of his illustrious relatives; and the mourning retinue of
the count took charge of his remains.

It is now high time that we should return to the ancient family
of Katzenellenbogen, who were impatient for their guest, and
still more for their dinner; and to the worthy little baron, whom
we left airing himself on the watchtower.

Night closed in, but still no guest arrived. The baron descended from the tower in despair. The banquet, which had been
delayed from hour to hour, could no longer be postponed. The
meats were already overdone; the cook in an agony; and the
whole household had the look of a garrison that had been reduced by famine. The baron was obliged reluctantly to give
orders for the feast without the presence of the guest. All were
seated at table, and just on the point of commencing when the
sound of a horn from without the gate gave notice of the approach of a stranger. Another long blast filled the old courts of
the castle with its echoes, and was answered by the warder from
the walls. The baron hastened to receive his future son-in-law.

The drawbridge had been let down, and the stranger was before the gate. He was a tall, gallant cavalier, mounted on a black steed. His countenance was pale, but he had a beaming, romantic eye, and an air of stately melancholy. The baron was a little mortified that he should have come in this simple, solitary style. His dignity for a moment was ruffled, and he felt disposed to consider it a want of proper respect for the important occasion and the important family with which he was to be connected. He pacified himself, however, with the conclusion that it must have been youthful impatience which had induced him thus to spur on sooner than his attendants.

"I am sorry," said the stranger, "to break in upon you thus unseasonably——"

Here the baron interrupted him with a world of compliments and greetings, for, to tell the truth, he prided himself upon his courtesy and eloquence. The stranger attempted, once or twice, to stem the torrent of words, but in vain, so he bowed his head and suffered it to flow on. By the time the baron had come to a pause, they had reached the inner court of the castle, and the stranger was again about to speak when he was once more interrupted by the appearance of the female part of the family, leading forth the shrinking and blushing bride. He gazed on her for a moment as one entranced; it seemed as if his whole soul beamed forth in the gaze, and rested upon that lovely form. One of the maiden aunts whispered something in her ear; she made an effort to speak; her moist blue eye was timidly raised, gave a shy glance of inquiry on the stranger, and was cast again to the ground. The words died away, but there was a sweet smile playing about her lips and a soft dimpling of the cheek that showed her glance had not been unsatisfactory. It was impossible for a girl of the fond age of eighteen, highly predisposed for love and matrimony, not to be pleased with so gallant a cavalier.

The late hour at which the guest had arrived left no time for parley. The baron was peremptory, and deferred all particular conversation until the morning, and led the way to the untasted banquet.

It was served up in the great hall of the castle. Around the walls hung the hard-favored portraits of the heroes of the house of Katzenellenbogen and the trophies which they had gained in the field and in the chase. Hacked corslets, splintered jousting spears, and tattered banners were mingled with the spoils of sylvan warfare; the jaws of the wolf and the tusks of the boar grinned horribly among cross-bows and battle-axes, and a huge pair of antlers branched immediately over the head of the youthful bridegroom.

The cavalier took but little notice of the company or the entertainment. He scarcely tasted the banquet, but seemed absorbed in admiration of his bride. He conversed in a low tone that could not be overheard—for the language of love is never loud; but where is the female ear so dull that it cannot catch the softest whisper of the lover? There was a mingled tenderness and gravity in his manner that appeared to have a powerful effect upon the young lady. Her color came and went as she listened with deep attention. Now and then she made some blushing reply, and when his eye was turned away, she would steal a sidelong glance at his romantic countenance and heave a gentle sigh of tender happiness. It was evident that the young couple were completely enamored. The aunts, who were deeply versed in the mysteries of the heart, declared that they had fallen in love with each other at first sight.

The feast went on merrily, or at least noisily, for the guests were all blessed with those keen appetites that attend upon light purses and mountain air. The baron told his best and longest stories, and never had he told them so well or with such great effect. If there was anything marvelous, his auditors were lost in astonishment; and if anything facetious, they were sure to laugh exactly in the right place. The baron, it is true, like most great men, was too dignified to utter any joke but a dull one; it was always enforced, however, by a bumper of excellent Hockheimer, and even a dull joke, at one's own table, served up with jolly old wine, is irresistible. Many good things were said by poorer and keener wits that would not bear repeating, except on similar occasions; many sly speeches whispered in ladies' ears that almost convulsed them with suppressed laughter; and a song or two roared out by a poor but merry and broad-faced cousin of the baron that absolutely made the maiden aunts hold up their fans.

Amidst all this revelry, the stranger guest maintained a most singular and unseasonable gravity. His countenance assumed a deeper cast of dejection as the evening advanced; and, strange as it may appear, even the baron's jokes seemed only to render him the more melancholy. At times he was lost in thought, and at times there was a perturbed and restless wandering of the eye that bespoke a mind but ill at ease. His conversations with the bride became more and more earnest and mysterious. Lowering clouds began to steal over the fair serenity of her brow, and tremors to run through her tender frame.

All this could not escape the notice of the company. Their

gaiety was chilled by the unaccountable gloom of the bridegroom; their spirits were infected; whispers and glances were interchanged, accompanied by shrugs and dubious shakes of the head. The song and the laugh grew less and less frequent; there were dreary pauses in the conversation, which were at length succeeded by wild tales and supernatural legends. One dismal story produced another still more dismal, and the baron nearly frightened some of the ladies into hysterics with the history of the goblin horseman that carried away the fair Leonora; a dreadful story, which has since been put into excellent verse, and is read and believed by all the world.

The bridegroom listened to this tale with profound attention. He kept his eyes steadily fixed on the baron, and, as the story drew to a close, began gradually to rise from his seat, growing taller and taller, until, in the baron's entranced eye, he seemed almost to tower into a giant. The moment the tale was finished, he heaved a deep sigh, and took a solemn farewell of the company. They were all amazement. The baron was perfectly thunderstruck.

"What! Going to leave the castle at midnight? Why, everything was prepared for his reception; a chamber was ready for him if he wished to retire."

The stranger shook his head mournfully and mysteriously. "I must lay my head in a different chamber tonight!"

There was something in this reply and the tone in which it was uttered that made the baron's heart misgive him, but he rallied his forces and repeated his hospitable entreaties.

The stranger shook his head silently, but positively, at every offer; and, waving his farewell to the company, stalked slowly out of the hall. The maiden aunts were absolutely petrified—the bride hung her head, and a tear stole to her eye.

The baron followed the stranger to the great court of the castle, where the black charger stood pawing the earth, and snorting with impatience. When they had reached the portal, whose deep archway was dimly lighted by a cresset, the stranger paused, and addressed the baron in a hollow tone of voice, which the vaulted roof rendered still more sepulchral.

"Now that we are alone," said he, "I will impart to you the reason of my going. I have a solemn, an indispensable engagement——"

"Why," said the baron, "cannot you send someone in your place?"

"It admits of no substitute—I must attend it in person—I must away to Würzburg cathedral——"

"Ay," said the baron, plucking up spirit, "but not until tomorrow—tomorrow you shall take your bride there."

"No! no!" replied the stranger, with tenfold solemnity, "my engagement is with no bride—the worms! The worms expect me! I am a dead man—I have been slain by robbers—my body lies at Würzburg—at midnight I am to be buried—the grave is waiting for me—I must keep my appointment!"

He sprang on his black charger, dashed over the drawbridge, and the clattering of his horse's hoofs was lost in the whistling of the night blast.

The baron returned to the hall in the utmost consternation and related what had passed. Two ladies fainted outright, others sickened at the idea of having banqueted with a specter. It was the opinion of some that this might be the wild huntsman, famous in German legend. Some talked of mountain sprites, of wood demons, and of other supernatural beings, with which the good people of Germany have been so grievously harassed since time immemorial. One of the poor relations ventured to suggest that it might be some sportive evasion of the young cavalier, and that the very gloominess of the caprice seemed to accord with so melancholy a personage. This, however, drew on him the indignation of the whole company, and especially of the baron, who looked upon him as little better than an infidel, so that he was fain to abjure his heresy as speedily as possible and come into the faith of the true believers.

But whatever may have been the doubts entertained, they were completely put to an end by the arrival, next day, of regular missives, confirming the intelligence of the young count's murder, and his interment in Würzburg cathedral.

The dismay at the castle may well be imagined. The baron shut himself up in his chamber. The guests, who had come to rejoice with him, could not think of abandoning him in his distress. They wandered about the courts, or collected in groups in the hall, shaking their heads and shrugging their shoulders at the troubles of so good a man; and sat longer than ever at table, and ate and drank more stoutly than ever, by way of keeping up their spirits. But the situation of the widowed bride was the most pitiable. To have lost a husband before she had even embraced him—and such a husband! If the very specter could be so gracious and noble, what must have been the living man? She filled the house with lamentations.

On the night of the second day of her widowhood, she had retired to her chamber, accompanied by one of her aunts, who insisted on sleeping with her. The aunt, who was one of the best tellers of ghost stories in all Germany, had just been recounting one of her longest, and had fallen asleep in the very midst of it. The chamber was remote, and overlooked a small garden. The niece lay pensively gazing at the beams of the rising moon, as they trembled on the leaves of an aspen tree before the lattice. The castle clock had just tolled midnight when a soft strain of music stole up from the garden. She rose hastily from her bed, and stepped lightly to the window. A tall figure stood among the shadows of the trees. As it raised its head, a beam of moonlight fell upon the countenance. Heaven and earth! She beheld the Specter Bridegroom! A loud shriek at that moment burst upon her ear, and her aunt, who had been awakened by the music and had followed her silently to the window, fell into her arms. When she looked again, the specter had disappeared.

Of the two females, the aunt now required the more soothing, for she was perfectly beside herself with terror. As to the young lady, there was something, even in the specter of her lover, that seemed endearing. There was still the semblance of manly beauty; and though the shadow of a man is but little calculated to satisfy the affections of a lovesick girl, yet, where the substance is not to be had, even that is consoling. The aunt declared she would never sleep in that chamber again; the niece, for once, was refractory, and declared as strongly that she would sleep in no other in the castle. The consequence was that she had to sleep in it alone; but she drew a promise from her aunt not to relate the story of the specter, lest she should be denied the only melancholy pleasure left her on earth—that of inhabiting the chamber over which the guardian shade of her lover kept its nightly vigils.

How long the good old lady would have observed this promise is uncertain, for she dearly loved to talk of the marvelous, and there is a triumph in being the first to tell a frightful story; it is, however, still quoted in the neighborhood, as a memorable instance of female secrecy, that she kept it to herself for a whole week, when she was suddenly absolved from all further restraint by intelligence brought to the breakfast table one morning that the young lady was not to be found. Her room was empty—the bed had not been slept in—the window was open, and the bird had flown!

The astonishment and concern with which the intelligence was received can only be imagined by those who have witnessed the agitation which the mishaps of a great man cause among his friends. Even the poor relations paused for a moment from the indefatigable labors of the trencher, when the aunt, who had at first been struck speechless, wrung her hands, and shrieked out, "The goblin! The goblin! She's carried away by the goblin."

In a few words she related the fearful scene of the garden, and concluded that the specter must have carried off his bride. Two of the domestics corroborated the opinion, for they had heard the clattering of a horse's hoofs down the mountain about midnight, and had no doubt that it was the specter on his black charger, bearing her away to the tomb. All present were struck with the direful probability, for events of the kind are extremely common in Germany, as many well-authenticated histories bear witness.

What a lamentable situation was that of the poor baron! What a heart-rending dilemma for a fond father, and a member of the great family of Katzenellenbogen! His only daughter had either been rapt away to the grave, or he was to have some wood demon for a son-in-law, and, perchance, a troop of goblin grandchildren. As usual, he was completely bewildered, and all the castle in an uproar. The men were ordered to take horse and scour every road and path and glen of the Odenwald. The baron himself had just drawn on his jack boots, girded on his sword, and was about to mount his steed to sally forth on the doubtful quest when he was brought to a pause by a new apparition. A lady was seen approaching the castle, mounted on a palfrey, attended by a cavalier on horseback. She galloped up to the gate, sprang from her horse, and, falling at the baron's feet, embraced his knees. It was his lost daughter and her companion—the Specter Bridegroom! The baron was astounded. He looked at his daughter, then at the specter, and almost doubted the evidence of his senses. The latter, too, was wonderfully improved in his appearance since his visit to the world of spirits. His dress was splendid, and set off a noble figure of manly symmetry. He was no longer pale and melancholy. His fine countenance was flushed with the glow of youth, and joy rioted in his large dark eye.

The mystery was soon cleared up. The cavalier (for, in truth, as you must have known all the while, he was no goblin) announced himself as Sir Herman Von Starkenfaust. He related his adventure with the young count. He told how he had hastened to the castle to deliver the unwelcome tidings, but that the eloquence of the baron had interrupted him in every attempt to tell his tale. How the sight of the bride had completely captivated him, and that to pass a few hours near her he had tacitly suffered the mistake to continue. How he had been sorely perplexed in what way to make a decent retreat, until the baron's goblin stories had suggested his eccentric exit. How, fearing the feudal hostility of the family, he had repeated his visits by stealth—had haunted the garden beneath the young lady's window—had wooed—had won—had borne away in triumph—and, in a word, had wedded the fair.

Under any other circumstances the baron would have been inflexible, for he was tenacious of paternal authority and devoutly obstinate in all family feuds; but he loved his daughter; he had lamented her as lost; he rejoiced to find her still alive; and, though her husband was of a hostile house, yet, thank Heaven, he was not a goblin. There was something, it must be acknowledged, that did not exactly accord with his notions of strict veracity, in the joke the knight had passed upon him of his being a dead man; but several old friends present, who had served in the wars, assured him that every stratagem was excusable in love, and that the cavalier was entitled to especial privilege, having lately served as a trooper.

Matters, therefore, were happily arranged. The baron pardoned the young couple on the spot. The revels at the castle were resumed. The poor relations overwhelmed this new member of the family with loving kindness; he was so gallant, so generous——and so rich. The aunts, it is true, were somewhat scandalized that their system of strict seclusion and passive obedience should be so badly exemplified, but attributed it all to their negligence in not having the windows grated. One of them was particularly mortified at having her marvelous story marred, and that the only specter she had ever seen should turn out a counterfeit; but the niece seemed perfectly happy at having found him substantial flesh and blood—and so the story ends.

Nathaniel Hawthorne
(1804–1864)

Son of a sea captain who died when the boy was four, Hawthorne lived an essentially reclusive youth. After graduating from Bowdoin College in 1825 he retired to his native Salem, Massachusetts, and began to write. Fanshaw, *a novel, appeared in 1828 (anonymously and printed at the author's own expense).* Twice-Told Tales *(1837; enlarged in 1842) established him as a writer, and thereafter he worked at editing, at the production of assorted potboilers, and for a time (1839–1841) in the Boston Custom House. Resident in Concord, Massachusetts, after 1841, he wrote the stories collected in* Mosses *from an Old Manse, from which ''Young Goodman Brown'' is taken.* The Scarlet Letter *appeared in 1850,* The House of the Seven Gables *in 1851, and* The Blithedale Romance *in 1852.* The Snow-Image and Other Twice-Told Tales, *1851, was his last major collection of stories;* The Marble Faun, *1860, written after some years spent abroad as U. S. consul at Liverpool, was his last completed novel.*

YOUNG GOODMAN BROWN

Young Goodman Brown came forth at sunset into the street at Salem village; but put his head back, after crossing the threshold, to exchange a parting kiss with his young wife. And Faith, as the wife was aptly named, thrust her own pretty head into the street, letting the wind play with the pink ribbons of her cap while she called to Goodman Brown.

"Dearest heart," whispered she, softly and rather sadly, when her lips were close to his ear, "prithee put off your journey until sunrise and sleep in your own bed to-night. A lone woman is troubled with such dreams and such thoughts that she's afeard of herself sometimes. Pray tarry with me this night, dear husband, of all nights in the year."

"My love and my Faith," replied young Goodman Brown, "of all nights in the year, this one night must I tarry away from thee. My journey, as thou callest it, forth and back again, must needs be done 'twixt now and sunrise. What, my sweet, pretty wife, dost thou doubt me already, and we but three months married?"

"Then God bless you!" said Faith, with the pink ribbons; "and may you find all well when you come back."

"Amen!" cried Goodman Brown. "Say thy prayers, dear Faith, and go to bed at dusk, and no harm will come to thee."

So they parted; and the young man pursued his way until, being about to turn the corner by the meeting-house, he looked back and saw the head of Faith still peeping after him with a melancholy air, in spite of her pink ribbons.

"Poor little Faith!" thought he, for his heart smote him. "What a wretch am I to leave her on such an errand! She talks of dreams, too. Methought as she spoke there was trouble in her face, as if a dream had warned her what work is to be done to-night. But no, no; 'twould kill her to think it. Well, she's a blessed angel on earth; and after this one night I'll cling to her skirts and follow her to heaven."

With this excellent resolve for the future, Goodman Brown felt himself justified in making more haste on his present evil purpose. He had taken a dreary road, darkened by all the gloomiest trees of the forest, which barely stood aside to let the narrow path creep through, and closed immediately behind. It was all as lonely as could be; and there is this peculiarity in such a solitude, that the traveller knows not who may be concealed by the innumerable trunks and the thick boughs overhead; so that with lonely footsteps he may yet be passing through an unseen multitude.

"There may be a devilish Indian behind every tree," said Goodman Brown to himself; and he glanced fearfully behind him as he added, "What if the devil himself should be at my very elbow!"

His head being turned back, he passed a crook of the road, and, looking forward again, beheld the figure of a man, in grave and decent attire, seated at the foot of an old tree. He arose at

Goodman Brown's approach and walked onward side by side
with him.

"You are late, Goodman Brown," said he. "The clock of the
Old South was striking as I came through Boston, and that is full
fifteen minutes agone."

"Faith kept me back a while," replied the young man, with a
tremor in his voice, caused by the sudden appearance of his
companion, though not wholly unexpected.

It was now deep dusk in the forest, and deepest in that part of
it where these two were journeying. As nearly as could be
discerned, the second traveller was about fifty years old, apparently in the same rank of life as Goodman Brown, and bearing a
considerable resemblance to him, though perhaps more in expression than features. Still they might have been taken for father
and son. And yet, though the elder person was as simply clad as
the younger, and as simple in manner too, he had an indescribable air of one who knew the world, and who would not have
felt abashed at the governor's dinner table or in King William's
court, were it possible that his affairs should call him thither. But
the only thing about him that could be fixed upon as remarkable
was his staff, which bore the likeness of a great black snake, so
curiously wrought that it might almost be seen to twist and
wriggle itself like a living serpent. This, of course, must have
been an ocular deception, assisted by the uncertain light.

"Come, Goodman Brown," cried his fellow-traveller, "this is
a dull place for the beginning of a journey. Take my staff, if you
are so soon weary."

"Friend," said the other, exchanging his slow pace for a full
stop, "having kept covenant by meeting thee here, it is my
purpose now to return whence I came. I have scruples touching
the matter thou wot'st of."

"Sayest thou so?" replied he of the serpent, smiling apart.
"Let us walk on, nevertheless, reasoning as we go; and if I
convince thee not thou shalt turn back. We are but a little way
in the forest yet."

"Too far! too far!" exclaimed the goodman, unconsciously
resuming his walk. "My father never went into the woods on
such an errand, nor his father before him. We have been a race
of honest men and good Christians since the days of the martyrs;
and shall I be the first of the name of Brown that ever took this
path and kept—"

"Such company, thou wouldst say," observed the elder person,
interpreting his pause. "Well said, Goodman Brown! I have
been as well acquainted with your family as with ever a one

among the Puritans; and that's no trifle to say. I helped your grandfather, the constable, when he lashed the Quaker woman so smartly through the streets of Salem; and it was I that brought your father a pitch-pine knot, kindled at my own hearth, to set fire to an Indian village, in King Philip's war. They were my good friends, both; and many a pleasant walk have we had along this path, and returned merrily after midnight. I would fain be friends with you for their sake.''

"If it be as thou sayest,'' replied Goodman Brown, "I marvel they never spoke of these matters; or, verily, I marvel not, seeing that the least rumor of the sort would have driven them from New England. We are a people of prayer, and good works to boot, and abide no such wickedness.''

"Wickedness or not,'' said the traveller with the twisted staff. "I have a very general acquaintance here in New England. The deacons of many a church have drunk the communion wine with me; the selectmen of divers towns make me their chairman; and a majority of the Great and General Court are firm supporters of my interest. The governor and I, too— But these are state secrets.''

"Can this be so?'' cried Goodman Brown, with a stare of amazement at his undisturbed companion. "Howbeit, I have nothing to do with the governor and council; they have their own ways, and are no rule for a simple husbandman like me. But, were I to go on with thee, how should I meet the eye of that good old man, our minister, at Salem village? Oh, his voice would make me tremble both Sabbath day and lecture day.''

Thus far the elder traveller had listened with due gravity; but now burst into a fit of irrepressible mirth, shaking himself so violently that his snake-like staff actually seemed to wriggle in sympathy.

"Ha!ha!ha!'' shouted he again and again; then composing himself, "Well, go on, Goodman Brown, go on; but, prithee, don't kill me with laughing.''

"Well, then, to end the matter at once,'' said Goodman Brown, considerably nettled, "there is my wife, Faith. It would break her dear little heart; and I'd rather break my own.''

"Nay, if that be the case,'' answered the other, "e'en go thy ways, Goodman Brown. I would not for twenty old women like the one hobbling before us that Faith should come to any harm.''

As he spoke he pointed his staff at a female figure on the path, in whom Goodman Brown recognized a very pious and exemplary dame, who had taught him his catechism in youth, and was still his moral and spiritual adviser, jointly with the minister and Deacon Gookin.

"A marvel, truly, that Goody Cloyse should be so far in the wilderness at nightfall," said he. "But with your leave, friend, I shall take a cut through the woods until we have left this Christian woman behind. Being a stranger to you, she might ask whom I was consorting with and whither I was going."

"Be it so," said his fellow-traveller. "Betake you to the woods, and let me keep the path."

Accordingly the young man turned aside, but took care to watch his companion, who advanced softly along the road until he had come within a staff's length of the old dame. She, meanwhile, was making the best of her way, with singular speed for so aged a woman, and mumbling some indistinct words—a prayer, doubtless—as she went. The traveller put forth his staff and touched her withered neck with what seemed the serpent's tail.

"The devil!" screamed the pious old lady.

"Then Goody Cloyse knows her old friend?" observed the traveller, confronting her and leaning on his writhing stick.

"Ah, forsooth, and is it your worship indeed?" cried the good dame. "Yea, truly is it, and in the very image of my old gossip, Goodman Brown, the grandfather of the silly fellow that now is. But—would your worship believe it?—my broomstick hath strangely disappeared, stolen, as I suspect, by that unhanged witch, Goody Cory, and that, too, when I was all anointed with the juice of smallage and cinquefoil and wolf's bane."

"Mingled with fine wheat and the fat of a new-born babe," said the shape of old Goodman Brown.

"Ah, your worship knows the recipe," cried the old lady, cackling aloud. "So, as I was saying, being all ready for the meeting, and no horse to ride on, I made up my mind to foot it; for they tell me there is a nice young man to be taken into communion to-night. But now your good worship will lend me your arm, and we shall be there in a twinkling."

"That can hardly be," answered her friend. "I may not spare you my arm, Goody Cloyse; but here is my staff, if you will."

So saying, he threw it down at her feet, where, perhaps, it assumed life, being one of the rods which its owner had formerly lent to the Egyptian magi. Of this fact, however, Goodman Brown could not take cognizance. He had cast up his eyes in astonishment, and, looking down again, beheld neither Goody Cloyse nor the serpentine staff, but his fellow-traveller alone, who waited for him as calmly as if nothing had happened.

"That old woman taught me my catechism," said the young man; and there was a world of meaning in this simple comment.

They continued to walk onward, while the elder traveller exhorted his companion to make good speed and persevere in the path, discoursing so aptly that his arguments seemed rather to spring up in the bosom of his auditor than to be suggested by himself. As they went, he plucked a branch of maple to serve for a walking stick, and began to strip it of the twigs and little boughs, which were wet with evening dew. The moment his fingers touched them they became strangely withered and dried up as with a week's sunshine. Thus the pair proceeded, at a good free pace, until suddenly, in a gloomy hollow of the road, Goodman Brown sat himself down on the stump of a tree and refused to go any farther.

"Friend," said he, stubbornly, "my mind is made up. Not another step will I budge on this errand. What if a wretched old woman do choose to go to the devil when I thought she was going to heaven: is that any reason why I should quit my dear Faith and go after her?"

"You will think better of this by and by," said his acquaintance, composedly. "Sit here and rest yourself a while; and when you feel like moving again, there is my staff to help you along."

Without more words, he threw his companion the maple stick, and was as speedily out of sight as if he had vanished into the deepening gloom. The young man sat a few moments by the roadside, applauding himself greatly, and thinking with how clear a conscience he should meet the minister in his morning walk, nor shrink from the eye of good old Deacon Gookin. And what calm sleep would be his that very night, which was to have been spent so wickedly, but so purely and sweetly now, in the arms of Faith! Amidst these pleasant and praiseworthy meditations, Goodman Brown heard the tramp of horses along the road, and deemed it advisable to conceal himself within the verge of the forest, conscious of the guilty purpose that had brought him thither, though now so happily turned from it.

On came the hoof tramps and the voices of the riders, two grave old voices, conversing soberly as they drew near. These mingled sounds appeared to pass along the road, within a few yards of the young man's hiding-place; but, owing doubtless to the depth of the gloom at that particular spot, neither the travellers nor their steeds were visible. Though their figures brushed the small boughs by the wayside, it could not be seen that they intercepted, even for a moment, the faint gleam from the strip of bright sky athwart which they must have passed. Goodman Brown alternately crouched and stood on tiptoe, pulling aside the branches and thrusting forth his head as far as he durst without discerning so much as a shadow. It vexed him the more, because he could have sworn, were such a thing possible, that he recognized the voices of the minister and Deacon Gookin, jogging along quietly, as they were wont to do, when bound to some ordination or ecclesiastical council. While yet within hearing, one of the riders stopped to pluck a switch.

"Of the two, reverend sir," said the voice like the deacon's, "I had rather miss an ordination dinner than to-night's meeting. They tell me that some of our community are to be here from Falmouth and beyond, and others from Connecticut and Rhode Island, besides several of the Indian powwows, who, after their fashion, know almost as much deviltry as the best of us. Moreover, there is a goodly young woman to be taken into communion."

"Mighty well, Deacon Gookin!" replied the solemn old tones of the minister. "Spur up, or we shall be late. Nothing can be done, you know, until I get on the ground."

The hoofs clattered again; and the voices, talking so strangely in the empty air, passed on through the forest, where no church had ever been gathered, nor solitary Christian prayed. Whither, then, could these holy men be journeying so deep into the heathen wilderness? Young Goodman Brown caught hold of a tree for support, being ready to sink down on the ground, faint and overburdened with the heavy sickness of his heart. He looked up to the sky, doubting whether there really was a heaven above him. Yet there was the blue arch, and the stars brightening in it.

"With heaven above and Faith below, I will yet stand firm against the devil!" cried Goodman Brown.

While he still gazed upward into the deep arch of the firmament and had lifted his hands to pray, a cloud, though no wind was stirring, hurried across the zenith and hid the brightening stars. The blue sky was still visible, except directly overhead, where this black mass of cloud was sweeping swiftly northward. Aloft in the air, as if from the depths of the cloud, came a confused and doubtful sound of voices. Once the listener fancied that he could distinguish the accents of towns-people of his own, men and women, both pious and ungodly, many of whom he had met at the communion table, and had seen others rioting at the tavern. The next moment, so indistinct were the sounds, he doubted whether he had heard aught but the murmur of the old forest, whispering without a wind. Then came a stronger swell of those familiar tones, heard daily in the sunshine at Salem village, but never until now from a cloud of night. There was one voice, of a young woman, uttering lamentations, yet with an uncertain sorrow, and entreating for some favor, which, perhaps, it would grieve her to obtain; and all the unseen multitude, both saints and sinners, seemed to encourage her onward.

"Faith!" shouted Goodman Brown, in a voice of agony and desperation; and the echoes of the forest mocked him, crying, "Faith! Faith!" as if bewildered wretches were seeking her all through the wilderness.

The cry of grief, rage, and terror was yet piercing the night, when the unhappy husband held his breath for a response. There was a scream, drowned immediately in a louder murmur of voices, fading into far-off laughter, as the dark cloud swept away, leaving the clear and silent sky above Goodman Brown. But something fluttered lightly down through the air and caught on the branch of a tree. The young man seized it, and beheld a pink ribbon.

"My Faith is gone!" cried he, after one stupefied moment. "There is no good on earth; and sin is but a name. Come, devil; for to thee is this world given."

And, maddened with despair, so that he laughed loud and long, did Goodman Brown grasp his staff and set forth again, at such a rate that he seemed to fly along the forest path rather than to walk or run. The road grew wilder and drearier and more faintly traced, and vanished at length, leaving him in the heart of the dark wilderness, still rushing onward with the instinct that guides mortal man to evil. The whole forest was peopled with frightful sounds—the creaking of the trees, the howling of wild beasts, and the yell of Indians; while sometimes the wind tolled like a distant church bell, and sometimes gave a broad roar around the traveller, as if all Nature were laughing him to scorn. But he was himself the chief horror of the scene, and shrank not from its other horrors.

"Ha! ha! ha!" roared Goodman Brown when the wind laughed at him. "Let us hear which will laugh loudest. Think not to frighten me with your deviltry. Come witch, come wizard, come Indian powwow, come devil himself, and here comes Goodman Brown. You may as well fear him as he fear you."

In truth, all through the haunted forest there could be nothing more frightful than the figure of Goodman Brown. On he flew among the black pines, brandishing his staff with frenzied gestures, now giving vent to an inspiration of horrid blasphemy, and now shouting forth such laughter as set all the echoes of the forest laughing like demons around him. The fiend in his own shape is less hideous than when he rages in the breast of man. Thus sped the demoniac on his course, until, quivering among the trees, he saw a red light before him, as when the felled trunks and branches of a clearing have been set on fire, and throw up their lurid blaze against the sky, at the hour of midnight. He paused, in a lull of the tempest that had driven him onward, and heard the swell of what seemed a hymn, rolling solemnly from a distance with the weight of many voices. He knew the tune; it was a familiar one in the choir of the village meeting-house. The verse died heavily away, and was lengthened by a chorus, not of human voices, but of all the sounds of the benighted wilderness pealing in awful harmony together. Goodman Brown cried out, and his cry was lost to his own ear by its unison with the cry of the desert.

In the interval of silence he stole forward until the light glared full upon his eyes. At one extremity of an open space, hemmed in by the dark wall of the forest, arose a rock, bearing some rude, natural resemblance either to an altar or a pulpit, and surrounded by four blazing pines, their tops aflame, their stems untouched, like candles at an evening meeting. The mass of foliage that had overgrown the summit of the rock was all on fire, blazing high into the night and fitfully illuminating the whole field. Each pendent twig and leafy festoon was in a blaze. As the red light arose and fell, a numerous congregation alternately shone forth, then disappeared in shadow, and again grew, as it were, out of the darkness, peopling the heart of the solitary woods at once.

"A grave and dark-clad company," quoth Goodman Brown.

In truth they were such. Among them, quivering to and fro between gloom and splendor, appeared faces that would be seen next day at the council board of the province, and others which, Sabbath after Sabbath, looked devoutly heavenward, and benignantly over the crowded pews, from the holiest pulpits in the land. Some affirm that the lady of the governor was there. At least there were high dames well known to her, and wives of honored husbands, and widows, a great multitude, and ancient maidens, all of excellent repute, and fair young girls, who trembled lest their mothers should espy them. Either the sudden gleams of light flashing over the obscure field bedazzled Goodman Brown, or he recognized a score of the church members of Salem village famous for their especial sanctity. Good old Deacon Gookin had arrived, and waited at the skirts of that venerable saint, his revered pastor. But, irreverently consorting with these grave, reputable, and pious people, these elders of the church, these chaste dames and dewy virgins, there were men of dissolute lives and women of spotted fame, wretches given over to all mean and filthy vice, and suspected even of horrid crimes. It was strange to see that the good shrank not from the wicked, nor were the sinners abashed by the saints. Scattered also among their pale-faced enemies were the Indian priests, or powwows, who had often scared their native forest with more hideous incantations than any known to English witchcraft.

"But where is Faith?" thought Goodman Brown; and, as hope came into his heart, he trembled.

Another verse of the hymn arose, a slow and mournful strain, such as the pious love, but joined to words which expressed all that our nature can conceive of sin, and darkly hinted at far more. Unfathomable to mere mortals is the lore of fiends. Verse after verse was sung; and still the chorus of the desert swelled between like the deepest tone of a mighty organ; and with the final peal of that dreadful anthem there came a sound, as if the roaring wind, the rushing streams, the howling beasts, and every other voice of the unconcerted wilderness were mingling and according with the voice of guilty man in homage to the prince of all. The four blazing pines threw up a loftier flame, and obscurely discovered shapes and visages of horror on the smoke wreaths above the impious assembly. At the same moment the fire on the rock shot redly forth and formed a glowing arch above its base, where now appeared a figure. With reverence be it spoken, the figure bore no slight similitude, both in garb and manner, to some grave divine of the New England churches.

"Bring forth the converts!" cried a voice that echoed through the field and rolled into the forest.

At the word, Goodman Brown stepped forth from the shadow of the trees and approached the congregation, with whom he felt a loathful brotherhood by the sympathy of all that was wicked in his heart. He could have well-nigh sworn that the shape of his own dead father beckoned him to advance, looking downward from a smoke wreath, while a woman, with dim features of despair, threw out her hand to warn him back. Was it his mother? But he had no power to retreat one step, nor to resist, even in thought, when the minister and good old Deacon Gookin seized his arms and led him to the blazing rock. Thither came also the slender form of a veiled female, led between Goody Cloyse, that pious teacher of the catechism, and Martha Carrier, who had received the devil's promise to be queen of hell. A rampant hag was she. And there stood the proselytes beneath the canopy of fire.

"Welcome, my children," said the dark figure, "to the communion of your race! Ye have found thus young your nature and your destiny. My children, look behind you!''

They turned; and flashing forth, as it were, in a sheet of flame, the fiend worshippers were seen; the smile of welcome gleamed darkly on every visage.

"There," resumed the sable form, "are all whom ye have reverenced from youth. Ye deemed them holier than yourselves, and shrank from your own sin, contrasting it with their lives of righteousness and prayerful aspirations heavenward. Yet here are they all in my worshipping assembly. This night it shall be granted you to know their secret deeds: how hoary-bearded elders of the church have whispered wanton words to the young maids of their households; how many a woman, eager for widow's weeds, has given her husband a drink at bedtime and let him sleep his last sleep in her bosom; how beardless youths have made haste to inherit their fathers' wealth; and how fair damsels—blush not, sweet ones—have dug little graves in the garden, and bidden me, the sole guest, to an infant's funeral. By the sympathy of your human hearts for sin ye shall scent out all the places—whether in church, bed-chamber, street, field, or forest—where crime has been committed, and shall exult to behold the whole earth one stain of guilt, one mighty blood spot. Far more than this. It shall be yours to penetrate, in every bosom, the deep mystery of sin, the fountain of all wicked arts, and which inexhaustibly supplies more evil impulses than human power—than my power at its utmost—can make manifest in deeds. And now, my children, look upon each other.''

They did so; and, by the blaze of the hell-kindled torches, the wretched man beheld his Faith, and the wife her husband, trembling before that unhallowed altar.

"Lo, there ye stand, my children," said the figure, in a deep and solemn tone, almost sad with its despairing awfulness, as if his once angelic nature could yet mourn for our miserable race. "Depending upon one another's hearts, ye had still hoped that virtue were not all a dream. Now are ye undeceived. Evil is the nature of mankind. Evil must be your only happiness. Welcome again, my children, to the communion of your race.''

"Welcome," repeated the fiend worshippers, in one cry of despair and triumph.

And there they stood, the only pair, as it seemed, who were yet hesitating on the verge of wickedness in this dark world. A basin was hollowed, naturally, in the rock. Did it contain water, reddened by the lurid light? or was it blood? or, perchance, a liquid flame? Herein did the shape of evil dip his hand and prepare to lay the mark of baptism upon their foreheads, that they might be partakers of the mystery of sin, more conscious of the secret guilt of others, both in deed and thought, than they could now be of their own. The husband cast one look at his pale wife, and Faith at him. What polluted wretches would the next glance show them to each other, shuddering alike at what they disclosed and what they saw!

"Faith! Faith!" cried the husband, "look up to heaven, and resist the wicked one."

Whether Faith obeyed he knew not. Hardly had he spoken when he found himself amid calm night and solitude, listening to a roar of the wind which died heavily away through the forest. He staggered against the rock, and felt it chill and damp; while a hanging twig, that had been all on fire, besprinkled his cheek with the coldest dew.

The next morning young Goodman Brown came slowly into the street of Salem village, staring around him like a bewildered man. The good old minister was taking a walk along the grave-yard to get an appetite for breakfast and meditate his sermon, and bestowed a blessing, as he passed, on Goodman Brown. He shrank from the venerable saint as if to avoid an anathema. Old Deacon Gookin was at domestic worship, and the holy words of his prayer were heard through the open window. "What God doth the wizard pray to?" quoth Goodman Brown. Goody Cloyse, that excellent old Christian, stood in the early sunshine at her own lattice, catechizing a little girl who had brought her a pint of morning's milk. Goodman Brown snatched away the child as from the grasp of the fiend himself. Turning the corner by the meeting-house, he spied the head of Faith, with the pink ribbons, gazing anxiously forth, and bursting into such joy at sight of him that she skipped along the street and almost kissed her husband before the whole village. But Goodman Brown looked sternly and sadly into her face, and passed on without a greeting.

Had Goodman Brown fallen asleep in the forest and only dreamed a wild dream of a witch-meeting?

Be it so if you will; but, alas! it was a dream of evil omen for young Goodman Brown. A stern, a sad, a darkly meditative, a distrustful, if not a desperate man did he become from the night of that fearful dream. On the Sabbath day, when the congregation were singing a holy psalm, he could not listen because an anthem of sin rushed loudly upon his ear and drowned all the blessed strain. When the minister spoke from the pulpit with power and fervid eloquence, and, with his hand on the open Bible, of the sacred truths of our religion, and of saint-like lives and triumphant deaths, and of future bliss or misery unutterable, then did Goodman Brown turn pale, dreading lest the roof should thunder down upon the gray blasphemer and his hearers. Often, awaking suddenly at midnight, he shrank from the bosom of Faith; and at morning or eventide, when the family knelt down at prayer, he scowled and muttered to himself, and gazed sternly at his wife, and turned away. And when he had lived long, and was borne to his grave a hoary corpse, followed by Faith, an aged woman, and children and grandchildren, a goodly procession, besides neighbors not a few, they carved no hopeful verse upon his tombstone, for his dying hour was gloom.

Edgar Allan Poe
(1809–1849)

Born in Boston, to a family of itinerant actors, Poe was more or less adopted and raised by a Virginia businessman, John Allan (from whose name Poe took his own middle name, which he began to use in 1824). John Allan took the young Poe to England in 1815, where he remained and attended school until 1820. Thereafter the relationship with Allan, and Poe's ability to maintain his own life on something of an even keel, steadily deteriorated. Poe gambled; more damagingly, in the long run, he drank to excess. Publication of his stories, poems, and essays began before he was twenty-one. Poe worked brilliantly but erratically as an editor, but could not keep any post long enough to produce stability in his personal existence. His young wife, Virginia, died of tuberculosis, after a period in which the couple came close to starvation. Poe's death came after a prolonged drinking bout. "The Gold Bug" won a prize when first published, in 1843, in a Philadelphia magazine.

THE GOLD BUG

What ho! what ho! this fellow is dancing mad!
He hath been bitten by the Tarantula.
ALL IN THE WRONG

Many years ago, I contracted an intimacy with a Mr. William Legrand. He was of an ancient Huguenot family, and had once been wealthy; but a series of misfortunes had reduced him to want. To avoid the mortification consequent upon his disasters,

58

he left New Orleans, the city of his forefathers, and took up his residence at Sullivan's Island, near Charleston, South Carolina.

This island is a very singular one. It consists of little else than the sea sand, and is about three miles long. Its breadth at no point exceeds a quarter of a mile. It is separated from the mainland by a scarcely perceptible creek, oozing its way through a wilderness of reeds and slime, a favorite resort of the marsh-hen. The vegetation, as might be supposed, is scant, or at least dwarfish. No trees of any magnitude are to be seen. Near the western extremity, where Fort Moultrie stands, and where are some miserable frame buildings, tenanted, during summer, by the fugitives from Charleston dust and fever, may be found, indeed, the bristly palmetto; but the whole island, with the exception of this western point, and a line of hard, white beach on the sea-coast, is covered with a dense undergrowth of the sweet myrtle so much prized by the horticulturists of England. The shrub here often attains the height of fifteen or twenty feet, and forms an almost impenetrable coppice, burdening the air with its fragrance.

In the inmost recesses of this coppice, not far from the eastern or more remote end of the island, Legrand had built himself a small hut, which he occupied when I first, by mere accident, made his acquaintance. This soon ripened into friendship—for there was much in the recluse to excite interest and esteem. I found him well educated, with unusual powers of mind, but infected with misanthropy, and subject to perverse moods of alternate enthusiasm and melancholy. He had with him many books, but rarely employed them. His chief amusements were gunning and fishing, or sauntering along the beach and through the myrtles, in quest of shells of entomological specimens;—his collection of the latter might have been envied by a Swammerdamm. In these excursions he was usually accompanied by an old negro, called Jupiter, who had been manumitted before the reverses of the family, but who could be induced, neither by threats nor by promises, to abandon what he considered his right of attendance upon the footsteps of his young "Massa Will." It is not improbable that the relatives of Legrand, conceiving him to be somewhat unsettled in intellect, had contrived to instill this obstinacy into Jupiter, with a view to the supervision and guardianship of the wanderer.

The winters in the latitude of Sullivan's Island are seldom very severe, and in the fall of the year it is a rare event indeed when a fire is considered necessary. About the middle of October, 18—, there occurred, however, a day of remarkable chilliness. Just

before sunset I scrambled my way through the evergreens to the
hut of my friend, whom I had not visited for several weeks—my
residence being, at that time, in Charleston, a distance of nine
miles from the island, while the facilities of passage and re-
passage were very far behind those of the present day. Upon
reaching the hut I rapped, as was my custom, and getting no
reply, sought for the key where I knew it was secreted, unlocked
the door, and went in. A fine fire was blazing upon the hearth. It
was a novelty, and by no means an ungrateful one. I threw off an
overcoat, took an arm-chair by the crackling logs, and awaited
patiently the arrival of my hosts.

Soon after dark they arrived, and gave me a most cordial
welcome. Jupiter, grinning from ear to ear, bustled about to
prepare some marsh-hens for supper. Legrand was in one of his
fits—how else shall I term them?—of enthusiasm. He had found
an unknown bivalve, forming a new genus, and, more than this,
he had hunted down and secured, with Jupiter's assistance a
scarabæus which he believed to be totally new, but in respect to
which he wished to have my opinion on the morrow.

"And why not to-night?" I asked, rubbing my hands over the
blaze, and wishing the whole tribe of *scarabæi* at the devil.

"Ah, if I had only known you were here!" said Legrand "but
it's so long since I saw you; and how could I foresee that you
would pay me a visit this very night of all others? As I was
coming home I met Lieutenant G——, from the fort, and, very
foolishly, I lent him the bug; so it will be impossible for you to
see it until the morning. Stay here to-night, and I will send Jup
down for it at sunrise. It is the loveliest thing in creation!"

"What?—sunrise?"

"Nonsense! no!—the bug. It is of a brilliant gold color—
about the size of a large hickory nut—with two jet black spots
near one extremity of the back, and another, somewhat longer, at
the other. The *antennæ* are—"

"Dey ain't *no* tin in him, Massa Will, I keep a tellin' on
you," here interrupted Jupiter "de bug is a goole-bug, solid,
ebery bit of him, inside and all, sep him wing—neber feel half
so hebby a bug in my life."

"Well, suppose it is, Jup," replied Legrand, somewhat more
earnestly, it seemed to me, than the case demanded; "is that any
reason for your letting the birds burn? The color"—here he
turned to me—"is really almost enough to warrant Jupiter's
idea. You never saw a more brilliant metallic lustre that the
scales emit—but of this you cannot judge till to-morrow. In the
meantime I can give you some idea of the shape." Saying this,

he seated himself at a small table, on which were a pen and ink, but no paper. He looked for some in a drawer, but found none.

"Never mind," he said at length, "this will answer;" and he drew from his waistcoat pocket a scrap of what I took to be very dirty foolscap, and made upon it a rough drawing with the pen. While he did this, I retained my seat by the fire, for I was still chilly. When the design was complete, he handed it to me without rising. As I received it, a loud growl was heard, succeeded by a scratching at the door. Jupiter opened it, and a large Newfoundland, belonging to Legrand, rushed in, leaped upon my shoulders, and loaded me with caresses; for I had shown him much attention during previous visits. When his gambols were over, I looked at the paper, and, to speak the truth, found myself not a little puzzled at what my friend had depicted.

"Well!" I said, after contemplating it for some minutes, "this *is* a strange *scarabæus*, I must confess; new to me; never saw anything like it before—unless it was a skull, or a death's-head, which it more nearly resembles than anything else that has come under *my* observation."

"A death's-head!" echoed Legrand. "Oh—yes—well, it has something of that appearance upon paper, no doubt. The two upper black spots look like eyes, eh? and the longer one at the bottom like a mouth—and then the shape of the whole is oval."

"Perhaps so," said I; "but, Legrand, I fear you are no artist. I must wait until I see the beetle itself, if I am to form any idea of its personal appearance."

"Well, I don't know," said he, a little nettled, "I draw tolerably—*should* do it at least—have had good masters, and flatter myself that I am not quite a blockhead."

"But, my dear fellow, you are joking, then," said I, "this is a very passable *skull*—indeed. I may say that it is a very *excellent* skull, according to the vulgar notions about such specimens of physiology—and your *scarabæus* must be the queerest *scarabæus* in the world if it resembles it. Why, we may get up a very thrilling bit of superstition upon this hint. I presume you will call the bug *scarabæus caput hominis*, or something of that kind—there are many similar titles in the Natural Histories. But where are the *antennæ* you spoke of?"

"The *antennæ*!" said Legrand, who seemed to be getting unaccountably warm upon the subject; "I am sure you must see the *antennæ*. I made them as distinct as they are in the original insect, and I presume that is sufficient."

"Well, well," I said, "perhaps you have—still I don't see them;" and I handed him the paper without additional remark, not wishing to ruffle his temper; but I was much surprised at the turn affairs had taken; his ill humor puzzled me—and, as for the drawing of the beetle, there were positively *no antennæ* visible, and the whole *did* bear a very close resemblance to the ordinary cuts of a death's-head.

He received the paper very peevishly, and was about to crumple it, apparently to throw it in the fire, when a casual glance at the design seemed suddenly to rivet his attention. In an instant his face grew violently red—in another excessively pale. For some minutes he continued to scrutinize the drawing minutely where he sat. At length he arose, took a candle from the table, and proceeded to seat himself upon a sea-chest in the farthest corner of the room. Here again he made an anxious examination of the paper; turning it in all directions. He said nothing however, and his conduct greatly astonished me; yet I thought it prudent not to exacerbate the growing moodiness of his temper by any comment. Presently he took from his coat-pocket a wallet, placed the paper carefully in it, and deposited both in a writing-desk, which he locked. He now grew more composed in his demeanor; but his original air of enthusiasm had quite disappeared. Yet he seemed not so much sulky as abstracted. As the evening wore away he became more and more absorbed in revery, from which no sallies of mine could arouse him. It had been my intention to pass the night at the hut, as I had frequently done before, but, seeing my host in this mood, I deemed it proper to take leave. He did not press me to remain, but, as I departed, he shook my hand with even more than his usual cordiality.

It was about a month after this (and during the interval I had seen nothing of Legrand) when I received a visit, at Charleston, from his man, Jupiter. I had never seen the good old negro look so dispirited, and I feared that some serious disaster had befallen my friend.

"Well, Jup," said I, "what is the matter now?—how is your master?"

"Why, to speak the troof, massa, him not so berry well as mought be."

"Not well! I am truly sorry to hear it. What does he complain of?"

"Dar! dat's it!—him neber plain of notin—but him berry sick for all dat."

"*Very* sick, Jupiter!—why didn't you say so at once? Is he confined to bed?"

"No, dat he aint!—he aint find nowhar—dat's just what he

shoe pinch—my mind is got to be berry hebby bout poor Massa Will.''

"Jupiter, I should like to understand what it is you are talking about. You say your master is sick. Hasn't he told you what ails him?''

"Why, massa, taint worf while for to git mad about de matter—Massa Will say noffin at all aint de matter wid him—but den what make him go about looking dis here way, wid he head down and he soldiers up, and as white as a gose? And den he keep a syphon all de time——''

"Keeps a what, Jupiter?''

"Keeps a syphon wid de figgurs on de slate—de queerest figgurs I ebber did see. Ise gittin to be skeered, I tell you. Hab for to keep mighty tight eye pon him noovers. Todder day he gib me slip fore de sun up and was gone de whole ob de blessed day. I had a big stick ready cut for to gib him deuced good beating when he did come—but Ise sich a fool dat I hadn't de heart arter all—he looked so berry poorly.''

"Eh?—what?—ah yes!—upon the whole I think you had better not be too severe with the poor fellow—don't flog him, Jupiter—he can't very well stand it—but can you form no idea of what has occasioned this illness, or rather this change of conduct? Has anything unpleasant happened since I saw you?''

"No, massa, dey aint bin noffin onpleasant *since* den—'twas *fore* den I'm feared—'twas be berry day you was dare.''

"How? what do you mean?''

"Why, massa, I mean de bug—dare now.''

"That what?''

"De bug—I'm berry sartain dat Massa Will bin bit somewhere 'bout he head by dat goole-bug.''

"And what cause have you, Jupiter, for such a supposition.''

"Claws enuff, massa, and mouff, too. I never did see sich a deuced bug—he kick and he bite ebery ting what cum near him. Massa Will cotch him fuss, but had for to let him go gin mighty quick, I tell you—den was de time he must ha got de bite. I didn't like de look ob de bug mouff, myself, no how, so I wouldn't take hold ob him wid my finger, but I cotch him wid a piece of paper dat I found. I rap him up in de paper and stuff a piece of it in he mouff—dat was de way.''

"And you think then, that your master was really bitten by the beetle, and that the bite made him sick?''

"I don't think noffin about it—I nose it. What make him dream bout de goole so much, if taint cause he bit by the goole-bug? Ise heered bout dem goole-bugs fore dis.''

"But how do you know he dreams about gold?"

"How I know? why, cause he talk about it in he sleep—dat's how I nose."

"Well, Jup, perhaps you are right; but to what fortunate circumstance am I to attribute the honor of a visit from you to-day?"

"What de matter, massa?"

"Did you bring any message from Mr. Legrand?"

"No, massa, I bring dis here pissel;" and here Jupiter handed me a note which ran thus:

"My Dear—

"Why have I not seen you for so long a time? I hope you have not been so foolish as to take offence at any little *brusquerie* of mine; but no, that is improbable.

"Since I saw you I have had great cause for anxiety. I have something to tell you, yet scarcely know how to tell it, or whether I should tell it at all.

"I have not been quite well for some days past, and poor old Jup annoys me, almost beyond endurance, by his well-meant attentions. Would you believe it?—he had prepared a huge stick, the other day, with which to chastise me for giving him the slip, and spending the day, *solus*, among the hills on the mainland. I verily believe that my ill looks alone saved me a flogging.

"I have made no addition to my cabinet since we met.

"If you can, in any way, make it convenient, come over with Jupiter. *Do* come. I wish to see you *to-night*, upon business of importance. I assure you that it is of the *highest* importance.

"Ever yours,
"WILLIAM LEGRAND."

There was something in the tone of this note which gave me great uneasiness. Its whole style differed materially from that of Legrand. What could he be dreaming of? What new crotchet possessed his excitable brain? What "business of the highest importance" could *he* possibly have to transact? Jupiter's account of him boded no good. I dreaded lest the continued pressure of misfortune had, at length, fairly unsettled the reason of my friend. Without a moment's hesitation, therefore, I prepared to accompany the negro.

Upon reaching the wharf, I noticed a scythe and three spades,

all apparently new, lying in the bottom of the boat in which we
were to embark.

"What is the meaning of all this, Jup?" I inquired.

"Him syfe, massa, and spade."

"Very true; but what are they doing here?"

"Him de syfe and de spade what Massa Will sis pon my
buying for him in de town, and de debbils own lot of money I
had to gib for em."

"But what, in the name of all that is mysterious, is your
'Massa Will' going to do with scythes and spades?"

"Dat's more dan *I* know, and debbil take me if I don't blieve
'tis more dan he know too. But it's all cum ob de bug."

Finding that no satisfaction was to be obtained of Jupiter,
whose whole intellect seemed to be absorbed by "de bug," I
now stepped into the boat, and made sail. With a fair and strong
breeze we soon ran into the little cove to the northward of Fort
Moultrie, and a walk of some two miles brought us to the hut. It
was about three in the afternoon when we arrived. Legrand had
been awaiting us in eager expectation. He grasped my hand with
a nervous *empressement* which alarmed me and strengthened the
suspicions already entertained. His countenance was pale even to
ghastliness, and his deep-set eyes glared with unnatural lustre.
After some inquiries respecting his health, I asked him, not
knowing what better to say, if he had yet obtained the *scarabæus*
from Lieutenant G——.

"Oh, yes," he replied, coloring violently, "I got it from him
the next morning. Nothing should tempt me to part with that
scarabæus. Do you know that Jupiter is quite right about it?"

"In what way?" I asked, with a sad foreboding at heart.

"In supposing it to be a bug of *real gold*." He said this with
an air of profound seriousness, and I felt inexpressibly shocked.

"This bug is to make my fortune," he continued, with a
triumphant smile; "to reinstate me in my family possessions. Is
it any wonder, then, that I prize it? Since Fortune has thought fit
to bestow it upon me, I have only to use it properly, and I shall
arrive at the gold of which it is the index. Jupiter, bring me that
scarabæus!"

"What! de bug, massa? I'd rudder not go fer trubble dat bug;
you must git him for your own self." Hereupon Legrand arose,
with a grave and stately air, and brought me the beetle from a
glass case in which it was enclosed. It was a beautiful *scarabæus*,
and, at that time, unknown to naturalists—of course a great prize
in a scientific point of view. There were two round black spots
near one extremity of the back, and a long one near the other.

The scales were exceedingly hard and glossy, with all the appearance of burnished gold. The weight of the insect was very remarkable, and, taking all things into consideration, I could hardly blame Jupiter for his opinion respecting it; but what to make of Legrand's concordance with that opinion, I could not, for the life of me, tell.

"I sent for you," said he, in a grandiloquent tone, when I had completed my examination of the beetle, "I sent for you that I might have your counsel and assistance in furthering the views of Fate and of the bug—"

"My dear Legrand," I cried, interrupting him, "you are certainly unwell, and had better use some little precautions. You shall go to bed, and I will remain with you a few days, until you get over this. You are feverish and—"

"Feel my pulse," said he.

I felt it, and, to say the truth, found not the slightest indication of fever.

"But you may be ill and yet have no fever. Allow me this once to prescribe for you. In the first place go to bed. In the next—"

"You are mistaken," he interposed, "I am as well as I can expect to be under the excitement which I suffer. If you really wish me well, you will relieve this excitement."

"And how is this to be done?"

"Very easily. Jupiter and myself are going upon an expedition into the hills, upon the main land, and, in this expedition, we shall need the aid of some person in whom we can confide. You are the only one we can trust. Whether we succeed or fail, the excitement which you now perceive in me will be equally allayed."

"I am anxious to oblige you in any way," I replied; "but do you mean to say that this infernal beetle has any connection with your expedition into the hills?"

"It has."

"Then, Legrand, I can become a party to no such absurd proceeding."

"I am sorry—very sorry—for we shall have to try it by ourselves."

"Try it by yourselves! The man is surely mad!—but stay! —how long do you propose to be absent?"

"Probably all night. We shall start immediately, and be back, at all events, by sunrise."

"And will you promise me, upon your honor, that when this freak of yours is over, and the bug business (good God!) settled to your satisfaction, you will then return home and follow my advice implicitly, as that of your physician?"

"Yes; I promise; and now let us be off, for we have no time to lose."

With a heavy heart I accompanied my friend. We started about four o'clock—Legrand, Jupiter, the dog, and myself. Jupiter had with him the scythe and spades—the whole of which he insisted upon carrying—more through fear, it seemed to me, of trusting either of the implements within reach of his master, than from any excess of industry or complaisance. His demeanor was dogged in the extreme, and "dat deuced bug" were the sole words which escaped his lips during the journey. For my own part, I had charge of a couple of dark lanterns, while Legrand contented himself with the *scarabæus*, which he carried attached to the end of a bit of whipcord: twirling it to and fro, with the air of a conjuror, as he went. When I observed this last, plain evidence of my friend's aberration of mind, I could scarcely refrain from tears. I thought it best, however, to humor his fancy, at least for the present, or until I could adopt some more energetic measures with a chance of success. In the meantime I endeavored, but all in vain, to sound him in regard to the object of the expedition. Having succeeded in inducing me to accompany him, he seemed unwilling to hold conversation upon any topic of minor importance, and to all my questions vouchsafed no other reply than "we shall see!"

We crossed the creek at the head of the island by means of a skiff, and, ascending the high grounds on the shore of the main land, proceeded in a northwesterly direction, through a tract of country excessively wild and desolate, where no trace of a human footstep was to be seen. Legrand led the way with decision; pausing only for an instant, here and there, to consult what appeared to be certain landmarks of his own contrivance upon a former occasion.

In this manner we journeyed for about two hours, and the sun was just setting when we entered a region infinitely more dreary than any yet seen. It was a species of tableland, near the summit of an almost inaccessible hill, densely wooded from base to pinnacle, and interspersed with huge crags that appeared to lie loosely upon the soil, and in many cases were prevented from precipitating themselves into the valleys below, merely by the support of the trees against which they reclined. Deep ravines, in various directions, gave an air of still sterner solemnity to the scene.

The natural platform to which we had clambered was thickly

overgrown with brambles, through which we soon discovered
that it would have been impossible to force our way but for the
scythe; and Jupiter, by direction of his master, proceeded to clear
for us a path to the foot of an enormously tall tulip-tree, which
stood, with some eight or ten oaks, upon the level, and far
surpassed them all, and all other trees which I had then ever
seen, in the beauty of its foliage and form, in the wide spread of
its branches, and in the general majesty of its appearance. When
we reached this tree, Legrand turned to Jupiter, and asked him if
he thought he could climb it. The old man seemed a little
staggered by the question, and for some moments made no reply.
At length he approached the huge trunk, walked slowly around
it, and examined it with minute attention. When he had completed his scrutiny, he merely said:

"Yes, massa, Jup climb any tree he ebber see in he life."

"Then up with you as soon as possible, for it will soon be too
dark to see what we are about."

"How far mus go up, massa?" inquired Jupiter.

"Get up the main trunk first, and then I will tell you which
way to go—and here—stop! take this beetle with you."

"De bug, Massa Will!—de goole-bug!" cried the negro, drawing back in dismay—"What for mus tote de bug way up de
tree?—d—n if I do!"

"If you are afraid, Jup, a great big negro like you, to take
hold of a hamless little dead beetle, why you can carry it up by
this string—but, if you do not take it up with you in some way, I
shall be under the necessity of breaking your head with this
shovel."

"What de matter now, massa?" said Jup, evidently shamed
into compliance; "always want for to raise fuss wid old nigger.
Was only funnin anyhow. *Me* feered de bug! what I keer for de
bug?" Here he took cautiously hold of the extreme end of the
string, and, maintaining the insect as far from his person as
circumstances would permit, prepared to ascend the tree.

In youth, the tulip-tree, or *Liriodendron Tulipiferum*, the most
magnificent of American foresters, has a trunk peculiarly smooth,
and often rises to a great height without lateral branches; but, in
its riper age, the bark becomes gnarled and uneven, while many
short limbs make their appearance on the stem. Thus the difficulty of ascension, in the present case, lay more in semblance
than in reality. Embracing the huge cylinder, as closely as
possible, with his arms and knees, seizing with his hands some
projections, and resting his naked toes upon others, Jupiter, after
one or two narrow escapes from falling, at length wriggled

himself into the first great fork, and seemed to consider the whole business as virtually accomplished. The *risk* of the achievement was, in fact, now over, although the climber was some sixty or seventy feet from the ground.

"Which way mus go now, Massa Will?" he asked.

"Keep up the largest branch—the one on this side," said Legrand. The negro obeyed him promptly, and apparently with but little trouble; ascending higher and higher, until no glimpse of his squat figure could be obtained through the dense foliage which enveloped it. Presently his voice was heard in a sort of halloo.

"How much fudder is got for go?"

"How high up are you?" asked Legrand.

"Ebber so fur," replied the negro; "can see de sky fru de top ob de tree."

"Never mind the sky, but attend to what I say. Look down the trunk and count the limbs below you on this side. How many limbs have you passed?"

"One, two, tree, four, fibe—I done pass fibe big limb, massa, pon dis side."

"Then go one limb higher."

In a few minutes the voice was heard again, announcing that the seventh limb was attained.

"Now, Jup," cried Legrand, evidently much excited, "I want you to work your way out upon that limb as far as you can. If you see anything strange let me know."

By this time what little doubt I might have entertained of my poor friend's insanity was put finally at rest. I had no alternative but to conclude him stricken with lunacy, and I became seriously anxious about getting him home. While I was pondering upon what was best to be done. Jupiter's voice was again heard.

"Mos feered for to ventur pon dis limb berry far—'tis dead limb putty much all de way."

"Did you say it was a *dead* limb, Jupiter?" cried Legrand in a quavering voice.

"Yes, massa, him dead as de doornail—done up for sartain—done departed dis here life."

"What in the name of heaven shall I do?" asked Legrand, seemingly in the greatest distress.

"Do!" said I, glad of an opportunity to interpose a word, "why come home and go to bed. Come now!—that's a fine fellow. It's getting late, and, besides, you remember your promise."

"Jupiter," cried he, without heeding me in the least, "do you hear me?"

"Yes, Massa Will, hear you ebber so plain."

"Try the wood well, then, with your knife, and see if you think it *very* rotten."

"Him rotten, massa, sure nuff," replied the negro in a few moments, "but not so berry rotten as mought be. Mought venture out leetle way pon de limb by myself, dat's true."

"By yourself!—what do you mean?"

"Why, I mean de bug. 'Tis *berry* hebby bug. Spose I drop him down fuss, and den de limb won't break wid just de weight of one nigger."

"You infernal scoundrel!" cried Legrand, apparently much relieved, "what do you mean by telling me such nonsense as that? As sure as you drop that beetle I'll break your neck. Look here, Jupiter, do you hear me?"

"Yess, massa, needn't hollo at poor nigger dat style."

"Well! now listen!—if you will venture out on the limb as far as you think safe, and not let go the beetle, I'll make you a present of a silver dollar as soon as you get down."

"I'm gwine, Massa Will—deed I is," replied the negro very promptly—"mos out to the eend now."

"Out to the end!" here fairly screamed Legrand; "do you say you are out to the end of that limb?"

"Soon be to de eend, massa—o-o-o-o-oh! Lor-gol-a-marcy! what *is* dis here pon de tree?"

"Well!" cried Legrand, highly delighted, "what is it?"

"Why 'taint noffin but a skull—somebody bin lef him head up de tree, and de crows done gobble ebery bit ob de meat off."

"A skull, you say!—very well,—how is it fastened to the limb?—what holds it on?"

"Sure nuff, massa; mus look. Why dis berry curious sarcumstance, pon my word—dare's a great big nail in de skull, what fastens ob it on to de tree."

"Well now, Jupiter, do exactly as I tell you—do you hear?"

"Yes, massa."

"Pay attention, then—find the left eye of the skull."

"Hum! hoo! dat's good! why dare ain't no eye lef at all."

"Curst your stupidity! do you know your right hand from your left?"

"Yes, I nose dat—nose all about dat—tis my lef hand what I chops de wood wid."

"To be sure! you are left-handed; and your left eye is on the same side as your left hand. Now, I suppose, you can find the left eye of the skull, or the place where the left eye has been. Have you found it?''

Here was a long pause. At length the negro asked.

''Is de lef eye of de skull pon de same side as de lef hand of de skull too?—cause de skull aint got not a bit ob a hand at all—nebber mind! I got de lef eye now—here de lef eye! what mus do wid it?''

''Let the beetle drop through it, as far as the string will reach—but be careful and not let go your hold of the string.''

''All dat done, Massa Will; mighty easy ting for to put de bug fru de hole—look out for him dare below!''

During this colloquy no portion of Jupiter's person could be seen; but the beetle, which he had suffered to descend, was now visible at the end of the string, and glistened, like a globe of burnished gold, in the last rays of the setting sun, some of which still faintly illumined the eminence upon which we stood. The *scarabæus* hung quite clear of any branches, and, if allowed to fall, would have fallen at our feet. Legrand immediately took the scythe, and cleared with it a circular space, three or four yards in diameter, just beneath the insect, and, having accomplished this, ordered Jupiter to let go the string and come down from the tree.

Driving a peg, with great nicety, into the ground, at the precise spot where the beetle fell, my friend now produced from his pocket a tape-measure. Fastening one end of this at that point of the trunk of the tree which was nearest the peg, he unrolled it till it reached the peg, and thence farther unrolled it, in the direction already established by the two points of the tree and the peg, for the distance of fifty feet—Jupiter clearing away the brambles with the scythe. At the spot thus attained a second peg was driven, and about this, as a centre, a rude circle, about four feet in diameter, described. Taking now a spade himself, and giving one to Jupiter and one to me, Legrand begged us to set about digging as quickly as possible.

To speak the truth, I had no special relish for such amusement at any time, and, at that particular moment, would willingly have declined it; for the night was coming on, and I felt much fatigued with the exercise already taken; but I saw no mode of escape, and was fearful of disturbing my poor friend's equanimity by a refusal. Could I have depended, indeed upon Jupiter's aid, I would have had no hesitation in attempting to get the lunatic home by force; but I was too well assured of the old negro's disposition, to hope that he would assist me, under any circumstances, in a personal contest with his master. I made no doubt that the latter had been infected with some of the innumerable Southern superstitions about money buried, and that his phantasy had received confirmation by the finding of the *scarabæus*, or, perhaps, by Jupiter's obstinacy in maintaining it to be "a bug of real gold." A mind disposed to lunacy would readily be led away by such suggestions—especially if chiming in with favorite preconceived ideas—and then I called to mind the poor fellow's speech about the beetle's being "the index of his fortune." Upon the whole, I was sadly vexed and puzzled, but, at length, I concluded to make a virtue of necessity—to dig with a good will, and thus the sooner to convince the visionary, by ocular demonstration, of the fallacy of the opinions he entertained.

The lanterns having been lit, we all fell to work with a zeal worthy a more rational cause; and, as the glare fell upon our persons and implements, I could not help thinking how picturesque a group we composed, and how strange and suspicious our labors must have appeared to any interloper who, by chance, might have stumbled upon our whereabouts.

We dug very steadily for two hours. Little was said; and our chief embarrassment lay in the yelpings of the dog, who took exceeding interest in our proceedings. He, at length, became so obstreperous that we grew fearful of his giving the alarm to some stragglers in the vicinity,—or, rather, this was the apprehension of Legrand;—for myself, I should have rejoiced at any interruption which might have enabled me to get the wanderer home. The noise was, at length, very effectually silenced by Jupiter, who, getting out of the hole with a dogged air of deliberation, tied the brute's mouth up with one of his suspenders, and then returned, with a grave chuckle, to his task.

When the time mentioned had expired, we had reached a depth of five feet, and yet no sign of any treasure became manifest. A general pause ensued, and I began to hope that the farce was at an end. Legrand, however, although evidently much disconcerted, wiped his brow thoughtfully and recommenced. We had excavated the entire circle of four feet diameter, and now we slightly enlarged the limit, and went to the farther depth of two feet. Still nothing appeared. The gold-seeker, whom I sincerely pitied, at length clambered from the pit, with the bitterest disappointment imprinted upon every feature, and proceeded, slowly and reluctantly, to put on his coat, which he had thrown off at the beginning of his labor. In the meantime I made no remark. Jupiter, at a signal from his master, began to gather up his tools. This done, and the dog having been unmuzzled, we turned in profound silence toward home.

We had taken, perhaps, a dozen steps in this direction, when, with a loud oath, Legrand strode up to Jupiter, and seized him by the collar. The astonished negro opened his eyes and mouth to the fullest extent, let fall the spades, and fell upon his knees.

"You scoundrel!" said Legrand, hissing out the syllables from between his clenched teeth—"you infernal black villain! —speak, I tell you!—answer me this instant, without prevarication! —which—which is your left eye?"

"Oh, my golly, Massa Will! aint dis here my lef eye for sartain?" roared the terrified Jupiter, placing his hand upon his *right* organ of vision, and holding it there with a desperate pertinacity, as if in immediate dread of his master's attempt at a gouge.

"I thought so!—I knew it! hurrah!" vociferated Legrand, letting the negro go and executing a series of curvets and caracols, much to the astonishment of his valet, who, arising from his knees, looked, mutely, from his master to myself, and then from myself to his master.

"Come! we must go back," said the latter, "the game's not up yet"; and he again led the way to the tulip-tree.

"Jupiter," said he, when we reached its foot, "come here! Was the skull nailed to the limb with the face outward, or with the face to the limb?"

"De face was out, massa, so dat de crows could get at de eyes good, widout any trouble."

"Well, then, was it this eye or that through which you dropped the beetle?" Here Legrand touched each of Jupiter's eyes.

"'Twas dis eye, massa—de lef eye—jis as you tell me," and here it was his right eye that the negro indicated.

"That will do—we must try it again."

Here my friend, about whose madness I now saw, or fancied that I saw, certain indications of method, removed the peg which marked the spot where the beetle fell, to a spot about three inches to the westward of its former position. Taking, now, the tape measure from the nearest point of the trunk to the peg, as before, and continuing the extension in a straight line to the distance of fifty feet, a spot was indicated, removed, by several yards, from the point at which we had been digging.

Around the new position a circle, somewhat larger than in the former instance, was now described, and we again set to work with the spades. I was dreadfully weary, but, scarcely understanding what had occasioned the change in my thoughts, I felt no longer any great aversion from the labor imposed. I had become most unaccountably interested—nay, even excited. Perhaps there was something, amid all the extravagant demeanor of Legrand—some air of forethought, or of deliberation, which impressed me. I dug eagerly, and now and then caught myself actually looking, with something that very much resembled expectation, for the fancied treasure, the vision of which had demented my unfortunate companion. At a period when such vagaries of thought most fully possessed me, and when we had been at work perhaps an hour and a half, we were again interrupted by the violent howlings of the dog. His uneasiness, in the first instance, had been, evidently, but the result of playfulness or caprice, but he now assumed a bitter and serious tone. Upon Jupiter's again attempting to muzzle him, he made furious resistance, and, leaping into the hole, tore up the mould frantically with his claws. In a few seconds he had uncovered a mass of human bones, forming two complete skeletons, intermingled with several buttons of metal, and what appeared to be the dust of decayed woolen. One or two strokes of a spade upturned the blade of a large Spanish knife, and, as we dug farther, three or four loose pieces of gold and silver coin came to light.

At sight of these the joy of Jupiter could scarcely be restrained, but the countenance of his master wore an air of extreme disappointment. He urged us, however, to continue our exertions, and the words were hardly uttered when I stumbled and fell forward, having caught the toe of my boot in a large ring of iron that lay half buried in the loose earth.

We now worked in earnest, and never did I pass ten minutes of more intense excitement. During this interval we had fairly unearthed an oblong chest of wood, which, from its perfect preservation and wonderful hardness, had plainly been subjected to some mineralizing process—perhaps that of the Bi-chloride of Mercury. This box was three feet and a half long, three feet broad, and two and a half feet deep. It was firmly secured by bands of wrought iron, riveted, and forming a kind of open trellis-work over the whole. On each side of the chest, near the top, were three rings of iron—six in all—by means of which a firm hold could be obtained by six persons. Our utmost united endeavors served only to disturb the coffer very slightly in its bed. We at once saw the impossibility of removing so great a weight. Luckily, the sole fastenings of the lid consisted of two sliding bolts. These we drew back—trembling and panting with anxiety. In an instant, a treasure of incalculable value lay gleaming before us. As the rays of the lanterns fell within the pit, there flashed upwards a glow and a glare, from a confused heap of gold and jewels, that absolutely dazzled our eyes.

I shall not pretend to describe the feelings with which I gazed. Amazement was, of course, predominant. Legrand appeared exhausted with excitement, and spoke very few words. Jupiter's countenance wore, for some minutes, as deadly a pallor as it is possible, in the nature of things, for any negro's visage to assume. He seemed stupefied—thunderstricken. Presently he fell upon his knees in the pit, and burying his naked arms up to the elbows in gold, let them there remain, as if enjoying the luxury of a bath. At length, with a deep sigh, he exclaimed, as if in a soliloquy:

"And dis all cum ob de goole-bug! de putty goole-bug! de poor little goole-bug, what I boosed in dat sabage kind ob style! Aint you shamed ob yourself, nigger?—answer me dat!"

It became necessary, at last, that I should arouse both master and valet to the expediency of removing the treasure. It was growing late, and it behooved us to make exertion, that we might get every thing housed before daylight. It was difficult to say what should be done, and much time was spent in deliberation—so confused were the ideas of all. We, finally, lightened the box by removing two-thirds of its contents, when we were enabled, with some trouble to raise it from the hole. The articles taken out were deposited among the brambles, and the dog left to guard them, with strict orders from Jupiter neither, upon any pretence, to stir from the spot, nor to open his mouth until our return. We then hurriedly made for home with the chest; reaching the hut in safety, but after excessive toil, at one o'clock in the morning. Worn out as we were, it was not in human nature to do more immediately. We rested until two, and had supper; starting for the hills immediately afterward, armed with three stout sacks, which, by good luck, were upon the premises. A little before four we arrived at the pit, divided the remainder of the booty, as equally as might be, among us, and, leaving the holes unfilled, again set out for the hut, at which, for the second time, we deposited our golden burthens, just as the first faint streaks of the dawn gleamed from over the tree-tops in the East.

We were now thoroughly broken down; but the intense excitement of the time denied us repose. After an unquiet slumber of some three or four hours' duration, we arose, as if by preconcert, to make examination of our treasure.

The chest had been full to the brim, and we spent the whole day, and the greater part of the next night, in a scrutiny of its contents. There had been nothing like order or arrangement.

Everything had been heaped in promiscuously. Having assorted
all with care we found ourselves possessed of even vaster wealth
than we had at first supposed. In coin there was rather more than
four hundred and fifty thousand dollars—estimating the value of
the pieces, as accurately as we could, by the tables of the period.
There was not a particle of silver. All was gold of antique date
and of great variety—French, Spanish, and German money, with
a few English guineas, and some counters, of which we had
never seen specimens before. There were several very large and
heavy coins, so worn that we could make nothing of their
inscriptions. There was no American money. The value of the
jewels we found more difficulty in estimating. There were
diamonds—some of them exceedingly large and fine—a hundred
and ten in all, and not one of them small; eighteen rubies of
remarkable brilliancy;—three hundred and ten emeralds, all very
beautiful; and twenty-one sapphires, with an opal. These stones
had all been broken from their settings and thrown loose in the
chest. The settings themselves, which we picked out from among
the other gold, appeared to have been beaten up with hammers,
as if to prevent identification. Besides all this, there was a vast
quantity of solid gold ornaments; nearly two hundred massive
finger and earrings; rich chains—thirty of these, if I remember;
eighty-three very large and heavy crucifixes; five gold censers of
great value; a prodigious golden punch-bowl, ornamented with
richly chased vine-leaves and Bacchanalian figures; with two
sword-handles exquisitely embossed, and many other smaller
articles which I cannot recollect. The weight of these valuables
exceeded three hundred and fifty pounds avoirdupois; and in this
estimate I have not included one hundred and ninety-seven superb gold watches; three of the number being worth each five
hundred dollars, if one. Many of them were very old, and as
timekeepers valueless; the works having suffered, more or less,
from corrosion—but all were richly jewelled and in cases of
great worth. We estimated the entire contents of the chest, that
night, at a million and a half of dollars; and upon the subsequent
disposal of the trinkets and jewels (a few being retained for our
own use), it was found that we had greatly under-valued the
treasure.

When, at length, we had concluded our examination, and the
intense excitement of the time had, in some measure, subsided,
Legrand, who saw that I was dying with impatience for a solution of this most extraordinary riddle, entered into a full detail of
all the circumstances connected with it.

"You remember," said he, "the night when I handed you the

rough sketch I had made of the *scarabæus*. You recollect also, that I became quite vexed at you for insisting that my drawing resembled a death's-head. When you first made this assertion I thought you were jesting; but afterwards I called to mind the peculiar spots on the back of the insect, and admitted to myself that your remark had some little foundation in fact. Still, the sneer at my graphic powers irritated me—for I am considered a good artist—and, therefore, when you handed me the scrap of parchment, I was about to crumple it up and throw it angrily into the fire.''

"The scrap of paper, you mean," said I.

"No; it had much of the appearance of paper, and at first I supposed it to be such, but when I came to draw upon it, I discovered it at once to be a piece of very thin parchment. It was quite dirty, you remember. Well, as I was in the very act of crumpling it up, my glance fell upon the sketch at which you had been looking, and you may imagine my astonishment when I perceived, in fact, the figure of a death's-head just where, it seemed to me, I had made the drawing of the beetle. For a moment I was too much amazed to think with accuracy. I knew that my design was very different in detail from this—although there was a certain similarity in general outline. Presently I took a candle, and seating myself at the other end of the room, proceeded to scrutinize the parchment more closely. Upon turning it over, I saw my own sketch upon the reverse, just as I had made it. My first idea, now, was mere surprise at the really remarkable similarity of outline—at the singular coincidence involved in the fact that, unknown to me, there should have been a skull upon the other side of the parchment, immediately beneath my figure of the *scarabæus*, and that this skull, not only in outline, but in size, should so closely resemble my drawing. I say the singularity of this coincidence absolutely stupefied me for a time. This is the usual effect of such coincidences. The mind struggles to establish a connexion—a sequence of cause and effect—and, being unable to do so, suffers a species of temporary paralysis. But, when I recovered from this stupor, there dawned upon me gradually a conviction which startled me even far more than the coincidence. I began distinctly, positively, to remember that there had been *no* drawing upon the parchment, when I made my sketch of the *scarabæus*. I became perfectly certain of this; for I recollected turning up first one side and then the other, in search of the cleanest spot. Had the skull been then there, of course I could not have failed to notice it. Here was indeed a mystery which I felt it impossible to explain; but, even at that early moment, there seemed to glimmer, faintly, within the most remote and secret chambers of my intellect, a glow-worm-like conception of that truth which last night's adventure brought to so magnificent a demonstration. I arose at once, and putting the parchment securely away, dismissed all further reflection until I should be alone.

"When you had gone, and when Jupiter was fast asleep, I betook myself to a more methodical investigation of the affair. In the first place I considered the manner in which the parchment had come into my possession. The spot where we discovered the *scarabæus* was on the coast of the mainland, about a mile eastward of the island, and but a short distance above high-water mark. Upon my taking hold of it, it gave me a sharp bite, which caused me to let it drop. Jupiter, with his accustomed caution, before seizing the insect, which had flown toward him, looked about him for a leaf, or something of that nature, by which to take hold of it. It was at this moment that his eyes, and mine also, fell upon the scrap of parchment, which I then supposed to be paper. It was lying half buried in the sand, a corner sticking up. Near the spot where we found it, I observed the remnants of the hull of what appeared to have been a ship's long boat. The wreck seemed to have been there for a very great while; for the resemblance to boat timbers could scarcely be traced.

"Well, Jupiter picked up the parchment, wrapped the beetle in it, and gave it to me. Soon afterward we turned to go home, and on the way met Lieutenant G——. I showed him the insect, and he begged me to let him take it to the fort. Upon my consenting, he thrust it forthwith into his waistcoat pocket, without the parchment in which it had been wrapped, and which I had continued to hold in my hand during his inspection. Perhaps he dreaded my changing my mind, and thought it best to make sure of the prize at once—you know how enthusiastic he is on all subjects connected with Natural History. At the same time, without being conscious of it, I must have deposited the parchment in my own pocket.

"You remember that when I went to the table, for the purpose of making a sketch of the beetle, I found no paper where it was usually kept. I looked in the drawer, and found none there. I searched my pockets, hoping to find an old letter, when my hand fell upon the parchment. I thus detail the precise mode in which it came into my possession; for the circumstances impressed me with a peculiar force.

"No doubt you will think me fanciful—but I had already established a kind of *connexion*. I had put together two links of a great chain. There was a boat lying upon a sea-coast, and not far from the boat was a parchment—*not a paper*—with a skull depicted upon it. You will, of course, ask 'where is the connexion?' I reply that the skull, or death's-head, is the well-known emblem of the pirate. The flag of the death's-head is hoisted in all engagements.

"I have said that the scrap was parchment, and not paper. Parchment is durable—almost imperishable. Matters of little moment are rarely consigned to parchment; since, for the mere ordinary purposes of drawing or writing, it is not nearly so well adapted as paper. This reflection suggested some meaning—some relevancy—in the death's-head. I did not fail to observe, also, the *form* of the parchment. Although one of its corners had been, by some accident, destroyed, it could be seen that the original form was oblong. It was just such a ship, indeed, as might have been chosen for a memorandum—for a record of something to be long remembered and carefully preserved."

"But," I interposed, "you say that the skull was *not* upon the parchment when you made the drawing of the beetle. How then do you trace any connexion between the boat and the skull—since this latter, according to your own admission, must have been designed (God only knows how or by whom) at some period subsequent to your sketching the *scarabæus*?"

"Ah, hereupon turns the whole mystery; although the secret, at this point, I had comparatively little difficulty in solving. My steps were sure, and could afford but a single result. I reasoned, for example, thus: When I drew the *scarabæus*, there was no skull apparent upon the parchment. When I had completed the drawing I gave it to you, and observed you narrowly until you returned it. *You*, therefore, did not design the skull, and no one else was present to do it. Then it was not done by human agency. And nevertheless it was done.

"At this stage of my reflections I endeavored to remember, and *did* remember, with entire distinctness, every incident which occurred about the period in question. The weather was chilly (oh, rare and happy accident!), and a fire was blazing upon the hearth. I was heated with exercise and sat near the table. You, however, had drawn a chair close to the chimney. Just as I placed the parchment in your hand, and as you were in the act of inspecting it, Wolf, the Newfoundland, entered, and leaped upon your shoulders. With your left hand you caressed him and kept him off, while your right, holding the parchment, was permtted to fall listlessly between your knees, and in close proximity to the fire. At one moment I thought the blaze had caught it, and was about to caution you, but, before I could speak, you had withdrawn it, and were engaged in its examination. When I considered all these particulars, I doubted not for a moment that *heat* had been the agent in bringing to light, upon the parchment, the skull which I saw designed upon it. You are well aware that chemical preparations exist, and have existed time out of mind, by means of which it is possible to write upon either paper or vellum, so that the characters shall become visible only when subjected to the action of fire. Zaffre, digested in *aqua regia*, and diluted with four times its weight of water, is sometimes employed; a green tint results. The regulus of cobalt, dissolved in spirit of nitre, gives a red. These colors disappear at longer or shorter intervals after the material written upon cools, but again become apparent upon the re-application of heat.

"I now scrutinized the death's-head with care. Its outer edges—the edges of the drawing nearest the edge of the vellum—were far more *distinct* than the others. It was clear that the action of the caloric had been imperfect or unequal. I immediately kindled a fire, and subjected every portion of the parchment to a glowing heat. At first, the only effect was the strengthening of the faint lines in the skull; but, upon persevering in the experiment, there became visible, at the corner of the slip, diagonally opposite to the spot in which the death's-head was delineated, the figure of what I at first supposed to be a goat. A closer scrutiny, however, satisfied me that it was intended for a kid."

"Ha! ha!" said I, "to be sure I have no right to laugh at you—a million and a half of money is too serious a matter for mirth—but you are not about to establish a third link in your chain—you will not find any especial connexion between your pirates and a goat—pirates, you know, have nothing to do with goats; they appertain to the farming interest."

"But I have just said that the figure was *not* that of a goat."

"Well, a kid then—pretty much the same thing."

"Pretty much, but not altogether," said Legrand. "You may have heard of one *Captain* Kidd. I at once looked upon the figure of the animal as a kind of punning or hieroglyphical signature. I say signature; because its position upon the vellum suggested this idea. The death's-head at the corner diagonally opposite, had, in the same manner, the air of a stamp, or seal. But I was sorely put out by the absence of all else—of the body to my imagined instrument—of the text for my context."

"I presume you expected to find a letter between the stamp and the signature."

"Something of that kind. The fact is, I felt irresistibly impressed with a presentiment of some vast good fortune impending. I can scarcely say why. Perhaps, after all, it was rather a desire than an actual belief;—but do you know that Jupiter's silly words, about the bug being of solid gold, had a remarkable effect upon my fancy? And then the series of accidents and coincidents—these were so *very* extraordinary. Do you observe how mere an accident it was that these events should have occurred upon the *sole* day of all the year in which it has been, or may be sufficiently cool for fire, and that without the fire, or without the intervention of the dog at the precise moment in which he appeared, I should never have become aware of the death's-head, and so never the possessor of the treasure.''

"But proceed—I am all impatience."

"Well; you have heard, of course, the many stories current— the thousand vague rumors afloat about money buried, some-where upon the Atlantic coast, by Kidd and his associates. These rumors must have had some foundation in fact. And that the rumors have existed so long and so continuous, could have resulted, it appeared to me, only from the circumstance of the buried treasures still *remaining* entombed. Had Kidd concealed his plunder for a time, and afterward reclaimed it, the rumors would scarcely have reached us in their present unvarying form. You will observe that the stories told are all about money-seekers, not about money-finders. Had the pirate recovered his money, there the affair would have dropped. It seemed to me that some accident—say the loss of a memorandum indicating its locality—had deprived him of the means of recovering it, and that this accident had become known to his followers, who otherwise might never have heard that the treasure had been concealed at all, and who, busying themselves in vain, because unguided, attempts to regain it, had given first birth, and then universal currency, to the reports which are now so common. Have you ever heard of any important treasure being unearthed along the coast?''

"Never."

"But that Kidd's accumulations were immense, is well known. I took it for granted, therefore, that the earth still held them; and you will scarcely be surprised when I tell you that I felt a hope, nearly amounting to certainty, that the parchment so strangely found involved a lost record of the place of deposit.''

"But how did you proceed?"

"I held the vellum again to the fire, after increasing the heat, but nothing appeared. I now thought it possible that the coating of dirt might have something to do with the failure: so I carefully rinsed the parchment by pouring warm water over it, and, having done this, I placed it in a tin pan, with the skull downward, and put the pan upon a furnace of lighted charcoal. In a few minutes, the pan having become thoroughly heated, I removed the slip, and, to my inexpressible joy, found it spotted, in several places, with what appeared to be figures arranged in lines. Again I placed it in the pan, and suffered it to remain another minute. Upon taking it off, the whole was just as you see it now.''

Here Legrand, having re-heated the parchment, submitted it to my inspection. The following characters were rudely traced, in a red tint, between the death's head and the goat:

        53   †305))6*;4826)4   .4);806*;48†8¶60))85;1
        (;: *8†83(88)5*†;46(;88*96*?;8)*‡(;485);5*†2:*‡(;4956*
        2(5*-4)8¶8*;4069285);)6†8)4   ;1(9;48081;8:8 1;
        48†85;4)485†528806*81(9;48;(88;4(?34;48)4 ;161;:
        188;   ?;

"But," said I, returning him the slip, "I am as much in the dark as ever. Were all the jewels of Golconda awaiting me upon my solution of this enigma, I am quite sure that I should be unable to earn them."

"And yet," said Legrand, "the solution is by no means so difficult as you might be led to imagine from the first hasty inspection of the characters. These characters, as any one might readily guess, form a cipher—that is to say, they convey a meaning; but then from what is known of Kidd, I could not suppose him capable of constructing any of the more abstruse cryptographs. I made up my mind, at once, that this was a simple species—such, however, as would appear, to the crude intellect of the sailor, absolutely insoluble without the key."

"And you really solved it?"

"Readily; I have solved others of an abstruseness ten thousand times greater. Circumstances, and a certain bias of mind, have led me to take interest in such riddles, and it may well be doubted whether human ingenuity can construct an enigma of the kind which human ingenuity may not, by proper application, resolve. In fact, having once established connected and legible characters, I scarcely gave a thought to the mere difficulty of developing their import.

"In the present case—indeed in all cases of secret writing— the first question regards the *language* of the cipher; for the principles of solution, so far, especially, as the more simple ciphers are concerned, depend upon, and are varied by, the genius of the particular idiom. In general, there is no alternative but experiment (directed by probabilities) of every tongue known to him who attempts the solution, until the true one be attained. But, with the cipher now before us all difficulty was removed by the signature. The pun upon the word 'Kidd' is appreciable in no other language than the English. But for this consideration I should have begun my attempts with the Spanish and French, as the tongues in which a secret of this kind would most naturally have been written by a pirate of the Spanish main. As it was, I assumed the cryptograph to be English.

"You observe there are no divisions between the words. Had there been divisions the task would have been comparatively easy. In such cases I should have commenced with a collation and analysis of the shorter words, and, had a word of a single letter occurred, as is most likely, (*a* or *I*, for example,) I should have considered the solution as assured. But, there being no division, my first step was to ascertain the predominant letters, as well as the least frequent. Counting all, I constructed a table thus:

Of the character 8 there are 33.

;	"	26.
4	"	19.
‡)	"	16.
*	"	13.
5	"	12.
6	"	11.
† 1	"	8.
0	"	6.

Of the character 9 2 there are are 5.

: 3	"	4.
?	"	3.
¶	"	2.
— .	"	1.

"Now, in English, the letter which most frequently occurs is *e*. Afterward, the succession runs thus: *a o i d h n r s t u y c f g l m w b k p q x z*. *E* predominates so remarkably, that an individual sentence of any length is rarely seen, in which it is not the prevailing character.

"Here, then, we have, in the very beginning, the groundwork for something more than a mere guess. The general use which may be made of the table is obvious—but, in this particular cipher, we shall only very partially require its aid. As our predominant character is 8, we will commence by assuming it as the *e* of the natural alphabet. To verify the supposition, let us observe if the 8 be seen often in couples—for *e* is doubled with great frequency in English—in such words, for example, as 'meet,' 'fleet,' 'speed,' 'seen,'' 'been,' 'agree,' &c. In the present instance we see it doubled no less than five times, although the cryptograph is brief.

"Let us assume 8, then, as *e*. Now, of all *words* in the language, 'the' is most usual; let us see, therefore, whether there are not repetitions of any three characters, in the same order of collocation, the last of them being 8. If we discover repetitions of such letters, so arranged, they will most probably represent the word 'the.' Upon inspection, we find no less than seven such arrangements, the characters being ;48. We may, therefore, assume that ; represents *t*, 4 represents *h*, and 8 represents *e*—the last being now well confirmed. Thus a great step has been taken.

"But, having established a single word, we are enabled to establish a vastly important point; that is to say, several commencements and terminations of other words. Let us refer, for example, to the last instance but one, in which the combination ;48 occurs—not far from the end of the cipher. We know that the ; immediately ensuing is the commencement of a word, and, of the six characters succeeding this 'the,' we are cognizant of no less than five. Let us set these characters down, thus, by the letters we know them to represent, leaving a space for the unknown—

t eeth

"Here we are enabled, at once, to discard the '*th*,' as forming no portion of the word commencing with the first *t;* since, by experiment of the entire alphabet for a letter adapted to the vacancy, we perceive that no word can be formed of which this *th* can be a part. We are thus narrowed into

t ee

and, going through the alphabet, if necessary, as before, we arrive at the word 'tree,' as the sole possible reading. We thus gain another letter, *r*, represented by (, with the words 'the tree' in juxtaposition.

"Looking beyond these words, for a short distance, we again see the combination ;48, and employ it by way of *termination* to what immediately precedes. We have thus this arrangement:

the tree ;4(≠ ?34 the,

or, substituting the natural letters, where known, it reads thus:

the tree thr ≠ ?3h the.

"Now, if, in place of the unknown characters, we leave blank spaces, or substitute dots, we read thus:

the tree thr. . .h the,

when the word '*through*' makes itself evident at once. But this discovery gives us three new letters, *o, u,* and *g,* represented by ≠ ,?, and 3.

"Looking now, narrowly, through the cipher for combinations of known characters, we find, not very far from the beginning, this arrangement,

83(88, or egree,

which plainly, is the conclusion of the word 'degree,' and gives us another letter, *d,* represented by †.

"Four letters beyond the word 'degree,' we perceive the combination

;46(;88.

"Translating the known characters, and representing the unknown by dots, as before, we read thus:

th.rtee

an arrangement immediately suggestive of the word 'thirteen,' and again furnishing us with two new characters, *i* and *n,* represented by 6 and *.

"Referring, now, to the beginning of the cryptograph, we find the combination,

53≠ ≠†.

"Translating as before, we obtain

.good,

which assures us that the first letter is *A*, and that the first two words are 'A good.'

"It is now time that we arrange our key, as far as discovered, in a tabular form, to avoid confusion. It will stand thus:

5	represents	a
†	"	d
8	"	e
3	"	g
4	"	h
6	"	i
*	"	n
‡	"	o
(	"	r
;	"	t

"We have therefore, no less than ten of the most important letters represented, and it will be unnecessary to proceed with the details of the solution. I have said enough to convince you that ciphers of this nature are readily soluble, and to give you some insight into the *rationale* of their development. But be assured that the specimen before us appertains to the very simplest species of cryptograph. It now only remains to give you the full translation of the characters upon the parchment, as unriddled. Here it is:

'A good glass in the bishop's hostel in the devil's seat forty-one degrees and thirteen minutes northeast and by north main branch seventh limb east side shoot from the left eye of the death's-head a bee line from the tree through the shot fifty feet out.' "

"But," said I, "the enigma seems still in as bad condition as ever. How is it possible to extort a meaning from all this jargon about 'devil's seats,' 'death's-heads,' and 'bishop's hotels?' "

"I confess," replied Legrand, "that the matter still wears a serious aspect, when regarded with a casual glance. My first endeavor was to divide the sentence into the natural division intended by the cryptographist."

"You mean, to punctuate it?"

"Something of that kind."

"But how was it possible to effect this?"

I reflected that it had been a *point* with the writer to run his words together without division, so as to increase the difficulty of solution. Now, a not over-acute man, in pursuing such an object, would be nearly certain to overdo the matter. When, in the course of his composition, he arrived at a break in his subject which would naturally require a pause, or a point, he would be exceedingly apt to run his characters, at this place, more than usually close together. If you will observe the MS., in the present instance, you will easily detect five such cases of unusual crowding. Acting upon this hint, I made the division thus:

"A good glass in the Bishop's hostel in the Devil's seat—forty-one degrees and thirteen minutes—northeast and by north—main branch seventh limb east side—shoot from the left eye of the death's-head—a bee-line from the tree through the shot fifty feet out."

"Even this division," said I, "leaves me still in the dark."

"It left me also in the dark," replied Legrand, "for a few days; during which I made diligent inquiry in the neighborhood of Sullivan's Island, for any building which went by the name of the 'Bishop's Hotel'; for, of course, I dropped the obsolete word 'hostel.' Gaining no information on the subject, I was on the point of extending my sphere of search, and proceeding in a more systematic manner, when, one morning, it entered into my head, quite suddenly, that this 'Bishop's Hostel' might have some reference to an old family, of the name of Bessop, which, time out of mind, had held possession of an ancient manor-house, about four miles to the northward of the island. I accordingly went over to the plantation, and re-instituted my inquiries among the older negroes of the place. At length one of the most aged of the women said that she had heard of such a place as *Bessop's Castle*, and thought that she could guide me to it, but that it was not a castle, nor a tavern, but a high rock.

"I offered to pay her well for her trouble, and, after some demur, she consented to accompany me to the spot. We found it without much difficulty, when, dismissing her, I proceeded to examine the place. The 'castle' consisted of an irregular assemblage of cliffs and rocks—one of the latter being quite remarkable for its height as well as for its insulated and artificial appearance. I clambered to its apex, and then felt much at a loss as to what should be next done.

"While I was busied in reflection, my eyes fell upon a narrow ledge in the eastern face of the rock, perhaps a yard below the summit upon which I stood. This ledge projected about eighteen inches, and was not more than a foot wide, while a niche in the cliff just above it gave it a rude resemblance to one of the hollow-backed chairs used by our ancestors. I made no doubt that here was the 'devil's-seat' alluded to in the MS., and now I seemed to grasp the full secret of the riddle.

"The 'good glass,' I knew, could have reference to nothing but a telescope; for the word 'glass' is rarely employed in any other sense by seamen. Now here, I at once saw, was a telescope to be used, and a definite point of view, *admitting no variation*, from which to use it. Nor did I hesitate to believe that the phrases 'forty-one degrees and thirteen minutes,' and 'northeast and by north,' were intended as directions for the levelling of the glass. Greatly excited by these discoveries, I hurried home, procured a telescope, and returned to the rock.

"I let myself down to the ledge, and found that it was impossible to retain a seat upon it except in one particular position. This fact confirmed my preconceived idea. I proceeded to use the glass. Of course, the 'forty-one degrees and thirteen minutes' could allude to nothing but elevation above the visible horizon, since the horizontal direction was clearly indicated by the words, 'northeast and by north.' This latter direction I at once established by means of a pocket-compass; then, pointing the glass as nearly at an angle of forty-one degrees of elevation as I could do it by guess, I moved it cautiously up or down, until my attention was arrested by a circular rift or opening in the foliage of a large tree that overtopped its fellows in the distance. In the centre of this rift I perceived a white spot, but could not, at first, distinguish what it was. Adjusting the focus of the telescope, I again looked, and now made it out to be a human skull.

"Upon this discovery I was so sanguine as to consider the enigma solved; for the phrase 'main branch, seventh limb, east side,' could refer only to the position of the skull upon the tree, while 'shoot from the left eye of the death's-head' admitted, also, of but one interpretation, in regard to a search for buried treasure. I perceived that the design was to drop a bullet from the left eye of the skull, and that a bee-line, or, in other words, a straight line, drawn from the nearest point of the trunk through 'the shot' (or the spot where the bullet fell), and thence extended to a distance of fifty feet, would indicate a definite point—and beneath this point I thought it at least *possible* that a deposit of value lay concealed."

"All this," I said, "is exceedingly clear, and, although ingenious, still simple and explicit. When you left the Bishop's Hotel, what then?"

"Why, having carefully taken the bearings of the tree, I

turned homeward. The instant that I left 'the devil's-seat,' however, the circular rift vanished; nor could I get a glimpse of it afterward, turn as I would. What seems to me the chief ingenuity in this whole business, is the fact (for repeated experiment has convinced me it *is* a fact) that the circular opening in question is visible from no other attainable point of view than that afforded by the narrow ledge upon the face of the rock.

"In this expedition to the 'Bishop's Hotel' I had been attended by Jupiter, who had, no doubt, observed, for some weeks past, the abstraction of my demeanor, and took special care not to leave me alone. But, on the next day, getting up very early, I contrived to give him the slip, and went into the hills in search of the tree. After much toil I found it. When I came home at night my valet proposed to give me a flogging. With the rest of the adventure I believe you are as well acquainted as myself."

"I suppose," said I, "you missed the spot, in the first attempt at digging, through Jupiter's stupidity in letting the bug fall through the right instead of through the left eye of the skull."

"Precisely. This mistake made a difference of about two inches and a half in the 'shot'—that is to say, in the position of the peg nearest the tree; and had the treasure been *beneath* the 'shot,' the error would have been of little moment; but 'the shot,' together with the nearest point of the tree, were merely two points for the establishment of a line of direction; of course the error, however trivial in the beginning, increased as we proceeded with the line, and by the time we had gone fifty feet threw us quite off the scent. But for my deep-seated impressions that treasure was here somewhere actually buried, we might have had all our labor in vain."

"But your grandiloquence, and your conduct in swinging the beetle—how excessively odd! I was sure you were mad. And why did you insist upon letting fall the bug, instead of a bullet, from the skull?"

"Why, to be frank, I felt somewhat annoyed by your evident suspicions touching my sanity, and so resolved to punish you quietly, in my own way, by a little bit of sober mystification. For this reason I swung the beetle, and for this reason I let it fall from the tree. An observation of yours about its great weight suggested the latter idea."

"Yes, I perceive; and now there is only one point which puzzles me. What are we to make of the skeletons found in the hole?"

"That is a question I am no more able to answer than yourself. There seems, however, only one plausible way of accounting for them—and yet it is dreadful to believe in such atrocity as my suggestion would imply. It is clear that Kidd—if Kidd indeed secreted this treasure, which I doubt not—it is clear that he must have had assistance in the labor. But this labor concluded, he may have thought it expedient to remove all participants in his secret. Perhaps a couple of blows with a mattock were sufficient, while his coadjutors were busy in the pit; perhaps it required a dozen—who shall tell?''

Herman Melville

(1819–1891)

Son of a bankrupt father, and the descendant of Dutch and English colonial families, Melville attended school only to the age of 15. After working at assorted odd jobs, in 1839 he went to sea as a cabin-boy; he taught school in upstate New York for a bit, then in 1841 returned to sea, this time as a sailor aboard a whaling ship. Jumping ship in the Marquesas, and thereafter working also in Tahiti, he enlisted in the U.S. Navy in 1843, being discharged in late 1844. These experiences provided the basis for his early and very successful books, Typee *(1846),* Omoo *(1847),* Mardi *(1849),* Redburn *(1849) and* White-Jacket *(1850). But when he left the adventure-novel genre, first with his greatest book,* Moby-Dick *(1851, dedicated to his friend Nathaniel Hawthorne), and then with* Pierre *(1852), he lost his audience and, with it, his livelihood.* Israel Potter *(1855) did nothing to improve matters; neither did* The Piazza Tales *(1856), from which "Bartleby the Scrivener" is taken, and with* The Confidence Man *(1857), his career as a writer of prose fiction was essentially over. Thereafter he worked as a New York customs inspector, writing poems and, toward the end of his life, the short novel,* Billy Budd.

BARTLEBY THE SCRIVENER

A STORY OF WALL STREET

I am a rather elderly man. The nature of my avocations, for the last thirty years, has brought me into more than ordinary contact with what would seem an interesting and somewhat singular set of men, of whom, as yet, nothing, that I know of, has ever been written—I mean, the law-copyists, or scriveners. I have known very many of them, professionally and privately, and, if I pleased, could relate divers histories, at which good-natured gentlemen might smile, and sentimental souls might weep. But I waive the biographies of all other scriveners, for a few passages in the life of Bartleby, who was a scrivener, the strangest I ever saw, or heard of. While, of other law-copyists, I might write the complete life, of Bartleby nothing of that sort can be done. I believe that no materials exist, for a full and satisfactory biography of this man. It is an irreparable loss to literature. Bartleby was one of those beings of whom nothing is ascertainable, except from the original sources, and, in his case, those are very small. What my own astonished eyes saw of Bartleby, *that* is all I know of him, except, indeed, one vague report, which will appear in the sequel.

Ere introducing the scrivener, as he first appeared to me, it is fit I make some mention of myself, my employés, my business, my chambers, and general surroundings; because some such description is indispensable to an adequate understanding of the chief character about to be presented. Imprimis: I am a man who, from his youth upward, has been filled with a profound conviction that the easiest way of life is the best. Hence, though I belong to a profession proverbially energetic and nervous, even to turbulence, at times, yet nothing of that sort have I ever suffered to invade my peace. I am one of those unambitious lawyers who never addresses a jury, or in any way draws down public applause; but, in the cool tranquillity of a snug retreat, do a snug business among rich men's bonds, and mortgages, and title-deeds. All who know me, consider me an eminently *safe* man. The late John Jacob Astor, a personage little given to poetic enthusiasm, had no hesitation in pronouncing my first grand point to be prudence; my next, method. I do not speak it in vanity, but simply record the fact, that I was not unemployed in my profession by the late John Jacob Astor; a name which, I admit, I love to repeat; for it hath a rounded and orbicular sound to it, and rings like unto bullion. I will freely add, that I was not insensible to the late John Jacob Astor's good opinion.

Some time prior to the period at which this little history begins, my avocations had been largely increased. The good old office, now extinct in the State of New York, of a Master in Chancery, had been conferred upon me. It was not a very arduous office, but very pleasantly remunerative. I seldom lose my temper; much more seldom indulge in dangerous indignation at wrongs and outrages; but, I must be permitted to be rash here, and declare, that I consider the sudden and violent abrogation of the office of Master of Chancery, by the new Constitution, as a—premature act; inasmuch as I had counted upon a life-lease of the profits, whereas I only received those of a few short years. But this is by the way.

My chambers were upstairs, at No.—Wall Street. At one end, they looked upon the white wall of the interior of a spacious skylight shaft, penetrating the building from top to bottom.

This view might have been considered rather tame than otherwise, deficient in what landscape painters call "life." But, if so, the view from the other end of my chambers offered, at least, a contrast, if nothing more. In that direction, my windows commanded an unobstructed view of a lofty brick wall, black by age and everlasting shade; which wall required no spy-glass to bring out its lurking beauties, but, for the benefit of all near-sighted spectators, was pushed up to within ten feet of my window panes. Owing to the great height of the surrounding buildings, and my chambers being on the second floor, the interval between this wall and mine not a little resembled a huge square cistern.

At the period just preceding the advent of Bartleby, I had two persons as copyists in my employment, and a promising lad as an office-boy. First, Turkey; second, Nippers; third, Ginger Nut. These may seem names, the like of which are not usually found in the Directory. In truth, they were nicknames, mutually conferred upon each other by my three clerks, and were deemed expressive of their respective persons or characters. Turkey was a short, pursy Englishman, of about my own age—that is, somewhere not far from sixty. In the morning, one might say, his face was of a fine florid hue, but after twelve o'clock, meridian—his dinner hour—it blazed like a grate full of Christmas coals; and continued blazing—but, as it were, with a gradual wane—till six o'clock, P.M., or thereabouts; after which, I saw no more of the proprietor of the face, which, gaining its meridian with the sun, seemed to set with it, to rise, culminate, and decline the following day, with the like regularity and undiminished glory. There are many singular coincidences I have known in the course of my life, not the least among which was the fact, that, exactly when Turkey displayed his fullest beams from his red and radiant countenance, just then, too, at that critical moment, began the daily period when I considered his business capacities as seriously disturbed for the remainder of the twenty-four hours. Not that he was absolutely idle, or averse to business, then; far from it. The difficulty was, he was apt to be altogether too energetic. There was a strange, inflamed, flurried, flighty recklessness of activity about him. He would be incautious in dipping his pen into his inkstand. All his blots upon my documents were dropped there after twelve o'clock, meridian. Indeed, not only would he be reckless, and sadly given to making blots in the afternoon, but, some days, he went further, and was rather noisy. At such times, too, his face flamed with augmented blazonry, as if cannel coal had been heaped on anthracite. He made an unpleasant racket with his chair; spilled his sand-box; in mending his pens, impatiently split them all to pieces, and threw them on the floor in a sudden passion; stood up, and leaned over his table, boxing his papers about in a most indecorous manner, very sad to behold in an elderly man like him. Nevertheless, as he was in many ways a most valuable person to me, and all the time before twelve o'clock, meridian, was the quickest, steadiest creature, too, accomplishing a great deal of work in a style not easily to be matched—for these reasons, I was willing to overlook his eccentricities, though, indeed, occasionally, I remonstrated with him. I did this very gently, however, because, though the civilest, nay, the blandest and most reverential of men in the morning, yet, in the afternoon, he was disposed, upon provocation, to be slightly rash with his tongue—in fact, insolent. Now, valuing his morning services as I did, and resolved not to lose them—yet, at the same time, made uncomfortable by his inflamed way after twelve o'clock— and being a man of peace, unwilling by my admonitions to call forth unseemly retorts from him, I took upon me, one Saturday noon (he was always worse on Saturdays) to hint to him, very kindly, that, perhaps, now that he was growing old, it might be well to abridge his labours; in short, he need not come to my chambers after twelve o'clock, but, dinner over, had best go home to his lodgings, and rest himself till tea-time. But no; he insisted upon his afternoon devotions. His countenance became intolerably fervid, as he oratorically assured me—gesticulating with a long ruler at the other end of the room—that if his services in the morning were useful, how indispensable, then, in the afternoon?

"With submission, sir," said Turkey, on this occasion, "I consider myself your right-hand man. In the morning I but marshal and deploy my columns; but in the afternoon I put myself at their head, and gallantly charge the foe, thus"—and he made a violent thrust with the ruler.

"But the blots, Turkey," intimated I.

"True; but, with submission, sir, behold these hairs! I am getting old. Surely, sir, a blot or two of a warm afternoon is not to be severely urged against gray hairs. Old age—even if it blot the page—is honourable. With submission, sir, we *both* are getting old."

This appeal to my fellow-feeling was hardly to be resisted. At all events, I saw that go he would not. So, I made up my mind to let him stay, resolving, nevertheless, to see to it that, during the afternoon, he had to do with my less important papers.

Nippers, the second on my list, was a whiskered, sallow, and, upon the whole, rather piratical-looking young man, of about five-and-twenty. I always deemed him the victim of two evil powers—ambition and indigestion. The ambition was evinced by a certain impatience of the duties of a mere copyist, an unwarrantable usurpation of strictly professional affairs, such as the original drawing up of legal documents. The indigestion seemed betokened in an occasional nervous testiness and grinning irritability, causing the teeth to audibly grind together over mistakes committed in copying; unnecessary maledictions, hissed, rather than spoken, in the heat of business; and especially by a continual discontent with the height of the table where he worked. Though of a very ingenious mechanical turn, Nippers could never get this table to suit him. He put chips under it, blocks of various sorts, bits of pasteboard, and at last went so far as to attempt an exquisite adjustment, by final pieces of folded blotting-paper. But no invention would answer. If, for the sake of easing his back, he brought the table lid at a sharp angle well up toward his chin, and wrote there like a man using the steep roof of a Dutch house for his desk, then he declared that it stopped the circulation in his arms. If now he lowered the table to his waistbands, and stooped over it in writing, then there was a sore aching in his back. In short, the truth of the matter was, Nippers knew not what he wanted. Or, if he wanted anything, it was to be rid of a scrivener's table altogether. Among the manifestations of his diseased ambition was a fondness he had for receiving visits from certain ambiguous-looking fellows in seedy coats, whom he called his clients. Indeed, I was aware that not only was he, at times, considerable of a ward-politician, but he occasionally did a little business at the Justices' courts, and was not unknown on the steps of the Tombs. I have good reason to believe, however, that one individual who called upon him at my chambers, and who, with a grand air, he insisted was his client, was no other than a dun, and the alleged title-deed, a bill. But, with all his failings, and the annoyances he caused me, Nippers, like his compatriot Turkey, was a very useful man to me; wrote a neat, swift hand; and, when he chose, was not deficient in a gentlemanly sort of deportment. Added to this, he always dressed in a gentlemanly sort of way; and so, incidentally, reflected credit upon my chambers. Whereas, with respect to Turkey, I had much ado to keep him from being a reproach to me. His clothes were apt to look oily, and smell of eating-houses. He wore his pantaloons very loose and baggy in summer. His coats were execrable; his hat not to be handled. But while the hat was a thing of indifference to me, inasmuch as his natural civility and deference, as a dependent Englishman, always led him to doff it the moment he entered the room, yet his coat was another matter. Concerning his coats, I reasoned with him; but with no effect. The truth was, I suppose, that a man with so small an income could not afford to sport such a lustrous face and a lustrous coat at one and the same time. As Nippers once observed, Turkey's money went chiefly for red ink. One winter day, I presented Turkey with a highly respectable-looking coat of my own—a padded gray coat, of a most comfortable warmth, and which buttoned straight up from the knee to the neck. I thought Turkey would appreciate the favour, and abate his rashness and obstreperousness of afternoons. But no; I verily believe that buttoning himself up in so downy and blanket-like a coat had a pernicious effect upon him—upon the same principle that too much oats are bad for horses. In fact, precisely as a rash, restive horse is said to feel his oats, so Turkey felt his coat. I made him insolent. He was a man whom prosperity harmed.

Though, concerning the self-indulgent habits of Turkey, I had my own private surmises, yet, touching Nippers, I was well persuaded that, whatever might be his faults in other respects, he was, at least, a temperate young man. But, indeed, nature herself seemed to have been his vintner, and, at his birth, charged him so thoroughly with an irritable, brandy-like disposition, that all subsequent potations were needless. When I consider how, amid the stillness of my chambers, Nippers would sometimes impatiently rise from his seat, and stooping over his table, spread his arms wide apart, seize the whole desk, and move it, and jerk it, with a grim, grinding motion on the floor, as if the table were a perverse voluntary agent, intent on thwarting and vexing him, I plainly perceive that, for Nippers, brandy-and-water were altogether superfluous.

It was fortunate for me that, owing to its peculiar cause—indigestion—the irritability and consequent nervousness of Nippers were mainly observable in the morning, while in the afternoon he was comparatively mild. So that, Turkey's paroxysms only coming on about twelve o'clock, I never had to do with their eccentricities at one time. Their fits relieved each other, like guards. When Nippers's was on, Turkey's was off; and *vice versa*. This was a good natural arrangement, under the circumstances.

Ginger Nut, the third on my list, was a lad, some twelve years old. His father was a carman, ambitious of seeing his son on the bench instead of a cart, before he died. So he sent him to my office, as student at law, errand-boy, cleaner and sweeper, at the rate of one dollar a week. He had a little desk to himself, but he did not use it much. Upon inspection, the drawer exhibited a great array of the shells of various sorts of nuts. Indeed, to this quick-witted youth, the whole noble science of the law was contained in a nut-shell. Not the least among the employments of Ginger Nut, as well as one which he discharged with the most alacrity, was his duty as cake and apple purveyor for Turkey and Nippers. Copying law-papers being proverbially a dry, husky sort of business, my two scriveners were fain to moisten their mouths very often with Spitzenbergs, to be had at the numerous stalls nigh the Custom House and Post Office. Also, they sent Ginger Nut very frequently for that peculiar cake—small, flat, round, and very spicy—after which he had been named by them. Of a cold morning, when business was but dull, Turkey would gobble up scores of these cakes, as if they were mere wafers—indeed, they sell them at the rate of six or eight for a penny—the scrape of his pen blending with the crunching of the crisp particles in his mouth. Of all the fiery afternoon blunders and flurried rashnesses of Turkey, was his once moistening a ginger-cake between his lips, and clapping it on to a mortgage, for a seal. I came within an ace of dismissing him then. But he mollified me by making an oriental bow, and saying—"With submission, sir, it was generous of me to find you in stationery on my own account."

Now my original business—that of a conveyancer and title-hunter, and drawer-up of recondite documents of all sorts—was considerably increased by receiving the master's office. There was now great work for scriveners. Not only must I push the clerks already with me, but I must have additional help.

In answer to my advertisement, a motionless young man one morning stood upon my office threshold, the door being open, for it was summer. I can see that figure now—pallidly neat, pitiably respectable, incurably forlorn! It was Bartleby.

After a few words touching his qualifications, I engaged him,

glad to have among my corps of copyists a man of so singularly
sedate an aspect, which I thought might operate beneficially
upon the flighty temper of Turkey, and the fiery one of Nippers.

I should have stated before that ground-glass folding-doors
divided my premises into two parts, one of which was occupied
by my scriveners, the other by myself. According to my humour,
I threw open these doors, or closed them. I resolved to assign
Bartleby a corner by the folding-doors, but on my side of them,
so as to have this quiet man within easy call, in case any trifling
thing was to be done. I placed his desk close up to a small
side-window in that part of the room, a window which originally
had afforded a lateral view of certain grimy backyards and
bricks, but which, owing to subsequent erections, commanded at
present no view at all, though it gave some light. Within three
feet of the panes was a wall, and the light came down from far
above, between two lofty buildings, as from a very small opening in a dome. Still further to a satisfactory arrangement, I
procured a high green folding-screen, which might entirely iso-
late Bartleby from my sight, though not remove him from my
voice. And thus, in a manner, privacy and society were conjoined.

At first, Bartleby did an extraordinary quantity of writing. As
if long famishing for something to copy, he seemed to gorge
himself on my documents. There was no pause for digestion. He
ran a day and night line, copying by sun-light and by candlelight. I should have been quite delighted with his application,
had he been cheerfully industrious. But he wrote on silently,
palely, mechanically.

It is, of course, an indispensable part of a scrivener's business
to verify the accuracy of his copy, word by word. Where there
are two or more scriveners in an office, they assist each other in
this examination, one reading from the copy, the other holding
the original. It is a very dull, wearisome, and lethargic affair. I
can readily imagine that, to some sanguine temperaments, it
would be altogether intolerable. For example, I cannot credit that
the mettlesome poet, Byron, would have contentedly sat down
with Bartleby to examine a law document of, say, five hundred
pages, closely written in a crimpy hand.

Now and then, in the haste of business, it had been my habit
to assist in comparing some brief document myself, calling
Turkey or Nippers for this purpose. One object I had, in placing
Bartleby so handy to me behind the screen, was, to avail myself
of his services on such trivial occasions. It was on the third day,
I think, of his being with me, and before any necessity had
arisen for having his own writing examined, that, being much

hurried to complete a small affair I had in hand, I abruptly called for Bartleby. In my haste and natural expectancy of instant compliance, I sat with my head bent over the original on my desk, and my right hand sideways, and somewhat nervously extended with the copy, so that, immediately upon emerging from his retreat, Bartleby might snatch it and proceed to business without the least delay.

In this very attitude did I sit when I called to him, rapidly stating what it was I wanted him to do—namely, to examine a small paper with me. Imagine my surprise, nay, my consternation, when, without moving from his privacy, Bartleby, in a singularly mild, firm voice, replied, "I would prefer not to."

I sat a while in perfect silence, rallying my stunned faculties. Immediately it occurred to me that my ears had deceived me, or Bartleby had entirely misunderstood my meaning. I repeated my request in the clearest tone I could assume; but in quite as clear a one came the previous reply, "I would prefer not to."

"Prefer not to," echoed I, rising in high excitement, and crossing the room with a stride. "What do you mean? Are you moon-struck? I want you to help me compare this sheet here— take it," and I thrust it toward him.

"I would prefer not to," said he.

I looked at him steadfastly. His face was leanly composed; his gray eye dimly calm. Not a wrinkle of agitation rippled him. Had there been the least uneasiness, anger, impatience, or impertinence in his manner; in other words, had there been anything ordinarily human about him, doubtless I should have violently dismissed him from the premises. But as it was, I should have as soon thought of turning my pale plaster-of-paris bust of Cicero out of doors. I stood gazing at him a while, as he went on with his own writing, and then reseated myself at my desk. This is very strange, thought I. What had one best do? But my business hurried me. I concluded to forget the matter for the present, reserving it for my future leisure. So calling Nippers from the other room, the paper was speedily examined.

A few days after this, Bartleby concluded four lengthy documents, being quadruplicates of a week's testimony taken before me in my High Court of Chancery. It became necessary to examine them. It was an important suit, and great accuracy was imperative. Having all things arranged, I called Turkey, Nippers, and Ginger Nut, from the next room, meaning to place the four copies in the hands of my four clerks, while I should read from the original. Accordingly, Turkey, Nippers, and Ginger Nut had taken their seats in a row, each with his document in his hand, when I called to Bartleby to join this interesting group.

"Bartleby! quick, I am waiting."

I heard a slow scrape of his chair legs on the uncarpeted floor, and soon he appeared standing at the entrance of his hermitage.

"What is wanted?" said he mildly.

"The copies, the copies," said I hurriedly. "We are going to examine them. There"—and I held toward him the fourth quadruplicate.

"I would prefer not to," he said, and gently disappeared behind the screen.

For a few moments I was turned into a pillar of salt, standing at the head of my seated column of clerks. Recovering myself, I advanced toward the screen, and demanded the reason for such extraordinary conduct.

"*Why* do you refuse?"

"I would prefer not to."

With any other man I should have flown outright into a dreadful passion, scorned all further words, and thrust him ignominiously from my presence. But there was something about Bartleby that not only strangely disarmed me, but, in a wonderful manner, touched and disconcerted me. I began to reason with him.

"These are your own copies we are about to examine. It is labour saving to you, because one examination will answer for your four papers. It is common usage. Every copyist is bound to help examine his copy. Is it not so? Will you not speak? Answer!"

"I prefer not to," he replied in a flute-like tone. It seemed to me that, while I had been addressing him, he carefully revolved every statement that I made; fully comprehended the meaning; could not gainsay the irresistible conclusion; but, at the same time, some paramount consideration prevailed with him to reply as he did.

"You are decided, then, not to comply with my request—a request made according to common usage and common sense?"

He briefly gave me to understand, that on that point my judgment was sound. Yes: his decision was irreversible.

It is not seldom the case that, when a man is browbeaten in some unprecedented and violently unreasonable way, he begins to stagger in his own plainest faith. He begins, as it were, vaguely to surmise that, wonderful as it may be, all the justice and all the reason is on the other side. Accordingly, if any disinterested persons are present, he turns to them for some reinforcement for his own faltering mind.

"Turkey," said I, "what do you think of this? Am I not right?"

"With submission, sir," said Turkey, in his blandest tone, "I think that you are."

"Nippers," said I, "what do *you* think of it?"

"I think I should kick him out of the office."

(The reader, of nice perceptions, will here perceive that, it being morning, Turkey's answer is couched in polite and tranquil terms, but Nippers's replies in ill-tempered ones. Or, to repeat a previous sentence, Nippers's ugly mood was on duty, and Turkey's off.)

"Ginger Nut," said I, willing to enlist the smallest suffrage in my behalf, "what do *you* think of it?"

"I think, sir, he's a little *luny*," replied Ginger Nut, with a grin.

"You hear what they say," said I, turning toward the screen, "come forth and do your duty."

But he vouchsafed no reply. I pondered a moment in sore perplexity. But once more business hurried me. I determined again to postpone the consideration of this dilemma to my future leisure. With a little trouble we made out to examine the papers without Bartleby, though at every page or two Turkey deferentially dropped his opinion, that this proceeding was quite out of the common; while Nippers, twitching in his chair with a dyspeptic nervousness, ground out, between his set teeth, occasional hissing maledictions against the stubborn oaf behind the screen. And for his (Nippers's) part, this was the first and the last time he would do another man's business without pay.

Meanwhile Bartleby sat in his hermitage, oblivious to everything but his own peculiar business there.

Some days passed, the scrivener being employed upon another lengthy work. His late remarkable conduct led me to regard his ways narrowly. I observed that he never went to dinner; indeed, that he never went anywhere. As yet I had never, of my personal knowledge, known him to be outside of my office. He was a perpetual sentry in the corner. At about eleven o'clock though, in the morning, I noticed that Ginger Nut would advance toward the opening in Bartleby's screen, as if silently beckoned thither by a gesture invisible to me where I sat. The boy would then leave the office, jingling a few pence, and reappear with a handful of ginger-nuts, which he delivered in the hermitage, receiving two of the cakes for his trouble.

He lives, then, on ginger-nuts, thought I; never eats a dinner, properly speaking; he must be a vegetarian, then; but no; he never eats even vegetables, he eats nothing but ginger-nuts. My mind then ran on in reveries concerning the probable effects upon the human constitution of living entirely on ginger-nuts. Ginger-nuts are so called, because they contain ginger as one of their peculiar constituents, and the final flavouring one. Now, what was ginger? A hot, spicy thing. Was Bartleby hot and spicy? Not at all. Ginger, then, had no effect upon Bartleby. Probably he preferred it should have none.

Nothing so aggravates an earnest person as a passive resistance. If the individual so resisted be of a not inhumane temper, and the resisting one perfectly harmless in his passivity, then, in the better moods of the former, he will endeavour charitably to construe to his imagination what proves impossible to be solved by his judgment. Even so, for the most part, I regarded Bartleby and his ways. Poor fellow! thought I, he means no mischief; it is plain he intends no insolence; his aspect sufficiently evinces that his eccentricities are involuntary. He is useful to me. I can get along with him. If I turn him away, the chances are he will fall in with some less-indulgent employer, and then he will be rudely treated, and perhaps driven forth miserably to starve. Yes. Here I can cheaply purchase a delicious self-approval. To befriend Bartleby; to humour him in his strange wilfulness, will cost me little or nothing, while I lay up in my soul what will eventually prove a sweet morsel for my conscience. But this mood was not invariable with me. The passiveness of Bartleby sometimes irritated me. I felt strangely goaded on to encounter him in new opposition—to elicit some angry spark from him answerable to my own. But, indeed, I might as well have essayed to strike fire with my knuckles against a bit of Windsor soap. But one afternoon the evil impulse in me mastered me, and the following little scene ensued:—

"Bartleby," said I, "when those papers are all copied, I will compare them with you."

"I would prefer not to."

"How? Surely you do not mean to persist in that mulish vagary?"

No answer.

I threw open the folding-doors near by, and, turning upon Turkey and Nippers, exclaimed:

"Bartleby a second time says, he won't examine his papers. What do you think of it, Turkey?"

It was afternoon, be it remembered. Turkey sat glowing like a brass boiler; his bald head steaming; his hands reeling among his blotted papers.

"Think of it?" roared Turkey; "I think I'll just step behind his screen, and black his eyes for him!"

So saying, Turkey rose to his feet and threw his arms into a pugilistic position. He was hurrying away to make good his promise, when I detained him, alarmed at the effect of incautiously rousing Turkey's combativeness after dinner.

"Sit down, Turkey," said I, "and hear what Nippers has to say. What do you think of it, Nippers? Would I not be justified in immediately dismissing Bartleby?"

"Excuse me, that is for you to decide, sir. I think his conduct quite unusual, and, indeed, unjust, as regards Turkey and myself. But it may only be a passing whim."

"Ah," exclaimed I, "you have strangely changed your mind, then—you speak very gently of him now."

"All beer," cried Turkey; "gentleness is effects of beer—Nippers and I dined together to-day. You see how gentle *I* am, sir. Shall I go and black his eyes?"

"You refer to Bartleby, I suppose. No, not to-day, Turkey," I replied; "pray, put up your fists."

I closed the doors, and again advanced toward Bartleby. I felt additional incentives tempting me to my fate. I burned to be rebelled against again. I remembered that Bartleby never left the office.

"Bartleby," said I, "Ginger Nut is away; just step around to the Post Office, won't you? (it was but a three minutes' walk), and see if there is anything for me."

"I would prefer not to."

"You *will* not?"

"I *prefer* not."

I staggered to my desk, and sat there in a deep study. My blind inveteracy returned. Was there any other thing in which I could procure myself to be ignominiously repulsed by this lean, penniless wight?—my hired clerk? What added thing is there, perfectly reasonable, that he will be sure to refuse to do?

"Bartleby!"

No answer.

"Bartleby," in a louder tone.

No answer.

"Bartleby," I roared.

Like a very ghost, agreeably to the laws of magical invocation, at the third summons, he appeared at the entrance of his hermitage.

"Go to the next room, and tell Nippers to come to me."

"I prefer not to," he respectfully and slowly said, and mildly disappeared.

"Very good, Bartleby," said I, in a quiet sort of serenely-severe self-possessed tone, intimating the unalterable purpose of some terrible retribution very close at hand. At the moment I half intended something of the kind. But upon the whole, as it was drawing toward my dinner-hour, I thought it best to put on my hat and walk home for the day, suffering much from perplexity and distress of mind.

Shall I acknowledge it? The conclusion of this whole business was, that it soon became a fixed fact of my chambers, that a pale young scrivener, by the name of Bartleby, had a desk there; that he copied for me at the usual rate of four cents a folio (one hundred words); but he was permanently exempt from examining the work done by him, that duty being transferred to Turkey and Nippers, out of compliment, doubtless to their superior acuteness; moreover, said Bartleby was never, on any account, to be dispatched on the most trivial errand of any sort; and that even if entreated to take upon him such a matter, it was generally understood that he would "prefer not to"—in other words, that he would refuse point-blank.

As days passed on, I became considerably reconciled to Bartleby. His steadiness, his freedom from all dissipation, his incessant industry (except when he chose to throw himself into a standing revery behind his screen), his great stillness, his unalterableness of demeanour under all circumstances, made him a valuable acquisition. One prime thing was this—*he was always there*—first in the morning, continually through the day, and the last at night. I had a singular confidence in his honesty. I felt my most precious papers perfectly safe in his hands. Sometimes, to be sure, I could not, for the very soul of me, avoid falling into sudden spasmodic passions with him. For it was exceeding difficult to bear in mind all the time those strange peculiarities, privileges, and unheard-of exemptions, forming the tacit stipulations on Bartleby's part under which he remained in my office. Now and then, in the eagerness of dispatching pressing business, I would inadvertently summon Bartleby, in a short, rapid tone, to put his finger, say, on the incipient tie of a bit of red tape with which I was about compressing some papers. Of course, from behind the screen the usual answer, "I prefer not to," was sure to come; and then, how could a human creature, with the common infirmities of our nature, refrain from bitterly exclaiming upon such perverseness—such unreasonableness. However, every added repulse of this sort which I received only tended to lessen the probability of my repeating the inadvertence.

Here it must be said, that according to the custom of most

legal gentlemen occupying chambers in densely populated law-buildings, there were several keys to my door. One was kept by a woman residing in the attic, which person weekly scrubbed and daily swept and dusted my apartments. Another was kept by Turkey for convenience sake. The third I sometimes carried in my own pocket. The fourth I knew not who had.

Now, one Sunday morning I happened to go to Trinity Church, to hear a celebrated preacher, and finding myself rather early on the ground I thought I would walk round to my chambers for a while. Luckily I had my key with me; but upon applying it to the lock, I found it resisted by something inserted from the inside. Quite surprised, I called out; when to my consternation a key was turned from within; and thrusting his lean visage at me, and holding the door ajar, the apparition of Bartleby appeared, in his shirt-sleeves, and otherwise in a strangely tattered dishabille, saying quietly that he was sorry, but he was deeply engaged just then, and—preferred not admitting me at present. In a brief word or two, he moreover added, that perhaps I had better walk round the block two or three times, and by that time he would probably have concluded his affairs.

Now, the utterly unsurmised appearance of Bartleby, tenanting my law-chambers of a Sunday morning, with his cadaverously gentlemanly nonchalance, yet withal firm and self-possessed, had such a strange effect upon me, that incontinently I slunk away from my own door, and did as desired. But not without sundry twinges of impotent rebellion against the mild effrontery of this unaccountable scrivener. Indeed, it was his wonderful mildness chiefly, which not only disarmed me, but unmanned me as it were. For I consider that one, for the time, is sort of unmanned when he tranquilly permits his hired clerk to dictate to him, and order him away from his own premises. Furthermore, I was full of uneasiness as to what Bartleby could possibly be doing in my office in his shirt-sleeves, and in an otherwise dismantled condition of a Sunday morning. Was anything amiss going on? Nay, that was out of the question. It was not to be thought of for a moment that Bartleby was an immoral person. But what could he be doing there?—copying? Nay again, what-ever might be his eccentricities, Bartleby was an eminently decorous person. He would be the last man to sit down to his desk in any state approaching to nudity. Besides, it was Sunday; and there was something about Bartleby that forbade the supposi-tion that he would by any secular occupation violate the proper-ties of the day.

Nevertheless, my mind was not pacified; and full of a restless curiosity, at last I returned to the door. Without hindrance I inserted my key, opened it, and entered. Bartleby was not to be seen. I looked round anxiously, peeped behind his screen; but it was very plain that he was gone. Upon more closely examining the place, I surmised that for an indefinite period Bartleby must have ate, dressed, and slept in my office, and that, too, without plate, mirror, or bed. The cushioned seat of a rickety old sofa in one corner bore the faint impress of a lean, reclining form. Rolled away under his desk, I found a blanket; under the empty grate a blacking box and brush; on a chair, a tin basin, with soap and a ragged towel; in a newspaper a few crumbs of ginger-nuts and a morsel of cheese. Yes, thought I, it is evident enough that Bartleby has been making his home here, keeping bachelor's hall all by himself. Immediately then the thought came sweeping across me, what miserable friendlessness and loneliness are here revealed! His poverty is great; but his solitude, how horrible! Think of it. Of a Sunday, Wall Street is deserted as Petra; and every night of every day it is an emptiness. This building, too, which of week-days hums with industry and life, at nightfall echoes with sheer vacancy, and all through Sunday is forlorn. And here Bartleby makes his home; sole spectator of a solitude which he has seen all-populous—a sort of innocent and transformed Marius brooding among the ruins of Carthage!

For the first time in my life a feeling of overpowering stinging melancholy seized me. Before, I had never experienced aught but a not unpleasing sadness. The bond of a common humanity now drew me irresistibly to gloom. A fraternal melancholy! For both I and Bartleby were sons of Adam. I remembered the bright silks and sparkling faces I had seen that day, in gala trim, swan-like sailing down the Mississippi of Broadway; and I contrasted them with the pallid copyist, and thought to myself, Ah, happiness courts the light, so we deem the world is gay; but misery hides aloof, so we deem that misery there is none. These sad fancyings—chimeras, doubtless, of a sick and silly brain—led on to other and more special thoughts, concerning the eccentricities of Bartleby. Presentiments of strange discoveries hovered round me. The scrivener's pale form appeared to me laid out, among uncaring strangers, in its shivering winding-sheet.

Suddenly I was attracted by Bartleby's closed desk, the key in open sight left in the lock.

I mean no mischief, seek the gratification of no heartless curiosity, thought I; besides, the desk is mine, and its contents, too, so I will make bold to look within. Everything was methodically arranged, the papers smoothly placed. The pigeon-holes were deep, and removing the files of documents, I groped into their recesses. Presently I felt something there, and dragged it out. It was an old bandanna handkerchief, heavy and knotted. I opened it, and saw it was a savings-bank.

I now recalled all the quiet mysteries which I had noted in the man. I remembered that he never spoke but to answer; that, though at intervals he had considerable time to himself, yet I had never seen him reading—no, not even a newspaper; that for long periods he would stand looking out, at his pale window behind the screen, upon the dead brick wall; I was quite sure he never visited any refectory or eating-house; while his pale face clearly indicated that he never drank beer like Turkey, or tea and coffee even, like other men; that he never went anywhere in particular that I could learn; never went out for a walk, unless, indeed, that was the case at present; that he had declined telling who he was, or whence he came, or whether he had any relatives in the world; that though so thin and pale, he never complained of ill health. And more than all, I remembered a certain unconscious air of pallid—how shall I call it?—of pallid haughtiness, say, or rather an austere reserve about him, which had positively awed me into my tame compliance with his eccentricities, when I had feared to ask him to do the slightest incidental thing for me, even though I might know, from his long-continued motionlessness, that behind his screen he must be standing in one of those dead-wall reveries of his.

Revolving all these things, and coupling them with the recently discovered fact, that he made my office his constant abiding-place and home, and not forgetful of his morbid moodiness; revolving all these things, a prudential feeling began to steal over me. My first emotions had been those of pure melancholy and sincerest pity; but just in proportion as the forlornness of Bartleby grew and grew to my imagination, did that same melancholy merge into fear, that pity into repulsion. So true it is, and so terrible, too, that up to a certain point the thought or sight of misery enlists our best affections; but, in certain special cases, beyond that point it does not. They err who would assert that invariably this is owing to the inherent selfishness of the human heart. It rather proceeds from a certain hopelessness of remedying excessive and organic ill. To a sensitive being, pity is not seldom pain. And when at last it is perceived that such pity cannot lead to effectual succour, common-sense bids the soul be rid of it. What I saw that morning persuaded me that the scrivener was the victim of innate and incurable disorder. I might give alms to his body; but his body did not pain him; it was his soul that suffered, and his soul I could not reach.

I did not accomplish the purpose of going to Trinity Church that morning. Somehow, the things I had seen disqualified me for the time for church-going. I walked homeward, thinking what I would do with Bartleby. Finally, I resolved upon this—I would put certain calm questions to him the next morning, touching his history, etc., and if he declined to answer them openly and unreservedly (and I supposed he would prefer not), then to give him a twenty-dollar bill over and above whatever I might owe him, and tell him his services were no longer required; but that if in any other way I could assist him, I would be happy to do so, especially if he desired to return to his native place, wherever that might be, I would willingly help to defray the expenses. Moreover, if, after reaching home, he found himself at any time in want of aid, a letter from him would be sure of a reply.

The next morning came.

"Bartleby," said I, gently calling to him behind his screen.

No reply.

"Bartleby," said I, in a still gentler tone, "come here; I am not going to ask you to do anything you would prefer not to do—I simply wish to speak to you."

Upon this he noiselessly slid into view.

"Will you tell me, Bartleby, where you were born."

"I would prefer not to."

"Will you tell me *anything* about yourself?"

"I would prefer not to."

"But what reasonable objection can you have to speak to me? I feel friendly toward you."

He did not look at me while I spoke, but kept his glance fixed upon my bust of Cicero, which, as I then sat, was directly behind me, some six inches above my head.

"What is your answer, Bartleby?" said I, after waiting a considerable time for a reply, during which his countenance remained immovable, only there was the faintest conceivable tremor of the white attenuated mouth.

"At present I prefer to give no answer," he said, and retired into his hermitage.

It was rather weak in me, I confess, but his manner, on this occasion, nettled me. Not only did there seem to lurk in it a certain calm disdain, but his perverseness seemed ungrateful, considering the undeniable good usage and indulgence he had received from me.

Again I sat ruminating what I should do. Mortified as I was at his behaviour, and resolved as I had been to dismiss him when I entered my office, nevertheless I strangely felt something superstitious knocking at my heart, and forbidding me to carry out my purpose, and denouncing me for a villain if I dared to breathe one bitter word against this forlornest of mankind. At last, familiarly drawing my chair behind his screen, I sat down and said: "Bartleby, never mind, then, about revealing your history; but let me entreat you, as a friend, to comply as far as may be with the usages of this office. Say now, you will help to examine papers to-morrow or next day: in short, say now, that in a day or two you will begin to be a little reasonable:—say so, Bartleby."

"At present I would prefer not to be a little reasonable," was his mildly cadaverous reply.

Just then the folding-doors opened, and Nippers approached. He seemed suffering from an unusually bad night's rest, induced by severer indigestion than common. He overheard those final words of Bartleby.

"*Prefer not*, eh?" gritted Nippers—"I'd *prefer* him, if I were you, sir," addressing me—"I'd *prefer* him; I'd give him preferences, the stubborn mule! What is it, sir, pray, that he *prefers* not to do now?"

Bartleby moved not a limb.

"Mr. Nippers," said I, "I'd prefer that you would withdraw for the present."

Somehow, of late, I had got into the way of involuntarily using this word "prefer" upon all sorts of not exactly suitable occasions. And I trembled to think that my contact with the scrivener had already and seriously affected me in a mental way. And what further and deeper aberration might it not yet produce? This apprehension had not been without efficacy in determining me to summary measures.

As Nippers, looking very sour and sulky, was departing, Turkey blandly and deferentially approached.

"With submission, sir," said he, "yesterday I was thinking about Bartleby here, and I think that if he would but prefer to take a quart of good ale everyday, it would do much toward mending him, and enabling him to assist in examining his papers."

"So you have got the word too," said I, slightly excited.

"With submission, what word, sir," asked Turkey, respectfully crowding himself into the contracted space behind the screen, and by so doing, making me jostle the scrivener. "What word, sir?"

"I would prefer to be left alone here," said Bartleby, as if offended at being mobbed in his privacy.

"*That's* the word, Turkey," said I—"*that's* it."

"Oh, *prefer?* oh yes—queer word. I never use it myself. But, sir, as I was saying, if he would but prefer——"

"Turkey," interrupted I, "you will please withdraw."

"Oh certainly, sir, if you prefer that I should."

As he opened the folding-door to retire, Nippers at his desk caught a glimpse of me, and asked whether I would prefer to have a certain paper copied on blue paper or white. He did not in the least roguishly accent the word prefer. It was plain that it involuntarily rolled from his tongue. I thought to myself, surely I must get rid of a demented man, who already has in some degree turned the tongues, if not the heads of myself and clerks. But I thought it prudent not to break the dismission at once.

The next day I noticed that Bartleby did nothing but stand at his window in his dead-wall revery. Upon asking him why he did not write, he said that he had decided upon doing no more writing.

"Why, how now? what next?" exclaimed I, "do no more writing?"

"No more."

"And what is the reason?"

"Do you not see the reason for yourself?" he indifferently replied.

I looked steadfastly at him, and perceived that his eyes looked dull and glazed. Instantly it occurred to me, that his unexampled diligence in copying by his dim window for the first few weeks of his stay with me might have temporarily impaired his vision.

I was touched. I said something in condolence with him. I hinted that of course he did wisely in abstaining from writing for a while; and urged him to embrace that opportunity of taking wholesome exercise in the open air. This, however, he did not do. A few days after this, my other clerks being absent, and being in a great hurry to dispatch certain letters by the mail, I thought that having nothing else earthly to do, Bartleby would surely be less inflexible than usual, and carry these letters to the Post Office. But he blankly declined. So, much to my inconvenience, I went myself.

Still added days went by. Whether Bartleby's eyes improved or not, I could not say. To all appearance, I thought they did. But when I asked him if they did, he vouchsafed no answer. At all events, he would do no copying. At last, in reply to my urgings, he informed me that he had permanently given up copying.

"What!" exclaimed I; "suppose your eyes should get entirely well—better than ever before—would you not copy then?"

"I have given up copying," he answered, and slid aside.

He remained as ever, a fixture in my chamber. Nay—if that were possible—he became still more of a fixture than before. What was to be done? He would do nothing in the office; why should he stay there? In plain fact, he had now become a millstone to me, not only useless as a necklace, but afflictive to bear. Yet I was sorry for him. I speak less than truth when I say that, on his own account, he occasioned me uneasiness. If he would but have named a single relative or friend, I would instantly have written, and urged their taking the poor fellow away to some convenient retreat. But he seemed alone, absolutely alone in the universe. A bit of wreck in the mid-Atlantic. At length, necessities connected with my business tyrannised over all other considerations. Decently as I could, I told Bartleby that in six days' time he must unconditionally leave the office. I warned him to take measures, in the interval, for procuring some other abode. I offered to assist him in this endeavour, if he himself would but take the first step toward a removal. "And when you finally quit me, Bartleby," added I, "I shall see that you go not away entirely unprovided. Six days from this hour, remember."

At the expiration of that period, I peeped behind the screen, and lo! Bartleby was there.

I buttoned up my coat, balanced myself; advanced slowly toward him, touched his shoulder, and said, "The time has come; you must quit this place; I am sorry for you; here is money; but you must go."

"I would prefer not," he replied, with his back still toward me.

"You *must*."

He remained silent.

Now I had an unbounded confidence in this man's common honesty. He had frequently restored to me sixpences and shillings carelessly dropped upon the floor, for I am apt to be very reckless in such shirt-button affairs. The proceeding, then, which followed will not be deemed extraordinary.

"Bartleby," said I, "I owe you twelve dollars on account; here are thirty-two; the odd twenty are yours—Will you take it?" and I handed the bills toward him.

But he made no motion.

"I will leave them here, then," putting them under a weight on the table. Then taking my hat and cane and going to the door, I tranquilly turned and added—"After you have removed your things from these offices, Bartleby, you will of course lock the door—since everyone is now gone for the day but you—and if you please, slip your key underneath the mat, so that I may have it in the morning. I shall not see you again; so good-bye to you. If, hereafter, in your new place of abode, I can be of any service to you, do not fail to advise me by letter. Good-bye, Bartleby, and fare you well."

But he answered not a word; like the last column of some ruined temple, he remained standing mute and solitary in the middle of the otherwise deserted room.

As I walked home in a pensive mood, my vanity got the better of my pity. I could not but highly plume myself on my masterly management in getting rid of Bartleby. Masterly I call it, and such it must appear to any dispassionate thinker. The beauty of my procedure seemed to consist in its perfect quietness. There was no vulgar bullying, no bravado of any sort, no choleric hectoring, and striding to and fro across the apartment, jerking out vehement commands for Bartleby to bundle himself off with his beggarly traps. Nothing of the kind. Without loudly bidding Bartleby depart—as an inferior genius might have done—I *assumed* the ground that depart he must; and upon that assumption built all I had to say. The more I thought over my procedure, the more I was charmed with it. Nevertheless, next morning, upon awakening, I had my doubts—I had somehow slept off the fumes of vanity. One of the coolest and wisest hours a man has, is just after he awakes in the morning. My procedure seemed as sagacious as ever—but only in theory. How it would prove in practice—there was the rub. It was truly a beautiful thought to have assumed Bartleby's departure; but, after all, that assumption was simply my own, and none of Bartleby's. The great point was, not whether I had assumed that he would quit me, but whether he would prefer so to do. He was more a man of preferences than assumptions.

After breakfast, I walked down town, arguing the probabilities *pro* and *con*. One moment I thought it would prove a miserable failure, and Bartleby would be found all alive at my office as usual; the next moment it seemed certain that I should find his chair empty. And so I kept veering about. At the corner of Broadway and Canal Street, I saw quite an excited group of people standing in earnest conversation.

"I'll take odds he doesn't," said a voice as I passed.

"Doesn't go?—done!" said I; "put up your money."

I was instinctively putting my hand in my pocket to produce my own, when I remembered that this was an election day. The words I had overheard bore no reference to Bartleby, but to the success or non-success of some candidate for the mayorality. In my intent frame of mind, I had, as it were, imagined that all Broadway shared in my excitement, and were debating the same question with me. I passed on, very thankful that the uproar of the street screened my momentary absent-mindedness.

As I had intended, I was earlier than usual at my office door. I stood listening for a moment. All was still. He must be gone. I tried the knob. The door was locked. Yes, my procedure had worked to a charm; he indeed must be vanished. Yet a certain melancholy mixed with this: I was almost sorry for my brilliant success. I was fumbling under the door-mat for the key, which Bartleby was to have left there for me, when accidentally my knee knocked against a panel, producing a summoning sound, and in response a voice came to me from within—"Not yet; I am occupied."

It was Bartleby.

I was thunderstruck. For an instant I stood like the man who, pipe in mouth, was killed one cloudless afternoon long ago in Virginia, by summer lightning; at his own warm open window he was killed, and remained leaning out there upon the dreamy afternoon, till someone touched him, when he fell.

"Not gone!" I murmured at last. But again obeying that wondrous ascendency which the inscrutable scrivener had over me, and from which ascendency, for all my chafing, I could not completely escape, I slowly went downstairs and out into the street, and while walking round the block, considered what I should next do in this unheard-of perplexity. Turn the man out by an actual thrusting I could not do; to drive him away by calling him hard names would not do; calling in the police was an unpleasant idea; and yet, permit him to enjoy his cadaverous triumph over me—this, too, I could not think of. What was to be done? or, if nothing could be done, was there anything further that I could *assume* in the matter? Yes, as before I had prospectively assumed that Bartleby would depart, so now I might retrospectively assume that departed he was. In the legitimate carrying out of this assumption, I might enter my office in a great hurry, and pretending not to see Bartleby at all, walk straight against him as if he were air. Such a proceeding would in a singular degree have the appearance of a homethrust. It was hardly possible that Bartleby could withstand such an application of the doctrine of assumptions. But upon second thoughts the success of the plan seemed rather dubious. I resolved to argue the matter over with him again.

"Bartleby," said I, entering the office, with a quietly severe expression, "I am seriously displeased. I am pained, Bartleby. I had thought better of you. I had imagined you of such a gentlemanly organisation, that in any delicate dilemma a slight hint would suffice—in short, an assumption. But it appears I am deceived. Why," I added, unaffectedly starting, "you have not even touched that money yet," pointing to it, just where I had left it the evening previous.

He answered nothing.

"Will you, or will you not, quit me?" I now demanded in a sudden passion, advancing close to him.

"I would prefer *not* to quit you," he replied, gently emphasizing the *not*.

"What earthly right have you to stay here? Do you pay any rent? Do you pay my taxes? Or is this property yours?"

He answered nothing.

"Are you ready to go on and write now? Are your eyes recovered? Could you copy a small paper for me this morning? or help examine a few lines? or step round to the Post Office? In a word, will you do anything at all, to give a colouring to your refusal to depart the premises?"

He silently retired into his hermitage.

I was now in such a state of nervous resentment that I thought it but prudent to check myself at present from further demonstrations. Bartleby and I were alone. I remembered the tragedy of the unfortunate Adams and the still more unfortune Colt in the solitary office of the latter; and how poor Colt, being dreadfully incensed by Adams, and imprudently permitting himself to get wildly excited, was at unawares hurried into his fatal act—an act which certainly no man could possibly deplore more than the actor himself. Often it had occurred to me in my ponderings upon the subject, that had that altercation taken place in the public street, or at a private residence, it would not have terminated as it did. It was the circumstance of being alone in a solitary office, upstairs, of a building entirely unhallowed by humanising domestic associations—an uncarpeted office, doubtless, of a dusty, haggard sort of appearance—this it must have been, which greatly helped to enhance the irritable desperation of the hapless Colt.

But when this old Adam of resentment rose in me and tempted me concerning Bartleby, I grappled him and threw him. How?

Why, simply by recalling the divine injunction: "A new commandment give I unto you, that ye love one another." Yes, this it was that saved me. Aside from higher considerations, charity often operates as a vastly wise and prudent principle—a great safeguard to its possessor. Men have committed murder for jealousy's sake, and anger's sake, and hatred's sake, and selfishness' sake, and spiritual pride's sake; but no man, that ever I heard of, ever committed a diabolical murder for sweet charity's sake. Mere self-interest, then, if no better motive can be enlisted, should, especially with high-tempered men, prompt all beings to charity and philanthropy. At any rate, upon the occasion in question, I strove to drown my exasperated feelings toward the scrivener by benevolently construing his conduct. Poor fellow, poor fellow! thought I, he don't mean anything; and besides, he has seen hard times, and ought to be indulged.

I endeavoured, also, immediately to occupy myself, and at the same time to comfort my despondency. I tried to fancy, that in the course of the morning, at such time as might prove agreeable to him, Bartleby, of his own free accord, would emerge from his hermitage and take up some decided line of march in the direction of the door. But no. Half-past twelve o'clock came; Turkey began to glow in the face, overturn his ink-stand, and become generally obstreperous; Nippers abated down into quietude and courtesy; Ginger Nut munched his noon apple; and Bartleby remained standing at his window in one of his profoundest dead-wall reveries. Will it be credited? Ought I to acknowledge it? That afternoon I left the office without saying one further word to him.

Some days now passed, during which, at leisure intervals, I looked a little into "Edwards on the Will," and "Priestley on Necessity." Under the circumstances, those books induced a salutary feeling. Gradually I slid into the persuasion that these troubles of mine, touching the scrivener, had been all predestinated from eternity, and Bartleby was billeted upon me for some mysterious purpose of an all-wise Providence, which it was not for a mere mortal like me to fathom. Yes, Bartleby, stay there behind your screen, thought I; I shall persecute you no more; you are harmless and noiseless as any of these old chairs; in short, I never feel so private as when I know you are here. At last I see it, I feel it; I penetrate to the predestinated purpose of my life. I am content. Others may have loftier parts to enact; but my mission in this world, Bartleby, is to furnish you with office-room for such period as you may see fit to remain.

I believe that this wise and blessed frame of mind would have continued with me, had it not been for the unsolicited and uncharitable remarks obtruded upon me by my professional friends who visited the rooms. But thus it often is, that the constant friction of illiberal minds wears out at last the best resolves of the more generous. Though to be sure, when I reflected upon it, it was not strange that people entering my office should be struck by the peculiar aspect of the unaccountable Bartleby, and so be tempted to throw out some sinister observations concerning him. Sometimes an attorney, having business with me, and calling at my office, and finding no one but the scrivener there, would undertake to obtain some sort of precise information from him touching my whereabouts; but without heeding his idle talk, Bartleby would remain standing immovable in the middle of the room. So after contemplating him in that position for a time, the attorney would depart, no wiser than he came.

Also, when a Reference was going on, and the room full of lawyers and witnesses, and business driving fast, some deeply occupied legal gentleman present, seeing Bartleby wholly unemployed, would request him to run round to his (the legal gentleman's) office and fetch some papers for him. Thereupon, Bartleby would tranquilly decline, and yet remain idle as before. Then the lawyer would give a great stare, and turn to me. And what could I say? At last I was made aware that all through the circle of my professional acquaintance, a whisper of wonder was running round, having reference to the strange creature I kept at my office. This worried me very much. And as the idea came upon me of his possibly turning out a long-lived man, and keep occupying my chambers, and denying my authority; and perplexing my visitors; and scandalising my professional reputation; and casting a general gloom over the premises; keeping soul and body together to the last upon his savings (for doubtless he spent but half a dime a day), and in the end perhaps outlive me, and claim possession of my office by right of his perpetual occupancy: as all these dark anticipations crowded upon me more and more, and my friends continually intruded their relentless remarks upon the apparition in my room; a great change was wrought in me. I resolved to gather all faculties together, and forever rid me of this intolerable incubus.

Ere revolving any complicated project, however, adapted to this end, I first simply suggested to Bartleby the propriety of his permanent departure. In a calm and serious tone, I commended the idea to his careful and mature consideration. But, having taken three days to meditate upon it, he apprised me, that his original determination remained the same; in short, that he still preferred to abide with me.

What shall I do? I now said to myself, buttoning up my coat to the last button. What shall I do? what ought I to do? what does conscience say I *should* do with this man, or, rather, ghost? Rid myself of him, I must; go, he shall. But how? You will not thrust him, the poor, pale, passive mortal—you will not thrust such a helpless creature out of your door? you will not dishonour yourself by such cruelty? No, I will not, I cannot do that. Rather would I let him live and die here, and then mason up his remains in the wall. What, then, will you do? For all your coaxing, he will not budge. Bribes he leaves under your own paperweight on your table; in short, it is quite plain that he prefers to cling to you.

Then something severe, something unusual must be done. What! surely you will not have him collared by a constable, and commit his innocent pallor to the common jail? And upon what ground could you procure such a thing to be done?—a vagrant, is he? What! he a vagrant, a wanderer, who refuses to budge? It is because he will *not* be a vagrant, then, that you seek to count him *as* a vagrant. This is too absurd. No visible means of support; there I have him. Wrong again: for indubitably he *does* support himself, and that is the only unanswerable proof that any man can show of his possessing the means so to do. No more, then. Since he will not quit me, I must quit him. I will change my offices; I will move elsewhere, and give him fair notice, that if I find him on my new premises I will then proceed against him as a common trespasser.

Acting accordingly, next day I thus addressed him: "I find these chambers too far from the City Hall; the air is unwholesome. In a word, I propose to remove my offices next week, and shall no longer require your services. I tell you this now, in order that you may seek another place."

He made no reply, and nothing more was said.

On the appointed day I engaged carts and men, proceeded to my chambers, and, having but little furniture, everything was removed in a few hours. Throughout, the scrivener remained standing behind the screen, which I directed to be removed the last thing. It was withdrawn; and, being folded up like a huge folio, left him the motionless occupant of a naked room. I stood in the entry watching him a moment, while something from within me upbraided me.

I re-entered, with my hand in my pocket—and—and my heart in my mouth.

"Good-bye, Bartleby, I am going—good-bye, and God some

way bless you; and take that," slipping something in his hand. But it dropped upon the floor, and then—strange to say—I tore myself from him whom I had so longed to be rid of.

Established in my new quarters, for a day or two I kept the door locked, and started at every footfall in the passages. When I returned to my rooms, after any little absence, I would pause at the threshold for an instant, and attentively listen ere applying my key. But these fears were needless. Bartleby never came nigh me.

I thought all was going well, when a perturbed-looking stranger visited me, inquiring whether I was the person who had recently occupied rooms at No.—Wall Street.

Full of forebodings, I replied that I was.

"Then, sir," said the stranger, who proved a lawyer, "you are responsible for the man you left there. He refuses to do any copying; he refuses to do anything; he says he prefers not to; and he refuses to quit the premises."

"I am very sorry, sir," said I, with assumed tranquillity, but an inward tremor, "but, really, the man you allude to is nothing to me—he is no relation or apprentice of mine, that you should hold me responsible for him."

"In mercy's name, who is he?"

"I certainly cannot inform you. I know nothing about him. Formerly I employed him as a copyist; but he has done nothing for me now for some time past."

"I shall settle him, then—good morning, sir."

Several days passed, and I heard nothing more; and, though I often felt a charitable prompting to call at the place and see poor Bartleby, yet a certain squeamishness, of I know not what, withheld me.

All is over with him, by this time, thought I, at last, when, through another week, no further intelligence reached me. But, coming to my room the day after, I found several persons waiting at my door in a high state of nervous excitement.

"That's the man—here he comes," cried the foremost one, whom I recognised as the lawyer who had previously called upon me alone.

"You must take him away, sir, at once," cried a portly person among them, advancing upon me, and whom I knew to be the landlord of No.—Wall Street. "These gentlemen, my tenants, cannot stand it any longer; Mr. B——," pointing to the lawyer, "has turned him out of his room, and he now persists in haunting the building generally, sitting upon the banisters of the stairs by day, and sleeping in the entry by night. Everybody is concerned;

clients are leaving the offices; some fears are entertained of a mob; something you must do, and that without delay.''

Aghast at this torrent, I fell back before it, and would fain have locked myself in my new quarters. In vain I persisted that Bartleby was nothing to me—no more than to anyone else. In vain—I was the last person known to have anything to do with him, and they held me to the terrible account. Fearful, then, of being exposed in the papers (as one person present obscurely threatened), I considered the matter, and, at length, said, that if the lawyer would give me a confidential interview with the scrivener, in his (the lawyer's) own room, I would, that afternoon, strive my best to rid them of the nuisance they complained of.

Going upstairs to my old haunt, there was Bartleby silently sitting upon the banister at the landing.

"What are you doing here, Bartleby?" said I.

"Sitting upon the banister," he mildly replied.

I motioned him into the lawyer's room, who then left us.

"Bartleby," said I, "are you aware that you are the cause of great tribulation to me, by persisting in occupying the entry after being dismissed from the office?"

No answer.

"Now one of two things must take place. Either you must do something, or something must be done to you. Now what sort of business would you like to engage in? Would you like to re-engage in copying for someone?"

"No; I would prefer not to make any change."

"Would you like a clerkship in a dry-goods store?"

"There is too much confinement about that. No, I would not like a clerkship; but I am not particular."

"Too much confinement," I cried, "why, you keep yourself confined all the time!"

"I would prefer not to take a clerkship," he rejoined, as if to settle that little item at once.

"How would a bar-tender's business suit you? There is no trying of the eyesight in that."

"I would not like it at all; though, as I said before, I am not particular."

His unwonted wordiness inspirited me. I returned to the charge.

"Well, then, would you like to travel through the country collecting bills for the merchants? That would improve your health."

"No, I would prefer to be doing something else."

"How, then, would going as a companion to Europe, to

entertain some young gentleman with your conversation—how would that suit you?"

"Not at all. It does not strike me that there is anything definite about that. I like to be stationary. But I am not particular,'

"Stationary you shall be, then," I cried, now losing all patience, and, for the first time in all my exasperating connection with him, fairly flying into a passion. "If you do not go away from these premises before night, I shall feel bound—indeed, I *am* bound—to—to quit the premises myself!" I rather absurdly concluded, knowing not with what possible threat to try to frighten his immobility into compliance. Despairing of all further efforts, I was precipitately leaving him, when a final thought occurred to me—one which had not been wholly unindulged before.

"Bartleby," said I, in the kindest tone I could assume under such exciting circumstances, "will you go home with me now—not to my office, but my dwelling—and remain there till we can conclude upon some convenient arrangement for you at our leisure? Come, let us start now, right away."

"No; at present I would prefer not to make any change at all."

I answered nothing; but, effectually dodging everyone by the suddenness and rapidity of my flight, rushed from the building, ran up Wall Street toward Broadway, and, jumping into the first omnibus, was soon removed from pursuit. As soon as tranquillity returned, I distinctly perceived that I had now done all that I possibly could, both in respect to the demands of the landlord and his tenants, and with regard to my own desire and sense of duty, to benefit Bartleby, and shield him from rude persecution. I now strove to be entirely carefree and quiescent; and my conscience justified me in the attempt; though, indeed, it was not so successful as I could have wished. So fearful was I of being again hunted out by the incensed landlord and his exasperated tenants, that, surrendering my business to Nippers, for a few days, I drove about the upper part of the town and through the suburbs, in my rockaway; crossed over to Jersey City and Hoboken, and paid fugitive visits to Manhattanville and Astoria. In fact, I almost lived in my rockaway for the time.

When again I entered my office, lo, a note from the landlord lay upon the desk. I opened it with trembling hands. It informed me that the writer had sent to the police, and had Bartleby removed to the Tombs as a vagrant. Moreover, since I knew more about him than anyone else, he wished me to appear at that place, and make a suitable statement of the facts. These tidings had a conflicting effect upon me. At first I was indignant; but, at last, almost approved. The landlord's energetic, summary disposition had led him to adopt a procedure which I do not think I would have decided upon myself; and yet, as a last resort, under such peculiar circumstances, it seemed the only plan.

As I afterward learned, the poor scrivener, when told that he must be conducted to the Tombs, offered not the slightest obstacle, but, in his pale, unmoving way, silently acquiesced.

Some of the compassionate and curious bystanders joined the party; and headed by one of the constables arm in arm with Bartleby, the silent procession filed its way through all the noise, and heat, and joy of the roaring throughfares at noon.

The same day I received the note, I went to the Tombs, or, to speak more properly, the Halls of Justice. Seeking the right officer, I stated the purpose of my call, and was informed that the individual I described was, indeed, within. I then assured the functionary that Bartleby was a perfectly honest man, and greatly to be compassionated, however unaccountably eccentric. I narrated all I knew, and closed by suggesting the idea of letting him remain in as indulgent confinement as possible, till something less harsh might be done—though, indeed, I hardly knew what. At all events, if nothing else could be decided upon, the almshouse must receive him. I then begged to have an interview.

Being under no disgraceful charge, and quite serene and harmless in all his ways, they had permitted him freely to wander about the prison, and, especially, in the enclosed grass-plotted yards thereof. And so I found him there, standing all alone in the quietest of the yards, his face toward a high wall, while all around, from the narrow slits of the jail windows, I thought I saw peering out upon him the eyes of murderers and thieves.

"Bartleby!"

"I know you," he said, without looking round—"and I want nothing to say to you."

"It was not I that brought you here, Bartleby," said I, keenly pained at his implied suspicion. "And to you, this should not be so vile a place. Nothing reproachful attaches to you by being here. And see, it is not so sad a place as one might think. Look, there is the sky, and here is the grass."

"I know where I am," he replied, but would say nothing more, and so I left him.

As I entered the corridor again, a broad meat-like man, in an apron, accosted me, and, jerking his thumb over his shoulder, said, "Is that your friend?"

"Yes."

"Does he want to starve? If he does, let him live on the prison fare, that's all."

"Who are you?" asked I, not knowing what to make of such an unofficially speaking person in such a place.

"I am the grub-man. Such gentlemen as have friends here, hire me to provide them with something good to eat."

"Is this so?" said I, turning to the turnkey.

He said it was.

"Well, then," said I, slipping some silver into the grub-man's hands (for so they called him), "I want you to give particular attention to my friend there; let him have the best dinner you can get. And you must be as polite to him as possible."

"Introduce me, will you?" said the grub-man, looking at me with an expression which seemed to say he was all impatient for an opportunity to give a specimen of his breeding.

Thinking it would prove of benefit to the scrivener, I acquiesced; and, asking the grub-man his name, went up with him to Bartleby.

"Bartleby, this is a friend; you will find him very useful to you."

"Your sarvant, sir, your sarvant," said the grub-man, making a low salutation behind his apron. "Hope you find it pleasant here, sir; nice grounds—cool apartments—hope you'll stay with us some time—try to make it agreeable. What will you have for dinner to-day?"

"I prefer not to dine to-day," said Bartleby, turning away. "It would disagree with me; I am unused to dinners." So saying, he slowly moved to the other side of the enclosure, and took up a position fronting the dead-wall.

"How's this?" said the grub-man, addressing me with a stare of astonishment. "He's odd, ain't he?"

"I think he is a little deranged," said I sadly.

"Deranged? deranged is it? Well, now, upon my word, I thought that friend of yourn was a gentleman forger; they are always pale and genteel-like, them forgers. I can't help pity 'em—can't help it, sir. Did you know Monroe Edwards?" he added touchingly, and paused. Then, laying his hand piteously on my shoulder, sighed, "he died of consumption at Sing-Sing. So you weren't acquainted with Monroe?"

"No, I was never socially acquainted with any forgers. But I cannot stop longer. Look to my friend yonder. You will not lose by it. I will see you again."

Some few days after this, I again obtained admission to the Tombs, and went through the corridors in quest of Bartleby; but without finding him.

"I saw him coming from his cell not long ago," said a turnkey, "maybe he's gone to loiter in the yards."

So I went in that direction.

"Are you looking for the silent man?" said another turnkey, passing me. "Yonder he lies—sleeping in the yard there. 'Tis not twenty minutes since I saw him lie down."

The yard was entirely quiet. It was not accessible to the common prisoners. The surrounding walls, of amazing thickness, kept off all sounds behind them. The Egyptian character of the masonry weighed upon me with its gloom. But a soft imprisoned turf grew under foot. The heart of the eternal pyramids, it seemed, wherein, by some strange magic, through the clefts, grass-seed, dropped by birds, had sprung.

Strangely huddled at the base of the wall, his knees drawn up, and lying on his side, his head touching the cold stones, I saw the wasted Bartleby. But nothing stirred. I paused; then went close up to him; stooped over, and saw that his dim eyes were open; otherwise he seemed profoundly sleeping. Something prompted me to touch him. I felt his hand, when a tingling shiver ran up my arm and down my spine to my feet.

The round face of the grub-man peered upon me now. "His dinner is ready. Won't he dine to-day, either? Or does he live without dining?"

"Lives without dining," said I, and closed the eyes.

"Eh!—He's asleep, ain't he?"

"With kings and counsellors," murmured I.

There would seem little need for proceeding further in this history. Imagination will readily supply the meagre recital of poor Bartleby's interment. But, ere parting with the reader, let me say, that if this little narrative has sufficiently interested him, to awaken curiosity as to who Bartleby was, and what manner of life he led prior to the present narrator's making his acquaintance, I can only reply, that in such curiosity I fully share, but am wholly unable to gratify it. Yet here I hardly know whether I should divulge one little item of rumour, which came to my ear a few months after the scrivener's decease. Upon what basis it rested I could never ascertain; and hence, how true it is I cannot now tell. But, inasmuch as this vague report has not been without a certain suggestive interest to me, however sad, it may prove the same with some others; and so I will briefly mention it. The report was this: that Bartleby had been a subordinate clerk in the Dead Letter Office at Washington, from which he had been suddenly removed by a change in the administration.

When I think over this rumour, hardly can I express the emotions which seize me. Dead letters! does it not sound like dead men? Conceive a man by nature and misfortune prone to a pallid hopelessness, can any business seem more fitted to heighten it than that of continually handling these dead letters, and assorting them for the flames? For by the cartload they are annually burned. Sometimes from out the folded paper the pale clerk takes a ring—the finger it was meant for, perhaps, moulders in the grave; a bank-note sent in swiftest charity—he whom it would relieve, nor eats nor hungers any more; pardon for those who died despairing; hope for those who died unhoping; good tidings for those who died stifled by unrelieved calamities. On errands of life, these letters speed to death.

Ah, Bartleby! Ah, humanity!

Harriet Beecher Stowe
(1811–1896)

Daughter of the famous Protestant minister, Lyman Beecher, she was married to a deservedly much less famous minister, Calvin E. Stowe, who had been employed at her father's seminary. Her first book, Uncle Tom's Cabin *(1852), was an immense success and guaranteed significant sales to anything and everything she wrote thereafter.* Dred, *another antislavery novel, appeared in 1856. In* The Minister's Wooing *(1859),* The Pearl of Orr's Island *(1862), and* Oldtown Folks *(1869), from which "Miss Asphyxia" is taken, she turned to her native New England, as she did in* Sam Lawson's Oldtown Fireside Stories *(1872) and* Poganuc People *(1878). Her later fiction, sometimes historical, sometimes contemporary (though not necessarily set in New England), neither did nor could essentially change her reputation, though she branched out in feminist directions and, in* Lady Byron Vindicated *(1870), launched an attack aimed at Lord Byron, charging him (probably correctly) with having committed incest with his half-sister, Augusta. For a time she resided in Connecticut, near the home of Mark Twain; she lived her last years in Florida.*

MISS ASPHYXIA

"There won't be no great profit in this 'ere these ten year."

The object denominated "this 'ere" was the golden-haired child whom we have spoken of before,—the little girl whose mother lay dying. That mother is dead now; and the thing to be settled is, What is to be done with the children? The morning

125

after the scene we have described looked in at the window and saw the woman, with a pale, placid face, sleeping as one who has found eternal rest, and the two weeping children striving in vain to make her hear.

Old Crab had been up early in his design of "carting the 'hull lot over to the poor-house," but made a solemn pause when his wife drew him into the little chamber. Death has a strange dignity, and whatsoever child of Adam he lays his hand on is for the time ennobled,—removed from the region of the earthly and commonplace to that of the spiritual and mysterious. And when Crab found, by searching the little bundle of the deceased, that there was actually money enough in it to buy a coffin and pay 'Zekiel Stebbins for digging the grave, he began to look on the woman as having made a respectable and edifying end, and the whole affair as coming to a better issue than he had feared.

And so the event was considered in the neighborhood, in a melancholy way, rather an interesting and auspicious one. It gave something to talk about in a region where exciting topics were remarkably scarce. The Reverend Jabez Periwinkle found in it a moving Providence which started him favorably on a sermon, and the funeral had been quite a windfall to all the gossips about; and now remained the question, What was to be done with the children?

"Now that we are diggin' the 'taters," said Old Crab, "that 'ere chap might be good for suthin', pickin' on 'em out o' the hills. Poor folks like us can't afford to keep nobody jest to look at, and so he'll have to step spry and work smart to airn his keep." And so at early dawn, the day after the funeral, the little boy was roused up and carried into the fields with the men.

But "this 'ere"—that is to say, a beautiful little girl of seven years—had greatly puzzled the heads of the worthy gossips of the neighborhood. Miss Asphyxia Smith, the elder sister of Old Crab, was at this moment turning the child around, and examining her through a pair of large horn spectacles, with a view to "taking her to raise," as she phrased it.

Now all Miss Asphyxia's ideas of the purpose and aim of human existence were comprised in one word,—work. She was herself a working machine, always wound up and going,—up at early cock-crowing, and busy till bedtime, with a rampant and fatiguing industry that never paused for a moment. She conducted a large farm by the aid of a hired man, and drove a flourishing dairy, and was universally respected in the neighborhood as a smart woman.

Latterly, as her young cousin, who had shared the toils of the house with her, had married and left her, Miss Asphyxia had talked of "takin' a child from the poor-house, and so raisin' her own help"; and it was with the view of this "raisin' her help," that she was thus turning over and inspecting the little article which we have spoken of.

Apparently she was somewhat puzzled, and rather scandalized, that Nature should evidently have expended so much in a merely ornamental way on an article which ought to have been made simply for service. She brushed up a handful of the clustering curls in her large, bony hand, and said, with a sniff, "These'll have to come right off to begin with; gracious me, what a tangle!"

"Mother always brushed them out every day," said the child.

"And who do you suppose is going to spend an hour every day brushing your hair, Miss Pert?" said Miss Asphyxia. "That ain't what I take ye for, I tell you. You've got to learn to work for your living; and you ought to be thankful if I'm willing to show you how."

The little girl did not appear particularly thankful. She bent her soft, pencilled eyebrows in a dark frown, and her great hazel eyes had gathering in them a cloud of sullen gloom. Miss Asphyxia did not mind her frowning,—perhaps did not notice it. She had it settled in her mind, as a first principle, that children never liked anything that was good for them, and that, of course, if she took a child, it would have to be made to come to her by forcible proceedings promptly instituted. So she set her little subject before her by seizing her by her two shoulders and squaring her round and looking in her face, and opened direct conversation with her in the following succinct manner.

"What's your name?"

Then followed a resolved and gloomy silence, as the large bright eyes surveyed, with a sort of defiant glance, the inquisitor.

"Don't you hear?" said Miss Asphyxia, giving her a shake.

"Don't be so ha'sh with her," said the little old woman. "Say, my little dear, tell Miss Asphyxia your name," she added, taking the child's hand.

"Eglantine Percival," said the little girl, turning towards the old woman, as if she disdained to answer the other party in the conversation.

"Wh—a—t?" said Miss Asphyxia. "If there ain't the beatin'est name ever I heard. Well, I tell you *I* ain't got time to fix *my* mouth to say all that 'ere every time I want ye, now I tell you."

"Mother and Harry called me Tina," said the child.

"Teny! Well, I should think so," said Miss Asphyxia. "That

showed she'd got a grain o' sense left, anyhow. She's tol'able strong and well-limbed for her age,'' added that lady, feeling of the child's arms and limbs; ''her flesh is solid. I think she'll make a strong woman, only put her to work early and keep her at it. I could rub out clothes at the wash-tub afore I was at her age.''

''O, she can do considerable many little chores,'' said Old Crab's wife.

''Yes,'' said Miss Asphyxia; ''there can a good deal be got of a child if you keep at 'em; hold 'em in tight, and never let 'em have their head a minute; push right hard on behind 'em, and you get considerable. That's the way I was raised.''

''But I want to play,'' said the little girl, bursting out in a sobbing storm of mingled fear and grief.

''Want to play, do you? Well, you must get over that. Don't you know that that's as bad as stealing? You haven't got any money, and if you eat folks's bread and butter, you've got to work to pay for it; and if folks buy your clothes, you've got to work to pay for them.''

''But I've got some clothes of my own,'' persisted the child, determined not to give up her case entirely.

''Well, so you have; but there ain't no sort of wear in 'em,'' said Miss Asphyxia, turning to Mrs. Smith. ''Them two dresses o' hern might answer for Sundays and sich, but I'll have to make her up a regular linsey working dress this fall, and check aprons; and she must set right about knitting every minute she isn't doing anything else. Did you ever learn how to knit?''

''No,'' said the child.

''Or to sew?'' said Miss Asphyxia.

''Yes; mother taught me to sew,'' said the child.

''No! Yes! Hain't you learned manners? Do you say yes and no to people?''

The child stood a moment, swelling with suppressed feeling, and at last she opened her great eyes full on Miss Asphyxia, and said, ''I don't like you. You ain't pretty, and I won't go with you.''

''O now,'' said Mrs. Smith, ''little girls mustn't talk so; that's naughty.''

''Don't like me?—ain't I pretty?'' said Miss Asphyxia, with a short, grim laugh. ''May be I ain't; but I know what I'm about, and you'd as goods know it first as last. I'm going to take ye right out with me in the waggin, and you'd best not have none of your cuttin's up. I keep a stick at home for naughty girls. Why, where do you suppose you're going to get your livin' if I don't take you?"

"I want to live with Harry," said the child, sobbing. "Where is Harry?"

"Harry's to work—and there's where he's got to be," said Miss Asphyxia. "He's got to work with the men in the fields, and you've got to come home and work with me."

"I want to stay with Harry,—Harry takes care of me," said the child, in a piteous tone.

Old Mother Smith now toddled to her milk-room, and, with a melting heart, brought out a doughnut. "There now, eat that," she said; "and mebbe, if you're good, Miss Asphyxia will bring you down here some time."

"O laws, Polly, you allers was a fool!" said Miss Asphyxia. "It's all for the child's good, and what's the use of fussin' on her up? She'll come to it when she knows she's got to. 'T ain't no more than I was put to at her age, only the child's been fooled with and babied."

The little one refused the doughnut, and seemed to gather herself up in silent gloom.

"Come, now, don't stand sulking; let me put your bonnet on," said Miss Asphyxia, in a brisk, metallic voice. "I can't be losin' the best part of my day with this nonsense!" And forthwith she clawed up the child in her bony grasp, as easily as an eagle might truss a chick-sparrow.

"Be a good little girl, now," said the little gray woman, who felt a strange swelling and throbbing in her poor old breast. To be sure, she knew she was a fool; her husband had told her so at least three times every day for years; and Miss Asphyxia only confirmed what she accepted familiarly as the truth. But yet she could not help these unprofitable longings to coddle and comfort something,—to do some of those little motherly tendernesses for children which go to no particular result, only to make them happy; so she ran out after the wagon with a tempting seed-cake, and forced it into the child's hand.

"Take it, do take it," she said; "eat it, and be a good girl, and do just as she tells you to."

"I'll see to that," said Miss Asphyxia, as she gathered up the reins and gave a cut to her horse, which started that quadruped from a dream of green grass into a most animated pace. Every creature in her service—horse, cow, and pig—knew at once the touch of Miss Asphyxia, and the necessity of being up and doing when she was behind them; and the horse, who under other hands would have been the slowest and most reflective of beasts, now made the little wagon spin and bounce over the rough, stony road, so that the child's short legs flew up in the air every few moments.

"You must hold on tight," was Miss Asphyxia's only comment on this circumstance. "If you fall out, you'll break your neck!"

It was a glorious day of early autumn, the sun shining as only an autumn sun knows how to shine. The blue fields of heaven were full of fleecy flocks of clouds, drifting hither and thither at their lazy will. The golden-rod and the aster hung their plumage over the rough, rocky road; and now and then it wound through a sombre piece of woods, where scarlet sumachs and maples flashed out among the gloomy green hemlocks with a solemn and gorgeous light. So very fair was the day, and so full of life and beauty was the landscape, that the child, who came of a beauty-loving lineage, felt her little heart drawn out from under its burden of troubles, and springing and bounding with that elastic habit of happiness which seems hard to kill in children.

Once she laughed out as a squirrel, with his little chops swelled with a nut on each side, sat upon the fence and looked after them, and then whisked away behind the stone wall; and once she called out, "O, how pretty!" at a splendid clump of blue fringed gentian, which stood holding up its hundred azure vases by the wayside. "O, I do wish I could get some of that!" she cried out, impulsively.

"Some of what?" said Miss Asphyxia.

"O, those *beautiful* flowers!" said the child, leaning far out to look back.

"O, that's nothing but gentian," said Miss Asphyxia; "can't stop for that. Them blows is good to dry for weakness," she added. "By and by, if you're good, mebbe I'll let you get some on 'em."

Miss Asphyxia had one word for all flowers. She called them all "blows," and they were divided in her mind, in a manner far more simple than any botanical system, into two classes; namely, blows that were good to dry, and blows that were not. Elder-blow, catnip, hoarhound, hardhack, gentian, ginseng, and various other vegetable tribes, she knew well and had a great respect for; but all the other little weeds that put on obtrusive colors and flaunted in the summer breeze, without any pretensions to further usefulness, Miss Asphyxia completely ignored. It would not be describing her state to say she had a contempt for them: she simply never saw or thought of them at all. The idea of beauty as connected with any of them never entered her mind,—it did not exist there.

The young cousin who shared her housework had, to be sure, planted a few flowers in a corner of the garden; there were some peonies and pinks and a rose-bush, which often occupied a spare hour of the girl's morning or evening; but Miss Asphyxia watched these operations with a sublime contempt, and only calculated the loss of potatoes and carrots caused by this unproductive beauty. Since the marriage of this girl, Miss Asphyxia had often spoken to her man about "clearing out them things"; but somehow he always managed to forget it, and the thriftless beauties still remained.

It wanted but about an hour of noon when Miss Asphyxia set down the little girl on the clean-scrubbed floor of a great kitchen, where everything was even desolately orderly and neat. She swung her at once into a chair. "Sit there," she said, "till I'm ready to see to ye." And then, marching up to her own room, she laid aside her bonnet, and, coming down, plunged into active preparations for the dinner.

An irrepressible feeling of desolation came over the child. The elation produced by the ride died away; and, as she sat dangling her heels from the chair, and watching the dry, grim form of Miss Asphyxia, a sort of terror of her began slowly to usurp the place of that courage which had at first inspired the child to rise up against the assertion of so uncongenial a power.

All the strange, dreadful events of the last few days mingled themselves, in her childish mind, in a weird mass of uncomprehended gloom and mystery. Her mother, so changed,—cold, stiff, lifeless, neither smiling nor speaking nor looking at her; the people coming to the house, and talking and singing and praying, and then putting her in a box in the ground, and saying that she was dead; and then, right upon that, to be torn from her brother, to whom she had always looked for protection and counsel,—all this seemed a weird, inexplicable cloud coming over her heart and darkening all her little life. Where was Harry? Why did he let them take her? Or perhaps equally dreadful people had taken him, and would never bring him back again.

There was a tall black clock in the corner of the kitchen, that kept its invariable monotone of tick-tack, tick-tack, with a persistence that made her head swim; and she watched the quick, decisive movements of Miss Asphyxia with somewhat of the same respectful awe with which one watches the course of a locomotive engine.

It was late for Miss Asphyxia's dinner preparations, but she instituted prompt measures to make up for lost time. She flew about the kitchen with such long-armed activity and fearful celerity, that the child began instinctively to duck and bob her little head when she went by, lest she should hit her and knock her off her chair.

Miss Asphyxia raked open the fire in the great kitchen chimney, and built it up with a liberal supply of wood; then she rattled into the back room, and a sound was heard of a bucket descending into a well with such frantic haste as only an oaken bucket under Miss Asphyxia's hands could be frightened into. Back she came with a stout black iron tea-kettle, which she hung over the fire; and then, flopping down a ham on the table, she cut off slices with a martial and determined air, as if she would like to see the ham try to help itself; and, before the child could fairly see what she was doing, the slices of ham were in the frying-pan over the coals, the ham hung up in its place, the knife wiped and put out of sight, and the table drawn out into the middle of the floor, and invested with a cloth for dinner.

During these operations the child followed every movement with awe-struck eyes, and studied with trembling attention every feature of this wonderful woman.

Miss Asphyxia was tall and spare. Nature had made her, as she often remarked of herself, entirely for use. She had allowed for her muscles no cushioned repose of fat, no redundant smoothness of outline. There was nothing to her but good, strong, solid bone, and tough, wiry, well-strung muscle. She was past fifty, and her hair was already well streaked with gray, and so thin that, when tightly combed and tied, it still showed bald cracks, not very sightly to the eye. The only thought that Miss Asphyxia ever had had in relation to the *coiffure* of her hair was that it was to be got out of her way. Hair she considered principally as something that might get into people's eyes, if not properly attended to; and accordingly, at a very early hour every morning, she tied all hers in a very tight knot, and then secured it by a horn comb on the top of her head. To tie this knot so tightly that, once done, it should last all day, was Miss Asphyxia's only art of the toilet, and she tried her work every morning by giving her head a shake, before she left her looking-glass, not unlike that of an unruly cow. If this process did not start the horn comb from its moorings, Miss Asphyxia was well pleased. For the rest, her face was dusky and wilted,—guarded by gaunt, high cheekbones, and watched over by a pair of small gray eyes of unsleeping vigilance. The shaggy eyebrows that overhung them were grizzled, like her hair.

It would not be proper to say that Miss Asphyxia looked ill-tempered; but her features could never, by any stretch of imagination, be supposed to wear an expression of tenderness. They were set in an austere, grim gravity, whose lines had become more deeply channelled by every year of her life. As related to her fellow-creatures, she was neither passionate nor cruel. We have before described her as a working machine, forever wound up to high-pressure working-point; and this being her nature, she trod down and crushed whatever stood in the way of her work, with as little compunction as if she had been a steam-engine or a power-loom.

Miss Asphyxia had a full conviction of what a recent pleasant writer has denominated the total depravity of matter. She was not given to many words, but it might often be gathered from her brief discourses that she had always felt herself, so to speak, sword in hand against a universe where everything was running to disorder,—everything was tending to slackness, shiftlessness, unthrift, and she alone was left on the earth to keep things in their places. Her hired men were always too late up in the morning,—always shirking,—always taking too long a nap at noon; everybody was watching to cheat her in every bargain; her horse, cow, pigs—all her possessions,—were ready at the slightest winking of her eye, or relaxing of her watch, to fall into all sorts of untoward ways and gyrations; and therefore she slept, as it were, in her armor, and spent her life as a sentinel on duty.

In taking a child, she had had her eyes open only to one patent fact,—that a child was an animal who would always be wanting to play, and that she must make all her plans and calculations to keep her from playing. To this end she had beforehand given out word to her brother, that, if she took the girl, the boy must be kept away. "Got enough on my hands now, without havin' a boy trainin' around my house, and upsettin' all creation," said the grim virgin.

"Wal, wal," said Old Crab, " 't ain't best; they'll be a consultin' together, and cuttin' up didos. I'll keep the boy tight enough, I tell you."

Little enough was the dinner that the child ate that day. There were two hulking, square-shouldered men at the table, who stared at her with great round eyes like oxen; and so, though Miss Asphyxia dumped down Indian pudding, ham, and fried potatoes before her, the child's eating was scarcely that of a blackbird.

Marvellous to the little girl was the celerity with which Miss Asphyxia washed and cleared up the dinner-dishes. How the dishes rattled, the knives and forks clinked, as she scraped and piled and washed and wiped and put everything in a trice back into such perfect place, that it looked as if nothing had ever been done on the premises!

After this Miss Asphyxia produced thimble, thread, needle, and scissors, and, drawing out of a closet a bale of coarse blue home-made cloth, proceeded to measure the little girl for a petticoat and short gown of the same. This being done to her mind, she dumped her into a chair beside her, and, putting a brown towel into her hands to be hemmed, she briefly said, "There, keep to work"; while she, with great despatch and resolution, set to work on the little garments aforesaid.

The child once or twice laid down her work to watch the chickens who came up round the door, or to note a bird which flew by with a little ripple of song. The first time, Miss Asphyxia only frowned, and said, "Tut, tut." The second time, there came three thumps of Miss Asphyxia's thimble down on the little head, with the admonition, "Mind your work." The child now began to cry, but Miss Asphyxia soon put an end to that by displaying a long birch rod, with a threatening movement, and saying succinctly, "Stop that, this minute, or I'll whip you." And the child was so certain of this that she swallowed her grief and stitched away as fast as her little fingers could go.

As soon as supper was over that night, Miss Asphyxia seized upon the child, and, taking her to a tub in the sink-room, proceeded to divest her of her garments and subject her to a most thorough ablution.

"I'm goin' to give you one good scrubbin' to start with," said Miss Asphyxia; and, truth to say, no word could more thoroughly express the character of the ablution than the term "scrubbing." The poor child was deluged with soap and water, in mouth, nose, ears, and eyes, while the great bony hands rubbed and splashed, twisted her arms, turned her ears wrong side out, and dashed on the water with unsparing vigor. Nobody can tell the torture which can be inflicted on a child in one of these vigorous old New England washings, which used to make Saturday night a terror in good families. But whatever they were, the little martyr was by this time so thoroughly impressed with the awful reality of Miss Asphyxia's power over her, that she endured all with only a few long-drawn and convulsed sighs, and an inaudible "O dear!"

When well scrubbed and wiped, Miss Asphyxia put on a coarse homespun nightgown, and, pinning a cloth round the child's neck, began with her scissors the work of cutting off her hair. Snip, snip, went the fatal shears, and down into the towel fell bright curls, once the pride of a mother's heart, till finally the small head was despoiled completely. Then Miss Asphyxia, shaking up a bottle of camphor, proceeded to rub some vigorously upon the child's head. "There," she said, "that's to keep ye from catchin' cold."

She then proceeded to the kitchen, raked open the fire, and shook the golden curls into the bed of embers, and stood grimly over them while they seethed and twisted and writhed, as if they had been living things suffering a fiery torture, meanwhile picking diligently at the cloth that had contained them, that no stray hair might escape.

"I wonder now," she said to herself, "if any of this will rise and get into the next pudding?" She spoke with a spice of bitterness, poor woman, as if it would be just the way things usually went on, if it did.

She buried the fire carefully, and then, opening the door of a small bedroom adjoining, which displayed a single bed, she said, "Now get into bed."

The child immediately obeyed, thankful to hide herself under the protecting folds of a blue checked coverlet, and feeling that at last the dreadful Miss Asphyxia would leave her to herself.

Miss Asphyxia clapped to the door, and the child drew a long breath. In a moment, however, the door flew open. Miss Asphyxia had forgotten something. "Can you say your prayers?" she demanded.

"Yes, ma'am," said the child.

"Say 'em, then," said Miss Asphyxia; and bang went the door again.

"There, now, if I hain't done up my duty to that child, then I don't know," said Miss Asphyxia.

Bret Harte
(1836–1902)

Born and raised in New York, the son of a professor of Greek, Harte went to California at the age of 18, worked as a teacher and as a miner and, two years later, became first a printer and then a journalist and literary critic. By 1870, his poems and stories of western life, and especially The Luck of Roaring Camp and Other Sketches *(1870), from which "The Iliad of Sandy Bar" is taken, had made him famous not only in the United States but all over the world. He was unable to live up to the reputation he had earned, however: most of the remainder of his writing was, in essence, either pale imitation of his earlier successes or dogged hackwork of no great interest. He wrote many stories, some novels, and a number of plays. He lived out his life in London, serving briefly as a U.S. consul in Germany and also at Glasgow.*

THE ILIAD OF SANDY BAR

Before nine o'clock it was pretty well known all along the river that the two partners of the "Amity Claim" had quarrelled and separated at daybreak. At that time the attention of their nearest neighbor had been attracted by the sounds of altercations and two consecutive pistol-shots. Running out, he had seen, dimly, in the gray mist that rose from the river, the tall form of Scott, one of the partners, descending the hill toward the *cañon*; a moment later, York, the other partner, had appeared from the cabin, and walked in an opposite direction toward the river, passing within a few feet of the curious watcher. Later it was discovered that a serious Chinaman, cutting wood before the cabin, had witnessed part of the quarrel. But John was stolid, indifferent, and reticent. "Me choppee wood, me no fightee," was his serene response to all anxious queries. "But what did they *say*, John?" John did not *sabe*. Colonel Starbottle deftly ran over the various popular epithets which a generous public sentiment might accept as reasonable provocation for an assault. But John did not recognize them. "And this yer's the cattle," said the Colonel, with some severity, "that some thinks oughter be allowed to testify ag'in' a White Man! Git—you heathen!"

Still the quarrel remained inexplicable. That two men, whose amiability and grave tact had earned for them the title of "The Peacemakers," in a community not greatly given to the passive virtues,—that these men, singularly devoted to each other, should suddenly and violently quarrel, might well excite the curiosity of the camp. A few of the more inquisitive visited the late scene of conflict, now deserted by its former occupants. There was no trace of disorder or confusion in the neat cabin. The rude table was arranged as if for breakfast; the pan of yellow biscuit still sat upon that hearth whose dead embers might have typified the evil passions that had raged there but an hour before. But Colonel Starbottle's eye—albeit somewhat bloodshot and rheumy—was more intent on practical details. On examination, a bullet-hole was found in the doorpost, and another, nearly opposite, in the casing of the window. The Colonel called attention to the fact that the one "agreed with" the bore of Scott's revolver, and the other with that of York's derringer. "They must hev stood about yer," said the Colonel, taking position; "not mor'n three feet apart, and—missed!" There was a fine touch of pathos in the falling inflection of the Colonel's voice, which was not without effect. A delicate perception of wasted opportunity thrilled his auditors.

But the Bar was destined to experience a greater disappointment. The two antagonists had not met since the quarrel, and it was vaguely rumored that, on the occasion of a second meeting, each had determined to kill the other "on sight." There was, consequently, some excitement—and, it is to be feared, no little gratification—when, at ten o'clock, York stepped from the Magnolia Saloon into the one long straggling street of the camp, at the same moment that Scott left the blacksmith's shop at the forks of the road. It was evident, at a glance, that a meeting could only be avoided by the actual retreat of one or the other.

In an instant the doors and windows of the adjacent saloons were filled with faces. Heads unaccountably appeared above the

river-banks and from behind bowlders. An empty wagon at the
cross-road was suddenly crowded with people, who seemed to
have sprung from the earth. There was much running and confusion on the hillside. On the mountain-road, Mr. Jack Hamlin had
reined up his horse, and was standing upright on the seat of his
buggy. And the two objects of this absorbing attention approached each other.

"York's got the sun," "Scott'll line him on that tree," "He's
waitin' to draw his fire," came from the cart; and then it was
silent. But above this human breathlessness the river rushed and
sang, and the wind rustled the tree-tops with an indifference that
seemed obtrusive. Colonel Starbottle felt it, and in a moment of
sublime preoccupation, without looking around, waved his cane
behind him, warningly to all nature, and said, "Shu!"

The men were now within a few feet of each other. A hen ran
across the road before one of them. A feathery seed-vessel,
wafted from a wayside tree, fell at the feet of the other. And,
unheeding this irony of nature, the two opponents came nearer,
erect and rigid, looked in each other's eyes, and—passed!

Colonel Starbottle had to be lifted from the cart. "This yer
camp is played out," he said, gloomily, as he affected to be
supported into the Magnolia. With what further expression he
might have indicated his feelings it was impossible to say, for at
that moment Scott joined the group. "Did you speak to me?" he
asked of the Colonel, dropping his hand, as if with accidental
familiarity, on that gentleman's shoulder. The Colonel, recogniz-
ing some occult quality in the touch, and some unknown quantity
in the glance of his questioner, contented himself by replying,
"No, sir," with dignity. A few rods away, York's conduct was
as characteristic and peculiar. "You had a mighty fine chance;
why didn't you plump him?" said Jack Hamlin, as York drew
near the buggy. "Because I hate him," was the reply, heard
only by Jack. Contrary to popular belief, this reply was not
hissed between the lips of the speaker, but was said in an
ordinary tone. But Jack Hamlin, who was an observer of mankind,
noticed that the speaker's hands were cold, and his lips dry, as
he helped him into the buggy, and accepted the seeming paradox
with a smile.

When Sandy Bar became convinced that the quarrel between
York and Scott could not be settled after the usual local methods,
it gave no further concern thereto. But presently it was rumored
that the "Amity Claim" was in litigation, and that its possession
would be expensively disputed by each of the partners. As it was

well known that the claim in question was "worked out" and worthless, and that the partners, whom it had already enriched, had talked of abandoning it but a day or two before the quarrel, this proceeding could only be accounted for as gratuitous spite. Later, two San Francisco lawyers made their appearance in this guileless Arcadia, and were eventually taken into the saloons, and—what was pretty much the same thing—the confidences of the inhabitants. The results of this unhallowed intimacy were many subpœnas; and, indeed, when the "Amity Claim" came to trial, all of Sandy Bar that was not in compulsory attendance at the county seat came there from curiosity. The gulches and ditches for miles around were deserted. I do not propose to describe that already famous trial. Enough that, in the language of the plaintiff's counsel, "it was one of no ordinary significance, involving the inherent rights of that untiring industry which had developed the Pactolian resources of his golden land"; and, in the homelier phrase of Colonel Starbottle, "A fuss that gentlemen might hev settled in ten minutes over a social glass, ef they meant business; or in ten seconds with a revolver, ef they meant fun." Scott got a verdict, from which York instantly appealed. It was said that he had sworn to spend his last dollar in the struggle.

In this way Sandy Bar began to accept the enmity of the former partners as a lifelong feud, and the fact that they had ever been friends was forgotten. The few who expected to learn from the trial the origin of the quarrel were disappointed. Among the various conjectures, that which ascribed some occult feminine influence as the cause was naturally popular, in a camp given to dubious compliment of the sex. "My word for it, gentlemen," said Colonel Starbottle, who had been known in Sacramento as a Gentleman of the Old School, "there's some lovely creature at the bottom of this." The gallant Colonel then proceeded to illustrate his theory, by divers sprightly stories, such as Gentlemen of the Old School are in the habit of repeating, but which, from deference to the prejudices of gentlemen of a more recent school, I refrain from transcribing here. But it would appear that even the Colonel's theory was fallacious. The only woman who personally might have exercised any influence over the partners was the pretty daughter of "old man Folinsbee," of Poverty Flat, at whose hospitable house—which exhibited some comforts and refinements rare in that crude civilization—both York and Scott were frequent visitors. Yet into this charming retreat York strode one evening, a month after the quarrel, and, beholding Scott sitting there, turned to the fair hostess with the abrupt query, "Do you love this man?" The young woman thus addressed returned that answer—at once spirited and evasive—which would occur to most of my fair readers in such an exigency. Without another word, York left the house. "Miss Jo" heaved the least possible sigh as the door closed on York's curls and square shoulders, and then, like a good girl, turned to her insulted guest. "But would you believe it, dear?" she afterward related to an intimate friend, "the other creature, after glowering at me for a moment, got upon its hind legs, took its hat, and left, too; and that's the last I've seen of either."

The same hard disregard of all other interests or feelings in the gratification of their blind rancor characterized all their actions. When York purchased the land below Scott's new claim, and obliged the latter, at a great expense, to make a long détour to carry a "tail-race" around it, Scott retaliated by building a dam that overflowed York's claim on the river. It was Scott, who, in conjunction with Colonel Starbottle, first organized that active opposition to the Chinamen, which resulted in the driving off of York's Mongolian laborers; it was York who built the wagon-road and established the express which rendered Scott's mules and pack-trains obsolete; it was Scott who called into life the Vigilance Committee which expatriated York's friend, Jack Hamlin; it was York who created the "Sandy Bar Herald," which characterized the act as "a lawless outrage," and Scott as a "Border Ruffian"; it was Scott, at the head of twenty masked men, who, one moonlight night, threw the offending "forms" into the yellow river, and scattered the type in the dusty road. These proceedings were received in the distant and more civilized outlying towns as vague indications of progress and vitality. I have before me a copy of the "Poverty Flat Pioneer," for the week ending August 12, 1856, in which the editor, under the head of "County Improvements," says: "The new Presbyterian Church on C Street, at Sandy Bar, is completed. It stands upon the lot formerly occupied by the Magnolia Saloon, which was so mysteriously burnt last month. The temple, which now rises like a Phœnix from the ashes of the Magnolia, is virtually the free gift of H. J. York, Esq., of Sandy Bar, who purchased the lot and donated the lumber. Other buildings are going up in the vicinity, but the most noticeable is the 'Sunny South Saloon,' erected by Captain Mat. Scott, nearly opposite the church. Captain Scott has spared no expense in the furnishing of this saloon, which promises to be one of the most agreeable places of resort in old Tuolumne. He has recently imported two new, first-class billiard-tables, with cork cushions. Our old friend, 'Mountain Jimmy,' will dispense liquors at the bar. We refer our readers to the advertisement in another column. Visitors to Sandy Bar cannot do better than give 'Jimmy' a call.'' Among the local items occurred the following: ''H. J. York, Esq., of Sandy Bar, has offered a reward of $100 for the detection of the parties who hauled away the steps of the new Presbyterian Chruch, C Street, Sandy Bar, during divine service on Sabbath evening last. Captain Scott adds another hundred for the capture of the miscreants who broke the magnificent plate-glass windows of the new saloon on the following evening. There is some talk of reorganizing the old Vigilance Committee at Sandy Bar.''

When, for many months of cloudless weather, the hard, unwinking sun of Sandy Bar had regularly gone down on the unpacified wrath of these men, there was some talk of mediation. In particular, the pastor of the church to which I have just referred—a sincere, fearless, but perhaps not fully enlightened man—seized gladly upon the occasion of York's liberality to attempt to reunite the former partners. He preached an earnest sermon on the abstract sinfulness of discord and rancor. But the excellent sermons of the Rev. Mr. Daws were directed to an ideal congregation that did not exist at Sandy Bar,—a congregation of beings of unmixed vices and virtues, of single impulses, and perfectly logical motives, of preternatural simplicity, of childlike faith, and grown-up responsibilities. As, unfortunately, the people who actually attended Mr. Daws's church were mainly very human, somewhat artful, more self-excusing than self-accusing, rather good-natured, and decidedly weak, they quietly shed that portion of the sermon which referred to themselves, and, accepting York and Scott— who were both in defiant attendance—as curious examples of those ideal beings above referred to, felt a certain satisfaction— which, I fear, was not altogether Christian-like—in their "raking-down.'' If Mr. Daws expected York and Scott to shake hands after the sermon, he was disappointed. But he did not relax his purpose. With that quiet fearlessness and determination which had won for him the respect of men who were too apt to regard piety as synonymous with effeminacy, he attacked Scott in his own house. What he said has not been recorded, but it is to be feared that it was part of his sermon. When he had concluded, Scott looked at him, not unkindly, over the glasses of his bar, and said, less irreverently than the words might convey, ''Young man, I rather like your style; but when you know York and me as well as you do God Almighty, it'll be time to talk.''

*   *   *

And so the feud progressed; and so, as in more illustrious examples, the private and personal enmity of two representative men led gradually to the evolution of some crude, half-expressed principle or belief. It was not long before it was made evident that those beliefs were identical with certain broad principles laid down by the founders of the American Constitution, as expounded by the statesmanlike A.; or were the fatal quicksands, on which the ship of state might be wrecked, warningly pointed out by the eloquent B. The practical result of all which was the nomination of York and Scott to represent the opposite factions of Sandy Bar in legislative councils.

For some weeks past, the voters of Sandy Bar and the adjacent camps had been called upon, in large type to "RALLY!" In vain the great pines at the cross-roads—whose trunks were compelled to bear this and other legends—moaned and protested from their windy watch-towers. But one day, with fife and drum, and flaming transparency, a procession filed into the triangular grove at the head of the gulch. The meeting was called to order by Colonel Starbottle, who, having once enjoyed legislative functions, and being vaguely known as a "war-horse," was considered to be a valuable partisan of York. He concluded an appeal for his friend, with an enunciation of principles, interspersed with one or two anecdotes so gratuitously coarse that the very pines might have been moved to pelt him with their cast-off cones, as he stood there. But he created a laugh, on which his candidate rode into popular notice; and when York rose to speak, he was greeted with cheers. But, to the general astonishment, the new speaker at once launched into bitter denunciation of his rival. He not only dwelt upon Scott's deeds and example, as known to Sandy Bar, but spoke of facts connected with his previous career, hitherto unknown to his auditors. To great precision of epithet and directness of statement, the speaker added the fascination of revelation and exposure. The crowd cheered, yelled, and were delighted, but when this astounding philippic was concluded, there was a unanimous call for "Scott!" Colonel Starbottle would have resisted this manifest impropriety, but in vain. Partly from a crude sense of justice, partly from a meaner craving for excitement, the assemblage was inflexible; and Scott was dragged, pushed, and pulled upon the platform.

As his frowsy head and unkempt beard appeared above the railing, it was evident that he was drunk. But it was also evident, before he opened his lips, that the orator of Sandy Bar—the one man who could touch the vagabond sympathies (perhaps because he was not above appealing to them)— stood before them. A consciousness of this power lent a certain dignity to his figure, and I am not sure but that his very physical condition impressed them as a kind of regal unbending and large condescension. Howbeit, when this unexpected Hector arose from the ditch, York's myrmidons trembled.

"There's naught, gentlemen," said Scott, leaning forward on the railing,—"there's naught as that man hez said as isn't true. I was run outer Cairo; I did belong to the Regulators; I did desert from the army; I did leave a wife in Kansas. But thar's one thing he didn't charge me with, and, maybe, he's forgotten. For three years, gentlemen, I was the man's pardner!—" Whether he intended to say more, I cannot tell; a burst of applause artistically rounded and enforced the climax, and virtually elected the speaker. That fall he went to Sacramento, York went abroad; and for the first time in many years, distance and a new atmosphere isolated the old antagonists.

With little of change in the green wood, gray rock, and yellow river, but with much shifting of human landmarks, and new faces in its habitations, three years passed over Sandy Bar. The two men, once so identified with its character, seemed to have been quite forgotten. "You will never return to Sandy Bar," said Miss Folinsbee, the "Lily of Poverty Flat," on meeting York in Paris, "for Sandy Bar is no more. They call it Riverside now; and the new town is built higher up on the river-bank. By the by, 'Jo' says that Scott has won his suit about the 'Amity Claim,' and that he lives in the old cabin, and is drunk half his time. O, I beg your pardon," added the lively lady, as a flush crossed York's sallow cheek; "but, bless me, I really thought that old grudge was made up. I'm sure it ought to be."

It was three months after this conversation, and a pleasant summer evening, that the Poverty Flat coach drew up before the veranda of the Union Hotel at Sandy Bar. Among its passengers was one, apparently a stranger, in the local distinction of well-fitting clothes and closely shaven face, who demanded a private room and retired early to rest. But before sunrise next morning he arose, and, drawing some clothes from his carpet-bag, proceeded to array himself in a pair of white duck trousers, a white duck overshirt, and straw hat. When his toilet was completed, he tied a red bandanna handkerchief in a loop and threw it loosely over his shoulders. The transformation was complete. As he crept softly down the stairs and stepped into the road, no one would have detected in him the elegant stranger of the previous night, and but few have recognized the face and figure of Henry York of Sandy Bar.

In the uncertain light of that early hour, and in the change that had come over the settlement, he had to pause for a moment to recall where he stood. The Sandy Bar of his recollection lay below him, nearer the river; the buildings around him were of later date and newer fashion. As he strode toward the river, he noticed here a schoolhouse and there a church. A little farther on, "The Sunny South" came in view, transformed into a restaurant, its gilding faded and its paint rubbed off. He now knew where he was; and, running briskly down a declivity, crossed a ditch, and stood upon the lower boundary of the Amity Claim.

The gray mist was rising slowly from the river, clinging to the tree-tops and drifting up the mountain-side, until it was caught among these rocky altars, and held a sacrifice to the ascending sun. At his feet the earth, cruelly gashed and scarred by his forgotten engines, had, since the old days, put on a show of greenness here and there, and now smiled forgivingly up at him, as if things were not so bad after all. A few birds were bathing in the ditch with a pleasant suggestion of its being a new and special provision of nature, and a hare ran into an inverted sluice-box, as he approached, as if it were put there for that purpose.

He had not yet dared to look in a certain direction. But the sun was now high enough to paint the little eminence on which the cabin stood. In spite of his self-control, his heart beat faster as he raised his eyes toward it. Its window and door were closed, no smoke came from its *adobe* chimney, but it was else unchanged. When within a few yards of it, he picked up a broken shovel, and, shouldering it with a smile, strode toward the door and knocked. There was no sound from within. The smile died upon his lips as he nervously pushed the door open.

A figure started up angrily and came toward him,—a figure whose bloodshot eyes suddenly fixed into a vacant stare, whose arms were at first outstretched and then thrown up in warning gesticulation,—a figure that suddenly gasped, choked, and then fell forward in a fit.

But before he touched the ground, York had him out into the open air and sunshine. In the struggle, both fell and rolled over on the ground. But the next moment York was sitting up, holding the convulsed frame of his former partner on his knee, and wiping the foam from his inarticulate lips. Gradually the tremor became less frequent, and then ceased; and the strong man lay unconscious in his arms.

For some moments York held him quietly thus, looking in his face. Afar, the stroke of a woodman's axe—a mere phantom of sound—was all that broke the stillness. High up the mountain, a wheeling hawk hung breathlessly above them. And then came voices, and two men joined them.

"A fight?" No, a fit; and would they help him bring the sick man to the hotel?

And there, for a week, the stricken partner lay, unconscious of aught but the visions wrought by disease and fear. On the eighth day, at sunrise, he rallied, and, opening his eyes, looked upon York, and pressed his hand; then he spoke:—

"And it's you. I thought it was only whiskey."

York replied by taking both of his hands, boyishly working them backward and forward, as his elbow rested on the bed, with a pleasant smile.

"And you've been abroad. How did you like Paris?"

"So, so. How did *you* like Sacramento?"

"Bully."

And that was all they could think to say. Presently Scott opened his eyes again.

"I'm mighty weak."

"You'll get better soon."

"Not much."

A long silence followed, in which they could hear the sounds of wood-chopping, and that Sandy Bar was already astir for the coming day. Then Scott slowly and with difficulty turned his face to York, and said,—

"I might hev killed you once."

"I wish you had."

They pressed each other's hands again, but Scott's grasp was evidently failing. He seemed to summon his energies for a special effort.

"Old man!"

"Old chap."

"Closer!"

York bent his head toward the slowly fading face.

"Do ye mind that morning?"

"Yes."

A gleam of fun slid into the corner of Scott's blue eye, as he whispered,—

"Old man, thar *was* too much saleratus in that bread!"

It is said that these were his last words. For when the sun, which had so often gone down upon the idle wrath of these foolish men, looked again upon them reunited, it saw the hand of Scott fall cold and irresponsive from the yearning clasp of his former partner, and it knew that the feud of Sandy Bar was at an end.

Bayard Taylor
(1825–1878)

Poet, journalist (for Greeley's Tribune *among others), and translator of Goethe's* Faust, *Taylor was best known in his lifetime as a writer of travel books and a lecturer on travel subjects. He wrote on England and Europe, on Egypt, Abyssinia, Turkey, on India and China, all of which he visited and toured. He wrote on Russia, where he was, for a time, secretary to the American legation in St. Petersburg. He wrote novels, he wrote parodies, and continued all his life to write poetry.* Beauty and the Beast *and* Tales of Home *(1872), from which "Who Was She?" is taken, was his only collection of short stories.*

WHO WAS SHE?

Come, now, there may as well be an end of this! Every time I meet your eyes squarely I detect the question just slipping out of them. If you had spoken it, or even boldly looked it; if you had shown in your motions the least sign of a fussy or fidgety concern on my account; if this were not the evening of my birthday, and you the only friend who remembered it; if confession were not good for the soul, though harder than sin to some people, of whom I am one,—well, if all reasons were not at this instant converged into a focus, and burning me rather violently in that region where the seat of emotion is supposed to lie, I should keep my trouble to myself.

Yes, I have fifty times had it on my mind to tell you the whole story. But who can be certain that his best friend will not smile—or, what is worse, cherish a kind of charitable pity ever

147

afterwards—when the external forms of a very serious kind of passion seem trivial, fantastic, foolish? And the worst of all is that the heroic part which I imagined I was playing proves to have been almost the reverse. The only comfort which I can find in my humiliation is that I am capable of feeling it. There isn't a bit of a paradox in this, as you will see; but I only mention it, now, to prepare you for, maybe, a little morbid sensitiveness of my moral nerves.

The documents are all in this portfolio, under my elbow. I had just read them again completely through, when you were announced. You may examine them as you like, afterwards: for the present, fill your glass, take another Cabaña, and keep silent until my "ghastly tale" has reached its most lamentable conclusion.

The beginning of it was at Wampsocket Springs three years ago last summer. I suppose most unmarried men who have reached, or passed, the age of thirty—and I was then thirty-three—experience a milder return of their adolescent warmth, a kind of fainter second spring, since the first has not fulfilled its promise. Of course, I wasn't clearly conscious of this at the time: who is? But I had had my youthful passion and my tragic disappointment, as you know: I had looked far enough into what Thackeray used to call the cryptic mysteries, to save me from the Scylla of dissipation, and yet preserved enough of natural nature to keep me out of the Pharisaic Charybdis. My devotion to my legal studies had already brought me a mild distinction; the paternal legacy was a good nest-egg for the incubation of wealth,—in short, I was a fair, respectable "party," desirable to the humbler mammas, and not to be despised by the haughty exclusives.

The fashionable hotel at the Springs holds three hundred, and it was packed. I had meant to lounge there for a fortnight and then finish my holiday at Long Branch; but eighty, at least, out of the three hundred, were young and moved lightly in muslin. With my years and experience I felt so safe, that to walk, talk, or dance with them became simply a luxury, such as I had never—at least so freely—possessed before. My name and standing, known to some families, were agreeably exaggerated to the others, and I enjoyed that supreme satisfaction which a man always feels when he discovers or imagines that he is popular in society. There is a kind of premonitory apology implied in my saying this, I am aware. You must remember that I am culprit and culprit's counsel at the same time.

You have never been at Wampsocket? Well, the hills sweep

around in a crescent on the northern side and four or five radiating glens descending from them unite just above the village. The central one leading to a waterfall (called "Minnehehe" by the irreverent young people, because there is so little of it), is the fashionable drive and promenade; but the second ravine on the left, steep, crooked, and cumbered with bowlders which have tumbled from somewhere and lodged in the most extraordinary groupings, became my favorite walk of a morning. There was a footpath in it, well-trodden at first, but gradually fading out as it became more like a ladder than a path, and I soon discovered that no other city feet than mine were likely to scale a certain rough slope which seemed the end of the ravine. With the aid of the tough laurel-stems I climbed to the top, passed through a cleft as narrow as a doorway, and presently found myself in a little upper dell, as wild and sweet and strange as one of the pictures that haunt us on the brink of sleep.

There was a pond—no, rather a bowl—of water in the centre; hardly twenty yards across, yet the sky in it was so pure and far down that the circle of rocks and summer foliage inclosing it seemed like a little planetary ring, floating off alone through space. I can't explain the charm of the spot, nor the selfishness which instantly suggested that I should keep the discovery to myself. Ten years earlier, I should have looked around for some fair spirit to be my "minister," but now—

One forenoon—I think it was the third or fourth time I had visited the place—I was startled to find the dint of a heel in the earth, half-way up the slope. There had been rain during the night, and the earth was still moist and soft. It was the mark of a woman's boot, only to be distinguished from that of a walking-stick by its semicircular form. A little higher, I found the outline of a foot, not so small as to awake an ecstasy, but with a suggestion of lightness, elasticity, and grace. If hands were thrust through holes in a board-fence, and nothing of the attached bodies seen, I can easily imagine that some would attract and others repel us: with footprints the impression is weaker, of course, but we cannot escape it. I am not sure whether I wanted to find the unknown wearer of the boot within my precious personal solitude; I was afraid I should see her, while passing through the rocky crevice, and yet was disappointed when I found no one.

But on the flat, warm rock overhanging the tarn—my special throne—lay some withering wildflowers, and a book! I looked up and down, right and left: there was not the slightest sign of

another human life than mine. Then I lay down for a quarter of
an hour, and listened; there were only the noises of bird and
squirrel, as before. At last I took up the book, the flat breadth of
which suggested only sketches. There were, indeed, some tolerable studies of rocks and trees on the first pages; a few not very
striking caricatures, which seemed to have been commenced as
portraits, but recalled no faces I knew; then a number of fragmen-
tary notes, written in pencil. I found no name, from first to last;
only, under the sketches, a monogram so complicated and laborious that the initials could hardly be discovered unless one already knew them.

The writing was a woman's, but it had surely taken its character from certain features of her own: it was clear, firm, individual.
It had nothing of that air of general debility which usually marks
the manuscript of young ladies, yet its firmness was far removed
from the stiff, conventional slope which all Englishwomen seem
to acquire in youth and retain through life. I don't see how any
man in my situation could have helped reading a few lines—if
only for the sake of restoring lost property. But I was drawn on,
and on, and finished by reading all: thence, since no further
harm could be done, I re-read, pondering over certain passages
until they stayed with me. Here they are, as I set them down,
that evening, on the back of a legal blank:

"It makes a great deal of difference whether we wear social
forms as bracelets or handcuffs."

"Can we not still be wholly our independent selves, even
while doing, in the main, as others do? I know two who are so;
but they are married."

"The men who admire these bold, dashing young girls treat
them like weaker copies of themselves. And yet they boast of
what they call 'experience!' "

"I wonder if any one felt the exquisite beauty of the noon as I
did, to-day? A faint appreciation of sunsets and storms is taught
us in youth, and kept alive by novels and flirtations; but the
broad, imperial splendor of this summer noon!—and myself
standing alone in it—yes, utterly alone!"

"The men I seek *must* exist: where are they? How make an
acquaintance, when one obsequiously bows himself away, as I
advance? The fault is surely not all on my side."

There was much more, intimate enough to inspire me with a
keen interest in the writer, yet not sufficiently so to make my
perusal a painful indiscretion. I yielded to the impulse of the
moment, took out my pencil, and wrote a dozen lines on one of
the blank pages. They ran something in this wise:

"IGNOTUS IGNOTÆ!—You have bestowed without intending it, and I have taken without your knowledge. Do not regret the accident which has enriched another. This concealed idyl of the hills was mine, as I supposed, but I acknowledge your equal right to it. Shall we share the possession, or will you banish me?"

There was a frank advance, tempered by a proper caution, I fancied, in the words I wrote. It was evident that she was unmarried, but outside of that certainty there lay a vast range of possibilities, some of them alarming enough. However, if any nearer acquaintance should arise out of the incident, the next step must be taken by her. Was I one of the men she sought? I almost imagined so—certainly hoped so.

I laid the book on the rock, as I had found it, bestowed another keen scrutiny on the lonely landscape, and then descended the ravine. That evening, I went early to the ladies' parlor, chatted more than usual with the various damsels whom I knew, and watched with a new interest those whom I knew not. My mind, involuntarily, had already created a picture of the unknown. She might be twenty-five, I thought: a reflective habit of mind would hardly be developed before that age. Tall and stately, of course; distinctly proud in her bearing, and somewhat reserved in her manners. Why she should have large dark eyes, with long dark lashes, I could not tell; but so I seemed to see her. Quite forgetting that I was (or had meant to be) *Ignotus*, I found myself staring rather significantly at one or the other of the young ladies, in whom I discovered some slight general resemblance to the imaginary character. My fancies, I must confess, played strange pranks with me. They had been kept in a coop so many years, that now, when I suddenly turned them loose, their rickety attempts at flight quite bewildered me.

No! there was no use in expecting a sudden discovery. I went to the glen betimes, next morning: the book was gone, and so were the faded flowers, but some of the latter were scattered over the top of another rock a few yards from mine. Ha! this means that I am not to withdraw, I said to myself: she makes room for me! But how to surprise her?—for by this time I was fully resolved to make her acquaintance, even though she might turn out to be forty, scraggy, and sandy-haired.

I knew no other way so likely as that of visiting the glen at all times of the day. I even went so far as to write a line of greeting, with a regret that our visits had not yet coincided, and laid it under a stone on the top of *her* rock. The note disappeared, but there was no answer in its place. Then I suddenly remembered her fondness for the noon hours, at which time she was "utterly alone." The hotel *table d'hôte* was at one o'clock, her family, doubtless, dined later, in their own rooms. Why, this gave me, at least, her place in society! The question of age, to be sure, remained unsettled; but all else was safe.

The next day I took a late and large breakfast and sacrificed my dinner. Before noon the guests had all straggled back to the hotel from glen and grove and lane, so bright and hot was the sunshine. Indeed, I could hardly have supported the reverberation of heat from the sides of the ravine, but for a fixed belief that I should be successful. While crossing the narrow meadow upon which it opened, I caught a glimpse of something white among the thickets higher up. A moment later, it had vanished, and I quickened my pace, feeling the beginning of an absurd nervous excitement in my limbs. At the next turn, there it was again! but only for another moment. I paused, exulting, and wiped my drenched forehead. "She cannot escape me!" I murmured between the deep draughts of cooler air I inhaled in the shadow of a rock.

A few hundred steps more brought me to the foot of the steep ascent, where I had counted on overtaking her. I was too late for that, but the dry, baked soil had surely been crumbled and dislodged, here and there, by a rapid foot. I followed, in reckless haste, snatching at the laurel-branches right and left, and paying little heed to my footing. About one third of the way up I slipped, fell, caught a bush which snapped at the root, slid, whirled over, and before I fairly knew what had happened, I was lying doubled up at the bottom of the slope.

I rose, made two steps forward, and then sat down with a groan of pain; my left ankle was badly sprained, in addition to various minor scratches and bruises. There was a revulsion of feeling, of course,—instant, complete, and hideous. I fairly hated the Unknown. "Fool that I was!" I exclaimed, in the theatrical manner, dashing the palm of my hand softly against my brow: "lured to this by the fair traitress! But, no!—not fair: she shows the artfulness of faded, desperate spinsterhood; she is all compact of enamel, 'liquid bloom of youth,' and hair-dye!"

There was a fierce comfort in this thought, but it couldn't help me out of the scrape. I dared not sit still, lest a sun-stroke should be added, and there was no resource but to hop or crawl down the rugged path, in the hope of finding a forked sapling from which I could extemporize a crutch. With endless pain and trouble I reached a thicket, and was feebly working on a branch with my penknife, when the sound of a heavy footstep surprised me.

A brown harvest-hand, in straw hat and shirtsleeves, presently appeared. He grinned when he saw me, and the thick snub of his nose would have seemed like a sneer at any other time.

"Are you the gentleman that got hurt?" he asked. "Is it pretty tolerable bad?"

"Who said I was hurt?" I cried in astonishment.

"One of your town-women from the hotel—I reckon she was. I was binding oats, in the field over the ridge; but I haven't lost no time in comin' here."

While I was stupidly staring at this announcement, he whipped out a big clasp knife, and in a few minutes fashioned me a practicable crutch. Then, taking me by the other arm, he set me in motion toward the village.

Grateful as I was for the man's help, he aggravated me by his ignorance. When I asked if he knew the lady, he answered: "It's more'n likely *you* know her better." But where did she come from? Down from the hill, he guessed, but it might ha' been up the road. How did she look? was she old or young? what was the color of her eyes? of her hair? There, now, I was too much for him. When a woman kept one o' them speckled veils over her face, turned her head away and held her parasol between, how were you to know her from Adam? I declare to you, I couldn't arrive at one positive particular. Even when he affirmed that she was tall, he added, the next instant: "Now I come to think on it, she stepped mighty quick; so I guess she must ha' been short."

By the time we reached the hotel, I was in a state of fever; opiates and lotions had their will of me for the rest of the day. I was glad to escape the worry of questions, and the conventional sympathy expressed in inflections of the voice which are meant to soothe, and only exasperate. The next morning, as I lay upon my sofa, restful, patient, and properly cheerful, the waiter entered with a bouquet of wild flowers.

"Who sent them?" I asked.

"I found them outside your door, sir. Maybe there's a card; yes, here's a bit o' paper."

I opened the twisted slip he handed me, and read: "From your dell—and mine." I took the flowers; among them were two or three rare and beautiful varieties, which I had only found in that one spot. Fool, again! I noiselessly kissed, while pretending to smell them, and had them placed on a stand within reach, and fell into a state of quiet and agreeable contemplation.

Tell me, yourself, whether any male human being is ever too old for sentiment, provided that it strikes him at the right time and in the right way! What did that bunch of wild flowers betoken? Knowledge, first; then, sympathy; and finally, encouragement, at least. Of course she had seen my accident, from above; of course she had sent the harvest laborer to aid me home. It was quite natural she should imagine some special romantic interest in the lonely dell, on my part, and the gift took additional value from her conjecture.

Four days afterward there was a hop in the large dining-room of the hotel. Early in the morning a fresh bouquet had been left at my door. I was tired of my enforced idleness, eager to discover the fair unknown (she was again fair, to my fancy!), and I determined to go down, believing that a cane and a crimson velvet slipper on the left foot would provoke a glance of sympathy from certain eyes, and thus enable me to detect them.

The fact was, the sympathy was much too general and effusive. Everybody, it seemed, came to me with kindly greetings; seats were vacated at my approach, even fat Mrs. Huxter insisting on my taking her warm place, at the head of the room. But Bob Leroy—you know him—as gallant a gentleman as ever lived, put me down at the right point, and kept me there. He only meant to divert me, yet gave me the only place where I could quietly inspect all the younger ladies, as dance or supper brought them near.

One of the dances was an old-fashioned cotillon, and one of the figures, the "coquette," brought every one, in turn, before me. I received a pleasant word or two from those whom I knew, and a long, kind, silent glance from Miss May Danvers. Where had been my eyes? She was tall, stately, twenty-five, had large dark eyes, and long dark lashes! Again the changes of the dance brought her near me; I threw (or strove to throw) unutterable meanings into my eyes, and cast them upon hers. She seemed startled, looked suddenly away, looked back to me, and—blushed. I knew her for what is called "a nice girl"—that is, tolerably frank, gently feminine, and not dangerously intelligent. Was it possible that I had overlooked so much character and intellect?

As the cotillon closed, she was again in my neighborhood, and her partner led her in my direction. I was rising painfully from my chair, when Bob Leroy pushed me down again, whisked another seat from somewhere, planted it at my side, and there she was!

She knew who was her neighbor, I plainly saw; but instead of turning toward me, she began to fan herself in a nervous way and to fidget with the buttons of her gloves. I grew impatient.

"Miss Danvers!" I said, at last.

"Oh!" was all her answer, as she looked at me for a moment.

"Where are your thoughts?" I asked.

Then she turned, with wide, astonished eyes, coloring softly up to the roots of her hair. My heart gave a sudden leap.

"How can you tell, if I cannot?" she asked.

"May I guess?"

She made a slight inclination of the head, saying nothing. I was then quite sure.

"The second ravine, to the left of the main drive?"

This time she actually started; her color became deeper, and a leaf of the ivory fan snapped between her fingers.

"Let there be no more a secret!" I exclaimed. "Your flowers have brought me your messages; I knew I should find you"—

Full of certainty, I was speaking in a low, impassioned voice. She cut me short by rising from her seat; I felt that she was both angry and alarmed. Fisher, of Philadelphia, jostling right and left in his haste, made his way toward her. She fairly snatched his arm, clung to it with a warmth I had never seen expressed in a ball-room, and began to whisper in his ear. It was not five minutes before he came to me, alone, with a very stern face, bent down, and said:

"If you have discovered our secret, you will keep silent. You are certainly a gentleman."

I bowed coldly and savagely. There was a draft from the open window; my ankle became suddenly weary and painful, and I went to bed. Can you believe that I didn't guess, immediately, what it all meant? In a vague way, I fancied that I had been premature in my attempt to drop our mutual incognito, and that Fisher, a rival lover, was jealous of me. This was rather flattering than otherwise; but when I limped down to the ladies' parlor, the next day, no Miss Danvers was to be seen. I did not venture to ask for her; it might seem importunate, and a woman of so much hidden capacity was evidently not to be wooed in the ordinary way.

So another night passed by; and then, with the morning, came a letter which made me feel, at the same instant, like a fool and a hero. It had been dropped in the Wampsocket post-office, was legibly addressed to me, and delivered with some other letters which had arrived by the night mail. Here it is; listen!

"Noto Ignota!—Haste is not a gift of the gods, and you have been impatient, with the usual result. I was almost prepared for this, and thus am not wholly disappointed. In a day or two more you will discover your mistake, which, so far as I can learn, has done no particular harm. If you wish to find *me*, there is only one way to seek me; should I tell you what it is, I should run the risk of losing you,—that is, I should preclude the manifestation of a certain quality which I hope to find in the man who may—or, rather, must—be my friend. This sounds enigmatical, yet you have read enough of my nature, as written in these random notes in my sketch-book, to guess, at least, how much I require. Only this let me add: mere guessing is useless.

"Being unknown, I can write freely. If you find me, I shall be justified; if not, I shall hardly need to blush, even to myself, over a futile experiment.

"It is possible for me to learn enough of your life, henceforth, to direct my relation toward you. This may be the end; if so, I shall know it soon. I shall also know whether you continue to seek me. Trusting in your honor as a man, I must ask you to trust in mine, as a woman."

I *did* discover my mistake, as the Unknown promised. There had been a secret betrothal between Fisher and Miss Danvers; and singularly enough, the momentous question and answer had been given in the very ravine leading to my upper dell! The two meant to keep the matter to themselves, but therein, it seems, I thwarted them; there was a little opposition on the part of their respective families, but all was amicably settled before I left Wampsocket.

The letter made a very deep impression upon me. What was the one way to find her? What could it be but the triumph that follows ambitious toil—the manifestation of all my best qualities, as a man? Be she old or young, plain or beautiful, I reflected, hers is surely a nature worth knowing, and its candid intelligence conceals no hazards for me. I have sought her rashly, blundered, betrayed that I set her lower, in my thoughts, than her actual self: let me now adopt the opposite course, seek her openly no longer, go back to my tasks, and, following my own aims vigorously and cheerfully, restore that respect which she seemed do be on the point of losing. For, consciously or not, she had communicated to me a doubt, implied in the very expression of her own strength and pride. She had meant to address me as an equal, yet, despite herself, took a stand a little above that which she accorded to me.

I came back to New York earlier than usual, worked steadily at my profession and with increasing success, and began to accept opportunities (which I had previously declined) of making myself personally known to the great, impressible, fickle, tyrannical public. One or two of my speeches in the hall of the Cooper Institute, on various occasions—as you may perhaps remember—gave me a good headway with the party, and were the chief cause of my nomination for the State office which I still hold. (There, on the table, lies a resignation, written to-day, but not yet signed. We'll talk of it afterwards.)

Several months passed by, and no further letter reached me. I gave up much of my time to society, moved familiarly in more than one province of the kingdom here, and vastly extended my acquaintance, especially among the women; but not one of them betrayed the mysterious something or other—really I can't explain precisely what it was!—which I was looking for. In fact, the more I endeavored quietly to study the sex, the more confused I became.

At last I was subjected to the usual onslaught from the strong-minded. A small but formidable committee entered my office one morning and demanded a categorical declaration of my principles. What my views on the subject were, I knew very well; they were clear and decided; and yet, I hesitated to declare them! It wasn't a temptation of Saint Anthony—that is, turned the other way—and the belligerent attitude of the dames did not alarm me in the least; but *she!* What was *her* position? How could I best please her? It flashed upon my mind, while Mrs. —— was making her formal speech, that I had taken no step for months without a vague, secret reference to *her*. So, I strove to be courteous, friendly, and agreeably non-committal; begged for further documents, and promised to reply by letter, in a few days.

I was hardly surprised to find the well-known hand on the envelope of a letter, shortly afterwards. I held it for a minute in my palm, with an absurd hope that I might sympathetically feel its character, before breaking the seal. Then I read it with a great sense of relief.

"I have never assumed to guide a man, except toward the full exercise of his powers. It is not opinion in action, but opinion in a state of idleness or indifference, which repels me. I am deeply glad that you have gained so much since you left the country. If, in shaping your course, you have thought of me, I will frankly say that, *to that extent*, you have drawn nearer. Am I mistaken in conjecturing that you wish to know my relation to the movement concerning which you were recently interrogated? In this, as in other instances which may come, I must beg you to consider me only as a spectator. The more my own views may seem likely to sway your action, the less I shall be inclined to declare them. If you find this cold or unwomanly, remember that it is not easy!''

Yes! I felt that I had certainly drawn much nearer to her. And from this time on, her imaginary face and form became other than they were. She was twenty-eight—three years older; a very little above the middle height, but not tall; serene, rather than stately, in her movements; with a calm, almost grave face, relieved by the sweetness of the full, firm lips; and finally eyes of pure, limpid gray, such as we fancy belonged to the Venus of Milo. I found her, thus, much more attractive than with the dark eyes and lashes—but she did not make her appearance in the circles which I frequented.

Another year slipped away. As an official personage, my importance increased, but I was careful not to exaggerate it to myself. Many have wondered (perhaps you among the rest) at my success, seeing that I possess no remarkable abilities. If I have any secret, it is simply this—doing faithfully, with all my might, whatever I undertake. Nine tenths of our politicians become inflated and careless, after the first few years, and are easily forgotten when they once lose place. I am a little surprised, now, that I had so much patience with the Unknown. I was too important, at least, to be played with; too mature to be subjected to a longer test; too earnest, as I had proved, to be doubted, or thrown aside without a further explanation.

Growing tired, at last, of silent waiting, I bethought me of advertising. A carefully-written ''Personal,'' in which *Ignotus* informed *Ignota* of the necessity of his communicating with her, appeared simultaneously in the Tribune, Herald, World, and Times. I renewed the advertisement as the time expired without an answer, and I think it was about the end of the third week before one came, through the post, as before.

Ah, yes! I had forgotten. See! my advertisement is pasted on the note, as a heading or motto for the manuscript lines. I don't know why the printed slip should give me a particular feeling of humiliation as I look at it, but such is the fact. What she wrote is all I need read to you:

''I could not, at first, be certain that this was meant for me. If I were to explain to you why I have not written for so long a time, I might give you one of the few clews which I insist on keeping

ould have been the end, had you really found me?
sincere, satisfying friendship. No mysterious mag-
as drawn you to me or held you near me, nor has my
inspired me with an interest which cannot be given
a personal pang. I am grieved, for the sake of all men
en. Yet, understand me! I mean no slightest reproach.
d honor you for what you are. Farewell!''

thing could be kinder in tone, nothing more humiliat-
ance. I was sore and offended for a few days; but I
to see, and ever more and more clearly, that she
right. I was sure, also, that any further attempt to
with her would be vain. It all comes of taking society
nd it, and supposing that conventional courtesy is the
ound on which men and women can meet.

s—there's no use in hiding it from myself (and I see,
, that the letter cuts into your own conscience)—she
urageous, independent character, and—I am not.
was she?

in my own hands. In your public capacity, you have been (so far as a woman may judge) upright, independent, wholly manly: in your relations with other men I learn nothing of you that is not honorable: toward women you are kind, chivalrous, no doubt, overflowing with the *usual* social refinements, but— Here, again, I run hard upon the absolute necessity of silence. The way to me, if you care to traverse it, is so simple, so very simple! Yet, after what I have written, I cannot even wave my hand in the direction of it, without certain self-contempt. When I feel free to tell you, we shall draw apart and remain unknown forever.

"You desire to write? I do not prohibit it. I have heretofore made no arrangement for hearing from you, in turn, because I could not discover that any advantage would accrue from it. But it seems only fair, I confess, and you dare not think me capricious. So, three days hence, at six o'clock in the evening, a trusty messenger of mine will call at your door. If you have anything to give her for me, the act of giving it must be the sign of a compact on your part, that you will allow her to leave immediately, unquestioned and unfollowed."

You look puzzled, I see: you don't catch the real drift of her words? Well—that's a melancholy encouragement. Neither did I, at the time: it was plain that I had disappointed her in some way, and my intercourse with, or manner toward, women, had something to do with it. In vain I ran over as much of my later social life as I could recall. There had been no special attention, nothing to mislead a susceptible heart; on the other side, certainly no rudeness, no want of "chivalrous" (she used the word!) respect and attention. What, in the name of all the gods, was the matter?

In spite of all my efforts to grow clearer, I was obliged to write my letter in a rather muddled state of mind. I had *so* much to say! sixteen folio pages, I was sure, would only suffice for an introduction to the case; yet, when the creamy vellum lay before me and the moist pen drew my fingers toward it, I sat stock dumb for half an hour. I wrote, finally, in a half-desperate mood, without regard to coherency or logic. Here's a rough-draft of a part of the letter, and a single passage from it will be enough:

"I can conceive of no simpler way to you than the knowledge of your name and address. I have drawn airy images of you, but they do not become incarnate, and I am not sure that I should recognize you in the brief moment of passing. Your nature is not of those which are instantly legible. As an abstract power, it has wrought in my life and it continually moves my heart with desires which are unsatisfactory because so vague and ignorant. Let me offer you, personally, my gratitude, my earnest friendship: you would laugh if I were *now* to offer more.''

Stay! here is another fragment, more reckless in tone:

''I want to find the woman whom I can love—who can love me. But this is a masquerade where the features are hidden, the voice disguised, even the hands grotesquely gloved. Come! I will venture more than I ever thought was possible to me. You shall know my deepest nature as I myself seem to know it. Then, give me the commonest chance of learning yours, through an inter-course which shall leave both free, should we not feel the closing of the inevitable bond!''

After I had written that, the pages filled rapidly. When the appointed hour arrived, a bulky epistle, in a strong linen envelope, sealed with five wax seals, was waiting on my table. Precisely at six there was an announcement: the door opened, and a little outside, in the shadow, I saw an old woman, in a threadbare dress of rusty black.

''Come in!'' I said.

''The letter!'' answered a husky voice. She stretched out a bony hand, without moving a step.

''It is for a lady—very important business,'' said I, taking up the letter; ''are you sure that there is no mistake?''

She drew her hand under the shawl, turned without a word, and moved toward the hall door.

''Stop!'' I cried; ''I beg a thousand pardons! Take it—take it! You are the right messenger!''

She clutched it, and was instantly gone.

Several days passed, and I gradually became so nervous and uneasy that I was on the point of inserting another ''Personal'' in the daily papers, when the answer arrived. It was brief and mysterious; you shall hear the whole of it.

''I thank you. Your letter is a sacred confidence which I pray you never to regret. Your nature is sound and good. You ask no more than is reasonable, and I have no real right to refuse. In the one respect which I have hinted, *I* may have been unskilful or too narrowly cautious: I must have the certainty of this. Therefore, as a generous favor, give me six months more! At the end of that time I will write to you again. Have patience with these brief lines: another word might be a word too much.''

You notice the change in her tone? The letter gave me the strongest impression of a new, warm, almost anxious interest on

her part. My fancies, as first at W
sorts of singular pranks: sometime
family, sometimes moderately poo
same calm, reposeful face and cle
for her in society, quite sure tha
nursed a wild expectation of sudde
in the most unlikely places and
However, the end of it all was pati

There's not much more to tell;
me to read. It came punctually, to
the last I began to dread the time,
due, and I had no funds to mee
when I broke the seal. The fact
once, but it was a long time be
became intelligible.

''The stipulated time has come,
an end. Had I taken this resoluti
saved me many vain hopes, and yo
Forgive me, first, if you can, and

''You wished for a personal int
but many. We have met, in soc
cussed the weather, the opera, toi
Long Branch and Newport, and
fashionable gossip; and you neve
by any deeper interest! I have
platitudes, and you were as smilir
them: I have let fall remarks wl
could not have escaped you, an
of sharp, honest, manly repr
unexceptionable, as it was to a
source of my disappointment,

''You appreciate, I canno
which men value in one anothe
high and earnest appreh
to seek them. It is not
is flattered by receiv
st men give to th
ives with her,
empty-heade
rstand som
avigatio
ho a
c

''What
Certainly
netic force
experimen
up without
and all wo
I esteem a

There. N
ing in sub
soon bega
was wholl
correspond
just as we
only safe g

The fact
by your fa
is a free, c
But who

Rose Terry Cooke

(1827–1892)

Born and raised in Connecticut, the daughter of a wealthy man who served in Congress, Rose Terry graduated from the Hartford Female Seminary in 1843. The school had been founded by Harriet Beecher Stowe's sister, Catherine Beecher; Rose and Mrs. Stowe were lifelong friends. Much of her early work was published under her maiden name, Rose Terry; she married Rollin Hillyer Cooke, an iron manufacturer, in 1873, and thereafter signed herself with the name she is today known by. Beginning as a teacher, she turned to literature, first as a poet (her first book, in 1860, was a collection of poems), and then as a regular contributor to magazines. By age 20 she had become a regular contributor to Putnam's; *later she was perhaps the leading contributor to* The Atlantic *during James Russell Lowell's editorship. Among her many collections of stories were* Somebody's Neighbors *(1881),* Root Bound *(1885),* The Sphynx's Children *(1886), and* Huckleberries Gathered From New England Hills *(1891), from which "Grit" is taken. She, Mrs. Stowe, Mary E. Wilkins Freeman, and Sarah O. Jewett were mutually influential one on the other, and were also friends and admirers of one another. Cooke lived all her life in New England, mostly in Connecticut.*

GRIT

"Look a-here, Phoebe, I won't hev no such goins'on here. That feller's got to make tracks. I don't want none o' Jake Potter's folks round, 'nd you may as well lay your account with it, 'nd fix accordin'."

Phoebe Fyler set her teeth together, and looked her father in the face with her steady gray eyes; but she said nothing, and the old man scrambled up into his rickety wagon and drove off.

"Fyler grit" was a proverb in Pasco, and old Reuben did credit to the family reputation. But his share of "grit" was not simply endurance, perseverance, dogged persistence, and courage, but a most unlimited obstinacy and full faith in his own wisdom. Phoebe was his own child, and when things came to an open struggle between them, it was hard to tell which would conquer.

There had been a long quarrel between the Fylers and Potters—such a quarrel as can only be found in little country villages, where people are thrown so near together and have so little to divert their minds that they become as belligerent as a company of passengers on a sailing vessel—fire easily and smoulder long. But Phoebe Fyler was a remarkably pretty girl, with great, clear gray eyes, a cheek like the wild rose, abundance of soft brown hair, and a sweet firm mouth and square cleft chin that told their own story of Fyler blood; and Tom Potter was a smart, energetic, fiery young fellow, ready to fight for his rights and then to shake hands with his enemy, whichever beat. There was no law to prevent his falling in love with Phoebe because their fathers had hated each other; indeed, that was rather an inducement. His honest, generous heart looked on the family feud with pity and regret. He would like to cancel it, especially if marrying Phoebe would do it.

And why should she hate him? Her father was an old tyrant in his family; and the feeble, pale mother, who had always trembled at his step since the girl could remember, had never taught her to love her father, because she did not love him herself. Obedience, indeed, was ground into Phoebe. It was obey or suffer in that family, and the rod hanging over the shelf was not in vain. But when she grew up, and left the childish instinct or habit behind her, and the Fyler grit developed, she had the sense to avoid an open conflict whenever she could, for her mother's sake.

This, however, was a matter of no small importance to Phoebe. She had met Tom Potter time after time at sewing societies, sleigh rides, huckleberryings, and other rustic amusements; they sat together in the singers' seat, they went to rehearsal; but Tom had never come home with her until lately, and then always parted at the doorsill. Now he had taken the decisive step; he had come Sunday evening to call, and every Pasco girl knew what that meant. It was a declaration. But while Phoebe's heart beat at

his clear whistle outside, and stood still at his knock, she saw
with dismay her father rise to open the door.

"Good evening, Mr. Fyler."

"How de do? how de do?" was the sufficiently cordial reply;
for the old man was half blind, and by the flicker of his tallow
candle could noway discern who his visitor might be.

"I don't really make out who ye be," he went on, peering
into the darkness.

"My name's Potter. Is Phoebe to home?"

"Jake Potter's son?"

"Yes, I be. Is Phoebe to home?"

An ominous flash from Tom's black eyes accentuated the
question this time, but old Reuben was too blind to see it. He
drew back the candle, and said, in a surly but decisive tone,—

" 'Tain't no matter to you ef she is or ef she ain't," and
calmly shut the door in his face.

For a moment Tom Potter was furious. Decency forbade that
he should take the door off its rackety hinges, like Samson at the
gates of Gaza, but he felt a strong impulse to do so, and then an
equally strong one to laugh, for the affair had its humorous side.
The result was that neither humor nor anger prevailed; but as he
strode away, a fixed purpose to woo and marry Phoebe, "whether
or no," took possession of him.

"I'll see ef Potter faculty can't match Fyler grit," he muttered
to himself; and not without reason, for the Potters had that trait
which conquers the world far more surely and subtly than grit,
—"faculty," *i.e.*, a clear head and a quick wit, and capacity of
adaptation that wrests from circumstance its stringent sceptre,
and is the talisman of what the world calls "luck."

In the mean time Phoebe, by the kitchen fire, sat burning with
rage. Her father came back chuckling.

"I've sent that spark up chimney pretty everlastin' quick."

Phoebe's red lips parted for a rude answer, but her mother
signaled to her from behind the fire-place, and the sad pale face
had its usual effect on her. She knew that sore heart would ache
beyond any sleep if she and her father came to words; so she
took up her candle to go to bed, but she did not escape.

"You've no need to be a-muggin' about that feller, Phoebe,"
cackled the old man after her. "He won't never darken my
doors, nor your'n nuther; so ye jest stop a-hankerin' arter him,
right off slap. The idee! a Potter a-comin' here arter you!"

Phoebe's eyes blazed. She stopped on the lower stair, and
spoke sharply,—

"Mebbe you'll find there's more things can go out o' the chimney than sparks," and then hurried up, banging the door behind her in very womanish fashion, and burst into tears as soon as she reached her room.

It was Tuesday morning when old Fyler drove from his door, hurling the words at the beginning of our story at Phoebe, on the doorstep.

He had found out that Tom Potter had gone to Hartford the day before for a week's stay, and took the chance to drive sixteen miles down the river on some business, sure that in his day's absence Tom could not go back to Pasco, and Phoebe would be safe.

But man proposes in vain sometimes. Mr. Fyler did his errand at Taunton, ate his dinner at the dirty little tavern, and set out for home. As he was jogging quietly along, laying plans for the easy discomfiture of Tom and Phoebe, a loud roll of wheels roused him, a muffled roar like a heavy pulse beat, a shriek as of ten thousand hysterical females, and right in the face and eyes of old Jerry appeared a locomotive under full headway, coming round a curve of the track, which the old man had either forgotten, or not known, ran beside the highway for nearly half a mile. Jerry was old and sober and steady, but what man even could bear the sudden and unforseen charge of a railway engine bearing down upon him face to face? The horse started, reared, jumped aside, and took to his heels for dear life; the wagon tilted up on a convenient stone, and threw the driver violently out; but in all the shock and terror the "Fyler grit" never failed. With horny hands he grasped the reins so powerfully that the horse could drag him but a few steps before he was stopped by the weight on the bit, and then, as Rueben tried to gather himself out of the dust and consider the situation, he found that one leg hung helpless from the knee, his cheek and forehead were well grazed, and his teeth—precious possession, over whose cost he had groaned and perspired as a necessary but dreadful expense—had disappeared entirely. This was the worst blow. Half blind, with a terrified horse and a broken leg, totally alone and seventy-seven years old, who else would have stopped to consider their false teeth? But he dragged himself over the ground, holding the reins with one hand, groping and fumbling in the dust, till fortunately the missing set was found, uninjured by wheel or stone, but considerably mixed up with kindred clay.

"Whoa, I tell ye! whoa!" shouted the old man to Jerry, who, with wild eyes and erect ears, stood quivering and eager to be off.

"Darn ye, stan' still!" and jerking the reins by way of comment, he crept and hitched himself toward the wagon. Jerry looked round, and seemed to understand the situation. He set down the pawing forefoot, lowered the pointed ears, and, though he trembled still, stood as a rock might, till, with pain and struggle, his master raised himself on one foot against the wheel, and, setting his lips tight, contrived to get into the wagon, and on to the seat. "Git up!" he said, and Jerry started with a spring that brought a dark flush of pain to the old man's cheek. But he did not stop nor stay for pain. "Git up, I tell ye! We've got to git as fur as Baxter, anyhow. Go 'long, Jerry." And on he drove, though the broken leg, beginning to swell and press on the stiff boot-leg, gave him exquisite pain. But a mile or two passed before he met any one, for it was just noon, and all the countryfolk were at their dinner. At last a man appeared in the distance, and Reuben drew up by the roadside, and shouted to him to stop. It proved to be an Irishman, on his way to a farm just below.

"Say, have ye got a jackknife?" was Reuben's salutation.

"Yis, surr, I have that; and a fuss-rate knoife as iver ye see. What's wantin'?"

"Will yer ole hoss stan' a spell?"

"Sure he'll stand still the day afther niver, av I'd let him. It's standin' he takes to far more than goin'."

"Then you git out, will ye, 'nd fetch yer knife over here 'nd cut my boot-leg down."

"What 'n the wurrld are ye afther havin' yer boot cut for?" queried the Irishman, clambering down to the ground.

"Well, I got spilt out a piece back. Hoss got skeert by one o' them pesky ingines, 'nd I expect I broke my leg. It's kinder useless, 'nd it's kep' a-swellin' ever sence, so's't it hurts like blazes, I tell ye."

"The divil an' all—broke yer leg, man alive? An' how did ye get back to the waggin?"

"Oh, I wriggled in somehow. Come, be quick! I want to get to Baxter right off."

"Why, is it mad ye are? Turn about, man. There's Kinney's farm just beyant a bit. Come in there. I'll fetch the docthor for yez."

"No, I won't stop. I must git to the tavern to Baxter fust; then I'll go home, if I can fix it."

"The Lord help ye, thin, ye poor old crathur!"

"You help me fust, and don't jaw no more."

And so snapped at, the astounded Irishman proceeded to cut the boot off—a slow and painful process, but of some relief

when over; and Jerry soon heard the word of command to start
forward. Three more hard uphill miles brought them to the
tavern, just at the entrance of Baxter, and Jerry stopped at the
backdoor.

"Hullo!" shouted the old man; and the man who kept the
house rose from his armchair with a yawn and sauntered leisurely to the piazza. But his steps quickened as soon as he found
out what was the matter, and with neighborly aid Mr. Fyler was
soon carried upstairs and laid on a bed, and the doctor sent for.

"Say, don't ye give Jerry no oats, now I tell ye. I won't pay for
'em. He's used to hay, 'nd he'll get a mess o' meal to-night arter
we get home."

"Why, you can't get home to-night!" exclaimed the landlord.

"Can't I? I will, anyhow, ye'd better believe. I've got to be
there whether or no. Where's that darned doctor? Brush the dirt
off'n my coat, will ye? 'nd here, jest rence off them teeth,"
handing them out of his pocket. "I lost 'em out, 'nd hed to
scrape round in the dirt quite a spell afore I found 'em."

"Well, I swan to man!" ejaculated the landlord. "Do you
mean to say you hunted round after them 'ere things after you'd
got a broke leg?"

"Sure's you live, sir. I hitched around just like a youngster
a-learnin' to creep, 'nd drawed my leg along back side o' me;
I'm kinder blind, ye see, or I should ha' found 'em quicker."

"By George! ef you hain't got the most grit!" And the
landlord went off to tell his tale in the office.

"Take him up a drink o' rum, Joe," was the comment of a
hearer. "I know him. He polishes his nose four time a week,
you bet; rum's kinder nateral to him. His dad kep' a corner
grocery. A drink'll do him good. I'll stan' treat, fur he's all-fired
close. He'd faint away afore he'd buy a drink, fur he 'stills his
own cider-brandy. But flesh an' blood can't allers go it on grit,
ef 'tis Fyler grit, 'nd he'll feel considerable mean afore the
doctor gets here. Fetch him up a good stiff sling, 'nd chalk it
down to me."

A kindly and timely tonic the sling seemed to be, and the old
fellow took it with great ease.

"Taste kinder nateral?" inquired the interested landlord, with
suspended spoon.

"It's reel refrashin'," was the long-delayed answer, as the
empty tumbler went back to join the unoccupied spoon. "Now
fetch on yer doctor." And without a groan or a word the old man
bore the examination, which revealed the fact that both bones of
the leg were fractured; or, as the landlord expressed it to a

gaping and expectant crowd outside, "His leg's broke short off
in two places." Without any more ado Reuben bore the setting
and splinting of the crushed limb, and accepted meekly another
dose of the "refrashin' " fluid from the bar-room. "Now, doctor,
I want to be a-travelin' right off."

"Traveling! where to?" demanded the doctor, glaring at him
over his spectacles.

"Where to! why, back to our folks's, to Pasco."

"You travel to the land of Nod, man. Go to sleep; you won't
see Pasco to-day nor to-morrow."

"I'm a-goin', anyhow. I tell ye I've got ter. Important bizness.
I wouldn't be kep' here for a thousand dollars."

The doctor saw a hot flush rise to his face, and an ominous
glitter invade the dull eye. He knew his man, and he knew what
determined opposition and helplessness might do for him. At
seventy-seven, a broken leg is no trifle; but if fever sets in,
matters become complicated.

"Well," he said, by way of humoring the refractory patient,
"if you're bound to go, you must go to-night; to-morrow'll be
harder for you to move." And with a friendly nod he left the
room, and the landlord followed him.

"Ye don't expect he's a-goin' to go, do ye, doctor?"

"Lord, man! he might as well stand on his head! Still, you
don't know old Reub Fyler, perhaps. He's as clear grit as a
grindstone, and if he is bound to go, he'll go; heaven nor earth
won't stop him, nor men neither." And the doctor stepped into
his sulky and drove off.

An hour afterward Reuben Fyler insisted on being sent home.
A neighbor from Pasco, who had come down after grain with a
long wagon, heard of the accident, and happened in.

"I'm bound to git home, John Barnes," said the old man.
"I've got ter; I've got bizness. Well, I might as well tell ye, that
darned Potter feller's a-snakin' 'nd a-sneakin' round arter Phoebe,
'nd ef I'm laid up here, he'll be hangin' round there as sure as
guns. Fust I know they'll up 'nd git merried. I'll see him hanged
fust! I'm goin' hum to-night. I can keep her under my thumb ef
I'm there; but ye know how 'tis: when the cat's away''—

"H'm!" said John Barnes—a man slow of speech, but
perceptive. "Well, ef you're bound to go, you can have my
waggin, 'nd I'll drive you'rn up."

"But change hosses; I can't drive no hoss but Jerry."

"You drive!" exclaimed John, in unfeigned astonishment.

"My arms ain't broke, I tell ye, 'nd I ain't a-goin' to pay
nobody for what I can do myself, you can jest swear to that."

And John Barnes retreated to hold council with the bar-room loungers. But remonstrance was in vain. About five o'clock the long wagon was brought up, the seat shoved quite back to the end, and an extempore bed made of flour bags, hay, and old buffalo-robes on the floor of the rickety vehicle; the old man was carried carefully down, packed in as well as the case allowed, his splinted and bandaged leg tied to one side to keep it steady, his head propped up with his overcoat rolled into a bundle, and an old carriage carpet thrown over him and tucked in. Then another "refrashin' " fluid was administered, and the reins being put into his hands, with a sharp chirrup to old Jerry, he started off at a quick trot, and before John Barnes could get into his wagon and follow, Fyler was round the corner, out of sight, speeded by the cheers and laughter of the spectators, and eulogized by the landlord, as he bit off the end of a fresh cigar, as "the darnedest piece of Fyler grit or any other grit I ever see!"

In the mean time Phoebe at home went about her daily work in a kind of sullen peace: peaceful, because her father was out of the way for one day at least; sullen, because she foresaw no end of trouble coming to her, but never for one moment had an idea of giving up Tom Potter, or of any way to achieve her freedom except by enduring obstinacy. Many another girl, quick-witted or well read in novels, would have enjoyed the situation with a certain zest, and already invented plenty of stratagems; but Phoebe had not been educated in modern style, and tact or cunning was not native to her; she could endure or resist to the death, but she could not elude or beguile, and her father knew it. Her mother was helpless to aid her; but, with the courage mothers have, she set herself out of the question, and having thought deeply all the morning, over the knitting-work, which was all she could do now, she surprised Phoebe in the midst of her potato-paring by suddenly saying:—

"Phoebe, I see what you're a-thinkin' of, and I want to say my say now, afore anybody comes in. I've heerd enough o' Tom Potter to know he's a reel likely young feller; he's stiddy, 'nd he's a professor besides, 'nd he's got a good trade; there ain't no reason on airth why you shouldn't keep company with him, ef you like him. It's clear senseless to hev your life spoiled because your folks 'nd his folks quarreled, away back, about a water right."

Phoebe dropped the potatoes, and gave her mother a speechless hug, that brought the tears into those pale blue eyes.

"Softly, dear! I don't mean to set ye ag'inst your pa, noways; but I don't think man nor woman hes a right to say their gal sha'n't marry a man that ain't bad nor shiftless, jest 'cause they don't fancy him; 'nd I don't want to leave ye here when I go, to live my life over agin.''

"Oh, mother," exclaimed Phoebe, almost dropping the pan again, "I think it would be awful mean of me to leave you here alone!"

" 'Twouldn't be no worse, Phoebe. I should miss ye, no doubt on 't; I should miss ye consider'ble, but then I shouldn't worry over your hard times here as I do, some, all the time.''

Poor saint! she fought her battle there by the fireside, and nobody saw it but the "cloud of witnesses," who had hung over many a martyrdom before that was not illustrated by fire or sword.

Phoebe choked a little, and her clear eyes softened; she was only a girl, and she did not fully understand what her mother had suffered and renounced for her, but she loved her with all her warm heart.

"I can't help ye none, Phoebe," Mrs. Fyler went on, with a patient smile, "but I can comfort ye, mebbe, and, as fur as my consent goes, you hev it, ef you want to marry Tom; but oh! Phoebe, be sure, sure as death, you *do* want to: don't marry him to get away from home. I'd ruther see ye drowned in Long Pond.''

Phoebe's cheek colored deeply and her bright eyes fell, for her mother's homely words were solemn in their meaning and tone.

"I *am* sure, mother," she said softly, and went away to fetch more wood for the fire; and neither of the women spoke again of the matter, but Phoebe's brow cleared of its trouble, and her mother lay back in her chair and prayed in her heart. Poor woman! she had mighty need of such a refuge.

So night came on, and after long delay they ate their supper, presuming that the head of the house was delayed by business, little thinking how he, strapped into John Barnes's wagon, was pursuing his homeward road in the gathering darkness and solitude; for though John caught up with him soon, after a mile or two some empty sacks fell out of the Barnes wagon, and no sooner did John miss them than he coolly turned back and left old Reuben to find his way alone. But the old man did not care; he had courage for anything; so he drove along as cheerily as ever, though his dim sight was darkened further by the darkening air, the overhanging trees, and the limit set to his vision by the horse's head, which from his position was all he could see before him.

About nine o'clock a benighted traveler driving toward Baxter from Pasco way, with his wife, discerned dimly an approaching horse and wagon, apparently without a driver. He reined his own horse and covered buggy into the ditch, to give room, but the road was narrow, and the other horse kept in the middle.

"Turn out! Turn out!" shouted the anxious man. "Are you asleep or drunk? Turn out, I tell you!"

But old Fyler heard the echo only of the strenuous voice, and turned out the wrong way, setting his own wheels right into the wheels of the stranger's buggy.

"You drunken idiot! back, back, I say! you've run right into me"—not without objurgations of a slightly profane character to emphasize his remark. "Back, I say! The devil! can't you hear?"

By this time both horses were excited; the horse in the ditch began to plunge, the other one to rear and back, till, what between the pull of his master on the reins and his own terror, Jerry backed his load down the steep bank at the roadside, and but for a tree that caught the wheel, horse, driver, and wagon would have gone headlong into a situation of fatal reverses, where even Fyler grit could not avail.

"Murder!" cried the old man. "I've broke my leg, 'nd I'm pitchin' over th' edge! Lordy massy! stop the cretur! Who be ye? Ketch his head, can't ye? Thunderation! I'm a-tippin', sure's ye live!"

"Let your horse alone, you old fool!" shouted the exasperated traveler, who was trying vainly to tie his own to some saplings by the roadside, while his wife scrambled out as best she might over the floundering wheels. But by the time the man succeeded, Fyler's horse had been so demonstrative that the wagon wheels were twisted and locked together, the wagon body tilted up to a dangerous degree, and the old man rolled down to the other side and half out, where he hung helpless, tied by the knee, sick with the pain of his wrenched leg, and unable to stir; but still he yelled for help.

"Can you hold this plaguy horse's head, Anne?" said the traveler. "I never can right the wheels while he plunges and rears like that."

"I'll try," was the quiet response; and being a woman of courage and weight, she hung on to the bridle, though Jerry made frantic efforts to lift her off the ground and stand on his hind-legs, till the wagon was righted, the groaning old man replaced, his story told, and he ready once more to shake the reins, which still were grasped in his hard hands.

"But you ain't going on alone in this dark?" asked the astonished traveler.

"Yes, I be, yes, I be—sartain. I shall git on well enough ef I don't meet nobody, 'nd I guess I sha'n't."

"But you met us."

"Well, it's a-growin' later 'nd later; there won't be many folks out to-night; they ginerly knows enough to stay to hum arter dark out our way." With which Parthian remark he chirruped to Jerry and trotted away, without a word of thanks or acknowledgment, aching and groaning, and muttering to himself, "Darned fool! what'd he want to be a-kitin' round in a narrer road this time o' night? Fixed me out, I guess; but I'll get hum, anyhow. Git up, Jerry!"

And Jerry got up to such a purpose that about twelve o'clock that night a loud shouting at the front door roused Phoebe and her mother, and they were forced to call in a couple of men from the next neighbor's, at least a quarter of a mile away, to get the old man into the house, undressed, and put to bed.

As might have been expected, fever set in; but he fought that with "Fyler grit." And though fever is a force of itself, there is a certain willful vitality and strength of will in some people that exert wonderful influence over physical maladies; and after a few days of pain and discomfort and anger with himself and everybody else, the old man grew more comfortable, and proceeded to rule his family as usual. By dint of questioning the daily visitors who always flock about the victim of an accident in a country village, he had kept himself posted as to Tom Potter's absence; but its limit was drawing to an end now, and he took alarm. He had not imagined that Tom might be as well informed on his part, and that more than one note had passed through the post-office already between the young couple. Nor did he know that the postmistress was a warm friend of Tom's; for he had rescued her only child from the threatening horns of his father's Ayrshire bull, when little Fanny had ventured to cross the pasture lot after strawberries, and her red shawl attracted that ill-conditioned quadruped's notice and aroused his wrath. Tom's correspondence was safe and secret in passing through aunty Leland's hands. But as soon as Reuben Fyler ceased to need doses from the drug store and ice from the tavern, Phoebe was kept within range of his eye and ear. Still, she knew Tom was at home now, and evening after evening his cheery whistle passed through the window as he sauntered by,— a signal to Phoebe to get outside if she could; but she never could.

However, "Potter faculty" was at work for her. When the county paper was sent over from the post-office by a small boy, he had directions from aunty Leland to give it at once into

Phoebe's hand, "and nobody else's." So he waited about till
Phoebe opened the kitchen door to sweep out the dust, and gave
it to her with a significant wink—not that he knew what his wink
signified at all, but, with the true *gamin* instinct, he gathered an
idea from the widow Leland's special instructions that "somethin'
wuz to pay," as he expressed it to himself.

And Phoebe, as she hastened in from the door to carry the
paper to her father's bedside, perceived on the margin, in a
well-known handwriting, these words, "Look out for lambs."
As she hung up her broom, she tore off the inscription and tossed
it into the fire; and then, while she patiently went through the
gossip, politics, religion, and weekly story of the "Slabtown
News," exercised herself mightily as to what that mystic sentence might mean; but not till the soft and fragrant darkness of
the June evening set in did she find a clew to the mystery.

Old Fyler had a few pure-blood merino sheep on his farm that
were the very apple of his eye. Not that he had ever bought such
expensive commodities; but a wealthy farmer in the next town
owned a small flock some years before, which the New England
nuisance of dogs at last succeeded in slaying or scattering. In
some panic of the sort, one had escaped to the woods, and, after
long straying, been found by Fyler, with a new-born pair of
lambs beside her, in a wood on the limit of Pasco township,
where he was cutting his winter supply. Of course this windfall
was too valuable to be neglected. The hay brought for Jerry's
dinner was made into a soft bed, and, with the help of an
Irishman, who was chopping also, the sheep and her family
lifted into the wagon and taken home. Pasco was not infested
with dogs; only two or three could be numbered in the village.
And after the old sheep was wonted to her quarters a little, fed
by hand, cosseted, and made at home, she was turned into a lot
with the cows. And woe betide any dog that intruded among the
beautiful Ayrshires! So the sheep increased year after year,
carefully sheltered in cold weather, as became their high breeding,
till now between thirty and forty ranged the sweet short pastures
of the Fyler farm, and their fleeces were the wonder and admiration of all the town.

Late that night—late, I mean, for Pasco, for the old-fashioned
nine-o'clock bell had but just rung, though Mrs. Fyler had gone
to bed upstairs an hour ago, and Phoebe was just spreading an
extempore bed on the lounge in the kitchen, to be where her
father might call her in case of need—a piteous bleat, unmistakably the bleat of a lamb in some kind of distress, was heard
outside. The old man started up from his pillow.

"What 'n thunder's that, Phoebe?"

"Sounds some like a lamb."

"Sounds like a lamb! Anybody'd think you was a durn fool. 'Tis a lamb, I tell ye. One o' them leetle creturs hez strayed away out o' the paddock. I 'xpect boys hez ben in there a-foolin' round 'cause I'm laid up abed. Lordy! I wish to the land I could smash that 'ere ingine. Go 'long out, gal, 'nd see to 't. It'll stray a mile mebbe ef ye don't. You've got ter look out for lambs. They don't know nothin'."

Phoebe started as her father repeated the very phrase penciled on the edge of the paper; the lamb kept bleating, and the dimple in the girl's rosy cheek deepened while she found her bonnet, and, turning the key of the kitchen door, stepped out into the starlit night. That lamb was evidently behind the woodshed, but so was somebody else; for Phoebe had hardly discerned its curly back in the shadow before she was grasped in a stringent embrace, and Tom Potter actually kissed her.

"Go 'long!" she whispered indignantly. But Tom did not seem to mind her, and probably she became resigned to the infliction, for at least ten minutes elapsed before that go-between of a lamb was restored to its anxious mother in the paddock, and full half the time was wasted in a whispered dialogue—with punctuation marks.

Very rosy indeed Miss Phoebe looked as she returned to the house.

"Seems to me ye was everlastin' long 'bout ketchin' that lamb," growled old Reuben.

"Well, I had to put it back, 'nd fix up the little gate. One hinge was off on 't, 'nd 'twas kinder canted round, so's't the lamb got out, 'nd was too simple to get back."

Oh, Phoebe! Well it was that no oath compelled the speaking of the whole truth—of who unhinged the gate, or who had the lamb safe by a long string, having previously captured it in the paddock for purposes of decoy, or how, indeed, a letter came to be in that calico pocket, making an alarming crackle whenever she moved, terribly loud to her, but silent to the sleepy old man in his bed.

Phoebe went about very thoughtful the next day. The letter contained an astounding proposition. It was an artful letter, too, for it began with a recital of all the difficulties that made the way of true love proverbially rugged, and convinced her of what she had unconsciously admitted before, that she could never marry her lover in the world with her father's consent and the pleasant observances of ordinary life. Then it went on to plead in tender

and manly fashion the writer's own affection; his ability to give
her a pleasant and happy home, for he had just bought out the
Pasco blacksmith shop, the owner thereof having moved to Hartford,
where Tom had spent that week settling up the matter, and the
smithy was a good business, being the only one in a wide radius.
And it wound up with a proposal that as soon as her father got
so much better that her mother could care for him alone, Phoebe
should slip out some fine night on to the roof, thence to the top
of the henhouse, and so to the ground, and meet Tom and his
sister, who would be with him, at Peter Green's wood, half a
mile away, and just at the edge of the Fyler farm. Phoebe was to
consider the matter fully and talk it over with her mother, and
when she had made up her mind, to put a letter in the corner of the
cow-shed, where she milked daily, under a stone, where she
would also find an answer, and probably other epistles thereafter.

Phoebe was not a girl to take such a proposal lightly. She did,
indeed, consider it long and in earnest. Day by day, as her father
grew better, with a rapidity astonishing in so old a man,—for
Reuben Fyler's adventures are literally true,—he became more
and more ill-tempered and exasperating. The pain of the knitting
bones, the bed-weariness, the constant fret over farm-work that
was either neglected or hired out, worked on his naturally growling temper, and made life unpleasant to all around him as well as
himself. Phoebe's mind was made up more by her father than
even her own affection for Tom, or her mother's gentle
encouragement. The old man vented his temper on Phoebe in the
matter of Tom Potter more and more frequently; he reviled the
Potter tribe, root and branch, in a radical and persistent way that
would have done credit to an ancient Israelite cursing Canaan; he
even taunted Phoebe with favoring such a chicken-hearted lover,
scared with one slam of a door in his face; and Phoebe's
inherited "grit" was taxed strongly to keep her tongue quiet lest
she should betray her own secret; yet angry as she was, there
was a glint of fun underlying her anger, to think how thoroughly
Tom had countermined her father, which set the deep, lovely
dimples in cheek and and chin alight, and sparkled in each steady
eye, almost belying the angry brow and set lips.

So it came about that she yielded to the inner pressure and the
outer persuasion. Her father was able now to get about a little on
crutches, and sit at the window overlooking the cow-shed; yet it
was there, right under his suspicious eyes, that Phoebe took the
time, while she was milking and her mother feeding a new-
weaned calf, to unfold her plans.

"Mother," she began, with eyes fixed on her pail, "I can't

stand it any longer; my mind's made up. I'm going to Tom, if you keep in the same mind you was.''

"Yes, dear; I think it is the best for both of us. But don't tell me any more about it than you can help. Tell me what you want me to do for you, but''—

"Yes, I know," answered Phoebe. "I don't want you to do anything, mother; only you'll know if you miss me.''

"Yes; and I want to tell you, Phoebe. Several years back I've kinder taken comfort a-fixin' for this time. I've hed a chance now 'nd then to sew a little, 'nd I've made ye a set o' things when you was off to school odd times, 'nd washed 'em up 'nd put 'em up chamber for ye in the old press drawers. Then I've laid up some little too, out of a dozen of eggs here, 'nd a little milk there, 'nd twenty gold dollars grandmother give me before she died. I guess there's nigh about fifty by this time; and the black silk dress aunt Sary sent me from York, arter her Sam spent that year here, never's ben cut. You better take that to Taunton tomorrer to be made.''

"Oh, mother!''

"Well, dear, you're all I've got. Why shouldn't I? Oh, that pesky calf!'' and just in time to divert sentiment into a safer channel, the calf threw up its head, knocked the good woman backward into the dirt, and with tail high in air, and its four feet apparently going four ways at once, began one of those wild canters about the yard which calves indulge in. Phoebe had to laugh, as her mother, indignant but unhurt, rose up from the ground, and old Fyler at the kitchen window grinned with amusement. So Phoebe transported her modest fitting-out little by little to Julia Potter, who was her only confidante in the matter, and could not even see Phoebe, but punctually went for the bundles, when Tom was notified that they would be left in the further barn, which opened on another road, for better convenience in haying. The black silk dress also was consigned to her care, with Phoebe's new bonnet, sent by express from Taunton along with the dress.

The day set for Phoebe's departure was the 3d of July, since the racket and wakefulness which pervade even country towns on this anniversary would make Tom's late drive less noticeable. In the afternoon of the sultry day ominous flashes of tempest began to play about the far horizon, whence all day long great "thundercaps" had rolled their still and solemn heights of rounded pearl and shadow upward through the stainless blue of heaven. Phoebe gave her mother a stringent hug and kiss on the stairs as she went up, little knowing how that mother's heart sank in her breast, or how dim were the sad eyes that dared not let a tear fall to relieve them. By nine o'clock the house was still, except for low mutterings of the storm and distant wheels hurrying through the night, which made Phoebe's heart beat wildly. She made a small bundle of needful things, wrapped it in a little shawl, put on her hat, and, taking her shoes in her hand, slipped softly out of the window to the shed roof, and thence to the ground. She felt like a guilty thing enough as she stole over the hencoop and roused the fluttering fowls, bringing out an untimely crow from one young rooster. But the thought of Tom and her father nerved her to action. Putting on her shoes hastily, she took a beeline for Green's wood, where, at the corner of a certain fence, she was to find Tom and Julia. The storm was coming up now rapidly, but Phoebe did not feel any fear; the frequent flashes blinded her, but the road was plain after she had passed through the home lots and found the highway; and she met no one, as she had feared, for even those irrepressible patriots, the boys, had sought shelter from probable rain that would spoil their powder and wet their firecrackers. But when Phoebe arrived at the rendezvous, her heart beat thick with trouble or fear, for no one was there. She knew Tom had got her letter; he had left a rapturous answer in its place, but what had kept him?

She sat down among the sweet-fern bushes and tufts of long grass to quiet herself and think, and being a cool-headed, reasonable girl, composed herself to the idea that something had delayed her lover, and she must have patience; but as the minutes went on long and slow enough, the thunder pealing loud and louder, the lightning darting swift lances from heaven to earth, and a sharp rush of rain rattling on the stiff oak leaves above her, Phoebe determined to go home; not without a certain indignation in her heart at the carelessness of the man who ought to have been not only ready, but waiting to receive her, but also a reserve of judgment, for she had a great trust in Tom. Drenched to the skin, and chilled by the cold wind that rose with the storm, she retraced her steps, and dragging a short ladder from the cow-shed, contrived to get back on the roof, wet and slippery as it was; but to her dismay and wonder the window of her room was not only shut, but tightly fastened, and the paper shade let down before it. Her father, waking with the noise of the heavy thunder, bethought himself of the lambs in the paddock, not being certain that Phoebe had remembered to fold them. He got up and hobbled to the stairs, calling her loudly, but with no reply. In vain his wife urged him to lie down while she called Phoebe; he wanted to scold her awake, and with pains and groans he drew himself up the stairs, only to find her bed untouched and her window open. At once the state of things flashed upon him; he did not swear, but setting his lips at their utmost vicious angle, shut and fastened the window, and let down the shade, fancying Phoebe had gone out to meet her lover, and would try to return.

"I've fixed the jade," was his first utterance, as he reentered his own room. "She's gone 'nd slipped out o' the winder for to meet that darned Potter feller. See ef she'll git in agin. A good wettin' down 'll sarve her right."

"Oh, Reuben!" remonstrated his wife.

"You shet up. She's got to ketch it, I tell ye," he growled back; and his wife, consoled by the belief that her darling was by that time in kindly hands, lay down again and slept, to be roused an hour after by a loud knocking at the back door.

"What ye want?" demanded the old man, who had not slept, but waited for this result.

"It's me, father," said Phoebe's resolute voice. "Let me in; I'm out in the rain."

Mrs. Fyler sprang from her bed, but Reuben caught her arm and pulled her back.

"You lie still, I tell ye," he growled; and then went on, in a louder key, "Folks don't come into my door by night unless they've gone out on 't."

"Let me in, father; it's me,—Phoebe. I'm wet through."

The poor mother made one more effort to rise, but was held with vise-like grasp, as her lord and master retorted,—

"No wet folks wanted here. You could ha' staid in ef you'd ha' wanted to keep dry."

Phoebe's spirit rose at the taunt. Had she been let in, even to receive the expected indignation and scolding, there would have been no second exploit of the kind, for she was thoroughly disgusted with herself and partially with her lover; but when steel strikes steel, it is only to elicit sparks. Her "Fyler grit" took possession of her. Picking up her soaked bundle, she set out for the Potter farm, which lay two long miles away, on a hillside, and was approached by a wood road as well as the highway. But the wood road was the shortest and most lonely. She was sure to meet no one in that grassy track. So she struck into it at once.

A weary walk it proved. The storm went on with unabated fury. Rain poured fiercely down. Her rough way was full of stones, of fallen boughs, and crossed by new-made brooks from the mountain springs, suddenly filled and overflowing. But, with stubborn courage, Phoebe kept on, though more than once she fell at length among the dripping weeds and grasses, and was sorely bruised by stones and jarred by the fall.

But it was a resolved and rosy face that presented itself when the kitchen door of the farm-house on Potter Hill opened to a firm, sharp knock. There were friendly lights in the windows, and Mrs. Potter's kind old countenance beamed with pity and surprise as she beheld Phoebe on the doorstep.

"Mercy's sakes alive, Phoebe! You be half drowned, child. Come in, come, quick! Where's Tom and Jule?"

"Well," said Phoebe, with a little laugh, "that's just what I'd like to know."

"You don't mean to say they hain't fetched ye? Why, how under the canopy did ye get here?"

So Phoebe told her tale of woe, while her wet clothes were taken off by the old lady (who was watching for the party, and had sent the "help" and the younger part of the family to bed hours ago), and was told, in her turn, how Tom and his sister had set off at half past eight, and how they had been expected back "ever 'nd ever so long," so that Phoebe was supposed to have come 'with them when she appeared.

"I'll bet a cent that colt's run away. Tom would take the colt. He thought the old hoss was kinder feeble 'nd slow-going'. But I'd ruther ha' took him—slow 'nd sure, ye know."

Here was food for anxiety; but it did not last long, for wheels rattled up from the highway side of the house, an angry "Whoa, whoa, I tell ye!" was heard outside, and in a moment Tom strode in half carrying his sister, wet with rain and crying.

"Take care o' Jule, mother; she's about dead. There ain't a cent's worth o' grit in her."

A low laugh stopped him very suddenly. He looked round, and there, by the little blaze in the chimney, which had been lit to warm her a cup of tea, sat Phoebe, rosy, smiling, and prettier than ever, in Julia's pink calico gown and a soft white shawl of his mother's.

"Tom! Tom! you'll get her all damp again!" screamed Mrs. Potter; from which it may be inferred what Tom was about.

However, Phoebe seemed to be used to dampness. Perhaps the night's experience had hardened her, for she made no effort to withdraw from this present second-hand shower, while Tom explained how the colt had been frightened, just as they drove by the post-office, at a giant cracker, and dashed off down the meadow road at full speed. This would not have mattered if a sudden jolt had not broken one side of the thills short off, whereupon the colt kicked and plunged till he broke the other, and with a sudden dash pulled Tom all but out of the wagon, tore the reins out of his hands, and set off at full speed, leaving them three miles from Green's wood, two from any house, with a broken wagon, no horse, and an approaching tempest. There was nothing to do but to walk back to the village, hire another "team," and through the pouring storm drive to Green's wood on the chance of seeing Phobe.

Naturally they did not see her; and then Tom in despair drove round to Reuben Fyler's house, whistled under Phoebe's window, rattled pebbles against the pane, and at last knocked at the door, but with no sign or answer to reward him. Then Julia insisted on being taken home, and Tom was forced to yield, since he was at his wits' end, and there he found Phoebe.

"Tom, be still!" was the irrelevant remark uttered by Phoebe at the end of the recital, and she blushed more rosily than ever as she said it.

But Mrs. Potter, with motherly sense, served the hot supper that had been covered up in the chimney-corner so long, and when it had been done justice to in the most unsentimental manner, sent the whole party peremptorily to their rooms.

In the morning the runaway colt was brought home bright and early, and Tom put him into the borrowed wagon and drove off with Phoebe, Julia, and his mother to the minister's house, where Parson Russell gave him undeniable rights to run away with Phoebe hereafter as much as he liked.

The news came quickly to her father's ears, and, strange to say, the old man chuckled. Perhaps his comments will explain. "Stumped it all the way up there in the dark, did she? thunderin' an' lightnin' too. Well, now, I tell ye, there ain't another gal in Pasco darst to ha' done it. She's clear Fyler. Our folks ain't made o' all dust; they're three quarter grit, you kin swear to 't. The darned little cretur! she beats all. Well! well! well! Wife, ain't you heerd what aunt Nabby's a-sayin'?"

"Yes, I did."

"Law, Mr. Fyler," put in aunt Nabby, "I thought ye'd be madder 'n a yaller hornet."

"So ye come to hear me buzz, did ye? 'Tain't safe to reckon on folks. Mis' Fyler, you fetch your bunnet; I'll tell Sam to harness up, 'nd you drive up to Potter's 'nd see the gal. She's a chip o' the old block. I guess I'll let her hev that 'ere brown 'nd white heifer for a settin' up. 'Tain't best, nuther, to fight with the blacksmith, when there ain't but one handy."

"Well, now, I am beat," muttered aunt Nabby. "I thought ye

'd ha' held out ugly to the day o' judgment, I've heern tell so much about Fyler grit.''

"I think it's likely," was the composed reply. "It's bad ye 're disapp'inted, ain't it? but didn't it never come to ye that it takes more grit to back down hill than to go 'long up it?"

"Mebbe it doos—mebbe it doos," said aunt Nabby, shaking her head with the wisdom of an owl.

Ambrose Bierce
(1842–1914)

*Born in Ohio, Bierce served in the Civil War—a pivotal experi-
ence in shaping his bitter, cynical mistrust of his fellow men—
and thereafter worked as a journalist in San Francisco. Part of
the 1870s were spent in England, as an editor and staff member
of the journal,* Fun. *The brittleness of his earliest work was
succeeded, in 1891, by the forceful, sardonic and distinctly
Poe-like stories of* In the Midst of Life: Tales of Soldiers and
Civilians, *from which "An Occurrence at Owl Creek Bridge" is
taken.* Fantastic Fables *(1899) and* The Devil's Dictionary *(1911)
are principal collections of his savage, socially-oriented humor.
Overwhelmed by disgust at civilization in general, and American
civilization in particular, he traveled to Mexico in 1913, a
country then ravaged by civil war and sometimes extraordinary
violence. There he vanished from sight; the date of his death,
and everything about his final years, is still entirely conjectural.*

AN OCCURRENCE
AT OWL CREEK BRIDGE

I

A man stood upon a railroad bridge in northern Alabama, looking down into the swift water twenty feet below. The man's
hands were behind his back, the wrists bound with a cord. A
rope loosely encircled his neck. It was attached to a stout cross-
timber above his head, and the slack fell to the level of his
knees. Some loose boards laid upon the sleepers supporting the
metals of the railway supplied a footing for him and his

executioners—two private soldiers of the Federal army, directed by a sergeant, who in civil life may have been a deputy sheriff. At a short remove upon the same temporary platform was an officer in the uniform of his rank, armed. He was a captain. A sentinel at each end of the bridge stood with with his rifle in the position known as "support," that is to say, vertical in front of the left shoulder, the hammer resting on the forearm thrown straight across the chest—a formal and unnatural position, enforcing an erect carriage of the body. It did not appear to be the duty of these two men to know what was occurring at the center of the bridge; they merely blockaded the two ends of the foot plank which traversed it.

Beyond one of the sentinels, nobody was in sight; the railroad ran straight away into a forest for a hundred yards, then, curving, was lost to view. Doubtless there was an outpost farther along. The other bank of the stream was open ground—a gentle acclivity crowned with a stockade of vertical tree trunks loopholed for rifles, with a single embrasure through which protruded the muzzle of a brass cannon commanding the bridge. Midway of the slope between bridge and fort were the spectators—a single company of infantry in line, at "parade rest," the butts of the rifles on the ground, the barrels inclining slightly backward against the right shoulder, the hands crossed upon the stock. A lieutenant stood at the right of the line, the point of his sword upon the ground, his left hand resting upon his right. Excepting the group of four at the center of the bridge, not a man moved. The company faced the bridge, staring stonily, motionless. The sentinels, facing the banks of the stream, might have been statues to adorn the bridge. The captain stood with folded arms, silent, observing the work of his subordinates, but making no sign. Death is a dignitary who when he comes announced is to be received with formal manifestations of respect, even by those most familiar with him. In the code of military etiquette silence and fixity are forms of deference.

The man who was engaged in being hanged was apparently about thirty-five years of age. He was a civilian, if one might judge from his dress, which was that of a planter. His features were good—a straight nose, firm mouth, broad forehead, from which his long, dark hair was combed straight back, falling behind his ears to the collar of his well-fitting frock coat. He wore a mustache and pointed beard, but no whiskers; his eyes were large and dark gray, and had a kindly expression which one would hardly have expected in one whose neck was in the hemp. Evidently this was no vulgar assassin. The liberal military code makes provision for hanging many kinds of people, and gentle-men are not excluded.

The preparations being complete, the two private soldiers stepped aside and each drew away the plank upon which he had been standing. The sergeant turned to the captain, saluted, and placed himself immediately behind that officer, who in turn moved apart one pace. These movements left the condemned man and the sergeant standing on the two ends of the same plank, which spanned three of the crossties of the bridge. The end upon which the civilian stood almost, but not quite, reached a fourth. This plank had been held in place by the weight of the captain; it was now held by that of the sergeant. At a signal from the former, the latter would step aside, the plank would tilt, and the condemned man go down between two ties. The arrangement commended itself to his judgment as simple and effective. His face had not been covered nor his eyes bandaged. He looked a moment at his "unsteadfast footing," then let his gaze wander to the swirling water of the stream racing madly beneath his feet. A piece of dancing driftwood caught his attention and his eyes followed it down the current. How slowly it appeared to move! What a sluggish stream!

He closed his eyes in order to fix his last thoughts upon his wife and children. The water, touched to gold by the early sun, the brooding mists under the banks at some distance down the stream, the fort, the soldiers, the piece of drift—all had dis-tracted him. And now he became conscious of a new disturbance. Striking through the thought of his dear ones was a sound which he could neither ignore nor understand, a sharp, distinct, metallic percussion like the stroke of a blacksmith's hammer upon the anvil; it had the same ringing quality. He wondered what it was, and whether immeasurably distant or near by—it seemed both. Its recurrence was regular, but as slow as the tolling of a death knell. He awaited each stroke with impatience and—he knew not why—apprehension. The intervals of silence grew progressively longer; the delays became maddening. With their greater infre-quency the sounds increased in strength and sharpness. They hurt his ear like the thrust of a knife; he feared he would shriek. What he heard was the ticking of his watch.

He unclosed his eyes and saw again the water below him. "If I could free my hands," he thought, "I might throw off the noose and spring into the stream. By diving I could evade the bullets, and, swimming vigorously, reach the bank, take to the woods, and get away home. My home, thank God, is as yet outside their lines; my wife and little ones are still beyond the invader's farthest advance.''

As these thoughts, which have here to be set down in words, were flashed into the doomed man's brain rather than evolved from it, the captain nodded to the sergeant. The sergeant stepped aside.

II

Peyton Farquhar was a well-to-do planter of an old and highly respected Alabama family. Being a slave owner and like other slave owners a politician, he was naturally an original secessionist and ardently devoted to the Southern cause. Circumstances of an imperious nature, which it is unnecessary to relate here, had prevented him from taking service with the gallant army which had fought the disastrous campaigns ending with the fall of Corinth, and he chafed under the inglorious restraint, longing for the release of his energies, the larger life of the soldier, the opportunity for distinction. That opportunity, he felt, would come, as it comes to all in war time. Meanwhile he did what he could. No service was too humble for him to perform in aid of the South, no adventure too perilous for him to undertake if consistent with the character of a civilian who was at heart a soldier, and who in good faith and without too much qualification assented to at least a part of the frankly villainous dictum that all is fair in love and war.

One evening while Farquhar and his wife were sitting on a rustic bench near the entrance to his grounds, a gray-clad soldier rode up to the gate and asked for a drink of water. Mrs Farquhar was only too happy to serve him with her own white hands. While she was gone to fetch the water, her husband approached the dusty horseman and inquired eagerly for news from the front.

''The Yanks are repairing the railroads,'' said the man, ''and are getting ready for another advance. They have reached the Owl Creek bridge, put it in order, and built a stockade on the north bank. The commandant has issued an order, which is posted everywhere, declaring that any civilain caught interfering with the railroad, its bridges, tunnels, or trains will be summarily hanged. I saw the order.''

''How far is it to the Owl Creek bridge?'' Farquhar asked.

''About thirty miles.''

''Is there no force on this side the creek?''

''Only a picket post half a mile out, on the railroad, a single sentinel at this end of the bridge.''

Peyton gets his idea.

"Suppose a man—a civilian and student of hanging—should elude the picket post and perhaps get the better of the sentinel," said Farquhar, smiling, "what could he accomplish?"

The soldier reflected. "I was there a month ago," he replied. "I observed that the flood of last winter had lodged a great quantity of driftwood against the wooden pier at this end of the bridge. It is now dry and would burn like tow."

The lady had now brought the water, which the soldier drank. He thanked her ceremoniously, bowed to her husband, and rode away. An hour later, after nightfall, he repassed the plantation, going northward in the direction from which he had come. He was a Federal scout.

III

As Peyton Farquhar fell straight downward through the bridge he lost consciousness and was as one already dead. From this state he was awakened—ages later, it seemed to him—by the pain of a sharp pressure upon his throat, followed by a sense of suffocation. Keen, poignant agonies seemed to shoot from his neck downward through every fiber of his body and limbs. These pains appeared to flash along well-defined lines a ramification and to beat with an inconceivably rapid periodicity. They seemed like streams of pulsating fire heating him to an intolerable temperature. As to his head, he was conscious of nothing but a feeling of fullness—of congestion. These sensations were unaccompanied by thought. The intellectual part of his nature was already effaced; he had power only to feel, and feeling was torment. He was conscious of motion. Encompassed in a luminous cloud, of which he was now merely the fiery heart, without material substance, he swung through unthinkable arcs of oscillation, like a vast pendulum. Then all at once, with terrible suddenness, the light about him shot upward with the noise of a loud splash; a frightful roaring was in his ears, and all was cold and dark. The power of thought was restored; he knew that the rope had broken and he had fallen into the stream. There was no additional strangulation; the noose about his neck was already suffocating him and kept the water from his lungs. To die of hanging at the bottom of a river!—the idea seemed to him ludicrous. He opened his eyes in the darkness and saw above him a gleam of light, but how distant, how inaccessible! He was still sinking, for the light became fainter and fainter until it was a mere glimmer. Then it began to grow and brighten, and he knew that he was rising toward the surface—knew it with reluctance, for he was now very comfortable. "To be hanged and drowned," he thought, "that is not so bad; but I do not wish to be shot. No, I will not be shot, that is not fair."

He was not conscious of an effort, but a sharp pain in his wrist apprised him that he was trying to free his hands. He gave the struggle his attention, as an idler might observe the feat of a juggler, without interest in the outcome. What splendid effort! —what magnificent, what super-human strength! Ah, that was a fine endeavor! Bravo! The cord fell away; his arms parted and floated upward, the hands dimly seen on each side in the growing light. He watched them with a new interest as first one and then the other pounced upon the noose at his neck. They tore it away and thrust it fiercely aside, its undulations resembling those of a water snake. "Put it back, put it back!" He thought he shouted these words to his hands, for the undoing of the noose had been succeeded by the direst pang that he had yet experienced. His neck ached horribly; his brain was on fire; his heart, which had been fluttering faintly, gave a great leap, trying to force itself out at his mouth. His whole body was racked and wrenched with an insupportable anguish! But his disobedient hands gave no heed to the command. They beat the water vigorously with quick, downward strokes, forcing him to the surface. He felt his head emerge; his eyes were blinded by the sunlight; his chest expanded convulsively, and with a supreme and crowning agony his lungs engulfed a great draught of air, which instantly he expelled in a shriek!

He was now in full possession of his physical senses. They were, indeed, preternaturally keen and alert. Something in the awful disturbance of his organic system had so exalted and refined them that they made record of things never before perceived. He felt the ripples upon his face and heard their separate sounds as they struck. He looked at the forest on the bank of the stream, saw the individual trees, the leaves and the veining of each leaf—saw the very insects upon them: the locusts, the brilliant-bodied flies, the gray spiders stretching their webs from twig to twig. He noted the prismatic colors in dewdrops upon a million blades of grass. The humming of the gnats that danced above the eddies of the stream, the beating of the dragonflies' wings, the strokes of the water spiders' legs, like oars which had lifted their boat—all these made audible music. A fish slid along beneath his eyes and he heard the rush of its body parting the water.

He had come to the surface facing down the stream; in a moment the visible world seemed to wheel slowly round, himself the pivotal point, and he saw the bridge, the fort, the soldiers upon the bridge, the captain, the sergeant, the two privates, his executioners. They were in silhouette against the blue sky. They shouted and gesticulated, pointing at him. The captain had drawn his pistol, but did not fire; the others were unarmed. Their movements were grotesque and horrible, their forms gigantic.

Suddenly he heard a sharp report and something struck the water smartly within a few inches of his head, spattering his face with spray. He heard the second report, and saw one of the sentinels with his rifle at his shoulder, a light cloud of blue smoke rising from the muzzle. The man in the water saw the eye of the man on the bridge gazing into his own through the sights of the rifle. He observed that it was a gray eye and remembered having read that gray eyes were keenest, and that all famous marksmen had them. Nevertheless, this one had missed.

A counterswirl had caught Farquhar and turned him half round; he was again looking into the forest on the bank opposite the fort. The sound of a clear, high voice in a monotonous singsong now rang out behind him and came across the water with distinctness that pierced and subdued all other sounds, even the beating of the ripples in his ears. Although no soldier, he had frequented camps enough to know the dread significance of that deliberate, drawling, aspirated chant; the lieutenant on shore was taking part in the morning's work. How coldly and pitilessly—with what an even, calm intonation, presaging and enforcing tranquillity in the men—with what accurately measured intervals fell those cruel words:

"Attention, company! . . . Shoulder arms! . . . Ready! . . . Aim! . . . Fire!"

Farquhar dived—dived as deeply as he could. The water roared in his ears like the voice of Niagara, yet he heard the dulled thunder of the volley and, rising again toward the surface, met shining bits of metal, singularly flattened, oscillating slowly downward. Some of them touched him on the face and hands, then fell away, continuing their descent. One lodged between his collar and his neck; it was uncomfortably warm and he snatched it out.

As he rose to the surface, gasping for breath, he saw that he had been a long time under water; he was perceptibly farther downstream—nearer to safety. The soldiers had almost finished reloading; the metal ramrods flashed all at once in the sunshine as they were drawn from the barrels, turned in the air, and thrust into their sockets. The two sentinels fired again, independently and ineffectually.

The hunted man saw all this over his shoulder; he was now swimming vigorously with the current. His brain was as energetic as his arms and legs; he thought with the rapidity of lightning.

"The officer," he reasoned, "will not make that martinet's error a second time. It is as easy to dodge a volley as a single shot. He has probably already given the command to fire at will. God help me, I cannot dodge them all!"

An appalling plash within two yards of him was followed by a loud, rushing sound, *diminuendo*, which seemed to travel back through the air to the fort and died in an explosion which stirred the very river to its deeps! A rising sheet of water, which curved over him, fell down upon him, blinded him, strangled him! The cannon had taken a hand in the game. As he shook his head free from the commotion of the smitten water, he heard the deflected shot humming through the air ahead, and in an instant it was cracking and smashing the branches in the forest beyond.

"They will not do that again," he thought; "the next time they will use a charge of grape. I must keep my eye upon the gun; the smoke will apprise me—the report arrives too late; it lags behind the missile. That is a good gun."

Suddenly he felt himself whirled round and round—spinning like a top. The water, the banks, the forests, the now distant bridge, fort, and men—all were commingled and blurred. Objects were represented by their colors only; circular horizontal streaks of color—that was all he saw. He had been caught in a vortex and was being whirled on with a velocity of advance and gyration which made him giddy and sick. In a few moments he was flung upon the gravel at the foot of the left bank of the stream—the southern bank—and behind a projecting point which concealed him from his enemies. The sudden arrest of his motion, the abrasion of one of his hands on the gravel, restored him, and he wept with delight. He dug his fingers into the sand, threw it over himself in handfuls, and audibly blessed it. It looked like gold, like diamonds, rubies, emeralds; he could think of nothing beautiful which it did not resemble. The trees upon the bank were giant garden plants; he noted a definite order in their arrangement, inhaled the fragrance of their blooms. A strange, roseate light shone through the spaces among their trunks and the wind made in their branches the music of aeolian harps. He had no wish to perfect his escape—was content to remain in that enchanting spot until retaken.

A whiz and rattle of grapeshot among the branches high above his head roused him from his dream. The baffled cannoneer had fired him a random farewell. He sprang to his feet, rushed up the sloping bank, and plunged into the forest.

All that day he traveled, laying his course by the rounding sun. The forest seemed interminable; nowhere did he discover a break in it, not even a woodman's road. He had not known that he lived in so wild a region. There was something uncanny in the revelation.

By nightfall he was fatigued, footsore, famishing. The thought of his wife and children urged him on. At last he found a road which led him in what he knew to be the right direction. It was wide and straight as a city street, yet it seemed untraveled. No fields bordered it, no dwelling anywhere. Not so much as the barking of a dog suggested human habitation. The black bodies of the great trees formed a straight wall on both sides, terminating on the horizon in a point, like a diagram in a lesson in perspective. Overhead, as he looked up through this rift in the wood, shone great golden stars looking unfamiliar and grouped in strange constellations. He was sure they were arranged in some order which had a secret and malign significance. The wood on either side was full of singular noises, among which—once, twice, and again—he distinctly heard whispers in an unknown tongue.

His neck was in pain and lifting his hand to it he found it horribly swollen. He knew that it had a circle of black where the rope had bruised it. His eyes felt congested; he could no longer close them. His tongue was swollen with thirst; he relieved its fever by thrusting it forward from between his teeth into the cool air. How softly the turf had carpeted the untraveled avenue—he could no longer feel the roadway beneath his feet!

Doubtless, despite his suffering, he had fallen asleep while walking, for now he sees another scene—perhaps he has merely recovered from a delirium. He stands at the gate of his own home. All is as he left it, and all bright and beautiful in the morning sunshine. He must have traveled the entire night. As he pushes open the gate and passes up the wide white walk, he sees a flutter of female garments; his wife, looking fresh and cool and sweet, steps down from the veranda to meet him. At the bottom of the steps she stands waiting, with a smile of ineffable joy, an attitude of matchless grace and dignity. Ah, how beautiful she is!

He springs forward with extended arms. As he is about to clasp her, he feels a stunning blow upon the back of the neck; a blinding white light blazes all about him with a sound like the shock of a cannon—then all is darkness and silence!

Peyton Farquhar was dead; his body, with a broken neck, swung gently from side to side beneath the timbers of the Owl Creek bridge.

Hamlin Garland
(1860–1940)

Born in Wisconsin, Garland spent some years studying in Boston, where he came under the influence of William Dean Howells (1837–1920, a novelist and editor whose influence on two generations of American writers, 1880–1920, is still inadequately understood or appreciated). Returning to the Midwest, determined to memorialize the reality of life in his native region, he wrote stories which were collected in Main-Travelled Roads *(1891), from which "The Return of a Private"—an autobiographical story written about his father's return from the Civil War—is taken. A* Son of the Middle Border *(1917), one of many autobiographical studies, remains perhaps his best-known book. He wrote voluminously on many social issues, as well as psychic research.*

THE RETURN OF A PRIVATE

The nearer the train drew toward La Crosse, the soberer the little group of "vets" became. On the long way from New Orleans they had beguiled tedium with jokes and friendly chaff; or with planning with elaborate detail what they were going to do now, after the war. A long journey, slowly, irregularly, yet persistently pushing northward. When they entered on Wisconsin territory they gave a cheer, and another when they reached Madison, but after that they sank into a dumb expectancy. Comrades dropped off at one or two points beyond, until there were only four or five left who were bound for La Crosse County.

Three of them were gaunt and brown, the fourth was gaunt and pale, with signs of fever and ague upon him. One had a great scar down his temple, one limped, and they all had unnaturally large, bright eyes, showing emaciation. There were no bands greeting them at the station, no banks of gayly dressed ladies waving handkerchiefs and shouting "Bravo!" as they came in on the caboose of a freight train into the towns that had cheered and blared at them on their way to war. As they looked out or stepped upon the platform for a moment, while the train stood at the station, the loafers looked at them indifferently. Their blue coats, dusty and grimy, were too familiar now to excite notice, much less a friendly word. They were the last of the army to return, and the loafers were surfeited with such sights.

The train jogged forward so slowly that it seemed likely to be midnight before they should reach La Crosse. The little squad grumbled and swore, but it was no use; the train would not hurry, and, as a matter of fact, it was nearly two o'clock when the engine whistled "down brakes."

All of the group were farmers, living in districts several miles out of the town, and all were poor.

"Now, boys," said Private Smith, he of the fever and ague, "we are landed in La Crosse in the night. We've got to stay somewhere till mornin'. Now I ain't got no two dollars to waste on a hotel. I've got a wife and children, so I'm goin' to roost on a bench and take the cost of a bed out of my hide."

"Same here," put in one of the other men. "Hide'll grow on again, dollars'll come hard. It's goin' to be mighty hot skirmishin' to find a dollar these days."

"Don't think they'll be a deputation of citizens waitin' to 'scort us to a hotel, eh?" said another. His sarcasm was too obvious to require an answer.

Smith went on, "Then at daybreak we'll start for home—at least, I will."

"Well, I'll be dummed if I'll take two dollars out o' *my* hide," one of the younger men said. "I'm goin' to a hotel, ef I don't never lay up a cent."

"That'll do f'r you," said Smith; "but if you had a wife an' three young uns dependin' on yeh—"

"Which I ain't, thank the Lord! and don't intend havin' while the court knows itself."

The station was deserted, chill, and dark, as they came into it at exactly a quarter to two in the morning. Lit by the oil lamps that flared a dull red light over the dingy benches, the waiting room was not an inviting place. The younger man went off to look up a hotel, while the rest remained and prepared to camp down on the floor and benches. Smith was attended to tenderly by the other men, who spread their blankets on the bench for him, and, by robbing themselves, made quite a comfortable bed, though the narrowness of the bench made his sleeping precarious.

It was chill, though August, and the two men, sitting with bowed heads, grew stiff with cold and weariness, and were forced to rise now and again and walk about to warm their stiffened limbs. It did not occur to them, probably, to contrast their coming home with their going forth, or with the coming home of the generals, colonels, or even captains—but to Private Smith, at any rate, there came a sickness at heart almost deadly as he lay there on his hard bed and went over his situation.

In the deep of the night, lying on a board in the town where he had enlisted three years ago, all elation and enthusiasm gone out of him, he faced the fact that with the joy of home-coming was already mingled the bitter juice of care. He saw himself sick, worn out, taking up the work on his half-cleared farm, the inevitable mortgage standing ready with open jaw to swallow half his earnings. He had given three years of his life for a mere pittance of pay, and now!—

Morning dawned at last, slowly, with a pale yellow dome of light rising silently above the bluffs, which stand like some huge storm-devastated castle, just east of the city. Out to the left the great river swept on its massive yet silent way to the south. Bluejays called across the water from hillside to hillside through the clear, beautiful air, and hawks begin to skim the tops of the hills. The older men were astir early, but Private Smith had fallen at last into a sleep, and they went out without waking him. He lay on his knapsack, his gaunt face turned toward the ceiling, his hands clasped on his breast, with a curious pathetic effect of weakness and appeal.

An engine switching near woke him at last, and he slowly sat up and stared about. He looked out of the window and saw that the sun was lightening the hills across the river. He rose and brushed his hair as well as he could, folded his blankets up, and went out to find his companions. They stood gazing silently at the river and at the hills.

"Looks natcher'l, don't it?" they said, as he came out.

"That's what it does," he replied. "An' it looks good. D' yeh see that peak?" He pointed at a beautiful symmetrical peak, rising like a slightly truncated cone, so high that it seemed the very highest of them all. It was touched by the morning sun and it glowed like a beacon, and a light scarf of gray morning fog was rolling up its shadowed side.

"My farm's just beyond that. Now, if I can only ketch a ride, we'll be home by dinner-time."

"I'm talkin' about breakfast," said one of the others.

"I guess it's one more meal o' hardtack f'r me," said Smith.

They foraged around, and finally found a restaurant with a sleepy old German behind the counter, and procured some coffee, which they drank to wash down their hardtack.

"Time'll come," said Smith, holding up a piece by the corner, "when this'll be a curiosity."

"I hope to God it will! I bet I've chawed hardtack enough to shingle every house in the coolly. I've chawed it when my lampers was down, and when they wasn't. I've took it dry, soaked, and mashed. I've had it wormy, musty, sour, and blue-mouldy. I've had it in little bits and big bits; 'fore coffee an' after coffee. I'm ready f'r a change. I'd like t' git holt jest about now o' some of the hot biscuits my wife c'n make when she lays herself out f'r company."

"Well, if you set there gabblin', you'll never *see* yer wife."

"Come on," said Private Smith. "Wait a moment, boys; less take suthin'. It's on me." He led them to the rusty tin dipper which hung on a nail beside the wooden water-pail, and they grinned and drank. Then shouldering their blankets and muskets, which they were "takin' home to the boys," they struck out on their last march.

"They called that coffee Jayvy," grumbled one of them, "but it never went by the road where government Jayvy resides. I reckon I know coffee from peas."

They kept together on the road along the turnpike, and up the winding road by the river, which they followed for some miles. The river was very lovely, curving down along its sandy beds, pausing now and then under broad basswood trees, or running in dark, swift, silent currents under tangles of wild grapevines, and drooping alders, and haw trees. At one of these lovely spots the three vets sat down on the thick green sward to rest, "on Smith's account." The leaves of the trees were as fresh and green as in June, the jays called cheery greetings to them, and kingfishers darted to and fro with swooping, noiseless flight.

"I tell yeh, boys, this knocks the swamps of Loueesiana into kingdom come."

"You bet. All they c'n raise down there is snakes, niggers, and p'rticler hell."

"An' fightin' men," put in the older man.

"An' fightin' men. If I had a good hook an' line I'd sneak a pick'rel out o' that pond. Say, remember that time I shot that alligator—''

"I guess we'd better be crawlin' along," interrupted Smith, rising and shouldering his knapsack, with considerable effort, which he tried to hide.

"Say, Smith, lemme give you a lift on that."

"I guess I c'n manage," said Smith, grimly.

"Course. But, yo' see, I may not have a chance right off to pay yeh back for the times you've carried my gun and hull caboodle. Say, now, gimme that gun, anyway."

"All right, if ye feel like it, Jim," Smith replied, and they trudged along doggedly in the sun, which was getting higher and hotter each half-mile.

"Ain't it queer there ain't no teams comin' along," said Smith, after a long silence.

"Well, no, seein's it's Sunday."

"By jinks, that's a fact. It *is* Sunday. I'll git home in time f'r dinner, sure!" he exulted. "She don't hev dinner usially till about *one* on Sundays." And he fell into a muse, in which he smiled.

"Well, I'll git home jest about six o'clock, jest about when the boys are milkin' the cows," said old Jim Cranby. "I'll step into the barn, an' then I'll say: "He*ah!* why ain't this milkin' done before this time o' day?' An' then won't they yell!" he added, slapping his thigh in great glee.

Smith went on. "I'll jest go up the path. Old Rover'll come down the road to meet me. He won't bark; he'll know me, an' he'll come down waggin' his tail an' showin' his teeth. That's his way of laughin'. An' so I'll walk up to the kitchen door, an' I'll say, 'Dinner f'r a hungry man!' And' then she'll jump up, an'—''

He couldn't go on. His voice choked at the thought of it. Saunders, the third man, hardly uttered a word, but walked silently behind the others. He had lost his wife the first year he was in the army. She died of pneumonia, caught in the autumn rains while working in the fields in his place.

They plodded along till at last they came to a parting of the ways. To the right the road continued up the main valley; to the left it went over the big ridge.

"Well, boys," began Smith, as they grounded their muskets and looked away up the valley, "here's where we shake hands. We've marched together a good many miles, an' now I s'pose we're done."

"Yes, I don't think we'll do any more of it f'r a while. I don't want to, I know."

"I hope I'll see yeh once in a while, boys, to talk over old times."

"Of course," said Saunders, whose voice trembled a little, too. "It ain't *exactly* like dyin'." They all found it hard to look at each other.

"But we'd ought'r go home with you," said Cranby. "You'll never climb that ridge with all them things on your back."

"Oh, I'm all right! Don't worry about me. Every step takes me nearer home, yeh see. Well, good-by, boys."

They shook hands. "Good-by. Good luck!"

"Same to you. Lemme know how you find things at home."

"Good-by."

"Good-by."

He turned once before they passed out of sight, and waved his cap, and they did the same, and all yelled. Then all marched away with their long, steady, loping, veteran step. The solitary climber in blue walked on for a time, with his mind filled with the kindness of his comrades, and musing upon the many wonderful days they had had together in camp and field.

He thought of his chum, Billy Tripp. Poor Billy! A "minie" ball fell into his breast one day, fell wailing like a cat, and tore a great ragged hole in his heart. He looked forward to a sad scene with Billy's mother and sweetheart. They would want to know all about it. He tried to recall all that Billy had said, and the particulars of it, but there was little to remember, just that wild wailing sound high in the air, a dull slap, a short, quick, expulsive groan, and the boy lay with his face in the dirt in the ploughed field they were marching across.

That was all. But all the scenes he had since been through had not dimmed the horror, the terror of that moment, when his boy comrade fell, with only a breath between a laugh and a death-groan. Poor handsome Billy! Worth millions of dollars was his young life.

These sombre recollections gave way at length to more cheerful feelings as he began to approach his home coolly. The fields and houses grew familiar, and in one or two he was greeted by people seated in the doorways. But he was in no mood to talk, and pushed on steadily, though he stopped and accepted a drink of milk once at the well-side of a neighbor.

The sun was burning hot on that slope, and his step grew slower, in spite of his iron resolution. He sat down several times to rest. Slowly he crawled up the rough, reddish-brown road, which wound along the hillside, under great trees, through dense groves of jack oaks, with tree-tops far below him on his left hand, and the hills far above him on his right. He crawled along like some minute, wingless variety of fly.

He ate some hardtack, sauced with wild berries, when he reached the summit of the ridge, and sat there for some time, looking down into his home coolly. *Romanticism*

Sombre, pathetic figure! His wide, round, gray eyes gazing down into the beautiful valley, seeing and not seeing, the splendid cloud-shadows sweeping over the western hills and across the green and yellow wheat far below. His head drooped forward on his palm, his shoulders took on a tired stoop, his cheek-bones showed painfully. An observer might have said, "He is looking down upon his own grave."

II

Sunday comes in a Western wheat harvest with such sweet and sudden relaxation to man and beast that it would be holy for that reason, if for no other, and Sundays are usually fair in harvest-time. As one goes out into the field in the hot morning sunshine, with no sound abroad save the crickets and the indescribably pleasant silken rustling of the ripened grain, the reaper and the very sheaves in the stubble seem to be resting, dreaming.

Around the house, in the shade of the trees, the men sit, smoking, dozing, or reading the papers, while the women, never resting, move about at the housework. The men eat on Sundays about the same as on other days, and breakfast is no sooner over and out of the way than dinner begins.

But at the Smith farm there were no men dozing or reading. Mrs. Smith was alone with her three children, Mary, nine, Tommy, six, and little Ted, just past four. Her farm, rented to a neighbor, lay at the head of a coolly or narrow gully, made at some far-off post-glacial period by the vast and angry floods of water which gullied these tremendous furrows in the level prairie—furrows so deep that undisturbed portions of the original level rose like hills on either side, rose to quite considerable mountains.

The chickens wakened her as usual that Sabbath morning from dreams of her absent husband, from whom she had not heard for weeks. The shadows drifted over the hills, down the slopes, across the wheat, and up the opposite wall in leisurely way, as if being Sunday, they could take it easy also. The fowls clustered about the housewife as she went out into the yard. Fuzzy little chickens swarmed out from the coops, where their clucking and perpetually disgruntled mothers tramped about, petulantly thrusting their heads through the spaces between the slats.

A cow called in a deep, musical bass, and a calf answered from a little pen near by, and a pig scurried guiltily out of the cabbages. Seeing all this, seeing the pig in the cabbages, the tangle of grass in the garden, the broken fence which she had mended again and again—the little woman, hardly more than a girl, sat down and cried. The bright Sabbath morning was only a mockery without him!

A few years ago they had bought this farm, paying part, mortgaging the rest in the usual way. Edward Smith was a man of terrible energy. He worked "nights and Sundays," as the saying goes, to clear the farm of its brush and of its insatiate mortgage! In the midst of his Herculean struggle came the call for volunteers, and with the grim and unselfish devotion to his country which made the Eagle Brigade able to "whip its weight in wild cats," he threw down his scythe and grub-axe, turned his cattle loose, and became a blue-coated cog in a vast machine for killing men, and not thistles. While the millionaire sent his money to England for safe-keeping, this man, with his girl-wife and three babies, left them on a mortgaged farm, and went away to fight for an idea. It was foolish, but it was sublime for all that.

That was three years before, and the young wife, sitting on the well-curb on this bright Sabbath harvest morning, was righteously rebellious. It seemed to her that she had borne her share of the country's sorrow. Two brothers had been killed, the renter in whose hands her husband had left the farm had proved a villain; one year the farm had been without crops, and now the overripe grain was waiting the tardy hand of the neighbor who had rented it, and who was cutting his own grain first.

About six weeks before, she had received a letter saying, "We'll be discharged in a little while." But no other word had come from him. She had seen by the papers that his army was being discharged, and from day to day other soldiers slowly percolated in blue streams back into the State and county, but still *her* hero did not return.

Each week she had told the children that he was coming, and she had watched the road so long that it had become unconscious; and as she stood at the well, or by the kitchen door, her eyes were fixed unthinkingly on the road that wound down the coolly.

Nothing wears on the human soul like waiting. If the stranded mariner, searching the sun-bright seas, could once give up hope of a ship, that horrible grinding on his brain would cease. It was this waiting, hoping, on the edge of despair, that gave Emma Smith no rest.

Neighbors said, with kind intentions: "He's sick, maybe, an' can't start north just yet. He'll come along one o' these days."

"Why don't he write?" was her question, which silenced them all. This Sunday morning it seemed to her as if she could not stand it longer. The house seemed intolerably lonely. So she dressed the little ones in their best calico dresses and home-made jackets, and, closing up the house, set off down the coolly to old Mother Gray's.

"Old Widder Gray" lived at the "mouth of the coolly." She was a widow woman with a large family of stalwart boys and laughing girls. She was the visible incarnation of hospitality and optimistic poverty. With Western open-heartedness she fed every mouth that asked food of her, and worked herself to death as cheerfully as her girls danced in the neighborhood harvest dances.

She waddled down the path to meet Mrs. Smith with a broad smile on her face.

"Oh, you little dears! Come right to your granny. Gimme a kiss! Come right in, Mis' Smith. How are yeh, anyway? Nice mornin', ain't it? Come in an' set down. Everything's in a clutter, but that won't scare you any."

She led the way into the best room, a sunny, square room, carpeted with a faded and patched rag carpet, and papered with white-and-green-striped wall-paper, where a few faded effigies of dead members of the family hung in variously sized oval walnut frames. The house resounded with singing, laughter, whistling, tramping of heavy boots, and riotous scufflings. Half-grown boys came to the door and crooked their fingers at the children, who ran out, and were soon heard in the midst of the fun.

"Don't s'pose you've heard from Ed?" Mrs. Smith shook her head. "He'll turn up some day, when you ain't lookin' for 'im." The good old soul had said that so many times that poor Mrs. Smith derived no comfort from it any longer.

"Liz heard from Al the other day. He's comin' some day this week. Anyhow, they expect him."

"Did he say anything of—"

"No, he didn't," Mrs. Gray admitted. "But then it was only a short letter, anyhow. Al ain't much for writin', anyhow.—But come out and see my new cheese. I tell yeh, I don't believe I ever had better luck in my life. If Ed should come, I want you should take him up a piece of this cheese."

It was beyond human nature to resist the influence of that noisy, hearty, loving household, and in the midst of the singing and laughing the wife forgot her anxiety, for the time at least, and laughed and sang with the rest.

About eleven o'clock a wagon-load more drove up to the door, and Bill Gray, the widow's oldest son, and his whole family, from Sand Lake Coolly, piled out amid a good-natured uproar. Every one talked at once, except Bill, who sat in the wagon with his wrists on his knees, a straw in his mouth, and an amused twinkle in his blue eyes.

"Ain't heard nothin' o' Ed, I s'pose?" he asked in a kind of bellow. Mrs. Smith shook her head. Bill, with a delicacy very striking in such a great giant, rolled his quid in his mouth, and said:

"Didn't know but you had. I hear two or three of the Sand Lake boys are comin'. Left New Orleenes some time this week. Didn't write nothin' about Ed, but no news is good news in such cases, mother always says."

"Well, go put out yer team," said Mrs. Gray, "an' go 'n bring me in some taters, an', Sim, you go see if you c'n find some corn. Sadie, you put on the water to bile. Come now, hustle yer boots, all o' yeh. If I feed this yer crowd, we've got to have some raw materials. If y' think I'm goin' to feed yeh on pie—you're jest mightily mistaken."

The children went off into the fields, the girls put dinner on to boil, and then went to change their dresses and fix their hair. "Somebody might come," they said.

"Land sakes, *I* hope not! I don't know where in time I'd set 'em, 'less they'd eat at the second table," Mrs. Gray laughed, in pretended dismay.

The two older boys, who had served their time in the army, lay out on the grass before the house, and whittled and talked desultorily about the war and the crops, and planned buying a threshing-machine. The older girls and Mrs. Smith helped enlarge the table and put on the dishes, talking all the time in that cheery, incoherent, and meaningful way a group of such women have,—a conversation to be taken for its spirit rather than for its letter, though Mrs. Gray at last got the ear of them all and dissertated at length on girls.

"Girls in love ain't no use in the whole blessed week," she said. "Sundays they're a-lookin' down the road, expectin' he'll *come*. Sunday afternoons they can't think o' nothin' else, 'cause he's *here*. Monday mornin's, they're sleepy and kind o' dreamy and slimpsy, and good f'r nothin' on Tuesday and Wednesday.

Thursday they git absent-minded, an' begin to look off toward Sunday agin, an' mope aroun' and let the dishwater git cold, right under their noses. Friday they break dishes, an' go off in the best room an' snivel, an' look out o' the winder. Saturdays they have queer spurts o' workin' like all p'ssessed, an' spurts o' frizzin' their hair. An' Sunday they begin it all over again."

The girls giggled and blushed, all through this tirade from their mother, their broad faces and powerful frames anything but suggestive of lackadaisical sentiment. But Mrs. Smith said:

"Now, Mrs. Gray, I hadn't ought to stay to dinner. You've got—"

"Now you set right down! If any of them girls' beaus comes, they'll have to take what's left, that's all. They ain't s'posed to have much appetite, nowhow. No, you're goin' to stay if they starve, an' they ain't no danger o' that."

At one o'clock the long table was piled with boiled potatoes, cords of boiled corn on the cob, squash and pumpkin pies, hot biscuit, sweet pickles, bread and butter, and honey. Then one of the girls took down a conch-shell from a nail, and going to the door, blew a long, fine, free blast, that showed there was no weakness of lungs in her ample chest.

Then the children came out of the forest of corn, out of the creek, out of the loft of the barn, and out of the garden.

"They come to their feed f'r all the world jest like the pigs when y' holler 'poo-ee!' See 'em scoot!" laughed Mrs. Gray, every wrinkle on her face shining with delight.

The men shut up their jack-knives, and surrounded the horse-trough to souse their faces in the cold, hard water, and in a few moments the table was filled with a merry crowd, and a row of wistful-eyed youngsters circled the kitchen wall, where they stood first on one leg and then on the other, in impatient hunger.

"Now pitch in, Mrs. Smith," said Mrs. Gray, presiding over the table. "You know these men critters. They'll eat every grain of it, if ye give 'em a chance. I swan, they're made o' India-rubber, their stomachs is, I know it."

"Haf to eat to work," said Bill, gnawing a cob with a swift, circular motion that rivalled a corn-sheller in results.

"More like workin' to eat," put in one of the girls with a giggle. "More eat 'n work with you."

"*You* needn't say anything, Net. Any one that'll eat seven ears—"

"I didn't, no such thing. You piled your cobs on my plate."

"That'll do to tell Ed Varney. It won't go down here where we know yeh."

"Good land! Eat all yeh want! They's plenty more in the
fiel's, but I can't afford to give you young uns tea. The tea is for
us womenfolks, and 'specially f'r Mis' Smith an' Bill's wife.
We're a-goin' to tell fortunes by it.''

One by one the men filled up and shoved back, and one by
one the children slipped into their places, and by two o'clock the
women alone remained around the débris-covered table, sipping
their tea and telling fortunes.

As they got well down to the grounds in the cup, they shook
them with a circular motion in the hand, and then turned them
bottom-side-up quickly in the saucer, then twirled them three or
four times one way, and three or four times the other, during a
breathless pause. Then Mrs. Gray lifted the cup, and, gazing into
it with profound gravity, pronounced the impending fate.

It must be admitted that, to a critical observer, she had abundant preparation for hitting close to the mark, as when she told
the girls that "somebody was comin'." "It's a man," she went
on gravely. "He is cross-eyed—"

"Oh, you hush!" cried Nettie.

"He has red hair, and is death on b'iled corn and hot biscuit."

The others shrieked with delight.

"But he's goin' to get the mitten, that red-headed feller is, for
I see another feller comin' up behind him."

"Oh, lemme see, lemme see!" cried Nettie.

"Keep off," said the priestess, with a lofty gesture. "His hair
is black. He don't eat so much, and he works more."

The girls exploded in a shriek of laughter, and pounded their
sister on the back.

At last came Mrs. Smith's turn, and she was trembling with
excitement as Mrs. Gray again composed her jolly face to what
she considered a proper solemnity of expression.

"Somebody is comin' to *you*," she said, after a long pause.
"He's got a musket on his back. He's a soldier. He's almost
here. See?''

She pointed at two little tea-stems, which really formed a faint
suggestion of a man with a musket on his back. He had climbed
nearly to the edge of the cup. Mrs. Smith grew pale with
excitement. She trembled so she could hardly hold the cup in her
hand as she gazed into it.

"It's Ed," cried the old woman. "He's on the way home.
Heavens an' earth! There he is now!" She turned and waved her
hand out toward the road. They rushed to the door to look where
she pointed.

A man in a blue coat, with a musket on his back, was toiling slowly up the hill on the sun-bright, dusty road, toiling slowly, with bent head half hidden by a heavy knapsack. So tired it seemed that walking was indeed a process of falling. So eager to get home he would not stop, would not look aside, but plodded on, amid the cries of the locusts, the welcome of the crickets, and the rustle of the yellow wheat. Getting back to God's country, and his wife and babies!

Laughing, crying, trying to call him and the children at the same time, the little wife, almost hysterical, snatched her hat and ran out into the yard. But the soldier had disappeared over the hill into the hollow beyond, and, by the time she had found the children, he was too far away for her voice to reach him. And, besides, she was not sure it was her husband, for he had not turned his head at her shouts. This seemed so strange. Why didn't he stop to rest at his old neighbor's house? Tortured by hope and doubt, she hurried up the coolly as fast as she could push the baby wagon, the blue-coated figure just ahead pushing steadily, silently forward up the coolly.

When the excited, panting little group came in sight of the gate they saw the blue-coated figure standing, leaning upon the rough rail fence, his chin on his palms, gazing at the empty house. His knapsack, canteen, blankets, and musket lay upon the dusty grass at his feet.

He was like a man lost in a dream. His wide, hungry eyes devoured the scene. The rough lawn, the little unpainted house, the field of clear yellow wheat behind it, down across which streamed the sun, now almost ready to touch the high hill to the west, the crickets crying merrily, a cat on the fence near by, dreaming, unmindful of the stranger in blue—

How peaceful it all was. O God! How far removed from all camps, hospitals, battle lines. A little cabin in a Wisconsin coolly, but it was majestic in its peace. How did he ever leave it for those years of tramping, thirsting, killing?

Trembling, weak with emotion, her eyes on the silent figure, Mrs. Smith hurried up to the fence. Her feet made no noise in the dust and grass, and they were close upon him before he knew of them. The oldest boy ran a little ahead. He will never forget that figure, that face. It will always remain as something epic, that return of the private. He fixed his eyes on the pale face covered with a ragged beard.

"Who *are* you, sir?" asked the wife, or, rather, started to ask, for he turned, stood a moment, and then cried:

"Emma!"

"Edward!"

The children stood in a curious row to see their mother kiss this bearded, strange man, the elder girl sobbing sympathetically with her mother. Illness had left the soldier partly deaf, and this added to the strangeness of his manner.

But the youngest child stood away, even after the girl had recognized her father and kissed him. The man turned then to the baby, and said in a curiously unpaternal tone:

"Come here, my little man; don't you know me?" But the baby backed away under the fence and stood peering at him critically.

"My little man!" What meaning in those words! This baby seemed like some other woman's child, and not the infant he had left in his wife's arms. The war had come between him and his baby—he was only a strange man to him, with big eyes; a soldier, with mother hanging to his arm, and talking in a loud voice.

"And this is Tom," the private said, drawing the oldest boy to him. *"He'll* come and see me. *He* knows his poor old pap when he comes home from the war."

The mother heard the pain and reproach in his voice and hastened to apologize.

"You've changed so, Ed. He can't know yeh. This is papa, Teddy; come and kiss him—Tom and Mary do. Come, won't you?" But Teddy still peered through the fence with solemn eyes, well out of reach. He resembled a half-wild kitten that hesitates, studying the tones of one's voice.

"I'll fix him," said the soldier, and sat down to undo his knapsack, out of which he drew three enormous and very red apples. After giving one to each of the older children, he said:

"Now I guess he'll come. Eh, my little man? Now come see your pap."

Teddy crept slowly under the fence, assisted by the overzealous Tommy, and a moment later was kicking and squalling in his father's arms. Then they entered the house, into the sitting room, poor, bare, art-forsaken little room, too, with its rag carpet, its square clock, and its two or three chromos and pictures from *Harper's Weekly* pinned about.

"Emma, I'm all tired out," said Private Smith, as he flung himself down on the carpet as he used to do, while his wife brought a pillow to put under his head, and the children stood about munching their apples.

"Tommy, you run and get me a pan of chips, and Mary, you get the tea-kettle on, and I'll go and make some biscuit."

And the soldier talked. Question after question he poured forth

about the crops, the cattle, the renter, the neighbors. He slipped
his heavy government brogan shoes off his poor, tired, blistered
feet, and lay out with utter, sweet relaxation. He was a free man
again, no longer a soldier under command. At supper he stopped
once, listened and smiled. "That's old Spot. I know her voice. I
s'pose that's her calf out there in the pen. I can't milk her
to-night, though. I'm too tired. But I tell you, I'd like a drink o'
her milk. What's become of old Rove?"

"He died last winter. Poisoned, I guess." There was a moment of sadness for them all. It was some time before the
husband spoke again, in a voice that trembled a little.

"Poor old feller! He'd 'a' known me half a mile away. I
expected him to come down the hill to meet me. It 'ud 'a' been
more like comin' home if I could 'a' seen him comin' down the
road an' waggin' his tail, an' laughin' that way he has. I tell
yeh, it kind o' took hold o' me to see the blinds down an' the
house shut up."

"But, yeh see, we—we expected you'd write again 'fore you
started. And then we thought we'd see you if you *did* come,"
she hastened to explain.

"Well, I ain't worth a cent on writin'. Besides, it's just as
well yeh didn't know when I was comin'. I tell you, it sounds
good to hear them chickens out there, an' turkeys, an' the
crickets. Do you know they don't have just the same kind o'
crickets down South? Who's Sam hired t' help cut yer grain?"

"The Ramsey boys."

"Looks like a good crop; but I'm afraid I won't do much
gettin' it cut. This cussed fever an' ague has got me down pretty
low. I don't know when I'll get rid of it. I'll bet I've took
twenty-five pounds of quinine if I've taken a bit. Gimme another
biscuit. I tell yeh, they taste good, Emma. I ain't had anything
like it— Say, if you'd 'a'hear'd me braggin' to th' boys about
your butter 'n' biscuits I'll bet your ears 'ud 'a' burnt."

The private's wife colored with pleasure. "Oh, you're always
a-braggin' about your things. Everybody makes good butter."

"Yes; old lady Snyder, for instance."

"Oh, well, she ain't to be mentioned. She's Dutch."

"Or old Mis' Snively. One more cup o' tea, Mary. That's my
girl! I'm feeling better already. I just b'lieve the matter with me
is, I'm *starved*."

This was a delicious hour, one long to be remembered. They
were like lovers again. But their tenderness, like that of a typical
American family, found utterance in tones, rather than in words.
He was praising her when praising her biscuit, and she knew it.

They grew soberer when he showed where he had been struck, one ball burning the back of his hand, one cutting away a lock of hair from his temple, and one passing through the calf of his leg. The wife shuddered to think how near she had come to being a soldier's widow. Her waiting no longer seemed hard. This sweet, glorious hour effaced it all.

Then they rose, and all went out into the garden and down to the barn. He stood beside her while she milked old Spot. They began to plan fields and crops for next year.

His farm was weedy and encumbered, a rascally renter had run away with his machinery (departing between two days), his children needed clothing, the years were coming upon him, he was sick and emaciated, but his heroic soul did not quail. With the same courage with which he had faced his Southern march he entered upon a still more hazardous future.

Oh, that mystic hour! The pale man with big eyes standing there by the well, with his young wife by his side. The vast moon swinging above the eastern peaks, the cattle winding down the pasture slopes with jangling bells, the crickets singing, the stars blooming out sweet and far and serene; the katydids rhythmically calling, the little turkeys crying querulously, as they settled to roost in the poplar tree near the open gate. The voices at the well drop lower, the little ones nestle in their father's arms at last, and Teddy falls asleep there.

The common soldier of the American volunteer army had returned. His war with the South was over, and his fight, his daily running fight with nature and against the injustice of his fellow-men, was begun again.

Mary Eleanor Wilkins Freeman
(1852–1930)

Born and raised in Massachusetts, Mrs. Freeman resided there until 1902, when she married a New Jersey physician. The editor of Harper's Bazar, Mary Louise Booth (1831–1889), launched Freeman's career in 1882. Thereafter Freeman published many of her stories either in Harper's Bazar *or in* Harper's; *her most notable collections were* A Humble Romance and Other Stories *(1887) and* A New England Nun and Other Stories *(1891), the title story of which is reprinted here. She wrote novels, which are not as effective as her stories, and tried her hand at plays as well. In 1903, she published a collection of supernatural tales,* Wind in the Rose Bush. *A posthumous collection,* Edgewater People *(1918), is in her best vein.*

A NEW ENGLAND NUN

It was late in the afternoon, and the light was waning. There was a difference in the look of the tree shadows out in the yard. Somewhere in the distance cows were lowing and a little bell was tinkling; now and then a farm-wagon tilted by, and the dust flew; some blue-shirted laborers with shovels over their shoulders plodded past; little swarms of flies were dancing up and down before the people's faces in the soft air. There seemed to be a gentle stir arising over everything for the mere sake of subsidence—a very premonition of rest and hush and night.

This soft diurnal commotion was over Louisa Ellis also. She had been peacefully sewing at her sitting-room window all the afternoon. Now she quilted her needle carefully into her work,

Louisa's Preciseness

which she folded precisely, and laid in a basket with her thimble
and thread and scissors. Louisa Ellis could not remember that
ever in her life she had mislaid one of these little feminine
appurtenances, which had become, from long use and constant
association, a very part of her personality.

Louisa tied a green apron round her waist, and got out a flat
straw hat with a green ribbon. Then she went into the garden
with a little blue crockery bowl, to pick some currants for her
tea. After the currants were picked she sat on the back door-step
and stemmed them, collecting the stems carefully in her apron,
and afterwards throwing them into the hen-coop. She looked
sharply at the grass beside the step to see if any had fallen there.

Louisa was slow and still in her movements; it took her a long
time to prepare her tea; but when ready it was set forth with as
much grace as if she had been a veritable guest to her own self.
The little square table stood exactly in the centre of the kitchen,
and was covered with a starched linen cloth whose border pattern
of flowers glistened. Louisa had a damask napkin on her tea-
tray, where were arranged a cut-glass tumbler full of teaspoons,
a silver cream-pitcher, a china sugar-bowl, and one pink china
cup and saucer. Louisa used china every day—something which
none of her neighbors did. They whispered about it among
themselves. Their daily tables were laid with common crockery,
their sets of best china stayed in the parlor closet, and Louisa
Ellis was no richer nor better bred than they. Still she would use
the china. She had for her supper a glass dish full of sugared
currants, a plate of little cakes, and one of light white biscuits.
Also a leaf or two of lettuce, which she cut up daintily. Louisa
was very fond of lettuce, which she raised to perfection in her
little garden. She ate quite heartily, though in a delicate, pecking
way; it seemed almost surprising that any considerable bulk of
the food should vanish.

After tea she filled a plate with nicely baked thin corn-cakes,
and carried them out into the back-yard.

"Cæsar!" she called. "Cæsar! Cæsar!"

There was a little rush, and the clank of a chain, and a large
yellow-and-white dog appeared at the door of his tiny hut, which
was half hidden among the tall grasses and flowers. Louisa
patted him and gave him the corn-cakes. Then she returned to the
house and washed the tea-things, polishing the china carefully.
The twilight had deepened; the chorus of the frogs floated in at
the open window wonderfully loud and shrill, and once in a while
a long sharp drone from a tree-toad pierced it. Louisa took off
her green gingham apron, disclosing a shorter one of pink and

white print. She lighted her lamp, and sat down again with her sewing.

In about half an hour Joe Dagget came. She heard his heavy step on the walk, and rose and took off her pink-and-white apron. Under that was still another—white linen with a little cambric edging on the bottom; that was Louisa's company apron. She never wore it without her calico sewing apron over it unless she had a guest. She had barely folded the pink and white one with methodical haste and laid it in a table-drawer when the door opened and Joe Dagget entered.

He seemed to fill up the whole room. A little yellow canary that had been asleep in his green cage at the south window woke up and fluttered wildly, beating his little yellow wings against the wires. He always did so when Joe Dagget came into the room.

"Good-evening," said Louisa. She extended her hand with a kind of solemn cordiality.

"Good-evening, Louisa," returned the man, in a loud voice.

She placed a chair for him, and they sat facing each other, with the table between them. He sat bolt-upright, toeing out his heavy feet squarely, glancing with a good-humored uneasiness around the room. She sat gently erect, folding her slender hands in her white-linen lap.

"Been a pleasant day," remarked Dagget.

"Real pleasant," Louisa assented, softly. "Have you been haying?" she asked, after a little while.

"Yes, I've been haying all day, down in the ten-acre lot. Pretty hot work."

"It must be."

"Yes, it's pretty hot work in the sun."

"Is your mother well to-day?"

"Yes, mother's pretty well."

"I suppose Lily Dyer's with her now?"
Dagget colored. "Yes, she's with her," he answered, slowly.

Dagget embarrassed

He was not very young, but there was a boyish look about his large face. Louisa was not quite as old as he, her face was fairer and smoother, but she gave people the impression of being older.

"I suppose she's a good deal of help to your mother," she said, further.

"I guess she is; I don't know how mother'd get along without her," said Dagget, with a sort of embarrassed warmth.

"She looks like a real capable girl. She's pretty-looking too," remarked Louisa.

"Yes, she is pretty fair-looking."

Presently Dagget began fingering the books on the table.

There was a square red autograph album, and a Young Lady's Gift-Book which had belonged to Louisa's mother. He took them up one after the other and opened them; then laid them down again, the album on the Gift-Book.

Louisa kept eying them with mild uneasiness. Finally she rose and changed the position of the books, putting the album underneath. That was the way they had been arranged in the first place. *Structured life; pickiness*

Dagget gave an awkward little laugh. "Now what difference did it make which book was on top?" said he.

Louisa looked at him with a deprecating smile. "I always keep them that way," murmured she.

"You do beat everything," said Dagget, trying to laugh again. His large face was flushed.

He remained about an hour longer, then rose to take leave. Going out, he stumbled over a rug, and trying to recover himself, hit Louisa's work-basket on the table, and knocked it on the floor.

He looked at Louisa, then at the rolling spools; he ducked himself awkwardly toward them, but she stopped him. "Never mind," said she; "I'll pick them up after you're gone."

She spoke with a mild stiffness. Either she was a little disturbed, or his nervousness affected her, and made her seem constrained in her effort to reassure him.

When Joe Dagget was outside he drew in the sweet evening air with a sigh, and felt much as an innocent and perfectly well-intentioned bear might after his exit from a china shop.

Louisa, on her part, felt much as the kind-hearted, long-suffering owner of the china shop might have done after the exit of the bear.

She tied on the pink, then the green apron, picked up all the scattered treasures and replaced them in her work-basket, and straightened the rug. Then she set the lamp on the floor, and began sharply examining the carpet. She even rubbed her fingers over it, and looked at them.

"He's tracked in a good deal of dust," she murmured. "I thought he must have."

Louisa got a dust-pan and brush, and swept Joe Dagget's track carefully.

If he could have known it, it would have increased his perplexity and uneasiness, although it would not have disturbed his loyalty in the least. He came twice a week to see Louisa Ellis, and every time, sitting there in her delicately sweet room, he felt as if surrounded by a hedge of lace. He was afraid to stir lest he should put a clumsy foot or hand through the fairy web, and he had always the consciousness that Louisa was watching fearfully lest he should.

Still the lace and Louisa commanded perforce his perfect respect and patience and loyalty. They were to be married in a month, after a singular courtship which had lasted for a matter of fifteen years. For fourteen out of the fifteen years the two had not once seen each other, and they had seldom exchanged letters. Joe had been all those years in Australia, where he had gone to make his fortune, and where he had stayed until he made it. He would have stayed fifty years if it had taken so long, and come home feeble and tottering, or never come home at all, to marry Louisa.

But the fortune had been made in the fourteen years, and he had come home now to marry the woman who had been patiently and unquestioningly waiting for him all that time.

Shortly after they were engaged he had announced to Louisa his determination to strike out into new fields, and secure a competency before they should be married. She had listened and assented with the sweet serenity which never failed her, not even when her lover set forth on that long and uncertain journey. Joe, buoyed up as he was by his sturdy determination, broke down a little at the last, but Louisa kissed him with a mild blush, and said good-by.

"It won't be for long," poor Joe had said, huskily; but it was for fourteen years.

In that length of time much had happened. Louisa's mother and brother had died, and she was all alone in the world. But greatest happening of all—a subtle happening which both were too simple to understand—Louisa's feet had turned into a path, smooth maybe under a calm, serene sky, but so straight and unswerving that it could only meet a check at her grave, and so narrow that there was no room for any one at her side.

Louisa's first emotion when Joe Dagget came home (he had not apprised her of his coming) was consternation, although she would not admit it to herself, and he never dreamed of it. Fifteen years ago she had been in love with him—at least she considered herself to be. Just at that time, gently acquiescing with and falling into the natural drift of girlhood, she had seen marriage ahead as a reasonable feature and a probable desirability of life. She had listened with calm docility to her mother's views upon the subject. Her mother was remarkable for her cool sense and sweet, even temperament. She talked wisely to her daughter

when Joe Dagget presented himself, and Louisa accepted him
with no hesitation. He was the first lover she had ever had.

She had been faithful to him all these years. She had never
dreamed of the possibility of marrying any one else. Her life,
especially for the last seven years, had been full of a pleasant
peace; she had never felt discontented nor impatient over her
lover's absence; still she had always looked forward to his return
and their marriage as the inevitable conclusion of things. However,
she had fallen into a way of placing it so far in the future that it
was almost equal to placing it over the boundaries of another
life.

When Joe came she had been expecting him, and expecting to
be married for fourteen years, but she was as much surprised
and taken aback as if she had never thought of it.

Joe's consternation came later. He eyed Louisa with an instant
confirmation of his old admiration. She had changed but little.
She still kept her pretty manner and soft grace, and was, he
considered, every whit as attractive as ever. As for himself, his
stent was done; he had turned his face away from fortune-
seeking, and the old winds of romance whistled as loud and
sweet as ever through his ears. All the song which he had been
wont to hear in them was Louisa; he had for a long time a loyal
belief that he heard it still, but finally it seemed to him that
although the winds sang always that one song, it had another
name. But for Louisa the wind had never more than murmured;
now it had gone down, and everything was still. She listened for
a little while with half-wistful attention; then she turned quietly
away and went to work on her wedding clothes.

Joe had made some extensive and quite magnificent alterations
in his house. It was the old homestead; the newly-married couple
would live there, for Joe could not desert his mother, who
refused to leave her old home. So Louisa must leave hers. Every
morning, rising and going about among her neat maidenly
possessions, she felt as one looking her last upon the faces of
dear friends. It was true that in a measure she could take them
with her, but, robbed of their old environments, they would
appear in such new guises that they would almost cease to be
themselves. Then there were some peculiar features of her happy
solitary life which she would probably be obliged to relinquish
altogether. Sterner tasks than these graceful but half-needless
ones would probably devolve upon her. There would be a large
house to care for; there would be company to entertain; there
would be Joe's rigorous and feeble old mother to wait upon; and
it would be contrary to all thrifty village traditions for her to

keep more than one servant. Louisa had a little still, and she used to occupy herself pleasantly in summer weather with distilling the sweet and aromatic essences from roses and peppermint and spearmint. By-and-by her still must be laid away. Her store of essences was already considerable, and there would be no time for her to distil for the mere pleasure of it. Then Joe's mother would think it foolishness; she had already hinted her own opinion in the matter. Louisa dearly loved to sew a linen seam, not always for use, but for the simple, mild pleasure which she took in it. She would have been loath to confess how more than once she had ripped a seam for the mere delight of sewing it together again. Sitting at her window during long sweet afternoons, drawing her needle gently through the dainty fabric, she was peace itself. But there was small chance of such foolish comfort in the future. Joe's mother, domineering, shrewd old matron that she was even in her old age, and very likely even Joe himself, with his honest masculine rudeness, would laugh and frown down all these pretty but senseless old maiden ways.

Louisa had almost the enthusiasm of an artist over the mere order and cleanliness of her solitary home. She had throbs of genuine triumph at the sight of the window-panes which she had polished until they shone like jewels. She gloated gently over her orderly bureau-drawers, with their exquisitely folded contents redolent with lavender and sweet clover and very purity. Could she be sure of the endurance of even this? She had visions, so startling that she half repudiated them as indelicate, of coarse masculine belongings strewn about in endless litter; of dust and disorder arising necessarily from a coarse masculine presence in the midst of all this delicate harmony.

Among her forebodings of disturbance, not the least was with regard to Cæsar. Cæsar was a veritable hermit of a dog. For the greater part of his life he had dwelt in his secluded hut, shut out from the society of his kind and all innocent canine joys. Never had Cæsar since his early youth watched at a woodchuck's hole; never had he known the delights of a stray bone at a neighbor's kitchen door. And it was all on account of a sin committed when hardly out of his puppyhood. No one knew the possible depth of remorse of which this mild-visaged, altogether innocent-looking old dog might be capable; but whether or not he had encountered remorse, he had encountered a full measure of righteous retribution. Old Cæsar seldom lifted up his voice in a growl or a bark; he was fat and sleepy; there were yellow rings which looked like spectacles around his dim old eyes; but there was a neighbor who bore on his hand the imprint of several of Cæsar's sharp white youthful teeth, and for that he had lived at the end of a chain, all alone in a little hut, for fourteen years. The neighbor, who was choleric and smarting with the pain of his wound, had demanded either Cæsar's death or complete ostracism. So Louisa's brother, to whom the dog had belonged, had built him his little kennel and tied him up. It was now fourteen years since, in a flood of youthful spirits, he had inflicted that memorable bite, and with the exception of short excursions, always at the end of the chain, under the strict guardianship of his master or Louisa, the old dog had remained a close prisoner. It is doubtful if, with his limited ambition, he took much pride in the fact, but it is certain that he was possessed of considerable cheap fame. He was regarded by all the children in the village and by many adults as a very monster of ferocity. St. George's dragon could hardly have surpassed in evil repute Louisa Ellis's old yellow dog. Mothers charged their children with solemn emphasis not to go too near to him, and the children listened and believed greedily, with a fascinated appetite for terror, and ran by Louisa's house stealthily, with many sidelong and backward glances at the terrible dog. If perchance he sounded a hoarse bark, there was a panic. Wayfarers chancing into Louisa's yard eyed him with respect, and inquired if the chain were stout. Cæsar at large might have seemed a very ordinary dog and excited no comment whatever; chained, his reputation overshadowed him, so that he lost his own proper outlines and looked darkly vague and enormous. Joe Dagget, however, with his good-humored sense and shrewdness, saw him as he was. He strode valiantly up to him and patted him on the head, in spite of Louisa's soft clamor of warning, and even attempted to set him loose. Louisa grew so alarmed that he desisted, but kept announcing his opinion in the matter quite forcibly at intervals. ''There ain't a better-natured dog in town,'' he would say, ''and it's downright cruel to keep him tied up there. Some day I'm going to take him out.''

Louisa had very little hope that he would not, one of these days, when their interests and possessions should be more completely fused in one. She pictured to herself Cæsar on the rampage through the quiet and unguarded village. She saw innocent children bleeding in his path. She was herself very fond of the old dog, because he had belonged to her dead brother, and he was always very gentle with her; still she had great faith in his ferocity. She always warned people not to go too near him. She fed him on ascetic fare of corn-mush and cakes, and never fired his dangerous temper with heating and sanguinary diet of flesh and bones. [Louisa looked at the old dog munching his simple fare, and thought of her approaching marriage and trembled. Still no anticipation of disorder and confusion in lieu of sweet peace and harmony, no forebodings of Cæsar on the rampage, no wild fluttering of her little yellow canary, were sufficient to turn her a hair's-breadth. Joe Dagget had been fond of her and working for her all these years. It was not for her, whatever came to pass, to prove untrue and break his heart. She put the exquisite little stitches into her wedding-garments, and the time went on until it was only a week before her wedding-day. It was a Tuesday evening, and the wedding was to be a week from Wednesday.

There was a full moon that night. About nine o'clock Louisa strolled down the road a little way. There were harvest-fields on either hand, bordered by low stone walls. Luxuriant clumps of bushes grew beside the wall, and trees—wild cherry and old apple-trees—at intervals. Presently Louisa sat down on the wall and looked about her with mildly sorrowful reflectiveness. Tall shrubs of blueberry and meadow-sweet, all woven together and tangled with blackberry vines and horsebriers, shut her in on either side. She had a little clear space between them. Opposite her, on the other side of the road, was a spreading tree; the moon shone between its boughs, and the leaves twinkled like silver. The road was bespread with a beautiful shifting dapple of silver and shadow; the air was full of a mysterious sweetness. "I wonder if it's wild grapes?" murmured Louisa. She sat there some time. She was just thinking of rising, when she heard footsteps and low voices, and remained quiet. It was a lonely place, and she felt a little timid. She thought she would keep still in the shadow and let the persons, whoever they might be, pass her.

But just before they reached her the voices ceased, and the footsteps. She understood that their owners had also found seats upon the stone wall. She was wondering if she could not steal away unobserved, when the voice broke the stillness. It was Joe Dagget's. She sat still and listened.

The voice was announced by a loud sigh, which was as familiar as itself. "Well," said Dagget, "you've made up your mind, then, I suppose?"

"Yes," returned another voice; "I'm going day after to-morrow."

"That's Lily Dyer," thought Louisa to herself. The voice embodied itself in her mind. She saw a girl tall and full-figured, with a firm, fair face, looking fairer and firmer in the moonlight, her strong yellow hair braided in a close knot. A girl full of a calm rustic strength and bloom, with a masterful way which might have beseemed a princess. Lily Dyer was a favorite with the village folk; she had just the qualities to arouse the admiration. She was good and handsome and smart. Louisa had often heard her praises sounded.

"Well," said Joe Dagget, "I ain't got a word to say."

"I don't know what you could say," returned Lily Dyer.

"Not a word to say," repeated Joe, drawing out the words heavily. Then there was a silence. "I ain't sorry," he began at last, "that that happened yesterday—that we kind of let on how we felt to each other. I guess it's just as well we knew. Of course I can't do anything any different. I'm going right on an' get married next week. I ain't going back on a woman that's waited for me fourteen years, an' break her heart." *Joe's dignity*

"If you should jilt her to-morrow, I wouldn't have you," spoke up the girl, with sudden vehemence.

"Well, I ain't going to give you the chance," said he; "but I don't believe you would, either."

"You'd see I wouldn't. Honor's honor, an' right's right. An' I'd never think anything of any man that went against 'em for me or any other girl; you'd find that out, Joe Dagget."

"Well, you'll find out fast enough that I ain't going against 'em for you or any other girl," returned he. Their voices sounded almost as if they were angry with each other. Louisa was listening eagerly.

"I'm sorry you feel as if you must go away," said Joe, "but I don't know but it's best."

"Of course it's best. I hope you and I have got common-sense."

"Well, I suppose you're right." Suddenly Joe's voice got an undertone of tenderness. "Say, Lily," said he, "I'll get along well enough myself, but I can't bear to think— You don't suppose you're going to fret much over it?"

"I guess you'll find out I sha'n' fret much over a married man."

"Well, I hope you won't—I hope you won't, Lily. God knows I do. And—I hope—one of these days—you'll—come across somebody else—"

"I don't see any reason why I shouldn't." Suddenly her tone changed. She spoke in a sweet, clear voice, so loud that she could have been heard across the street. "No, Joe Dagget," said she, "I'll never marry any other man as long as I live. I've got good sense, an' I ain't going to break my heart nor make a fool of myself; but I'm never going to be married, you can be sure of that. I ain't that sort of a girl to feel this way twice."

Louisa heard an exclamation and a soft commotion behind the

If marriage happens, all 3 people will be unhappy

bushes; then Lily spoke again—the voice sounded as if she had risen. "This must be put a stop to," said she. "We've stayed here long enough. I'm going home."

Louisa sat there in a daze, listening to their retreating steps. After a while she got up and slunk softly home herself. The next day she did her housework methodically; that was as much a matter of course as breathing; but she did not sew on her wedding-clothes. She sat at her window and meditated. In the evening Joe came. Louisa Ellis had never known that she had any diplomacy in her, but when she came to look for it that night she found it, although meek of its kind, among her little feminine weapons. Even now she could hardly believe that she had heard aright, and that she would not do Joe a terrible injury should she break her troth-plight. She wanted to sound him without betraying too soon her own inclinations in the matter. She did it successfully, and they finally came to an understanding; but it was a difficult thing, for he was as afraid of betraying himself as she.

She never mentioned Lily Dyer. She simply said that while she had no cause of complaint against him, she had lived so long in one way that she shrank from making a change.

"Well, I never shrank, Louisa," said Dagget. "I'm going to be honest enough to say that I think maybe it's better this way; but if you'd wanted to keep on, I'd have stuck to you till my dying day. I hope you know that."

"Yes, I do," said she.

That night she and Joe parted more tenderly than they had done for a long time. Standing in the door, holding each other's hands, a last great wave of regretful memory swept over them.

"Well, this ain't the way we've thought it was all going to end, is it, Louisa?" said Joe.

She shook her head. There was a little quiver on her placid face.

"You let me know if there's ever anything I can do for you," said he. "I ain't ever going to forget you, Louisa." Then he kissed her, and went down the path.

Louisa, all alone by herself that night, wept a little, she hardly knew why; but the next morning, on waking, she felt like a queen who, after fearing lest her domain be wrested away from her, sees it firmly insured in her possession.

Now the tall weeds and grasses might cluster around Cæsar's little hermit hut, the snow might fall on its roof year in and year out, but he never would go on a rampage through the unguarded village. Now the little canary might turn itself into a peaceful yellow ball night after night, and have no need to wake and flutter with wild terror against its bars. Louisa could sew linen seams, and distil roses, and dust and polish and fold away in lavender, as long as she listed. That afternoon she sat with her needle-work at the window, and felt fairly steeped in peace. Lily Dyer, tall and erect and blooming, went past; but she felt no qualm. If Louisa Ellis had sold her birthright she did not know it, the taste of the pottage was so delicious, and had been her sole satisfaction for so long. Serenity and placid narrowness had become to her as the birthright itself. She gazed ahead through a long reach of future days strung together like pearls in a rosary, every one like the others, and all smooth and flawless and innocent, and her heart went up in thankfulness. Outside was the fervid summer afternoon; the air was filled with the sounds of the busy harvest of men and birds and bees; there were halloos, metallic clatterings, sweet calls, and long hummings. Louisa sat, prayerfully numbering her days, like an uncloistered nun.

Religious Images

Henry James
(1843–1916)

Son of a wealthy writer and lecturer on religious and social subjects, Henry James, Sr. (1811–1882), and younger brother of the philosopher and psychologist, William James (1842–1910), Henry James was born in New York City but was educated, and grew up, literally all over the map. Briefly a student at the Harvard Law School (1862–1863), his drive toward social observation and analysis led him to begin writing—essays, reviews, travel notes, short stories, novelettes, and then, in 1876, his first novel, Roderick Hudson. Inherited wealth underwrote his early years as a writer; thereafter he depended on his literary work to earn at least a part of his livelihood. Much of his subject matter centers on the relative positions, social, sexual, and moral, of Europeans and Americans. The American (1877), The Europeans (1878), Daisy Miller (1879), and The Portrait of a Lady (1881, the first of his masterpieces) are all written around aspects of this European-American contrast and comparison. After an unsuccessful attempt at playwrighting, James wrote increasingly complex and subtle, sometimes overly subtle, novels and stories on a wide variety of themes, including What Maisie Knew (1897), a story seen through the eyes of a young girl, "The Turn of the Screw" (1898), a fine tale of the supernatural, and The Awkward Age (1899), a novel largely in dialogue. Of his last major novels, The Wings of the Dove (1902), The Ambassadors (1903), and The Golden Bowl (1904), the last-named is almost diaphanously oversubtle, the first-named is more vital but still somewhat overwritten, and The Ambassadors is arguably the greatest novel he ever produced. His The American Scene (1907), a travel book about his native country, is alternately brilliantly incisive and tediously literary.

James lived much of his life abroad, settling finally in London.

THE REAL THING

When the porter's wife (she used to answer the house-bell) announced "A gentleman—with a lady, sir," I had, as I often had in those days, for the wish was father to the thought, an immediate vision of sitters. Sitters my visitors in this case proved to be; but not in the sense I should have preferred. However, there was nothing at first to indicate that they might not have come for a portrait. The gentleman, a man of fifty, very high and very straight, with a moustache slightly grizzled and a dark grey walking-coat admirably fitted, both of which I noted professionally—I don't mean as a barber or yet as a tailor—would have struck me as a celebrity if celebrities often were striking. It was a truth of which I had for some time been conscious that a figure with a good deal of frontage was, as one might say, almost never a public institution. A glance at the lady helped to remind me of this paradoxical law: she also looked too distinguished to be a "personality." Moreover one would scarcely come across two variations together.

Neither of the pair spoke immediately—they only prolonged the preliminary gaze which suggested that each wished to give the other a chance. They were visibly shy; they stood there letting me take them in—which, as I afterwards perceived, was the most practical thing they could have done. In this way their embarrassment served their cause. I had seen people painfully reluctant to mention that they desired anything so gross as to be represented on canvas; but the scruples of my new friends appeared almost insurmountable. Yet the gentleman might have said "I should like a portrait of my wife," and the lady might have said "I should like a portrait of my husband." Perhaps they were not husband and wife—this naturally would make the matter more delicate. Perhaps they wished to be done together—in which case they ought to have brought a third person to break the news.

"We come from Mr. Rivet," the lady said at last, with a dim smile which had the effect of a moist sponge passed over a "sunk" piece of painting, as well as of a vague allusion to vanished beauty. She was as tall and straight, in her degree, as her companion, and with ten years less to carry. She looked as sad as a woman could look whose face was not charged with expression; that is her tinted oval mask showed friction as an exposed surface shows it. The hand of time had played over her freely, but only to simplify. She was slim and stiff, and so well-dressed, in dark cloth, with lappets and pockets and buttons, that it was clear she employed the same tailor as her husband. The couple had an indefinable air of prosperous thrift—they evidently got a good deal of luxury for their money. If I was to be one of their luxuries it would behove me to consider my terms.

"Ah, Claude Rivet recommended me?" I inquired; and I added that it was very kind of him, though I could reflect that, as he only painted landscape, this was not a sacrifice.

The lady looked very hard at the gentleman, and the gentleman looked round the room. Then staring at the floor a moment and stroking his moustache, he rested his pleasant eyes on me with the remark: "He said you were the right one."

"I try to be, when people want to sit."

"Yes, we should like to," said the lady anxiously.

"Do you mean together?"

My visitors exchanged a glance. "If you could do anything with *me*, I suppose it would be double," the gentleman stammered.

"Oh yes, there's naturally a higher charge for two figures than for one."

"We should like to make it pay," the husband confessed.

"That's very good of you," I returned, appreciating so unwonted a sympathy—for I supposed he meant pay the artist.

A sense of strangeness seemed to dawn on the lady. "We mean for the illustrations—Mr. Rivet said you might put one in."

"Put one in—an illustration?" I was equally confused.

"Sketch her off, you know," said the gentleman, colouring.

It was only then that I understood the service Claude Rivet had rendered me; he had told them that I worked in black and white, for magazines, for story-books, for sketches of contemporary life, and consequently had frequent employment for models. These things were true, but it was not less true (I may confess it now—whether because the aspiration was to lead to everything or to nothing I leave the reader to guess), that I couldn't get the honours, to say nothing of the emoluments, of a great painter of portraits out of my head. My "illustrations" were my potboilers; I looked to a different branch of art (far and away the most interesting it had always seemed to me), to perpetuate my fame. There was no shame in looking to it also to make my fortune; but that fortune was by so much further from being made from the moment my visitors wished to be "done" for nothing. I was disappointed; for in the pictorial sense I had immediately *seen* them. I had seized their type—I had already settled what I would do with it. Something that wouldn't absolutely have pleased them, I afterwards reflected.

"Ah, you're—you're—a—?" I began, as soon as I had mastered my surprise. I couldn't bring out the dingy word "models"; it seemed to fit the case so little.

"We haven't had much practice," said the lady.

"We've got to *do* something, and we've thought that an artist in your line might perhaps make something of us," her husband threw off. He further mentioned that they didn't know many artists and that they had gone first, on the off-chance (he painted views of course, but sometimes put in figures—perhaps I remembered), to Mr. Rivet, whom they had met a few years before at a place in Norfolk where he was sketching.

"We used to sketch a little ourselves," the lady hinted.

"It's very awkward, but we absolutely *must* do something," her husband went on.

"Of course, we're not so *very* young," she admitted, with a wan smile.

With the remark that I might as well know something more about them, the husband had handed me a card extracted from a neat new pocket-book (their appurtenances were all of the freshest) and inscribed with the words "Major Monarch." Impressive as these words were they didn't carry my knowledge much further; but my visitor presently added: "I've left the army, and we've had the misfortune to lose our money. In fact our means are dreadfully small."

"It's an awful bore," said Mrs. Monarch.

They evidently wished to be discreet—to take care not to swagger because they were gentlefolks. I perceived they would have been willing to recognise this as something of a drawback, at the same time that I guessed at an underlying sense—their consolation in adversity—that they *had* their points. They certainly had; but these advantages struck me as preponderantly social; such for instance as would help to make a drawing-room look well. However, a drawing-room was always, or ought to be, a picture.

In consequence of his wife's allusion to their age Major

Monarch observed: "Naturally, it's more for the figure that we thought of going in. We can still hold ourselves up." On the instant I saw that the figure was indeed their strong point. His "naturally" didn't sound vain, but it lighted up the question. "*She* has got the best," he continued, nodding at his wife, with a pleasant after-dinner absence of circumlocution. I could only reply, as if we were in fact sitting over our wine, that this didn't prevent his own from being very good; which led him in turn to rejoin: "We thought that if you ever have to do people like us, we might be something like it. *She*, particularly—for a lady in a book, you know."

I was so amused by them that, to get more of it, I did my best to take their point of view; and though it was an embarrassment to find myself appraising physically, as if they were animals on hire or useful blacks, a pair whom I should have expected to meet only in one of the relations in which criticism is tacit, I looked at Mrs. Monarch judicially enough to be able to exclaim, after a moment, with conviction: "Oh yes, a lady in a book!" She was singularly like a bad illustration.

"We'll stand up, if you like," said the Major; and he raised himself before me with a really grand air.

I could take his measure at a glance—he was six feet two and a perfect gentleman. It would have paid any club in process of formation and in want of a stamp to engage him at a salary to stand in the principal window. What struck me immediately was that in coming to me they had rather missed their vocation; they could surely have been turned to better account for advertising purposes. I couldn't of course see the thing in detail, but I could see them make someone's fortune—I don't mean their own. There was something in them for a waistcoat-maker, an hotel-keeper or a soap-vendor. I could imagine "We always use it" pinned on their bosoms with the greatest effect; I had a vision of the promptitude with which they would launch a table d'hôte.

Mrs. Monarch sat still, not from pride but from shyness, and presently her husband said to her: "Get up my dear and show how smart you are." She obeyed, but she had no need to get up to show it. She walked to the end of the studio, and then she came back blushing, with her fluttered eyes on her husband. I was reminded of an incident I had accidentally had a glimpse of in Paris—being with a friend there, a dramatist about to produce a play—when an actress came to him to ask to be intrusted with a part. She went through her paces before him, walked up and down as Mrs. Monarch was doing. Mrs. Monarch did it quite as well, but I abstained from applauding. It was very odd to see such people apply for such poor pay. She looked as if she had ten thousand a year. Her husband had used the word that described her: she was, in the London current jargon, essentially and typically "smart." Her figure was, in the same order of ideas, conspicuously and irreproachably "good." For a woman of her age her waist was surprisingly small; her elbow moreover had the orthodox crook. She held her head at the conventional angle; but why did she come to *me?* She ought to have tried on jackets at a big shop. I feared my visitors were not only destitute, but "artistic"—which would be a great complication. When she sat down again I thanked her, observing that what a draughtsman most valued in his model was the faculty of keeping quiet.

"Oh, *she* can keep quiet," said Major Monarch. Then he added, jocosely: "I've always kept her quiet."

"I'm not a nasty fidget, am I?" Mrs. Monarch appealed to her husband.

He addressed his answer to me. "Perhaps it isn't out of place to mention—because we ought to be quite businesslike, oughtn't we?—that when I married her she was known as the Beautiful Statue."

"Oh dear!" said Mrs. Monarch, ruefully.

"Of course I should want a certain amount of expression," I rejoined.

"Of *course!*" they both exclaimed.

"And then I suppose you know that you'll get awfully tired."

"Oh, we *never* get tired!" they eagerly cried.

"Have you had any kind of practice?"

They hesitated—they looked at each other. "We've been photographed, *immensely*," said Mrs. Monarch.

"She means the fellows have asked us," added the Major.

"I see—because you're so good-looking."

"I don't know what they thought, but they were always after us."

"We always got our photographs for nothing," smiled Mrs. Monarch.

"We might have brought some, my dear," her husband remarked.

"I'm not sure we have any left. We've given quantities away," she explained to me.

"With our autographs and that sort of thing," said the Major.

"Are they to be got in the shops?" I inquired, as a harmless pleasantry.

"Oh, yes; *hers*—they used to be."

"Not now," said Mrs. Monarch, with her eyes on the floor.

II

I could fancy the "sort of thing" they put on the presentation-copies of their photographs, and I was sure they wrote a beautiful hand. It was odd how quickly I was sure of everything that concerned them. If they were now so poor as to have to earn shillings and pence, they never had had much of a margin. Their good looks had been their capital, and they had good-humouredly made the most of the career that this resource marked out for them. It was in their faces, the blankness, the deep intellectual repose of the twenty years of country-house visiting which had given them pleasant intonations. I could see the sunny drawing-rooms, sprinkled with periodicals she didn't read, in which Mrs. Monarch had continuously sat; I could see the wet shrubberies in which she had walked, equipped to admiration for their exercise. I could see the rich covers the Major had helped to shoot and the wonderful garments in which, late at night, he repaired to the smoking-room to talk about them. I could imagine their leggings and waterproofs, their knowing tweeds and rugs, their rolls of sticks and cases of tackle and neat umbrellas; and I could evoke the exact appearance of their servants and the compact variety of their luggage on the platforms of country stations.

They gave small tips, but they were liked; they didn't do anything themselves, but they were welcome. They looked so well everywhere; they gratified the general relish for stature, complexion and "form." They knew it without fatuity or vulgarity, and they respected themselves in consequence. They were not superficial; they were thorough and kept themselves up—it had been their line. People with such a taste for activity had to have some line. I could feel how, even in a dull house, they could have been counted upon for cheerfulness. At present something had happened—it didn't matter what, their little income had grown less, it had grown least—and they had to do something for pocket-money. Their friends liked them, but didn't like to support them. There was something about them that represented credit—their clothes, their manners, their type; but if credit is a large empty pocket in which an occasional chink reverberates, the chink at least must be audible. What they wanted of me was to help to make it so. Fortunately they had no children—I soon divined that. They would also perhaps wish our relations to be kept secret: this was why it was "for the figure"—the reproduction of the face would betray them.

I liked them—they were so simple; and I had no objection to

them if they would suit. But, somehow, with all their perfections I didn't easily believe in them. After all they were amateurs, and the ruling passion of my life was the detestation of the amateur. Combined with this was another perversity—an innate preference for the represented subject over the real one: the defect of the real one was so apt to be a lack of representation. I liked things that appeared; then one was sure. Whether they *were* or not was a subordinate and almost always a profitless question. There were other considerations, the first of which was that I already had two or three people in use, notably a young person with big feet, in alpaca, from Kilburn, who for a couple of years had come to me regularly for my illustrations and with whom I was still—perhaps ignobly—satisfied. I frankly explained to my visitors how the case stood; but they had taken more precautions than I supposed. They had reasoned out their opportunity, for Claude Rivet had told them of the projected *édition de luxe* of one of the writers of our day—the rarest of the novelists—who, long neglected by the multitudinous vulgar and dearly prized by the attentive (need I mention Philip Vincent?) had had the happy fortune of seeing, late in life, the dawn and then the full light of a higher criticism—an estimate in which, on the part of the public, there was something really of expiation. The edition in question, planned by a publisher of taste, was practically an act of high reparation; the woodcuts with which it was to be enriched were the homage of English art to one of the most independent representatives of English letters. Major and Mrs. Monarch confessed to me that they had hoped I might be able to work *them* into my share of the enterprise. They knew I was to do the first of the books, "Rutland Ramsay," but I had to make clear to them that my participation in the rest of the affair—this first book was to be a test—was to depend on the satisfaction I should give. If this should be limited my employers would drop me without a scruple. It was therefore a crisis for me and naturally I was making special preparations, looking about for new people, if they should be necessary, and securing the best types. I admitted however that I should like to settle down to two or three good models who would do for everything.

"Should we have often to—a—put on special clothes?" Mrs. Monarch timidly demanded.

"Dear, yes—that's half the business."

"And should we be expected to supply our own costumes?"

"Oh, no; I've got a lot of things. A painter's models put on—or put off—anything he likes."

"And do you mean—a—the same?"

"The same?"

Mrs. Monarch looked at her husband again.

"Oh, she was just wondering," he explained, "if the costumes are in *general* use." I had to confess that they were, and I mentioned further that some of them (I had a lot of genuine, greasy last-century things), had served their time, a hundred years ago, on living, world-stained men and women. "We'll put on anything that *fits*," said the Major.

"Oh, I arrange that—they fit in the pictures."

"I'm afraid I should do better for the modern books. I would come as you like," said Mrs. Monarch.

"She has got a lot of clothes at home: they might do for contemporary life," her husband continued.

"Oh, I can fancy scenes in which you'd be quite natural." And indeed I could see the slipshod rearrangements of stale properties—the stories I tried to produce pictures for without the exasperation of reading them—whose sandy tracts the good lady might help to people. But I had to return to the fact that for this sort of work—the daily mechanical grind—I was already equipped; the people I was working with were fully adequate.

"We only thought we might be more like *some* characters," said Mrs. Monarch mildly, getting up.

Her husband also rose; he stood looking at me with a dim wistfulness that was touching in so fine a man. "Wouldn't it be rather a pull sometimes to have—a—to have—?" He hung fire; he wanted me to help him by phrasing what he meant. But I couldn't—I didn't know. So he brought it out, awkwardly: "The *real* thing; a gentleman, you know, or a lady." I was quite ready to give a general assent—I admitted that there was a great deal in that. This encouraged Major Monarch to say, following up his appeal with an unacted gulp: "It's awfully hard—we've tried everything." The gulp was communicative; it proved too much for his wife. Before I knew it Mrs. Monarch had dropped again upon a divan and burst into tears. Her husband sat down beside her, holding one of her hands; whereupon she quickly dried her eyes with the other, while I felt embarrassed as she looked up at me. "There isn't a confounded job I haven't applied for—waited for—prayed for. You can fancy we'd be pretty bad first. Secretaryships and that sort of thing? You might as well ask for a peerage. I'd be *anything*—I'm strong; a messenger or a coalheaver. I'd put on a gold-laced cap and open carriage-doors in front of the haberdasher's; I'd hang about a station, to carry portmanteaus; I'd be a postman. But they won't *look* at you; there are thousands, as good as yourself, already on the ground. *Gentlemen*, poor beggars, who have drunk their wine, who have kept their hunters!''

I was as reassuring as I knew how to be, and my visitors were presently on their feet again while, for the experiment, we agreed on an hour. We were discussing it when the door opened and Miss Churm came in with a wet umbrella. Miss Churm had to take the omnibus to Maida Vale and then walk half-a-mile. She looked a trifle blowsy and slightly splashed. I scarcely ever saw her come in without thinking afresh how odd it was that, being so little in herself, she should yet be so much in others. She was a meagre little Miss Churm, but she was an ample heroine of romance. She was only a freckled cockney, but she could represent everything, from a fine lady to a shepherdess; she had the faculty, as she might have had a fine voice or long hair. She couldn't spell, and she loved beer, but she had two or three ''points,'' and practice, and a knack, and mother-wit, and a kind of whimsical sensibility, and a love of the theatre, and seven sisters, and not an ounce of respect, especially for the *h*. The first thing my visitors saw was that her umbrella was wet, and in their spotless perfection they visibly winced at it. The rain had come on since their arrival.

''I'm all in a soak; there *was* a mess of people in the 'bus. I wish you lived near a styion,'' said Miss Churm. I requested her to get ready as quickly as possible, and she passed into the room in which she always changed her dress. But before going out she asked me what she was to get into this time.

''It's the Russian princess, don't you know?'' I answered; ''the one with the 'golden eyes,' in black velvet, for the long thing in the *Cheapside*.''

''Golden eyes? I *say!*'' cried Miss Churm, while my companions watched her with intensity as she withdrew. She always arranged herself, when she was late, before I could turn round; and I kept my visitors a little, on purpose, so that they might get an idea, from seeing her, what would be expected of themselves. I mentioned that she was quite my notion of an excellent model— she was really very clever.

''Do you think she looks like a Russian princess?'' Major Monarch asked, with lurking alarm.

''When I make her, yes.''

''Oh, if you have to *make* her—!'' he reasoned, acutely.

''That's the most you can ask. There are so many that are not makeable.''

''Well now, *here's* a lady''—and with a persuasive smile he passed his arm into his wife's—''who's already made!''

"Oh, I'm not a Russian princess," Mrs. Monarch protested, a little coldly. I could see that she had known some and didn't like them. There, immediately, was a complication of a kind that I never had to fear with Miss Churm.

This young lady came back in black velvet—the gown was rather rusty and very low on her lean shoulders—and with a Japanese fan in her red hands. I reminded her that in the scene I was doing she had to look over someone's head. "I forget whose it is; but it doesn't matter. Just look over a head."

"I'd rather look over a stove," said Miss Churm; and she took her station near the fire. She fell into position, settled herself into a tall attitude, gave a certain backward inclination to her head and a certain forward droop to her fan, and looked, at least to my prejudiced sense, distinguished and charming, foreign and dangerous. We left her looking so, while I went down-stairs with Major and Mrs. Monarch.

"I think I could come about as near it as that," said Mrs. Monarch.

"Oh, you think she's shabby, but you must allow for the alchemy of art."

However, they went off with an evident increase of comfort, founded on their demonstrable advantage in being the real thing. I could fancy them shuddering over Miss Churm. She was very droll about them when I went back, for I told her what they wanted.

"Well, if *she* can sit I'll tyke to bookkeeping," said my model.

"She's very lady-like," I replied, as an innocent form of aggravation.

"So much the worse for *you*. That means she can't turn round."

"She'll do for the fashionable novels."

"Oh yes, she'll *do* for them!" my model humorously declared. "Ain't they bad enough without her?" I had often sociably denounced them to Miss Churm.

III

It was for the elucidation of a mystery in one of these works that I first tried Mrs. Monarch. Her husband came with her, to be useful if necessary—it was sufficiently clear that as a general thing he would prefer to come with her. At first I wondered if this were for "propriety's" sake—if he were going to be jealous and meddling. The idea was too tiresome, and if it had been confirmed it would speedily have brought our acquaintance to a close. But I soon saw there was nothing in it and that if he accompanied Mrs. Monarch it was (in addition to the chance of being wanted), simply because he had nothing else to do. When she was away from him his occupation was gone—she never *had* been away from him. I judged, rightly, that in their awkward situation their close union was their main comfort and that this union had no weak spot. It was a real marriage, an encouragement to the hesitating, a nut for pessimists to crack. Their address was humble (I remember afterwards thinking it had been the only thing about them that was really professional), and I could fancy the lamentable lodgings in which the Major would have been left alone. He could bear them with his wife—he couldn't bear them without her.

He had too much tact to try and make himself agreeable when he couldn't be useful; so he simply sat and waited, when I was too absorbed in my work to talk. But I liked to make him talk—it made my work, when it didn't interrupt it, less sordid, less special. To listen to him was to combine the excitement of going out with the economy of staying at home. There was only one hindrance: that I seemed not to know any of the people he and his wife had known. I think he wondered extremely, during the term of our intercourse, whom the deuce I *did* know. He hadn't a stray sixpence of an idea to fumble for; so we didn't spin it very fine—we confined ourselves to questions of leather and even of liquor (saddlers and breeches-makers and how to get good claret cheap), and matters like "good trains" and habits of small game. His lore on these last subjects was astonishing, he managed to interweave the stationmaster with the ornithologist. When he couldn't talk about greater things he could talk cheerfully about smaller, and since I couldn't accompany him into reminiscences of the fashionable world he could lower the conversation without a visible effort to my level.

So earnest a desire to please was touching in a man who could so easily have knocked one down. He looked after the fire and had an opinion on the draught of the stove, without my asking him, and I could see that he thought many of my arrangements not half clever enough. I remember telling him that if I were only rich I would offer him a salary to come and teach me how to live. Sometimes he gave a random sigh, of which the essence was: "Give me even such a bare old barrack as *this*, and I'd do something with it!" When I wanted to use him he came alone; which was an illustration of the superior courage of women. His wife could bear her solitary second floor, and she was in general

more discreet; showing by various small reserves that she was
alive to the propriety of keeping our relations markedly professional—not letting them slide into sociability. She wished it
to remain clear that she and the Major were employed, not
cultivated, and if she approved of me as a superior, who could
be kept in his place, she never thought me quite good enough for
an equal.

She sat with great intensity, giving the whole of her mind to
it, and was capable of remaining for an hour almost as motionless as if she were before a photographer's lens. I could see she
had been photographed often, but somehow the very habit that
made her good for that purpose unfitted her for mine. At first I
was extremely pleased with her lady-like air, and it was a
satisfaction, on coming to follow her lines, to see how good they
were and how far they could lead the pencil. But after a few
times I began to find her too insurmountably stiff; do what I
would with it my drawing looked like a photograph or a copy of
a photograph. Her figure had no variety of expression—she
herself had no sense of variety. You may say that this was my
business, was only a question of placing her. I placed her in
every conceivable position, but she managed to obliterate their
differences. She was always a lady certainly, and into the bargain was always the same lady. She was the real thing, but
always the same thing. There were moments when I was op-
pressed by the serenity of her confidence that she *was* the real
thing. All her dealings with me and all her husband's were an
implication that this was lucky for *me*. Meanwhile I found
myself trying to invent types that approached her own, instead of
making her own transform itself—in the clever way that was not
impossible, for instance, to poor Miss Churm. Arrange as I
would and take the precautions I would, she always, in my
pictures, came out too tall—landing me in the dilemma of having
represented a fascinating woman as seven feet high, which, out
of respect perhaps to my own very much scantier inches, was far
from my idea of such a personage.

The case was worse with the Major—nothing I could do
would keep *him* down, so that he became useful only for the
representation of brawny giants. I adored variety and range, I
cherished human accidents, the illustrative note; I wanted to
characterise closely, and the thing in the world I most hated was
the danger of being ridden by a type. I had quarrelled with some
of my friends about it—I had parted company with them for
maintaining that one *had* to be, and that if the type was beautiful
(witness Raphael and Leonardo), the servitude was only a gain. I

was neither Leonardo nor Raphael; I might only be a presumptuous young modern searcher, but I held that everything was to be sacrificed sooner than character. When they averred that the haunting type in question could easily *be* character, I retorted, perhaps superficially: ''Whose?'' It couldn't be everybody's—it might end in being nobody's.

After I had drawn Mrs. Monarch a dozen times I perceived more clearly than before that the value of such a model as Miss Churm resided precisely in the fact that she had no positive stamp, combined of course with the other fact that what she did have was a curious and inexplicable talent for imitation. Her usual appearance was like a curtain which she could draw up at request for a capital performance. This performance was simply suggestive; but it was a word to the wise—it was vivid and pretty. Sometimes, even, I thought it, though she was plain herself, too insipidly pretty; I made it a reproach to her that the figures drawn from her were monotonously (*bêtement*, as we used to say) graceful. Nothing made her more angry; it was so much her pride to feel that she could sit for characters that had nothing in common with each other. She would accuse me at such moments of taking away her ''reputytion.''

It suffered a certain shrinkage, this queer quantity, from the repeated visits of my new friends. Miss Churm was greatly in demand, never in want of employment, so I had no scruple in putting her off occasionally, to try them more at my ease. It was certainly amusing at first to do the real thing—it was amusing to do Major Monarch's trousers. They *were* the real thing, even if he did come out colossal. It was amusing to do his wife's back hair (it was so mathematically neat,) and the particular ''smart'' tension of her tight stays. She lent herself especially to positions in which the face was somewhat averted or blurred; she abounded in lady-like back views and *profils perdus*. When she stood erect she took naturally one of the attitudes in which court-painters represented queens and princesses; so that I found myself wondering whether, to draw out this accomplishment, I couldn't get the editor of the *Cheapside* to publish a really royal romance, ''A Tale of Buckingham Palace.'' Sometimes, however, the real thing and the make-believe came into contact; by which I mean that Miss Churm, keeping an appointment or coming to make one on days when I had much work in hand, encountered her invidious rivals. The encounter was not on their part, for they noticed her no more than if she had been the housemaid; not from intentional loftiness, but simply because, as yet, professionally, they didn't know how to fraternise, as I could guess that they would have liked—or at least that the Major would. They couldn't talk about the omnibus—they always walked; and they didn't know what else to try—she wasn't interested in good trains or cheap claret. Besides, they must have felt—in the air—that she was amused at them, secretly derisive of their ever knowing how. She was not a person to conceal her scepticism if she had had a chance to show it. On the other hand Mrs. Monarch didn't think her tidy; for why else did she take pains to say to me (it was going out of the way, for Mrs. Monarch), that she didn't like dirty women?

One day when my young lady happened to be present with my other sitters (she even dropped in, when it was convenient, for a chat), I asked her to be so good as to lend a hand in getting tea—a service with which she was familiar and which was one of a class that, living as I did in a small way, with slender domestic resources, I often appealed to my models to render. They liked to lay hands on my property, to break the sitting, and sometimes the china—I made them feel Bohemian. The next time I saw Miss Churm after this incident she surprised me greatly by making a scene about it—she accused me of having wished to humiliate her. She had not resented the outrage at the time, but had seemed obliging and amused, enjoying the comedy of asking Mrs. Monarch, who sat vague and silent, whether she would have cream and sugar, and putting an exaggerated simper into the question. She had tried intonations—as if she too wished to pass for the real thing; till I was afraid my other visitors would take offence.

Oh, *they* were determined not to do this; and their touching patience was the measure of their great need. They would sit by the hour, uncomplaining, till I was ready to use them; they would come back on the chance of being wanted and would walk away cheerfully if they were not. I used to go to the door with them to see in what magnificent order they retreated. I tried to find other employment for them—I introduced them to several artists. But they didn't "take," for reasons I could appreciate, and I became conscious, rather anxiously, that after such disappointments they fell back upon me with a heavier weight. They did me the honour to think that it was I who was most *their* form. They were not picturesque enough for the painters, and in those days there were not so many serious workers in black and white. Besides, they had an eye to the great job I had mentioned to them—they had secretly set their hearts on supplying the right essence for my pictorial vindication of our fine novelist. They knew that for this undertaking I should want no costume-effects, none of the frippery of past ages—that it was a case in which everything would be contemporary and satirical and, presumably, genteel. If I could work them into it their future would be assured, for the labour would of course be long and the occupation steady.

One day Mrs. Monarch came without her husband—she explained his absence by his having had to go to the City. While she sat there in her usual anxious stiffness there came, at the door, a knock which I immediately recognised as the subdued appeal of a model out of work. It was followed by the entrance of a young man whom I easily perceived to be a foreigner and who proved in fact an Italian acquainted with no English word but my name, which he uttered in a way that made it seem to include all others. I had not then visited his country, nor was I proficient in his tongue; but as he was not so meanly constituted— what Italian is?—as to depend only on that member for expression he conveyed to me, in familiar but graceful mimicry, that he was in search of exactly the employment in which the lady before me was engaged. I was not struck with him at first, and while I continued to draw I emitted rough sounds of discouragement and dismissal. He stood his ground, however, not importunately, but with a dumb, dog-like fidelity in his eyes which amounted to innocent impudence—the manner of a devoted servant (he might have been in the house for years), unjustly suspected. Suddenly I saw that this very attitude and expression made a picture, whereupon I told him to sit down and wait till I should be free. There was another picture in the way he obeyed me, and I observed as I worked that there were others still in the way he looked wonderingly, with his head thrown back, about the high studio. He might have been crossing himself in St. Peter's. Before I finished I said to myself: "The fellow's a bankrupt orange-monger, but he's a treasure."

When Mrs. Monarch withdrew he passed across the room like a flash to open the door for her, standing there with the rapt, pure gaze of the young Dante spellbound by the young Beatrice. As I never insisted, in such situations, on the blankness of the British domestic, I reflected that he had the making of a servant (and I needed one, but couldn't pay him to be only that), as well as of a model; in short I made up my mind to adopt my bright adventurer if he would agree to officiate in the double capacity. He jumped at my offer, and in the event my rashness (for I had known nothing about him), was not brought home to me. He proved a sympathetic though desultory ministrant, and had in a wonderful degree the *sentiment de la pose*. It was uncultivated, instinctive; a part of the happy instinct which had guided him to my door and helped him to spell out my name on the card nailed to it. He had had no other introduction to me than a guess, from the shape of my high north window, seen outside, that my place was a studio, and that as a studio it would contain an artist. He had wandered to England in search of fortune, like other itinerants, and had embarked, with a partner and a small green handcart, on the sale of penny ices. The ices had melted away and the partner had dissolved in their train. My young man wore tight yellow trousers with reddish stripes and his name was Oronte. He was sallow but fair, and when I put him into some old clothes of my own he looked like an Englishman. He was as good as Miss Churm, who could look, when required, like an Italian.

IV

I thought Mrs. Monarch's face slightly convulsed when, on her coming back with her husband, she found Oronte installed. It was strange to have to recognise in a scrap of a lazzarone a competitor to her magnificent Major. It was she who scented danger first, for the Major was anecdotically unconscious. But Oronte gave us tea, with a hundred eager confusions (he had never seen such a queer process), and I think she thought better of me for having at last an "establishment." They saw a couple of drawings that I had made of the establishment, and Mrs. Monarch hinted that it never would have struck her that he had sat for them. "Now the drawings you make from *us*, they look exactly like us," she reminded me, smiling in triumph; and I recognised that this was indeed just their defect. When I drew the Monarchs I couldn't, somehow, get away from them—get into the character I wanted to represent; and I had not the least desire my model should be discoverable in my picture. Miss Churm never was, and Mrs. Monarch thought I hid her, very properly, because she was vulgar; whereas if she was lost it was only as the dead who go to heaven are lost—in the gain of an angel the more.

By this time I had got a certain start with "Rutland Ramsay," the first novel in the great projected series; that is I had produced a dozen drawings, several with the help of the Major and his wife, and I had sent them in for approval. My understanding with the publishers, as I have already hinted, had been that I was to be left to do my work, in this particular case, as I liked, with the whole book committed to me; but my connection with the rest of the series was only contingent. There were moments when, frankly, it *was* a comfort to have the real thing under one's hand; for there were characters in "Rutland Ramsay" that were very much like it. There were people presumably as straight as the Major and women of as good a fashion as Mrs. Monarch. There was a great deal of country-house life—treated, it is true, in a fine, fanciful, ironical, generalised way—and there was a considerable implication of knickerbockers and kilts. There were certain things I had to settle at the outset; such things for instance as the exact appearance of the hero, the particular bloom of the heroine. The author of course gave me a lead, but there was a margin for interpretation. I took the Monarchs into my confidence, I told them frankly what I was about, I mentioned my embarrassments and alternatives. "Oh, take *him!*" Mrs. Monarch murmured sweetly, looking at her husband; and "What could you want better than my wife?" the Major inquired, with the comfortable candour that now prevailed between us.

I was not obliged to answer these remarks—I was only obliged to place my sitters. I was not easy in mind, and I postponed, a little timidly perhaps, the solution of the question. The book was a large canvas, the other figures were numerous, and I worked off at first some of the episodes in which the hero and the heroine were not concerned. When once I had set *them* up I should have to stick to them—I couldn't make my young man seven feet high in one place and five feet nine in another. I inclined on the whole to the latter measurement, though the Major more than once reminded me that *he* looked about as young as anyone. It was indeed quite possible to arrange him, for the figure, so that it would have been difficult to detect his age. After the spontaneous Oronte had been with me a month, and after I had given him to understand several different times that his native exuberance would presently constitute an insurmountable barrier to our further intercourse, I waked to a sense of his heroic capacity. He was only five feet seven, but the remaining inches were latent. I tried him almost secretly at first, for I was really rather afraid of the judgment my other models would pass on such a choice. If they regarded Miss Churm as little better than a snare, what would they think of the representation by a person so little the real thing as an Italian street-vendor of a protagonist formed by a public school?

If I went a little in fear of them it was not because they bullied me, because they had got an oppressive foothold, but because in their really pathetic decorum and mysteriously permanent newness they counted on me so intensely. I was therefore very glad when Jack Hawley came home: he was always of such good counsel.

He painted badly himself, but there was no one like him for putting his finger on the place. He had been absent from England for a year; he had been somewhere—I don't remember where—to get a fresh eye. I was in a good deal of dread of any such organ, but we were old friends; he had been away for months and a sense of emptiness was creeping into my life. I hadn't dodged a missile for a year.

He came back with a fresh eye, but with the same old black velvet blouse, and the first evening he spent in my studio we smoked cigarettes till the small hours. He had done no work himself, he had only got the eye; so the field was clear for the production of my little things. He wanted to see what I had done for the *Cheapside*, but he was disappointed in the exhibition. That at least seemed the meaning of two or three comprehensive groans which, as he lounged on my big divan, on a folded leg, looking at my latest drawings, issued from his lips with the smoke of the cigarette.

"What's the matter with you?" I asked.

"What's the matter with *you?*"

"Nothing save that I'm mystified."

"You are indeed. You're quite off the hinge. What's the meaning of this new fad?" And he tossed me, with visible irreverence, a drawing in which I happened to have depicted both my majestic models. I asked if he didn't think it good, and he replied that it struck him as execrable, given the sort of thing I had always represented myself to him as wishing to arrive at; but I let that pass, I was so anxious to see exactly what he meant. The two figures in the picture looked colossal, but I supposed this was *not* what he meant, inasmuch as, for aught he knew to the contrary, I might have been trying for that. I maintained that I was working exactly in the same way as when he last had done me the honour to commend me. "Well, there's a big hole somewhere," he answered; "wait a bit and I'll discover it." I depended upon him to do so: where else was the fresh eye? But he produced at last nothing more luminous than "I don't know—I don't like your types." This was lame, for a critic who had never consented to discuss with me anything but the question of execution, the direction of strokes and the mystery of values.

"In the drawings you've been looking at I think my types are very handsome."

"Oh, they won't do!"

"I've had a couple of new models."

"I see you have. *They* won't do."

"Are you very sure of that?"

"Absolutely—they're stupid."

"You mean *I* am—for I ought to get round that."

"You *can't*—with such people. Who are they?"

I told him, as far as was necessary, and he declared, heartlessly:
"Ce sont des gens qu'il faut mettre à la porte."

"You've never seen them; they're awfully good," I compassionately objected.

"Not seen them? Why, all this recent work of yours drops to
pieces with them. It's all I want to see of them."

"No one else has said anything against it—the *Cheapside*
people are pleased."

"Everyone else is an ass, and the *Cheapside* people the biggest asses of all. Come, don't pretend, at this time of day, to
have pretty illusions about the public, especially about publishers
and editors. It's not for *such* animals you work—it's for those
who know, *coloro che sanno;* so keep straight for *me* if you
can't keep straight for yourself. There's a certain sort of thing
you tried for from the first—and a very good thing it is. But this
twaddle isn't *in* it." When I talked with Hawley later about
"Rutland Ramsay" and its possible successors he declared that I
must get back into my boat again or I would go to the bottom.
His voice in short was the voice of warning.

I noted the warning, but I didn't turn my friends out of doors.
They bored me a good deal; but the very fact that they bored me
admonished me not to sacrifice them—if there was anything to
be done with them—simply to irritation. As I look back at this
phase they seem to me to have pervaded my life not a little. I
have a vision of them as most of the time in my studio, seated,
against the wall, on an old velvet bench to be out of the way,
and looking like a pair of patient courtiers in a royal ante-
chamber. I am convinced that during the coldest weeks of the
winter they held their ground because it saved them fire. Their
newness was losing its gloss, and it was impossible not to feel
that they were objects of charity. Whenever Miss Churm arrived
they went away, and after I was fairly launched in "Rutland
Ramsay" Miss Churm arrived pretty often. They managed to
express to me tacitly that they supposed I wanted her for the low
life of the book, and I let them suppose it, since they had
attempted to study the work—it was lying about the studio—
without discovering that it dealt only with the highest circles.
They had dipped into the most brilliant of our novelists without
deciphering many passages. I still took an hour from them, now
and again, in spite of Jack Hawley's warning: it would be time
enough to dismiss them, if dismissal should be necessary, when

the rigour of the season was over. Hawley had made their
acquaintance—he had met them at my fireside—and thought
them a ridiculous pair. Learning that he was a painter they tried
to approach him, to show him too that they were the real thing;
but he looked at them, across the big room, as if they were miles
away: they were a compendium of everything that he most
objected to in the social system of his country. Such people as
that, all convention and patent-leather, with ejaculations that
stopped conversation, had no business in a studio. A studio was
a place to learn to see, and how could you see through a pair of
feather beds?

The main inconvenience I suffered at their hands was that, at
first, I was shy of letting them discover how my artful little
servant had begun to sit to me for "Rutland Ramsay." They
knew that I had been odd enough (they were prepared by this
time to allow oddity to artists,) to pick a foreign vagabond out of
the streets, when I might have had a person with whiskers and
credentials; but it was some time before they learned how high I
rated his accomplishments. They found him in an attitude more
than once, but they never doubted I was doing him as an
organ-grinder. There were several things they never guessed, and
one of them was that for a striking scene in the novel, in which a
footman briefly figured, it occurred to me to make use of Major
Monarch as the menial. I kept putting this off, I didn't like to ask
him to don the livery—besides the difficulty of finding a livery
to fit him. At last, one day late in the winter, when I was at work
on the despised Oronte (he caught one's idea in an instant), and was
in the glow of feeling that I was going very straight, they came
in, the Major and his wife, with their society laugh about nothing
(there was less and less to laugh at), like country-callers—they
always reminded me of that—who have walked across the park
after church and are presently persuaded to stay to luncheon.
Luncheon was over, but they could stay to tea—I knew they
wanted it. The fit was on me, however, and I couldn't let my
ardour cool and my work wait, with the fading daylight, while
my model prepared it. So I asked Mrs. Monarch if she would
mind laying it out—a request which, for an instant, brought all
the blood to her face. Her eyes were on her husband's for a
second, and some mute telegraphy passed between them. Their
folly was over the next instant; his cheerful shrewdness put an
end to it. So far from pitying their wounded pride, I must add, I
was moved to give it as complete a lesson as I could. They
bustled about together and got out the cups and saucers and made
the kettle boil. I know they felt as if they were waiting on my

servant, and when the tea was prepared I said: "He'll have a cup, please—he's tired." Mrs. Monarch brought him one where he stood, and he took it from her as if he had been a gentleman at a party, squeezing a crush-hat with an elbow.

Then it came over me that she had made a great effort for me—made it with a kind of nobleness—and that I owed her a compensation. Each time I saw her after this I wondered what the compensation could be. I couldn't go on doing the wrong thing to oblige them. Oh, it *was* the wrong thing, the stamp of the work for which they sat—Hawley was not the only person to say it now. I sent in a large number of the drawings I had made for "Rutland Ramsay," and I received a warning that was more to the point than Hawley's. The artistic adviser of the house for which I was working was of opinion that many of my illustrations were not what had been looked for. Most of these illustrations were the subjects in which the Monarchs had figured. Without going into the question of what *had* been looked for, I saw at this rate I shouldn't get the other books to do. I hurled myself in despair upon Miss Churm, I put her through all her paces. I not only adopted Oronte publicly as my hero, but one morning when the Major looked in to see if I didn't require him to finish a figure for the *Cheapside,* for which he had begun to sit the week before, I told him that I had changed my mind—I would do the drawing from my man. At this my visitor turned pale and stood looking at me. "Is *he* your idea of an English gentleman?" he asked.

I was disappointed, I was nervous, I wanted to get on with my work; so I replied with irritation: "Oh, my dear Major—I can't be ruined for *you!*"

He stood another moment; then, without a word, he quitted the studio. I drew a long breath when he was gone, for I said to myself that I shouldn't see him again. I had not told him definitely that I was in danger of having my work rejected, but I was vexed at his not having felt the catastrophe in the air, read with me the moral of our fruitless collaboration, the lesson that, in the deceptive atmosphere of art, even the highest respectability may fail of being plastic.

I didn't owe my friends money, but I did see them again. They re-appeared together, three days later, and under the circumstances there was something tragic in the fact. It was a proof to me that they could find nothing else in life to do. They had threshed the matter out in a dismal conference—they had digested the bad news that they were not in for the series. If they were not useful to me even for the *Cheapside* their function

seemed difficult to determine, and I could only judge at first that
they had come, forgivingly, decorously, to take a last leave. This
made me rejoice in secret that I had little leisure for a scene; for I
had placed both my other models in position together and I was
pegging away at a drawing from which I hoped to derive glory.
It had been suggested by the passage in which Rutland Ramsay,
drawing up a chair to Artemisia's piano-stool, says extraordinary
things to her while she ostensibly fingers out a difficult piece of
music. I had done Miss Churm at the piano before—it was an
attitude in which she knew how to take on an absolutely poetic
grace. I wished the two figures to "compose" together, intensely,
and my little Italian had entered perfectly into my conception.
The pair were vividly before me, the piano had been pulled out;
it was a charming picture of blended youth and murmured love,
which I had only to catch and keep. My visitors stood and
looked at it, and I was friendly to them over my shoulder.

They made no response, but I was used to silent company and
went on with my work, only a little disconcerted (even though
exhilarated by the sense that *this* was at least the ideal thing), at
not having got rid of them after all. Presently I heard Mrs.
Monarch's sweet voice beside, or rather above me: " I wish her
hair was a little better done." I looked up and she was staring
with a strange fixedness at Miss Churm, whose back was turned
to her. "Do you mind my just touching it?" she went on—a
question which made me spring up for an instant, as with the
instinctive fear that she might do the young lady a harm. But she
quieted me with a glance I shall never forget—I confess I should
like to have been able to paint *that*—and went for a moment to
my model. She spoke to her softly, laying a hand upon her
shoulder and bending over her; and as the girl, understanding,
gratefully assented, she disposed her rough curls, with a few
quick passes, in such a way as to make Miss Churm's head twice
as charming. It was one of the most heroic personal services I
have ever seen rendered. Then Mrs. Monarch turned away with a
low sigh and, looking about her as if for something to do,
stooped to the floor with a noble humility and picked up a dirty
rag that had dropped out of my paint-box.

The Major meanwhile had also been looking for something to
do and, wandering to the other end of the studio, saw before him
my breakfast things, neglected, unremoved. "I say, can't I be
useful *here?*" he called out to me with an irrepressible quaver. I
assented with a laugh that I fear was awkward and for the next
ten minutes, while I worked, I heard the light clatter of china
and the tinkle of spoons and glass. Mrs. Monarch assisted her

husband—they washed up my crockery, they put it away. They wandered off into my little scullery, and I afterwards found that they had cleaned my knives and that my slender stock of plate had an unprecedented surface. When it came over me, the latent eloquence of what they were doing, I confess that my drawing was blurred for a moment—the picture swam. They had accepted their failure, but they couldn't accept their fate. They had bowed their heads in bewilderment to the perverse and cruel law in virtue of which the real thing could be so much less precious than the unreal; but they didn't want to starve. If my servants were my models, my models might be my servants. They would reverse the parts—the others would sit for the ladies and gentlemen, and *they* would do the work. They would still be in the studio—it was an intense dumb appeal to me not to turn them out. "Take us on," they wanted to say—"we'll do *anything*."

When all this hung before me the *afflatus* vanished—my pencil dropped from my hand. My sitting was spoiled and I got rid of my sitters, who were also evidently rather mystified and awestruck. Then, alone with the Major and his wife, I had a most uncomfortable moment. He put their prayer into a single sentence: "I say, you know—just let *us* do for you, can't you?" I couldn't—it was dreadful to see them emptying my slops; but I pretended I could, to oblige them, for about a week. Then I gave them a sum of money to go away; and I never saw them again. I obtained the remaining books, but my friend Hawley repeats that Major and Mrs. Monarch did me a permanent harm, got me into a second-rate trick. If it be true I am content to have paid the price—for the memory.

Charlotte Perkins Gilman
(1860–1935)

Born in Connecticut, Gilman's father was a grandson of Lyman Beecher (and a nephew of Henry Ward Beecher and of Harriet Beecher Stowe). He abandoned his family shortly after her birth; her mother lived a poverty-stricken and isolated life, an influence of obvious significance on Gilman's own life and career. Married at 24, to a painter, Charles Walter Stetson, Gilman suffered so severely from depression that she was placed under the care of the Philadelphia psychologist, Silas Weir Mitchell, himself a fine writer. His treatment was notably successful. She literally ran from her husband and her marriage, living in California for some years (and there supporting her mother). Many years later, in 1900, she married George Houghton Gilman, a first cousin and also a descendant of Lyman Beecher.

Much of her career was as a lecturer and writer on feminist themes. She published Women and Economics *(1898),* Concerning Children *(1900),* The Home: Its Work and Influence *(1903),* Human Work *(1904),* Manmade World *(1911), and* His Religion and Hers: A study of the Faith of Our Fathers and the Work of Our Mothers *(1923). ''The Yellow Wallpaper'' appeared in* The Forerunner, *a monthly magazine she edited and for which she wrote all the copy (1909-1916).* Herland, *a feminist utopian novel, appeared in 1915.*

THE YELLOW WALLPAPER

It is very seldom that mere ordinary people like John and myself secure ancestral halls for the summer.

A colonial mansion, a hereditary estate, I would say a haunted house and reach the height of romantic felicity—but that would be asking too much of fate!

Still I will proudly declare that there is something queer about it.

Else, why should it be let so cheaply? And why have stood so long untenanted?

John laughs at me, of course, but one expects that.

John is practical in the extreme. He has no patience with faith, an intense horror of superstition, and he scoffs openly at any talk of things not to be felt and seen and put down in figures.

John is a physician, and *perhaps*—(I would not say it to a living soul, of course, but this is dead paper and a great relief to my mind)—*perhaps* that is one reason I do not get well faster.

You see, he does not believe I am sick! And what can one do?

If a physician of high standing, and one's own husband, assures friends and relatives that there is really nothing the matter with one but temporary nervous depression—a slight hysterical tendency—what is one to do?

My brother is also a physician, and also of high standing, and he says the same thing.

So I take phosphates or phosphites—whichever it is—and tonics, and air and exercise, and journeys, and am absolutely forbidden to ''work'' until I am well again.

Personally, I disagree with their ideas.

Personally, I believe that congenial work, with excitement and change, would do me good.

But what is one to do?

I did write for a while in spite of them; but it *does* exhaust me a good deal—having to be so sly about it, or else meet with heavy opposition.

I sometimes fancy that in my condition, if I had less opposition and more society and stimulus—but John says the very worst thing I can do is to think about my condition, and I confess it always makes me feel bad.

So I will let it alone and talk about the house.

The most beautiful place! It is quite alone, standing well back from the road, quite three miles from the village. It makes me think of English places that you read about, for there are hedges and walls and gates that lock, and lots of separate little houses for the gardeners and people.

There is a *delicious* garden! I never saw such a garden—large and shady, full of box-bordered paths, and lined with long grape-covered arbors with seats under them.

There were greenhouses, but they are all broken now.

There was some legal trouble, I believe, something about the heirs and co-heirs; anyhow, the place has been empty for years.

That spoils my ghostliness, I am afraid, but I don't care—there is something strange about the house—I can feel it.

I even said so to John one moonlight evening, but he said what I felt was a draught, and shut the window.

I get unreasonably angry with John sometimes. I'm sure I never used to be so sensitive. I think it is due to this nervous condition.

But John says if I feel so I shall neglect proper self-control; so I take pains to control myself—before him, at least, and that makes me very tired.

I don't like our room a bit. I wanted one downstairs that opened onto the piazza and had roses all over the window, and such pretty old-fashioned chintz hangings! But John would not hear of it.

He said there was only one window and not room for two beds, and no near room for him if he took another.

He is very careful and loving, and hardly lets me stir without special direction.

I have a schedule prescription for each hour in the day; he takes all care from me, and so I feel basely ungrateful not to value it more.

He said he came here solely on my account, that I was to have perfect rest and all the air I could get. "Your exercise depends on your strength, my dear," said he, "and your food somewhat on your appetite; but air you can absorb all the time." So we took the nursery at the top of the house.

It is a big, airy room, the whole floor nearly, with windows that look all ways, and air and sunshine galore. It was nursery first, and then playroom and gymnasium, I should judge, for the windows are barred for little children, and there are rings and things in the walls.

The paint and paper look as if a boys' school had used it. It is stripped off—the paper—in great patches all around the head of my bed, about as far as I can reach, and in a great place on the other side of the room low down. I never saw a worse paper in my life. One of those sprawling, flamboyant patterns committing every artistic sin.

It is dull enough to confuse the eye in following, pronounced enough constantly to irritate and provoke study, and when you follow the lame uncertain curves for a little distance they suddenly commit suicide—plunge off at outrageous angles, destroy themselves in unheard-of contradictions.

The color is repellent, almost revolting: a smouldering unclean yellow, strangely faded by the slow-turning sunlight. It is a dull yet lurid orange in some places, a sickly sulphur tint in others.

No wonder the children hated it! I should hate it myself if I had to live in this room long.

There comes John, and I must put this away—he hates to have me write a word.

We have been here two weeks, and I haven't felt like writing before, since that first day.

I am sitting by the window now, up in this atrocious nursery, and there is nothing to hinder my writing as much as I please, save lack of strength.

John is away all day, and even some nights when his cases are serious.

I am glad my case is not serious!

But these nervous troubles are dreadfully depressing.

John does not know how much I really suffer. He knows there is no reason to suffer, and that satisfies him.

Of course it is only nervousness. It does weigh on me so not to do my duty in any way!

I meant to be such a help to John, such a real rest and comfort, and here I am a comparative burden already!

Nobody would believe what an effort it is to do what little I am able—to dress and entertain, and order things.

It is fortunate Mary is so good with the baby. Such a dear baby!

And yet I *cannot* be with him, it makes me so nervous.

I suppose John never was nervous in his life. He laughs at me so about this wallpaper!

At first he meant to repaper the room, but afterward he said that I was letting it get the better of me, and that nothing was worse for a nervous patient than to give way to such fancies.

He said that after the wallpaper was changed it would be the heavy bedstead, and then the barred windows, and then that gate at the head of the stairs, and so on.

"You know the place is doing you good," he said, "and really, dear, I don't care to renovate the house just for a three months' rental."

"Then do let us go downstairs," I said. "There are such pretty rooms there."

Then he took me in his arms and called me a blessed little goose, and said he would go down cellar, if I wished, and have it whitewashed into the bargain.

But he is right enough about the beds and windows and things.

It is as airy and comfortable a room as anyone need wish, and, of course, I would not be so silly as to make him uncomfortable just for a whim.

I'm really getting quite fond of the big room, all but that horrid paper.

Out of one window I can see the garden—those mysterious deep-shaded arbors, the riotous old-fashioned flowers, and bushes and gnarly trees.

Out of another I get a lovely view of the bay and a little private wharf belonging to the estate. There is a beautiful shaded lane that runs down there from the house. I always fancy I see people walking in these numerous paths and arbors, but John has cautioned me not to give way to fancy in the least. He says that with my imaginative power and habit of story-making, a nervous weakness like mine is sure to lead to all manner of excited fancies, and that I ought to use my will and good sense to check the tendency. So I try.

I think sometimes that if I were only well enough to write a little it would relieve the press of ideas and rest me.

But I find I get pretty tired when I try.

It is so discouraging not to have any advice and companionship about my work. When I get really well, John says we will ask Cousin Henry and Julia down for a long visit; but he says he would as soon put fireworks in my pillow-case as to let me have those stimulating people about now.

I wish I could get well faster.

But I must not think about that. This paper looks to me as if it *knew* what a vicious influence it had!

There is a recurrent spot where the pattern lolls like a broken neck and two bulbous eyes stare at you upside down.

I get positively angry with the impertinence of it and the everlastingness. Up and down and sideways they crawl, and those absurd unblinking eyes are everywhere. There is one place where two breadths didn't match, and the eyes go all up and down the line, one a little higher than the other.

I never saw so much expression in an inanimate thing before, and we all know how much expression they have! I used to lie awake as a child and get more entertainment and terror out of blank walls and plain furniture than most children could find in a toy-store.

I remember what a kindly wink the knobs of our big old bureau used to have, and there was one chair that always seemed like a strong friend.

I used to feel that if any of the other things looked too fierce I could always hop into that chair and be safe.

The furniture in this room is no worse than inharmonious, however, for we had to bring it all from downstairs. I suppose when this was used as a playroom they had to take the nursery things out, and no wonder! I never saw such ravages as the children have made here.

The wallpaper, as I said before, is torn off in spots, and it sticketh closer than a brother—they must have had perseverance as well as hatred.

Then the floor is scratched and gouged and splintered, the plaster itself is dug out here and there, and this great heavy bed, which is all we found in the room, looks as if it had been through the wars.

But I don't mind it a bit—only the paper.

There comes John's sister. Such a dear girl as she is, and so careful of me! I must not let her find me writing.

She is a perfect and enthusiastic housekeeper, and hopes for no better profession. I verily believe she thinks it is the writing which made me sick!

But I can write when she is out, and see her a long way off from these windows.

There is one that commands the road, a lovely shaded winding road, and one that just looks off over the country. A lovely country, too, full of great elms and velvet meadows.

This wallpaper has a kind of sub-pattern in a different shade, a particularly irritating one, for you can only see it in certain lights, and not clearly then.

But in the places where it isn't faded and where the sun is just so—I can see a strange, provoking, formless sort of figure that seems to skulk about behind that silly and conspicuous front design.

There's sister on the stairs!

Well, the Fourth of July is over! The people are all gone, and I am tired out. John thought it might do me good to see a little company, so we just had Mother and Nellie and the children down for a week.

Of course I didn't do a thing. Jennie sees to everything now.

But it tired me all the same.

John says if I don't pick up faster he shall send me to Weir Mitchell in the fall.

But I don't want to go there at all. I had a friend who was in his hands once, and she says he is just like John and my brother, only more so!

Besides, it is such an undertaking to go so far.

I don't feel as if it was worthwhile to turn my hand over for anything, and I'm getting dreadfully fretful and querulous.

I cry at nothing, and cry most of the time.

Of course I don't when John is here, or anybody else, but when I am alone.

And I am alone a good deal just now. John is kept in town very often by serious cases, and Jennie is good and lets me alone when I want her to.

So I walk a little in the garden or down that lovely lane, sit on the porch under the roses, and lie down up here a good deal.

I'm getting really fond of the room in spite of the wallpaper. Perhaps *because* of the wallpaper.

It dwells in my mind so!

I lie here on this great immovable bed—it is nailed down, I believe—and follow that pattern about by the hour. It is as good as gymnastics, I assure you. I start, we'll say, at the bottom, down in the corner over there where it has not been touched, and I determine for the thousandth time that I *will* follow that point-less pattern to some sort of a conclusion.

I know a little of the principle of design, and I know this thing was not arranged on any laws of radiation, or alternation, or repetition, or symmetry, or anything else that I ever heard of.

It is repeated, of course, by the breadths, but not otherwise.

Looked at in one way, each breadth stands alone; the bloated curves and flourishes—a kind of "debased Romanesque" with delirium tremens—go waddling up and down in isolated columns of fatuity.

But, on the other hand, they connect diagonally, and the sprawling outlines run off in great slanting waves of optic horror, like a lot of wallowing sea-weeds in full chase.

The whole thing goes horizontally, too, at least it seems so, and I exhaust myself trying to distinguish the order of its going in that direction.

They have used a horizontal breadth for a frieze, and that adds wonderfully to the confusion.

There is one end of the room where it is almost intact, and there, when the crosslights fade and the low sun shines directly upon it, I can almost fancy radiation after all—the interminable grotesque seems to form around a common center and rush off in headlong plunges of equal distraction.

It makes me tired to follow it. I will take a nap, I guess.

I don't know why I should write this.

I don't want to.

I don't feel able.

And I know John would think it absurd. But I *must* say what I feel and think in some way—it is such a relief!

But the effort is getting to be greater than the relief.

Half the time now I am awfully lazy, and lie down ever so much. John says I mustn't lose my strength, and has me take cod liver oil and lots of tonics and things, to say nothing of ale and wine and rare meat.

Dear John! He loves me very dearly, and hates to have me sick. I tried to have a real earnest reasonable talk with him the other day, and tell him how I wish he would let me go and make a visit to Cousin Henry and Julia.

But he said I wasn't able to go, nor able to stand it after I got there; and I did not make out a very good case for myself, for I was crying before I had finished.

It is getting to be a great effort for me to think straight. Just this nervous weakness, I suppose.

And dear John gathered me up in his arms, and just carried me upstairs and laid me on the bed, and sat by me and read to me till it tired my head.

He said I was his darling and his comfort and all he had, and that I must take care of myself for his sake, and keep well.

He says no one but myself can help me out of it, that I must use my will and self-control and not let any silly fancies run away with me.

There's one comfort—the baby is well and happy, and does not have to occupy this nursery with the horrid wallpaper.

If we had not used it, that blessed child would have! What a fortunate escape! Why, I wouldn't have a child of mine, an impressionable little thing, live in such a room for worlds.

I never thought of it before, but it is lucky that John kept me here after all; I can stand it so much easier than a baby, you see.

Of course I never mention it to them any more—I am too wise—but I keep watch for it all the same.

There are things in that wallpaper that nobody knows about but me, or ever will.

Behind that outside pattern the dim shapes get clearer every day.

It is always the same shape, only very numerous.

And it is like a woman stooping down and creeping about behind that pattern. I don't like it a bit. I wonder—I begin to think—I wish John would take me away from here!

It is so hard to talk with John about my case, because he is so wise, and because he loves me so.

But I tried it last night.

It was moonlight. The moon shines in all around just as the sun does.

I hate to see it sometimes, it creeps so slowly, and always comes in by one window or another.

John was asleep and I hated to waken him, so I kept still and watched the moonlight on that undulating wallpaper till I felt creepy.

The faint figure behind seemed to shake the pattern, just as if she wanted to get out.

I got up softly and went to feel and see if the paper *did* move and when I came back John was awake.

"What is it, little girl?" he said. "Don't go walking about like that—you'll get cold."

I thought it was a good time to talk, so I told him that I really was not gaining here, and that I wished he would take me away.

"Why, darling!" said he. "Our lease will be up in three weeks, and I can't see how to leave before.

"The repairs are not done at home, and I cannot possibly leave town just now. Of course, if you were in any danger, I could and would, but you really are better, dear, whether you can see it or not. I am a doctor, dear, and I know. You are gaining flesh and color, your appetite is better, I feel really much easier about you."

"I don't weigh a bit more," said I, "nor as much; and my appetite may be better in the evening when you are here but it is worse in the morning when you are away!"

"Bless her little heart!" said he with a big hug. "She shall be as sick as she pleases! But now let's improve the shining hours by going to sleep, and talk about it in the morning!"

"And you won't go away?" I asked gloomily.

"Why, how can I, dear? It is only three weeks more and then we will take a nice little trip of a few days while Jennie is getting the house ready. Really, dear, you are better!"

"Better in body perhaps—" I began, and stopped short, for he sat up straight and looked at me with such a stern, reproachful look that I could not say another word.

"My darling," said he, "I beg of you, for my sake and for our child's sake, as well as for your own, that you will never for one instant let that idea enter your mind! There is nothing so dangerous, so fascinating, to a temperament like yours. It is a false and foolish fancy. Can you not trust me as a physician when I tell you so?"

So of course I said no more on that score, and we went to sleep before long. He thought I was asleep first, but I wasn't, and lay there for hours trying to decide whether that front pattern and the back pattern really did move together or separately.

On a pattern like this, by daylight, there is a lack of sequence, a defiance of law, that is a constant irritant to a normal mind.

The color is hideous enough, and unreliable enough, and infuriating enough, but the pattern is torturing.

You think you have mastered it, but just as you get well under way in following, it turns a back-somersault and there you are. It slaps you in the face, knocks you down, and tramples upon you. It is like a bad dream.

The outside pattern is a florid arabesque, reminding one of a fungus. If you can imagine a toadstool in joints, an interminable string of toadstools, budding and sprouting in endless convolutions—why, that is something like it.

That is, sometimes!

There is one marked peculiarity about this paper, a thing nobody seems to notice but myself, and that is that it changes as the light changes.

When the sun shoots in through the east window—I always watch for that first long, straight ray—it changes so quickly that I never can quite believe it.

That is why I watch it always.

By moonlight—the moon shines in all night when there is a moon—I wouldn't know it was the same paper.

At night in any kind of light, in twilight, candlelight, lamplight, and worst of all by moonlight, it becomes bars! The outside pattern, I mean, and the woman behind it as plain as can be.

I didn't realize for a long time what the thing was that showed behind, that dim sub-pattern, but now I am quite sure it is a woman.

By daylight she is subdued, quiet. I fancy it is the pattern that keeps her so still. It is so puzzling. It keeps me quiet by the hour.

I lie down ever so much now. John says it is good for me, and to sleep all I can.

Indeed he started the habit by making me lie down for an hour after each meal.

It is a very bad habit, I am convinced, for you see, I don't sleep.

And that cultivates deceit, for I don't tell them I'm awake—oh, no!

The fact is I am getting a little afraid of John.

He seems very queer sometimes, and even Jennie has an inexplicable look.

It strikes me occasionally, just as a scientific hypothesis, that perhaps it is the paper!

I have watched John when he did not know I was looking, and come into the room suddenly on the most innocent excuses, and I've caught him several times *looking at the paper!* And Jennie too. I caught Jennie with her hand on it once.

She didn't know I was in the room, and when I asked her in a quiet, a very quiet voice, with the most restrained manner possible, what she was doing with the paper, she turned around as if she had been caught stealing, and looked quite angry—asked me why I should frighten her so!

Then she said that the paper stained everything it touched, that she had found yellow smooches on all my clothes and John's and she wished we would be more careful!

Did not that sound innocent? But I know she was studying that pattern, and I am determined that nobody shall find it out but myself!

Life is very much more exciting now than it used to be. You see, I have something more to expect, to look forward to, to watch. I really do eat better, and am more quiet than I was.

John is so pleased to see me improve! He laughed a little the other day, and said I seemed to be flourishing in spite of my wallpaper.

I turned it off with a laugh. I had no intention of telling him it was *because* of the wallpaper—he would make fun of me. He might even want to take me away.

I don't want to leave now until I have found it out. There is a week more, and I think that will be enough.

I'm feeling so much better!

I don't sleep much at night, for it is so interesting to watch developments; but I sleep a good deal during the daytime.

In the daytime it is tiresome and perplexing.

There are always new shoots on the fungus, and new shades of yellow all over it. I cannot keep count of them, though I have tried conscientiously.

It is the strangest yellow, that wallpaper! It makes me think of all the yellow things I ever saw—not beautiful ones like buttercups, but old, foul, bad yellow things.

But there is something else about that paper—the smell! I noticed it the moment we came into the room, but with so much air and sun it was not bad. Now we have had a week of fog and rain, and whether the windows are open or not, the smell is here.

It creeps all over the house.

I find it hovering in the dining-room, skulking in the parlor, hiding in the hall, lying in wait for me on the stairs.

It gets into my hair.

Even when I go to ride, if I turn my head suddenly and surprise it—there is that smell!

Such a peculiar odor, too! I have spent hours in trying to analyze it, to find what it smelled like.

It is not bad—at first—and very gentle, but quite the subtlest, most enduring odor I ever met.

In this damp weather it is awful. I wake up in the night and find it hanging over me.

It used to disturb me at first. I thought seriously of burning the house—to reach the smell.

But now I am used to it. the only thing I can think of that it is like is the *color* of the paper! A yellow smell.

There is a very funny mark on this wall, low down, near the mopboard. A streak that runs round the room. It goes behind every piece of furniture, except the bed, a long, straight, even *smooch*, as if it had been rubbed over and over.

I wonder how it was done and who did it, and what they did it for. Round and round and round—round and round and round—it makes me dizzy!

I really have discovered something at last.

Through watching so much at night, when it changes so, I have finally found out.

The front pattern *does* move—and no wonder! The woman behind shakes it!

Sometimes I think there are a great many women behind, and sometimes only one, and she crawls around fast, and her crawling shakes it all over.

Then in the very bright spots she keeps still, and in the very shady spots she just takes hold of the bars and shakes them hard.

And she is all the time trying to climb through. But nobody could climb through that pattern—it strangles so; I think that is why it has so many heads.

They get through, and then the pattern strangles them off and turns them upside down, and makes their eyes white!

If those heads were covered or taken off it would not be half so bad.

I think that woman gets out in the daytime!

And I'll tell you why—privately—I've seen her!

I can see her out of every one of my windows!

It is the same woman, I know, for she is always creeping, and most women do not creep by daylight.

I see her in that long shaded lane, creeping up and down. I see her in those dark grape arbors, creeping all around the garden.

I see her on that long road under the trees, creeping along, and when a carriage comes she hides under the blackberry vines.

I don't blame her a bit. It must be very humiliating to be caught creeping by daylight!

I always lock the door when I creep by daylight. I can't do it at night, for I know John would suspect something at once.

And John is so queer now that I don't want to irritate him. I wish he would take another room! Besides, I don't want anybody to get that woman out at night but myself.

I often wonder if I could see her out of all the windows at once.

But, turn as fast as I can, I can only see out of one at one time.

And though I always see her, she *may* be able to creep faster than I can turn! I have watched her sometimes away off in the open country, creeping as fast as a cloud shadow in a wind.

If only that top pattern could be gotten off from the under one! I mean to try it, little by little.

I have found out another funny thing, but I shan't tell it this time! It does not do to trust people too much.

There are only two more days to get this paper off, and I

believe John is beginning to notice. I don't like the look in his eyes.

And I heard him ask Jennie a lot of professional questions about me. She had a very good report to give.

She said I slept a good deal in the daytime.

John knows I don't sleep very well at night, for all I'm so quiet!

He asked me all sorts of questions, too, and pretended to be very loving and kind.

As if I couldn't see through him!

Still, I don't wonder he acts so, sleeping under this paper for three months.

It only interests me, but I feel sure John and Jennie are affected by it.

Hurrah! This is the last day, but it is enough. John is to stay in town over night, and won't be out until this evening.

Jennie wanted to sleep with me—the sly thing; but I told her I should undoubtedly rest better for a night all alone.

That was clever, for really I wasn't alone a bit! As soon as it was moonlight and that poor thing began to crawl and shake the pattern, I got up and ran to help her.

I pulled and she shook, I shook and she pulled, and before morning we had peeled off yards of that paper.

A strip about as high as my head and half around the room.

And then when the sun came and that awful pattern began to laugh at me, I declared I would finish it today!

We go away tomorrow, and they are moving all my furniture down again to leave things as they were before.

Jennie looked at the wall in amazement, but I told her merrily that I did it out of pure spite at the vicious thing.

She laughed and said she wouldn't mind doing it herself, but I must not get tired.

How she betrayed herself that time!

But I am here, and no person touches this paper but Me—not *alive*!

She tried to get me out of the room—it was too patent! But I said it was so quiet and empty and clean now that I believed I would lie down again and sleep all I could, and not to wake me even for dinner—I would call when I woke.

So now she is gone, and the servants are gone, and the things are gone, and there is nothing left but that great bedstead nailed down, with the canvas mattress we found on it.

We shall sleep downstairs tonight, and take the boat home tomorrow.

I quite enjoy the room, now it is bare again.

How those children did tear about here!

This bedstead is fairly gnawed!

But I must get to work.

I have locked the door and thrown the key down into the front path.

I don't want to go out, and I don't want to have anybody come in, till John comes.

I want to astonish him.

I've got a rope up here that even Jennie did not find. If that woman does get out, and tries to get away, I can tie her!

But I forgot I could not reach far without anything to stand on!

This bed will *not* move!

I tried to lift and push it until I was lame, and then I got so angry I bit off a little piece at one corner—but it hurt my teeth.

Then I peeled off all the paper I could reach standing on the floor. It sticks horribly and the pattern just enjoys it! All those strangled heads and bulbous eyes and waddling fungus growths just shriek with derision!

I am getting angry enough to do something desperate. To jump out of the window would be admirable exercise, but the bars are too strong even to try.

Besides I wouldn't do it. Of course not. I know well enough that a step like that is improper and might be misconstrued.

I don't like to *look* out of the windows even—there are so many of those creeping women, and they creep so fast.

I wonder if they all come out of that wallpaper as I did?

But I am securely fastened now by my well-hidden rope—you don't get *me* out in the road there!

I suppose I shall have to get back behind the pattern when it comes night, and that is hard!

It is so pleasant to be out in this great room and creep around as I please!

I don't want to go outside. I won't, even if Jennie asks me to.

For outside you have to creep on the ground, and everything is green instead of yellow.

But here I can creep smoothly on the floor, and my shoulder just fits in that long smooch around the wall, so I cannot lose my way.

Why, there's John at the door!

It is no use, young man, you can't open it!

How he does call and pound!

Now he's crying to Jennie for an axe.

It would be a shame to break down that beautiful door!

"John, dear!" said I in the gentlest voice. "The key is down by the front steps, under a plantain leaf!"

That silenced him for a few moments.

Then he said, very quietly indeed, "Open the door, my darling!"

"I can't," said I. "The key is down by the front door under a plantain leaf!" And then I said it again, several times, very gently and slowly, and said it so often that he had to go and see, and he got it of course, and came in. He stopped short by the door.

"What is the matter?" he cried. "For God's sake, what are you doing!"

I kept on creeping just the same, but I looked at him over my shoulder.

"I've got out at last," said I, "in spite of you and Jane. And I've pulled off most of the paper, so you can't put me back!"

Now why should that man have fainted? But he did, and right across my path by the wall, so that I had to creep over him every time!

Sarah Orne Jewett
(1849–1909)

Born and raised in Maine, the daughter of a physician, Jewett published her first story, "Shore House," in The Atlantic *at age 19. She has recorded that much of her literary inspiration came from her reading of Harriet Beecher Stowe.* Deephaven *(1877), a collection of local color tales, established her reputation;* Play Days, *a book of stories for children, followed in 1878; and from 1879 to 1899 she published ten volumes of stories, including* A White Heron and Other Stories *(1886),* A Native of Winby and Other Tales *(1893), from which "The Flight of Betsey Lane" is taken, and her most famous book,* The Country of the Pointed Firs *(1896). In addition to poetry, collected posthumously as* Verses *(1916), she wrote a number of novels, including* A Country Doctor *(1884),* A Marsh Island *(1885), and a historical romance,* The Tory Lover *(1901). Her influence on other women writers was large: part of the technical underpinning of that influence can be seen in an 1871 diary entry, recording a bit of advice given her by her father. " 'A story should be managed so that it should suggest interesting things to the reader instead of the author's doing all the thinking for him' . . ." A slogan from Flaubert, posted where she could see it whenever she wrote, is also illuminating: "Ecrire la vie ordinaire comme on ecrit l'histoire." [Write ordinary life as one writes history.]*

THE FLIGHT
OF BETSEY LANE

I

One windy morning in May, three old women sat together near an open window in the shed chamber of Byfleet Poor-house. The wind was from the northwest, but their window faced the southeast, and they were only visited by an occasional pleasant waft of fresh air. They were close together, knee to knee, picking over a bushel of beans, and commanding a view of the dandelion-starred, green yard below, and of the winding, sandy road that led to the village, two miles away. Some captive bees were scolding among the cobwebs of the rafters overhead, or thumping against the upper panes of glass; two calves were bawling from the barnyard, where some of the men were at work loading a dump-cart and shouting as if every one were deaf. There was a cheerful feeling of activity, and even an air of comfort, about the Byfleet Poor-house. Almost every one was possessed of a most interesting past, though there was less to be said about the future. The inmates were by no means distressed or unhappy; many of them retired to this shelter only for the winter season, and would go out presently, some to begin such work as they could still do, others to live in their own small houses; old age had impoverished most of them by limiting their power of endurance; but far from lamenting the fact that they were town charges, they rather liked the change and excitement of a winter residence on the poor-farm. There was a sharp-faced, hard-worked young widow with seven children, who was an exception to the general level of society, because she deplored the change in her fortunes. The older women regarded her with suspicion, and were apt to talk about her in moments like this, when they happened to sit together at their work.

The three bean-pickers were dressed alike in stout brown ginghams, checked by a white line, and all wore great faded aprons of blue drilling, with sufficient pockets convenient to the right hand. Miss Peggy Bond was a very small, belligerent-looking person, who wore a huge pair of steel-bowed spectacles,

262

holding her sharp chin well up in air, as if to supplement an inadequate nose. She was more than half blind, but the spectacles seemed to face upward instead of square ahead, as if their wearer were always on the sharp lookout for birds. Miss Bond had suffered much personal damage from time to time, because she never took heed where she planted her feet, and so was always tripping and stubbing her bruised way through the world. She had fallen down hatchways and cellarways, and stepped composedly into deep ditches and pasture brooks; but she was proud of stating that she was upsighted, and so was her father before her. At the poor-house, where an unusual malady was considered a distinction, upsightedness was looked upon as a most honorable infirmity. Plain rheumatism, such as afflicted Aunt Lavina Dow, whose twisted hands found even this light work difficult and tiresome,—plain rheumatism was something of every-day occurrence, and nobody cared to hear about it. Poor Peggy was a meek and friendly soul, who never put herself forward; she was just like other folks, as she always loved to say, but Mrs. Lavina Dow was a different sort of person altogether, of great dignity and, occasionally, almost aggressive behavior. The time had been when she could do a good day's work with anybody: but for many years now she had not left the town-farm, being too badly crippled to work; she had no relations or friends to visit, but from an innate love of authority she could not submit to being one of those who are forgotten by the world. Mrs. Dow was the hostess and social lawgiver here, where she remembered every inmate and every item of interest for nearly forty years, besides an immense amount of town history and biography for three or four generations back.

She was the dear friend of the third woman. Betsey Lane; together they led thought and opinion—chiefly opinion—and held sway, not only over Byfleet Poor-farm, but also the selectmen and all others in authority. Betsey Lane had spent most of her life as aid-in-general to the respected household of old General Thornton. She had been much trusted and valued, and, at the breaking up of that once large and flourishing family, she had been left in good circumstances, what with legacies and her own comfortable savings; but by sad misfortune and lavish generosity everything had been scattered, and after much illness, which ended in a stiffened arm and more uncertainty, the good soul had sensibly decided that it was easier for the whole town to support her than for a part of it. She had always hoped to see something of the world before she died; she came of an adventurous, seafaring stock, but had never made a longer jour-

ney than to the towns of Danby and Northville, thirty miles
away.

They were all old women; but Betsey Lane, who was sixty-
nine, and looked much older, was the youngest. Peggy Bond
was far on in the seventies, and Mrs. Dow was at least ten years
older. She made a great secret of her years; and as she sometimes spoke of events prior to the Revolution with the assertion
of having been an eye-witness, she naturally wore an air of vast
antiquity. Her tales were an inexpressible delight to Betsey Lane,
who felt younger by twenty years because her friend and comrade was so unconscious of chronological limitations.

The bushel basket of cranberry beans was within easy reach and
each of the pickers had filled her lap from it again and again.
The shed chamber was not an unpleasant place in which to sit at
work, with its traces of seed corn hanging from the brown
crossbeams, its spare churns, and dusty loom, and rickety wool-
wheels, and a few bits of old furniture. In one far corner was a
wide board of dismal use and suggestion, and close beside it an
old cradle. There was a battered chest of drawers where the
keeper of the poor-house kept his garden-seeds, with the withered
remains of three seed cucumbers ornamenting the top. Nothing
beautiful could be discovered, nothing interesting, but there was
something usable and homely about the place. It was the favorite
and untroubled bower of the bean-pickers, to which they might
retreat unmolested from the public apartments of this rustic
institution.

Betsey Lane blew away the chaff from her handful of beans.
The spring breeze blew the chaff back again, and sifted it over
her face and shoulders. She rubbed it out of her eyes impatiently,
and happened to notice old Peggy holding her own handful high,
as if it were an oblation, and turning her queer, up-tilted head
this way and that, to look at the beans sharply, as if she were
first cousin to a hen.

"There, Miss Bond, 't is kind of botherin' work for you, ain't
it?" Betsey inquired compassionately.

"I feel to enjoy it, anything that I can do my own way so,"
responded Peggy. "I like to do my part. Ain't that old Mis'
Fales comin' up the road? It sounds like her step."

The others looked, but they were not farsighted, and for a
moment Peggy had the advantage. Mrs. Fales was not a favorite.

"I hope she ain't comin' here to put up this spring. I guess she
won't now, it's gettin' so late," said Betsey Lane. "She likes to
go rovin' soon as the roads is settled."

" 'T is Mis' Fales!" said Peggy Bond, listening with solemn anxiety. "There, do let's pray her by!"

"I guess she's headin' for her cousin's folks up Beech Hill way," said Betsey presently. "If she'd left her daughter's this mornin', she'd have got just about as far as this. I kind o' wish she had stepped in just to pass the time o'day, long's she wa'n't going to make no stop."

There was a silence as to further speech in the shed chamber; and even the calves were quiet in the barnyard. The men had all gone away to the field where corn-planting was going on. The beans clicked steadily into the wooden measure of the pickers' feet. Betsey Lane began to sing a hymn, and the others joined in as best they might, like autumnal crickets; their voices were sharp and cracked, with now and then a few low notes of plaintive tone. Betsey herself could sing pretty well, but the others could only make a kind of accompaniment. Their voices ceased altogether at the higher notes.

"Oh my! I wish I had the means to go to the Centennial," mourned Betsey Lane, stopping so suddenly that the others had to go on croaking and shrilling without her for a moment before they could stop. "It seems to me as if I can't die happy 'less I do," she added; "I ain't never seen nothin' of the world, an' here I be."

"What if you was as old as I be?" suggested Mrs. Dow pompously. "You've got time enough yet, Betsey; don't you go an' despair. I knowed of a woman that went clean round the world four times when she was past eighty, an' enjoyed herself real well. Her folks followed the sea; she had three sons an' a daughter married,—all shipmasters, and she'd been with her own husband when they was young. She was left a widder early, and fetched up her family herself,—a real stirrin', smart woman. After they'd got married off, an' settled, an' was doing well, she come to be lonesome; and first she tried to stick it out alone, but she wa'n't one that could; an' she got a notion she hadn't nothin' before her but her last sickness, and she wa'n't a person that enjoyed havin' other folks do for her. So one of her boys—I guess 't was the oldest—said he was going to take her to sea; there was ample room, an' he was sailin' a good time o' year for the Cape o' Good Hope an' way up to some o' them tea-ports in the Chiny Seas. She was all high to go, but it made a sight o' talk at her age; an' the minister made it a subject o' prayer the last Sunday, and all the folks took a last leave; but she said to some she'd fetch 'em home something real pritty, and so did. An' then they come home t' other way, round the Horn, an' she done so well, an' was such a sight o' company, the other child'n was jealous, an' she promised she'd go a v'y'ge long o' each on 'em. She was as sprightly a person as ever I see; an' could speak well o' what she'd seen.''

"Did she die to sea?" asked Peggy, with interest.

"No, she died to home between v'y'ges, or she'd gone to sea again. I was to her funeral. She liked her son George's ship the best; 't was the one she was going on to Callao. They said the men aboard all called her 'gran'ma'am,' an' she kep' 'em mended up, an' would go below and tend to 'em if they was sick. She might 'a' been alive an' enjoyin' of herself a good many years but for the kick of a cow; 't was a new cow out of a drove, a dreadful unruly beast.''

Mrs. Dow stopped for breath, and reached down for a new supply of beans; her empty apron was gray with soft chaff. Betsey Lane, still pondering on the Centennial, began to sing another verse of her hymn, and again the old women joined her. At this moment some strangers came driving round into the yard from the front of the house. The turf was soft, and our friends did not hear the horses' steps. Their voices cracked and quavered; it was a funny little concert, and a lady in an open carriage just below listened with sympathy and amusement.

II

"Betsey! Betsey! Miss Lane!" a voice called eagerly at the foot of the stairs that led up from the shed. "Betsey! There's a lady here wants to see you right away.''

Betsey was dazed with excitement, like a country child who knows the rare pleasure of being called out of school. "Lor', I ain't fit to go down, be I?" she faltered, looking anxiously at her friends; but Peggy was gazing even nearer to the zenith than usual, in her excited effort to see down into the yard, and Mrs. Dow only nodded somewhat jealously, and said that she guessed 't was nobody would do her any harm. She rose ponderously, while Betsey hesitated, being, as they would have said, all of a twitter. "It is a lady, certain," Mrs. Dow assured her; " 't ain't often there's a lady comes here.''

"While there was any of Mis' Gen'ral Thornton's folks left, I wa'n't without visits from the gentry," said Betsey Lane, turning back proudly at the head of the stairs, with a touch of old-world pride and sense of high station. Then she disappeared, and closed the door behind her at the stair-foot with a decision quite unwelcome to the friends above.

"She needn't 'a' been so dreadful 'fraid anybody was goin' to listen. I guess we've got folks to ride an' see us, or had once, if we hain't now," said Miss Peggy Bond, plaintively.

"I expect 't was only the wind shoved it to," said Aunt Lavina. "Betsey is one that gits flustered easier than some. I wish 't was somebody to take her off an' give her a kind of a good time; she's young to settle down 'long of old folks like us. Betsey's got a notion o' rovin' such as ain't my natur', but I should like to see her satisfied. She'd been a very understandin' person, if she had the advantages that some does."

" 'T is so," said Peggy Bond, tilting her chin high. "I suppose you can't hear nothin' they're saying? I feel my hearin' ain't up to whar it was. I can hear things close to me well as ever; but there, hearin' ain't everything; 't ain't as if we lived where there was more goin' on to hear. Seems to me them folks is stoppin' a good while."

"They surely be," agreed Lavina Dow.

"I expect it's somethin' particular. There ain't none of the Thornton folks left, except one o' the gran'darters, an' I've often heard Betsey remark that she should never see her more, for she lives to London. Strange how folks feels contented in them strayaway places off to the ends of the airth."

The flies and bees were buzzing against the hot windowpanes; the handfuls of beans were clicking into the brown wooden measure. A bird came and perched on the windowsill, and then flitted away toward the blue sky. Below, in the yard, Betsey Lane stood talking with the lady. She had put her blue drilling apron over her head, and her face was shining with delight.

"Lor', dear," she said, for at least the third time, "I remember ye when I first see ye; an awful pritty baby you was, an' they all said you looked just like the old gen'ral. Be you goin' back to foreign parts right away?"

"Yes, I'm going back; you know that all my children are there. I wish I could take you with me for a visit," said the charming young guest. "I'm going to carry over some of the pictures and furniture from the old house; I didn't care half so much for them when I was younger as I do now. Perhaps next summer we shall all come over for a while. I should like to see my girls and boys playing under the pines."

"I wish you re'lly was livin' to the old place," said Betsey Lane. Her imagination was not swift; she needed time to think over all that was being told her, and she could not fancy the two strange houses across the sea. The old Thornton house was to her mind the most delightful and elegant in the world.

"Is there anything I can do for you?" asked Mrs. Strafford kindly,—"anything that I can do for you myself, before I go away? I shall be writing to you, and sending some pictures of the children, and you must let me know how you are getting on."

"Yes, there is one thing, darlin'. If you could stop in the village an' pick me out a pritty, little, small lookin'-glass, that I can keep for my own an' have to remember you by. 'T ain't that I want to set me above the rest o' the folks, but I was always used to havin' my own when I was to your grandma's. There's very nice folks here, some on 'em, and I'm better off than if I was able to keep house; but sence you ask me, that's the only thing I keep cropin' about. What be you goin' right back for? ain't you goin' to see the great fair to Pheladelphy, that everybody talks about?"

"No," said Mrs. Strafford, laughing at this eager and almost convicting question. "No; I'm going back next week. If I were, I believe that I should take you with me. Good-by, dear old Betsey; you make me feel as if I were a little girl again; you look just the same."

For full five minutes the old woman stood out in the sunshine, dazed with delight, and majestic with a sense of her own consequence. She held something tight in her hand, without thinking what it might be; but just as the friendly mistress of the poor-farm came out to hear the news, she tucked the roll of money into the bosom of her brown gingham dress. " 'T was my dear Mis' Katy Strafford," she turned to say proudly. "She come way over from London; she's been sick; they thought the voyage would do her good. She said most the first thing she had on her mind was to come an' find me, and see how I was, an' if I was comfortable; an' now she's goin' right back. She's got two splendid houses; an' said how she wished I was there to look after things,—she remembered I was always her gran'ma's right hand. Oh, it does so carry me back, to see her! Seems if all the rest on 'em must be there together to the old house. There, I must go right up an' tell Mis' Dow an' Peggy."

"Dinner's all ready; I was just goin' to blow the horn for the men-folks," said the keeper's wife. "They'll be right down. I expect you've got along smart with them beans,—all three of you together;" but Betsey's mind roved so high and so far at that moment that no achievements of bean-picking could lure it back.

III

The long table in the great kitchen soon gathered its company of waifs and strays,—creatures of improvidence and misfortune, and the irreparable victims of old age. The dinner was satisfactory, and there was not much delay for conversation. Peggy Bond and Mrs. Dow and Betsey Lane always sat together at one end, with an air of putting the rest of the company below the salt. Betsey was still flushed with excitement; in fact, she could not eat as much as usual, and she looked up from time to time expectantly, as if she were likely to be asked to speak of her guest; but everybody was hungry, and even Mrs. Dow broke in upon some attempted confidences by asking inopportunely for a second potato. There were nearly twenty at the table, counting the keeper and his wife and two children, noisy little persons who had come from school with the small flock belonging to the poor widow, who sat just opposite our friends. She finished her dinner before any one else, and pushed her chair back; she always helped with the housework,—a thin, sorry, bad-tempered-looking poor soul, whom grief had sharpened instead of softening. "I expect you feel too fine to set with common folks," she said enviously to Betsey.

"Here I be a-settin'," responded Betsey calmly. "I don' know's I behave more unbecomin' than usual." Betsey prided herself upon her good and proper manners; but the rest of the company, who would have liked to hear the bit of morning news, were now defrauded of that pleasure. The wrong note had been struck; there was a silence after the clatter of knives and plates, and one by one the cheerful town charges disappeared. The bean-picking had been finished, and there was a call for any of the women who felt like planting corn; so Peggy Bond, who could follow the line of hills pretty fairly, and Betsey herself, who was still equal to anybody at that work, and Mrs. Dow, all went out to the field together. Aunt Lavina labored slowly up the yard, carrying a light splint-bottomed kitchen chair and her knitting-work, and sat near the stone wall on a gentle rise, where she could see the pond and the green country, and exchange a word with her friends as they came and went up and down the rows. Betsey vouchsafed a word now and then about Mrs. Strafford, but you would have thought that she had been suddenly elevated to Mrs. Strafford's own cares and the responsibilities attending them, and had little in common with her old associates. Mrs. Dow and Peggy knew well that these high-feeling times never lasted long, and so they waited with as much patience as they could muster. They were by no means without that true tact which is only another word for unselfish sympathy.

The strip of corn land ran along the side of a great field; at the upper end of it was a field-corner thicket of young maples and walnut saplings, the children of a great nut-tree that marked the boundary. Once, when Betsey Lane found herself alone near this shelter at the end of her row, the other planters having lagged behind beyond the rising ground, she looked stealthily about, and then put her hand inside her gown, and for the first time took out the money that Mrs. Strafford had given her. She turned it over and over with an astonished look: there were new bank-bills for a hundred dollars. Betsey gave a funny little shrug of her shoulders, came out of the bushes, and took a step or two on the narrow edge of turf, as if she were going to dance; then she hastily tucked away her treasure, and stepped discreetly down into the soft harrowed and hoed land, and began to drop corn again, five kernels to a hill. She had seen the top of Peggy Bond's head over the knoll, and now Peggy herself came entirely into view, gazing upward to the skies, and stumbling more or less, but counting the corn by touch and twisting her head about anxiously to gain advantage over her uncertain vision. Betsey made a friendly, inarticulate little sound as they passed; she was thinking that somebody said once that Peggy's eyesight might be remedied if she could go to Boston to the hospital; but that was so remote and impossible an undertaking that no one had ever taken the first step. Betsey Lane's brown old face suddenly worked with excitement, but in a moment more she regained her usual firm expression, and spoke carelessly to Peggy as she turned and came alongside.

The high spring wind of the morning had quite fallen; it was a lovely May afternoon. The woods about the field to the northward were full of birds, and the young leaves scarcely hid the solemn shapes of a company of crows that patiently attended the corn-planting. Two of the men had finished their hoeing, and were busy with the construction of a scarecrow; they knelt in the furrows, chuckling, and looking over some forlorn, discarded garments. It was a time-honored custom to make the scarecrow resemble one of the poor-house family; and this year they intended to have Mrs. Lavina Dow protect the field in effigy; last year it was the counterfeit of Betsey Lane who stood on guard, with an easily recognized quilted hood and the remains of a valued shawl that one of the calves had found airing on a fence and chewed to pieces. Behind the men was the foundation for this rustic attempt at statuary,—an upright stake and bar in the form of a cross. This stood on the highest part of the field; and as the men knelt near it, and the quaint figures of the corn-planters went and came, the scene gave a curious suggestion of foreign life. It was not like New England; the presence of the rude cross appealed strangely to the imagination.

IV

Life flowed so smoothly, for the most part, at the Byfleet Poor-farm, that nobody knew what to make, later in the summer, of a strange disappearance. All the elder inmates were familiar with illness and death, and the poor pomp of a town-pauper's funeral. The comings and goings and the various misfortunes of those who composed this strange family, related only through its disasters, hardly served for the excitement and talk of a single day. Now that the June days were at their longest, the old people were sure to wake earlier than ever; but one morning, to the astonishment of every one, Betsey Lane's bed was empty; the sheets and blankets, which were her own, and guarded with jealous care, were carefully folded and placed on a chair not too near the window, and Betsey had flown. Nobody had heard her go down the creaking stairs. The kitchen door was unlocked, and the old watch-dog lay on the step outside in the early sunshine, wagging his tail and looking wise, as if he were left on guard and meant to keep the fugitive's secret.

"Never knowed her to do nothin' afore 'thout talking it over a fortnight, and paradin' off when we could all see her," ventured a spiteful voice. "Guess we can wait till night to hear 'bout it."

Mrs. Dow looked sorrowful and shook her head. "Betsey had an aunt on her mother's side that went and drownded of herself; she was a pritty-appearing woman as ever you see."

"Perhaps she's gone to spend the day with Decker's folks," suggested Peggy Bond. "She always takes an extra early start; she was speakin' lately o' going up their way;" but Mrs. Dow shook her head with a most melancholy look. "I'm impressed that something's befell her," she insisted. "I heard her a-groanin' in her sleep. I was wakeful the fore-part o' the night,—'t is very unusual with me, too."

" 'T wa'n't like Betsey not to leave us any word," said the other old friend, with more resentment than melancholy. They sat together almost in silence that morning in the shed chamber. Mrs. Dow was sorting and cutting rags, and Peggy braided them into long ropes, to be made into mats at a later date. If they had only known where Betsey Lane had gone, they might have talked about it until dinner-time at noon; but failing this new subject, they could take no interest in any of their old ones. Out in the field the corn was well up, and the men were hoeing. It was a hot morning in the shed chamber, and the woolen rags were dusty and hot to handle.

v

Byfleet people knew each other well, and when this mysteriously absent person did not return to the town-farm at the end of a week, public interest became much excited; and presently it was ascertained that Betsey Lane was neither making a visit to her friends the Deckers on Birch Hill, nor to any nearer acquaintances; in fact, she had disappeared altogether from her wonted haunts. Nobody remembered to have seen her pass, hers had been such an early flitting; and when somebody thought of her having gone away by train, he was laughed at for forgetting that the earliest morning train from South Byfleet, the nearest station, did not start until long after eight o'clock; and if Betsey had designed to be one of the passengers, she would have started along the road at seven, and been seen and known of all women. There was not a kitchen in that part of Byfleet that did not have windows toward the road. Conversation rarely left the level of the neighborhood gossip: to see Betsey Lane, in her best clothes, at that hour in the morning, would have been the signal for much exercise of imagination; but as day after day went by without news, the curiosity of those who knew her best turned slowly into fear, and at last Peggy Bond again gave utterance to the belief that Betsey had either gone out in the early morning and put an end to her life, or that she had gone to the Centennial. Some of the people at table were moved to loud laughter,—it was at supper-time on a Sunday night,—but others listened with great interest.

"She never'd put on her good clothes to drownd herself," said the widow. "She might have thought 't was good as takin' 'em with her, though. Old folks has wandered off an' got lost in the woods afore now."

Mrs. Dow and Peggy resented this impertinent remark, but deigned to take no notice of the speaker. "She wouldn't have wore her best clothes to the Centennial, would she?" mildly inquired Peggy, bobbing her head toward the ceiling. " 'T would be a shame to spoil your best things in such a place. An' I don't know of her havin' any money; there's the end o' that."

"You're bad as old Mis' Bland, that used to live neighbor to our folks," said one of the old men. "She was dreadful precise; an' she so begretched to wear a good alapaca dress that was left to her, that it hung in a press forty year, an' baited the moths at last."

"I often seen Mis' Bland a-goin' in to meetin' when I was a young girl," said Peggy Bond approvingly. "She was a good-appearin' woman, an' she left property."

"Wish she'd left it to me, then," said the poor soul opposite, glancing at her pathetic row of children: but it was not good manners at the farm to deplore one's situation, and Mrs. Dow and Peggy only frowned. "Where do you suppose Betsey can be?" said Mrs. Dow, for the twentieth time. "She didn't have no money. I know she ain't gone far, if it's so that she's yet alive. She's b'en real pinched all the spring."

"Perhaps that lady that come one day give her some," the keeper's wife suggested mildly.

"Then Betsey would have told me," said Mrs. Dow, with injured dignity.

VI

On the morning of her disappearance, Betsey rose even before the pewee and the English sparrow, and dressed herself quietly, though with trembling hands, and stole out of the kitchen door like a plunderless thief. The old dog licked her hand and looked at her anxiously; the tortoise-shell cat rubbed against her best gown, and trotted away up the yard, then she turned anxiously and came after the old woman, following faithfully until she had to be driven back. Betsey was used to long country excursions afoot. She dearly loved the early morning; and finding that there was no dew to trouble her, she began to follow pasture paths and short cuts across the fields, surprising here and there a flock of sleepy sheep, or a startled calf that rustled out from the bushes. The birds were pecking their breakfast from bush and turf; and hardly any of the wild inhabitants of that rural world were enough alarmed by her presence to do more than flutter away if they chanced to be in her path. She stepped along, light-footed and eager as a girl, dressed in her neat old straw bonnet and black gown, and carrying a few belongings in her best bundle-handkerchief, one that her only brother had brought home from the East Indies fifty years before. There was an old crow perched as sentinel on a small, dead pine-tree, where he could warn friends who were pulling up the sprouted corn in a field close by;

but he only gave a contemptuous caw as the adventurer appeared, and she shook her bundle at him in revenge, and laughed to see him so clumsy as he tried to keep his footing on the twigs.

"Yes, I be," she assured him. "I'm a-goin' to Pheladelphy, to the Centennial, same's other folks. I'd jest as soon tell ye's not, old crow;" and Betsey laughed aloud in pleased content with herself and her daring, as she walked along. She had only two miles to go to the station at South Byfleet, and she felt for the money now and then, and found it safe enough. She took great pride in the success of her escape, and especially in the long concealment of her wealth. Not a night had passed since Mrs. Strafford's visit that she had not slept with the roll of money under her pillow by night, and buttoned safe inside her dress by day. She knew that everybody would offer advice and even commands about the spending or saving of it; and she brooked no interference.

The last mile of the foot-path to South Byfleet was along the railway track; and Betsey began to feel in haste, though it was still nearly two hours to train time. She looked anxiously forward and back along the rails every few minutes, for fear of being run over; and at last she caught sight of an engine that was apparently coming toward her, and took flight into the woods before she could gather courage to follow the path again. The freight train proved to be at a standstill, waiting at a turnout; and some of the men were straying about, eating their early breakfast comfortably in this time of leisure. As the old woman came up to them, she stopped too, for a moment of rest and conversation.

"Where be ye goin'?" she asked pleasantly; and they told her. It was to the town where she had to change cars and take the great through train; a point of geography which she had learned from evening talks between the men at the farm.

"What'll ye carry me there for?"

"We don't run no passenger cars," said one of the young fellows, laughing. "What makes you in such a hurry?"

"I'm startin' for Pheladelphy, an' it's a gre't ways to go."

"So 't is; but you're consid'able early, if you're makin' for the eight-forty train. See here! you haven't got a needle an' thread 'long of you in that bundle, have you? If you'll sew me on a couple o' buttons, I'll give ye a free ride. I'm in a sight o' distress, an' none o' the fellows is provided with as much as a bent pin."

"You poor boy! I'll have you seen to, in half a minute. I'm troubled with a stiff arm, but I'll do the best I can."

The obliging Betsey seated herself stiffly on the slope of the embankment, and found her thread and needle with utmost haste. Two of the train-men stood by and watched the careful stitches, and even offered her a place as spare brakeman, so they might keep her near; and Betsey took the offer with considerable seriousness, only thinking it necessary to assure them that she was getting most too old to be out in all weathers. An express went by like an earthquake, and she was presently hoisted on board an empty box-car by two of her new and flattering acquaintances, and found herself before noon at the end of the first stage of her journey, without having spent a cent, and furnished with any amount of thrifty advice. One of the young men, being compassionate of her unprotected state as a traveler, advised her to find out the widow of an uncle of his in Philadelphia, saying despairingly that he couldn't tell her just how to find the house; but Miss Betsey Lane said that she had an English tongue in her head, and should be sure to find whatever she was looking for. This unexpected incident of the freight train was the reason why everybody about the South Byfleet station insisted that no such person had taken passage by the regular train that same morning, and why there were those who persuaded themselves that Miss Betsey Lane was probably lying at the bottom of the poor-farm pond.

VII

"Land sakes!" said Miss Betsey Lane, as she watched a Turkish person parading by in his red fez, "I call the Centennial somethin' like the day o' judgment! I wish I was goin' to stop a month, but I dare say 't would be the death o' my poor old bones."

She was leaning against the barrier of a patent pop-corn establishment, which had given her a sudden reminder of home, and of the winter nights when the sharp-kerneled little red and yellow ears were brought out, and Old Uncle Eph Flanders sat by the kitchen stove, and solemnly filled a great wooden chopping-tray for the refreshment of the company. She had wandered and loitered and looked until her eyes and head had grown numb and unreceptive; but it is only unimaginative persons who can be really astonished. The imagination can always outrun the possible and actual sights and sounds of the world; and this plain old body from Byfleet rarely found anything rich and splendid enough to surprise her. She saw the wonders of the West and the splendors of the East with equal calmness and satisfaction; she had always known that there was an amazing world outside the boundaries of Byfleet. There was a piece of paper in her pocket on which was marked, in her clumsy handwriting, "If Betsey Lane should meet with accident, notify the selectmen of Byfleet;" but having made this slight provision for the future, she had thrown herself boldly into the sea of strangers, and then she had made the joyful discovery that friends were to be found at every turn.

There was something delightfully companionable about Betsey; she had a way of suddenly looking up over her big spectacles with a reassuring and expectant smile, as if you were going to speak to her, and you generally did. She must have found out where hundreds of people came from, and whom they had left at home, and what they thought of the great show, as she sat on a bench to rest, or leaned over the railings where free luncheons were afforded by the makers of hot waffles and molasses candy and fried potatoes; and there was not a night when she did not return to her lodgings with a pocket crammed with samples of spool cotton and nobody knows what. She had already collected small presents for almost everybody she knew at home, and she was such a pleasant, beaming old country body, so unmistakably appreciative and interested, that nobody ever thought of wishing that she would move on. Nearly all the busy people of the Exhibition called her either Aunty or Grandma at once, and made little pleasures for her as best they could. She was a delightful contrast to the indifferent, stupid crowd that drifted along, with eyes fixed at the same level, and seeing, even on that level, nothing for fifty feet at a time. "What be you making here, dear?" Betsey Lane would ask joyfully, and the most perfunctory guardian hastened to explain. She squandered money as she had never had the pleasure of doing before, and this hastened the day when she must return to Byfleet. She was always inquiring if there were any spectacle-sellers at hand, and received occasional directions; but it was a difficult place for her to find her way about in, and the very last day of her stay arrived before she found an exhibitor of the desired sort, an oculist and instrument-maker.

"I called to get some specs for a friend that's upsighted," she gravely informed the salesman, to his extreme amusement. "She's dreadful troubled, and jerks her head up like a hen a-drinkin'. She's got a blur a-growin' an' spreadin', an' sometimes she can see out to one side on 't, and more times she can't."

"Cataracts," said a middle-aged gentleman at her side; and Betsey Lane turned to regard him with approval and curiosity.

" 'T is Miss Peggy Bond I was mentioning, of Byfleet Poor-farm," she explained. "I count on gettin' some glasses to relieve her trouble, if there's any to be found."

"Glasses won't do her any good," said the stranger. "Suppose you come and sit down on this bench, and tell me all about it. First, where is Byfleet?" and Betsey gave the directions at length.

"I thought so," said the surgeon. "How old is this friend of yours?"

Betsey cleared her throat decisively, and smoothed her gown over her knees as if it were an apron; then she turned to take a good look at her new acquaintance as they sat on the rustic bench together. "Who be you, sir, I should like to know?" she asked, in a friendly tone.

"My name's Dunster."

"I take it you're a doctor," continued Betsey, as if they had overtaken each other walking from Byfleet to South Byfleet on a summer morning.

"I'm a doctor; part of one at least," said he. "I know more or less about eyes; and I spend my summers down on the shore at the mouth of your river; some day I'll come up and look at this person. How old is she?"

"Peggy Bond is one that never tells her age; 't ain't come quite up to where she'll begin to brag of it, you see," explained Betsey reluctantly; "but I know her to be nigh to seventy-six, one way or t' other. Her an' Mrs. Mary Ann Chick was same year's child'n, and Peggy knows I know it, an' two or three times when we've be'n in the buryin'-ground where Mary Ann lays an' has her dates right on her headstone, I couldn't bring Peggy to take no sort o' notice. I will say she makes, at times, a convenience of being upsighted. But there, I feel for her, —everybody does; it keeps her stubbin' an' trippin' against everything, beakin' and gazin' up the way she has to."

"Yes, yes," said the doctor, whose eyes were twinkling. "I'll come and look after her, with your town doctor, this summer, —some time in the last of July or first of August."

"You'll find occupation," said Betsey, not without an air of patronage. "Most of us to the Byfleet Farm has got our ails, now I tell ye. You ain't got no bitters that'll take a dozen years right off an ol' lady's shoulders?"

The busy man smiled pleasantly, and shook his head as he went away. "Dunster," said Betsey to herself, soberly committing the new name to her sound memory. "Yes, I mustn't forget to speak of him to the doctor, as he directed. I do' know now as Peggy would vally herself quite so much accordin' to, if she had her eyes fixed same as other folks. I expect there wouldn't been a smarter woman in town, though, if she'd had a proper chance. Now I've done what I set to do for her, I do believe, an' 't wa'n't glasses, neither. I'll git her a pritty little shawl with that money I laid aside. Peggy Bond ain't got a pritty shawl. I always wanted to have a real good time, an' now I'm havin' it.''

VIII

Two or three days later, two pathetic figures might have been seen crossing the slopes of the poor-farm field, toward the low shores of Byfleet pond. It was early in the morning, and the stubble of the lately mown grass was wet with rain and hindering to old feet. Peggy Bond was more blundering and liable to stray in the wrong direction than usual; it was one of the days when she could hardly see at all. Aunt Lavina Dow was unusually clumsy of movement, and stiff in the joints; she had not been so far from the house for three years. The morning breeze filled the gathers of her wide gingham skirt, and aggravated the size of her unwieldy figure. She supported herself with a stick, and trusted beside to the fragile support of Peggy's arm. They were talking together in whispers.

"Oh, my sakes!" exclaimed Peggy, moving her small head from side to side. "Hear you wheeze, Mis' Dow! This may be the death o' you; there, do go slow! You set here on the side-hill, an' le' me go try if I can see.''

"It needs more eyesight than you've got," said Mrs. Dow, panting between the words. "Oh! to think how spry I was in my young days, an' here I be now, the full of a door, an' all my complaints so aggravated by my size. 'T is hard! 't is hard! but I'm a-doin' of all this for pore Betsey's sake. I know they've all laughed, but I look to see her ris' to the top o' the pond this day,—'t is just nine days since she departed; an' say what they may, I know she hove herself in. It run in her family; Betsey had an aunt that done just so, an' she ain't be'n like herself, a-broodin' an' hivin' away alone, an' nothin' to say to you an' me that was always sich good company all together. Somethin' sprung her mind, now I tell ye, Mis' Bond.''

"I feel to hope we sha'n't find her, I must say," faltered Peggy. It was plain that Mrs. Dow was the captain of this doleful expedition. "I guess she ain't never thought o' drowndin' of herself, Mis' Dow; she's gone off a-visitin' way over to the other side o' South Byfleet; some thinks she's gone to the Centennial even now!''

"She hadn't no proper means, I tell ye," wheezed Mrs. Dow indignantly; "an' if you prefer that others should find her floatin' to the top this day, instid of us that's her best friends, you can step back to the house."

They walked on in aggrieved silence. Peggy Bond trembled with excitement, but her companion's firm grasp never wavered, and so they came to the narrow, gravelly margin and stood still. Peggy tried in vain to see the glittering water and the pond-lilies that starred it; she knew that they must be there; once, years ago, she had caught fleeting glimpses of them, and she never forgot what she had once seen. The clear blue sky overhead, the dark pine-woods beyond the pond, were all clearly pictured in her mind. "Can't you see nothin'?" she faltered; "I believe I'm wuss'n upsighted this day. I'm going to be blind."

"No," said Lavina Dow solemnly; "no, there ain't nothin' whatever, Peggy. I hope to mercy she ain't"—

"Why, whoever'd expected to find you 'way out here!" exclaimed a brisk and cheerful voice. There stood Betsey Lane herself, close behind them, having just emerged from a thicket of alders that grew close by. She was following the short way homeward from the railroad.

"Why, what's the matter, Mis' Dow? You ain't overdoin', be ye? an' Peggy's all of a flutter. What in the name o' natur' ails ye?"

"There ain't nothin' the matter, as I knows on," responded the leader of this fruitless expedition. "We only thought we'd take a stroll this pleasant mornin'," she added, with sublime self-possession. "Where've you be'n, Betsey Lane?"

"To Pheladelphy, ma'am," said Betsey, looking quite young and gay, and wearing a townish and unfamiliar air that upheld her words. "All ought to go that can; why, you feel's if you'd be'n all round the world. I guess I've got enough to think of and tell ye for the rest o' my days. I've always wanted to go somewheres. I wish you'd be'n there, I do so. I've talked with folks from Chiny an' the back o' Pennsylvany; and I see folks way from Australy that 'peared as well as anybody; an' I see how they made spool cotton, an' sights o' other things; an' I spoke with a doctor that lives down to the beach in the summer, an' he offered to come up 'long in the first of August, an' see what he can do for Peggy's eyesight. There was di'monds there as big as pigeon's eggs; an' I met with Mis' Abby Fletcher from South Byfleet depot; an' there was hogs there that weighed risin' thirteen hunderd"—

"I want to know," said Mrs. Lavina Dow and Peggy Bond, together.

"Well, 't was a great exper'ence for a person," added Lavina, turning ponderously, in spite of herself, to give a last wistful look at the smiling waters of the pond.

"I don't know how soon I be goin' to settle down," proclaimed the rustic sister of Sindbad. "What's for the good o' one's for the good of all. You just wait till we're setting together up in the old shed chamber! You know, my dear Mis' Katy Strafford give me a han'some present o' money that day she come to see me; and I'd be'n a-dreamin' by night an' day o' seein' that Centennial; and when I come to think on 't I felt sure somebody ought to go from this neighborhood, if 't was only for the good o' the rest; and I thought I'd better be the one. I wa'n't goin' to ask the selec'men neither. I've come back with one-thirty-five in money, and I see everything there, an' I fetched ye all a little somethin'; but I'm full o' dust now, an' pretty nigh beat out. I never see a place more friendly than Pheladelphy; but 't ain't natural to a Byfleet person to be always walkin' on a level. There, now, Peggy, you take my bundle-handkercher and the basket, and let Mis' Dow sag on to me. I'll git her along twice as easy."

With this the small elderly company set forth triumphant toward the poor-house, across the wide green field.

Grace Elizabeth King
(1851–1932)

Born and educated in New Orleans, at a French Creole school, King spoke English at home but drew much of her inspiration from such French writers as Guy de Maupassant. Something of an unreconstructed Confederate, she was fiercely Southern: she had been only 9 years old when her family fled from Northern-occupied New Orleans, and only 13 when the family returned, to years of comparative hard circumstances. Her fiction seems to have begun as a way of answering what she saw as the treachery of George W. Cable, who had, she said, "stabbed [New Orleans] in the back . . . in a dastardly way to please the Northern press." Using her Southern charm consciously and actively, she persuaded the visiting Charles Dudley Warner (1829-1900, friend and collaborator of Mark Twain, with whom, in 1873, he had written The Gilded Age*) to help her gain entry to that same Northern press, notably* Harper's. *"I am not a romanticist," she declared, "I am a realist* a la mode de la Nouvelle-Orleans *[according to the fashion/style of New Orleans]." Her stories are collected in* Monsieur Motte *(1888),* Tales of a Time and Place *(1892), and* Balcony Stories *(1893), from which "La Grande Demoiselle" is taken. She wrote novels, notably* The Pleasant Ways of St. Medard *(1916) and also a number of biographical and historical works, including* New Orleans, the Place and the People *(1895).*

LA GRANDE DEMOISELLE

That was what she was called by everybody as soon as she was
seen or described. Her name, besides baptismal titles, was Idalie
Sainte Foy Mortemart des Islets. When she came into society, in
the brilliant little world of New Orleans, it was the event of the
season, and after she came in, whatever she did became also
events. Whether she went, or did not go; what she said, or did
not say; what she wore, and did not wear—all these became
important matters of discussion, quoted as much or more than
what the president said, or the governor thought. And in those
days, the days of '59, New Orleans was not, as it is now, a
one-heiress place, but it may be said that one could find heir-
esses then as one finds typewriting girls now.

Mademoiselle Idalie received her birth, and what education
she had, on her parents' plantation, the famed old Reine Sainte
Foy place, and it is no secret that, like the ancient kings of
France, her birth exceeded her education.

It was a plantation, the Reine Sainte Foy, the richness and
luxury of which are really well described in those perfervid
pictures of tropical life, at one time the passion of philanthropic
imaginations, excited and exciting over the horrors of slavery.
Although these pictures were then often accused of being purposely
exaggerated, they seem now to fall short of, instead of surpassing,
the truth. Stately walls, acres of roses, miles of oranges, unmeas-
ured fields of cane, colossal sugar-house—they were all there,
and all the rest of it, with the slaves, slaves, slaves everywhere,
whole villages of Negro cabins. And there were also, most
noticeable to the natural, as well as to the visionary, eye—there
were the ease, idleness, extravagance, self-indulgence, pomp,
pride, arrogance, in short the whole enumeration, the moral *sine
qua non,* as some people considered it, of the wealthy slaveholder
of aristocratic descent and tastes.

What Mademoiselle Idalie cared to learn she studied, what she
did not she ignored; and she followed the same simple rule
untrammeled in her eating, drinking, dressing, and comportment
generally; and whatever discipline may have been exercised on
the place, either in fact or fiction, most assuredly none of it,

even so much as in a threat, ever attained her sacred person. When she was just turned sixteen, Mademoiselle Idalie made up her mind to go into society. Whether she was beautiful or not, it is hard to say. It is almost impossible to appreciate properly the beauty of the rich, the very rich. The unfettered development, the limitless choice of accessories, the confidence, the self-esteem, the sureness of expression, the simplicity of purpose, the ease of execution—all these produce a certain effect of beauty behind which one really cannot get to measure length of nose, or brilliancy of eye. This much can be said: there was nothing in her that positively contradicted any assumption of beauty on her part, or credit of it on the part of others. She was very tall and very thin with small head, long neck, black eyes, and abundant straight black hair,—for which her hair-dresser deserved more praise than she,—good teeth, of course, and a mouth that, even in prayer, talked nothing but commands; that is about all she had *en fait d'ornements,* as the modistes say. It may be added that she walked as if the Reine Sainte Foy plantation extended over the whole earth, and the soil of it were too vile for her tread. Of course she did not buy her toilets in New Orleans. Everything was ordered from Paris, and came as regularly through the custom-house as the modes and robes to the milliners. She was furnished by a certain house there, just as one of a royal family would be at the present day. As this had lasted from her layette up to her sixteenth year, it may be imagined what took place when she determined to make her début. Then it was literally, not metaphorically, *carte blanche,* at least so it got to the ears of society. She took a sheet of notepaper, wrote the date at the top, added, "I make my début in November," signed her name at the extreme end of the sheet, addressed it to her dressmaker in Paris, and sent it.

It was said that in her dresses the very handsomest silks were used for linings, and that real lace was used where others put imitation—around the bottoms of the skirts, for instance,—and silk ribbons of the best quality served the purposes of ordinary tapes; and sometimes the buttons were of real gold and silver, sometimes set with precious stones. Not that she ordered these particulars, but the dressmakers, when given *carte blanche* by those who do not condescend to details, so soon exhaust the outside limits of garments that perforce they take to plastering them inside with gold, so to speak, and, when the bill goes in, they depend upon the furnishings to carry out a certain amount of the contract in justifying the price. And it was said that these costly dresses, after being worn once or twice, were cast aside, thrown upon the floor, given to the Negroes—anything to get them out of sight. Not an inch of the real lace, not one of the jeweled buttons, not a scrap of ribbon, was ripped off to save. And it was said that if she wanted to romp with her dogs in all her finery, she did it; she was known to have ridden horseback, one moonlight night, all around the plantation in a white silk dinner-dress flounced with Alençon. And at night, when she came from the balls, tired, tired to death as only balls can render one, she would throw herself down upon her bed in her tulle skirts,—on top, or not, of the exquisite flowers, she did not care,—and make her maid undress her in that position; often having her bodices cut off her, because she was too tired to turn over and have them unlaced.

That she was admired, raved about, loved even, goes without saying. After the first month she held the refusal of half the beaux of New Orleans. Men did absurd, undignified, preposterous things for her; and she? Love? Marry? The idea never occurred to her. She treated the most exquisite of her pretenders no better than she treated her Paris gowns, for the matter of that. She could not even bring herself to listen to a proposal patiently; whistling to her dogs, in the middle of the most ardent protestations, or jumping up and walking away with a shrug of the shoulders, and a "Bah!"

Well! Every one knows what happened after '59. There is no need to repeat. The history of one is the history of all. But there was this difference—for there is every shade of difference in misfortune, as there is every shade of resemblance in happiness. Mortemart des Islets went off to fight. That was natural; his family had been doing that, he thought, or said, ever since Charlemagne. Just as naturally he was killed in the first engagement. They, his family, were always among the first killed; so much so that it began to be considered assassination to fight a duel with any of them. All that was in the ordinary course of events. One difference in their misfortunes lay in that after the city was captured, their plantation, so near, convenient, and rich in all kinds of provisions, was selected to receive a contingent of troops—a colored company. If it had been a colored company raised in Louisana it might have been different; and these Negroes mixed with the Negroes in the neighborhood,—and Negroes are no better than whites, for the proportion of good and bad among them,—and the officers were always off duty when they should have been on, and on when they should have been off.

One night the dwelling caught fire. There was an immediate

rush to save the ladies. Oh, there was no hesitation about that! They were seized in their beds, and carried out in the very arms of their enemies; carried away off to the sugar-house, and deposited there. No danger of their doing anything but keep very quiet and still in their *chemises de nuit*, and their one sheet apiece, which was about all that was saved from the conflagration—that is, for them. But it must be remembered that this is all hearsay. When one has not been present, one knows nothing of one's own knowledge; one can only repeat. It has been repeated, however, that although the house was burned to the ground, and everything in it destroyed, wherever, for a year afterward, a man of that company or of that neighborhood was found, there could have been found also, without search-warrant, property that had belonged to the Des Islets. That is the story; and it is believed or not, exactly according to prejudice.

How the ladies ever got out of the sugar-house, history does not relate; nor what they did. It was not a time for sociability, either personal or epistolary. At one offensive word your letter, and you, very likely, examined; and Ship Island for a hotel, with soldiers for hostesses! Madame Des Islets died very soon after the accident—of rage, they say; and that was about all the public knew.

Indeed, at that time the society of New Orleans had other things to think about than the fate of the Des Islets. As for *la grande demoiselle*, she had prepared for her own oblivion in the hearts of her female friends. And the gentlemen,—her *preux chevaliers*,—they were burning with other passions than those which had driven them to her knees, encountering a little more serious response than "bahs" and shrugs. And, after all, a woman seems the quickest thing forgotten when once the important affairs of life come to men for consideration.

It might have been ten years according to some calculations, or ten eternities,—the heart and the almanac never agree about time,—but one morning old Champigny (they used to call him Champignon) was walking along his levee front, calculating how soon the water would come over, and drown him out, as the Louisianians say. It was before a seven-o'clock breakfast, cold, wet, rainy, and discouraging. The road was knee-keep in mud, and so broken up with hauling that it was like walking upon waves to get over it. A shower poured down. Old Champigny was hurrying in when he saw a figure approaching. He had to stop to look at it, for it was worth while. The head was hidden by a green *barège* veil, which the showers had plentifully besprinkled with dew, a tall, thin figure. Figure! No; not even could it be called a figure: straight up and down, like a finger or a post; high-shouldered, and a step—a step like a plow-man's. No umbrella; no—nothing more, in fact. It does not sound so peculiar as when first related—something must be forgotten. The feet—oh, yes, the feet—they were like waffle-irons, or frying-pans, or anything of that shape.

Old Champigny did not care for women—he never had; they simply did not exist for him in the order of nature. He had been married once, it is true, about a half century before; but that was not reckoned against the existence of his prejudice, because he was *célibataire* to his finger-tips, as any one could see a mile away. But that woman intrigued him.

He had no servant to inquire from. He performed all of his own domestic work in the wretched little cabin that replaced his old home. For Champigny also belonged to the great majority of the *nouveaux pauvres*. He went out into the rice-field, where were one or two hands that worked on shares with him, and he asked them. They knew immediately; there is nothing connected with the parish that a field-hand does not know at once. She was the teacher of the colored public school some three or four miles away. "Ah," thought Champigny, "some Northern lady on a mission." He watched to see her return in the evening, which she did, of course; in a blinding rain. Imagine the green *barège* veil then; for it remained always down over her face.

Old Champigny could not get over it that he had never seen her before. But he must have seen her, and, with his abstraction and old age, not have noticed her, for he found out from the Negroes that she had been teaching four or five years there. And he found out also—how, is not important—that she was Idalie Sainte Foy Mortemart des Islets. *La grande demoiselle!* He had never known her in the old days, owing to his uncomplimentary attitude toward women, but he knew of her, of course, and of her family. It should have been said that his plantation was about fifty miles higher up the river, and on the opposite bank to Reine Sainte Foy. It seemed terrible. The old gentleman had had reverses of his own, which would bear the telling, but nothing was more shocking to him than this—that Idalie Sainte Foy Mortemart des Islets should be teaching a public colored school for—it makes one blush to name it—seven dollars and a half a month. For seven dollars and a half a month to teach a set of—well! He found out where she lived, a little cabin—not so much worse than his own, for that matter—in the corner of a field; no companion, no servant, nothing but food and shelter. Her clothes have been described.

Only the good God himself knows what passed in Champigny's mind on the subject. We know only the results. He went and married *la grande demoiselle*. How? Only the good God knows that too. Every first of the month, when he goes to the city to buy provisions, he takes her with him—in fact, he takes her everywhere with him.

Passengers on the railroad know them well, and they always have a chance to see her face. When she passes her old plantation *la grande demoiselle* always lifts her veil for one instant— the inevitable green *barège* veil. What a face! Thin, long, sallow, petrified! And the neck! If she would only tie something around the neck! And her plain, coarse cottonade gown! The Negro women about her were better dressed than she.

Poor old Champignon! It was not an act of charity to himself, no doubt cross and disagreeable, besides being ugly. And as for love, gratitude!

Harold Frederic
(1856–1898)

Son of a New York Central freight conductor who was killed in an accident when the boy was only 2, Frederic was raised in Utica and trained as a printer and photographer. From 1873 to 1875, he studied art and photography in Boston; later that year he became a journalist, a profession he practiced to the end of his life, becoming editor of the Albany, N.Y., Evening Journal *in 1882 (a paper founded by the famous editor-politician, Thurlow Weed [1797-1882]), and after 1884 the London correspondent of the New York* Times. *His novels include* Seth's Brother's Wife *(1887),* The Lawton Girl *(1890),* The Damnation of Theron Ware *(1896, his most famous book), and* The Market Place *(1899). "The War Widow" is taken from* The Copperhead and Other Stories *(1894). Frederic also wrote* The Young Emperor: William II of Germany *(1891) and* The New Exodus: A Study of Israel in Russia *(1892), the latter such an effective piece of reporting that the Czar personally banned Frederic from ever traveling again in his country.*

THE WAR WIDOW

I

Although we had been one man short all day, and there was a plain threat of rain in the hot air, everybody left the hayfield long before sundown. It was too much to ask of human nature to stay off up in the remote meadows, when such remarkable things were happening down around the house.

Marcellus Jones and I were in the pasture, watching the dog get the cows together for the homeward march. He did it so well and, withal, so willingly, that there was no call for us to trouble ourselves in keeping up with him. We waited instead at the open bars until the hay-waggon had passed through, rocking so heavily in the ancient pitch-hole as it did so that the driver was nearly thrown off his perch on the top of the high load. Then we put up the bars, and fell in close behind the haymakers. A rich cloud of dust far ahead on the road suggested that the dog was doing his work even too willingly, but for the once we feared no rebuke. Almost anything might be condoned that day.

Five grown-up men walked abreast down the highway, in the shadow of the towering waggon mow, clad much alike in battered straw hats, grey woollen shirts open at the neck, and rough old trousers bulging over the swollen, creased ankles of thick boots. One had a scythe on his arm; two others bore forks over their shoulders. By request, Hi Tuckerman allowed me to carry his sickle.

Although my present visit to the farm had been of only a few days' duration—and those days of strenuous activity darkened by a terrible grief—I had come to be very friendly with Mr. Tuckerman. He took a good deal more notice of me than the others did; and, when chance and leisure afforded, addressed the bulk of his remarks to me. This favouritism, though it fascinated me, was not without its embarrassing side. Hi Tuckerman had taken part in the battle of Gaines' Mill two years before, and had been shot straight through the tongue. One could still see the deep scar on each of his cheeks, a sunken and hairless pit in among his sandy beard. His heroism in the war, and his good qualities as a citizen, had earned for him the esteem of his neighbours, and they saw to it that he never wanted for work. But their present respect for him stopped short of the pretence that they enjoyed hearing him talk. Whenever he attempted conversation, people moved away, or began boisterous dialogues with one another to drown him out. Being a sensitive man, he had come to prefer silence to these rebuffs among those he knew. But he still had a try at the occasional polite stranger—and I suppose it was in this capacity that I won his heart. Though I never of my own initiative understood a word he said, Marcellus sometimes interpreted a sentence or so for me, and I listened to all the rest with a fraudulently wise face. To give only a solitary illustration of the tax thus levied on our friendship, I may mention that when Hi Tuckerman said "*Aah!*-ah-*aah*!-uh," he meant "Rappahannock," and he did this rather better than a good many other words.

"Rappahannock," alas! was a word we heard often enough in those days, along with Chickahominy and Rapidan, and that odd Chattahoochee, the sound of which raised always in my boyish mind the notion that the geography-makers must have achieved it in their baby-talk period. These strange Southern river names, and many more, were as familiar to the ears of these four other untravelled Dearborn County farmers as the noise of their own shallow Nedahma rattling over its pebbles in the valley yonder. Only when their slow fancy fitted substance to these names they saw in mind's eye dark, sinister, swampy currents, deep and silent and discoloured with human blood.

Two of these men who strode along behind the waggon were young half-uncles of mine, Myron and Warren Turnbull, stout, thick-shouldered, honest fellows not much out of their teens, who worked hard, said little, and were always lumped together in speech by their family, the hired help, and the neighbours as "the boys." They asserted themselves so rarely, and took everything as it came with such docility, that I myself, being in my eleventh year, thought of them as very young indeed. Next them walked a man, hired just for the haying, named Philleo, and then, scuffling along over the uneven humps and hollows on the outer edge of the road, came Si Hummaston, with the empty ginger-beer pail knocking against his knees.

As Tuckermann's "Hi" stood for Hiram, so I assume the other's "Si" meant Silas, or possibly Cyrus. I daresay no one, not even his mother, had ever called him by his full name. I know that my companion, Marcellus Jones, who wouldn't be thirteen until after Thanksgiving, habitually addressed him as Si, and almost daily I resolved that I would do so myself. He was a man of more than fifty, I should think, tall, lean, and what Marcellus called "bible-backed." He had a short iron-grey beard and long hair. Whenever there was any very hard or steady work going, he generally gave out and went to sit in the shade, holding a hand flat over his heart, and shaking his head dolefully. This kept a good many from hiring him, and even in haying-time, when everybody on two legs is of some use, I fancy he would often have been left out if it hadn't been for my grandparents. They respected him on account of his piety and his moral character, and always had him down when extra work began. He was said to be the only hired man in the township who could not be goaded in some way into swearing. He looked at one slowly, with the mild expression of a heifer calf.

We had come to the crown of the hill, and the waggon started down the steeper incline, with a great groaning of the brake. The men, by some tacit understanding, halted and overlooked the scene.

The big old stone farmhouse—part of which is said to date almost to the Revolutionary times—was just below us, so near, indeed, that Marcellus said he had once skipped a scaling-stone from where we stood to its roof. The dense, big-leafed foliage of a sap-bush, sheltered in the basin which dipped from our feet, pretty well hid this roof now from view. Further on, heavy patches of a paler, brighter green marked the orchard, and framed one side of a cluster of barns and stables, at the end of which three or four belated cows were loitering by the trough. It was so still that we could hear the clatter of the stanchions as the rest of the herd sought their places inside the milking-barn.

The men, though, had no eyes for all this, but bent their gaze fixedly on the road, down at the bottom. For a long way this thoroughfare was bordered by a row of tall poplars, which, as we were placed, receded from the vision in so straight a line that they seemed one high, fat tree. Beyond these one saw only a line of richer green, where the vine-wrapped rail-fences cleft their way between the ripening fields.

"I'd a' took my oath it was them," said Philleo. "I can spot them greys as fur's I can see 'em. They turned by the school-house, there, or I'll eat it, school-ma'am 'n' all. And the buggy was follerin' 'em too."

"Yes, I thought it was them," said Myron, shading his eyes with his brown hand.

"But they ought to got past the poplars by this time, then," remarked Warren.

"Why, they'll be drivin' as slow as molasses in January," put in Si Hummaston. "When you come to think of it, it *is* pretty nigh the same as a regular funeral. You mark my words, your father'll have walked them greys every step of the road. I s'pose he'll drive himself—he wouldn't trust bringin' Alvy home to nobody else, would he? I know I wouldn't, if the Lord had given *me* such a son; but then He didn't!"

"No, He didn't!" commented the first speaker, in an unnaturally loud tone of voice, to break in upon the chance that Hi Tuckerman was going to try to talk. But Hi only stretched out his arm, pointing the forefinger toward the poplars.

Sure enough, something was in motion down at the base of the shadows on the road. Then it crept forward, out in the sunlight, and separated itself into two vehicles. A farm waggon came first, drawn by a team of grey horses. Close after it followed a buggy, with its black top raised. Both advanced so slowly that they seemed scarcely to be moving at all.

"Well, I swan!" exclaimed Si Hummaston, after a minute, "it's Dana Pillsbury drivin' the waggon after all! Well—I dunno— yes, I guess that's probably what I'd 'a' done too, if I'd be'n your father. Yes, it does look more correct, his follerin' on behind, like that. I s'pose that's Alvy's widder in the buggy there with him."

"Yes, that's Serena—it looks like her little girl with her," said Myron, gravely.

"I s'pose we might's well be movin' along down," observed his brother, and at that we all started.

We walked more slowly now, matching our gait to the snail- like progress of those coming toward us. As we drew near to the gate, the three hired men instinctively fell behind the brothers, and in that position the group halted on the grass, facing our drive-way where it left the main road. Not a word was uttered by any one. When at last the waggon came up, Myron and Warren took off their hats, and the others followed suit, all holding them poised at the level of their shoulders.

Dana Pillsbury, carrying himself rigidly upright on the box- seat, drove past us with eyes fixed straight ahead, and a face as coldly expressionless as that of a wooden Indian. The waggon was covered all over with rubber blankets, so that whatever it bore was hidden. Only a few paces behind came the buggy, and my grandfather, old Arphaxed Turnbull, went by in his turn with the same averted, far-away gaze, and the same resolutely stolid countenance. He held the restive young carriage horse down to a decorous walk, a single firm hand on the tight reins, without so much as looking at it. The strong yellow light of the declining sun poured full upon his long grey beard, his shaven upper lip, his dark-skinned, lean, domineering face—and made me think of some hard and gloomy old Prophet seeing a vision in the back part of the Old Testament. If that woman beside him, swathed in heavy black raiment, and holding a child up against her arm, was my Aunt Serena, I should never have guessed it.

We put on our hats again, and walked up the drive-way with measured step behind the carriage till it stopped at the side- piazza stoop. The waggon had passed on towards the big new red barn—and crossing its course I saw my Aunt Em, bare- headed and with her sleeves rolled up, going to the cow-barn with a milking-pail in her hand. She was walking quickly, as if in a great hurry.

"There's your Ma," I whispered to Marcellus, assuming that he would share my surprise at her rushing off like this, instead of waiting to say "How-d'-do" to Serena. He only nodded knowingly, and said nothing.

No one else said much of anything. Myron and Warren shook hands in stiff solemnity with the veiled and craped sister-in-law, when their father had helped her and her daughter from the buggy, and one of them remarked in a constrained way that the hot spell seemed to keep up right along. The newcomers ascended the steps to the open door, and the woman and child went inside. Old Arphaxed turned on the threshold, and seemed to behold us for the first time.

"After you've put out the horse," he said, "I want the most of yeh to come up to the new barn. Si Hummaston and Marcellus can do the milkin'."

"I kind o' rinched my wrist this forenoon," put in Si, with a note of entreaty in his voice. He wanted sorely to be one of the party at the red barn.

"Mebbe milkin' 'll be good for it," said Arphaxed, curtly. "You and Marcellus do what I say, and keep Sidney with you." With this he, too, went into the house.

II

It wasn't an easy matter for even a member of the family like myself to keep clearly and untangled in his head all the relationships which existed under this patriarchial Turnbull roof.

Old Arphaxed had been married twice. His first wife was the mother of two children, who grew up, and the older of these was my father, Wilbur Turnbull. He never liked farm-life, and left home early, not without some hard feeling, which neither father nor son ever quite forgot. My father made a certain success of it as a business man in Albany until, in the thirties, his health broke down. He died when I was seven, and, although he left some property, my mother was forced to supplement this help by herself going to work as forewoman in a large store. She was too busy to have much time for visiting, and I don't think there was any great love lost between her and the people on the farm; but it was a good healthy place for me to be sent to when the summer vacation came, and withal inexpensive, and so the first of July each year generally found me out at the homestead, where, indeed, nobody pretended to be heatedly fond of me, but where I was still treated well and enjoyed myself. This year it was understood that my mother was coming out to bring me home later on.

The other child of that first marriage was a girl who was spoken of in youth as Emelline, but whom I knew now as Aunt Em'. She was a silent, tough-fibred, hard-working creature, not at all good-looking, but relentlessly neat, and the best cook I ever knew. Even when the house was filled with extra hired men, no one ever thought of getting in any female help, so tireless and so resourceful was Em. She did all the housework there was to do, from cellar to garret, was continually lending a hand in the men's chores, made more butter than the household could eat up, managed a large kitchen-garden, and still had a good deal of spare time, which she spent in sitting out in the piazza in a starched pink calico gown, knitting the while she watched who went up and down the road. When you knew her, you understood how it was that the original Turnbulls had come into that part of the country just after the Revolution, and in a few years chopped down all the forests, dug up all the stumps, drained the swail-lands, and turned the entire place from a wilderness into a flourishing and fertile home for civilised people. I used to feel, when I looked at her that she would have been quite equal to doing the whole thing herself.

All at once, when she was something over thirty, Em had up and married a mowing-machine agent named Abel Jones, whom no one knew anything about, and who, indeed, had only been in the neighbourhood for a week or so. The family was struck dumb with amazement. The idea of Em's dallying with the notion of matrimony had never crossed anybody's mind. As a girl she had never had any patience with husking-bees or dances or sleigh-ride parties. No young man had ever seen her home from anywhere, or had had the remotest encouragement to hang around the house. She had never been pretty—so my mother told me—and as she got along in years grew dumpy and thick in figure, with a plain, fat face, a rather scowling brow, and an abrupt, ungracious manner. She had no conversational gifts whatever, and through years of increasing taciturnity and confirmed unsociability, built up in everybody's mind the conviction that, if there could be a man so wild and unsettled in intellect as to suggest a tender thought to Em, he would get his ears cuffed off his head for his pains.

Judge, then, how like a thunderbolt the episode of the mowing-machine agent fell upon the family. To bewildered astonishment there soon enough succeeded rage. This Jones was a curly-headed man, with a crinkly black beard like those of Joseph's brethren in the Bible picture. He had no home and no property, and didn't seem to amount to much even as a salesman of other people's goods. His machine was quite the worst then in the market, and it could not be learned that he had sold a single one in the county. But he had married Em, and it was calmly proposed that he should henceforth regard the farm as his home. After this point had been sullenly conceded, it turned out that Jones was a widower, and had a boy nine or ten years old, named Marcellus, who was in a sort of orphan asylum in Vermont. There were more angry scenes between father and daughter, and a good deal more bad blood, before it was finally agreed that the boy also should come and live on the farm.

All this had happened in 1860 or 1861. Jones had somewhat improved on acquaintance. He knew about lightning rods, and had been able to fit out all the farm buildings with them at cost price. He had turned a little money now and again in trades with hop-poles, butter-firkins, shingles, and the like, and he was very ingenious in mending and fixing up odds and ends. He made shelves, and painted the woodwork, and put a tar roof on the summer kitchen. Even Martha, the second Mrs. Turnbull, came finally to admit that he was handy about a house.

This Martha became the head of the household while Em was still a little girl. She was a heavy woman, mentally as well as bodily, rather prone to a peevish view of things, and greatly given to pride in herself and her position, but honest, charitable in her way, and not unkindly at heart. On the whole, she was a good stepmother, and Em probably got on quite as well with her as she would have done with her own mother—even in the matter of the mowing-machine agent.

To Martha three sons were born. The two younger ones, Myron and Warren, have already been seen. The eldest boy, Alva, was the pride of the family, and for that matter, of the whole section.

Alva was the first Turnbull to go to college. From his smallest boyhood it had been manifest that he had great things before him, so handsome and clever and winning a lad was he. Through each of his schooling years he was the honour-man of his class, and he finished in a blaze of glory by taking the Clark Prize, and practically everything else within reach in the way of academic distinctions. He studied law at Octavius, in the office of Judge Schermerhorn, and in a little time was not only that distinguished man's partner, but distinctly the more important figure in the firm. At the age of twenty-five he was sent to the Assembly. The next year they made him District Attorney, and it was quite understood that it rested with him whether he should be sent to

Congress later on, or be presented by the Dearborn County bar
for the next vacancy on the Supreme Court bench.

At this point in his brilliant career he married Miss Serena
Wadsworth, of Wadsworth's Falls. The wedding was one of the
most imposing social events the county had known, so it was
said, since the visit of Lafayette. The Wadsworths were an older
family, even, than the Fairchilds, and infinitely more fastidious
and refined. The daughters of the household, indeed, carried
their refinement to such a pitch that they lived an almost solitary
life, and grew to the parlous verge of old-maidhood, simply
because there was nobody good enough to marry them. Alva
Turnbull was, however, up to the standard. It could not be said,
of course, that his home surroundings quite matched those of his
bride; but, on the other hand, she was nearly two years his
senior, and this was held to make matters about even.

In a year or so came the War, and nowhere in the North did
patriotic excitement run higher than in this old Abolition strong-
hold of upper Dearborn. Public meetings were held, and nearly a
whole regiment was raised in Octavius and the surrounding
towns alone. Alva Turnbull made the most stirring and important
speech at the first big gathering, and sent a thrill through the
whole countryside by claiming the privilege of heading the list of
volunteers. He was made a Captain by general acclaim, and went
off with his company in time to get chased from the field of Bull
Run. When he came home on a furlough in 1863 he was a
Major, and later on he rose to be Lieutenant-Colonel. We understood vaguely that he might have climbed vastly higher in promotion but for the fact that he was too moral and conscientious to
get on very well with his immediate superior, General Boyce, of
Thessaly, who was notoriously a drinking man.

It was glory enough to have him at the farm, on that visit of
his, even as a Major. His old parents literally abased themselves
at his feet, quite tremulous in their awed pride at his greatness. It
made it almost too much to have Serena there also, this fair,
thin-faced, prim-spoken daughter of the Wadsworths, and actually to call her by her first name. It was haying time, I remember,
but the hired men that year did not eat their meals with the
family, and there was even a question whether Marcellus and I
were socially advanced enough to come to the table, where
Serena and her husband were feeding themselves in state with a
novel kind of silver implement called a four-tined fork. If Em
hadn't put her foot down, out to the kitchen we should both have
gone, I fancy. As it was, we sat decorously at the far end of the
table, and asked with great politeness to have things passed to us

which by standing up we could have reached as well as not. It was slow, but it made us feel immensely respectable, almost as if we had been born Wadsworths ourselves.

We agreed that Serena was "stuck-up," and Marcellus reported Aunt Em as feeling that her bringing along with her a nursemaid to be waited on hand and foot, just to take care of a baby, was an imposition bordering upon the intolerable. He said that that was the sort of thing the English did until George Washington rose and drove them out. But we both felt that Alva was splendid.

He was a fine creature physically—taller even than old Arphaxed, with huge square shoulders and a mighty frame. I could recall him as without whiskers, but now he had a waving, lustrous brown beard, the longest and biggest I ever saw. He didn't pay much attention to us boys, it was true; but he was affable when we came in his way, and he gave Myron and Warren each a dollar bill when they went to Octavius to see the Fourth of July doings. In the evening some of the more important neighbours would drop in, and then Alva would talk about the War, and patriotism, and saving the Union, till it was like listening to Congress itself. He had a rich, big voice which filled the whole room, so that the hired men could hear every word out in the kitchen; but it was even more affecting to see him walking with his father down under the poplars, with his hands making orator's gestures as he spoke and old Arphaxed looking at him and listening with shining eyes.

Well, then, he and his wife went away to visit her folks, and then we heard he had left to join his regiment. From time to time he wrote to his father—letters full of high and loyal sentiments, which were printed next week in the Octavius *Transcript*, and the week after in the Thessaly *Banner of Liberty*. Whenever any of us thought about the War—and who thought much of anything else?—it was always with Alva as the predominant figure in every picture.

Sometimes the arrival of a letter for Aunt Em, or a chance remark about a broken chair or a clock hopelessly out of kilter, would recall for the moment the fact that Abel Jones was also at the seat of war. He had enlisted on that very night when Alva headed the roll of honour, and he had marched away in Alva's company. Somehow he got no promotion, but remained in the ranks. Not even the members of the family were shown the letters Aunt Em received, much less the printers of the newspapers. They were indeed poor misspelled scrawls, about which no one displayed any interest or questioned Aunt Em. Even Marcellus rarely spoke of his father, and seemed to share to the full the family's concentration of thought upon Alva.

Thus matters stood when Spring began to play at being Summer in the year of '64. The birds came and the trees burst forth into green, the sun grew hotter and the days longer, the strawberries hidden under the big leaves in our yard started into shape where the blossoms had been, quite in the ordinary, annual way, with us up North. But down where that dread thing they called "The War" was going on, this coming of warm weather meant more awful massacre, more tortured hearts and desolated homes than ever before. I can't be at all sure how much later reading and associations have helped out and patched up what seemed to be my boyish recollections of this period; but it is, at all events, much clearer in my mind than are the occurrences of the week before last.

We heard a good deal about how deep the mud was in Virginia that Spring. All the photographs and tin-types of officers which found their way to relatives at home now, showed them in boots that came up to their thighs. Everybody understood that as soon as this mud dried up a little, there were to be most terrific doings. The two great lines of armies lay scowling at each other, still on that blood-soaked fighting ground between Washington and Richmond where they were three years before. Only now things were to go differently. A new General was at the head of affairs, and he was going in, with jaws set and nerves of steel, to smash, kill, burn, annihilate, sparing nothing, looking neither right or left, till the red road had been hewed through to Richmond. In the first week of May this thing began—a push forward all along the line—and the North, with scared eyes and fluttering heart, held its breath.

My chief personal recollection of those historic forty days is that one morning I was awakened early by a noise in my bedroom and saw my mother looking over the contents of the big chest of drawers which stood against the wall. She was getting out some black articles of apparel. When she discovered that I was awake, she told me in a low voice that my Uncle Alva had been killed. Then a few weeks later my school closed, and I was packed off to the farm for the vacation. It will be better to tell what had happened as I learned it there from Marcellus and the others.

Along about the middle of May, the weekly paper came up from Octavius, and old Arphaxed Turnbull, as was his wont, read it over out on the piazza before supper. Presently he called his wife to him, and showed her something in it. Martha went out into the kitchen, where Aunt Em was getting the meal ready, and told her, as gently as she could, that there was very bad news for her; in fact, her husband, Abel Jones, had been killed in the first day's battle in the Wilderness, something like a week before. Aunt Em said she didn't believe it, and Martha brought in the paper and pointed out the fatal line to her. It was not quite clear whether this convinced Aunt Em or not. She finished getting supper, and sat silently through the meal, afterwards, but she went upstairs to her room before family prayers. The next day she was about as usual, doing the work and saying nothing. Marcellus told me that to the best of his belief no one had said anything to her on the subject. The old people were a shade more ceremonious in their manner towards her, and "the boys" and the hired men were on the look-out to bring in water for her from the well, and to spare her as much as possible in the routine of chores, but no one talked about Jones. Aunt Em did not put on mourning. She made a black necktie for Marcellus to wear to church, but stayed away from meeting herself.

A little more than a fortnight afterwards, Myron was walking down the road from the meadows one afternoon, when he saw a man on horseback coming up from the poplars, galloping like mad in a cloud of dust. The two met at the gate. The man was one of the hired helps of the Wadsworths, and he had ridden as hard as he could pelt from the Falls, fifteen miles away, with a message, which now he gave Myron to read. Both man and beast dripped sweat, and trembled with fatigued excitement. The youngster eyed them, and then gazed meditatively at the sealed envelope in his hand.

"I s'pose you know what's inside?" he asked, looking up at last.

The man in the saddle nodded, with a tell-tale look on his face, and breathing heavily.

Myron handed the letter back, and pushed the gate open. "You'd better go up and give it to father yourself," he said. "I ain't got the heart to face him—jest now, at any rate."

Marcellus was fishing that afternoon, over in the creek which ran through the woods. Just as at last he was making up his mind that it must be about time to go after the cows, he saw Myron sitting on a log beside the forest path, whittling mechanically, and staring at the foliage before him, in an obvious brown study. Marcellus went up to him, and had to speak twice before Myron turned his head and looked up.

"Oh! it's you, eh, Bubb?" he remarked dreamily, and began gazing once more into the thicket.

"What's the matter?" asked the puzzled boy.

"I guess Alvy's dead," replied Myron. To the lad's comments and questions he made small answer. "No," he said at last, "I don't feel much like goin' home jest now. Lea' me alone here; I'll prob'ly turn up later on." And Marcellus went alone to the pasture, and thence, at the tail of his bovine procession, home.

When he arrived he regretted not having remained with Myron in the woods. It was like coming into something which was prison, hospital, and tomb in one. The household was paralysed with horror and fright. Martha had gone to bed, or rather had been put there by Em, and all through the night, when he woke up, he heard her broken and hysterical voice in moans and screams. The men had hitched up the greys, and Arphaxed Turnbull was getting into the buggy to drive to Octavius for news when the boy came up. He looked twenty years older than he had at noon—all at once turned into a chalk-faced, trembling, infirm old man—and could hardly see to put his foot on the carriage-step. His son Warren had offered to go with him, and had been rebuffed almost with fierceness. Warren and the others silently bowed their heads before this mood; instinct told them that nothing but Arphaxed's show of temper held him from collapse—from falling at their feet and grovelling on the grass with cries and sobs of anguish, perhaps even dying in a fit. After he had driven off they forebore to talk to one another, but went about noiselessly with drooping chins and knotted brows.

"It jest took the tuck out of everything," said Marcellus, relating these tragic events to me. There was not much else to tell. Martha had had what they call brain-fever, and had emerged from this some weeks afterward a pallid and dim-eyed ghost of her former self, sitting for hours together in her rocking-chair in the unused parlour, her hands idly in her lap, her poor thoughts glued ceaselessly to that vague far-off Virginia which folks told about as hot and sunny, but which her mind's eye saw under the gloom of an endless and dreadful night. Arphaxed had gone South, still defiantly alone, to bring back the body of his boy. An acquaintance wrote to them of his being down sick in Washington, prostrated by the heat and strange water; but even from his sickbed he had sent on orders to an undertaking firm out at the front, along with a hundred dollars, their price in advance for embalming. Then, recovering, he had himself pushed down to headquarters, or as near them as civilians might approach, only to learn that he had passed the precious freight on the way. He posted back again, besieging the railroad officials at every point with inquiries, scolding, arguing, beseeching in turn, until at last he overtook his quest at Juno Mills Junction, only a score of miles from home.

Then only he wrote, telling people his plans. He came first to Octavius, where a funeral service was held in the forenoon, with military honours, the Wadsworths as the principal mourners, and a memorable turn-out of distinguished citizens. The town-hall was draped with mourning, and so was Alva's pew in the Episcopal Church, which he had deserted his ancestral Methodism to join after his marriage. Old Arphaxed listened to the novel burial service of his son's communion, and watched the clergyman in his curious white and black vestments, with sombre pride. He himself needed and deserved only a plain and homely religion, but it was fitting that his boy should have organ music and flowers, and a ritual.

Dana Pillsbury had arrived in town early in the morning with the greys, and a neighbour's boy had brought in the buggy. Immediately after dinner Arphaxed had gathered up Alva's widow and little daughter, and started the funeral cortège upon its final homeward stage.

And so I saw them arrive on that July afternoon.

III

For so good and patient a man, Si Hummaston bore himself rather vehemently during the milking. It was hotter in the barn than it was outside in the sun, and the stifling air swarmed with flies, which seemed to follow Si perversely from stall to stall and settle on his cow. One beast put her hoof square in his pail, and another refused altogether to "give down," while the rest kept up a tireless slapping and swishing of their tails very hard to bear, even if one had the help of profanity. Marcellus and I listened carefully to hear him at last provoked to an oath, but the worst thing he uttered, even when the cow stepped in the milk, was "Dum your buttons!" which Marcellus said might conceivably be investigated by a church committee, but was hardly out-and-out swearing.

I remember Si's groans and objurgations, his querulous "Hyst there, will ye!" his hypocritical "So-boss! So-boss!" his despondent "They never will give down for me!" because presently there was crossed upon this woof of peevish impatience the web of a curious conversation.

Si had been so slow in his headway against flapping tails and restive hoofs that before he had got up to the end of the row, Aunt Em had finished her side. She brought over her stool and pail, and seated herself at the next cow to Hummaston's. For a little, one heard only the resonant din of the stout streams against the tin; then as the bottom was covered, there came the ploughing plash of milk on milk, and Si could hear himself talk.

"S'pose you know S'reny's come, 'long with your father,'' he remarked, ingratiatingly.

"I saw 'em drive in," replied Em.

"Whoa! Hyst there! Hole still, can't ye? I didn't know if you quite made out who she was, you was scootin' 'long so fast. They ain't—*Whoa there!*—they ain't nothin' the matter 'twixt you and her, is they?''

"I don't know as there is," said Em, curtly. "The world's big enough for both of us—we ain't no call to bunk into each other.''

"No, of course—*Now you stop it!*—but it looked kind o' curious to me, your pikin off like that, without waitin' to say 'Howd'-do?' Of course, I never had no relation by marriage that was stuck-up at all, or looked down on me—*Stiddy there, now!*—but I guess I can reelize pretty much how you feel about it. I'm a good deal of a hand at that. It's what they call imagination. It's a gift, you know, like good looks, or preachin', or the knack o' makin' money. But you can't help what you're born with, can you? I'd been a heap better off if my gift 'd be'n in some other direction; but, as I tell 'em, it ain't my fault. And my imagination—*Hi, there! git over, will ye?*—it's downright cur'ous sometimes, how it works. Now I could tell, you see, that you 'n S'reny didn't pull together. I s'pose she never writ a line to you, when your husband was killed?''

"Why should she?" demanded Em. "We never did correspond. What'd be the sense of beginning then? She minds her affairs, 'n I mind mine. Who wanted her to write?''

"Oh, of course not," said Si lightly. "Prob'ly you'll git along better together, though, now that you'll see more of one another. I s'pose S'reny's figurin' on stayin' here right along now, her 'n her little girl. Well, it'll be nice for the old folks to have somebody they're fond of. They jest worshipped the ground Alvy walked on—and I s'pose they won't be anything in this wide world too good for that little girl of his. Le's see, she must be comin' on three now, ain't she?''

"I don't know anything about her!" snapped Aunt Em, with emphasis.

"Of course, it's natural the old folks should feel so—she bein' Alvy's child. I hain't noticed anything special, but does it— *Well, I swan! Hyst there!*—does it seem to you that they're as good to Marcellus, quite, as they used to be? I don't hear 'em sayin' nothin' about his goin' to school next winter.''

Aunt Em said nothing, too, but milked doggedly on. Si told her about the thickness and profusion of Serena's mourning, guardedly hinted at the injustice done him by not allowing him to go to the red barn with the others, speculated on the likelihood of the Wadsworths contributing to their daughter's support, and generally exhibited his interest in the family through a monologue which finished only with the milking; but Aunt Em made no response whatever.

When the last pails had been emptied into the big cans at the door—Marcellus and I had let the cows out one by one into the yard, as their individual share in the milking ended—Si and Em saw old Arphaxed wending his way across from the house to the red barn. He appeared more bent than ever but he walked with a slowness which seemed born of reluctance even more than of infirmity.

"Well, now," mused Si aloud, "Brother Turnbull an' me's be'n friends for a good long spell. I don't believe he'd be mad if I cut over now to the red barn, too, seein' the milkin's all out of the way. Of course I don't want to do what ain't right—what d'you think now, Em, honest? Think it 'ud rile him?''

"I don't know anything about it?'' my aunt replied with increased vigour of emphasis. "But for the land sake go somewhere! Don't hang around botherin' me. I got enough else to think of besides your everlasting cackle.''

Thus rebuffed, Si meandered sadly into the cow-yard, shaking his head as he came. Seeing us seated on an upturned plough, over by the fence, from which point we had a perfect view of the red barn, he sauntered towards us, and, halting at our side, looked to see if there was room enough for him to sit also. But Marcellus, in quite a casual way, remarked: "Oh! wheeled the milk over to the house already, Si?'' and at this the doleful man lounged off again in new despondency, got out the wheelbarrow, and, with ostentatious groans of travail, hoisted a can upon it and started off.

"He's takin' advantage of Arphaxed's being so worked up to play 'ole soldier' on him,'' said Marcellus. "All of us have to stir him up the whole time to keep him from takin' root somewhere. I told him this afternoon 't if there had to be any settin' around under the bushes an' cryin', the fam'ly 'd do it.''

We talked in hushed tones as we sat there watching the shut doors of the red barn, in boyish conjecture about what was going on behind them. I recall much of this talk with curious distinctness, but candidly it jars now upon my maturer nerves. The individual man looks back upon his boyhood with much the same amused amazement that the race feels in contemplating the memorials of its own cave-dwelling or bronze period. What strange savages we were! In those days Marcellus and I used to find our very highest delight in getting off on Thursdays, and going over to Dave Bushnell's slaughterhouse, to witness with stony hearts, and from as close a coign of vantage as might be, the slaying of some score of barnyard animals—the very thought of which now revolts our grown-up minds. In the same way we sat there on the plough, and criticised old Arphaxed's meanness in excluding us from the red barn, where the men-folks were coming in final contact with "the pride of the family." Some of the cows wandering toward us, began to "moo" with impatience for the pasture, but Marcellus said there was no hurry.

All at once we discovered that Aunt Em was standing a few yards away from us, on the other side of the fence. We could see her from where we sat by only turning a little—a motionless, stout upright figure, with a pail in her hand, and a sternly impassive look on her face. She, too, had her gaze fixed upon the red barn, and, though the declining sun was full in her eyes, seemed incapable of blinking, but just stared coldly, straight ahead.

Suddenly an unaccustomed voice fell upon our ears. Turning, we saw that a black-robed woman, with a black wrap of some sort about her head, had come up to where Aunt Em stood, and was at her shoulder. Marcellus nudged me, and whispered, "It's S'reny. Look out for squalls!" And then we listened in silence.

"Won't you speak to me at all, Emmeline?" we heard this new voice say.

Aunt Em's face, sharply outlined in profile against the sky, never moved. Her lips were pressed into a single line, and she kept her eyes on the barn.

"If there's anything I've done, tell me," pursued the other. "In such a hour as this—when both our hearts are bleeding so, and—and every breath we draw is like a curse upon us—it doesn't seem a fit time for us—for us to——" The voice faltered and broke, leaving the speech unfinished.

Aunt Em kept silence so long that we fancied this appeal, too, had failed. Then abruptly, and without moving her head, she dropped a few ungracious words as it were over her shoulder: "If I had anything special to say, most likely I'd say it," she remarked.

We could hear the sigh that Serena drew. She lifted her

shawled head, and for a moment seemed as if about to turn. Then she changed her mind, apparently, for she took a step nearer to the other.

"See here, Emmeline," she said, in a more confident tone. "Nobody in the world knows better than I do how thoroughly good a woman you are, how you have done your duty, and more than your duty, by your parents and your brothers, and your little stepson. You have never spared yourself for them, day or night. I have said often to—to him who has gone—that I didn't believe there was anywhere on earth a worthier or more devoted woman than you, his sister. And—now that he is gone—and we are both more sisters than ever in affliction—why in Heaven's name should you behave like this to me?"

Aunt Em spoke more readily this time. "I don't know as I've done anything to you," she said in defence. "I've just let you alone, that's all. An' that's doin' as I'd like to be done by." Still she did not turn her head, or lift her steady gaze from those closed doors.

"Don't let us split words!" entreated the other, venturing a thin, white hand upon Aunt Em's shoulder. "That isn't the way we two ought to stand to each other. Why, you were friendly enough when I was here before. Can't it be the same again? What has happened to change it? Only to-day, on our way up here, I was speaking to your father about you, and my deep sympathy for you, and——"

Aunt Em wheeled like a flash. "Yes, 'n' what did *he* say? Come, don't make up anything! Out with it! What did he say?" She shook off the hand on her shoulder as she spoke.

Gesture and voice and frowning vigour of mien were all so imperative and rough that they seemed to bewilder Serena. She, too, had turned now, so that I could see her wan and delicate face, framed in the laced festoons of black, like the fabulous countenance of "The Lady Iñez" in my mother's "Album of Beauty." She bent her brows in hurried thought, and began stammering, "Well, he said—Let's see, he said——"

"Oh, yes!" broke in Aunt Em, with raucous irony. "I know well enough what he said! He said I was a good worker—that they'd never had to have a hired girl since I was big enough to wag a churn dash, an' they wouldn't known what to do without me. I know all that; I've heard it on an' off for twenty years. What I'd like to hear is, did he tell you that he went down South to bring back *your* husband, an' that he never so much as give a thought to fetchin' *my* husband, who was just as good a soldier and died just as bravely as yours did? I'd like to know—did he tell you that.''

What could Serena do but shake her head, and bow it in silence before this bitter gale of words?

"An' tell me this, too,'' Aunt Em went on, lifting her harsh voice mercilessly, "when you was settin' there in church this forenoon, with the soldiers out, an' the bells tollin' an' all that—did he say 'This is some for Alvy, an' some for Abel, who went to the war together, an' was killed together, or within a month o' one another?' Did he say that, or look for one solitary minute as if he thought it? I'll bet he didn't!''

Serena's head sank lower still, and she put up, in a blinded sort of a way, a little white handkerchief to her eyes. "But why blame *me?*'' she asked.

Aunt Em heard her own voice so seldom that the sound of it now seemed to intoxicate her. "No!'' she shouted. "It's like the Bible. One was taken an' the other left. It was always Alvy this an' Alvy that, nothin' for anyone but Alvy. That was all right; nobody complained: prob'ly he deserved it all; at any rate, we didn't begrudge him any of it, while he was livin'. But there ought to be a limit somewhere. When a man's dead, he's pretty much about on an equality with other dead men, one would think. But it ain't so. One man gets hunted after, when he's shot, an' there's a hundred dollars for embalmin' him, an' a journey after him, an' bringin' him home, an' two big funerals, an' crape for his widow that'd stand by itself. The *other* man—he can lay where he fell! Them that's lookin' for the first one are right close by—it ain't more'n a few miles from the Wilderness to Cold Harbour, so Hi Tuckerman tells me, 'an he was all over the ground two years ago—but nobody looks for this other man! Oh, no! Nobody so much as remembers to think of him! They ain't no hundred dollars, no, not so much as fifty cents, for embalmin' *him*! No—*he* could be shovelled in anywhere, or maybe burned up when the woods got on fire that night, the night of the sixth. They ain't no funeral for him—no bells tolled—unless it may be a cowbell up in the pasture that he hammered out himself. An' *his* widow can go around, week days an' Sundays, in her old calico dresses. Nobody ever mentions the word 'mournin' crape' to her, or asks her if she'd like to put on black. I 'spose they thought if they gave me the money for some mournin' I'd buy *candy* with it instead!''

With this climax of flaming sarcasm Aunt Em stopped, her eyes aglow, her thick breast heaving in a flurry of breathlessness.

She had never talked so much or so fast before in her life. She swung the empty tin-pail now defiantly at her side to hide the fact that her arms were shaking with excitement. Every instant it looked as if she was going to begin again.

Serena had taken the handkerchief down from her eyes and held her arms stiff and straight by her side. Her chin seemed to have grown longer or to be thrust forward more. When she spoke it was in a colder voice—almost mincing in the way it cut off the words.

"All this is not my doing," she said. "I am to blame for nothing of it. As I tried to tell you, I sympathise deeply with your grief. But grief ought to make people at least fair, even if it cannot make them gentle and soften their hearts. I shall trouble you with no more offers of friendship. I—I think I will go back to the house now—to my little girl."

Even as she spoke, there came from the direction of the red barn a shrill, creaking noise which we all knew. At the sound Marcellus and I stood up, and Serena forgot her intention to go away. The barn doors, yelping as they moved on their dry rollers, had been pushed wide open.

IV

The first one to emerge from the barn was Hi Tuckerman. He started to make for the house, but when he caught sight of our group, came running towards us at the top of his speed, uttering incoherent shouts as he advanced, and waving his arms excitedly. It was apparent that something out of the ordinary had happened.

We were but little the wiser as to this something, when Hi had come to a halt before us, and was pouring out a volley of explanations, accompanied by earnest grimaces and strenuous gestures. Even Marcellus could make next to nothing of what he was trying to convey, but Aunt Em, strangely enough, seemed to understand him. Still slightly trembling, and with a little occasional catch in her breath, she bent an intent scrutiny upon Hi, and nodded comprehendingly from time to time, with encouraging exclamations, "He did, eh!" "Is that so?" and "I expected as much." Listening and watching, I formed the uncharitable conviction that she did not really understand Hi at all, but was only pretending to do so in order further to harrow Serena's feelings.

Doubtless I was wrong, for presently she turned, with an

effort, to her sister-in-law, and remarked: "P'rhaps you don't quite follow what he's sayin'?"

"Not a word!" said Serena, eagerly. "Tell me, please, Emmeline!"

Aunt Em seemed to hesitate. "He was shot through the mouth at Gaines' Mills, you know—that's right near Cold Harbour and—the Wilderness," she said, obviously making talk.

"That isn't what he's saying," broke in Serena. "What *is* it, Emmeline?"

"Well," rejoined the other, after an instant's pause, "if you want to know—he says that ain't Alvy at all that they've got there in the barn."

Serena turned swiftly, so that we could not see her face.

"He says it's some strange man," continued Em, "a yaller-headed man, all packed an' stuffed with charcoal, so't his own mother wouldn't know him. Who it is nobody knows, but it ain't Alvy."

"They're a pack of robbers 'n' swindlers!" cried old Arphaxed, shaking his long grey beard with wrath.

He had come up without our noticing his approach, so rapt had been our absorption in the strange discovery reported by Hi Tuckerman. Behind him straggled the boys and the hired men, whom Si Hummaston had scurried across from the house to join. No one said anything now, but tactily deferred to the old man's principal right to speak. It was a relief to hear that terrible silence of his broken at all.

"They ought to all be hung!" he cried, in a voice to which the excess of passion over physical strength gave a melancholy quaver. "I paid 'em what they asked—they took a hundred dollars o' my money—an' they ain't sent me *him* at all! There I went, at my age, all through the Wilderness, almost clear to Cold Harbour, an' that, too, gittin' up from a sick bed in Washington, and then huntin' for the box at New York an' Albany, an' all the way back, an' holdin' a funeral over it only this very day—an' here it ain't *him* at all! I'll have the law on 'em though, if it costs the last cent I've got in the world!"

Poor old man! These weeks of crushing grief and strain had fairly broken him down. We listened to his fierce outpourings with sympathetic silence, almost thankful that he had left strength and vitality enough still to get angry and shout. He had been always a hard and gusty man; we felt by instinct, I suppose, that his best chance of weathering this terrible month of calamity was to batter his way furiously through it, in a rage with everything and everybody.

"If there's any justice in the land," put in Si Hummaston, "you'd ought to get your hundred dollars back. I shouldn't wonder if you could, too, if you sued 'em afore a Jestice that was a friend of yours."

"Why, the man's a fool!" burst forth Arphaxed, turning towards him with a snort. "I don't want the hundred dollars—I wouldn't 'a' begrudged a thousand—if only they'd dealt honestly by me. I paid 'em their own figure, without beatin' 'em down a penny. If it 'd be'n double, I'd 'a' paid it. What *I* wanted was *my boy*! It ain't so much their cheatin' *me* I mind, either, if it'd be'n about anything else. But to think of Alvy—*my boy*—after all the trouble I took, an' the journey, an' my sickness there among strangers—to think that after it all he's buried down there, no one knows where, p'raps in some trench with private soldiers, shovelled in anyhow—Oh-h! they ought to be hung!"

The two women had stood motionless, with their gaze on the grass; Aunt Em lifted her head at this.

"If a place is good enough for private soldiers to be buried in," she said vehemently, "it's good enough for the best man in the army. On Resurrection Day, do you think them with shoulder-straps 'll be called fust an' given all the front places? I reckon the men that carried a musket are every whit as good, there in the trench, as them that wore swords. They gave their lives as much as the others did, an' the best man that ever stepped couldn't do no more."

Old Arphaxed bent upon her a long look, which had in it much surprise and some elements of menace. Reflection seemed, however, to make him think better of an attack on Aunt Em. He went on, instead, with rambling exclamations to his auditors at large.

"Makin' me the butt of the whole county!" he cried. "There was that funeral to-day—with a parade an' a choir of music an' so on—an' now it'll come out in the papers that it wasn't Alvy at all I brought back with me, but only some perfect stranger—by what you can make out from his clothes, not even an officer at all. I tell you the War's a jedgment on this country for its wickedness, for its cheatin' an' robbin' of honest men! They wa'n't no sense in that battle at Cold Harbour anyway—everybody admits that!—it was murder an' massacre in cold blood;—fifty thousand men mowed down, an' nothin' gained by it!—an' then not even to git my boy's dead body back! I say hangin's too good for 'em!"

"Yes, father," said Myron, soothingly; "but do you stick to what you said about the—the box? Wouldn't it look better——"

"No!" shouted Arphaxed, with emphasis. "Let Dana do what I told him—take it down this very night to the poor-master, an' let him bury it where he likes. It's no affair of mine. I wash my hands of it. There won't be no funeral held here!"

It was then that Serena spoke. Strangely enough, old Arphaxed had not seemed to notice her presence in our group, and his jaw visibly dropped as he beheld her now standing before him. He made a gesture signifying his disturbance at finding her among his hearers, and would have spoken, but she held up her hand.

"Yes, I heard it all," she said, in answer to his deprecatory movement. "I am glad I did. It has given me time to get over the shock of learning—our mistake—and it gives me the chance now to say something which I—I feel keenly. The poor man you have brought home was, you say, a private soldier. Well, isn't this a good time to remember that there was a private soldier who went out from this farm—belonging right to this family—and who, as a private, laid down his life as nobly as General Sedgwick or General Wadsworth; or even our dear Alva, or any one else? I never met Emmeline's husband, but Alva liked him, and spoke to me often of him. Men who fall in the ranks don't get identified, or brought home, but they deserve funerals as much as the others—just as much. Now this is my idea—let us feel that the mistake which has brought this poor stranger to us is God's way of giving us a chance to remember and do honour to Abel Jones. Let him be buried in the family lot up yonder, where we had thought to lay Alva, and let us do it reverently, in the name of Emmeline's husband, and of all others who have fought and died for our country—and with sympathy in our hearts for the women who, somewhere in the North, are mourning, just as we mourn here, for the stranger there in the red barn."

Arphaxed had watched her intently. He nodded now, and blinked at the moisture gathering in his old eyes. "I could e'en a'most 'a' thought it was Alvy talkin'," was what he said. Then he turned abruptly, but we all knew, without further words, that what Serena had suggested was to be done.

The men-folk, wondering doubtless much among themselves, moved slowly off toward the house or the cow-barns, leaving the two women alone. A minute of silence passed, before we saw Serena creep gently up to Aunt Em's side, and lay the thin white hand again upon her shoulder. This time it was not shaken off, but stretched itself forward, little by little, until its palm rested against Aunt Em's further cheek. We heard the tin-pail fall resonantly against the stones under the rail-fence, and there was a confused movement as if the two women were somehow melting into one.

"Come on, Sid!" said Marcellus Jones to me "let's start them cows along. If there's anything I hate to see it's women cryin' on each other's necks."

Kate O'Flaherty Chopin
(1851–1904)

Born in St. Louis, daughter of a businessman who had married a French woman of aristocratic family, Chopin was privately and exclusively educated. In 1870 she married Oscar Chopin, a New Orleans Creole of wealth and social standing; in the twelve years of their marriage she bore six children. From early 1883, when her husband died suddenly of swamp fever, until 1884, she managed the Chopin plantation. In 1884, she returned to St. Louis, living in her mother's home. Her mother died in 1885, and Chopin, for the first time, began writing seriously. At Fault, a novel, appeared in 1890, and The Awakening, her major work, was published in 1899. A collection of stories, Bayou Folk, appeared in 1894, and "Madame Célestin's Divorce" is taken from this volume. Another collection, A Night in Acadie, was published in 1897. Her literary career was effectively ended by the outrage created by The Awakening, a novel frankly and openly about matters sexual. "The purport of the story can hardly be described in language fit for publication," wrote one critic; "an essentially vulgar story," wrote another; even the young Willa Cather hoped "that Miss Chopin will devote that flexible iridescent style of hers to a better cause" in her next book. But Chopin lived the last five years of her life in virtual literary silence, frozen into deep discouragement; no next book was ever written.

MADAME CÉLESTIN'S DIVORCE

Madame Célestin always wore a neat and snugly fitting calico wrapper when she went out in the morning to sweep her small gallery. Lawyer Paxton thought she looked pretty in the gray one that was made with a graceful Watteau fold at the back: and with which she invariably wore a bow of pink ribbon at the throat. She was always sweeping her gallery when lawyer Paxton passed by in the morning on his way to his office in St. Denis Street.

Sometimes he stopped and leaned over the fence to say good-morning at his ease; to criticise or admire her rosebushes; or, when he had time enough, to hear what she had to say. Madame Célestin usually had a good deal to say. She would gather up the train of her calico wrapper in one hand, and balancing the broom gracefully in the other, would go tripping down to where the lawyer leaned, as comfortably as he could, over her picket fence.

Of course she had talked to him of her troubles. Every one knew Madame Célestin's troubles.

"Really, madame," he told her once, in his deliberate, calculating, lawyer-tone, "it's more than human nature—woman's nature—should be called upon to endure. Here you are, working your fingers off"—she glanced down at two rosy finger-tips that showed through the rents in her baggy doeskin gloves—"taking in sewing; giving music lessons; doing God knows what in the way of manual labor to support yourself and those two little ones"—Madame Célestin's pretty face beamed with satisfaction at this enumeration of her trials.

"You right, Judge. Not a picayune, not one, not one, have I lay my eyes on in the pas' fo' months that I can say Célestin give it to me or sen' it to me."

"The scoundrel!" muttered lawyer Paxton in his beard.

"An' *pourtant*," she resumed, "they say he's making money down roun' Alexandria w'en he wants to work."

"I dare say you haven't seen him for months?" suggested the lawyer.

"It's good six month' since I see a sight of Célestin," she admitted.

"That's it, that's what I say; he has practically deserted you;

313

fails to support you. It wouldn't surprise me a bit to learn that he has ill treated you.''

''Well, you know, Judge,'' with an evasive cough, ''a man that drinks—w'at can you expec'? An' if you would know the promises he has made me! Ah, if I had as many dolla' as I had promise from Célestin, I would n' have to work, *je vous garantis*.''

''And in my opinion, madame, you would be a foolish woman to endure it longer, when the divorce court is there to offer you redress.''

''You spoke about that befo', Judge; I'm goin' think about that divo'ce. I believe you right.''

Madame Célestin thought about the divorce and talked about it, too; and lawyer Paxton grew deeply interested in the theme.

''You know, about that divo'ce, Judge,'' Madame Célestin was waiting for him that morning, ''I been talking to my family an' my frien's, an' it's me that tells you, they all plumb agains' that divo'ce.''

''Certainly, to be sure; that's to be expected, madame, in this community of Creoles. I warned you that you would meet with opposition, and would have to face it and brave it.''

''Oh, don't fear, I'm going to face it! Maman says it's a disgrace like it's neva been in the family. But it's good for Maman to talk, her. W'at trouble she ever had? She says I mus' go by all means consult with Père Duchéron—it's my confessor, you undastan'— Well, I'll go, Judge, to please Maman. But all the confessor' in the worl' ent goin' make me put up with that conduc' of Célestin any longa.''

A day or two later, she was there waiting for him again. ''You know, Judge, about that divo'ce.''

''Yes, yes,'' responded the lawyer, well pleased to trace a new determination in her brown eyes and in the curves of her pretty mouth. ''I suppose you saw Père Duchéron and had to brave it out with him, too.''

''Oh, fo' that, a perfec' sermon. I assho you. A talk of giving scandal an' bad example that I thought would neva en'! He says, fo' him, he wash' his hands; I mus' go see the bishop.''

''You won't let the bishop dissuade you, I trust,'' stammered the lawyer more anxiously than he could well understand.

''You don't know me yet, Judge,'' laughed Madame Célestin with a turn of the head and a flirt of the broom which indicated that the interview was at an end.

''Well, Madame Célestin! And the bishop!'' Lawyer Paxton was standing there holding to a couple of the shaky pickets. She had not seen him. ''Oh, it's you, Judge?'' and she hastened towards him with an *empressement* that could not but have been flattering.

"Yes, I saw Monseigneur," she began. The lawyer had already gathered from her expressive countenance that she had not wavered in her determination. "Ah, he's a eloquent man. It's not a mo' eloquent man in Natchitoches parish. I was fo'ced to cry, the way he talked to me about my troubles; how he undasta's them, an' feels for me. It would move even you, Judge, to hear how he talk' about that step I want to take; its danga, its temptation. How it is the duty of a Catholic to stan' everything till the las' extreme. An' that life of retirement an' self-denial I would have to lead,—he told me all that."

"But he hasn't turned you from your resolve, I see," laughed the lawyer complacently.

"For that, no," she returned emphatically. "The bishop don't know what it is to be married to a man like Célestin, an' have to endu' that conduc' like I have to endu' it. The Pope himse'f can't make me stan' that any longer, if you say I got the right in the law to sen' Célestin sailing."

A noticeable change had come over lawyer Paxton. He discarded his work-day coat and began to wear his Sunday one to the office. He grew solicitous as to the shine of his boots, his collar, and the set of his tie. He brushed and trimmed his whiskers with a care that had not before been apparent. Then he fell into a stupid habit of dreaming as he walked the streets of the old town. It would be very good to take unto himself a wife, he dreamed. And he could dream of no other than pretty Madame Célestin filling that sweet and sacred office as she filled his thoughts, now. Old Natchitoches would not hold them comfortably, perhaps; but the world was surely wide enough to live in, outside of Natchitoches town.

His heart beat in a strangely irregular manner as he neared Madame Célestin's house one morning, and discovered her behind the rosebushes, as usual plying her broom. She had finished the gallery and steps and was sweeping the little brick walk along the edge of the violet border.

"Good-morning, Madame Célestin."

"Ah, it's you, Judge? Good-morning." He waited. She seemed to be doing the same. Then she ventured, with some hesitancy, "You know, Judge, about that divo'ce. I been thinking,—I reckon you betta neva mind about that divo'ce." She was making deep rings in the palm of her gloved hand with the end of the broomhandle, and looking at them critically. Her face seemed to the lawyer to be unusually rosy; but maybe it was only the

reflection of the pink bow at the throat. "Yes, I reckon you need
n' mine. You see, Judge, Célestin came home las' night. An'
he's promise me on his word an' honor he's going to turn ova a
new leaf."

Stephen Crane
(1871–1900)

Born in New Jersey, raised in upstate New York, Crane briefly attended first Lafayette College and then Syracuse University; he then moved to New York City and began to write, both as a journalist and as a novelist. His first book, Maggie: A Girl of the Streets *(1893), which he published himself, won him the acclaim and support of William Dean Howells; by 1895, when he published his most famous book,* The Red Badge of Courage, *his reputation was established. In the same year appeared a collection of free verse,* The Black Riders, *inspired by his reading of Emily Dickinson's poetry. After a certain amount of hackwork, Crane in 1898 brought out* The Open Boat and Other Tales of Adventure *and in 1899* The Monster and Other Stories, *from which "The Blue Hotel" is taken. Having become an immensely successful war reporter, Crane was sent on expeditions to Mexico, to Cuba (the key episodes of* The Open Boat *were based on his experiences when leaving Cuba), and to Greece. His health seriously compromised, he traveled to England, where he lived for a very short time as a celebrated writer. A desperate trip to a sanitorium in Germany could not save him; he died of tuberculosis.*

THE BLUE HOTEL

I

The Palace Hotel at Fort Romper was painted a light blue, a shade that is on the legs of a kind of heron, causing the bird to declare its position against any background. The Palace Hotel,

then, was always screaming and howling in a way that made the
dazzling winter landscape of Nebraska seem only a gray, swampish
hush. It stood alone on the prairie, and when the snow was
falling, the town two hundred yards away was not visible. But
when the traveler alighted at the railway station, he was obliged
to pass the Palace Hotel before he could come upon the company
of low, clapboard houses which composed Fort Romper, and it
was not to be thought that any traveler could pass the Palace
Hotel without looking at it. Pat Scully, the proprietor, had
proved himself a master of strategy when he chose his paints. It
is true that on clear days, when the great transcontinental expresses,
long lines of swaying Pullmans, swept through Fort Romper,
passengers were overcome at the sight, and the cult that knows
the brown-reds and the subdivisions of the dark greens of the
East expressed shame, pity, horror, in a laugh. But to the
citizens of this prairie town and to the people who would naturally stop there, Pat Scully had performed a feat. With this
opulence and splendor, these creeds, classes, egotisms that
streamed through Romper on the rails day after day, they had no
color in common.

As if the displayed delights of such a blue hotel were not
sufficiently enticing, it was Scully's habit to go every morning
and evening to meet the leisurely trains that stopped at Romper
and work his seductions upon any man that he might see wavering,
gripsack in hand.

One morning, when a snow-crusted engine dragged its long
string of freight cars and its one passenger coach to the station,
Scully performed the marvel of catching three men. One was a
shaky and quick-eyed Swede, with a great, shining, cheap valise;
one was a tall, bronzed cowboy, who was on his way to a ranch
near the Dakota line; one was a little, silent man from the East,
who didn't look it, and didn't announce it. Scully practically
made them prisoners. He was so nimble and merry and kindly
that each probably felt it would be the height of brutality to try to
escape. They trudged off over the creaking board sidewalks in
the wake of the eager little Irishman. He wore a heavy fur cap
squeezed tightly down on his head. It caused his two red ears to
stick out stiffly, as if they were made of tin.

At last, Scully, elaborately, with boisterous hospitality, conducted them through the portals of the blue hotel. The room
which they entered was small. It seemed to be merely a proper
temple for an enormous stove, which, in the center, was humming with godlike violence. At various points on its surface the
iron had become luminous and glowed yellow from the heat.

Beside the stove, Scully's son Johnnie was playing high-five with an old farmer who had whiskers both gray and sandy. They were quarreling. Frequently the old farmer turned his face toward a box of sawdust—colored brown from tobacco juice—that was behind the stove, and spat with an air of great impatience and irritation. With a loud flourish of words, Scully destroyed the game of cards, and bustled his son upstairs with part of the baggage of the new guests. He himself conducted them to three basins of the coldest water in the world. The cowboy and the Easterner burnished themselves fiery red with this water, until it seemed to be some kind of metal polish. The Swede, however, merely dipped his fingers gingerly and with trepidation. It was notable that throughout this series of small ceremonies, the three travelers were made to feel that Scully was very benevolent. He was conferring great favors upon them. He handed the towel from one to another with an air of philanthropic impulse.

Afterward they went to the first room, and sitting about the stove, listened to Scully's officious clamor at his daughters, who were preparing the midday meal. They reflected in the silence of experienced men who tread carefully amid new people. Nevertheless, the old farmer, stationary, invincible in his chair near the warmest part of the stove, turned his face from the sawdust box frequently and addressed a glowing commonplace to the strangers. Usually he was answered in short but adequate sentences by either the cowboy or the Easterner. The Swede said nothing. He seemed to be occupied in making furtive estimates of each man in the room. One might have thought that he had the sense of silly suspicion which comes to guilt. He resembled a badly frightened man.

Later, at dinner, he spoke a little, addressing his conversation entirely to Scully. He volunteered that he had come from New York, where for ten years he had worked as a tailor. These facts seemed to strike Scully as fascinating, and afterward he volunteered that he had lived at Romper for fourteen years. The Swede asked about the crops and the price of labor. He seemed barely to listen to Scully's extended replies. His eyes continued to rove from man to man.

Finally, with a laugh and a wink, he said that some of these Western communities were very dangerous; and after his statement, he straightened his legs under the table, tilted his head, and laughed again, loudly. It was plain that the demonstration had no meaning to the others. They looked at him wondering and in silence.

II

As the men trooped heavily back into the front room, the two little windows presented views of a turmoiling sea of snow. The huge arms of the wind were making attempts—mighty, circular, futile—to embrace the flakes as they sped. A gatepost like a still man with a blanched face stood aghast amid this profligate fury. In a hearty voice Scully announced the presence of a blizzard. The guests of the blue hotel, lighting their pipes, assented with grunts of lazy, masculine contentment. No island of the sea could be exempt in the degree of this little room with its humming stove. Johnnie, son of Scully, in a tone which defined his opinion of his ability as a card-player, challenged the old farmer of both gray and sandy whiskers to a game of high-five. The farmer agreed with a contemptuous and bitter scoff. They sat close to the stove, and squared their knees under a wide board. The cowboy and the Easterner watched the game with interest. The Swede remained near the window, aloof, but with a countenance that showed signs of an inexplicable excitement.

The play of Johnnie and the graybeard was suddenly ended by another quarrel. The old man arose while casting a look of heated scorn at his adversary. He slowly buttoned his coat, and then stalked with fabulous dignity from the room. In the discreet silence of all the other men, the Swede laughed. His laughter rang somehow childish. Men by this time had begun to look at him askance, as if they wished to inquire what ailed him.

A new game was formed jocosely. The cowboy volunteered to become the partner of Johnnie, and they all then turned to ask the Swede to throw in his lot with the little Easterner. He asked some questions about the game, and learning that it wore many names, and that he had played it when it was under an alias, he accepted the invitation. He strode toward the men nervously, as if he expected to be assaulted. Finally, seated, he gazed from face to face and laughed shrilly. This laugh was so strange that the Easterner looked up quickly, the cowboy sat intent and with his mouth open, and Johnnie paused, holding the cards with still fingers.

Afterward there was a short silence. Then Johnnie said, "Well, let's get at it. Come on now!" They pulled their chairs forward until their knees were bunched under the board. They began to play, and their interest in the game caused the others to forget the manner of the Swede.

The cowboy was a board-whacker. Each time that he held

superior cards, he whanged them, one by one, with exceeding force, down upon the improvised table, and took the tricks with a glowing air of prowess and pride that sent thrills of indignation into the hearts of his opponents. A game with a board-whacker in it is sure to become intense. The countenances of the Easterner and the Swede were miserable whenever the cowboy thundered down his aces and kings, while Johnnie, his eyes gleaming with joy, chuckled and chuckled.

Because of the absorbing play, none considered the strange ways of the Swede. They paid strict heed to the game. Finally, during a lull caused by a new deal, the Swede suddenly addressed Johnnie: "I suppose there have been a good many men killed in this room." The jaws of the others dropped and they looked at him.

"What in hell are you talking about?" said Johnnie.

The Swede laughed again his blatant laugh, full of a kind of false courage and defiance. "Oh, you know what I mean, all right," he answered.

"I'm a liar if I do!" Johnnie protested. The card was halted, and the men stared at the Swede. Johnnie evidently felt that as the son of the proprietor he should make a direct inquiry. "Now what might you be drivin' at, mister?" he asked. The Swede winked at him. It was a wink full of cunning. His fingers shook on the edge of the board. "Oh, maybe you think I have been to nowheres. Maybe you think I'm a tenderfoot?"

"I don't know nothin' about you," answered Johnnie, "and I don't give a damn where you've been. All I got to say is that I don't know what you're driving at. There hain't never been nobody killed in this room."

The cowboy, who had been steadily gazing at the Swede, then spoke: "What's wrong with you, mister?"

Apparently it seemed to the Swede that he was formidably menaced. He shivered and turned white near the corners of his mouth. He sent an appealing glance in the direction of the little Easterner. During these moments, he did not forget to wear his air of advanced pot valor. "They say they don't know what I mean," he remarked mockingly to the Easterner.

The latter answered after prolonged and cautious reflection. "I don't understand you," he said impassively.

The Swede made a movement then which announced that he thought he had encountered treachery from the only quarter where he had expected sympathy, if not help. "Oh, I see you are all against me. I see—"

The cowboy was in a state of deep stupefaction. "Say," he

cried, as he tumbled the deck violently down upon the board. "Say, what are you gittin' at, hey?"

The Swede sprang up with the celerity of a man escaping from a snake on the floor. "I don't want to fight!" he shouted. "I don't want to fight!"

The cowboy stretched his long legs indolently and deliberately. His hands were in his pockets. He spat into the sawdust box. "Well, who the hell thought you did?" he inquired.

The Swede backed rapidly toward a corner of the room. His hands were out protectingly in front of his chest, but he was making an obvious struggle to control his fright. "Gentlemen," he quavered, "I suppose I am going to be killed before I can leave this house! I suppose I am going to be killed before I can leave this house!" In his eyes was the dying-swan look. Through the windows could be seen the snow turning blue in the shadow of dusk. The wind tore at the house, and some loose thing beat regularly against the clapboards like a spirit tapping.

A door opened, and Scully himself entered. He paused in surprise as he noted the tragic attitude of the Swede. Then he said, "What's the matter here?"

The Swede answered him swiftly and eagerly: "These men are going to kill me."

"Kill you!" ejaculated Scully. "Kill you! What are you talkin'?"

The Swede made the gesture of a martyr.

Scully wheeled sternly upon his son. "What is this, Johnnie?"

The lad had grown sullen. "Damned if I know," he answered. "I can't make no sense to it." He began to shuffle the cards, fluttering them together with an angry snap. "He says a good many men have been killed in this room, or something like that. And he says he's going to be killed here, too. I don't know what ails him. He's crazy, I shouldn't wonder."

Scully then looked for explanation to the cowboy, but the cowboy simply shrugged his shoulders.

"Kill you?" said Scully again to the Swede. "Kill you? Man, you're off your nut."

"Oh, I know," burst out the Swede. "I know what will happen. Yes, I'm crazy—yes. Yes, of course, I'm crazy—yes. But I know one thing—" There was a sort of sweat of misery and terror upon his face. "I know I won't get out of here alive."

The cowboy drew a deep breath, as if his mind was passing into the last stages of dissolution. "Well, I'm doggoned," he whispered to himself.

Scully wheeled suddenly and faced his son. "You've been troublin' this man!"

Johnnie's voice was loud with its burden of grievance. "Why, good Gawd, I ain't done nothin' to 'im."

The Swede broke in. "Gentlemen, do not disturb yourselves. I will leave this house. I will go away, because"—he accused them dramatically with his glance—"because I do not want to be killed."

Scully was furious with his son. "Will you tell me what is the matter, you young divil? What's the matter, anyhow? Speak out!"

"Blame it!" cried Johnnie in despair. "Don't I tell you I don't know? He—he says we want to kill him, and that's all I know. I can't tell what ails him."

The Swede continued to repeat, "Never mind, Mr. Scully; never mind. I will leave this house. I will go away, because I do not wish to be killed. Yes, of course, I am crazy—yes. But I know one thing! I will go away. I will leave this house. Never mind, Mr. Scully; never mind. I will go away."

"You will not go 'way," said Scully. "You will not go 'way until I hear the reason of this business. If anybody has troubled you, I will take care of him. This is my house. You are under my roof, and I will not allow any peaceable man to be troubled here." He cast a terrible eye upon Johnnie, the cowboy, and the Easterner.

"Never mind, Mr. Scully; never mind. I will go away. I do not wish to be killed." The Swede moved toward the door which opened upon the stairs. It was evidently his intention to go at once for his baggage.

"No, no," shouted Scully peremptorily; but the white-faced man slid by him and disappeared. "Now," said Scully severely, "what does this mane?"

Johnnie and the cowboy cried together. "Why, we didn't do nothin' to 'im!"

Scully's eyes were cold. "No," he said, "you didn't?"

Johnnie swore a deep oath. "Why, this is the wildest loon I ever see. We didn't do nothin' at all. We were jest sittin' here playin' cards, and he—"

The father suddenly spoke to the Easterner. "Mr. Blanc," he asked, "what has these boys been doin'?"

The Easterner reflected again. "I didn't see anything wrong at all," he said at last, slowly.

Scully began to howl. "But what does it mane?" He stared

ferociously at his son. "I have a mind to lather you for this, me boy."

Johnnie was frantic. "Well, what have I done?" he bawled at his father.

III

"I think you are tongue-tied," said Scully finally to his son, the cowboy, and the Easterner; and at the end of this scornful sentence, he left the room.

Upstairs the Swede was swiftly fastening the straps of his great valise. Once his back happened to be half turned toward the door, and hearing a noise there, he wheeled and sprang up, uttering a loud cry. Scully's wrinkled visage showed grimly in the light of the small lamp he carried. This yellow effulgence, streaming upward, colored only his prominent features, and left his eyes, for instance, in mysterious shadow. He resembled a murderer.

"Man! Man!" he exclaimed. "Have you gone daffy?"

"Oh, no! Oh, no!" rejoined the other. "There are people in this world who know pretty nearly as much as you do—understand?"

For a moment they stood gazing at each other. Upon the Swede's deathly pale cheeks were two spots brightly crimson and sharply edged, as if they had been carefully painted. Scully placed the light on the table and sat himself on the edge of the bed. He spoke ruminatively. "By cracky, I never heard of such a thing in my life. It's a complete muddle. I can't, for the soul of me, think how you ever got this idea into your head." Presently he lifted his eyes and asked, "And did you sure think they were going to kill you?"

The Swede scanned the old man as if he wished to see into his mind. "I did," he said at last. He obviously suspected that this answer might precipitate an outbreak. As he pulled on a strap, his whole arm shook, the elbow wavering like a bit of paper.

Scully banged his hand impressively on the footboard of the bed. "Why, man, we're goin' to have a line of ilictric streetcars in this town next spring."

" 'A line of electric streetcars,' " repeated the Swede stupidly.

"And," said Scully, "there's a new railroad goin' to be built down from Broken Arm to here. Not to mention the four churches and the smashin'-big brick schoolhouse. Then there's the big factory, too. Why, in two years, Romper'll be a met-tro-*pol*-is."

Having finished the preparation of his baggage, the Swede

straightened himself. "Mr. Scully," he said, with sudden hardihood, "how much do I owe you?"

"You don't owe me anythin'," said the old man angrily.

"Yes, I do," retorted the Swede. He took seventy-five cents from his pocket and tendered it to Scully; but the latter snapped his fingers in disdainful refusal. However, it happened that they both stood gazing in a strange fashion at three silver pieces on the Swede's open palm.

"I'll not take your money," said Scully at last. "Not after what's been goin' on here." Then a plan seemed to strike him. "Here," he cried, picking up his lamp and moving toward the door. "Here! Come with me a minute."

"No," said the Swede, in overwhelming alarm.

"Yes," urged the old man. "Come on! I want you to come and see a picter—just across the hall—in my room."

The Swede must have concluded that his hour was come. His jaw dropped and his teeth showed like a dead man's. He ultimately followed Scully across the corridor, but he had the step of one hung in chains.

Scully flashed the light high on the wall of his own chamber. There was revealed a ridiculous photograph of a little girl. She was leaning against a balustrade of gorgeous decoration, and the formidable bang to her hair was prominent. The figure was as graceful as an upright sled stake, and, withal, it was of the hue of lead. "There," said Scully tenderly, "that's the picter of my little girl that died. Her name was Carrie. She had the purtiest hair you ever saw! I was that fond of her, she—"

Turning then, he saw that the Swede was not contemplating the picture at all, but instead, was keeping keen watch on the gloom in the rear.

"Look, man!" cried Scully heartily. "That's the picter of my little gal that died. Her name was Carrie. And then here's the picter of my oldest boy, Michael. He's a lawyer in Lincoln, an' doin' well. I gave that boy a grand eddication, and I'm glad for it now. He's a fine boy. Look at 'im now. Ain't he bold as blazes, him there in Lincoln, an honored an' respicted gintleman! An honored and respicted gintleman," concluded Scully with a flourish. And so saying, he smote the Swede jovially on the back.

The Swede faintly smiled.

"Now," said the old man, "there's only one more thing." He dropped suddenly to the floor and thrust his head beneath the bed. The Swede could hear his muffled voice. "I'd keep it under me piller if it wasn't for that boy Johnnie. Then there's the old woman— Where is it now? I never put it twice in the same place. Ah, now come out with you!''

Presently he backed clumsily from under the bed, dragging with him an old coat rolled into a bundle. ''I've fetched him,'' he muttered. Kneeling on the floor, he unrolled the coat and extracted from its heart a large, yellow-brown whisky bottle.

His first maneuver was to hold the bottle up to the light. Reassured, apparently, that nobody had been tampering with it, he thrust it with a generous movement toward the Swede.

The weak-kneed Swede was about to eagerly clutch this element of strength, but he suddenly jerked his hand away and cast a look of horror upon Scully.

''Drink,'' said the old man affectionately. He had risen to his feet, and now stood facing the Swede.

There was a silence. Then again Scully said, ''Drink!''

The Swede laughed wildly. He grabbed the bottle, put it to his mouth; and as his lips curled absurdly around the opening and his throat worked, he kept his glance, burning with hatred, upon the old man's face.

IV

After the departure of Scully, the three men, with the cardboard still upon their knees, preserved for a long time an astounded silence. Then Johnnie said, ''That's the dod-dangedest Swede I ever see.''

''He ain't no Swede,'' said the cowboy scornfully.

''Well, what is he, then?'' cried Johnnie. ''What is he then?''

''It's my opinion,'' replied the cowboy deliberately, ''he's some kind of a Dutchman.'' It was a venerable custom of the country to entitle as Swedes all light-haired men who spoke with a heavy tongue. In consequence, the idea of the cowboy was not without its daring. ''Yes, sir,'' he repeated. ''It's my opinion this feller is some kind of a Dutchman.''

''Well, he says he's a Swede, anyhow,'' muttered Johnnie sulkily. He turned to the Easterner: ''What do you think, Mr. Blanc?''

''Oh, I don't know,'' replied the Easterner.

''Well, what do you think makes him act that way?'' asked the cowboy.

''Why, he's frightened.'' The Easterner knocked his pipe against a rim of the stove. ''He's clear frightened out of his boots.''

''What at?'' cried Johnnie and the cowboy together.

The Easterner reflected over his answer.

"What at?" cried the others again.

"Oh, I don't know, but it seems to me this man has been reading dime novels, and he thinks he's right out in the middle of it—the shootin' and stabbin' and all."

"But," said the cowboy, deeply scandalized, "this ain't Wyoming, ner none of them places. This is Nebrasker."

"Yes," added Johnnie, "an' why don't he wait till he gits *out West?*"

The traveled Easterner laughed. "It isn't different there even—not in these days. But he thinks he's right in the middle of hell."

Johnnie and the cowboy mused long.

"It's awful funny," remarked Johnnie at last.

"Yes," said the cowboy. "This is a queer game. I hope we don't git snowed in, because then we'd have to stand this here man bein' around with us all the time. That wouldn't be no good."

"I wish Pop would throw him out," said Johnnie.

Presently they heard a loud stamping on the stairs, accompanied by ringing jokes in the voice of old Scully, and laughter, evidently from the Swede. The men around the stove stared vacantly at each other. "Gosh!" said the cowboy. The door flew open, and old Scully, flushed and anecdotal, came into the room. He was jabbering at the Swede, who followed him, laughing bravely. It was the entry of two roisterers from a banquet hall.

"Come now," said Scully sharply to the three seated men, "move up and give us a chance at the stove." The cowboy and the Easterner obediently sidled their chairs to make room for the newcomers. Johnnie, however, simply arranged himself in a more indolent attitude, and then remained motionless.

"Come! Git over, there," said Scully.

"Plenty of room on the other side of the stove," said Johnnie.

"Do you think we want to sit in the draught?" roared the father.

But the Swede here interposed with a grandeur of confidence. "No, no. Let the boy sit where he likes," he cried in a bullying voice to the father.

"All right! All right!" said Scully deferentially. The cowboy and the Easterner exchanged glances of wonder.

The five chairs were formed in a crescent about one side of the stove. The Swede began to talk; he talked arrogantly, profanely, angrily. Johnnie, the cowboy, and the Easterner maintained a morose silence, while old Scully appeared to be receptive and eager, breaking in constantly with sympathetic ejaculations.

Finally the Swede announced that he was thirsty. He moved in his chair, and said that he would go for a drink of water.

"I'll git it for you," cried Scully at once.

"No," said the Swede contemptuously. "I'll get it for myself." He arose and stalked with the air of an owner off into the executive parts of the hotel.

As soon as the Swede was out of hearing, Scully sprang to his feet and whispered intensely to the others, "Upstairs he thought I was tryin' to poison 'im."

"Say," said Johnnie, "this makes me sick. Why don't you throw 'im out in the snow?"

"Why, he's all right now," declared Scully. "It was only that he was from the East, and he thought this was a tough place. That's all. He's all right now."

The cowboy looked with admiration upon the Easterner. "You were straight," he said. "You were on to that there Dutchman."

"Well," said Johnnie to his father, "he may be all right now, but I don't see it. Other time he was scared, but now he's too fresh."

Scully's speech was always a combination of Irish brogue and idiom, Western twang and idiom, and scraps of curiously formal diction taken from the storybooks and newspapers. He now hurled a strange mass of language at the head of his son. "What do I keep? What do I keep? What do I keep?" he demanded in a voice of thunder. He slapped his knee impressively, to indicate that he himself was going to make reply, and that all should heed. "I keep a hotel," he shouted, "A hotel, do you mind? A guest under my roof has sacred privileges. He is to be intimidated by none. Not one word shall he hear that would prijudice him in favor of goin' away. I'll not have it. There's no place in this here town where they can say they iver took in a guest of mine because he was afraid to stay here." He wheeled suddenly upon the cowboy and the Easterner. "Am I right?"

"Yes, Mr. Scully," said the cowboy, "I think you're right."

"Yes, Mr. Scully," said the Easterner, "I think you're right."

v

At six-o'clock supper, the Swede fizzed like a fire wheel. He sometimes seemed on the point of bursting into riotous song, and in all his madness he was encouraged by old Scully. The Easterner was encased in reserve; the cowboy sat in wide-mouthed amazement, forgetting to eat, while Johnnie wrathily demolished great plates of food. The daughters of the house, when they were obliged to replenish the biscuits, approached as warily as Indians, and having succeeded in their purpose, fled with ill-concealed trepidation. The Swede domineered the whole feast, and he gave it the appearance of a cruel bacchanal. He seemed to have grown suddenly taller; he gazed, brutally disdainful, into every face. His voice rang through the room. Once when he jabbed out harpoon-fashion with his fork to pinion a biscuit, the weapon nearly impaled the hand of the Easterner, which had been stretched quietly out for the same biscuit.

After supper, as the men filed toward the other room, the Swede smote Scully ruthlessly on the shoulder. "Well, old boy, that was a good, square meal." Johnnie looked hopefully at his father; he knew that shoulder was tender from an old fall; and indeed, it appeared for a moment as if Scully was going to flame out over the matter, but in the end he smiled a sickly smile and remained silent. The others understood from his manner that he was admitting his responsibility for the Swede's new viewpoint.

Johnnie, however, addressed his parent in an aside. "Why don't you license somebody to kick you downstairs?" Scully scowled darkly by way of reply.

When they were gathered about the stove, the Swede insisted on another game of high-five. Scully gently deprecated the plan at first, but the Swede turned a wolfish glare upon him. The old man subsided, and the Swede canvassed the others. In his tone there was always a great threat. The cowboy and the Easterner both remarked indifferently that they would play. Scully said that he would presently have to go to meet the six fifty-eight train, and so the Swede turned menacingly upon Johnnie. For a moment their glances crossed like blades, and then Johnnie smiled and said, "Yes, I'll play."

They formed a square, with the little board on their knees. The Easterner and the Swede were again partners. As the play went on, it was noticeable that the cowboy was not board-whacking as usual. Meanwhile Scully, near the lamp, had put on his spectacles, and with an appearance curiously like an old priest, was reading a newspaper. In time he went out to meet the six fifty-eight train, and despite his precautions, a gust of polar wind whirled into the room as he opened the door. Besides scattering the cards, it chilled the players to the marrow. The Swede cursed frightfully. When Scully returned, his entrance disturbed a cosy and friendly scene. The Swede again cursed. But presently they were once more intent, their heads bent forward and their hands moving swiftly. The Swede had adopted the fashion of board-whacking.

Scully took up his paper and for a long time remained immersed in matters which were extraordinarily remote from him. The lamp burned badly, and once he stopped to adjust the wick. The newspaper, as he turned from page to page, rustled with a slow and comfortable sound. Then suddenly he heard three terrible words: "You are cheatin'!"

Such scenes often prove that there can be little of dramatic import in environment. Any room can present a tragic front; any room can be comic. This little den was now hideous as a torture chamber. The new faces of the men themselves had changed it upon the instant. The Swede held a huge fist in front of Johnnie's face, while the latter looked steadily over it into the blazing orbs of his accuser. The Easterner had grown pallid; the cowboy's jaw had dropped in that expression of bovine amazement which was one of his important mannerisms. After the three words, the first sound in the room was made by Scully's paper as it floated forgotten to his feet. His spectacles had also fallen from his nose, but by a clutch he had saved them in air. His hand, grasping the spectacles, now remained poised awkwardly and near his shoulder. He stared at the card-players.

Probably the silence was while a second elapsed. Then, if the floor had been suddenly twitched out from under the men, they could not have moved quicker. The five had projected themselves headlong toward a common point. It happened that Johnnie, in rising to hurl himself upon the Swede, had stumbled slightly because of his curiously instinctive care for the cards and the board. The loss of the moment allowed time for the arrival of Scully, and also allowed the cowboy time to give the Swede a great push which sent him staggering back. The men found tongue together, and hoarse shouts of rage, appeal, or fear burst from every throat. The cowboy pushed and jostled feverishly at the Swede, and the Easterner and Scully clung wildly to Johnnie; but through the smoky air, above the swaying bodies of the peace-compellers, the eyes of the two warriors ever sought each other in glances of challenge that were at once hot and steely.

Of course the board had been overturned, and now the whole company of cards was scattered over the floor, where the boots of the men trampled the fat and painted kings and queens as they gazed with their silly eyes at the war that was waging above them.

Scully's voice was dominating the yells. "Stop, now! Stop, I say! Stop, now—"

Johnnie, as he struggled to burst through the rank formed by Scully and the Easterner, was crying, "Well, he says I cheated! He says I cheated! I won't allow no man to say I cheated! If he says I cheated, he's a —— ——!"

The cowboy was telling the Swede, "Quit, now! Quit, d'ye hear—"

The screams of the Swede never ceased: "He did cheat! I saw him! I saw him—"

As for the Easterner, he was importuning in a voice that was not heeded: "Wait a moment, can't you? Oh, wait a moment. What's the good of a fight over a game of cards? Wait a moment—"

In this tumult, no complete sentences were clear. "Cheat"— "Quit"—"He says"—these fragments pierced the uproar and rang out sharply. It was remarkable that, whereas Scully undoubtedly made the most noise, he was the least heard of any of the riotous band.

Then suddenly there was a great cessation. It was as if each man had paused for breath; and although the room was still lighted with the anger of men, it could be seen that there was no danger of immediate conflict, and at once Johnnie, shouldering his way forward, almost succeeded in confronting the Swede. "What did you say I cheated for? What did you say I cheated for? I don't cheat, and I won't let no man say I do!"

The Swede said, "I saw you! I saw you!"

"Well," cried Johnnie, "I'll fight any man what says I cheat!"

"No, you won't," said the cowboy. "Not here."

"Ah, be still, can't you?" said Scully, coming between them.

The quiet was sufficient to allow the Easterner's voice to be heard. He was repeating, "Oh, wait a moment, can't you? What's the good of a fight over a game of cards? Wait a moment!"

Johnnie, his red face appearing above his father's shoulder, hailed the Swede again. "Did you say I cheated?"

The Swede showed his teeth. "Yes."

"Then," said Johnnie, "we must fight."

"Yes, fight," roared the Swede. He was like a demoniac. "Yes, fight! I'll show you what kind of a man I am! I'll show you who you want to fight! Maybe you think I can't fight! Maybe you think I can't! I'll show you, you skin, you card-sharp! Yes, you cheated! You cheated! You cheated!"

"Well, let's go at it, then, mister," said Johnnie coolly.

The cowboy's brow was beaded with sweat from his efforts

in intercepting all sorts of raids. He turned in despair to Scully.
"What are you goin' to do now?"

A change had come over the Celtic visage of the old man. He
now seemed all eagerness; his eyes glowed.

"We'll let them fight," he answered stalwartly. "I can't put
up with it any longer. I've stood this damned Swede till I'm
sick. We'll let them fight."

VI

The men prepared to go out of doors. The Easterner was so
nervous that he had great difficulty in getting his arms into the
sleeves of his new leather coat. As the cowboy drew his fur cap
down over his ears, his hands trembled. In fact, Johnnie and old
Scully were the only ones who displayed no agitation. These
preliminaries were conducted without words.

Scully threw open the door. "Well, come on," he said.
Instantly a terrific wind caused the flame of the lamp to struggle
at its wick, while a puff of black smoke sprang from the chimney
top. The stove was in midcurrent of the blast, and its voice
swelled to equal the roar of the storm. Some of the scarred and
bedabbled cards were caught up from the floor and dashed
helplessly against the farther wall. The men lowered their heads
and plunged into the tempest as into a sea.

No snow was falling, but great whirls and clouds of flakes,
swept up from the ground by the frantic winds, were streaming
southward with the speed of bullets. The covered land was blue
with the sheen of an unearthly satin, and there was no other hue
save where, at the low, black railway station—which seemed
incredibly distant—one light gleamed like a tiny jewel. As
the men floundered into a thigh-deep drift, it was known that the
Swede was bawling out something. Scully went to him, put a
hand on his shoulder, and projected an ear. "What's that you
say?" he shouted.

"I say," bawled the Swede again, "I won't stand much show
against this gang. I know you'll all pitch on me."

Scully smote him reproachfully on the arm. "Tut, man!" he
yelled. The wind tore the words from Scully's lips and scattered
them far alee.

"You are all a gang of—" boomed the Swede, but the storm
also seized the remainder of this sentence.

Immediately turning their backs upon the wind, the men had
swung around a corner to the sheltered side of the hotel. It was
the function of the little house to preserve here, amid this great

devastation of snow, an irregular V-shape of heavily encrusted grass, which crackled beneath the feet. One could imagine the great drifts piled against the windward side. When the party reached the comparative peace of this spot, it was found that the Swede was still bellowing.

"Oh, I know what kind of a thing this is! I know you'll all pitch on me. I can't lick you all!"

Scully turned upon him panther-fashion. "You'll not have to whip all of us. You'll have to whip my son Johnnie. An' the man that troubles you durin' that time will have me to dale with."

The arrangements were swiftly made. The two men faced each other, obedient to the harsh commands of Scully, whose face, in the subtly luminous gloom, could be seen in the austere, impersonal lines that are pictured on the countenances of the Roman veterans. The Easterner's teeth were chattering, and he was hopping up and down like a mechanical toy. The cowboy stood rocklike.

The contestants had not stripped off any clothing. Each was in his ordinary attire. Their fists were up, and they eyed each other in a calm that had the elements of leonine cruelty in it.

During this pause, the Easterner's mind, like a film, took lasting impressions of three men—the iron-nerved master of the ceremony; the Swede, pale, motionless, terrible; and Johnnie, serene yet ferocious, brutish yet heroic. The entire prelude had in it a tragedy greater than the tragedy of action, and this aspect was accentuated by the long, mellow cry of the blizzard, as it sped the tumbling and wailing flakes into the black abyss of the south.

"Now!" said Scully.

The two combatants leaped forward and crashed together like bullocks. There was heard the cushioned sound of blows, and of a curse squeezing out from between the tight teeth of one.

As for the spectators, the Easterner's pent-up breath exploded from him with a pop of relief, absolute relief from the tension of the preliminaries. The cowboy bounded into the air with a yowl. Scully was immovable as from supreme amazement and fear at the fury of the fight which he himself had permitted and arranged.

For a time the encounter in the darkness was such a perplexity of flying arms that it presented no more detail than would a swiftly revolving wheel. Occasionally a face, as if illumined by a flash of light, would shine out, ghastly and marked with pink spots. A moment later, the men might have been known as shadows, if it were not for the involuntary utterance of oaths that came from them in whispers.

Suddenly a holocaust of warlike desire caught the cowboy, and he bolted forward with the speed of a bronco. "Go it, Johnnie! Go it! Kill him! Kill him!"

Scully confronted him. "Kape back," he said; and by his glance the cowboy could tell that this man was Johnnie's father.

To the Easterner there was a monotony of unchangeable fighting that was an abomination. This confused mingling was eternal to his sense, which was concentrated in a longing for the end, the priceless end. Once the fighters lurched near him, and as he scrambled hastily backward, he heard them breathe like men on the rack.

"Kill him, Johnnie! Kill him! Kill him! Kill him!" The cowboy's face was contorted like one of those agony masks in museums.

"Keep still," said Scully icily.

Then there was a sudden loud grunt, incomplete, cut short, and Johnnie's body swung away from the Swede and fell with sickening heaviness to the grass. The cowboy was barely in time to prevent the mad Swede from flinging himself upon his prone adversary. "No, you don't," said the cowboy, interposing an arm. "Wait a second."

Scully was at his son's side. "Johnnie! Johnnie, me boy!" His voice had a quality of melancholy tenderness. "Johnnie! Can you go on with it?" He looked anxiously down into the bloody, pulpy face of his son.

There was a moment of silence, and then Johnnie answered in his ordinary voice, "Yes, I—it—yes."

Assisted by his father, he struggled to his feet. "Wait a bit now till you git your wind," said the old man.

A few paces away, the cowboy was lecturing the Swede. "No, you don't! Wait a second!"

The Easterner was plucking at Scully's sleeve. "Oh, this is enough," he pleaded. "This is enough! Let it go as it stands. This is enough!"

"Bill," said Scully, "git out of the road." The cowboy stepped aside. "Now." The combatants were actuated by a new caution as they advanced toward collision. They'd glared at each other, and then the Swede aimed a lightning blow that carried with it his entire weight. Johnnie was evidently half stupid from weakness, but he miraculously dodged, and his fist sent the overbalanced Swede sprawling.

The cowboy, Scully, and the Easterner burst into a cheer that was like a chorus of triumphant soldiery, but before its conclusion the Swede had scuffled agilely to his feet and come in berserk abandon at his foe. There was another perplexity of flying arms, and Johnnie's body again swung away and fell, even as a bundle might fall from a roof. The Swede instantly staggered to a little wind-waved tree and leaned upon it, breathing like an engine, while his savage and flame-lit eyes roamed from face to face as the men bent over Johnnie. There was a splendor of isolation in his situation at this time which the Easterner felt once when, lifting his eyes from the man on the ground, he beheld that mysterious and lonely figure, waiting.

"Are you any good yet, Johnnie?" asked Scully in a broken voice.

The son gasped and opened his eyes languidly. After a moment, he answered, "No—I ain't—any good—any—more." Then, from shame and bodily ill, he began to weep, the tears furrowing down through the bloodstains on his face. "He was too—too—too heavy for me."

Scully straightened and addressed the waiting figure. "Stranger," he said evenly, "it's all up with our side." Then his voice changed into that vibrant huskiness which is commonly the tone of the most simple and deadly announcements. "Johnnie is whipped."

Without replying, the victor moved off on the route to the front door of the hotel.

The cowboy was formulating new and unspellable blasphemies. The Easterner was startled to find that they were out in a wind that seemed to come direct from the shadowed Arctic floes. He heard again the wail of the snow as it was flung to its grave in the south. He knew now that all this time the cold had been sinking into him deeper and deeper, and he wondered that he had not perished. He felt indifferent to the condition of the vanquished man.

"Johnnie, can you walk?" asked Scully.

"Did I hurt—hurt him any?" asked the son.

"Can you walk, boy? Can you walk?"

Johnnie's voice was suddenly strong. There was a robust impatience in it. "I asked you whether I hurt him any!"

"Yes, yes, Johnnie," answered the cowboy consolingly, "he's hurt a good deal."

They raised him from the ground, and as soon as he was on his feet, he went tottering off, rebuffing all attempts at assistance. When the party rounded the corner, they were fairly blinded by the pelting of the snow. It burned their faces like fire. The cowboy carried Johnnie through the drift to the door. As they entered, some cards again rose from the floor and beat against the wall.

The Easterner rushed to the stove. He was so profoundly chilled that he almost dared to embrace the glowing iron. The Swede was not in the room. Johnnie sank into a chair, and folding his arms on his knees, buried his face in them. Scully, warming one foot and then the other at a rim of the stove, muttered to himself with Celtic mournfulness. The cowboy had removed his fur cap, and with a dazed and rueful air, he was running one hand through his tousled locks. From overhead they could hear the creaking of boards, as the Swede tramped here and there in his room.

The sad quiet was broken by the sudden flinging open of a door that led toward the kitchen. It was instantly followed by an inrush of women. They precipitated themselves upon Johnnie amid a chorus of lamentation. Before they carried their prey off to the kitchen, there to be bathed and harangued with that mixture of sympathy and abuse which is a feat of their sex, the mother straightened herself and fixed old Scully with an eye of stern reproach. "Shame be upon you, Patrick Scully!" she cried. "Your own son, too. Shame be upon you!"

"There now! Be quiet now!" said the old man weakly.

"Shame be upon you, Patrick Scully!" The girls, rallying to this slogan, sniffed disdainfully in the direction of those trembling accomplices, the cowboy and the Easterner. Presently they bore Johnnie away, and left the three men to dismal reflection.

VII

"I'd like to fight this here Dutchman myself," said the cowboy, breaking a long silence.

Scully wagged his head sadly. "No, that wouldn't do. It wouldn't be right. It wouldn't be right."

"Well, why wouldn't it?" argued the cowboy. "I don't see no harm in it."

"No," answered Scully with mournful heroism. "It wouldn't be right. It was Johnnie's fight, and now we mustn't whip the man just because he whipped Johnnie."

"Yes, that's true enough," said the cowboy, "but—he better not get fresh with me, because I couldn't stand no more of it."

"You'll not say a word to him," commanded Scully, and even then they heard the tread of the Swede on the stairs. His entrance was made theatric. He swept the door back with a bang and swaggered to the middle of the room. No one looked at him. "Well," he cried insolently at Scully, "I s'pose you'll tell me now how much I owe you?"

The old man remained stolid. "You don't owe me nothin'."

"Huh!" said the Swede. "Huh! Don't owe 'im nothin'."

The cowboy addressed the Swede. "Stranger, I don't see how you come to be so gay around here."

Old Scully was instantly alert. "Stop!" he shouted, holding his hand forth, fingers upward. "Bill, you shut up!"

The cowboy spat carelessly into the sawdust box. "I didn't say a word, did I?" he asked.

"Mr. Scully," called the Swede, "how much do I owe you?" It was seen that he was attired for departure, and that he had his valise in his hand.

"You don't owe me nothin'," repeated Scully in the same imperturbable way.

"Huh!" said the Swede. "I guess you're right. I guess if it was any way at all, you'd owe me somethin'. That's what I guess." He turned to the cowboy. " 'Kill him! Kill him! Kill him!' " he mimicked, and then guffawed victoriously. " 'Kill him!' " He was convulsed with ironical humor.

But he might have been jeering the dead. The three men were immovable and silent, staring with glassy eyes at the stove.

The Swede opened the door and passed into the storm, giving one derisive glance backward at the still group.

As soon as the door was closed, Scully and the cowboy leaped to their feet and began to curse. They trampled to and fro, waving their arms and smashing into the air with their fists. "Oh, but that was a hard minute!" wailed Scully. "That was a hard minute! Him there leerin' and scoffin'! One bang at his nose was worth forty dollars to me that minute! How did you stand it, Bill?"

"How did I stand it?" cried the cowboy in a quivering voice. "How did I stand it? Oh!"

The old man burst into sudden brogue. "I'd loike to take that Swede," he wailed, "and hould 'im down on a shtone flure and bate 'im to a jelly wid a shtick!"

The cowboy groaned in sympathy. "I'd like to git him by the neck and ha-ammer him"—he brought his hand down on a chair with a noise like a pistol shot—"hammer that there Dutchman until he couldn't tell himself from a dead coyote!"

"I'd bate 'im until he—"

"I'd show *him* some things—"

And then together they raised a yearning, fanatic cry: "Oh-o-oh! if we only could—"

"Yes!"

"Yes!"

"And then I'd—"

"O-o-oh!"

VIII

The Swede, tightly gripping his valise, tacked across the face of the storm as if he carried sails. He was following a line of little naked, gasping trees which, he knew, must mark the way of the road. His face, fresh from the pounding of Johnnie's fists, felt more pleasure than pain in the wind and the driving snow. A number of square shapes loomed upon him finally, and he knew them as the houses of the main body of the town. He found a street and made travel along it, leaning heavily upon the wind whenever, at a corner, a terrific blast caught him.

He might have been in a deserted village. We picture the world as thick with conquering and elate humanity, but here, with the bugles of the tempest pealing, it was hard to imagine a peopled earth. One viewed the existence of man then as a marvel, and conceded a glamour of wonder to these lice which were caused to cling to a whirling, fire-smitten, ice-locked, disease-stricken, space-lost bulb. The conceit of man was explained by this storm to be the very engine of life. One was a coxcomb not to die in it. However, the Swede found a saloon.

In front of it an indomitable red light was burning, and the snowflakes were made blood color as they flew through the circumscribed territory of the lamp's shining. The Swede pushed open the door of the saloon and entered. A sanded expanse was before him, and at the end of it four men sat about a table drinking. Down one side of the room extended a radiant bar, and its guardian was leaning upon his elbows listening to the talk of the men at the table. The Swede dropped his valise upon the floor, and smiling fraternally upon the barkeeper, said, "Gimme some whisky, will you?" The man placed a bottle, a whisky glass, and a glass of ice-thick water upon the bar. The Swede poured himself an abnormal portion of whisky and drank it in three gulps. "Pretty bad night," remarked the bartender indifferently. He was making the pretension of blindness which is usually a distinction of his class; but it could have been seen that he was furtively studying the half-erased bloodstains on the face of the Swede. "Bad night," he said again.

"Oh, it's good enough for me," replied the Swede hardily, as he poured himself some more whisky. The barkeeper took his coin and maneuvered it through its reception by the highly nickeled cash machine. A bell rang; a card labeled "20 cts." had appeared.

"No," continued the Swede, "this isn't too bad weather. It's good enough for me."

"So?" murmured the barkeeper languidly.

The copious drams made the Swede's eyes swim, and he breathed a trifle heavier. "Yes, I like this weather. I like it. It suits me." It was apparently his design to impart a deep significance to these words.

"So?" murmured the bartender again. He turned to gaze dreamily at the scroll-like birds and birdlike scrolls which had been drawn with soap upon the mirrors in back of the bar.

"Well, I guess I'll take another drink," said the Swede presently. "Have something?"

"No, thanks; I'm not drinkin'," answered the bartender. Afterward he asked, "How did you hurt your face?"

The Swede immediately began to boast loudly. "Why, in a fight. I thumped the soul out of a man down here at Scully's hotel."

The interest of the four men at the table was at last aroused.

"Who was it?" said one.

"Johnnie Scully," blustered the Swede. "Son of the man what runs it. He will be pretty near dead for some weeks, I can tell you. I made a nice thing of him, I did. He couldn't get up. They carried him in the house. Have a drink?"

Instantly the men in some subtle way encased themselves in reserve. "No, thanks," said one. The group was of curious formation. Two were prominent local businessmen; one was the district attorney; and one was a professional gambler of the kind known as "square." But a scrutiny of the group would not have enabled an observer to pick the gambler from the men of more reputable pursuits. He was, in fact, a man so delicate in manner, when among people of fair class, and so judicious in his choice of victims, that in the strictly masculine part of the town's life he had come to be explictly trusted and admired. People called him a thoroughbred. The fear and contempt with which his craft was regarded were undoubtedly the reason why his quiet dignity shone conscpicuous above the quiet dignity of men who might be merely hatters, billiard-markers, or grocery clerks. Beyond an occasional unwary traveler who came by rail, this gambler was supposed to prey solely upon reckless and senile farmers, who, when flush with good crops, drove into town in all the pride and confidence of an absolutely invulnerable stupidity. Hearing at times in circuitous fashion of the despoilment of such a farmer, the important men of Romper invariably laughed in contempt of the victim, and if they thought of the wolf at all, it was with a kind of pride at the knowledge that he would never dare think of attacking their wisdom and courage. Besides, it was popular that this gambler had a real wife and two real children in a neat cottage in a suburb, where he led an exemplary home life; and when anyone even suggested a discrepancy in his character, the crowd immediately vociferated descriptions of this virtuous family circle. Then men who led exemplary home lives, and men who did not lead exemplary home lives, all subsided in a bunch, remarking that there was nothing more to be said.

However, when a restriction was placed upon him—as, for instance, when a strong clique of members of the new Pollywog Club refused to permit him, even as a spectator, to appear in the rooms of the organization—the candor and gentleness with which he accepted the judgment disarmed many of his foes and made his friends more desperately partisan. He invariably distinguished between himself and a respectable Romper man so quickly and frankly that his manner actually appeared to be a continual broadcast compliment.

And one must not forget to declare the fundamental fact of his entire position in Romper. It is irrefutable that in all affairs outside his business, in all matters that occur eternally and commonly between man and man, this thieving card-player was so generous, so just, so moral, that in a contest, he could have put to flight the consciences of nine-tenths of the citizens of Romper.

And so it happened that he was seated in this saloon with the two prominent local merchants and the district attorney.

The Swede continued to drink raw whisky, meanwhile babbling at the barkeeper and trying to induce him to indulge in potations. "Come on. Have a drink. Come on. What—no? Well, have a little one, then. By gawd, I've whipped a man tonight, and I want to celebrate. I whipped him good, too. Gentlemen," the Swede cried to the men at the table, "have a drink?"

"Ssh!" said the barkeeper.

The group at the table, although furtively attentive, had been pretending to be deep in talk, but now a man lifted his eyes toward the Swede and said, shortly, "Thanks. We don't want any more."

At this reply, the Swede ruffled out his chest like a rooster.

"Well," he exploded, "it seems I can't get anybody to drink with me in this town. Seems so, don't it? Well!"

"Ssh!" said the barkeeper.

"Say," snarled the Swede, "don't you try to shut me up. I won't have it. I'm a gentleman, and I want people to drink with me. And I want 'em to drink with me now. *Now*—do you understand?" He rapped the bar with his knuckles.

Years of experience had calloused the bartender. He merely grew sulky. "I hear you," he answered.

"Well," cried the Swede, "listen hard then. See those men over there? Well, they're going to drink with me, and don't you forget it. Now you watch."

"Hi!" yelled the barkeeper. "This won't do!"

"Why won't it?" demanded the Swede. He stalked over to the table, and by chance laid his hand upon the shoulder of the gambler. "How about this?" he asked wrathfully. "I asked you to drink with me."

The gambler simply twisted his head and spoke over his shoulder. "My friend, I don't know you."

"Oh, hell!" answered the Swede, "come and have a drink."

"Now, my boy," advised the gambler kindly, "take your hand off my shoulder and go 'way and mind your own business." He was a little, slim man, and it seemed strange to hear him use this tone of heroic patronage to the burly Swede. The other men at the table said nothing.

"What! You won't drink with me, you little dude? I'll make you, then! I'll make you!" The Swede had grasped the gambler frenziedly at the throat, and was dragging him from his chair. The other men sprang up. The barkeeper dashed around the corner of his bar. There was a great tumult, and then was seen a long blade in the hand of the gambler. It shot forward, and a human body, this citadel of virtue, wisdom, power, was pierced as easily as if it had been a melon. The Swede fell with a cry of supreme astonishment.

The prominent merchants and the district attorney must have at once tumbled out of the place backward. The bartender found himself hanging limply to the arm of a chair and gazing into the eyes of a murderer.

"Henry," said the latter, as he wiped his knife on one of the towels that hung beneath the bar rail, "you tell 'em where to find me. I'll be home, waiting for 'em." Then he vanished. A moment afterward the barkeeper was in the street dinning through the storm for help and, moreover, companionship.

The corpse of the Swede, alone in the saloon, had its eyes

fixed upon a dreadful legend that dwelt atop of the cash-machine: "This registers the amount of your purchases."

IX

Months later, the cowboy was frying pork over the stove of a little ranch near the Dakota line, when there was a quick thud of hoofs outside, and presently the Easterner entered with the letters and the papers.

"Well," said the Easterner at once, "the chap that killed the Swede has got three years. Wasn't much, was it?"

"He has? Three years?" The cowboy poised his pan of pork, while he ruminated upon the news. "Three years. That ain't much."

"No. It was a light sentence," replied the Easterner as he unbuckled his spurs. "Seems there was a good deal of sympathy for him in Romper."

"If the bartender had been any good," observed the cowboy, thoughtfully, "he would have gone in and cracked that there Dutchman on the head with a bottle in the beginnin' of it and stopped all this here murderin'."

"Yes, a thousand things might have happened," said the Easterner, tartly.

The cowboy returned his pan of pork to the fire, but his philosophy continued. "It's funny, ain't it? If he hadn't said Johnnie was cheatin' he'd be alive this minute. He was an awful fool. Game played for fun, too. Not for money. I believe he was crazy."

"I feel sorry for that gambler," said the Easterner.

"Oh, so do I," said the cowboy. "He don't deserve none of it for killin' who he did."

"The Swede might not have been killed if everything had been square."

"Might not have been killed?" exclaimed the cowboy. "Everythin' square? Why, when he said that Johnnie was cheatin' and acted like such a jackass? And then in the saloon he fairly walked up to git hurt?" With these arguments the cowboy browbeat the Easterner and reduced him to rage.

"You're a fool!" cried the Easterner, viciously. "You're a bigger jackass than the Swede by a million majority. Now let me tell you one thing. Let me tell you something. Listen! Johnnie *was* cheating!"

" 'Johnnie,' " said the cowboy, blankly. There was a minute

of silence, and then he said, robustly, "Why, no. The game was only for fun."

"Fun or not," said the Easterner, "Johnnie was cheating. I saw him. I know it. I saw him. And I refused to stand up and be a man. I let the Swede fight it out alone. And you—you were simply puffing around the place and wanting to fight. And then old Scully himself! We are all in it! This poor gambler isn't even a noun. He is kind of an adverb. Every sin is the result of a collaboration. We, five of us, have collaborated in the murder of this Swede. Usually there are from a dozen to forty women really involved in every murder, but in this case it seems to be only five men—you, I, Johnnie, old Scully; and that fool of an unfortunate gambler came merely as a culmination, the apex of a human movement, and gets all the punishment."

The cowboy, injured and rebellious, cried out blindly into this fog of mysterious theory: "Well, I didn't do anythin', did I?"

Edith Newbold Jones Wharton
(1862–1937)

Born and educated in the social aristocracy of New York, Wharton was introduced to society in 1879, married to Boston-bred Edward Robbins Wharton in 1885, and quickly discovered that neither her life nor her handsome, aristocratic, but unintellectual and totally unvocational husband suited her. She had been writing all her life; she turned to serious writing in the late 1880s, and by 1899, when her first collection of stories appeared (The Greater Inclination, *from which "A Journey" is taken), she was becoming established. Her novel,* The Valley of Decision *(1902) added to her reputation;* The House of Mirth *(1905), an intense study of an aristocratic girl ruined and eventually killed by her unwillingness to adhere to social convention, was for many months the best-selling novel of its day and was an enormous critical success as well. Wharton had begun under the influence of Henry James: she now stood on her own feet as a major literary figure. And she followed her early successes with such books as* Ethan Frome *(1911),* The Custom of the Country *(1913), and* The Age of Innocence *(1920), as well as a number of collections of stories, notably* Tales of Men and Ghosts *(1910) and* Xingu *(1916). Most of the fiction she wrote after 1920 is thin, but in her last decade or so she produced two more books of enduring value,* The Writing of Fiction *(1925) and an autobiography,* A Backward Glance *(1934). Her* Collected Short Stories, *in two volumes, was published in 1968, edited by her biographer, R.W.B. Lewis.*

A JOURNEY

As she lay in her berth, staring at the shadows overhead, the rush of the wheels was in her brain, driving her deeper and deeper into circles of wakeful lucidity. The sleeping car had sunk into its night silence. Through the wet windowpane she watched the sudden lights, the long stretches of hurrying blackness. Now and then she turned her head and looked through the opening in the hangings at her husband's curtains across the aisle. . . .

She wondered restlessly if he wanted anything and if she could hear him if he called. His voice had grown very weak within the last months and it irritated him when she did not hear. This irritability, this increasing childish petulance seemed to give expression to their imperceptible estrangement. Like two faces looking at one another through a sheet of glass they were close together, almost touching, but they could not hear or feel each other: the conductivity between them was broken. She, at least, had this sense of separation, and she fancied sometimes that she saw it reflected in the look with which he supplemented his failing words. Doubtless the fault was hers. She was too impenetrably healthy to be touched by the irrelevancies of disease. Her self-reproachful tenderness was tinged with the sense of his irrationality: she had a vague feeling that there was a purpose in his helpless tyrannies. The suddenness of the change had found her so unprepared. A year ago their pulses had beat to one robust measure; both had the same prodigal confidence in an exhaustless future. Now their energies no longer kept step: hers still bounded ahead of life, pre-empting unclaimed regions of hope and activity, while his lagged behind, vainly struggling to overtake her.

When they married, she had such arrears of living to make up: her days had been as bare as the whitewashed schoolroom where she forced innutritious facts upon reluctant children. His coming had broken in on the slumber of circumstance, widening the present till it became the enclosure of remotest chances. But imperceptibly the horizon narrowed. Life had a grudge against her: she was never to be allowed to spread her wings.

At first the doctors had said that six weeks of mild air would

set him right; but when he came back this assurance was explained as having of course included a winter in a dry climate.
They gave up their pretty house, storing the wedding presents
and new furniture, and went to Colorado. She had hated it there
from the first. Nobody knew her or cared about her; there was no
one to wonder at the good match she had made, or to envy her
the new dresses and the visiting cards which were still a surprise
to her. And he kept growing worse. She felt herself beset with
difficulties too evasive to be fought by so direct a temperament.
She still loved him, of course; but he was gradually, undefinably
ceasing to be himself. The man she had married had been strong,
active, gently masterful: the male whose pleasure it is to clear a
way through the material obstructions of life; but now it was she
who was the protector, he who must be shielded from importuni-
ties and given his drops or his beef juice though the skies were
falling. The routine of the sickroom bewildered her; this punctual
administering of medicine seemed as idle as some uncomprehended religious mummery.

There were moments, indeed, when warm gushes of pity
swept away her instinctive resentment of his condition, when she
still found his old self in his eyes as they groped for each other
through the dense medium of his weakness. But these moments
had grown rare. Sometimes he frightened her: his sunken expressionless face seemed that of a stranger; his voice was weak and
hoarse; his thin-lipped smile a mere muscular contraction. Her
hand avoided his damp soft skin, which had lost the familiar
roughness of health: she caught herself furtively watching him as
she might have watched a strange animal. It frightened her to
feel that this was the man she loved; there were hours when to
tell him what she suffered seemed the one escape from her fears.
But in general she judged herself more leniently, reflecting that
she had perhaps been too long alone with him, and that she
would feel differently when they were at home again, surrounded
by her robust and buoyant family. How she had rejoiced when
the doctors at last gave their consent to his going home! She
knew, of course, what the decision meant; they both knew. It
meant that he was to die; but they dressed the truth in hopeful
euphemisms, and at times, in the joy of preparation, she really
forgot the purpose of their journey, and slipped into an eager
allusion to next year's plans.

At last the day of leaving came. She had a dreadful fear that
they would never get away; that somehow at the last moment he
would fail her; that the doctors held one of their accustomed
treacheries in reserve; but nothing happened. They drove to the

station, he was installed in a seat with a rug over his knees and a cushion at his back, and she hung out of the window waving unregretful farewells to the acquaintances she had really never liked till then.

The first twenty-four hours had passed off well. He revived a little and it amused him to look out of the window and to observe the humors of the car. The second day he began to grow weary and to chafe under the dispassionate stare of the freckled child with the lump of chewing gum. She had to explain to the child's mother that her husband was too ill to be disturbed: a statement received by that lady with a resentment visibly supported by the maternal sentiment of a whole car. . . .

That night he slept badly and the next morning his temperature frightened her: she was sure he was growing worse. The day passed slowly, punctuated by the small irritations of travel. Watching his tired face, she traced in its contractions every rattle and jolt of the train, till her own body vibrated with sympathetic fatigue. She felt the others observing him too, and hovered restlessly between him and the line of interrogative eyes. The freckled child hung about him like a fly; offers of candy and picture books failed to dislodge her: she twisted one leg around the other and watched him imperturbably. The porter, as he passed, lingered with vague proffers of help, probably inspired by philanthropic passengers swelling with the sense that "something ought to be done"; and one nervous man in a skull cap was audibly concerned as to the possible effect on his wife's health.

The hours dragged on in a dreary inoccupation. Towards dusk she sat down beside him and he laid his hand on hers. The touch startled her. He seemed to be calling her from far off. She looked at him helplessly and his smile went through her like a physical pang.

"Are you very tired?" she asked.

"No, not very."

"We'll be there soon now."

"Yes, very soon."

"This time tomorrow—"

He nodded and they sat silent. When she had put him to bed and crawled into her own berth she tried to cheer herself with the thought that in less than twenty-four hours they would be in New York. Her people would all be at the station to meet her—she pictured their round unanxious faces pressing through the crowd. She only hoped they would not tell him too loudly that he was looking splendidly and would be all right in no time: the subtler sympathies developed by long contact with suffering were making her aware of a certain coarseness of texture in the family sensibilities.

Suddenly she thought she heard him call. She parted the curtains and listened. No, it was only a man snoring at the other end of the car. His snores had a greasy sound, as though they passed through tallow. She lay down and tried to sleep. . . . Had she not heard him move? She started up trembling. . . . The silence frightened her more than any sound. He might not be able to make her hear—he might be calling her now. . . . What made her think of such things? It was merely the familiar tendency of an overtired mind to fasten itself on the most intolerable chance within the range of its forebodings. . . . Putting her head out, she listened; but she could not distinguish his breathing from that of the other pairs of lungs about her. She longed to get up and look at him, but she knew the impulse was a mere vent for her restlessness, and the fear of disturbing him restrained her. . . . The regular movement of his curtain reassured her, she knew not why; she remembered that he had wished her a cheerful good night; and the sheer inability to endure her fears a moment longer made her put them from her with an effort of her whole sound-tired body. She turned on her side and slept.

She sat up stiffly, staring out at the dawn. The train was rushing through a region of bare hillocks huddled against a lifeless sky. It looked like the first day of creation. The air of the car was close, and she pushed up her window to let in the keen wind. Then she looked at her watch: it was seven o'clock, and soon the people about her would be stirring. She slipped into her clothes, smoothed her disheveled hair and crept to the dressing room. When she had washed her face and adjusted her dress she felt more hopeful. It was always a struggle for her not to be cheerful in the morning. Her cheeks burned deliciously under the coarse towel and the wet hair about her temples broke into strong upward tendrils. Every inch of her was full of life and elasticity. And in ten hours they would be at home!

She stepped to her husband's berth: it was time for him to take his early glass of milk. The window shade was down, and in the dusk of the curtained enclosure she could just see that he lay sideways, with his face away from her. She leaned over him and drew up the shade. As she did so she touched one of his hands. It felt cold. . . .

She bent closer, laying her hand on his arm and calling him by name. He did not move. She spoke again more loudly; she grasped his shoulder and gently shook it. He lay motionless. She caught hold of his hand again: it slipped from her limply, like a dead thing. A dead thing?

Her breath caught. She must see his face. She leaned forward, and hurriedly, shrinkingly, with a sickening reluctance of the flesh, laid her hands on his shoulders and turned him over. His head fell back; his face looked small and smooth; he gazed at her with steady eyes.

She remained motionless for a long time, holding him thus; and they looked at each other. Suddenly she shrank back: the longing to scream, to call out, to fly from him, had almost overpowered her. But a strong hand arrested her. Good God! If it were known that he was dead they would be put off the train at the next station—

In a terrifying flash of remembrance there arose before her a scene she had once witnessed in traveling, when a husband and wife, whose child had died in the train, had been thrust out at some chance station. She saw them standing on the platform with the child's body between them; she had never forgotten the dazed look with which they followed the receding train. And this was what would happen to her. Within the next hour she might find herself on the platform of some strange station, alone with her husband's body. . . . Anything but that! It was too horrible— She quivered like a creature at bay.

As she cowered there, she felt the train moving more slowly. It was coming then—they were approaching a station! She saw again the husband and wife standing on the lonely platform; and with a violent gesture she drew down the shade to hide her husband's face.

Feeling dizzy, she sank down on the edge of the berth, keeping away from his outstretched body, and pulling the curtains close, so that he and she were shut into a kind of sepulchral twilight. She tried to think. At all costs she must conceal the fact that he was dead. But how? Her mind refused to act: she could not plan, combine. She could think of no way but to sit there, clutching the curtains, all day long. . . .

She heard the porter making up her bed; people were beginning to move about the car; the dressing-room door was being opened and shut. She tried to rouse herself. At length with a supreme effort she rose to her feet, stepping into the aisle of the car and drawing the curtains tight behind her. She noticed that they still parted slightly with the motion of the car, and finding a pin in her dress she fastened them together. Now she was safe. She looked round and saw the porter. She fancied he was watching her.

"Ain't he awake yet?" he inquired.

"No," she faltered.

"I got his milk all ready when he wants it. You know you told me to have it for him by seven."

She nodded silently and crept into her seat.

At half-past eight the train reached Buffalo. By this time the other passengers were dressed and the berths had been folded back for the day. The porter, moving to and fro under his burden of sheets and pillows, glanced at her as he passed. At length he said: "Ain't he going to get up? You know we're ordered to make up the berths as early as we can."

She turned cold with fear. They were just entering the station.

"Oh, not yet," she stammered. "Not till he's had his milk. Won't you get it, please?"

"All right. Soon as we start again."

When the train moved on he reappeared with the milk. She took it from him and sat vaguely looking at it: her brain moved slowly from one idea to another, as though they were stepping-stones set far apart across a whirling flood. At length she became aware that the porter still hovered expectantly.

"Will I give it to him?" he suggested.

"Oh, no," she cried, rising. "He—he's asleep yet, I think—"

She waited till the porter had passed on; then she unpinned the curtains and slipped behind them. In the semiobscurity her husband's face stared up at her like a marble mask with agate eyes. The eyes were dreadful. She put out her hand and drew down the lids. Then she remembered the glass of milk in her other hand: what was she to do with it? She thought of raising the window and throwing it out; but to do so she would have to lean across his body and bring her face close to his. She decided to drink the milk.

She returned to her seat with the empty glass and after a while the porter came back to get it.

"When'll I fold up his bed?" he asked.

"Oh, not now—not yet; he's ill—he's very ill. Can't you let him stay as he is? The doctor wants him to lie down as much as possible."

He scratched his head. "Well, if he's *really* sick—"

He took the empty glass and walked away, explaining to the passengers that the party behind the curtains was too sick to get up just yet.

She found herself the center of sympathetic eyes. A motherly woman with an intimate smile sat down beside her.

"I'm real sorry to hear your husband's sick. I've had a

remarkable amount of sickness in my family and maybe I could assist you. Can I take a look at him?"

"Oh, no—no, please! He mustn't be disturbed."

The lady accepted the rebuff indulgently.

"Well, it's just as you say, of course, but you don't look to me as if you'd had much experience in sickness and I'd have been glad to assist you. What do you generally do when your husband's taken this way?"

"I—I let him sleep."

"Too much sleep ain't any too healthful either. Don't you give him any medicine?"

"Y—yes."

"Don't you wake him to take it?"

"Yes."

"When does he take the next dose?"

"Not for—two hours—"

The lady looked disappointed. "Well, if I was you I'd try giving it oftener. That's what I do with my folks."

After that many faces seemed to press upon her. The passengers were on their way to the dining car, and she was conscious that as they passed down the aisle they glanced curiously at the closed curtains. One lantern-jawed man with prominent eyes stood still and tried to shoot his projecting glance through the division between the folds. The freckled child, returning from breakfast, waylaid the passers with a buttery clutch, saying in a loud whisper, "He's sick"; and once the conductor came by, asking for tickets. She shrank into her corner and looked out of the window at the flying trees and houses, meaningless hieroglyphs of an endlessly unrolled papyrus.

Now and then the train stopped, and the newcomers on entering the car stared in turn at the closed curtains. More and more people seemed to pass—their faces began to blend fantastically with the images surging in her brain. . . .

Later in the day a fat man detached himself from the mist of faces. He had a creased stomach and soft pale lips. As he pressed himself into the seat facing her she noticed that he was dressed in black broadcloth, with a soiled white tie.

"Husband's pretty bad this morning, is he?"

"Yes."

"Dear, dear! Now that's terribly distressing, ain't it?" An apostolic smile revealed his gold-filled teeth. "Of course you know there's no sech thing as sickness. Ain't that a lovely thought? Death itself is but a deloosion of our grosser senses. On'y lay yourself open to the influx of the sperrit, submit

yourself passively to the action of the divine force, and disease
and dissolution will cease to exist for you. If you could indooce
your husband to read this little pamphlet—''

The faces about her again grew indistinct. She had a vague
recollection of hearing the motherly lady and the parent of the
freckled child ardently disputing the relative advantages of trying
several medicines at once, or of taking each in turn; the motherly
lady maintaining that the competitive system saved time; the
other objecting that you couldn't tell which remedy had effected
the cure; their voices went on and on, like bell buoys droning
through a fog. . . . The porter came up now and then with
questions that she did not understand, but somehow she must
have answered since he went away again without repeating them;
every two hours the motherly lady reminded her that her husband
ought to have his drops; people left the car and others replaced
them. . . .

Her head was spinning and she tried to steady herself by
clutching at her thoughts as they swept by, but they slipped away
from her like bushes on the side of a sheer precipice down which
she seemed to be falling. Suddenly her mind grew clear again
and she found herself vividly picturing what would happen when
the train reached New York. She shuddered as it occurred to her
that he would be quite cold and that someone might perceive he
had been dead since morning.

She thought hurriedly: ''If they see I am not surprised they
will suspect something. They will ask questions, and if I tell
them the truth they won't believe me—no one would believe me!
It will be terrible''—and she kept repeating to herself—''I must
pretend I don't know. I must pretend I don't know. When they
open the curtains I must go up to him quite naturally—and then I
must scream!'' She had an idea that the scream would be very
hard to do.

Gradually new thoughts crowded upon her, vivid and urgent:
she tried to separate and restrain them, but they beset her
clamorously, like her school children at the end of a hot day,
when she was too tired to silence them. Her head grew confused,
and she felt a sick fear of forgetting her part, of betraying herself
by some unguarded word or look.

''I must pretend I don't know,'' she went on murmuring. The
words had lost their significance, but she repeated them
mechanically, as though they had been a magic formula, until
suddenly she heard herself saying: ''I can't remember, I can't
remember!''

Her voice sounded very loud, and she looked about her in terror; but no one seemed to notice that she had spoken.

As she glanced down the car her eye caught the curtains of her husband's berth, and she began to examine the monotonous arabesques woven through their heavy folds. The pattern was intricate and difficult to trace; she gazed fixedly at the curtains and as she did so the thick stuff grew transparent and through it she saw her husband's face—his dead face. She struggled to avert her look, but her eyes refused to move and her head seemed to be held in a vise. At last, with an effort that left her weak and shaking, she turned away; but it was of no use, close in front of her, small and smooth, was her husband's face. It seemed to be suspended in the air between her and the false braids of the woman who sat in front of her. With an uncontrollable gesture she stretched out her hand to push the face away, and suddenly she felt the touch of his smooth skin. She repressed a cry and half started from her seat. The woman with the false braids looked around, and feeling that she must justify her movement in some way she rose and lifted her traveling bag from the opposite seat. She unlocked the bag and looked into it; but the first object her hand met was a small flask of her husband's, thrust there at the last moment, in the haste of departure. She locked the bag and closed her eyes . . . his face was there again, hanging between her eyeballs and lids like a waxen mask against a red curtain. . . .

She roused herself with a shiver. Had she fainted or slept? Hours seemed to have elapsed; but it was still broad day, and the people about her were sitting in the same attitudes as before.

A sudden sense of hunger made her aware that she had eaten nothing since morning. The thought of food filled her with disgust, but she dreaded a return of faintness, and remembering that she had some biscuits in her bag she took one out and ate it. The dry crumbs choked her, and she hastily swallowed a little brandy from her husband's flask. The burning sensation in her throat acted as a counterirritant, momentarily relieving the dull ache of her nerves. Then she felt a gently-stealing warmth, as though a soft air fanned her, and the swarming fears relaxed their clutch, receding through the stillness that enclosed her, a stillness soothing as the spacious quietude of a summer day. She slept.

Through her sleep she felt the impetuous rush of the train. It seemed to be life itself that was sweeping her on with headlong inexorable force—sweeping her into darkness and terror, and the awe of unknown days.—Now all at once everything was still—

not a sound, not a pulsation. . . . She was dead in her turn, and lay beside him with smooth upstaring face. How quiet it was! —and yet she heard feet coming, the feet of the men who were to carry them away. . . . She could feel too—she felt a sudden prolonged vibration, a series of hard shocks, and then another plunge into darkness: the darkness of death this time—a black whirlwind on which they were both spinning like leaves, in wild uncoiling spirals, with millions and millions of the dead. . . .

She sprang up in terror. Her sleep must have lasted a long time, for the winter day had paled and the lights had been lit. The car was in confusion, and as she regained her self-possession she saw that the passengers were gathering up their wraps and bags. The woman with the false braids had brought from the dressing room a sickly ivy plant in a bottle, and the Christian Scientist was reversing his cuffs. The porter passed down the aisle with his impartial brush. An impersonal figure with a gold-banded cap asked for her husband's ticket. A voice shouted "Baiggage *ex*press!" and she heard the clicking of metal as the passengers handed over their checks.

Presently her window was blocked by an expanse of sooty wall, and the train passed into the Harlem tunnel. The journey was over; in a few minutes she would see her family pushing their joyous way through the throng at the station. Her heart dilated. The worst terror was past. . . .

"We'd better get him up now, hadn't we?" asked the porter, touching her arm.

He had her husband's hat in his hand and was meditatively revolving it under his brush.

She looked at the hat and tried to speak; but suddenly the car grew dark. She flung up her arms, struggling to catch at something, and fell face downward, striking her head against the dead man's berth.

Mark Twain
(Samuel Langhorne Clemens)
(1835–1910)

Born and raised in Missouri, Twain left school at age 12, after the death of his father, to be apprenticed to a printer. At about the same time, he began writing for newspapers. From 1856 to the outbreak of the Civil War, he was a successful Mississippi steamboat pilot. After brief service in the war, on the Confederate side, Twain migrated west and quickly became a famous and well-paid humorist. A superb public performer, he added vastly both to his income and to his reputation by immensely successful lecture tours. Most of his early work was humorous and nonfictional, including such popular travel books as The Innocents Abroad *(1869) and* Roughing It *(1872), though in 1867 he had published* The Celebrated Jumping Frog of Calaveras County and Other Sketches. *His first novel,* The Gilded Age *(1873, written with Charles Dudley Warner), was followed in 1876 by* The Adventures of Tom Sawyer, *which in turn led, some years later, to his greatest book,* The Adventures of Huckleberry Finn *(1884). Other major books include* A Connecticut Yankee in King Arthur's Court *(1889),* The Tragedy of Pudd'nhead Wilson *(1894), and* The Man That Corrupted Hadleyburg and Other Stories and Essays *(1900), the title story of which is here reprinted.*

THE MAN
THAT CORRUPTED HADLEYBURG

I

It was many years ago. Hadleyburg was the most honest and upright town in all the region around about. It had kept that reputation unsmirched during three generations, and was prouder of it than of any other of its possessions. It was so proud of it, and so anxious to insure its perpetuation, that it began to teach the principles of honest dealing to its babies in the cradle, and made the like teachings the staple of their culture thenceforward through all the years devoted to their education. Also, throughout the formative years temptations were kept out of the way of the young people, so that their honesty could have every chance to harden and solidify, and become a part of their very bone. The neighboring towns were jealous of this honorable supremacy, and affected to sneer at Hadleyburg's pride in it and call it vanity; but all the same they were obliged to acknowledge that Hadleyburg was in reality an incorruptible town; and if pressed they would also acknowledge that the mere fact that a young man hailed from Hadleyburg was all the recommendation he needed when he went forth from his natal town to seek for responsible employment.

But at last, in the drift of time, Hadleyburg had the ill luck to offend a passing stranger—possibly without knowing it, certainly without caring, for Hadleyburg was sufficient unto itself, and cared not a rap for strangers or their opinions. Still, it would have been well to make an exception in this one's case, for he was a bitter man and revengeful. All through his wanderings during a whole year he kept his injury in mind, and gave all his leisure moments to trying to invent a compensating satisfaction for it. He contrived many plans, and all of them were good, but none of them was quite sweeping enough; the poorest of them would hurt a great many individuals, but what he wanted was a plan which would comprehend the entire town, and not let so much as one person escape unhurt. At last he had a fortunate idea, and when it fell into his brain it lit up his whole head with an evil joy. He began to form a plan at once, saying to himself, "That is the thing to do—I will corrupt the town."

Six months later he went to Hadleyburg, and arrived in a buggy at the house of the old cashier of the bank about ten at night. He got a sack out of the buggy, shouldered it, and staggered with it through the cottage yard, and knocked at the door. A woman's voice said "Come in," and he entered, and set his sack behind the stove in the parlor, saying politely to the old lady who sat reading the *Missionary Herald* by the lamp:

"Pray keep your seat, madam, I will not disturb you. There— now it is pretty well concealed; one would hardly know it was there. Can I see your husband a moment, madam?"

No, he was gone to Brixton, and might not return before morning.

"Very well, madam, it is no matter. I merely wanted to leave that sack in his care, to be delivered to the rightful owner when he shall be found. I am a stranger; he does not know me; I am merely passing through the town to-night to discharge a matter which has been long in my mind. My errand is now completed, and I go pleased and a little proud, and you will never see me again. There is a paper attached to the sack which will explain everything. Good night, madam."

The old lady was afraid of the mysterious big stranger, and was glad to see him go. But her curiosity was roused, and she went straight to the sack and brought away the paper. It began as follows:

TO BE PUBLISHED; *or, the right man sought out by private inquiry— either will answer. This sack contains gold coin weighing a hundred and sixty pounds four ounces—*

"Mercy on us, and the door not locked!"

Mrs. Richards flew to it all in a tremble and locked it, then pulled down the window-shades and stood frightened, worried, and wondering if there was anything else she could do toward making herself and the money more safe. She listened awhile for burglars, then surrendered to curiosity and went back to the lamp and finished reading the paper:

I am a foreigner, and am presently going back to my own country, to remain there permanently. I am grateful to America for what I have received at her hands during my long stay under her flag; and to one of her citizens—a citizen of Hadleyburg—I am especially grateful for a great kindness done me a year or two ago. Two great kindnesses, in fact. I will explain. I was a gambler. I say I was. I was a ruined gambler. I arrived in this village at night, hungry and without a penny. I asked for help—in the dark; I was ashamed to beg in the light. I begged of the right man. He gave me twenty dollars—that is to say, he gave me life, as I considered it. He also gave me fortune; for out of that money I have made myself rich at the gaming-table. And finally, a remark which he made to me has remained with me to this day, and has at last conquered me; and in conquering has saved the remnant of my morals; I shall gamble no more. Now I have no idea who that man was, but I want him found, and I want him to have this money, to give away, throw away, or keep, as he pleases. It is merely my way of testifying my gratitude to him. If I could stay, I would find him myself; but no matter, he will be found. This is an honest town, an incorruptible town, and I know I can trust it without fear. This man can be identified by the remark which he made to me; I feel persuaded that he will remember it.

And now my plan is this: If you prefer to conduct the inquiry privately, do so. Tell the contents of this present writing to any one who is likely to be the right man. If he shall answer, 'I am the man; the remark I made was so-and-so,' apply the test—to wit: open the sack, and in it you will find a sealed envelope containing that remark. If the remark mentioned by the candidate tallies with it, give him the money, and ask no further questions, for he is certainly the right man.

But if you shall prefer a public inquiry, then publish this present writing in the local paper—with these instructions added, to wit: Thirty days from now, let the candidate appear at the town-hall at eight in the evening (Friday), and hand his remark, in a sealed envelope, to the Rev. Mr. Burgess (if he will be kind enough to act); and let Mr. Burgess there and then destroy the seals of the sack, open it, and see if the remark is correct; if correct, let the money be delivered with my sincere gratitude, to my benefactor thus identified.

Mrs. Richards sat down, gently quivering with excitement, and was soon lost in thinkings—after this pattern: "What a strange thing it is! . . . And what a fortune for that kind man who set his bread afloat upon the waters! . . . If it had only been my husband that did it!—for we are so poor, so old and poor! . . ." Then, with a sigh—"But it was not my Edward; no, it was not he that gave a stranger twenty dollars. It is pity, too; I see it now. . . ." Then, with a shudder—"But it is *gambler's*

money! the wages of sin: we couldn't take it; we couldn't touch
it. I don't like to be near it; it seems a defilement." She moved
to a farther chair. . . . "I wish Edward would come and take it
to the bank; a burglar might come at any moment; it is dreadful
to be here all alone with it."

At eleven Mr. Richards arrived, and while his wife was
saying, "I am *so* glad you've come!" he was saying, "I'm so
tired—tired clear out; it is dreadful to be poor, and have to make
these dismal journeys at my time of life. Always at the grind,
grind, grind, on a salary—another man's slave, and he sitting at
home in his slippers, rich and comfortable."

"I am so sorry for you, Edward, you know that; but be
comforted: we have our livelihood; we have our good name—"

"Yes, Mary, and that is everything. Don't mind my talk—it's
just a moment's irritation and doesn't mean anything. Kiss me—
there, it's all gone now, and I am not complaining any more.
What have you been getting? What's in the sack?"

Then his wife told him the great secret. It dazed him for a
moment; then he said:

"It weighs a hundred and sixty pounds? Why, Mary, it's
for-ty thousand dollars—think of it—a whole fortune! Not ten
men in this village are worth that much. Give me the paper."

He skimmed through it and said:

"Isn't it an adventure! Why, it's a romance; it's like the
impossible things one reads about in books, and never sees in
life." He was well stirred up now; cheerful, even gleeful. He
tapped his old wife on the cheek, and said, humorously, "Why,
we're rich, Mary, rich; all we've got to do is to bury the money
and burn the papers. If the gambler ever comes to inquire, we'll
merely look coldly upon him and say: 'What is this nonsense
you are talking! We have never heard of you and your sack of
gold before'; and then he would look foolish, and—"

"And in the mean time, while you are running on with your
jokes, the money is still here, and it is fast getting along toward
burglar-time."

"True. Very well, what shall we do—make the inquiry private?
No, not that; it would spoil the romance. The public method is
better. Think what a noise it will make! And it will make all the
other towns jealous; for no stranger would trust such a thing to
any town but Hadleyburg, and they know it. It's a great card for
us. I must get to the printing-office now, or I shall be too late."

"But stop—stop—don't leave me here alone with it, Edward!"

But he was gone. For only a little while, however. Not far
from his own house he met the editor-proprietor of the paper,

and gave him the document, and said, "Here is a good thing for you, Cox—put it in."

"It may be too late, Mr. Richards, but I'll see."

At home again he and his wife sat down to talk the charming mystery over; they were in no condition for sleep. The first question was, Who could the citizen have been who gave the stranger the twenty dollars? It seemed a simple one; both answered it in the same breath:

"Barclay Goodson."

"Yes," said Richards, "he could have done it, and it would have been like him, but there's not another in the town."

"Everybody will grant that, Edward—grant it privately, anyway. For six months, now, the village has been its own proper self once more—honest, narrow, self-righteous, and stingy."

"It is what he always called it, to the day of his death—said it right out publicly, too."

"Yes, and he was hated for it."

"Oh, of course; but he didn't care. I reckon he was the best-hated man among us, except the Reverend Burgess."

"Well, Burgess deserves it—he will never get another congregation here. Mean as the town is, it knows how to estimate *him*. Edward, doesn't it seem odd that the stranger should appoint Burgess to deliver the money?"

"Well, yes—it does. That is—that is—"

"Why so much that-*is*-ing? Would *you* select him?"

"Mary, maybe the stranger knows him better than this village does."

"Much *that* would help Burgess!"

The husband seemed perplexed for an answer; the wife kept a steady eye upon him, and waited. Finally Richards said, with the hesitancy of one who is making a statement which is likely to encounter doubt:

"Mary, Burgess is not a bad man."

His wife was certainly surprised.

"Nonsense!" she exclaimed.

"He is not a bad man. I know. The whole of his unpopularity had its foundation in that one thing—the thing that made so much noise."

"That 'one thing,' indeed! As if that 'one thing' wasn't enough, all by itself."

"Plenty. Plenty. Only he wasn't guilty of it."

"How you talk! Not guilty of it! Everybody knows he *was* guilty."

"Mary, I give you my word—he was innocent."

"I can't believe it, and I don't. How do you know?"

"It is a confession. I am ashamed, but I will make it. I was the only man who knew he was innocent. I could have saved him, and—and—well, you know how the town was wrought up—I hadn't the pluck to do it. It would have turned everybody against me. I felt mean, ever so mean; but I didn't dare; I hadn't the manliness to face that."

Mary looked troubled, and for a while was silent. Then she said, stammeringly:

"I—I don't think it would have done for you to—to— One mustn't—er—public opinion—one has to be so careful—so—" It was a difficult road, and she got mired; but after a little she got started again. "It was a great pity, but— Why, we couldn't afford it, Edward—we couldn't indeed. Oh, I wouldn't have had you do it for anything!"

"It would have lost us the good will of so many people, Mary; and then—and then—"

"What troubles me now is, what *he* thinks of us, Edward."

"He? *He* doesn't suspect that I could have saved him."

"Oh," exclaimed the wife, in a tone of relief, "I am glad of that! As long as he doesn't know that you could have saved him, he—he—well, that makes it a great deal better. Why, I might have known he didn't know, because he is always trying to be friendly with us, as little encouragement as we give him. More than once people have twitted me with it. There's the Wilsons, and the Wilcoxes, and the Harknesses, they take a mean pleasure in saying, '*Your friend* Burgess,' because they know it pesters me. I wish he wouldn't persist in liking us so; I can't think why he keeps it up."

"I can explain it. It's another confession. When the thing was new and hot, and the town made a plan to ride him on a rail, my conscience hurt me so that I couldn't stand it, and I went privately and gave him notice, and he got out of the town and staid out till it was safe to come back."

"Edward! If the town had found it out—"

"*Don't!* It scares me yet, to think of it. I repented of it the minute it was done; and I was even afraid to tell you, lest your face might betray it to somebody. I didn't sleep any that night, for worrying. But after a few days I saw that no one was going to suspect me, and after that I got to feeling glad I did it. And I feel glad yet, Mary—glad through and through."

"So do I, now, for it would have been a dreadful way to treat him. Yes, I'm glad; for really you did owe him that, you know. But, Edward, suppose it should come out yet, some day!"

"It won't."

"Why?"

"Because everybody thinks it was Goodson."

"Of course they would!"

"Certainly. And of course *he* didn't care. They persuaded poor old Sawlsberry to go and charge it on him, and he went blustering over there and did it. Goodson looked him over, like as if he was hunting for a place on him that he could despise the most, then he says, 'So you are the Committee of Inquiry, are you?' Sawlsberry said that was about what he was. 'Hm. Do they require particulars, or do you reckon a kind of a *general* answer will do?' 'If they require particulars, I will come back, Mr. Goodson; I will take the general answer first.' 'Very well, then, tell them to go to hell—I reckon that's general enough. And I'll give you some advice, Sawlsberry; when you come back for the particulars, fetch a basket to carry the relics of yourself home in.'

"Just like Goodson; it's got all the marks. He had only one vanity: he thought he could give advice better than any other person."

"It settled the business, and saved us, Mary. The subject was dropped."

"Bless you, I'm not doubting *that*."

Then they took up the gold-sack mystery again, with strong interest. Soon the conversation began to suffer breaks—interruptions caused by absorbed thinkings. The breaks grew more and more frequent. At last Richards lost himself wholly in thought. He sat long, gazing vacantly at the floor, and by and by he began to punctuate his thoughts with little nervous movements of his hands that seemed to indicate vexation. Meantime his wife too had relapsed into a thoughtful silence, and her movements were beginning to show a troubled discomfort. Finally Richards got up and strode aimlessly about the room, plowing his hands through his hair, much as a somnambulist might do who was having a bad dream. Then he seemed to arrive at a definite purpose; and without a word he put on his hat and passed quickly out of the house. His wife sat brooding, with a drawn face, and did not seem to be aware that she was alone. Now and then she murmured, "Lead us not into t— . . . but—but—we are so poor, so poor! . . . Lead us not into . . . Ah, who would be hurt by it?—and no one would ever know. . . . Lead us . . ." The voice died out in mumblings. After a little she glanced up and muttered in a half-frightened, half-glad way:

"He is gone! But, oh dear, he may be too late—too late. . . .

Maybe not—maybe there is still time.'' She rose and stood thinking, nervously clasping and unclasping her hands. A slight shudder shook her frame, and she said, out of a dry throat, "God forgive me—it's awful to think such things—but . . . Lord, how we are made—how strangely we are made!''

She turned the light low, and slipped stealthily over and kneeled down by the sack and felt of its ridgy sides with her hands, and fondled them lovingly; and there was a gloating light in her poor old eyes. She fell into fits of absence; and came half out of them at times to mutter, "If we had only waited!—oh, if we had only waited a little, and not been in such a hurry!''

Meantime Cox had gone home from his office and told his wife all about the strange thing that had happened, and they had talked it over eagerly, and guessed that the late Goodson was the only man in the town who could have helped a suffering stranger with so noble a sum as twenty dollars. Then there was a pause, and the two became thoughtful and silent. And by and by nervous and fidgety. At last the wife said, as if to herself:

"Nobody knows this secret but the Richardses . . . and us . . . nobody.''

The husband came out of his thinkings with a slight start, and gazed wistfully at his wife, whose face was become very pale; then he hesitatingly rose, and glanced furtively at his hat, then at his wife—a sort of mute inquiry. Mrs. Cox swallowed once or twice, with her hand at her throat, then in place of speech she nodded her head. In a moment she was alone, and mumbling to herself.

And now Richards and Cox were hurrying through the deserted streets, from opposite directions. They met, panting, at the foot of the printing-office stairs; by the night light there they read each other's face. Cox whispered:

"Nobody knows about this but us?''

The whispered answer was,

"Not a soul—on honor, not a soul!''

"If it isn't too late to—''

The men were starting up-stairs; at this moment they were overtaken by a boy, and Cox asked:

"Is that you, Johnny?''

"Yes, sir.''

"You needn't ship the early mail—nor *any* mail; wait till I tell you.''

"It's already gone, sir.''

"Gone?" It had the sound of an unspeakable disappointment in it.

"Yes, sir. Time-table for Brixton and all the towns beyond changed to-day, sir—had to get the papers in twenty minutes earlier than common. I had to rush; if I had been two minutes later—"

The men turned and walked slowly away, not waiting to hear the rest. Neither of them spoke during ten minutes; then Cox said, in a vexed tone:

"What possessed you to be in such a hurry, *I* can't make out."

The answer was humble enough:

"I see it now, but somehow I never thought, you know, until it was too late. But the next time—"

"Next time be hanged! It won't come in a thousand years."

Then the friends separated without a good night, and dragged themselves home with the gait of mortally stricken men. At their homes their wives sprang up with an eager "Well?"—then saw the answer with their eyes and sank down sorrowing, without waiting for it to come in words. In both houses a discussion followed of a heated sort—a new thing; there had been discussions before, but not heated ones, not ungentle ones. The discussions to-night were a sort of seeming plagiarisms of each other. Mrs. Richards said,

"If you had only waited, Edward—if you had only stopped to think; but no, you must run straight to the printing-office and spread it all over the world."

"It *said* publish it."

"That is nothing; it also said do it privately, if you liked. There, now—is that true, or not?"

"Why, yes—yes, it is true; but when I thought what stir it would make, and what a compliment it was to Hadleyburg that a stranger should trust it so—"

"Oh, certainly, I know all that; but if you had only stopped to think, you would have seen that you *couldn't* find the right man, because he is in his grave, and hasn't left chick nor child nor relation behind him; and as long as the money went to somebody that awfully needed it, and nobody would be hurt by it, and—and—"

She broke down, crying. Her husband tried to think of some comforting thing to say, and presently came out with this:

"But after all, Mary, it must be for the best—it *must* be; we know that. And we must remember that it was so ordered—"

"Ordered! Oh, everything's *ordered*, when a person has to find some way out when he has been stupid. Just the same, it was *ordered* that the money should come to us in this special way, and it was you that must take it on yourself to go meddling with the designs of Providence—and who gave you the right? It was wicked, that is what it was—just blasphemous presumption, and no more becoming to a meek and humble professor of—"

"But, Mary, you know how we have been trained all our lives long, like the whole village, till it is absolutely second nature to us to stop not a single moment to think when there's an honest thing to be done—"

"Oh, I know it, I know it—it's been one everlasting training and training and training in honesty—honesty shielded, from the very cradle, against every possible temptation, and so it's *artificial* honesty, and weak as water when temptation comes, as we have seen this night. God knows I never had shade nor shadow of a doubt of my petrified and indestructible honesty until now—and now, under the very first big and real temptation, I—Edward, it is my belief that this town's honesty is as rotten as mine is; as rotten as yours is. It is a mean town, a hard, stingy town, and hasn't a virtue in the world but this honesty it is so celebrated for and so conceited about; and so help me, I do believe that if ever the day comes that its honesty falls under great temptation, its grand reputation will go to ruin like a house of cards. There, now, I've made confession, and I feel better; I am a humbug, and I've been one all my life, without knowing it. Let no man call me honest again—I will not have it."

"I—well, Mary, I feel a good deal as you do; I certainly do. It seems strange, too, so strange. I never could have believed it—never."

A long silence followed; both were sunk in thought. At last the wife looked up and said:

"I know what you are thinking, Edward."

Richards had the embarrassed look of a person who is caught.

"I am ashamed to confess it, Mary, but—"

"It's no matter, Edward, I was thinking the same question myself."

"I hope so. State it."

"You were thinking, if a body could only guess out *what the remark was* that Goodson made to the stranger."

"It's perfectly true. I feel guilty and ashamed. And you?"

"I'm past it. Let us make a pallet here; we've got to stand watch till the bank vault opens in the morning and admits the sack. . . . Oh dear, oh dear—if we hadn't made the mistake!"

The pallet was made, and Mary said:

"The open sesame—what could it have been? I do wonder what that remark could have been? But come; we will get to bed now."

"And sleep?"

"No: think."

"Yes, think."

By this time the Coxes too had completed their spat and their reconciliation, and were turning in—to think, to think, and toss, and fret, and worry over what the remark could possibly have been which Goodson made to the stranded derelict; that golden remark; that remark worth forty thousand dollars, cash.

The reason that the village telegraph-office was open later than usual that night was this: The foreman of Cox's paper was the local representative of the Associated Press. One might say its honorary representative, for it wasn't four times a year that he could furnish thirty words that would be accepted. But this time it was different. His despatch stating what he had caught got an instant answer:

Send the whole thing—all the details—twelve hundred words.

A colossal order! The foreman filled the bill; and he was the proudest man in the State. By breakfast-time the next morning the name of Hadleyburg the Incorruptible was on every lip in America, from Montreal to the Gulf, from the glaciers of Alaska to the orange-groves of Florida; and millions and millions of people were discussing the stranger and his money-sack, and wondering if the right man would be found, and hoping some more news about the matter would come soon—right away.

II

Hadleyburg village woke up world-celebrated—astonished—happy—vain. Vain beyond imagination. Its nineteen principal citizens and their wives went about shaking hands with each other, and beaming, and smiling, and congratulating, and saying *this* thing adds a new word to the dictionary—*Hadleyburg,* synonym for *incorruptible*—destined to live in dictionaries forever! And the minor and unimportant citizens and their wives went around acting in much the same way. Everybody ran to the bank to see the gold-sack; and before noon grieved and envious crowds began to flock in from Brixton and all neighboring towns; and that afternoon and next day reporters began to arrive from everywhere to verify the sack and its history and write the whole thing up anew, and make dashing free-hand pictures of the sack, and of Richards's house, and the bank, and the Presbyterian church, and the Baptist church, and the public square, and the town-hall where the test would be applied and the money delivered; and damnable portraits of the Richardses, and Pinkerton the banker, and Cox, and the foreman, and Reverend Burgess, and the postmaster—and even of Jack Halliday, who was the loafing, good-natured, no-account, irreverent fisherman, hunter, boys' friend, stray-dogs' friend, typical "Sam Lawson" of the town. The little mean, smirking, oily Pinkerton showed the sack to all comers, and rubbed his sleek palms together pleasantly, and enlarged upon the town's fine old reputation for honesty and upon this wonderful indorsement of it, and hoped and believed that the example would now spread far and wide over the American world, and be epoch-making in the matter of moral regeneration. And so on, and so on.

By the end of a week things had quieted down again; the wild intoxication of pride and joy had sobered to a soft, sweet, silent delight—a sort of deep, nameless, unutterable content. All faces bore a look of peaceful, holy happiness.

Then a change came. It was a gradual change: so gradual that its beginnings were hardly noticed; maybe were not noticed at all, except by Jack Halliday, who always noticed everything; and always made fun of it, too, no matter what it was. He began to throw out chaffing remarks about people not looking quite so happy as they did a day or two ago; and next he claimed that the new aspect was deepening to positive sadness; next, that it was taking on a sick look; and finally he said that everybody was become so moody, thoughtful, and absentminded that he could rob the meanest man in town of a cent out of the bottom of his breeches pocket and not disturb his revery.

At this stage—or at about this stage—a saying like this was dropped at bedtime—with a sigh, usually—by the head of each of the nineteen principal households: "Ah, what could have been the remark that Goodson made?"

And straightway—with a shudder—came this, from the man's wife:

"Oh, *don't!* What horrible thing are you mulling in your mind? Put it away from you, for God's sake!"

But that question was wrung from those men again the next night—and got the same retort. But weaker.

And the third night the men uttered the question yet again—with anguish, and absently. This time—and the following night—the wives fidgeted feebly, and tried to say something. But didn't.

And the night after that they found their tongues and responded—longingly:

"Oh, if we *could* only guess!"

Halliday's comments grew daily more and more sparklingly

disagreeable and disparaging. He went diligently about, laughing at the town, individually and in mass. But his laugh was the only one left in the village: it fell upon a hollow and mournful vacancy and emptiness. Not even a smile was findable anywhere. Halliday carried a cigar-box around on a tripod, playing that it was a camera, and halted all passers and aimed the thing and said, "Ready!—now look pleasant, please," but not even this capital joke could surprise the dreary faces into any softening.

So three weeks passed—one week was left. It was Saturday evening—after supper. Instead of the aforetime Saturday-evening flutter and bustle and shopping and larking, the streets were empty and desolate. Richards and his old wife sat apart in their little parlor—miserable and thinking. This was become their evening habit now: the lifelong habit which had preceded it, of reading, knitting, and contented chat, or receiving or paying neighborly calls, was dead and gone and forgotten, ages ago— two or three weeks ago; nobody talked now, nobody read, nobody visited—the whole village sat at home, sighing, worrying, silent. Trying to guess out that remark.

The postman left a letter. Richards glanced listlessly at the superscription and the postmark—unfamiliar, both—and tossed the letter on the table and resumed his might-have-beens and his hopeless dull miseries where he had left them off. Two or three hours later his wife got wearily up and was going away to bed without a good night—custom now—but she stopped near the letter and eyed it awhile with a dead interest, then broke it open, and began to skim it over. Richards, sitting there with his chair tilted back against the wall and his chin between his knees, heard something fall. It was his wife. He sprang to her side, but she cried out:

"Leave me alone, I am too happy. Read the letter—read it!"

He did. He devoured it, his brain reeling. The letter was from a distant state, and it said:

> *I am a stranger to you, but no matter: I have something to tell. I have just arrived home from Mexico, and learned about that episode. Of course you do not know who made that remark, but I know, and I am the only person living who does know. It was* GOODSON. *I knew him well, many years ago. I passed through your village that very night, and was his guest till the midnight train came along. I overheard him make that remark to the stranger in the dark—it was in Hale Alley. He and I talked of it the rest of the way home, and while smoking in his house. He men-*

tioned many of your villagers in the course of his talk—most of them in a very uncomplimentary way, but two or three favorably; among these latter yourself. I say "favorably"— nothing stronger. I remember his saying he did not actually LIKE *any person in the town—not one; but that you—I* THINK *he said you—am almost sure—had done him a very great service once, possibly without knowing the full value of it, and he wished he had a fortune, he would leave it to you when he died, and a curse apiece for the rest of the citizens. Now, then, if it was you that did him that service, you are his legitimate heir, and entitled to the sack of gold. I know that I can trust to your honor and honesty, for in a citizen of Hadleyburg these virtues are an unfailing inheritance, and so I am going to reveal to you the remark, well satisfied that if you are not the right man you will seek and find the right one and see that poor Goodson's debt of gratitude for the service referred to is paid. This is the remark:* "YOU ARE FAR FROM BEING A BAD MAN: GO, AND REFORM."

HOWARD L. STEPHENSON

"Oh, Edward, the money is ours, and I am so grateful, oh, so grateful—kiss me, dear, it's forever since we kissed—and we needed it so—the money—and now you are free of Pinkerton and his bank and nobody's slave any more; it seems to me I could fly for joy."

It was a happy half-hour that the couple spent there on the settee caressing each other; it was the old days come again— days that had begun with their courtship and lasted without a break till the stranger brought the deadly money. By and by the wife said:

"Oh, Edward, how lucky it was you did him that grand service, poor Goodson! I never liked him, but I love him now. And it was fine and beautiful of you never to mention it or brag about it." Then, with a touch of reproach, "But you ought to have told *me*, Edward, you ought to have told your wife, you know."

"Well, I—er—well, Mary, you see—"

"Now stop hemming and hawing, and tell me about it, Edward. I always loved you, and now I'm proud of you. Everybody believes there was only one good generous soul in this village, and now it turns out that you— Edward, why don't you tell me?"

"Well—er—er—Why, Mary, I can't!"

"You *can't*? *Why* can't you?"

"You see, he—well, he—he made me promise I wouldn't."

The wife looked him over, and said, very slowly:

"Made—you—promise? Edward, what do you tell me that for?"

"Mary, do you think I would lie?"

She was troubled and silent for a moment, then she laid her hand within his and said:

"No . . . no. We have wandered far enough from our bearings—God spare us that! In all your life you have never uttered a lie. But now—now that the foundations of things seem to be crumbling from under us, we—we—" She lost her voice for a moment, then said, brokenly, "Lead us not into temptation. . . . I think you made the promise, Edward. Let it rest so. Let us keep away from that ground. Now—that is all gone by; let us be happy again; it is no time for clouds."

Edward found it something of an effort to comply, for his mind kept wandering—trying to remember what the service was that he had done Goodson.

The couple lay awake the most of the night, Mary happy and busy, Edward busy but not so happy. Mary was planning what she would do with the money. Edward was trying to recall that service. At first his conscience was sore on account of the lie he had told Mary—if it was a lie. After much reflection—suppose it *was* a lie? What then? Was it such a great matter? Aren't we always *acting* lies? Then why not tell them? Look at Mary—look what she had done. While he was hurrying off on his honest errand, what was she doing? Lamenting because the papers hadn't been destroyed and the money kept! Is theft better than lying?

That point lost its sting—the lie dropped into the background and left comfort behind it. The next point came to the front: *Had* he rendered that service? Well, here was Goodson's own evidence as reported in Stephenson's letter; there could be no better evidence than that—it was even *proof* that he had rendered it. Of course. So that point was settled. . . . No, not quite. He recalled with a wince that this unknown Mr. Stephenson was just a trifle unsure as to whether the performer of it was Richards or some other—and, oh dear, he had put Richards on his honor! He must himself decide whither that money must go—and Mr. Stephenson was not doubting that if he was the wrong man he would go honorably and find the right one. Oh, it was odious to put a man in such a situation—ah, why couldn't Stephenson have left out that doubt! What did he want to intrude that for?

Further reflection. How did it happen that *Richards's* name remained in Stephenson's mind as indicating the right man, and not some other man's name? That looked good. Yes, that looked very good. In fact, it went on looking better and better, straight along—until by and by it grew into positive *proof*. And then Richards put the matter at once out of his mind, for he had a private instinct that a proof once established is better left so.

He was feeling reasonably comfortable now, but there was still one other detail that kept pushing itself on his notice: of course he had done that service—that was settled; but what *was* that service? He must recall it—he would not go to sleep till he had recalled it; it would make his peace of mind perfect. And so he thought and thought. He thought of a dozen things—possible services, even probable services—but none of them seemed adequate, none of them seemed large enough, none of them seemed worth the money—worth the fortune Goodson had wished he could leave in his will. And besides, he couldn't remember having done them, anyway. Now, then—now, then—what *kind* of a service would it be that would make a man so inordinately grateful? Ah—the saving of his soul! That must be it. Yes, he could remember, now, how he once set himself the task of converting Goodson, and labored at it as much as—he was going to say three months; but upon closer examination it shrunk to a month, then to a week, then to a day, then to nothing. Yes, he remembered now, and with unwelcome vividness, that Goodson had told him to go to thunder and mind his own business—*he* wasn't hankering to follow Hadleyburg to heaven!

So that solution was a failure—he hadn't saved Goodson's soul. Richards was discouraged. Then after a little came another idea: had he saved Goodson's property? No, that wouldn't do—he hadn't any. His life? That is it! Of course. Why, he might have thought of it before. This time he was on the right track, sure. His imagination-mill was hard at work in a minute, now.

Thereafter during a stretch of two exhausting hours he was busy saving Goodson's life. He saved it in all kinds of difficult and perilous ways. In every case he got it saved satisfactorily up to a certain point; then, just as he was beginning to get well persuaded that it had really happened, a troublesome detail would turn up which made the whole thing impossible. As in the matter of drowning, for instance. In that case he had swum out and tugged Goodson ashore in an unconscious state with a great crowd looking on and applauding, but when he had got it all thought out and was just beginning to remember all about it, a whole swarm of disqualifying details arrived on the ground: the town would have known of the circumstance, Mary would have known of it, it would glare like a limelight in his own memory instead of being an inconspicuous service which he had possibly rendered "without knowing its full value." And at this point he remembered that he couldn't swim, anyway.

Ah—*there* was a point which he had been overlooking from the start: it had to be a service which he had rendered "possibly without knowing the full value of it." Why, really, that ought to be an easy hunt—much easier than those others. And sure enough, by and by he found it. Goodson, years and years ago, came near marrying a very sweet and pretty girl, named Nancy Hewitt, but in some way or other the match had been broken off; the girl died, Goodson remained a bachelor, and by and by became a soured one and a frank despiser of the human species. Soon after the girl's death the village found out, or thought it had found out, that she carried a spoonful of negro blood in her veins. Richards worked at these details a good while, and in the end he thought he remembered things concerning them which must have gotten mislaid in his memory through long neglect. He seemed to dimly remember that it was *he* that found out about the negro blood; that it was he that told the village; that the village told Goodson where they got it; that he thus saved Goodson from marrying the tainted girl; that he had done him this great service "without knowing the full value of it," in fact without knowing that he *was* doing it; but that Goodson knew the value of it, and what a narrow escape he had had, and so went to his grave grateful to his benefactor and wishing he had a fortune to leave him. It was all clear and simple now, and the more he went over it the more luminous and certain it grew; and at last, when he nestled to sleep satisfied and happy, he remembered the whole thing just as if it had been yesterday. In fact, he dimly remembered Goodson's *telling* him his gratitude once. Meantime Mary had spent six thousand dollars on a new house for herself and a pair of slippers for her pastor, and then had fallen peacefully to rest.

That same Saturday evening the postman had delivered a letter to each of the other principal citizens—nineteen letters in all. No two of the envelopes were alike, and no two of the superscriptions were in the same hand, but the letters inside were just like each other in every detail but one. They were exact copies of the letter received by Richards—handwriting and all—and were all signed by Stephenson, but in place of Richard's name each receiver's own name appeared.

All night long eighteen principal citizens did what their caste-brother Richards was doing at the same time—they put in their energies trying to remember what notable service it was that they had unconsciously done Barclay Goodson. In no case was it a holiday job; still they succeeded.

And while they were at this work, which was difficult, their wives put in the night spending the money, which was easy. During that one night the nineteen wives spent an average of seven thousand dollars each out of the forty thousand in the sack—a hundred and thirty-three thousand altogether.

Next day there was a surprise for Jack Halliday. He noticed that the faces of the nineteen chief citizens and their wives bore that expression of peaceful and holy happiness again. He could not understand it, neither was he able to invent any remarks about it that could damage it or disturb it. And so it was his turn to be dissatisfied with life. His private guesses at the reasons for the happiness failed in all instances, upon examination. When he met Mrs. Wilcox and noticed the placid ecstasy in her face, he said to himself, "Her cat has had kittens"—and went and asked the cook: it was not so; the cook had detected the happiness, but did not know the cause. When Halliday found the duplicate ecstasy in the face of "Shadbelly" Billson (village nickname), he was sure some neighbor of Billson's had broken his leg, but inquiry showed that this had not happened. The subdued ecstasy in Gregory Yates's face could mean but one thing—he was a mother-in-law short: it was another mistake. "And Pinkerton—Pinkerton—he has collected ten cents that he thought he was going to lose." And so on, and so on. In some cases the guesses had to remain in doubt, in the others they proved distinct errors. In the end Halliday said to himself, "Anyway it foots up that there's nineteen Hadleyburg families temporarily in heaven: I don't know how it happened; I only know Providence is off duty to-day."

An architect and builder from the next state had lately ventured to set up a small business in this unpromising village, and his sign had now been hanging out a week. Not a customer yet; he was a discouraged man, and sorry he had come. But his weather changed suddenly now. First one and then another chief citizen's wife said to him privately:

"Come to my house Monday week—but say nothing about it for the present. We think of building."

He got eleven invitations that day. That night he wrote his daughter and broke off her match with her student. He said she could marry a mile higher than that.

Pinkerton the banker and two or three other well-to-do men planned country-seats—but waited. That kind don't count their chickens until they are hatched.

The Wilsons devised a grand new thing—a fancy-dress ball. They made no actual promises, but told all their acquaintance-ship in confidence that they were thinking the matter over and thought they should give it—"and if we do, you will be invited, of course." People were surprised, and said, one to another, "Why, they are crazy, those poor Wilsons, they can't afford it." Several among the nineteen said privately to their husbands, "It is a good idea: we will keep still till their cheap thing is over, then *we* will give one that will make it sick."

The days drifted along, and the bill of future squanderings rose higher and higher, wilder and wilder, more and more fool-ish and reckless. It began to look as if every member of the nineteen would not only spend his whole forty thousand dollars before receiving-day, but be actually in debt by the time he got the money. In some cases light-headed people did not stop with planning to spend, they really spent—on credit. They bought land, mortgages, farms, speculative stocks, fine clothes, horses, and various other things, paid down the bonus, and made them-selves liable for the rest—at ten days. Presently the sober second thought came, and Halliday noticed that a ghastly anxiety was beginning to show up in a good many faces. Again he was puzzled, and didn't know what to make of it. "The Wilcox kittens aren't dead, for they weren't born; nobody's broken a leg; there's no shrinkage in mother-in-laws; *nothing* has happened—it is an unsolvable mystery."

There was another puzzled man, too—the Rev. Mr. Burgess. For days, wherever he went, people seemed to follow him or to be watching out for him; and if he ever found himself in a retired spot, a member of the nineteen would be sure to appear, thrust an envelope privately into his hand, whisper "To be opened at the town-hall Friday evening," then vanish away like a guilty thing. He was expecting that there might be one claimant for the sack—doubtful, however, Goodson being dead—but it never occurred to him that all this crowd might be claimants. When the great Friday came at last, he found that he had nineteen envelopes.

III

The town-hall had never looked finer. The platform at the end of it was backed by a showy draping of flags; at intervals along the walls were festoons of flags; the gallery fronts were clothed in flags; the supporting columns were swathed in flags; all this was to impress the stranger, for he would be there in consider-able force, and in a large degree he would be connected with the press. The house was full. The 412 fixed seats were occupied; also the 68 extra chairs which had been packed into the aisles; the steps of the platform were occupied; some distinguished strangers were given seats on the platform; at the horseshoe of tables which fenced the front and sides of the platform sat a strong force of special correspondents who had come from everywhere. It was the best-dressed house the town had ever produced. There were some tolerably expensive toilets there, and in several cases the ladies who wore them had the look of being unfamiliar with that kind of clothes. At least the town thought they had that look, but the notion could have arisen from the town's knowledge of the fact that these ladies had never inhabited such clothes before.

The gold-sack stood on a little table at the front of the platform where all the house could see it. The bulk of the house gazed at it with a burning interest, a mouth-watering interest, a wistful and pathetic interest; a minority of nineteen couples gazed at it tenderly, lovingly, proprietarily, and the male half of this minority kept saying over to themselves the moving little impromptu speeches of thankfulness for the audience's applause and congratulations which they were presently going to get up and deliver. Every now and then one of these got a piece of paper out of his vest pocket and privately glanced at it to refresh his memory.

Of course there was a buzz of conversation going on—there always is; but at last when the Rev. Mr. Burgess rose and laid his hand on the sack he could hear his microbes gnaw, the place was so still. He related the curious history of the sack, then went on to speak in warm terms of Hadleyburg's old and well-earned reputation for spotless honesty, and of the town's just pride in this reputation. He said that this reputation was a treasure of priceless value; that under Providence its value had now become inestimably enhanced, for the recent episode had spread this fame far and wide, and thus had focused the eyes of the American world upon this village, and made its name for all time, as he hoped and believed, a synonym for commercial incorruptibility. [*Applause.*] "And who is to be the guardian of this noble treasure—the community as a whole? No! The responsibility is individual, not communal. From this day forth each and every one of you is in his own person its special guardian, and individually responsible that no harm shall come to it. Do you—does each of you—accept this great trust? [*Tumultuous assent.*] Then all is well. Transmit it to your children and to your children's children. To-day your purity is beyond reproach—see to it that it shall remain so. To-day there is not a person in your community who could be beguiled to touch a penny not his own—see to it that you abide in this grace. [*"We will! we will!"*] This is not the place to make comparisons between ourselves and other communities—some of them ungracious toward us; they have their ways, we have ours; let us be content. [*Applause.*] I am done. Under my hand, my friends, rests a stranger's eloquent recognition of what we are; through him the world will always henceforth know what we are. We do not know who he is, but in your name I utter your gratitude, and ask you to raise your voices in indorsement."

The house rose in a body and made the walls quake with the thunders of its thankfulness for the space of a long minute. Then it sat down, and Mr. Burgess took an envelope out of his pocket. The house held its breath while he slit the envelope open and took from it a slip of paper. He read its contents—slowly and impressively—the audience listening with tranced attention to this magic document, each of whose words stood for an ingot of gold:

" *'The remark which I made to the distressed stranger was this. "You are very far from being a bad man: go, and reform."' "* Then he continued:

"We shall know in a moment now whether the remark here quoted corresponds with the one concealed in the sack; and if that shall prove to be so—and it undoubtedly will—this sack of gold belongs to a fellow-citizen who will henceforth stand before the nation as the symbol of the special virtue which has made our town famous throughout the land—Mr. Billson!"

The house had gotten itself all ready to burst into the proper tornado of applause; but instead of doing it, it seemed stricken with a paralysis; there was a deep hush for a moment or two, then a wave of whispered murmurs swept the place—of about this tenor: *"Billson!* oh, come, this is too thin! Twenty dollars to a stranger—or *anybody—Billson!* tell it to the marines!" And now at this point the house caught its breath all of a sudden in a new access of astonishment, for it discovered that whereas in one part of the hall Deacon Billson was standing up with his head meekly bowed, in another part of it Lawyer Wilson was doing the same. There was a wondering silence now for a while.

Everybody was puzzled, and nineteen couples were surprised and indignant.

Billson and Wilson turned and stared at each other. Billson asked, bitingly:

"Why do *you* rise, Mr. Wilson?"

"Because I have a right to. Perhaps you will be good enough to explain to the house why *you* rise?"

"With great pleasure. Because I wrote that paper."

"It is an impudent falsity! I wrote it myself."

It was Burgess's turn to be paralyzed. He stood looking vacantly at first one of the men and then the other, and did not seem to know what to do. The house was stupefied. Lawyer Wilson spoke up, now, and said,

"I ask the Chair to read the name signed to that paper."

That brought the Chair to itself, and it read out the name:

" 'John Wharton *Billson*.' "

"There!" shouted Billson, "what have you got to say for yourself, now? And what kind of apology are you going to make to me and to this insulted house for the imposture which you have attempted to play here?"

"No apologies are due, sir; and as for the rest of it, I publicly charge you with pilfering my note from Mr. Burgess and substituting a copy of it signed with your own name. There is no other way by which you could have gotten hold of the test-remark; I alone, of living men, possessed the secret of its wording."

There was likely to be a scandalous state of things if this went on; everybody noticed with distress that the shorthand scribes were scribbling like mad; many people were crying "Chair, Chair! Order! order!" Burgess rapped with his gavel, and said:

"Let us not forget the proprieties due. There has evidently been a mistake somewhere, but surely that is all. If Mr. Wilson gave me an envelope—and I remember now that he did—I still have it."

He took one out of his pocket, opened it, glanced at it, looked surprised and worried, and stood silent a few moments. Then he waved his hand in a wandering and mechanical way, and made an effort or two to say something, then gave it up, despondently. Several voices cried out:

"Read it! read it! What is it?"

So he began in a dazed and sleep-walker fashion:

" *'The remark which I made to the unhappy stranger was this: "You are far from being a bad man.* [The house gazed at him, marveling.] *Go, and reform.' "* [Murmurs: "Amazing! what can this mean?"] This one," said the Chair, "is signed Thurlow G. Wilson."

"There!" cried Wilson. "I reckon that settles it! I knew perfectly well my note was purloined."

"Purloined!" retorted Billson. "I'll let you know that neither you nor any man of your kidney must venture to—"

THE CHAIR "Order, gentlemen, order! Take your seats, both of you, please."

They obeyed, shaking their heads and grumbling angrily. The house was profoundly puzzled; it did not know what to do with this curious emergency. Presently Thompson got up. Thompson was the hatter. He would have liked to be a Nineteener; but such was not for him: his stock of hats was not considerable enough for the position. He said:

"Mr. Chairman, if I may be permitted to make a suggestion, can both of these gentlemen be right? I put it to you, sir, can both have happened to say the very same words to the stranger? It seems to me—"

The tanner got up and interrupted him. The tanner was a disgruntled man; he believed himself entitled to be a Nineteener, but he couldn't get recognition. It made him a little unpleasant in his ways and speech. Said he:

"Sho, *that's* not the point! *That* could happen—twice in a hundred years—but not the other thing. *Neither* of them gave the twenty dollars!"

[*A ripple of applause.*]

BILLSON "*I* did!"

WILSON "*I* did!"

Then each accused the other of pilfering.

THE CHAIR "Order! Sit down, if you please—both of you. Neither of the notes has been out of my possession at any moment."

A VOICE "Good—that settles *that!*"

THE TANNER "Mr. Chairman, one thing is now plain: one of these men have been eavesdropping under the other one's bed, and filching family secrets. If it is not unparliamentary to suggest it, I will remark that both are equal to it. [*The Chair.* "Order! order!"] I withdraw the remark, sir, and will confine myself to suggesting that *if* one of them has overheard the other reveal the test-remark to his wife, we shall catch him now."

A VOICE "How?"

THE TANNER "Easily. The two have not quoted the remark in exactly the same words. You would have noticed that, if there hadn't been a considerable stretch of time and an exciting quarrel inserted between the two readings."

A VOICE "Name the difference."

THE TANNER "The word *very* is in Billson's note, and not in the other."

MANY VOICES "That's so—he's right!"

THE TANNER "And so, if the Chair will examine the test-remark in the sack, we shall know which of these two frauds—[*The Chair*. "Order!"]—which of these two adventurers—[*The Chair*. "Order! order!"]—which of these two gentlemen—[*laughter and applause*]—is entitled to wear the belt as being the first dishonest blatherskite ever bred in this town—which he has dishonored, and which will be a sultry place for him from now out!" [*Vigorous applause*.]

MANY VOICES "Open it!—open the sack!"

Mr. Burgess made a slit in the sack, slid his hand in and brought out an envelope. In it were a couple of folded notes. He said:

"One of these is marked, 'Not to be examined until all written communications which have been addressed to the Chair—if any—shall have been read.' The other is marked '*The Test*.' Allow me. It is worded—to wit:

" 'I do not require that the first half of the remark which was made to me by my benefactor shall be quoted with exactness, for it was not striking, and could be forgotten; but its closing fifteen words are quite striking, and I think easily rememberable; unless *these* shall be accurately reproduced, let the applicant be regarded as an impostor. My benefactor began by saying he seldom gave advice to any one, but that it always bore the hall-mark of high value when he did give it. Then he said this—and it has never faded from my memory: *"You are far from being a bad man—"* ' "

FIFTY VOICES "That settles it—the money's Wilson's! Wilson! Wilson! Speech! Speech!"

People jumped up and crowded around Wilson, wringing his hand and congratulating fervently—meantime the Chair was hammering with the gavel and shouting:

"Order, gentlemen! Order! Order! Let me finish reading, please." When quiet was restored, the reading was resumed—as follows:

" ' "Go, and reform—or, mark my words—some day, for your sins, you will die and go to hell or Hadleyburg—TRY AND MAKE IT THE FORMER." ' "

A ghastly silence followed. First an angry cloud began to settle darkly upon the faces of the citizenship; after a pause the cloud began to rise, and a tickled expression tried to take its place; tried so hard that it was only kept under with great and painful difficulty; the reporters, the Brixtonites, and other strangers bent their heads down and shielded their faces with their hands, and managed to hold in by main strength and heroic courtesy. At this most inopportune time burst upon the stillness the roar of a solitary voice—Jack Halliday's:

"*That's* got the hall-mark on it!"

Then the house let go, strangers and all. Even Mr. Burgess's gravity broke down presently, then the audience considered itself officially absolved from all restraint, and it made the most of its privilege. It was a good long laugh, and a tempestuously whole-hearted one, but it ceased at last—long enough for Mr. Burgess to try to resume, and for the people to get their eyes partially wiped; then it broke out again; and afterward yet again; then at last Burgess was able to get out these serious words:

"It is useless to try to disguise the fact—we find ourselves in the presence of a matter of grave import. It involves the honor of your town, it strikes at the town's good name. The difference of a single word between the test-remarks offered by Mr. Wilson and Mr. Billson was itself a serious thing, since it indicated that one or the other of these gentlemen had committed a theft—"

The two men were sitting limp, nerveless, crushed; but at these words both were electrified into movement, and started to get up—

"Sit down!" said the Chair, sharply, and they obeyed. "That, as I have said, was a serious thing. And it was—but for only one of them. But the matter has become graver; for the honor of *both* is now in formidable peril. Shall I go even further, and say in inextricable peril? *Both* left out the crucial fifteen words." He paused. During several moments he allowed the pervading stillness to gather and deepen its impressive effects, then added: "There would seem to be but one way whereby this could happen. I ask these gentlemen—Was there *collusion?—agreement?*"

A low murmur sifted through the house; its import was, "He's got them both."

Billson was not used to emergencies; he sat in a helpless collapse. But Wilson was a lawyer. He struggled to his feet, pale and worried, and said:

"I ask the indulgence of the house while I explain this most painful matter. I am sorry to say what I am about to say, since it must inflict irreparable injury upon Mr. Billson, whom I have always esteemed and respected until now, and in whose invulnerability to temptation I entirely believed—as did you all. But for the preservation of my own honor I must speak—and with frankness. I confess with shame—and I now beseech your pardon for it—that I said to the ruined stranger all of the words contained in the test-remark, including the disparaging fifteen.

[*Sensation.*] When the late publication was made I recalled them, and I resolved to claim the sack of coin, for by every right I was entitled to it. Now I will ask you to consider this point, and weigh it well: that stranger's gratitude to me that night knew no bounds; he said himself that he could find no words for it that were adequate, and that if he should ever be able he would repay me a thousandfold. Now, then, I ask you this: Could I expect—could I believe—could I even remotely imagine—that, feeling as he did, he would do so ungrateful a thing as to add those quite unnecessary fifteen words to his test?—set a trap for me?—expose me as a slanderer of my own town before my own people assembled in a public hall? It was preposterous; it was impossible. His test would contain only the kindly opening clause of my remark. Of that I had no shadow of doubt. You would have thought as I did. You would not have expected a base betrayal from one whom you had befriended and against whom you had committed no offense. And so, with perfect confidence, perfect trust, I wrote on a piece of paper the opening words—ending with 'Go, and reform,'—and signed it. When I was about to put it in an envelope I was called into my back office, and without thinking I left the paper lying open on my desk.'' He stopped, turned his head slowly toward Billson, waited a moment, then added: ''I ask you to note this: when I returned, a little later, Mr. Billson was retiring by my street door.'' [*Sensation.*]

In a moment Billson was on his feet and shouting:

''It's a lie! It's an infamous lie!''

THE CHAIR ''Be seated, sir! Mr. Wilson has the floor.''

Billson's friends pulled him into his seat and quieted him, and Wilson went on:

''Those are the simple facts. My note was now lying in a different place on the table from where I had left it. I noticed that, but attached no importance to it, thinking a draught had blown it there. That Mr. Billson would read a private paper was a thing which could not occur to me; he was a honorable man, and he would be above it. If you will allow me to say it, I think his extra word '*very*' stands explained; it is attributable to a defect of memory. I was the only man in the world who could furnish here any detail of the test-remark—by *honorable* means. I have finished.''

There is nothing in the world like a persuasive speech to fuddle the mental apparatus and upset the convictions and debauch the emotions of an audience not practised in the tricks and delusions of oratory. Wilson sat down victorious. The house submerged him in tides of approving applause; friends swarmed to him and shook him by the hand and congratulated him, and Billson was shouted down and not allowed to say a word. The Chair hammered and hammered with its gavel, and kept shouting:

"But let us proceed, gentlemen, let us proceed!"

At last there was a measurable degree of quiet, and the hatter said:

"But what is there to proceed with, sir, but to deliver the money?"

VOICES "That's it! That's it! Come forward, Wilson!"

THE HATTER "I move three cheers for Mr. Wilson, Symbol of the special virtue which—"

The cheers burst forth before he could finish; and in the midst of them—and in the midst of the clamor of the gavel also—some enthusiasts mounted Wilson on a big friend's shoulder and were going to fetch him in triumph to the platform. The Chair's voice now rose above the noise—

"Order! To your places! You forget that there is still a document to be read." When quiet had been restored he took up the document, and was going to read it, but laid it down again, saying, "I forgot; this is not to be read until all written communications received by me have first been read." He took an envelope out of his pocket, removed its inclosure, glanced at it—seemed astonished—held it out and gazed at it—stared at it.

Twenty or thirty voices cried out:

"What is it? Read it! read it!"

And he did—slowly, and wondering:

" *'The remark which I made to the stranger—*[Voices. "Hello! how's this?"]*—was this: "You are far from being a bad man."* [Voices. "Great Scott!"] *Go, and reform."* [Voices. "Oh, saw my leg off!"] Signed by Mr. Pinkerton, the banker."

The pandemonium of delight which turned itself loose now was of a sort to make the judicious weep. Those whose withers were unwrung laughed till the tears ran down; the reporters, in throes of laughter, set down disordered pot-hooks which would never in the world be decipherable; and a sleeping dog jumped up, scared out of its wits, and barked itself crazy at the turmoil. All manner of cries were scattered through the din: "We're getting rich—*two* Symbols of Incorruptibility!—without counting Billson!" "*Three!*—count Shadbelly in—we can't have too many!" "All right—Billson's elected!" "Alas, poor Wilson—victim of *two* thieves!"

A POWERFUL VOICE "Silence! The Chair's fishing up something more out of its pocket."

VOICES "Hurrah! Is it something fresh? Read it! read! read!"

THE CHAIR [*reading*] " '*The remark which I made,*' *etc.*; " '*You are far from being a bad man. "Go,*' " *etc.* Signed, 'Gregory Yates.' "

TORNADO OF VOICES "Four Symbols!" " 'Rah for Yates!" "Fish again!"

The house was in a roaring humor now, and ready to get all the fun out of the occasion that might be in it. Several Nineteeners, looking pale and distressed, got up and began to work their way toward the aisles, but a score of shouts went up:

"The doors, the doors—close the doors; no Incorruptible shall leave this place! Sit down, everybody!"

The mandate was obeyed.

"Fish again! Read! read!"

The Chair fished again, and once more the familiar words began to fall from its lips—" '*You are far from being a bad man.*' "

"Name! name! What's his name?"

" 'L. Ingoldsby Sargent.' "

"Five elected! Pile up the Symbols! Go on, go on!"

" '*You are far from being a bad—*' "

"Name! name!"

" 'Nicholas Whitworth.' "

"Hooray! hooray! it's a symbolical day!"

Somebody wailed in, and began to sing this rhyme (leaving out "it's") to the lovely "Mikado" tune of "When a man's afraid, a beautiful maid—"; the audience joined in, with joy; then, just in time, somebody contributed another line—

And don't you this forget—

The house roared it out. A third line was at once furnished—

Corruptibles far from Hadleyburg are—

The house roared that one too. As the last note died, Jack Halliday's voice rose high and clear, freighted with a final line—

But the Symbols are here, you bet!

That was sung, with booming enthusiasm. Then the happy house started in at the beginning and sang the four lines through twice, with immense swing and dash, and finished up with a crashing three-times-three and a tiger for "Hadleyburg the Incorruptible and all Symbols of it which we shall find worthy to receive the hall-mark to-night.''

Then the shoutings at the Chair began again, all over the place:

"Go on! go on! Read! read some more! Read all you've got!"

"That's it—go on! We are winning eternal celebrity!"

A dozen men got up now and began to protest. They said that this farce was the work of some abandoned joker, and was an insult to the whole community. Without a doubt these signatures were all forgeries—

"Sit down! sit down! Shut up! You are confessing. We'll find *your* names in the lot."

"Mr. Chairman, how many of those envelopes have you got?"

The Chair counted.

"Together with those that have been already examined, there are nineteen."

A storm of derisive applause broke out.

"Perhaps they all contain the secret. I move that you open them all and read every signature that is attached to a note of that sort—and read also the first eight words of the note."

"Second the motion!"

It was put and carried—uproariously. Then poor old Richards got up, and his wife rose and stood at his side. Her head was bent down, so that none might see that she was crying. Her husband gave her his arm, and so supporting her, he began to speak in a quavering voice:

"My friends, you have known us two—Mary and me—all our lives, and I think you have liked us and respected us—"

The Chair interrupted him:

"Allow me. It is quite true—that which you are saying, Mr. Richards: this town *does* know you two; it *does* like you, it *does* respect you; more—it honors you and *loves* you—"

Halliday's voice rang out:

"That's the hall-marked truth, too! If the Chair is right, let the house speak up and say it. Rise! Now, then—hip! hip! hip!—all together!"

The house rose in mass, faced toward the old couple eagerly, filled the air with a snow-storm of waving handkerchiefs, and delivered the cheers with all its affectionate heart.

The Chair then continued:

"What I was going to say is this: We know your good heart, Mr. Richards, but this is not a time for the exercise of charity toward offenders. [*Shouts of "Right! right!"*] I see your generous purpose in your face, but I cannot allow you to plead for these men—''

"But I was going to—"

"Please take your seat, Mr. Richards. We must examine the rest of these notes—simple fairness to the men who have already been exposed requires this. As soon as that has been done—I give you my word for this—you shall be heard."

MANY VOICES "Right!—the Chair is right—no interruption can be permitted at this stage! Go on!—the names! the names! —according to the terms of the motion!"

The old couple sat reluctantly down, and the husband whispered to the wife, "It is pitifully hard to have to wait; the shame will be greater than ever when they find we were only going to plead for *ourselves*."

Straightway the jollity broke loose again with the reading of the names.

" 'You are far from being a bad man—' " Signature, 'Robert J. Titmarsh.'

" 'You are far from being a bad man—' " Signature, 'Eliphalet Weeks.'

" 'You are far from being a bad man—' " Signature, 'Oscar B. Wilder.'

At this point the house lit upon the idea of taking the eight words out of the Chairman's hands. He was not unthankful for that. Thenceforward he held up each note in its turn, and waited. The house droned out the eight words in a massed and measured and musical deep volume of sound (with a daringly close resemblance to a well-known church chant)—" 'You are f-a-r from being a b-a-a-a-d man.' " Then the Chair said, "Signature, 'Archibald Wilcox.' " And so on, and so on, name after name, and everybody had an increasingly and gloriously good time except the wretched Nineteen. Now and then, when a particularly shining name was called, the house made the Chair wait while it chanted the whole of the test-remark from the beginning to the closing words, "And go to hell or Hadleyburg— try and make it the for-or-m-e-r!" and in these special cases they added a grand and agonized and imposing "A-a-a-a-*men!*"

The list dwindled, dwindled, dwindled, poor old Richards keeping tally of the count, wincing when a name resembling his own was pronounced, and waiting in miserable suspense for the time to come when it would be his humiliating privilege to rise with Mary and finish his plea, which he was intending to word thus: ". . . for until now we have never done any wrong thing, but have gone our humble way unreproached. We are very poor,

we are old, and have no chick nor child to help us; we were
sorely tempted, and we fell. It was my purpose when I got up
before to make confession and beg that my name might not be
read out in this public place, for it seemed to us that we could
not bear it; but I was prevented. It was just; it was our place to
suffer with the rest. It has been hard for us. It is the first time we
have ever heard our name fall from any one's lips—sullied. Be
merciful—for the sake of the better days; make our shame as
light to bear as in your charity you can." At this point in his
revery Mary nudged him, perceiving that his mind was absent.
The house was chanting, "You are f-a-r," etc.

"Be ready," Mary whispered. "Your name comes now; he
has read eighteen."

The chant ended.

"Next! next! next!" came volleying from all over the house.

Burgess put his hand into his pocket. The old couple, trembling,
began to rise. Burgess fumbled a moment, then said,

"I find I have read them all."

Faint with joy and surprise, the couple sank into their seats,
and Mary whispered:

"Oh, bless God, we are saved!—he has lost ours—I wouldn't
give this for a hundred of those sacks!"

The house burst out with its "Mikado" travesty, and sang it
three times with ever-increasing enthusiasm, rising to its feet
when it reached for the third time the closing line—

But there's one Symbol left, you bet!

and finishing up with cheers and a tiger for "Hadleyburg purity
and our eighteen immortal representatives of it."

Then Wingate, the saddler, got up and proposed cheers "for
the cleanest man in town, the one solitary important citizen in it
who didn't try to steal that money—Edward Richards."

They were given with great and moving heartiness; then somebody proposed that Richards be elected sole guardian and Symbol of the now Sacred Hadleyburg Tradition, with power and
right to stand up and look the whole sarcastic world in the face.

Passed, by acclamation; then they sang the "Mikado" again,
and ended it with:

And there's one Symbol left, you bet!

There was a pause; then—

A VOICE "Now, then, who's to get the sack?"

THE TANNER *(with bitter sarcasm)* "That's easy. The money has to be divided among the eighteen Incorruptibles. They gave the suffering stranger twenty dollars apiece—and that remark—each in his turn—it took twenty-two minutes for the procession to move past. Staked the stranger—total contribution, $360. All they want is just the loan back—and interest—forty thousand dollars altogether."

MANY VOICES *[derisively]* "That's it! Divvy! divvy! Be kind to the poor—don't keep them waiting!"

THE CHAIR "Order! I now offer the stranger's remaining document. It says: 'If no claimant shall appear *[grand chorus of groans]* I desire that you open the sack and count out the money to the principal citizens of your town, they to take it in trust *[cries of "Oh! Oh! Oh!"]*, and use it in such ways as to them shall seem best for the propagation and preservation of your community's noble reputation for incorruptible honesty *[more cries]*—a reputation to which their names and their efforts will add a new and far-reaching luster.' *[Enthusiastic outburst of sarcastic applause.]* That seems to be all. No—here is a postscript:

'P. S.—CITIZENS OF HADLEYBURG: *There is no test-remark—nobody made one.* [Great sensation.] *There wasn't any pauper stranger, nor any twenty-dollar contribution, nor any accompanying benediction and compliment—these are all inventions.* [General buzz and hum of astonishment and delight.] *Allow me to tell my story—it will take but a word or two. I passed through your town at a certain time, and received a deep offense which I had not earned. Any other man would have been content to kill one or two of you and call it square, but to me that would have been a trivial revenge, and inadequate; for the dead do not suffer. Besides, I could not kill you all—and, anyway, made as I am, even that would not have satisfied me. I wanted to damage every man in the place, and every woman—and not in their bodies or in their estate, but in their vanity—the place where feeble and foolish people are most vulnerable. So I disguised myself and came back and studied you. You were easy game. You had an old and lofty reputation for honesty, and naturally you were proud of it—it was your treasure of treasures, the very apple of your eye. As soon as I found out that you carefully and vigilantly kept yourselves and your children out of temptation, I knew how to proceed. Why, you simple creatures, the weakest of all weak things is a virtue which has not been tested in the fire. I laid a plan, and gathered a list of names. My project was to corrupt Hadleyburg the Incorruptible. My idea was to make liars and*

*thieves of nearly half a hundred smirchless men and women who
had never in their lives uttered a lie or stolen a penny. I was
afraid of Goodson. He was neither born nor reared in Hadleyburg.
I was afraid that if I started to operate my scheme by getting my
letter laid before you, you would say to yourselves, "Goodson is
the only man among us who would give away twenty dollars to a
poor devil"—and then you might not bite at my bait. But Heaven
took Goodson; then I knew I was safe, and I set my trap and
baited it. It may be that I shall not catch all the men to whom I
mailed the pretended test secret, but I shall catch the most of
them, if I know Hadleyburg nature.* [Voices. "*Right—he got
every last one of them.*"] *I believe they will even steal ostensible
gamble-money, rather than miss, poor, tempted, and mistrained
fellows. I am hoping to eternally and everlastingly squelch your
vanity and give Hadleyburg a new renown—one that will stick—
and spread far. If I have succeeded, open the sack and summon
the Committee on Propagation and Preservation of the Hadleyburg
Reputation.*'

A CYCLONE OF VOICES "Open it! Open it! The Eighteen to the
front! Committee on Propagation of the Tradition! Forward—the
Incorruptibles!"

The Chair ripped the sack wide, and gathered up a handful of
bright, broad, yellow coins, shook them together, then examined
them—

"Friends, they are only gilded disks of lead!"

There was a crashing outbreak of delight over this news, and
when the noise had subsided, the tanner called out:

"By right of apparent seniority in this business, Mr. Wilson is
Chairman of the Committee on Propagation of the Tradition. I
suggest that he step forward on behalf of his pals, and receive in
trust the money."

A HUNDRED VOICES "Wilson! Wilson! Wilson! Speech! Speech!"

WILSON [*in a voice trembling with anger*] "You will allow me
to say, and without apologies for my language, *damn* the money!"

A VOICE "Oh, and him a Baptist!"

A VOICE "Seventeen Symbols left! Step up, gentlemen, and
assume your trust!"

There was a pause—no response.

THE SADDLER "Mr. Chairman, we've got *one* clean man left,
anyway, out of the late aristocracy; and he needs money, and
deserves it. I move that you appoint Jack Halliday to get up there
and auction off that sack of gilt twenty-dollar pieces, and give

the result to the right man—the man whom Hadleyburg delights to honor—Edward Richards.''

This was received with great enthusiasm, the dog taking a hand again; the saddler started the bids at a dollar, the Brixton folk and Barnum's representative fought hard for it, the people cheered every jump that the bids made, the excitement climbed moment by moment higher and higher, the bidders got on their mettle and grew steadily more and more daring, more and more determined, the jumps went from a dollar up to five, then to ten, then to twenty, then fifty, then to a hundred, then—

At the beginning of the auction Richards whispered in distress to his wife: "O Mary, can we allow it? It—it—you see, it is an honor-reward, a testimonial to purity of character, and—and—can we allow it do? Hadn't I better get up and—O Mary, what ought we to do?—what do you think we—[*Halliday's voice. "Fifteen I'm bid!—fifteen for the sack!—twenty!—ah, thanks! —thirty—thanks again! Thirty, thirty, thirty!—do I heard forty? —forty it is! Keep the ball rolling, gentlemen, keep it rolling!—fifty! thanks, noble Roman! going at fifty, fifty, fifty!—seventy!—ninety! —splendid!—a hundred!—pile it up, pile it up!—hundred and twenty—forty!—just in time!—hundred and fifty!—*TWO *hundred! —superb! Do I hear two h—thanks!—two hundred and fifty!—*''*]*

"It is another temptation, Edward—I'm all in a tremble—but, oh,, we've escaped *one* temptation, and that ought to warn us to—[*"Six did I hear?—thanks!—six-fifty, six-f—*SEVEN *hundred!"*] And yet, Edward, when you think—nobody susp—[*"Eight hundred dollars!—hurrah!—make it nine!—Mr. Parsons, did I hear you say—thanks—nine!—this noble sack of virgin lead going at only nine hundred dollars, gilding and all—come! do I hear—a thousand!—gratefully yours!—did some one say eleven?—a sack which is going to be the most celebrated in the whole Uni—*] O Edward" (beginning to sob), "we are *so* poor!—but—but—do as you think best—do as you think best."

Edward fell—that is, he sat still; sat with a conscience which was not satisfied, but which was overpowered by circumstances.

Meantime a stranger, who looked like an amateur detective gotten up as an impossible English earl, had been watching the evening's proceedings with manifest interest, and with a contented expression in his face; and he had been privately commenting to himself. He was now soliloquizing somewhat like this: "None of the Eighteen are bidding; that is not satisfactory; I must change that—the dramatic unities require it; they must buy the sack they tried to steal; they must pay a heavy price, too— some of them are rich. And another thing, when I make a mistake in Hadleyburg nature the man that puts that error upon me is entitled to a high honorarium, and some one must pay it. This poor old Richards has brought my judgment to shame; he is an honest man:—I don't understand it, but I acknowledge it. Yes, he saw my deuces *and* with a straight flush, and by rights the pot is his. And it shall be a jack-pot, too, if I can manage it. He disappointed me, but let that pass.''

He was watching the bidding. At a thousand, the market broke; the prices tumbled swiftly. He waited—and still watched. One competitor dropped out; then another, and another. He put in a bid or two, now. When the bids had sunk to ten dollars, he added a five; some one raised him a three; he waited a moment, then flung in a fifty-dollar jump, and the sack was his—at $1,282. The house broke out in cheers—then stopped; for he was on his feet, and had lifted his hand. He began to speak.

''I desire to say a word, and ask a favor. I am a speculator in rarities, and I have dealings with persons interested in numismatics all over the world. I can make a profit on this purchase, just as it stands; but there is a way, if I can get your approval, whereby I can make every one of these leaden twenty-dollar pieces worth its face in gold, and perhaps more. Grant me that approval, and I will give part of my gains to your Mr. Richards, whose invulnerable probity you have so justly and so cordially recognized to-night; his share shall be ten thousand dollars, and I will hand him the money to-morrow. [*Great applause from the house.* But the ''invulnerable probity'' made the Richardses blush prettily; however, it went for modesty, and did no harm.] If you will pass my proposition by a good majority—I would like a two-thirds vote—I will regard that as the town's consent, and that is all I ask. Rarities are always helped by any device which will rouse curiosity and compel remark. Now if I may have your permission to stamp upon the faces of each of these ostensible coins the names of the eighteen gentlemen who—''

Nine-tenths of the audience were on their feet in a moment— dog and all—and the proposition was carried with a whirlwind of approving applause and laughter.

They sat down, and all the Symbols except ''Dr.'' Clay Harkness got up, violently protesting against the proposed outrage, and threatening to—

''I beg you not to threaten me,'' said the stranger, calmly. ''I know my legal rights, and am not accustomed to being frightened at bluster.'' [*Applause.*] He sat down. ''Dr.'' Harkness saw an opportunity here. He was one of the two very rich men of the place, and Pinkerton was the other. Harkness was proprietor of a mint; that is to say, a popular patent medicine. He was running for the legislature on one ticket, and Pinkerton on the other. It was a close race and a hot one, and getting hotter every day. Both had strong appetites for money; each had bought a great tract of land, with a purpose; there was going to be a new railway, and each wanted to be in the legislature and help locate the route to his own advantage; a single vote might make the decision, and with it two or three fortunes. The stake was large, and Harkness was a daring speculator. He was sitting close to the stranger. He leaned over while one or another of the other Symbols was entertaining the house with protests and appeals, and asked, in a whisper.

"What is your price for the sack?"

"Forty thousand dollars."

"I'll give you twenty."

"No."

"Twenty-five."

"No."

"Say thirty."

"The price is forty thousand dollars; not a penny less."

"All right, I'll give it. I will come to the hotel at ten in the morning. I don't want it known: will see you privately."

"Very good." Then the stranger got up and said to the house:

"I find it late. The speeches of these gentlemen are not without merit, not without interest, not without grace; yet if I may be excused I will take my leave. I thank you for the great favor which you have shown me in granting my petition. I ask the Chair to keep the sack for me until to-morrow, and to hand these three five-hundred-dollar notes to Mr. Richards." They were passed up to the Chair. "At nine I will call for the sack, and at eleven will deliver the rest of the ten thousand to Mr. Richards in person, at his home. Good night."

Then he slipped out, and left the audience making a vast noise which was composed of a mixture of cheers, the "Mikado" song, dog-disapproval, and the chant, "You are f-a-r from being a b-a-a-d man—a-a-a-a-men!"

IV

At home the Richardses had to endure congratulations and compliments until midnight. Then they were left to themselves. They looked a little sad, and they sat silent and thinking. Finally Mary sighed and said,

"Do you think we are to blame, Edward—*much* to blame?"

and her eyes wandered to the accusing triplet of big banknotes lying on the table, where the congratulators had been gloating over them and reverently fingering them. Edward did not answer at once; then he brought out a sigh and said, hesitatingly:

"We—we couldn't help it, Mary. It—well, it was ordered. *All* things are."

Mary glanced up and looked at him steadily, but he didn't return the look. Presently she said:

"I thought congratulations and praises always tasted good. But—it seems to me, now—Edward?"

"Well?"

"Are you going to stay in the bank?"

"N-no."

"Resign?"

"In the morning—by note."

"It does seem best."

Richards bowed his head in his hands and muttered:

"Before, I was not afraid to let oceans of people's money pour through my hands, but—Mary, I am so tired, so tired—"

"We will go to bed."

At nine in the morning the stranger called for the sack and took it to the hotel in a cab. At ten Harkness had a talk with him privately. The stranger asked for and got five checks on a metropolitan bank—drawn to "Bearer"—four for $1,500 each, and one for $34,000. He put one of the former in his pocketbook, and the remainder, representing $38,500, he put in an envelope, and with these he added a note, which he wrote after Harkness was gone. At eleven he called at the Richards house and knocked. Mrs. Richards peeped through the shutters, then went and received the envelope, and the stranger disappeared without a word. She came back flushed and a little unsteady on her legs, and gasped out:

"I am sure I recognized him! Last night it seemed to me that maybe I had seen him somewhere before."

"He is the man that brought the sack here?"

"I am almost sure of it."

"Then he is the ostensible Stephenson, too, and sold every important citizen in this town with his bogus secret. Now if he has sent checks instead of money, we are sold, too, after we thought we had escaped. I was beginning to feel fairly comfortable once more, after my night's rest, but the look of that envelope makes me sick. It isn't fat enough; $8,500 in even the largest bank-notes makes more bulk than that."

"Edward, why do you object to checks?"

"Checks signed by Stephenson! I am resigned to take the $8,500 if it could come in bank-notes—for it does seem that it was so ordered, Mary—but I have never had much courage, and I have not the pluck to try to market a check signed with that disastrous name. It would be a trap. That man tried to catch me; we escaped somehow or other; and now he is trying a new way. If it is checks—"

"Oh, Edward, it is *too* bad!" and she held up the checks and began to cry.

"Put them in the fire! quick! we mustn't be tempted. It is a trick to make the world laugh at *us*, along with the rest, and—Give them to *me*, since you can't do it!" He snatched them and tried to hold his grip till he could get to the stove; but he was human, he was a cashier, and he stopped a moment to make sure of the signature. Then he came near to fainting.

"Fan me, Mary, fan me! They are the same as gold!"

"Oh, how lovely, Edward! Why?"

"Signed by Harkness. What can the mystery of that be, Mary?"

"Edward, do you think—"

"Look here—look at this! Fifteen—fifteen—fifteen—thirty-four. Thirty-eight thousand five hundred! Mary, the sack isn't worth twelve dollars, and Harkness—apparently—has paid about par for it."

"And does it all come to us, do you think—instead of the ten thousand?"

"Why, it looks like it. And the checks are made to 'Bearer,' too."

"Is that good, Edward? What is it for?"

"A hint to collect them at some distant bank, I reckon. Perhaps Harkness doesn't want the matter known. What is that—a note?"

"Yes. It was with the checks."

It was in the "Stephenson" handwriting, but there was no signature. It said:

"I am a disappointed man. Your honesty is beyond the reach of temptation. I had a different idea about it, but I wronged you in that, and I beg pardon, and do it sincerely. I honor you—and that is sincere too. This town is not worthy to kiss the hem of your garment. Dear sir, I made a square bet with myself that there were nineteen debauchable men in your self-righteous community. I have lost. Take the whole pot, you are entitled to it."

Richards drew a deep sigh, and said:

"It seems written with fire—it burns so. Mary—I am miserable again."

"I, too. Ah, dear, I wish—"

"To think, Mary—he *believes* in me."

"Oh, don't, Edward—I can't bear it."

"If those beautiful words were deserved, Mary—and God knows I believed I deserved them once—I think I could give the forty thousand dollars for them. And I would put that paper away, as representing more than gold and jewels, and keep it always. But now— We could not live in the shadow of its accusing presence, Mary."

He put it in the fire.

A messenger arrived and delivered an envelope.

Richards took from it a note and read it; it was from Burgess.

"You saved me, in a difficult time. I saved you last night. It was at cost of a lie, but I made the sacrifice freely, and out of a grateful heart. None in this village knows so well as I know how brave and good and noble you are. At bottom you cannot respect me, knowing as you do of that matter of which I am accused, and by the general voice condemned; but I beg that you will at least believe that I am grateful man; it will help me to bear my burden."

[*Signed*]

BURGESS

"Saved, once more. And on such terms!" He put the note in the fire. "I—I wish I were dead, Mary, I wish I were out of it all."

"Oh, these are bitter, bitter days, Edward. The stabs, through their very generosity, are so deep—and they come so fast!"

Three days before the election each of two thousand voters suddenly found himself in possession of a prized memento—one of the renowned bogus double-eagles. Around one of its faces was stamped these words: "THE REMARK I MADE TO THE POOR STRANGER WAS—" Around the other face was stamped these: "GO, AND REFORM. [SIGNED] PINKERTON." Thus the entire remaining refuse of the renowned joke was emptied upon a single head, and with calamitous effect. It revived the recent vast laugh and concentrated it upon Pinkerton; and Harkness's election was a walkover.

Within twenty-four hours after the Richardses had received their checks their consciences were quieting down, discouraged; the old couple were learning to reconcile themselves to the sin which they had committed. But they were to learn, now, that a sin takes on new and real terrors when there seems a chance that it is going to be found out. This gives it a fresh and most substantial and important aspect. At church the morning sermon was of the usual pattern; it was the same old things said in the same old way; they had heard them a thousand times and found them innocuous, next to meaningless, and easy to sleep under; but now it was different: the sermon seemed to bristle with accusations; it seemed aimed straight and specially at people who were concealing deadly sins. After church they got away from the mob of congratulators as soon as they could, and hurried homeward, chilled to the bone at they did not know what—vague, shadowy, indefinite fears. And by chance they caught a glimpse of Mr. Burgess as he turned a corner. He paid no attention to their nod of recognition! He hadn't seen it; but they did not know that. What could his conduct mean? It might mean—it might mean—oh, a dozen dreadful things. Was it possible that he knew that Richards could have cleared him of guilt in that bygone time, and had been silently waiting for a chance to even up accounts? At home, in their distress they got to imagining that their servant might have been in the next room listening when Richards revealed the secret to his wife that he knew of Burgess's innocence; next, Richards began to imagine that he had heard the swish of a gown in there at that time; next, he was sure he *had* heard it. They would call Sarah in, on a pretext, and watch her face: if she had been betraying them to Mr. Burgess, it would show in her manner. They asked her some questions—questions which were so random and incoherent and seemingly purposeless that the girl felt sure that the old people's minds had been affected by their sudden good fortune; the sharp and watchful gaze which they bent upon her frightened her, and that completed the business. She blushed, she became nervous and confused, and to the old people these were plain signs of guilt—guilt of some fearful sort or other—without doubt she was a spy and a traitor. When they were alone again they began to piece many unrelated things together and get horrible results out of the combination. When things had got about to the worst, Richards was delivered of a sudden gasp, and his wife asked:

"Oh, what is it?—what is it?"

"The note—Burgess's note! Its language was sarcastic, I see it now." He quoted: " 'At bottom you cannot respect me, *knowing*, as you do, of *that matter* of which I am accused'—oh, it is perfectly plain, now, God help me! He knows that I know!

You see the ingenuity of the phrasing. It was a trap—and like a fool, I walked into it. And Mary—?"

"Oh, it is dreadful—I know what you are going to say—he didn't return your transcript of the pretended test-remark."

"No—kept it to destroy us with. Mary, he has exposed us to some already. I know it—I know it well. I saw it in a dozen faces after church. Ah, he wouldn't answer our nod of recognition—*he* knew what he had been doing!"

In the night the doctor was called. The news went around in the morning that the old couple were rather seriously ill—prostrated by the exhausting excitement growing out of their great windfall, the congratulations, and the late hours, the doctor said. The town was sincerely distressed; for these old people were about all it had left to be proud of, now.

Two days later the news was worse. The old couple were delirious, and were doing strange things. By witness of the nurses, Richards had exhibited checks—for $8,500? No—for an amazing sum—$38,500! What could be the explanation of this gigantic piece of luck?

The following day the nurses had more news—and wonderful. They had concluded to hide the checks, lest harm come to them; but when they searched they were gone from under the patient's pillow—vanished away. The patient said:

"Let the pillow alone; what do you want?"

"We thought it best that the checks—"

"You will never see them again—they are destroyed. They came from Satan. I saw the hell-brand on them, and I knew they were sent to betray me to sin." Then he fell to gabbling strange and dreadful things which were not clearly understandable, and which the doctor admonished them to keep to themselves.

Richards was right; the checks were never seen again.

A nurse must have talked in her sleep, for within two days the forbidden gabblings were the property of the town; and they were of a surprising sort. They seemed to indicate that Richards had been a claimant for the sack himself, and that Burgess had concealed that fact and then maliciously betrayed it.

Burgess was taxed with this and stoutly denied it. And he said it was not fair to attach weight to the chatter of a sick old man who was out of his mind. Still, suspicion was in the air, and there was much talk.

After a day or two it was reported that Mrs. Richards's delirious deliveries were getting to be duplicates of her husband's. Suspicion flamed up into conviction, now, and the town's pride in the purity of its one undiscredited important citizen began to dim down and flicker toward extinction.

Six days passed, then came more news. The old couple were dying. Richards's mind cleared in his latest hour, and sent for Burgess. Burgess said:

"Let the room be cleared. I think he wishes to say something in privacy."

"No!" said Richards: "I want witnesses. I want you all to hear my confession, so that I may die a man, and not a dog. I was clean—artificially—like the rest; and like the rest I fell when temptation came. I signed a lie, and claimed the miserable sack. Mr. Burgess remembered that I had done him a service, and in gratitude (and ignorance) he suppressed my claim and saved me. You know the thing that was charged against Burgess years ago. My testimony, and mine alone, could have cleared him, and I was a coward, and left him to suffer disgrace—"

"No—no—Mr. Richards, you—"

"My servant betrayed my secret to him—"

"No one has betrayed anything to me—"

—"and then he did a natural and justifiable thing, he repented of the saving kindness which he had done me, and he *exposed* me—as I deserved—"

"Never!—I make oath—"

"Out of my heart I forgive him."

Burgess's impassioned protestations fell upon deaf ears; the dying man passed away without knowing that once more he had done poor Burgess a wrong. The old wife died that night.

The last of the sacred Nineteen had fallen a prey to the fiendish sack; the town was stripped of the last rag of its ancient glory. Its mourning was not showy, but it was deep.

By act of the Legislature—upon prayer and petition—Hadleyburg was allowed to change its name to (never mind what—I will not give it away), and leave one word out of the motto that for many generations had graced the town's official seal.

It is an honest town once more, and the man will have to rise early that catches it napping again.

Jack London
(1876–1916)

Born in San Francisco, of uncertain parentage, London left school at age 14; in 1893, he sailed to Japan on a sealing voyage. Thereafter he tramped across the United States, briefly attended the University of California, and, in 1897, joined the gold rush to the Klondike. By 1898, he was back in Oakland, California, and trying to write of the many things he had seen and experienced. The Overland Monthly *and the* Atlantic Monthly, *among other magazines, accepted his work; by 1900, his first book,* The Son of the Wolf, *began to establish his reputation. A Socialist and dedicated reformer, he traveled to London, gathering material for* The People of the Abyss *(1903). The Call of the Wild (1903) and* The Sea-Wolf *(1904), powerful novels of the wild, were followed by* White Fang *(1906) and his best novel,* Martin Eden *(1909), a semi-autobiographical recounting of his early career as a writer. Much of his work, and especially his later work, is polemical.*

ALL GOLD CANYON

It was the green heart of the canyon, where the walls swerved back from the rigid plan and relieved their harshness of line by making a little sheltered nook and filling it to the brim with sweetness and roundness and softness. Here all things rested. Even the narrow stream ceased its turbulent downrush long enough to form a quiet pool. Knee-deep in the water, with drooping head and half-shut eyes, drowsed a red-coated, many-antlered buck.

On one side, beginning at the very lip of the pool, was a tiny meadow, a cool, resilient surface of green that extended to the base of the frowning wall. Beyond the pool a gentle slope of earth ran up and up to meet the opposing wall. Fine grass covered the slope—grass that was spangled with flowers, with here and there patches of color, orange and purple and golden. Below, the canyon was shut in. There was no view. The walls leaned together abruptly and the canyon ended in a chaos of rocks, moss-covered and hidden by a green screen of vines and creepers and boughs of trees. Up the canyon rose far hills and peaks, the big foothills, pine-covered and remote. And far beyond, like clouds upon the border of the sky, towered minarets of white, where the Sierra's eternal snows flashed austerely the blazes of the sun.

There was no dust in the canyon. The leaves and flowers were clean and virginal. The grass was young velvet. Over the pool three cottonwoods sent their snowy fluffs fluttering down the quiet air. On the slope the blossoms of the wine-wooded manzanita filled the air with springtime odors, while the leaves, wise with experience, were already beginning their vertical twist against the coming aridity of summer. In the open spaces on the slope, beyond the farthest shadow-reach of the manzanita, poised the maripose lilies, like so many flights of jeweled moths suddenly arrested and on the verge of trembling into flight again. Here and there that woods harlequin, the madroña, permitting itself to be caught in the act of changing its pea-green trunk to madder red, breathed its fragrance into the air from great clusters of waxen bells. Creamy white were these bells, shaped like lilies of the valley, with the sweetness of perfume that is of the springtime.

There was not a sigh of wind. The air was drowsy with its weight of perfume. It was a sweetness that would have been cloying had the air been heavy and humid. But the air was sharp and thin. It was as starlight transmuted into atmosphere, shot through and warmed by sunshine, and flower-drenched with sweetness.

An occasional butterfly drifted in and out through the patches of light and shade. And from all about rose the low and sleepy hum of mountain bees—feasting sybarites that jostled one another good-naturedly at the board, nor found time for rough discourtesy. So quietly did the little stream drip and ripple its way through the canyon that it spoke only in faint and occasional gurgles. The voice of the stream was as a drowsy whisper, ever interrupted by dozings and silences, ever lifted again in the awakenings.

The motion of all things was a drifting in the heart of the canyon. Sunshine and butterflies drifted in and out among the trees. The hum of the bees and the whisper of the stream were a drifting of sound. And the drifting sound and drifting color seemed to weave together in the making of a delicate and intangible fabric which was the spirit of the place. It was a spirit of peace that was not of death, but of smooth-pulsing life, of quietude that was not silence, of movement that was not action, of repose that was quick with existence without being violent with struggle and travail. The spirit of the place was the spirit of the peace of the living, somnolent with the easement and content of prosperity, and undisturbed by rumors of far wars.

The red-coated, many-antlered buck acknowledged the lordship of the spirit of the place and dozed knee-deep in the cool, shaded pool. There seemed no flies to vex him and he was languid with rest. Sometimes his ears moved when the stream awoke and whispered; but they moved lazily, with foreknowledge that it was merely the stream grown garrulous at discovery that it had slept.

But there came a time when the buck's ears lifted and tensed with swift eagerness for sound. His head was turned down the canyon. His sensitive, quivering nostrils scented the air. His eyes could not pierce the green screen through which the stream rippled away, but to his ears came the voice of a man. It was a steady, monotonous, singsong voice. Once the buck heard the harsh clash of metal upon rock. At the sound he snorted with a sudden start that jerked him through the air from water to meadow, and his feet sank into the young velvet, while he pricked his ears and again to listen, and faded away out of the canyon like a wraith, soft-footed and without sound.

The clash of steel-shod soles against the rocks began to be heard, and the man's voice grew louder. It was raised in a sort of chant and became distinct with nearness, so that the words could be heard:

> Tu'n around an' tu'n yo' face
> Untoe them sweet hills of grace.
>   (D' pow'rs of sin yo' am scornin'!)
> Look about an' look aroun',
> Fling yo' sin pack on d' groun'.
>   (Yo' will meet wid d' Lord in d' mornin'!)

A sound of scrambling accompanied the song, and the spirit of the place fled away on the heels of the red-coated buck. The green screen was burst asunder, and a man peered out at the meadow and the pool and the sloping sidehill. He was a deliberate sort of man. He took in the scene with one embracing glance, then ran his eyes over the details to verify the general impression. Then, and not until then, did he open his mouth in vivid and solemn approval.

"Smoke of life an' snakes of purgatory! Will you just look at that! Wood an' water an' grass an' a sidehill! A pocket hunter's delight an' a cayuse's paradise! Cool green for tired eyes! Pink pills for pale people ain't in it. A secret pasture for prospectors and a resting place for tired burros, by damn!"

He was a sandy-complexioned man in whose face geniality and humor seemed the salient characteristics. It was a mobile face, quick-changing to inward mood and thought. Thinking was in him a visible process. Ideas chased across his face like windflaws across the surface of a lake. His hair, sparse and unkempt of growth, was as indeterminate and colorless as his complexion. It would seem that all the color of his frame had gone into his eyes, for they were startlingly blue. Also they were laughing and merry eyes, within them much of the naïveté and wonder of the child; and yet, in an unassertive way, they contained much of calm self-reliance and strength of purpose founded upon self-experience and experience of the world.

From out the screen of vines and creepers he flung ahead of him a miner's pick and shovel and gold pan. Then he crawled out himself into the open. He was clad in faded overalls and black cotton shirt, with hobnailed brogans on his feet, and on his head a hat whose shapelessness and stains advertised the rough usage of wind and rain and sun and camp smoke. He stood erect, seeing wide-eyed the secrecy of the scene and sensuously inhaling the warm, sweet breath of the canyon garden through nostrils that dilated and quivered with delight. His eyes narrowed to laughing slits of blue, his face wreathed itself in joy, and his mouth curled in a smile as he cried aloud:

"Jumping dandelions and happy hollyhocks, but that smells good to me! Talk about your attar o' roses an' cologne factories! They ain't in it!"

He had the habit of soliloquy. His quick-changing facial expressions might tell every thought and mood, but the tongue, perforce, ran hard after, repeating, like a second Boswell.

The man lay down on the lip of the pool and drank long and deep of its water. "Tastes good to me," he murmured, lifting his head and gazing across the pool at the sidehill, while he wiped his mouth with the back of his hand. The sidehill attracted his attention. Still lying on his stomach, he studied the hill formation long and carefully. It was a practiced eye that traveled up the slope to the crumbling canyon wall and back and down again to the edge of the pool. He scrambled to his feet and favored the sidehill with a second survey.

"Looks good to me," he concluded, picking up his pick and shovel and gold pan.

He crossed the stream below the pool, stepping agilely from stone to stone. Where the sidehill touched the water he dug up a shovelful of dirt and put it into the gold pan. He squatted down, holding the pan in his two hands, and partly immersing it in the stream. Then he imparted to the pan a deft circular motion that sent the water sluicing in and out through the dirt and gravel. The larger and the lighter particles worked to the surface, and these, by a skillful dipping movement of the pan, he spilled out and over the edge. Occasionally, to expedite matters, he rested the pan and with his fingers raked out the large pebbles and pieces of rock.

The contents of the pan diminished rapidly until only fine dirt and the smallest bits of gravel remained. At this stage he began to work very deliberately and carefully. It was fine washing, and he washed fine and finer, with a keen scrutiny and delicate and fastidious touch. At last the pan seemed empty of everything but water; but with a quick semicircular flirt that sent the water flying over the shallow rim into the stream he disclosed a layer of black sand on the bottom of the pan. So thin was this layer that it was like a streak of paint. He examined it closely. In the midst of it was a tiny golden speck. He dribbled a little water in over the depressed edge of the pan. With a quick flirt he sent the water sluicing across the bottom, turning the grains of black sand over and over. A second tiny golden speck rewarded his effort.

The washing had now become very fine—fine beyond all need of ordinary placer mining. He worked the black sand, a small portion at a time, up the shallow rim of the pan. Each small portion he examined sharply, so that his eyes saw every grain of it before he allowed it to slide over the edge and away. Jealously, bit by bit, he let the black sand slip away. A golden speck, no larger than a pinpoint, appeared on the rim, and by his manipulation of the water it returned to the bottom of the pan. And in such fashion another speck was disclosed, and another. Great was his care of them. Like a shepherd he herded his flock of golden specks so that not one should be lost. At last, of the pan of dirt nothing remained but his golden herd. He counted it, and then, after all his labor, sent it flying out of the pan with one final swirl of water.

But his blue eyes were shining with desire as he rose to his feet. "Seven," he muttered aloud, asserting the sum of the specks for which he had toiled so hard and which he had so wantonly thrown away. "Seven," he repeated, with the emphasis of one trying to impress a number on his memory.

He stood still a long while, surveying the hillside. In his eyes was a curiosity, new-aroused and burning. There was an exultance about his bearing and a keenness like that of a hunting animal catching the fresh scent of game.

He moved down the stream a few steps and took a second panful of dirt.

Again came the careful washing, the jealous herding of the golden specks, and the wantonness with which he sent them flying into the stream when he had counted their number.

"Five," he muttered, and repeated, "five."

He could not forbear another survey of the hill before filling the pan farther down the stream. His golden herds diminished. "Four, three, two, two, one," were his memory tabulations as he moved down the stream. When but one speck of gold rewarded his washing he stopped and built a fire of dry twigs. Into this he thrust the gold pan and burned it till it was blue-black. He held up the pan and examined it critically. Then he nodded approbation. Against such a color background he could defy the tiniest yellow speck to elude him.

Still moving down the stream, he panned again. A single speck was his reward. A third pan contained no gold at all. Not satisfied with this, he panned three times again, taking his shovels of dirt within a foot of one another. Each pan proved empty of gold, and the fact, instead of discouraging him, seemed to give him satisfaction. His elation increased with each barren washing, until he arose, exclaiming jubilantly:

"If it ain't the real thing, may God knock off my head with sour apples!"

Returning to where he had started operations, he began to pan up the stream. At first his golden herds increased—increased prodigiously. "Fourteen, eighteen, twenty-one, twenty-six," ran his memory tabulations. Just above the pool he struck his richest pan—thirty-five colors.

"Almost enough to save," he remarked regretfully as he allowed the water to sweep them away.

The sun climbed to the top of the sky. The man worked on.

Pan by pan he went up the stream, the tally of results steadily decreasing.

"It's just booful, the way it peters out," he exulted when a shovelful of dirt contained no more than a single speck of gold.

And when no specks at all were found in several pans he straightened up and favored the hillside with a confident glance.

"Aha! Mr. Pocket!" he cried out as though to an auditor hidden somewhere above him beneath the surface of the slope. "Aha! Mr. Pocket! I'm a-comin', I'm a-comin', an' I'm shorely gwine to get yer! You heah me, Mr. Pocket? I'm gwine to get yer as shore as punkins ain't cauliflowers!"

He turned and flung a measuring glance at the sun poised above him in the azure of the cloudless sky. Then he went down the canyon, following the line of shovel holes he had made in filling the pans. He crossed the stream below the pool and disappeared through the green screen. There was little opportunity for the spirit of the place to return with its quietude and repose, for the man's voice, raised in ragtime song, still dominated the canyon with possession.

After a time, with a greater clashing of steel-shod feet on rock, he returned. The green screen was tremendously agitated. It surged back and forth in the throes of a struggle. There was a loud grating and clanging of metal. The man's voice leaped to a higher pitch and was sharp with imperativeness. A large body plunged and panted. There was a snapping and ripping and rending, and amid a shower of falling leaves a horse burst through the screen. On its back was a pack, and from this trailed broken vines and torn creepers. The animal gazed with astonished eyes at the scene into which it had been precipitated, then dropped its head to the grass and began contentedly to graze. A second horse scrambled into view, slipping once on the mossy rocks and regaining equilibrium when its hoofs sank into the yielding surface of the meadow. It was riderless, though on its back was a high-horned Mexican saddle, scarred and discolored by long usage.

The man brought up the rear. He threw off pack and saddle, with an eye to camp location, and gave the animals their freedom to graze. He unpacked his food and got out frying pan and coffeepot. He gathered an armful of dry wood, and with a few stones made a place for his fire.

"My," he said, "but I've got an appetite! I could scoff iron filings an' horseshoe nails an' thank you kindly, ma'am, for a second helpin'."

He straightened up, and while he reached for matches in the

pocket of his overalls his eyes traveled across the pool to the sidehill. His fingers had clutched the matchbox, but they relaxed their hold and the hand came out empty. The man wavered perceptibly. He looked at his preparations for cooking and he looked at the hill.

"Guess I'll take another whack at her," he concluded, starting to cross the stream.

"They ain't no sense in it, I know," he mumbled apologetically. "But keepin' grub back an hour ain't goin' to hurt none, I reckon."

A few feet back from his first line of test pans he started a second line. The sun dropped down on the western sky, the shadows lengthened, but the man worked on. He began a third line of test pans. He was crosscutting the hillside, line by line, as he ascended. The center of each line produced the richest pans, while the ends came where no colors showed in the pan. And as he ascended the hillside the lines grew perceptibly shorter. The regularity with which their length diminished served to indicate that somewhere up the slope the last line would be so short as to have scarcely length at all, and that beyond could come only a point. The design was growing into an inverted V. The converging sides of this V marked the boundaries of the gold-bearing dirt.

The apex of the V was evidently the man's goal. Often he ran his eye along the converging sides and on up the hill, trying to divine the apex, the point where the gold-bearing dirt must cease. Here resided "Mr. Pocket"—for so the man familiarly addressed the imaginary point above him on the slope, crying out:

"Come down out o' that, Mr. Pocket! Be right smart an' agreeable, an' come down!"

"All right," he would add later, in a voice resigned to determination. "All right, Mr. Pocket. It's plain to me I got to come right up an' snatch you out bald-headed. An' I'll do it! I'll do it!" he would threaten still later.

Each pan he carried down to the water to wash, and as he went higher up the hill the pans grew richer, until he began to save the gold in an empty bakingpowder can which he carried carelessly in his lap pocket. So engrossed was he in his toil that he did not notice the long twilight of oncoming night. It was not until he tried vainly to see the gold colors in the bottom of the pan that he realized the passage of time. He straightened up abruptly. An expression of whimsical wonderment and awe overspread his face as he drawled:

"Gosh darn my bottons, if I didn't plumb forget dinner!"

He stumbled across the stream in the darkness and lighted his long-delayed fire. Flapjacks and bacon and warmed-over beans constituted his supper. Then he smoked a pipe by the smoldering coals, listening to the night noises and watching the moonlight stream through the canyon. After that he unrolled his bed, took off his heavy shoes, and pulled the blankets up to his chin. His face showed white in the moonlight, like the face of a corpse. But it was a corpse that knew its resurrection, for the man rose suddenly on one elbow and gazed across at his hillside.

"Good night, Mr. Pocket," he called sleepily. "Good night."

He slept through the early gray of morning until the direct rays of the sun smote his closed eyelids, when he awoke with a start and looked about him until he had established the continuity of his existence and identified his present self with the days previously lived.

To dress, he had merely to buckle on his shoes. He glanced at his fireplace and at his hillside, wavered, but fought down the temptation and started the fire.

"Keep yer shirt on, Bill; keep yer shirt on," he admonished himself. "What's the good of rushin'? No use in gettin' all het up an' sweaty. Mr. Pocket'll wait for you. He ain't a-runnin' away before you can get yer breakfast. Now what you want, Bill, is something fresh in yer bill o' fare. So it's up to you to go an' get it."

He cut a short pole at the water's edge and drew from one of his pockets a bit of line and a draggled fly that had once been a royal coachman.

"Mebbe they'll bite in the early morning," he muttered as he made his first cast into the pool. And a moment later he was gleefully crying: "What'd I tell you, eh? What'd I tell you?"

He had no reel or any inclination to waste time, and by main strength, and swiftly, he drew out of the water a flashing ten-inch trout. Three more, caught in rapid succession, furnished his breakfast. When he came to the steppingstones on his way to his hillside, he was struck by a sudden thought, and paused.

Fore-
shadow

"I'd just better take a hike downstream a ways," he said. "There's no tellin' what cuss may be snoopin' around."

But he crossed over on the stones, and with a "I really oughter take that hike" the need of the precaution passed out his mind and he fell to work.

At nightfall he straightened up. The small of his back was stiff from stooping toil, and as he put his hand behind him to soothe the protesting muscles he said:

"Now what d'ye think of that, by damn? I clean forgot my dinner again! If I don't watch out I'll sure be degeneratin' into a two-meal-a-day crank."

"Pockets is the damnedest things I ever see for makin' a man absent-minded," he communed that night as he crawled into his blankets. Nor did he forget to call up the hillside, "Good night, Mr. Pocket! Good night!"

Rising with the sun, and snatching a hasty breakfast, he was early at work. A fever seemed to be growing in him, nor did the increasing richness of the test pans allay this fever. There was a flush in his cheek other than that made by the heat of the sun, and he was oblivious to fatigue and the passage of time. When he filled a pan with dirt he ran down the hill to wash it; nor could he forbear running up the hill again, panting and stumbling profanely, to refill the pan.

He was now a hundred yards from the water, and the inverted V was assuming definite proportions. The width of the pay dirt steadily decreased, and the man extended in his mind's eye the sides of the V to their meeting place far up the hill. This was his goal, the apex of the V, and he panned many times to locate it.

"Just about two yards above that manzanita bush an' a yard to the right," he finally concluded.

Then the temptation seized him. "As plain as the nose on your face," he said as he abandoned his laborious crosscutting and climbed to the indicated apex. He filled a pan and carried it down the hill to wash. It contained no trace of gold. He dug deep, and he dug shallow, filling and washing a dozen pans, and was unrewarded even by the tiniest golden specks. He was enraged at having yielded to the temptation, and cursed himself blasphemously and pridelessly. Then he went down the hill and took up the crosscutting.

"Slow an' certain, Bill; slow an' certain," he crooned. "Short cuts to fortune ain't in your line, an' it's about time you know it. Get wise, Bill; get wise. Slow an' certain's the only hand you can play; so go to it, an' keep to it, too."

As the crosscuts decreased, showing that the sides of the V were converging, the depth of the V increased. The gold trace was dipping into the hill. It was only at thirty inches beneath the surface that he could get colors in his pan. The dirt he found at twenty-five inches from the surface, and at thirty-five inches, yielded barren pans. At the base of the V, by the water's edge, he had found the gold colors at the grass roots. The higher he went up the hill, the deeper the gold dipped. To dig a hole three feet deep in order to get one test pan was a task of no mean magnitude; while between the man and the apex intervened an untold number of such holes to be dug. "An' there's no tellin' how much deeper it'll pitch," he sighed in a moment's pause, while his fingers soothed his aching back.

Feverish with desire, with aching back and stiffening muscles, with pick and shovel gouging and mauling the soft brown earth, the man toiled up the hill. Before him was the smooth slope, spangled with flowers and made sweet with their breath. Behind him was devastation. It looked like some terrible eruption breaking out on the smooth skin of the hill. His slow progress was like that of a slug, be-fouling beauty with a monstrous trail.

[margin note: Values of Nature]

Though the dipping gold trace increased the man's work, he found consolation in the increasing richness of the pans. Twenty cents, thirty cents, fifty cents, sixty cents, were the values of the gold found in the pans, and at nightfall he washed his banner pan, which gave him a dollar's worth of gold dust from a shovelful of dirt.

"I'll just bet it's my luck to have some inquisitive cuss come buttin' in here on my pasture," he mumbled sleepily that night as he pulled the blankets up to his chin.

[margin note: Fore-Shadow]

Suddenly he sat upright. "Bill!" he called sharply. "Now listen to me, Bill; d'ye hear! It's up to you, tomorrow mornin', to mosey round an' see what you can see. Understand? Tomorrow morning, an' don't you forget it!"

He yawned and glanced across at his sidehill. "Good night, Mr. Pocket," he called.

In the morning he stole a march on the sun, for he had finished breakfast when its first rays caught him, and he was climbing the wall of the canyon where it crumbled away and gave footing. From the outlook at the top he found himself in the midst of loneliness. As far as he could see, chain after chain of mountains heaved themselves into his vision. To the east his eyes, leaping the miles between range and range and between many ranges, brought up at last against the white-peaked Sierras— the main crest, where the backbone of the Western world reared itself against the sky. To the north and south he could see more distinctly the cross systems that broke through the main trend of the sea of mountains. To the west the ranges fell away, one behind the other, diminishing and fading into the gentle foothills that, in turn, descended into the great valley which he could not see.

And in all that mighty sweep of earth he saw no sign of man nor of the handiwork of man—save only the torn bosom of the hillside at his feet. The man looked long and carefully. Once, far down his own canyon, he thought he saw in the air a faint hint of smoke. He looked again and decided that it was the purple haze of the hills made dark by a convolution of the canyon wall at its back.

"Hey, you, Mr. Pocket!" he called down into the canyon. "Stand out from under! I'm a-comin', Mr. Pocket! I'm a-comin'!"

The heavy brogans on the man's feet made him appear clumsy-footed, but he swung down from the giddy height as lightly and airily as a mountain goat. A rock, turning under his foot on the edge of the precipice, did not disconcert him. He seemed to know the precise time required for the turn to culminate in disaster, and in the meantime he utilized the false footing itself for the momentary earth contact necessary to carry him on into safety. Where the earth sloped so steeply that it was impossible to stand for a second upright, the man did not hesitate. His foot pressed the impossible surface for but a fraction of the fatal second and gave him the bound that carried him onward. Again, where even the fraction of a second's footing was out of the question, he would swing his body past by a moment's handgrip on a jutting knob of rock, a crevice, or a precariously rooted shrub. At last, with a wild leap and yell, he exchanged the face of the wall for an earth slide and finished the descent in the midst of several tons of sliding earth and gravel.

His first pan of the morning washed out over two dollars in coarse gold. It was from the center of the V. To either side the diminution in the values of the pans was swift. His lines of crosscutting holes were growing very short. The converging sides of the inverted V were only a few yards apart. Their meeting point was only a few yards above him. But the pay streak was dipping deeper and deeper into the earth. By early afternoon he was sinking the test holes five feet before the pans could show the gold trace.

For that matter the gold trace had become something more than a trace; it was a placer mine in itself, and the man resolved to come back after he had found the pocket and work over the ground. But the increasing richness of the pans began to worry him. By late afternoon the worth of the pans had grown to three and four dollars. The man scratched his head perplexedly and looked a few feet up the hill at the manzanita bush that marked approximately the apex of the V. He nodded his head and said oracularly:

"It's one o' two things, Bill; one o' two things. Either Mr. Pocket's spilled himself all out an' down the hill, or else Mr. Pocket's that damned rich you maybe won't be able to carry him all away with you. And that'd be hell, wouldn't it, now?" He chuckled at contemplation of so pleasant a dilemma.

Nightfall found him by the edge of the stream, his eyes wrestling with the gathering darkness over the washing of a five-dollar pan.

"Wisht I had an electric light to go on working," he said.

He found sleep difficult that night. Many times he composed himself and closed his eyes for slumber to overtake him; but his blood pounded with too strong desire, and as many times his eyes opened and he murmured wearily, "Wisht it was sunup."

Sleep came to him in the end, but his eyes were open with the first paling of the stars, and the gray of dawn caught him with breakfast finished and climbing the hillside in the direction of the secret abiding place of Mr. Pocket.

The first crosscut the man made, there was space for only three holes, so narrow had become the pay streak and so close was he to the fountainhead of the golden stream he had been following for four days.

"Be ca'm, Bill; be ca'm," he admonished himself as he broke ground for the final hole where the sides of the V had at last come together in a point.

"I've got the almighty cinch on you, Mr. Pocket, an' you can't lose me," he said many times as he sank the hole deeper and deeper.

Four feet, five feet, six feet, he dug his way down into the earth. The digging grew harder. His pick grated on broken rock. He examined the rock. "Rotten quartz," was his conclusion as, with the shovel, he cleared the bottom of the hole of loose dirt. He attacked the crumbling quartz with the pick, bursting the disintegrating rock asunder with every stroke.

He thrust his shovel into the loose mass. His eye caught a gleam of yellow. He dropped the shovel and squatted suddenly on his heels. As a farmer rubs the clinging earth from fresh-dug potatoes, so the man, a piece of rotten quartz held in both hands, rubbed the dirt away.

"Sufferin' Sardanopolis!" he cried. "Lumps an' chunks of it! Lumps an' chunks of it!"

It was only half rock he held in his hand. The other half was virgin gold. He dropped it into his pan and examined another piece. Little yellow was to be seen, but with his strong fingers he crumbled the rotten quartz away till both hands were filled with glowing yellow. He rubbed the dirt away from fragment after fragment, tossing them into the gold pan. It was a treasure hole. So much had the quartz rotted away that there was less of it than there was of gold. Now and again he found a piece to which no rock clung—a piece that was all gold. A chunk, where the pick had laid open the heart of the gold, glittered like a handful of yellow jewels, and he cocked his head at it and slowly turned it around and over to observe the rich play of the light upon it.

"Talk about yer Too Much Gold diggin's!" the man snorted contemptuously. "Why, this diggin'd make it look like thirty cents. This diggin' is all gold. An' right here an' now I name this yere canyon 'All Gold Canyon,' b' gosh!"

Still squatting on his heels, he continued examining the fragments and tossing them into the pan. Suddenly there came to him a premonition of danger. It seemed a shadow had fallen upon him. But there was no shadow. His heart had given a great jump up into his throat and was choking him. Then his blood slowly chilled and he felt the sweat of his shirt cold against his flesh.

He did not spring up nor look around. He did not move. He was considering the nature of the premonition he had received, trying to locate the source of the mysterious force that had warned him, striving to sense the imperative presence of the unseen thing that threatened him. There is an aura of things hostile, made manifest by messengers too refined for the senses to know; and this aura he felt, but knew not how he felt it. His was the feeling as when a cloud passes over the sun. It seemed that between him and life had passed something dark and smothering and menacing; a gloom, as it were, that swallowed up life and made for death—his death.

Every force of his being impelled him to spring up and confront the unseen danger, but his soul dominated the panic, and he remained squatting on his heels, in his hands a chunk of gold. He did not dare to look around, but he knew by now that there was something behind him and above him. He made believe to be interested in the gold in his hand. He examined it critically, turned it over and over, and rubbed the dirt from it. And all the time he knew that something behind him was looking at the gold over his shoulder.

Still feigning interest in the chunk of gold in his hand, he listened intently and he heard the breathing of the thing behind him. His eyes searched the ground in front of him for a weapon, but they saw only the uprooted gold, worthless to him now in his extremity. There was his pick, a handy weapon on occasion; but this was not such an occasion. The man realized his

predicament. He was in a narrow hole that was seven feet deep.
His head did not come to the surface of the ground. He was in a
trap.

He remained squatting on his heels. He was quite cool and
collected; but his mind, considering every factor, showed him
only his helplessness. He continued rubbing the dirt from the
quartz fragments and throwing the gold into the pan. There was
nothing else for him to do. Yet he knew that he would have to
rise up, sooner or later, and face the danger that breathed at his
back. The minutes passed, and with the passage of each minute
he knew that by so much he was nearer the time when he must
stand up or else—and his wet shirt went cold against his flesh
again at the thought—or else he might receive death as he
stooped there over his treasure.

Still he squatted on his heels, rubbing dirt from gold and
debating in just what manner he should rise up. He might rise up
with a rush and claw his way out of the hole to meet whatever
threatened on the even footing aboveground. Or he might rise up
slowly and carelessly, and feign casually to discover the thing
that breathed at his back. His instinct and every fighting fiber of
his body favored the mad, clawing rush to the surface. His
intellect, and the craft thereof, favored the slow and cautious
meeting with the thing that menaced and which he could not see.
And while he debated, a loud, crashing noise burst on his ear. At
the same instant he received a stunning blow on the left side of
the back, and from the point of impact felt a rush of flame
through his flesh. He sprang up in the air, but halfway to his feet
collapsed. His body crumpled in like a leaf withered in sudden
heat, and he came down, his chest across his pan of gold, his
face in the dirt and rock, his legs tangled and twisted because of
the restricted space at the bottom of the hole. His legs twitched
convulsively several times. His body was shaken as with a
mighty ague. There was a slow expansion of the lungs, accompanied by a deep sigh. Then the air was slowly, very slowly,
exhaled, and his body as slowly flattened itself down into inertness.

Above, revolver in hand, a man was peering down over the
edge of the hole. He peered for a long time at the prone and
motionless body beneath him. After a while the stranger sat
down on the edge of the hole so that he could see into it, and
rested the revolver on his knee. Reaching his hand into a pocket,
he drew out a wisp of brown paper. Into this he dropped a few
crumbs of tobacco. The combination became a cigarette, brown
and squat, with the ends turned in. Not once did he take his eyes
from the body at the bottom of the hole. He lighted the cigarette

and drew its smoke into his lungs with a caressing intake of the breath. He smoked slowly. Once the cigarette went out and he relighted it. And all the while he studied the body beneath him.

In the end he tossed the cigarette stub away and rose to his feet. He moved to the edge of the hole. Spanning it, a hand resting on each edge, and with the revolver still in the right hand, he muscled his body down into the hole. While his feet were yet a yard from the bottom he released his hands and dropped down.

At the instant his feet struck bottom he saw the pocket miner's arm leap out, and his own legs knew a swift, jerking grip that overthrew him. In the nature of the jump his revolver hand was above his head. Swiftly as the grip had flashed about his legs, just as swiftly he brought the revolver down. He was still in the air, his fall in process of completion, when he pulled the trigger. The explosion was deafening in the confined space. The smoke filled the hole so that he could see nothing. He struck the bottom on his back, and like a cat's the pocket miner's body was on top of him. Even as the miner's body passed on top, the stranger crooked in his right arm to fire; and even in that instant the miner, with a quick thrust of elbow, struck his wrist. The muzzle was thrown up and the bullet thudded into the dirt of the side of the hole.

The next instant the stranger felt the miner's hand grip his wrist. The struggle was now for the revolver. Each man strove to turn it against the other's body. The smoke in the hole was clearing. The stranger, lying on his back, was beginning to see dimly. But suddenly he was blinded by a handful of dirt deliberately flung into his eyes by his antagonist. In that moment he felt a smashing darkness descend upon his brain, and in the midst of the darkness even the darkness ceased.

But the pocket miner fired again and again, until the revolver was empty. Then he tossed it from him and, breathing heavily, sat down on the dead man's legs.

The miner was sobbing and struggling for breath. "Measly skunk!" he panted; "a-campin' on my trail an' lettin' me do the work, an' then shootin' me in the back!"

He was half crying from anger and exhaustion. He peered at the face of the dead man. It was sprinkled with loose dirt and gravel, and it was difficult to distinguish the features.

"Never laid eyes on him before," the miner concluded his scrutiny. "Just a common an' ordinary thief, damn him! An' he shot me in the back! He shot me in the back!"

He opened his shirt and felt himself, front and back, on his left side.

"Went clean through, and no harm done!" he cried jubilantly. "I'll bet he aimed all right, all right; but he drew the gun over when he pulled the trigger—the cuss! But I fixed 'm! Oh, I fixed 'm!"

His fingers were investigating the bullet hole in his side, and a shade of regret passed over his face. "It's goin' to be stiffer'n hell," he said. "An' it's up to me to get mended an' get out o' here."

He crawled out of the hole and went down the hill to his camp. Half an hour later he returned, leading his pack horse. His open shirt disclosed the rude bandages with which he had dressed his wound. He was slow and awkward with his left-hand movements, but that did not prevent his using the arm.

The bight of the pack rope under the dead man's shoulders enabled him to heave the body out of the hole. Then he set to work gathering up his gold. He worked steadily for several hours, pausing often to rest his stiffening shoulder and to exclaim:

"He shot me in the back, the measly skunk! He shot me in the back!"

When his treasure was quite cleaned up and wrapped securely into a number of blanket-covered parcels, he made an estimate of its value.

"Four hundred pounds, or I'm a Hottentot," he concluded. "Say two hundred in quartz an' dirt—that leaves two hundred pounds of gold. Bill! Wake up! Two hundred pounds of gold! Forty thousand dollars! An' it's yourn—all yourn!"

He scratched his head delightedly and his fingers blundered into an unfamiliar groove. They quested along it for several inches. It was a crease through his scalp where the second bullet had plowed.

He walked angrily over to the dead man.

"You would, would you?" he bullied. "You would, eh? Well, I fixed you good an' plenty, an' I'll give you decent burial, too. That's more'n you'd have done for me."

He dragged the body to the edge of the hole and toppled it in. It struck the bottom with a dull crash, on its side, the face twisted up to the light. The miner peered down at it.

"An' you shot me in the back!" he said accusingly.

With pick and shovel he filled the hole. Then he loaded the gold on his horse. It was too great a load for the animal, and when he had gained his camp he transferred part of it to his saddle horse. Even so, he was compelled to abandon a portion of his outfit—pick and shovel and gold pan, extra food and cooking utensils, and divers odds and ends.

The sun was at the zenith when the man forced the horses at the screen of vines and creepers. To climb the huge boulders the animals were compelled to uprear and struggle blindly through the tangled mass of vegetation. Once the saddle horse fell heavily and the man removed the pack to get the animal on its feet. After it started on its way again the man thrust his head out from among the leaves and peered up at the hillside.

"The measly skunk!" he said, and disappeared.

There was a ripping and tearing of vines and boughs. The trees surged back and forth, marking the passage of the animals through the midst of them. There was a clashing of steel-shod hoofs on stone, and now and again an oath or a sharp cry of command. Then the voice of the man was raised in song:

> Tu'n around an' tu'n yo' face
> Untoe them sweet hills of grace.
>   (D' pow'rs of sin yo' am scornin'!)
> Look about an' look aroun',
> Fling yo' sin pack on d' groun'.
>   (Yo' will meet wid d' Lord in d' mornin'!)

The song grew faint and fainter, and through the silence crept back the spirit of the place. The stream once more drowsed and whispered; the hum of the mountain's bees rose sleepily. Down through the perfume-weighted air fluttered the snowy fluffs of the cottonwoods. The butterflies drifted in and out among the trees, and over all blazed the quiet sunshine. Only remained the hoofmarks in the meadow and the torn hillside to mark the boisterous trail of the life that had broken the peace of the place and passed on.

Peace of Nature returned to normal like beginning

Francis Hopkinson Smith
(1838–1915)

Born and raised in Baltimore, Smith spent the first 50 years of his life as an engineer, with painting as an avocation. His first books were travel volumes which he illustrated himself. Colonel Carter of Cartersville *(1891) marked his debut as a serious writer of fiction. It was followed by a series of novels and collections of stories, notably* Tom Grogan *(1896),* The Fortunes of Oliver Horn *(1902), perhaps his best novel, and* Kennedy Square *(1911). "The Rajah of Bungpore" is taken from his 1905 collection,* At Close Range.

THE RAJAH OF BUNGPORE

It was the crush hour at Sherry's. A steady stream of men and women in smart toilettes—the smartest the town afforded—had flowed in under the street awning, through the doorway guarded by flunkeys, past the dressing-rooms and coat-racks, and were now banked up in the spacious hall waiting for tables, the men standing about, the women resting on the chairs and divans listening to the music of the Hungarian band or chatting with one another. The two cafés were full—had been since seven o'clock, every table being occupied except two. One of these had been reserved that morning by my dear friend Marny, the distinguished painter of portraits—I being his guest—and the other, so the head-waiter told us, awaited the arrival of Mr. John Stirling, who would entertain a party of six.

When Marny was a poor devil of an illustrator, and worked for the funny column of the weekly papers—we had studios in the same building—we used to dine at Porcelli's, the price of the two meals equalling the value of one American trade dollar, and including one bottle of vin ordinaire. Now that Marny wears a ribbon in his button-hole, has a suite of rooms that look like a museum, man-servants and maid-servants, including an English butler whose principal business is to see that Marny is not disturbed, a line of carriages before his door on his reception days, and refuses two portraits a week at his own prices—we sometimes dine at Sherry's.

As I am still a staid old landscape painter living up three flights of stairs with no one to wait on me but myself and the ten-year-old daughter of the janitor, I must admit that these occasional forays into the whirl of fashionable life afford me not only infinite enjoyment, but add greatly to my knowledge of human nature.

As we followed the waiter into the café, a group of half a dozen men, all in full dress, emerged from a side room and preceded us into the restaurant, led by a handsome young fellow of thirty. The next moment they grouped themselves about the other reserved table, the young fellow seating his guests himself, drawing out each chair with some remark that kept the whole party laughing.

When we had settled into our own chairs, and my host had spread his napkin and looked about him, the young fellow nodded his head at Marny, clasped his two hands together, shook them together heartily, and followed this substitute for a closer welcome by kissing his hand at him.

Marny returned the courtesy by a similar handshake, and bending his head said in a low voice, "The Rajah must be in luck to-night."

"Who?" I asked. My acquaintance with foreign potentates is necessarily limited.

"The Rajah—Jack Stirling. Take a look at him. You'll never see his match; nobody has yet."

I shifted my chair a little, turned my head in the opposite direction, and then slowly covering Stirling with my gaze—the polite way of staring at a stranger—got a full view of the man's face and figure; rather a difficult thing on a crowded night at Sherry's, unless the tables are close together. What I saw was a well-built, athletic-looking young man with a smooth-shaven face, laughing eyes, a Cupid mouth, curly brown hair, and a fresh ruddy complexion; a Lord Byron sort of a young fellow with a modern up-to-date training. He was evidently charming his guests, for every man's head was bent forward seemingly hanging on each word that fell from his lips.

"A rajah, is he? He don't look like an Oriental."

"He isn't. He was born in New Jersey."

"Is he an artist?"

"Yes, five or six different kinds; he draws better than I do; plays on three instruments, and speaks five languages."

"Rich?"

"No—dead broke half the time."

I glanced at the young fellow's faultless appearance and the group of men he was entertaining. My eye took in the array of bottles, the number of wineglasses of various sizes, and the mass of roses that decorated the centre of the table. Such appointments and accompaniments are not generally the property of the poor. Then, again, I remembered we were at Sherry's.

"What does he do for a living, then?" I asked.

"Do for a living? He doesn't do anything for a living. He's a purveyor of cheerfulness. He wakes up every morning with a fresh stock of happiness, more than he can use himself, and he trades it off during the day for anything he can get."

"What kind of things?" I was a little hazy over Marny's meaning.

"Oh, dinners—social, of course—board bills, tailor's bills, invitations to country houses, voyages on yachts—anything that comes along and of which he may be in need at the time. Most interesting man in town. Everybody loves him. Known all over the world. If a fellow gets sick, Stirling waltzes in, fires out the nurse, puts on a linen duster, starts an alcohol lamp for gruel, and never leaves till you are out again. All this time he is pumping laughs into you and bracing you up so that you get well twice as quick. Did it for me once for five weeks on a stretch, when I was laid up in my studio with inflammatory rheumatism, with my grub bills hung up in the restaurant downstairs, and my rent three months overdue. Fed me on the fat of the land, too. Soup from Delmonico's, birds from some swell house up the Avenue, where he had been dining—sent that same night with the compliments of his hostess with a 'Please forgive me, but dear Mr. Stirling tells me how ill you have been, and at his suggestion, and with every sympathy for your sufferings—please accept.' Oh, I tell you he's a daisy!"

Here a laugh sounded from Stirling's table.

"Who's he got in tow now?" I asked, as my eyes roamed over the merry party.

"That fat fellow in eyeglasses is Crofield the banker, and the hatchet-faced man with white whiskers is John Riggs from Denver, President of the C. A.—worth ten millions. I don't know the others—some bored-to-death fellows, perhaps, starving for a laugh. Jack ought to go slow, for he's dead broke—told me so yesterday.''

"Perhaps Riggs is paying for the dinner." This was an impertinent suggestion, I know; but then sometimes I can be impertinent—especially when some of my pet theories have to be defended.

"Not if Jack invited him. He's the last man in the world to sponge on anybody. Inviting a man to dinner and leaving his pocketbook in his other coat is not Jack's way. If he hasn't got the money in his own clothes, he'll find it somehow, but not in *their* clothes."

"Well, but at times he *must* have ready money," I insisted. "He can't be living on credit all the time." I have had to work for all my pennies, am of a practical turn of mind, and often live in constant dread of the first of every month—that fatal pay-day from which there is no escape. The success, therefore, of another fellow along different and more luxurious lines naturally irritates me.

"Yes, now and then he does need money. But that never bothers Jack. When his tailor, or his shoemaker, or his landlord gets him into a corner, he sends the bill to some of his friends to pay for him. They never come back—anybody would do Stirling a favor, and they know that he never calls on them unless he is up against it solid.''

I instinctively ran over in my mind which of my own friends I would approach, in a similar emergency, and the notes I would receive in reply. Stirling must know rather a stupid lot of men or they couldn't be buncoed so easily, I thought.

Soup was now being served, and Marny and the waiter were discussing the merits of certain vintages, my host insisting on a bottle of '84 in place of the '82, then in the waiter's hand.

During the episode I had the opportunity to study Stirling's table. I noticed that hardly a man entered the room who did not stop and lay his hand affectionately on Stirling's shoulder, bending over and joining in the laugh. His guests, too—those about his table—seemed equally loyal and happy. Riggs's hard business face—evidently a man of serious life—was beaming with merriment and twice as wide, under Jack's leadership, and Crofield and the others were leaning forward, their eyes fixed on their host, waiting for the point of his story, then breaking out together in a simultaneous laugh that could be heard all over our part of the room.

When Marny had received the wine he wanted—it's extraordinary how critical a man's palate becomes when his income is thousands a year instead of dollars—I opened up again with my battery of questions. His friend had upset all my formulas and made a laughing-stock of my most precious traditions. "Pay as you go and keep out of debt" seemed to belong to a past age.

"Speaking of your friend, the Rajah, as you call him," I asked, "and his making his friends pay his bills—does he ever pay back?"

"Always, when he gets it."

"Well, where *does* he get it—cards?" It seemed to me now that I saw some comforting light ahead, dense as I am at times.

"Cards! Not much—never played a game in his life. Not that kind of a man."

"How, then?" I wanted the facts. There must be some way in which a man like Stirling could live, keep out of jail, and keep his friends—friends like Marny.

"Same way. Just chucks around cheerfulness to everybody who wants it, and 'most everybody does. As to ready money, there's hardly one of his rich friends in the Street who hasn't a Jack Stirling account on his books. And they are always lucky, for what they buy for Jack Stirling is sure to go up. Got to be a superstition, really. I know one broker who sent him over three thousand dollars last fall—made it for him out of a rise in some coal stock. Wrote him a note and told him he still had two thousand dollars to his credit on his books, which he would hold as a stake to make another turn on next time he saw a sure thing in sight. I was with Jack when he opened the letter. What do you think he did? He pulled out his bureau drawer, found a slip of paper containing a list of his debts, sat down and wrote out a check for each one of his creditors and enclosed them in the most charming little notes with marginal sketches—some in watercolor—which every man of them preserves now as souvenirs. I've got one framed in my studio—regular little Fortuny—and the check is framed in with it. Never cashed it and never will. The Rajah, I tell you, old man, is very punctilious about his debts, no matter how small they are. Gave me fifteen shillings last time I went to Cairo to pay some duffer that lived up a street back of Shepheard's, a red-faced Englishman who had helped Jack out of a hole the year before, and who would have pensioned the Rajah for life if he could have induced him to pass the rest of his years with him. And he only saw him for two days! That's the funny thing about Jack. He never forgets his creditors, and his creditors never forget him. I'll tell you about this old Cairo lobster—that's what he looked like—red and claw-y.

"When I found him he was stretched in a chair trying to cool off; he didn't even have the decency to get on his feet.

" 'Who?' he snapped out. Just as if I had been a book agent.

" 'Mr. John Stirling of New York.'

" 'Owes *me* fifteen shillings?'

" 'That's what he said, and here it is,' and I handed him the silver.

" 'Young man,' he says, glowering at me, 'I don't know what your game is, but I'll tell you right here you can't play it on me. Never heard of *Mister*-John-Stirling-of-New-York in my life. So you can put your money back.' I wasn't going to be whipped by the old shell-fish, and then I didn't like the way he spoke of Jack. I knew he was the right man, for Jack doesn't make mistakes—not about things like that. So I went at him on another tack.

" 'Weren't you up at Philæ two years ago in a dahabieh?'

" 'Yes.'

" 'And didn't you meet four or five young Americans who came up on the steamer, and who got into a scrape over their fare?'

" 'I might—I can't recollect everybody I meet—don't want to—half of 'em—' All this time I was standing, remember.

" 'And didn't you—' I was going on to say, but he jumped from his chair and was fumbling about a bookcase.

" 'Ah, here it is!' he cried out. 'Here's a book of photographs of a whole raft of young fellows I met up the Nile on that trip. Most of 'em owed me something and still do. Pick out the man now you say owes me fifteen shillings and wants to pay it.'

" 'There he is—one of those three.'

"The old fellow adjusted his glasses.

" 'The Rajah! That man! Know him? Best lad I ever met in my life. I'm damned if I take his money, and you can go home and tell him so.' He did, though, and I sat with him until three o'clock in the morning talking about Jack, and I had all I could do getting away from him then. Wanted me to move in next day bag and baggage, and stay a month with him. He wasn't so bad when I came to know him, if he was red and claw-y."

I again devoted my thoughts to the dinner—what I could spare from the remarkable personage Marny had been discussing, and who still sat within a few tables of us. My friend's story had opened up a new view of life, one that I had never expected to see personified in any one man. The old-fashioned rules by which I had been brought up—the rules of "An eye for an eye," and "Earn thy bread by the sweat of thy brow," etc.—seemed to have lost their meaning. The Rajah's method, it seemed to me, if persisted in, might help solve the new problem of the day—"the joy of living"—always a colossal joke with me. I determined to know something more of this lazy apostle in a dress suit who dispensed sweetness and light at some other fellow's expense.

"Why do you call him 'The Rajah,' Marny?" I asked.

"Oh, he got that in India. A lot of people like that old lobster in Cairo don't know him by any other name."

"What did he do in India?"

"Nothing in particular—just kept on being himself—just as he does everywhere."

"Tell me about it."

"Well, I got it from Ashburton, a member of the Alpine Club in London. But everybody knows the story—wonder you haven't heard it. You ought to come out of your hole, old man, and see what's going on in the world. You live up in that den of yours, and the procession goes by and you don't even hear the band. You ought to know Jack—he'd do you a lot of good," and Marny looked at me curiously—as a physician would, who, when he prescribes for you, tells you only one-half of your ailment.

I did not interrupt my friend—I wasn't getting thousands for a child's head, and twice that price for the mother in green silk and diamonds. And I couldn't afford to hang out my window and watch any kind of procession, figurative or otherwise. Nor could I afford to exchange dinners with John Stirling.

"Do you want me to tell you about that time the Rajah had in India? Well, move your glass this way," and my host picked up the '84. "Ashburton," continued Marny, and he filled my glass to the brim, "is one of those globe-trotters who does mountain-tops for exercise. He knows the Andes as well as he does the glaciers in Switzerland; has been up the Matterhorn and Mont Blanc, and every other snow-capped peak within reach, and so he thought he'd try the Himalayas. You know how these Englishmen are—the rich ones. At twenty-five a good many of them have exhausted life. Some shoot tigers, some fit out cara-vans and cross deserts, some get lost in African jungles, and some come here and go out West for big game; anything that will keep them from being bored to death before they are thirty-five years of age. Ashburton was that kind.

"He had only been home ten days—he had spent two years in

Yucatan looking up Toltec ruins—when this Himalaya trip got into his head. Question was, whom could he get to go with him, for these fellows hate to be alone. Some of the men he wanted hadn't returned from their own wild-goose chases; others couldn't get away—one was running for Parliament, I think—and so Ashburton, cursing his luck, had about made up his mind to try it alone, when he ran across Jack one day in the club.

" 'Hello, Stirling! Thought you'd sailed for America.'

" 'No,' said Jack, 'I go next week. What are you doing here? Thought you had gone to India.'

" 'Can't get anybody to go with me,' answered Ashburton.

" 'Where do you go first?'

" 'To Calcutta by steamer, and then strike in and up to the foot-hills.'

" 'For how long?'

" 'About a year. Come with me like a decent man.'

" 'Can't. Only got money enough to get home, and I don't like climbing.'

" 'Money hasn't got anything to do with it—you go as my guest. As to climbing, you won't have to climb an inch. I'll leave you at the foot-hills in a bungalow, with somebody to take care of you, and you can stay there until I come back.'

" 'How long will you be climbing?'

" 'About two months.'

" 'When do you start?'

" 'To-morrow, at daylight.'

" 'All right, I'll be on board.'

"Going out, Jack got up charades and all sorts of performances; rescued a man overboard, striking the water about as soon as the man did, and holding on to him until the lifeboat reached them; studied navigation and took observations every day until he learned how; started a school for the children—there were a dozen on board—and told them fairy tales by the hour; and by the time the steamer reached Calcutta every man, woman, and child had fallen in love with him. One old Maharajah, who was on board, took such a fancy to him that he insisted on Jack's spending a year with him, and there came near being a precious row when he refused, which of course he had to do, being Ashburton's guest.

"When the two got to where Jack was to camp out and wait for Ashburton's return from his climb—it was a little spot called Bungpore—the Englishman fitted up a place just as he said he would; left two men to look after him—one to cook and the other to wait on him—fell on Jack's neck, for he hated the worst kind to leave him, and disappeared into the brush with his retainers—or whatever he did disappear into and with—I never climbed the Himalayas, and so I'm a little hazy over these details. And that's the last Ashburton saw of Jack until he returned two months later.''

Marny emptied his glass, flicked the ashes from his cigarette, beckoned to the waiter, and gave him an order for a second bottle of '84. During the break in the story I made another critical examination of the hero, as he sat surrounded by his guests, his face beaming, the light falling on his immaculate shirt-front. I noted the size of his arm and the depth of his chest, and his lithe, muscular thighs. I noticed, too, how quickly he gained his feet when welcoming a friend, who had just stopped at his table. I understood now how the drowning sailor came to be saved.

The wine matter settled, Marny took some fresh cigarettes from his silver case, passed one to me, and held a match to both in turn. Between the puffs I again brought the talk back to the man who now interested me intensely. I was afraid we would be interrupted and I have to wait before finding out why his friend was called the "Rajah."

"I should think he would have gone with him instead of staying behind and living off his bounty,'' I ventured.

"Yes—I know you would, old man, but Jack thought differently, not being built along your lines. You've got to know him—I tell you, he'll do you a lot of good. Stirling saw that, if he went, it would only double Ashburton's expense account, and so he squatted down to wait with just money enough to get along those two months, and not another cent. Told Ashburton he wanted to learn Hindustanee, and he couldn't do it if he was sliding down glaciers and getting his feet wet—it would keep him from studying.''

"And was Stirling waiting for him when Ashburton came back?''

"Waiting for him! Well, I guess! First thing Ashburton ran up against was one of the blackamoors he had hired to take care of Jack. When he had left the fellow he was clothed in a full suit of yellow dust with a rag around his loins. Now he was gotten up in a red turban and pajamas trimmed with gewgaws. The blacka-moor prostrated himself and began kowtowing backward toward a marquee erected on a little knoll under some trees and sur-rounded by elephants in gorgeous trappings. 'The Rajah of Bungpore'—that was Jack—'had sent him,' he said, 'to conduct his Royal Highness into the presence of his illustrious master!'

"When Ashburton reached the door of the marquee and peered in, he saw Jack lying back on an Oriental couch at the other end smoking the pipe of the country—whatever that was—and surrounded by a collection of Hottentots of various sizes and colors, who fell on their foreheads every time Jack crooked his finger. At his feet knelt two Hindoo merchants displaying their wares— pearls, ivories, precious stones, arms, porcelains—stuffs of a quality and price, Ashburton told me, that took his breath away. Jack kept on—he made out he didn't see Ashburton—his slaves bearing the purchases away and depositing them on a low inlaid table—teakwood, I guess—in one corner of the marquee, while a confidential Lord of the Treasury took the coin of the realm from a bag or gourd—or whatever he did take it from—and paid the shot.

"When the audience was over, Jack waved everybody outside with a commanding gesture, and still lolling on his rugs—or maybe his tiger skins—told his Grand Vizier to conduct the strange man to his august presence. Then Jack rose from his throne, dismissed the Grand Vizier, and fell into Ashburton's arms roaring with laughter."

"And Ashburton had to foot the bills, I suppose," I blurted out. It is astonishing how suspicious and mean a man gets sometimes who mixes as little as I do with what Marny calls "the swim."

"Ashburton foot the bills! Not much! Listen, you six by nine! Stirling hadn't been alone more than a week when along comes the Maharajah he had met on the steamer. He lived up in that part of the country, and one of his private detectives had told him that somebody was camping out on his lot. Down he came in a white heat, with a bag of bowstrings and a squad of the 'Finest' in pink trousers and spears. I get these details all wrong, old man—they might have been in frock-coats for all I know or care—but what I'm after is the Oriental atmosphere—a sort of property background with my principal figure high up on the canvas—and one costume is as good as another.

"When the old Maharajah found out it was Jack instead of some squatter, he fell all over himself with joy. Wanted to take him up to his marble palace, open up everything, unlock a harem, trot out a half-dozen chorus girls in bangles and mosquito-net bloomers, and do a lot of comfortable things for him. But Jack said No. He was put here to stay, and here he was going to stay if he had to call out every man in his army. The old fellow saw the joke and said all right, here he *should* stay; and before night he had moved down a tent, and a bodyguard, and an elephant or two for local color, so as to make it real Oriental for Jack, and the next day he sent him down a bag of gold, and servants, and a cook. Every pedler who appeared after that he passed along to Jack, and before Ashburton turned up Stirling had a collection of curios worth a fortune. One-half of them he gave to Ashburton and the other half he brought home to his friends. That inlaid elephant's tusk hanging up in my studio is one of them—you remember it.''

As Marny finished, one of the waiters who had been serving Stirling and his guests approached our table under the direction of the Rajah's finger, and, bending over Marny, whispered something in his ear. He had the cashier's slip in his hand and Stirling's visiting card.

Marny laid the bill beside his plate, glanced at the card with a laugh, his face lighting up, and then passed it to me. It read as follows: "Not a red and no credit. Sign it for Jack.''

Marny raised his eyes, nodded his head at Stirling, kissed his finger-tips at him, fished up his gold chain, slid out a pencil dangling at its end, wrote his name across the slip, and said in a whisper to the waiter: "Take this to the manager and have him charge it to my account.''

When we had finished our dinner and were passing out abreast of Stirling's table, the Rajah rose to his feet, his guests all standing about him, their glasses in their hands—Riggs's whiskers stood straight, he was so happy—and, waving his own glass toward my host, said: "Gentlemen, I give you Marny, the Master, the Velasquez of modern times!''

•   •   •   •   •   •   •

Some weeks later I called at Marny's studio. He was out. On the easel stood a full-length portrait of Riggs, the millionaire, his thin, hatchet-shaped face and white whiskers in high relief against a dark background. Scattered about the room were smaller heads bearing a strong resemblance to the great president. Jack had evidently corralled the entire family—and all out of that dinner at Sherry's.

I shut the door of Marny's studio softly behind me, tiptoed downstairs, dropped into a restaurant under the sidewalk, and dined alone.

Marny is right. The only way to hear the band is to keep up with the procession.

My philosophy is a failure.

Zona Gale
(1874–1938)

Born and raised in Wisconsin, Miss Gale set herself the task of recording as faithfully as possible the realities of midwestern life. Friendship Village *(1909), from which "Nobody Sick, Nobody Poor" is taken, the* Yellow Gentians and Blue *(1927) are her chief collections of stories. Her novels include* Miss Lulu Bett *(1920, her dramatization of which won a Pulitzer Prize),* Faint Perfume *(1923),* Preface to a Life *(1926), and* Papa La Fleur *(1933). She also published a book of poems,* The Secret Way *(1921), and two volumes of autobiography,* When I Was a Little Girl *(1913) and* Portage, Wisconsin *(1928).*

NOBODY SICK, NOBODY POOR

Two days before Thanksgiving the air was already filled with white turkey feathers, and I stood at a window and watched until the loneliness of my still house seemed like something pointing a mocking finger at me. When I could bear it no longer I went out in the snow, and through the soft drifts I fought my way up the Plank Road toward the village.

I had almost passed the little bundled figure before I recognized Calliope. She was walking in the middle of the road, as in Friendship we all walk in winter; and neither of us had umbrellas. I think that I distrust people who put up umbrellas on a country road in a fall of friendly flakes.

Instead of inquiring perfunctorily how I did, she greeted me with a fragment of what she had been thinking—which is always

427

as if one were to open a door of his mind to you instead of signing you greeting from a closed window.

"I just been tellin' myself," she looked up to say without preface, "that if I could see one more good old-fashion' Thanksgivin', life'd sort o' smooth out. An' land knows, it needs some smoothin' out for me."

With this I remember that it was as if my own loneliness spoke for me. At my reply Calliope looked at me quickly—as if I, too, had opened a door.

"Sometimes Thanksgivin' *is* some like seein' the sun shine when you're feeling rill rainy yourself," she said thoughtfully.

She held out her blue-mittened hand and let the flakes fall on it in stars and coronets.

"I wonder," she asked evenly, "if you'd help me get up a Thanksgivin' dinner for a few poor sick folks here in Friendship?"

In order to keep my self-respect, I recall that I was as ungracious as possible. I think I said that the day meant so little to me that I was willing to do anything to avoid spending it alone. A statement which seems to me now not to bristle with logic.

"That's nice of you," Calliope replied genially. Then she hesitated, looking down Daphne Street, which the Plank Road had become, toward certain white houses. There were the homes of Mis' Mayor Uppers, Mis' Holcomb-that-was-Mame-Bliss, and the Liberty sisters,—all substantial dignified houses, typical of the simple prosperity of the countryside.

"The only trouble," she added simply, "is that in Friendship I don't know a soul rill sick, nor a soul what you might call poor."

At this I laughed, unwillingly enough. Dear Calliope! Here indeed was a drawback to her project.

"Honestly," she said reflectively, "Friendship can't seem to do anything like any other town. When the new minister come here, he give out he was goin' to do settlement work. An' his second week in the place he come to me with a reg'lar hang-dog look. 'What kind of a town is this?' he says to me, disgusted. 'They ain't nobody sick in it an' they ain't nobody poor!' I guess he could 'a' got along without the poor—most of us can. But we mostly like to hev a few sick to carry the flowers off our house plants to, an' now an' then a tumbler o' jell. An' yet I've known weeks at a time when they wasn't a soul rill flat down sick in Friendship. It's so now. An' that's hard, when you're young an' enthusiastic, like the minister."

"But where are you going to find your guests then, Calliope?" I asked curiously.

"Well," she said brightly, "I was just plannin' as you come up with me. An' I says to myself: 'God give me to live in a little bit of a place where we've all got enough to get along on, an' Thanksgivin' finds us all in health. It looks like He'd afflicted us by lettin' us hev nobody to do for.' An' then it come to me that if we was to get up the dinner,—with all the misery an' hunger they is in the world,—God in His goodness would let some of it come our way to be fed. 'In the wilderness a cedar,' you know—as Liddy Ember an' I was always tellin' each other when we kep' shop together. An' so to-day I said to myself I'd go to work an' get up the dinner an' trust there'd be eaters for it."

"Why, Calliope," I said, "Calliope!"

"I ain't got much to do with, myself," she added apologetically; "the most I've got in my sullar, I guess, is a gallon jar o' watermelon pickles. I could give that. You don't think it sounds irreverent—connectin' God with a big dinner, so?" she asked anxiously.

And, at my reply:—

"Well, then," she said briskly, "let's step in an' see a few folks that might be able to tell us of somebody to do for. Let's ask Mis' Mayor Uppers an' Mis' Holcomb-that-was-Mame-Bliss, an' the Liberty girls."

Because I was lonely and idle, and because I dreaded inexpressibly going back to my still house, I went with her. Her ways were a kind of entertainment, and I remember that I believed my leisure to be infinite.

We turned first toward the big shuttered house of Mis' Mayor Uppers, to whom, although her husband had been a year ago removed from office, discredited, and had not since been seen in Friendship, we yet gave her old proud title, as if she had been Former Lady Mayoress. For the present mayor, Authority Hubblethwaite, was, as Calliope said, "unconnect.'"

I watched Mis' Uppers in some curiosity while Calliope explained that she was planning a dinner for the poor and sick, —"the lame and the sick that's comfortable enough off to eat,"—and could she suggest some poor and sick to ask? Mis' Uppers was like a vinegar cruet of mine, slim and tall, with a little grotesquely puckered face for a stopper, as if the whole known world were sour.

"I'm sure," she said humbly, "it's a nice i-dee. But I declare, I'm put to it to suggest. We ain't got nobody sick nor nobody poor in Friendship, you know."

"Don't you know of anybody kind o' hard up? Or somebody

that, if they ain't down sick, feels sort o' spindlin'?'' Calliope asked anxiously.

Mis' Uppers thought, rocking a little and running a pin in and out of a fold of her skirt.

"No," she said at length, "I don't know a soul. I think the church'd give a good deal if a real poor family'd come here to do for. Since the Cadozas went, we ain't known which way to look for poor. Mis' Ricker gettin' her fortune so puts her beyond the wolf. An' Peleg Bemus, you can't *get* him to take anything. No, I don't know of anybody real decently poor."

"An' nobody sick?" Calliope pressed her wistfully.

"Well, there's Mis' Crawford," admitted Mis' Uppers; "she had a spell o' lumbago two weeks ago, but I see her pass the house to-day. Mis' Brady was laid up with toothache, too, but the *Daily* last night said she'd had it out. An' Mis' Doctor Helman did have one o' her stomach attacks this week, an' Elzabella got out her dyin' dishes an' her dyin' linen from the still-room—you know how Mis' Doctor always brings out her nice things when she's sick, so't if she should die an' the neighbours come in, it'd all be shipshape. But she got better this time an' helped put 'em back. I declare it's hard to get up anything in the charity line here."

Calliope sat smiling a little, and I knew that it was because of her secret certainty that "some o' the hunger" would come her way, to be fed.

"I can't help thinkin'," she said quietly, "that we'll find somebody. An' I tell you what: if we do, can I count on you to help some?"

Mis' Uppers flushed with quick pleasure.

"Me, Calliope?" she said. And I remembered that they had told me how the Friendship Married Ladies' Cemetery Improvement Sodality had been unable to tempt Mis' Uppers to a single meeting since the mayor ran away. "Oh, but I couldn't though," she said wistfully.

"No need to go to the table if you don't want," Calliope told her. "Just bake up somethin' for us an' bring it over. Make a couple o' your cherry pies—did you get hold of any cherries to put up this year? Well, a couple o' your cherry pies an' a batch o' your nice drop sponge cakes," she directed. "Could you?"

Mis' Mayor Uppers looked up with a kind of light in her eyes.

"Why, yes," she said, "I could, I guess. I'll bake 'em Thanksgivin' mornin'. I—I was wonderin' how I'd put in the day."

When we stepped out in the snow again, Calliope's face was

shining. Sometimes now, when my faith is weak in any good thing, I remember her look that November morning. But all that I thought then was how I was being entertained that lonely day.

The dear Liberty sisters were next, Lucy and Viny and Libbie Liberty. We went to the side door,—there were houses in Friendship whose front doors we tacitly understood that we were never expected to use,—and we found the sisters down cellar, with shawls over their head, feeding their hens through the cellar window, opening on the glassed-in coop under the porch.

In Friendship it is a point of etiquette for a morning caller never to interrupt the employment of a hostess. So we obeyed the summons of the Liberty sister to "come right down"; and we sat on a firkin and an inverted tub while Calliope told her plan and the hens fought for delectable morsels.

"My grief!" said Libbie Liberty tartly, "where you goin' to *get* your sick an' poor?"

Mis' Viny, balancing on the window ledge to reach for eggs, looked back at us.

"Friendship's so comfortable that way," she said, "I don't see how you can get up much of anything."

And little Miss Lucy, kneeling on the floor of the cellar to measure more feed, said without looking up:—

"You know, since mother died we ain't never done anything for holidays. No—we can't seem to want to think about Thanksgiving or Christmas or like that."

They all turned their grave lined faces toward us.

"We want to let the holidays just slip by without noticin'," Miss Viny told us. "Seems like it hurts less that way."

Libbie Liberty smiled wanly.

"Don't you know," she said, "when you hold your hand still in hot water, you don't feel how hot the water really is? But when you move around in it some, it begins to burn you. Well, when we let Thanksgiving an' Christmas alone, it ain't so bad. But when we start to move around in 'em—"

Her voice faltered and stopped.

"We miss mother terrible," Miss Lucy said simply.

Calliope put her blue mitten to her mouth, but her eyes she might not hide, and they were soft with sympathy.

"I know—I know," she said. "I remember the first Christmas after my mother died—I ached like the toothache all over me, an' I couldn't bear to open my presents. Nor the next year I couldn't either—I couldn't open my presents with any heart. But—" Calliope hesitated, "that second year," she said, "I found somethin' I could do. I saw I could fix up little things for other folks an' take some comfort in it. Like mother would of.''

She was silent for a moment, looking thoughtfully at the three lonely figures in the dark cellar of their house.

"Your mother," she said abruptly, "stuffed the turkey for a year ago the last harvest home."

"Yes," they said.

"Look here," said Calliope; "if I can get some poor folks together,—or even *one* poor folk, or hungry,—will you three come to my house an' stuff the turkey? The way—I can't help thinkin' the way your mother would of, if she'd been here. An' then," Calliope went on briskly, "could you bring some fresh eggs an' make a pan o' custard over to my house? An' mebbe one o' you'd stir up a sunshine cake. You must know how to make your mother's sunshine cake?"

There was another silence in the cellar when Calliope had done, and for a minute I wondered if, after all, she had not failed, and if the bleeding of the three hearts might be so stanched. It was not self-reliant Libbie Liberty who spoke first; it was gentle Miss Lucy.

"I guess," she said, "I could, if we all do it. I know mother would of."

"Yes," Miss Viny nodded, "mother would of."

Libbie Liberty stood for a moment with compressed lips.

"It seems like not payin' respect to mother," she began; and then shook her head. "It ain't that," she said; "it's only missin' her when we begin to step around the kitchen, bakin' up for a holiday."

"I know—I know," Calliope said again. "That's why I said for you to come over in my kitchen. You come over there an' stir up the sunshine cake, too, an' bake it in my oven, so's we can hev it et hot. Will you do that?"

And after a little time they consented. If Calliope found any sick or poor, they would do that.

"We ain't gettin' many i-dees for guests," Calliope said, as we reached the street, "but we're gettin' helpers, anyway. An' some dinner, too."

Then we went to the house of Mis' Holcomb-that-was-Mame-Bliss—called so, of course, to distinguish her from the "Other" Holcombs.

"Don't you be shocked at her," Calliope warned me, as we closed Mis' Holcomb's gate behind us, "she's dreadful diff'r'nt an' bitter since Abigail was married last month. She's got hold o' some kind of a Persian book, in a decorated cover, from the

City; an' now she says your soul is like when you look in a lookin'-glass—that there ain't really nothin' there. An' that the world's some wind an' the rest water, an' they ain't no God only your own breath—oh, poor Mis' Holcomb!" said Calliope. "I guess she ain't rill balanced. But we ought to go to see her. We always consult Mis' Holcomb about everything."

Poor Mis' Holcom-that-was-Mame-Bliss! I can see her now in her comfortable dining room, where she sat cleaning her old silver, her thin, veined hands as fragile as her grandmother's spoons.

"Of course, you don't know," she said, when Calliope had unfolded her plans, "how useless it all seems to me. What's the use—I keep sayin' to myself now'-days; what's the use? You put so much pains on somethin', an' then it goes off an' leaves you. Mebbe it dies, an' everything's all wasted. There ain't anything to tie to. It's like lookin' in a glass all the while. It's seemin', it ain't bein'. We ain't certain o' nothin' but our breath, an' when that goes, what hev you got? What's the use o' plannin' Thanksgivin' for anybody?"

"Well, if you're hungry, it's kind o' nice to get fed up," said Calliope, crisply. "Don't you know a soul that's hungry, Mame Bliss?"

She shook her head.

"No," she said, "I don't. Nor nobody sick in body."

"Nobody sick in body," Calliope repeated absently.

"Soul-sick an' soul-hungry you can't feed up," Mis' Holcomb added.

"I donno," said Calliope thoughtfully, "I donno but you can."

"No," Mis' Holcomb went on; "your soul's like yourself in the glass: they ain't anything there."

"I donno," Calliope said again; "some mornin's when I wake up with the sun shinin' in, I can feel my soul in me just as plain as plain."

Mis' Holcomb sighed.

"Life looks dreadful footless to me," she said.

"Well," said Calliope, "sometimes life *is* some like hearin' firecrackers go off when you don't feel up to shootin' 'em yourself. When I'm like that, I always think if I'd go out an' buy a bunch or two, an' get somebody to give me a match, I could see more sense to things. Look here, Mame Bliss; if I get hold o' any folks to give the dinner for, will you help me some?"

"Yes," Mis' Holcomb assented half-heartedly, "I'll help you. I ain't nobody much in family, now Abigail's done what she has.

They's only Eppleby, an' he won't be home Thanksg'vin this year. So I ain't nothin' else to do.''

"That's the i-dee," said Calliope heartily; "if everything's foolish, it's just as foolish doin' nothin' as doin' somethin'. Will you bring over a kettleful o' boiled potatoes to my house Thanksgivin' noon? An' mash 'em an' whip 'em in my kitchen? I'll hev the milk to put in. You—you don't cook as much as some, do you, Mame?''

Did Calliope ask her that purposely? I am almost sure that she did. Mis' Holcomb's neck stiffened a little.

"I guess I can cook a thing or two beside mash' potatoes," she said, and thought for a minute. "How'd you like a pan o' 'scalloped oysters an' some baked marcaroni with plenty o' cheese?" she demanded.

"Sounds like it'd go down awful easy," admitted Calliope, smiling. "It's just what we need to carry the dinner off full sail," she added earnestly.

"Well, I ain't nothin' else to do an' I'll make 'em," Mis' Holcomb promised. "Only it beats me who you can find to do for. If you don't get anybody, let me know before I order the oysters."

Calliope stood up, her little wrinkled face aglow; and I wondered at her confidence.

"You just go ahead an' order your oysters," she said. "That dinner's goin' to come off Thanksgivin' noon at twelve o'clock. An' you be there to help feed the hungry, Mame."

When we were on the street again, Calliope looked at me with her way of shy eagerness.

"Could you hev the dinner up to your house," she asked me, "if I do every bit o' the work?"

"Why, Calliope," I said, amazed at her persistence, "have it there, of course. But you haven't any guests yet."

She nodded at me through the falling flakes.

"You say you ain't got much to be thankful for," she said, "so I thought mebbe you'd put in the time that way. Don't you worry about folks to eat the dinner. I'll tell Mis' Holcomb an' the others to come to your house—an' I'll get the food an' the folks. Don't you worry! An' I'll bring my watermelon pickles an' a bowl o' cream for Mis' Holcomb's potatoes, an' I'll furnish the turkey—a big one. The rest of us'll get the dinner in your kitchen Thanksgivin' mornin'. My!" she said, "seems though life's smoothin' out fer me a'ready. Goodby—it's 'most noon.''

She hurried up Daphne Street in the snow, and I turned toward my lonely house. But I remember that I was planning how I would make my table pretty, and how I would add a delicacy or two from the City for this strange holiday feast. And I found myself hurrying to look over certain long-disused linen and silver, and to see whether my Cloth-o'-Gold rose might be counted on to bloom by Thursday noon.

II

"We'll set the table for seven folks," said Calliope, at my house on Thanksgiving morning.

"Seven!" I echoed. "But where in the world did you ever find seven, Calliope?"

"I found 'em," she answered. "I knew I could find hungry folks to do for if I tried, an' I found 'em. You'll see. I sha'n't say another word. They'll be here by twelve sharp. Did the turkey come?"

Yes, the turkey had come, and almost as she spoke the dear Liberty sisters arrived to dress and stuff it, and to make ready the pan of custard, and to "stir up" the sunshine cake. I could guess how the pleasant bustle in my kitchen would hurt them by its holiday air, and I carried them off to see my Cloth-o'-Gold rose which had opened in the night, to the very crimson heart of it. And I told them of the seven guests whom, after all, Calliope had actually contrived to marshal to her dinner. And in the midst of our almost gay speculation on this, they went at their share of the task.

The three moved about their office gravely at first, Libbie Liberty keeping her back to us as she worked, Miss Viny scrupulously intent on the delicate clatter of the egg-beater, Miss Lucy with eyes downcast on the sage she rolled. I noted how Calliope made little excuses to pass near each of them, with now a touch of the hand and now a pat on a shoulder, and all the while she talked briskly of ways and means and recipes, and should there be onions in the dressing or should there not be? We took a vote on this and were about to chop the onions in when Mis' Holcomb's little maid arrived at my kitchen door with a bowl of oysters which Mis' Holcomb had left from the 'scallop, an' wouldn't we like 'em in the stuffin'? Roast turkey stuffed with oysters! I saw Libbie Liberty's eyes brighten so delightedly that I brought out a jar of seedless raisins and another of preserved cherries to add to the custard, and then a bag of sweet almonds to be blanched and split for the cake o' sunshine. Surely, one of us said, the seven guests could be preparing for their Thanksgiving dinner with no more zest than we were putting into that dinner for their sakes. "Seven guests!" we said over and again.

"Calliope, how did you do it! When everybody says there's nobody in Friendship that's either sick or poor?"

"Nobody sick, nobody poor!" Calliope exclaimed, piling a dish with watermelon pickles. "Land, you might think that was the town motto. Well, the town don't know everything. Don't you ask me so many questions."

Before eleven o'clock Mis' Mayor Uppers tapped at my back door, with two deep-dish cherry pies in a basket, and a row of her delicate, feathery sponge cakes and a jar of pineapple and pie-plant preserves "to chink in.' She drew a deep breath and stood looking about the kitchen.

"Throw off your things an' help, Mis' Uppers," Calliope admonished her, one hand on the cellar door. "I'm just goin' down for some sweet potatoes Mis' Holcomb sent over this morning, an' you might get 'em ready, if you will. We ain't goin' to let you off now, spite of what you've done for us."

So Mis' Mayor Uppers hung up her shawl and washed the sweet potatoes. And my kitchen was fragrant with spices and flavourings and an odorous oven, and there was no end of savoury business to be at. I found myself glad of the interest of these others in the day and glad of the stirring in my lonely house. Even if their bustle could not lessen my own loneliness, it was pleasant, I said to myself, to see them quicken with interest; and the whole affair entertained my infinite leisure. After all, I was not required to be thankful. I merely loaned my house, cosey in its glittering drifts of turkey feathers, and the day was no more and no less to me than before, though I own that I did feel more than an amused interest in Calliope's guests. Whom, in Friendship, had she found "to do for," I detected myself speculating with real interest as in the dining room, with one and another to help me, I made ready my table. My prettiest dishes and silver, the Cloth-o'-Gold rose, and my yellow-shaded candles made little auxiliary welcomes. Whoever Calliope's guests were, we would do them honour and give them the best we had. And in the midst of all came from the City the box with my gift of hothouse fruit and a rosebud for every plate. "Calliope!" I cried, as I went back to the kitchen, "Calliope, it's nearly twelve now. Tell us who the guests are, or we won't finish dinner!"

Calliope laughed and shook her head and opened the door for Mis' Holcomb-that-was-Mame-Bliss, who entered, followed by her little maid, both laden with good things.

"I prepared for seven," Mis' Holcomb said. "That was the

word you sent me—but where you got your seven sick an' poor in Friendship beats me. I'll stay an' help for a while—but to me it all seems like so much monkey work."

We worked with a will that last half-hour, and the spirit of the kitchen came upon them all. I watched them, amused and pleased at Mis' Mayor Uppers's flushed anxiety over the sweet potatoes, at Libbie Liberty furiously basting the turkey, and at Miss Lucy exclaiming with delight as she unwrapped the rosebuds from their moss. But I think that Mis' Holcomb pleased me most, for with the utensils of housewifery in her hands she seemed utterly to have forgotten that there is no use in anything at all. This was not wonderful in the presence of such a feathery cream of mashed potatoes and such aromatic coffee as she made. *There* was something to tie to. Those were real, at any rate, and beyond all seeming.

Just before twelve Calliope caught off her apron and pulled down her sleeves.

"Now," she said, "I'm going to welcome the guests. I can—can't I?" she begged me. "Everything's all ready but putting on. I won't need to come out here again; when I ring the bell on the sideboard, dish it up an' bring it in, all together—turkey ahead an' vegetables followin'. Mis' Holcomb, you help 'em, won't you? An' then you can leave if you want. Talk about an old-fashion' Thanksgivin'. My!"

"Who *has* she got?" Libbie Liberty burst out, basting the turkey. "I declare, I'm nervous as a witch, I'm so curious!"

And then the clock struck twelve, and a minute after we heard Calliope tinkle a silvery summons on the call-bell.

I remember that it was Mis' Holcomb herself—to whom nothing mattered—who rather lost her head as we served our feast, and who was about putting in dishes both her oysters and her macaroni instead of carrying in the fair, brown, smoking bake pans. But at last we were ready—Mis' Holcomb at our head with the turkey, the others following with both hands filled, and I with the coffee-pot. As they gave the signal to start, something—it may have been the mystery before us, or the good things about us, or the mere look of the Thanksgiving snow on the window-sills—seemed to catch at the hearts of them all, and they laughed a little, almost joyously, those five for whom joy had seemed done, and I found myself laughing too.

So we six filed into the dining room to serve whomever Calliope had found "to do for." I wonder that I had not guessed before. There stood Calliope at the foot of the table, with its lighted candles and its Cloth-o'-Gold rose, and the other six chairs were quite vacant.

"Sit down!" Calliope cried to us, with tears and laughter in her voice. "Sit down, all six of you. Don't you see? Didn't you know? Ain't we soul-sick an' soul-hungry, all of us? An' I tell you, this is goin' to do our souls good—an' our stomachs too!"

Nobody dropped anything, even in the flood of our amazement. We managed to get our savoury burden on the table, and some way we found ourselves in the chairs—I at the head of my table where Calliope led me. And we all talked at once, exclaiming and questioning, with sudden thanksgiving in our hearts that in the world such things may be.

"I was hungry an' sick," Calliope was telling, "for an old-fashion' Thanksgivin'—or anything that'd smooth life out some. But I says to myself, 'It looks like God had afflicted us by not givin' us anybody to do for.' An' then I started out to find some poor an' some sick—an' each one o' you knows what I found. An' I ask' myself before I got home that day, 'Why not them an' me?' There's lots o' kinds o' things to do on Thanksgivin' Day. Are you ever goin' to forgive me?"

I think that we all answered at once. But what we all meant was what Mis' Holcomb-that-was-Mame-Bliss said, as she sat flushed and smiling behind the coffee cups:—

"I declare, I feel something like I ain't felt since I don't know when!"

And Calliope nodded at her.

"I guess that's your soul, Mame Bliss," she said. "You can always feel it if you go to work an' act as if you got one. I'll take my coffee clear."

And as we laughed, and as I looked down my table at my guests, I felt with a wonder that was like belief. How my heart leaped up within me and how it glowed! And I knew a mist of tears in my eyes, and something like happiness possessed me.

And I understood, with infinite thanksgiving, that, if I would have it so, my little house need never be wholly lonely any more.

O. Henry
(William Sydney Porter)

(1862–1910)

Born in North Carolina, O. Henry was largely raised by an aunt who ran a private school. His formal education was over at age 15, when he began to work in his uncle's drugstore; his aunt informally encouraged his passion for reading. His mother had died of tuberculosis when O. Henry was 3 and when, in 1882, he too showed signs of the disease, he was sent to a sheep farm in Texas, where he met cowboys and heard tales of cattle thieves and other desperadoes. In 1884, he moved to Austin, Texas, took a job as teller in a bank, married, and began to write The Rolling Stone, *a humorous magazine which he founded and for which he wrote most of the copy, did not last long; he wrote, too, for a Houston newspaper. In 1896, he was indicted for embezzling bank funds: no one knows whether he was guilty, but he ran off to New Orleans and then to Honduras, returning only in 1898 after learning that his wife was dying of tuberculosis. He was sentenced to five years in the penitentiary and served something over three. And while in jail, he began to write the stories that soon made him famous. Released in 1901, he came to New York in 1902 and thereafter wrote at a furious pace, mostly for newspapers and new, popular magazines like* Everybody's, McClure's, *and* The Cosmopolitan. *By December, 1903, the* New York World *had put him on salary as a writer of stories—one a week—for its Sunday edition and he proceeded to write 113 stories in about 30 months. His first collection was* Cabbages and Kings *(1904). Many others followed, including* The Four Million *(1906),* The Trimmed Lamp *(1907),* Heart of the West *(1907),* The Voice of the City *(1908),* Roads of Destiny *(1909),* Options *(1909). Other volumes appeared posthumously, including, in 1936, a volume of sketches culled from the files of the* Houston Post.

ONE THOUSAND DOLLARS

"One thousand dollars," repeated Lawyer Tolman, solemnly and severely, "and here is the money."

Young Gillian gave a decidedly amused laugh as he fingered the thin package of new fifty-dollar notes.

"It's such a confoundedly awkward amount," he explained, genially, to the lawyer. "If it had been ten thousand a fellow might wind up with a lot of fireworks and do himself credit. Even fifty dollars would have been less trouble."

"You heard the reading of your uncle's will," continued Lawyer Tolman, professionally dry in his tones. "I do not know if you paid much attention to its details. I must remind you of one. You are required to render to us an account of the manner of expenditure of this $1,000 as soon as you have disposed of it. The will stipulates that. I trust that you will so far comply with the late Mr. Gillian's wishes."

"You may depend upon it," said the young man, politely, "in spite of the extra expense it will entail. I may have to engage a secretary. I was never good at accounts."

Gillian went to his club. There he hunted out one whom he called Old Bryson.

Old Bryson was calm and forty and sequestered. He was in a corner reading a book, and when he saw Gillian approaching he sighed, laid down his book and took off his glasses.

"Old Bryson, wake up," said Gillian. "I've a funny story to tell you."

"I wish you would tell it to someone in the billiard room," said Old Bryson. "You know how I hate your stories."

"This is a better one than usual," said Gillian, rolling a cigarette; "and I'm glad to tell it to you. It's too sad and funny to go with the rattling of billiard balls. I've just come from my late uncle's firm of legal corsairs. He leaves me an even thousand dollars. Now, what can a man possibly do with a thousand dollars?"

"I thought," said Old Bryson, showing as much interest as a bee shows in a vinegar cruet, "that the late Septimus Gillian was worth something like half a million."

"He was," assented Gillian, joyously, "and that's where the joke comes in. He's left his whole cargo of doubloons to a microbe. That is, part of it goes to the man who invents a new bacillus and the rest to establish a hospital for doing away with it again. There are one or two trifling bequests on the side. The butler and the housekeeper get a seal ring and $10 each. His nephew gets $1,000."

"You've always had plenty of money to spend," observed Old Bryson.

"Tons," said Gillian. "Uncle was the fairy godmother as far as an allowance was concerned."

"Any other heirs?" asked Old Bryson.

"None." Gillian frowned at his cigarette and kicked the upholstered leather of a divan uneasily. "There is a Miss Hayden, a ward of my uncle, who lived in his house. She's a quiet thing—musical—the daughter of somebody who was unlucky enough to be his friend. I forgot to say that she was in on the seal ring and $10 joke, too. I wish I had been. Then I could have had two bottles of brut, tipped the waiter with the ring, and had the whole business off my hands. Don't be superior and insulting, Old Bryson—tell me what a fellow can do with a thousand dollars."

Old Bryson rubbed his glasses and smiled. And when Old Bryson smiled, Gillian knew that he intended to be more offensive than ever.

"A thousand dollars" he said, "means much or little. One man may buy a happy home with it and laugh at Rockefeller. Another could send his wife South with it and save her life. A thousand dollars would buy pure milk for one hundred babies during June, July, and August and save fifty of their lives. You could count upon a half hour's diversion with it at faro in one of the fortified art galleries. It would furnish an education to an ambitious boy. I am told that a genuine Corot was secured for that amount in an auction room yesterday. You could move to a New Hampshire town and live respectably two years on it. You could rent Madison Square Garden for one evening with it, and lecture your audience, if you should have one, on the precariousness of the profession of heir presumptive."

"People might like you, Old Bryson," said Gillian, almost unruffled, "if you wouldn't moralize. I asked you to tell me what I could do with a thousand dollars."

"You?" said Bryson, with a gentle laugh. "Why, Bobby Gillian, there's only one logical thing you could do. You can go buy Miss Lotta Lauriere a diamond pendant with the money, and then take yourself off to Idaho and inflict your presence upon a ranch. I advise a sheep ranch, as I have a particular dislike for sheep."

"Thanks," said Gillian, rising. "I thought I could depend upon you, Old Bryson. You hit on the very scheme. I wanted to chuck the money in a lump, for I've got to turn in an account for it, and I hate itemizing."

Gillian phoned for a cab and said to the driver:

"The stage entrance of the Columbine Theatre."

Miss Lotta Lauriere was assisting nature with a powder puff, almost ready for her call at a crowded matinée, when her dresser mentioned the name of Mr. Gillian.

"Let it in," said Miss Lauriere. "Now, what is it, Bobby? I'm going on in two minutes."

"Rabbit-foot your right ear a little," suggested Gillian, critically. "That's better. It won't take two minutes for me. What do you say to a little thing in the pendant line? I can stand three ciphers with a figure one in front of 'em."

"Oh, just as you say," carolled Miss Lauriere.

"My right glove, Adams. Say, Bobby, did you see that necklace Della Stacey had on the other night? Twenty-two hundred dollars it cost at Tiffany's. But, of course—pull my sash a little to the left, Adams."

"Miss Lauriere for the opening chorus!" cried the call boy without.

Gillian strolled out to where his cab was waiting.

"What would you do with a thousand dollars if you had it?" he asked the driver.

"Open a s'loon," said the cabby promptly and huskily. "I know a place I could take money in with both hands. It's a four-story brick on a corner. I've got it figured out. Second story—Chinks and chop suey; third floor—manicures and foreign missions; fourth floor—poolroom. If you was thinking of putting up the cap——"

"Oh, no," said Gillian, "I merely asked from curiosity. I take you by the hour. Drive till I tell you to stop."

Eight blocks down Broadway Gillian poked up the trap with his cane and got out. A blind man sat upon a stool on the sidewalk selling pencils. Gillian went out and stood before him.

"Excuse me," he said, "but would you mind telling me what you would do if you had a thousand dollars?"

"You got out of that cab that just drove up, didn't you?" asked the blind man.

"I did," said Gillian.

"I guess you are all right," said the pencil dealer, "to ride in a cab by daylight. Take a look at that, if you like."

He drew a small book from his coat pocket and held it out. Gillian opened it and saw that it was a bank deposit book. It showed a balance of $1,785 to the blind man's credit.

Gillian returned the book and got into the cab.

"I forgot something," he said. "You may drive to the law offices of Tolman & Sharp, at——Broadway."

Lawyer Tolman looked at him hostilely and inquiringly through his gold-rimmed glasses.

"I beg your pardon," said Gillian, cheerfully, "but may I ask you a question? It is not an impertinent one, I hope. Was Miss Hayden left anything by my uncle's will besides the ring and the $10?"

"Nothing," said Mr. Tolman.

"I thank you very much, sir," said Gillian, and out he went to his cab. He gave the driver the address of his late uncle's home.

Miss Hayden was writing letters in the library. She was small and slender and clothed in black. But you would have noticed her eyes. Gillian drifted in with his air of regarding the world as inconsequent.

"I've just come from old Tolman's," he explained. "They've been going over the papers down there. They found a"—Gillian searched his memory for a legal term—"they found an amendment or a postscript or something to the will. It seemed that the old boy loosened up a little on second thoughts and willed you a thousand dollars. I was driving up this way and Tolman asked me to bring you the money. Here it is. You'd better count it to see if it's right." Gillian laid the money beside her hand on the desk.

Miss Hayden turned white. "Oh!" she said, and again "Oh!"

Gillian half turned and looked out of the window.

"I suppose, of course," he said, in a low voice, "that you know I love you."

"I am sorry," said Miss Hayden, taking up her money.

"There is no use?" asked Gillian, almost light-heartedly.

"I am sorry," she said again.

"May I write a note?" asked Gillian, with a smile. He seated himself at the big library table. She supplied him with paper and pen, and then went back to her secrétaire.

Gillian made out his account of his expenditure of the thousand dollars in these words:

"Paid by the black sheep, Robert Gillian, $1,000 on account

of the eternal happiness, owed by Heaven to the best and dearest woman on earth.''

Gillian slipped his writing into an envelope, bowed and went his way.

His cab stopped again at the offices of Tolman & Sharp.

"I have expended the thousand dollars," he said, cheerily, to Tolman of the gold glasses, "and I have come to render account of it, as I agreed. There is quite a feeling of summer in the air—do you not think so, Mr. Tolman?" He tossed a white envelope on the lawyer's table. "You will find there a memorandum, sir, of the *modus operandi* of the vanishing of the dollars.''

Without touching the envelope, Mr. Tolman went to a door and called his partner, Sharp. Together they explored the caverns of an immense safe. Forth they dragged as trophy of their search a big envelope sealed with wax. This they forcibly invaded, and wagged their venerable heads together over its contents. Then Tolman became spokesman.

"Mr. Gillian," he said, formally, "there was a codicil to your uncle's will. It was intrusted to us privately, with instructions that it be not opened until you had furnished us with a full account of your handling of the $1,000 bequest in the will. As you have fulfilled the conditions, my partner and I have read the codicil. I do not wish to encumber your understanding with its legal phraseology, but I will acquaint you with the spirit of its contents.

"In the event that your disposition of the $1,000 demonstrates that you possess any of the qualifications that deserve reward, much benefit will accrue to you. Mr. Sharp and I are named as the judges, and I assure you that we will do our duty strictly according to justice—with liberality. We are not at all unfavorably disposed toward you, Mr. Gillian. But let us return to the letter of the codicil. If your disposal of the money in question has been prudent, wise, or unselfish, it is in our power to hand you over bonds to the value of $50,000, which have been placed in our hands for that purpose. But if—as our client, the late Mr. Gillian, explicitly provides—you have used this money as you have used money in the past—I quote the late Mr. Gillian—in reprehensible dissipation among disreputable associates—the $50,000 is to be paid to Miriam Hayden, ward of the late Mr. Gillian, without delay. Now, Mr. Gillian, Mr. Sharp and I will examine your account in regard to the $1,000. You submit it in writing, I believe. I hope you will repose confidence in our decision.''

Mr. Tolman reached for the envelope. Gillian was a little the quicker in taking it up. He tore the account and its cover leisurely into strips and dropped them into his pocket.

"It's all right," he said, smilingly. "There isn't a bit of need to bother you with this. I don't suppose you'd understand these itemized bets, anyway. I lost the thousand dollars on the races. Good-day to you, gentlemen."

Tolman & Sharp shook their heads mournfully at each other when Gillian left, for they heard him whistling gayly in the hallways as he waited for the elevator.

Sherwood Anderson
(1876–1941)

Born in Ohio, and raised there in the small town of Clyde (population about 3,000, and later to be made famous as "Winesburg"), Anderson was the son of a harness maker and house painter of no great talents and little stability, who was rather too fond of drink. His mother died in 1895; by 1896, Anderson was living and working in Chicago. In 1898, he enlisted and served in the Spanish-American War. Thereafter he settled in Ohio, married, and worked as an advertising copywriter, meanwhile beginning a modest career as a freelance journalist. In 1907, he founded the Anderson Manufacturing Company, which in 1908 became not only a retailer but also a manufacturer of house paint. In December, 1912, he suffered a mental breakdown, later leaving for Chicago and, once again, a career as a copywriter. His journalistic writing had already begun to turn to fiction-writing: his first novel, Windy McPherson's Son, appeared in 1916, his second, Marching Men, came out in 1917. Winesburg, Ohio (1919), his most famous book, from which "Queer" is taken, established his reputation. Other books include Poor White (1920), Many Marriages (1923), Dark Laughter (1925), a book about black life in America, and Tar, A Midwest Childhood (1926), a fictionalized version of his own life. Anderson also wrote poetry, essays, and criticism. In the late 1920s, he moved to Virginia, where he worked as a journalist and editor. His Memoirs and Letters were published posthumously, in 1942 and 1953, respectively.

"QUEER"

From his seat on a box in the rough board shed that stuck like a burr on the rear of Cowley & Son's store in Winesburg, Elmer Cowley, the junior member of the firm, could see through a dirty window into the printshop of the *Winesburg Eagle*. Elmer was putting new shoelaces in his shoes. They did not go in readily and he had to take the shoes off. With the shoes in his hand he sat looking at a large hole in the heel of one of his stockings. Then looking quickly up he saw George Willard, the only newspaper reporter in Winesburg, standing at the back door of the *Eagle* printshop and staring absent-mindedly about. "Well, well, what next!" exclaimed the young man with the shoes in his hand, jumping to his feet and creeping away from the window.

A flush crept into Elmer Cowley's face and his hands began to tremble. In Cowley & Son's store a Jewish traveling salesman stood by the counter talking to his father. He imagined the reporter could hear what was being said and the thought made him furious. With one of the shoes still held in his hand he stood in a corner of the shed and stamped with a stockinged foot upon the board floor.

Cowley & Son's store did not face the main street of Winesburg. The front was on Maumee Street and beyond it was Voight's wagon shop and a shed for the sheltering of farmers' horses. Beside the store an alleyway ran behind the main street stores and all day drays and delivery wagons, intent on bringing in and taking out goods, passed up and down. The store itself was indescribable. Will Henderson once said of it that it sold everything and nothing. In the window facing Maumee Street stood a chunk of coal as large as an apple barrel, to indicate that orders for coal were taken, and beside the black mass of the coal stood three combs of honey grown brown and dirty in their wooden frames.

The honey had stood in the store window for six months. It was for sale as were also the coat hangers, patent suspender buttons, cans of roof paint, bottles of rheumatism cure and a substitute for coffee that companioned the honey in its patient willingness to serve the public.

Ebenezer Cowley, the man who stood in the store listening to the eager patter of words that fell from the lips of the traveling man, was tall and lean and looked unwashed. On his scrawny neck was a large wen partially covered by a grey beard. He wore a long Prince Albert coat. The coat had been purchased to serve as a wedding garment. Before he became a merchant Ebenezer was a farmer and after his marriage he wore the Prince Albert coat to church on Sundays and on Saturday afternoons when he came into town to trade. When he sold the farm to become a merchant he wore the coat constantly. It had become brown with age and was covered with grease spots, but in it Ebenezer always felt dressed up and ready for the day in town.

As a merchant Ebenezer was not happily placed in life and he had not been happily placed as a farmer. Still he existed. His family, consisting of a daughter named Mabel and the son, lived with him in rooms above the store and it did not cost them much to live. His troubles were not financial. His unhappiness as a merchant lay in the fact that when a traveling man with wares to be sold came in at the front door he was afraid. Behind the counter he stood shaking his head. He was afraid, first that he would stubbornly refuse to buy and thus lose the opportunity to sell again; second that he would not be stubborn enough and would in a moment of weakness buy what could not be sold.

In the store on the morning when Elmer Cowley saw George Willard standing and apparently listening at the back door of the *Eagle* printshop, a situation had arisen that always stirred the son's wrath. The traveling man talked and Ebenezer listened, his whole figure expressing uncertainty. "You see how quickly it is done," said the traveling man who had for sale a small flat metal substitute for collar buttons. With one hand he quickly unfastened a collar from his shirt and then fastened it on again. He assumed a flattering wheedling tone. "I tell you what, men have come to the end of all this fooling with collar buttons and you are the man to make money out of the change that is coming. I am offering you the exclusive agency for this town. Take twenty dozen of these fasteners and I'll not visit any other store. I'll leave the field to you."

The traveling man leaned over the counter and tapped with his finger on Ebenezer's breast. "It's an opportunity and I want you to take it," he urged. "A friend of mine told me about you. 'See that man Cowley,' he said. 'He's a live one.'"

The traveling man paused and waited. Taking a book from his pocket he began writing out the order. Still holding the shoe in his hand Elmer Cowley went through the store, past the two absorbed men, to a glass show case near the front door. He took a cheap revolver from the case and began to wave it about. "You get out of here!" he shrieked. "We don't want any collar fasteners here." An idea came to him. "Mind, I'm not making any threat," he added. "I don't say I'll shoot. Maybe I just took this gun out of the case to look at it. But you better get out. Yes sir, I'll say that. You better grab up your things and get out."

The young storekeeper's voice rose to a scream and going behind the counter he began to advance upon the two men. "We're through being fools here!" he cried. "We ain't going to buy any more stuff until we begin to sell. We ain't going to keep on being queer and have folks staring and listening. You get out of here!"

The traveling man left. Raking the samples of collar fasteners off the counter into a black leather bag, he ran. He was a small man and very bow-legged and he ran awkwardly. The black bag caught against the door and he stumbled and fell. "Crazy, that's what he is—crazy!" he sputtered as he arose from the sidewalk and hurried away.

In the store Elmer Cowley and his father stared at each other. Now that the immediate object of his wrath had fled, the younger man was embarrassed. "Well, I meant it. I think we've been queer long enough," he declared, going to the showcase and replacing the revolver. Sitting on a barrel he pulled on and fastened the shoe he had been holding in his hand. He was waiting for some word of understanding from his father but when Ebenezer spoke his words only served to reawaken the wrath in the son and the young man ran out of the store without replying. Scratching his grey beard with his long dirty fingers, the merchant looked at his son with the same wavering uncertain stare with which he had confronted the traveling man. "I'll be starched," he said softly. "Well, well, I'll be washed and ironed and starched!"

Elmer Cowley went out of Winesburg and along a country road that paralleled the railroad track. He did not know where he was going or what he was going to do. In the shelter of a deep cut where the road, after turning sharply to the right, dipped under the tracks he stopped and the passion that had been the cause of his outburst in the store began to again find expression. "I will not be queer—one to be looked at and listened to," he declared aloud. "I'll be like other people. I'll show that George Willard. He'll find out. I'll show him!"

The distraught young man stood in the middle of the road and glared back at the town. He did not know the reporter George

Willard and had no special feeling concerning the tall boy who
ran about town gathering the town news. The reporter had
merely come, by his presence in the office and in the printshop
of the *Winesburg Eagle,* to stand for something in the young
merchant's mind. He thought the boy who passed and repassed
Cowley & Son's store and who stopped to talk to people in the
street must be thinking of him and perhaps laughing at him.
George Willard, he felt, belonged to the town, typified the town,
represented in his person the spirit of the town. Elmer Cowley
could not have believed that George Willard had also his days of
unhappiness, that vague hungers and secret unnamable desires
visited also his mind. Did he not represent public opinion and
had not the public opinion of Winesburg condemned the Cow-
leys to queerness? Did he not walk whistling and laughing
through Main Street? Might not one by striking his person strike
also the greater enemy—the thing that smiled and went its own
way—the judgment of Winesburg?

Elmer Cowley was extraordinarily tall and his arms were long
and powerful. His hair, his eyebrows, and the downy beard that
had begun to grow upon his chin, were pale almost to whiteness.
His teeth protruded from between his lips and his eyes were blue
with the colorless blueness of the marbles called "aggies" that
the boys of Winesburg carried in their pockets. Elmer had lived
in Winesburg for a year and had made no friends. He was, he
felt, one condemned to go through life without friends and he
hated the thought.

Sullenly the tall young man tramped along the road with his
hands stuffed into his trouser pockets. The day was cold with a
raw wind, but presently the sun began to shine and the road
became soft and muddy. The tops of the ridges of frozen mud
that formed the road began to melt and the mud clung to Elmer's
shoes. His feet became cold. When he had gone several miles he
turned off the road, crossed a field and entered a wood. In the
wood he gathered sticks to build a fire by which he sat trying to
warm himself, miserable in body and in mind.

For two hours he sat on the log by the fire and then, arising
and creeping cautiously through a mass of underbrush, he went
to a fence and looked across fields to a small farmhouse surrounded by low sheds. A smile came to his lips and he began
making motions with his long arms to a man who was husking
corn in one of the fields.

In his hour of misery the young merchant had returned to the
farm where he had lived through boyhood and where there was
another human being to whom he felt he could explain himself.

The man on the farm was a half-witted old fellow named Mook. He had once been employed by Ebenezer Cowley and had stayed on the farm when it was sold. The old man lived in one of the unpainted sheds back of the farmhouse and puttered about all day in the fields.

Mook the half-wit lived happily. With childlike faith he believed in the intelligence of the animals that lived in the sheds with him, and when he was lonely held long conversations with the cows, the pigs, and even with the chickens that ran about the barnyard. He it was who had put the expression regarding being "laundered" into the mouth of his former employer. When excited or surprised by anything he smiled vaguely and muttered: "I'll be washed and ironed. Well, well, I'll be washed and ironed and starched."

When the half-witted old man left his husking of corn and came into the wood to meet Elmer Cowley, he was neither surprised nor especially interested in the sudden appearance of the young man. His feet also were cold and he sat on the log by the fire, grateful for the warmth and apparently indifferent to what Elmer had to say.

Elmer talked earnestly and with great freedom, walking up and down and waving his arms about. "You don't understand what's the matter with me so of course you don't care," he declared. "With me it's different. Look how it has always been with me. Father is queer and mother was queer, too. Even the clothes mother used to wear were not like other people's clothes, and look at that coat in which father goes about there in town, thinking he's dressed up, too. Why don't he get a new one? It wouldn't cost much. I'll tell you why. Father doesn't know and when mother was alive she didn't know either. Mabel is different. She knows but she won't say anything. I will, though. I'm not going to be stared at any longer. Why look here, Mook, father doesn't know that his store there in town is just a queer jumble, that he'll never sell the stuff he buys. He knows nothing about it. Sometimes he's a little worried that trade doesn't come and then he goes and buys something else. In the evenings he sits by the fire upstairs and says trade will come after a while. He isn't worried. He's queer. He doesn't know enough to be worried."

The excited young man became more excited. "He don't know but I know," he shouted, stopping to gaze down into the dumb, unresponsive face of the half-wit. "I know too well. I can't stand it. When we lived out here it was different. I worked and at night I went to bed and slept. I wasn't always seeing people and thinking as I am now. In the evening, there in town, I go to the post office or to the depot to see the train come in, and no one says anything to me. Everyone stands around and laughs and they talk but they say nothing to me. Then I feel so queer that I can't talk either. I go away. I don't say anything. I can't.''

The fury of the young man became uncontrollable. "I won't stand it," he yelled, looking up at the bare branches of the trees. "I'm not made to stand it."

Maddened by the dull face of the man on the log by the fire, Elmer turned and glared at him as he had glared back along the road at the town of Winesburg. "Go on back to work," he screamed. "What good does it do me to talk to you?" A thought came to him and his voice dropped. "I'm a coward too, eh?" he muttered. "Do you know why I came clear out here afoot? I had to tell someone and you were the only one I could tell. I hunted out another queer one, you see. I ran away, that's what I did. I couldn't stand up to someone like that George Willard. I had to come to you. I ought to tell him and I will."

Again his voice arose to a shout and his arms flew about. "I will tell him. I won't be queer. I don't care what they think. I won't stand it."

Elmer Cowley ran out of the woods leaving the half-wit sitting on the log before the fire. Presently the old man arose and climbing over the fence went back to his work in the corn. "I'll be washed and ironed and starched," he declared. "Well, well, I'll be washed and ironed." Mook was interested. He went along a lane to a field where two cows stood nibbling at a straw stack. "Elmer was here," he said to the cows. "Elmer is crazy. You better get behind the stack where he don't see you. He'll hurt someone yet, Elmer will."

At eight o'clock that evening Elmer Cowley put his head in at the front door of the office of the *Winesburg Eagle* where George Willard sat writing. His cap was pulled down over his eyes and a sullen determined look was on his face. "You come on outside with me," he said, stepping in and closing the door. He kept his hand on the knob as though prepared to resist anyone else coming in. "You just come along outside. I want to see you."

George Willard and Elmer Cowley walked through the main street of Winesburg. The night was cold and George Willard had on a new overcoat and looked very spruce and dressed up. He thrust his hands into the overcoat pockets and looked inquiringly at his companion. He had long been wanting to make friends with the young merchant and find out what was in his mind. Now he thought he saw a chance and was delighted. "I wonder what he's up to? Perhaps he thinks he has a piece of news for the paper. It can't be a fire because I haven't heard the fire bell and there isn't anyone running," he thought.

In the main street of Winesburg, on the cold November evening, but few citizens appeared and these hurried along bent on getting to the stove at the back of some store. The windows of the stores were frosted and the wind rattled the tin sign that hung over the entrance to the stairway leading to Doctor Welling's office. Before Hearn's Grocery a basket of apples and a rack filled with new brooms stood on the sidewalk. Elmer Cowley stopped and stood facing George Willard. He tried to talk and his arms began to pump up and down. His face worked spasmodically. He seemed about to shout. "Oh, you go on back," he cried. "Don't stay out here with me. I ain't got anything to tell you. I don't want to see you at all."

For three hours the distracted young merchant wandered through the resident streets of Winesburg blind with anger, brought on by his failure to declare his determination not to be queer. Bitterly the sense of defeat settled upon him and he wanted to weep. After the hours of futile sputtering at nothingness that had occupied the afternoon and his failure in the presence of the young reporter, he thought he could see no hope of a future for himself.

And then a new idea dawned for him. In the darkness that surrounded him he began to see a light. Going to the now darkened store, where Cowley & Son had for over a year waited vainly for trade to come, he crept stealthily in and felt about in a barrel that stood by the stove at the rear. In the barrel beneath shavings lay a tin box containing Cowley & Son's cash. Every evening Ebenezer Cowley put the box in the barrel when he closed the store and went upstairs to bed. "They wouldn't never think of a careless place like that," he told himself, thinking of robbers.

Elmer took twenty dollars, two ten dollar bills, from the little roll containing perhaps four hundred dollars, the cash left from the sale of the farm. Then replacing the box beneath the shavings he went quietly out at the front door and walked again in the streets.

The idea that he thought might put an end to all of his unhappiness was very simple. "I will get out of here, run away from home," he told himself. He knew that a local freight train passed through Winesburg at midnight and went on to Cleveland where it arrived at dawn. He would steal a ride on the local and when he got to Cleveland would lose himself in the crowds there. He would get work in some shop and become friends with the other workmen. Gradually he would become like other men and would be indistinguishable. Then he could talk and laugh.

He would no longer be queer and would make friends. Life would begin to have warmth and meaning for him as it had for others.

The tall awkward young man, striding through the streets, laughed at himself because he had been angry and had been half afraid of George Willard. He decided he would have his talk with the young reporter before he left town, that he would tell him about things, perhaps challenge him, challenge all of Winesburg through him.

Aglow with new confidence Elmer went to the office of the New Willard House and pounded on the door. A sleep-eyed boy slept on a cot in the office. He received no salary but was fed at the hotel table and bore with pride the title of "night clerk." Before the boy Elmer was bold, insistent. "You wake him up," he commanded. "You tell him to come down by the depot. I got to see him and I'm going away on the local. Tell him to dress and come on down. I ain't got much time."

The midnight local had finished its work in Winesburg and the trainsmen were coupling cars, swinging lanterns and preparing to resume their flight east. George Willard, rubbing his eyes and again wearing the new overcoat, ran down to the station platform afire with curiosity. "Well, here I am. What do you want? You've got something to tell me, eh?" he said.

Elmer tried to explain. He wet his lips with his tongue and looked at the train that had begun to groan and get under way. "Well, you see," he began, and then lost control of his tongue, "I'll be washed and ironed. I'll be washed and ironed and starched," he muttered half incoherently.

Elmer Cowley danced with fury beside the groaning train in the darkness on the station platform. Lights leaped into the air and bobbed up and down before his eyes. Taking the two ten dollar bills from his pocket he thrust them into George Willard's hand. "Take them," he cried. "I don't want them. Give them to father. I stole them." With a snarl of rage he turned and his long arms began to flay the air. Like one struggling for release from hands that held him he struck out, hitting George Willard blow after blow on the breast, the neck, the mouth. The young reporter rolled over on the platfom half unconscious, stunned by the terrific force of the blows. Springing aboard the passing train and running over the top of cars, Elmer sprang down to a flat car and lying on his face looked back, trying to see the fallen man in the darkness. Pride surged up in him. "I showed him," he cried. "I guess I showed him. I ain't so queer. I guess I showed him I ain't so queer."

Ernest Hemingway

(1899–1961)

   *Born in Illinois, the son of a physician, Hemingway and his
father hunted and fished together in northern Michigan, the
background for his first story, "Up in Michigan," here reprinted.
Rejected for military service in 1917 because of poor vision, he
began his journalistic career with the Kansas City* Star, *then
volunteered for and served with the Red Cross in Italy, where he
was badly wounded by a mortar shell. In 1920, he became a
reporter for the Toronto* Star, *for which paper, in late 1921, he
went to Paris. His first book,* Three Stories and Ten Poems *(from
which "Up in Michigan" is taken), appeared in 1923, followed
by* In Our Time *(1924),* The Torrents of Spring *(1926), and the
first of his major books,* The Sun Also Rises *(1926), which
began to make his name. A collection of stories,* Men Without
Women, *appeared in 1927, and then* A Farewell to Arms, *also in
1927, the latter not only solidifying his reputation but also
selling extremely well.* Death in the Afternoon *(1932),* Winner
Take Nothing *(1933),* Green Hills of Africa *(1935), and* The
Fifth Column and the First Forty-nine Stories *(1938), were followed by his most sensational (if not his best) novel,* For Whom
the Bell Tolls *(1940). His career declined, thereafter.* Across the
River and Into the Trees *(1950) received and deserved poor
reviews;* The Old Man and the Sea *(1952) received but did not
deserve extravagantly good reviews. He won the Nobel Prize in
1954. In 1961 he shot himself, just as, some thirty-odd years
earlier, his own father had done.*

UP IN MICHIGAN

Jim Gilmore came to Hortons Bay from Canada. He bought the blacksmith shop from old man Horton. Jim was short and dark with big mustaches and big hands. He was a good horseshoer and did not look much like a blacksmith even with his leather apron on. He lived upstairs above the blacksmith shop and took his meals at D. J. Smith's.

Liz Coates worked for Smith's. Mrs. Smith, who was a very large clean woman, said Liz Coates was the neatest girl she'd ever seen. Liz had good legs and always wore clean gingham aprons and Jim noticed that her hair was always neat behind. He liked her face because it was so jolly but he never thought about her.

Liz liked Jim very much. She liked it the way he walked over from the shop and often went to the kitchen door to watch for him to start down the road. She liked it about his mustache. She liked it about how white his teeth were when he smiled. She liked it very much that he didn't look like a blacksmith. She liked it how much D. J. Smith and Mrs. Smith liked Jim. One day she found that she liked it the way the hair was black on his arms and how white they were above the tanned line when he washed up in the washbasin outside the house. Liking that made her feel funny.

Hortons Bay, the town, was only five houses on the main road between Boyne City and Charlevoix. There was the general store and post office with a high false front and maybe a wagon hitched out in front, Smith's house, Stroud's house, Dillworth's house, Horton's house and Van Hoosen's house. The houses were in a big grove of elm trees and the road was very sandy. There was farming country and timber each way up the road. Up the road a ways was the Methodist church and down the road the other direction was the township school. The blacksmith shop was painted red and faced the school.

A steep sandy road ran down the hill to the bay through the timber. From Smith's back door you could look out across the woods that ran down to the lake and across the bay. It was very beautiful in the spring and summer, the bay blue and bright and usually whitecaps on the lake out beyond the point from the breeze blowing from Charlevoix and Lake Michigan. From Smith's back door Liz could see ore barges way out in the lake going toward Boyne City. When she looked at them they didn't seem to be moving at all but if she went in and dried some more dishes and then came out again they would be out of sight beyond the point.

All the time now Liz was thinking about Jim Gilmore. He didn't seem to notice her much. He talked about the shop to D. J. Smith and about the Republican Party and about James G. Blaine. In the evenings he read *The Toledo Blade* and the Grand Rapids paper by the lamp in the front room or went out spearing fish in the bay with a jacklight with D. J. Smith. In the fall he and Smith and Charley Wyman took a wagon and tent, grub, axes, their rifles and two dogs and went on a trip to the pine plains beyond Vanderbilt deer hunting. Liz and Mrs. Smith were cooking for four days for them before they started. Liz wanted to make something special for Jim to take but she didn't finally because she was afraid to ask Mrs. Smith for the eggs and flour and afraid if she bought them Mrs. Smith would catch her cooking. It would have been all right with Mrs. Smith but Liz was afraid.

All the time Jim was gone on the deer hunting trip Liz thought about him. It was awful while he was gone. She couldn't sleep well from thinking about him but she discovered it was fun to think about him too. If she let herself go it was better. The night before they were to come back she didn't sleep at all, that is she didn't think she slept because it was all mixed up in a dream about not sleeping and really not sleeping. When she saw the wagon coming down the road she felt weak and sick sort of inside. She couldn't wait till she saw Jim and it seemed as though everything would be all right when he came. The wagon stopped outside under the big elm and Mrs. Smith and Liz went out. All the men had beards and there were three deer in the back of the wagon, their thin legs sticking stiff over the edge of the wagon box. Mrs. Smith kissed D. J. and he hugged her. Jim said "Hello, Liz," and grinned. Liz hadn't known just what would happen when Jim got back but she was sure it would be something. Nothing had happened. The men were just home, that was all. Jim pulled the burlap sacks off the deer and Liz looked at them. One was a big buck. It was stiff and hard to lift out of the wagon.

"Did you shoot it, Jim?" Liz asked.

"Yeah. Ain't it a beauty?" Jim got it onto his back to carry to the smokehouse.

That night Charley Wyman stayed to supper at Smith's. It was too late to get back to Charlevoix. The men washed up and waited in the front room for supper.

"Ain't there something left in that crock, Jimmy?" D. J. Smith asked, and Jim went out to the wagon in the barn and fetched in the jug of whiskey the men had taken hunting with them. It was a four-gallon jug and there was quite a little slopped back and forth in the bottom. Jim took a long pull on his way back to the house. It was hard to lift such a big jug up to drink out of it. Some of the whiskey ran down on his shirt front. The two men smiled when Jim came in with the jug. D. J. Smith sent for glasses and Liz brought them. D. J. poured out three big shots.

"Well, here's looking at you, D. J.," said Charley Wyman.

"That damn big buck, Jimmy," said D. J.

"Here's all the ones we missed, D. J.," said Jim, and downed his liquor.

"Tastes good to a man."

"Nothing like it this time of year for what ails you."

"How about another, boys?"

"Here's how, D. J."

"Down the creek, boys."

"Here's to next year."

Jim began to feel great. He loved the taste and the feel of whiskey. He was glad to be back to a comfortable bed and warm food and the shop. He had another drink. The men came in to supper feeling hilarious but acting very respectable. Liz sat at the table after she put on the food and ate with the family. It was a good dinner. The men ate seriously. After supper they went into the front room again and Liz cleaned off with Mrs. Smith. Then Mrs. Smith went upstairs and pretty soon Smith came out and went upstairs too. Jim and Charley were still in the front room. Liz was sitting in the kitchen next to the stove pretending to read a book and thinking about Jim. She didn't want to go to bed yet because she knew Jim would be coming out and she wanted to see him as he went out so she could take the way he looked up to bed with her.

She was thinking about him hard and then Jim came out. His eyes were shining and his hair was a little rumpled. Liz looked down at her book. Jim came over back of her chair and stood there and she could feel him breathing and then he put his arms around her. Her breasts felt plump and firm and the nipples were erect under his hands. Liz was terribly frightened, no one had ever touched her, but she thought, "He's come to me finally. He's really come."

She held herself stiff because she was so frightened and did not know anything else to do and then Jim held her tight against the chair and kissed her. It was such a sharp, aching, hurting feeling that she thought she couldn't stand it. She felt Jim right through the back of the chair and she couldn't stand it and then something clicked inside of her and the feeling was warmer and softer. Jim held her tight hard against the chair and she wanted it now and Jim whispered, "Come on for a walk."

Liz took her coat off the peg on the kitchen wall and they went out the door. Jim had his arm around her and every little way they stopped and pressed against each other and Jim kissed her. There was no moon and they walked ankle-deep in the sandy road through the trees down to the dock and the warehouse on the bay. The water was lapping in the piles and the point was dark across the bay. It was cold but Liz was hot all over from being with Jim. They sat down in the shelter of the warehouse and Jim pulled Liz close to him. She was frightened. One of Jim's hands went inside her dress and stroked over her breast and the other hand was in her lap. She was very frightened and didn't know how he was going to go about things but she snuggled close to him. Then the hand that felt so big in her lap went away and was on her leg and started to move up it.

"Don't, Jim," Liz said. Jim slid the hand further up.

"You mustn't, Jim. You mustn't." Neither Jim nor Jim's big hand paid any attention to her.

The boards were hard. Jim had her dress up and was trying to do something to her. She was frightened but she wanted it. She had to have it but it frightened her.

"You mustn't do it, Jim. You mustn't."

"I got to. I'm going to. You know we got to."

"No we haven't, Jim. We ain't got to. Oh, it isn't right. Oh, it's so big and it hurts so. You can't. Oh, Jim. Jim. Oh."

The hemlock planks of the dock were hard and splintery and cold and Jim was heavy on her and he had hurt her. Liz pushed him, she was so uncomfortable and cramped. Jim was asleep. He wouldn't move. She worked out from under him and sat up and straightened her skirt and coat and tried to do something with her hair. Jim was sleeping with his mouth a little open. Liz leaned over and kissed him on the cheek. He was still asleep. She lifted his head a little and shook it. He rolled his head over and swallowed. Liz started to cry. She walked over to the edge of the dock and looked down to the water. There was a mist coming up from the bay. She was cold and miserable and everything felt gone. She walked back to where Jim was lying and shook him once more to make sure. She was crying.

"Jim," she said, "Jim. Please, Jim."

Jim stirred and curled a little tighter. Liz took off her coat and leaned over and covered him with it. She tucked it around him neatly and carefully. Then she walked across the dock and up the steep sandy road to go to bed. A cold mist was coming up through the woods from the bay.

John Dos Passos

(1896–1970)

*Born in Chicago, son of a prominent lawyer who was unable
to marry his son's mother until 1910, Dos Passos and his mother
spent the early years of his life in Europe, sometimes joined by
his father. He returned to the U.S. in 1906, attending the Choate
School, spending 1911–1912 in Europe and then entering Harvard in 1912. Graduating in 1916, he journeyed to Spain to
study architecture, but soon enlisted in the French ambulance
service; the experience of World War One led to his first book,*
One Man's Initiation—1917 *(1920), which was followed in 1921
by his first mature novel, still insufficiently appreciated,* Three
Soldiers, *a powerful and bitter attack on war and its effects on
human character.* Manhattan Transfer *(1925), part novel, part
collective portrait of New York City, a section of which, "Great
Lady on a White Horse," is here reprinted, was followed in
1930, 1932, and 1936 by the three volumes of his massive
trilogy,* U.S.A., *again a pioneering and vastly influential book
neither the merits nor the importance of which has been properly
recognized. Dos Passos also published poetry and plays, as well
as travel books, historical and biographical accounts, and political essays (collected in* The Theme Is Freedom *[1956] and*
Occasions and Protests *[1964]). His later fiction, like Edith
Wharton's, is significantly less important than his earlier work.*

GREAT LADY
ON A WHITE HORSE

Morning clatters with the first L train down Allen Street. Daylight rattles through the windows, shaking the old brick houses, splatters the girders of the L structure with bright confetti.

The cats are leaving the garbage cans, the chinches are going back into the walls, leaving sweaty limbs, leaving the grimetender necks of little children asleep. Men and women stir under blankets and bedquilts on mattresses in the corners of rooms, clots of kids begin to untangle to scream and kick.

At the corner of Riverton the old man with the hempen beard who sleeps where nobody knows is putting out his picklestand. Tubs of gherkins, pimentos, melonrind, piccalilli give out twining vines and cold tendrils of dank pepperyfragrance that grow like a marshgarden out of the musky bedsmells and the rancid clangor of the cobbled awakening street.

The old man with the hempen beard who sleeps where nobody knows sits in the midst of it like Jonah under his gourd.

Jimmy Herf walked up four creaky flights and knocked at a white door fingermarked above the knob where the name *Sunderland* appeared in old English characters on a card neatly held in place by brass thumbtacks. He waited a long while beside a milkbottle, two creambottles and a copy of the Sunday *Times*. There was a rustle behind the door and the creak of a step, then no more sound. He pushed a white button in the doorjamb.

"An he said, Margie I've got a crush on you so bad, and she said, Come in outa the rain, you're all wet. . . ." Voices coming down the stairs, a man's feet in button shoes, a girl's feet in sandals, pink silk legs; the girl in a fluffy dress and a Spring Maid hat; the young man had white edging on his vest and a green, blue, and purple striped necktie.

"But you're not that kind of a girl."

"How do you know what kind of a girl I am?"

The voices trailed out down the stairs.

Jimmy Herf gave the bell another jab.

"Who is it?" came a lisping female voice through a crack in the door.

"I want to see Miss Prynne please."

Glimpse of a blue kimono held up to the chin of a fluffy face. "Oh I dont know if she's up yet."

"She said she would be."

"Look will you please wait a second to let me make my getaway," she tittered behind the door. "And then come in. Excuse us but Mrs. Sunderland thought you were the rent collector. They sometimes come on Sunday just to fool you." A smile coyly bridged the crack in the door.

"Shall I bring in the milk?"

"Oh do and sit down in the hall and I'll call Ruth." The hall was very dark; smelled of sleep and toothpaste and massagecream; across one corner a cot still bore the imprint of a body on its rumpled sheets. Straw hats, silk eveningwraps, and a couple of men's dress overcoats hung in a jostling tangle from the staghorns of the hatrack. Jimmy picked a corsetcover off a rockingchair and sat down. Women's voices, a subdued rustling of people dressing, Sunday newspaper noises seeped out through the partitions of the different rooms.

The bathroom door opened; a stream of sunlight reflected out of a pierglass cut the murky hall in half, out of it came a head of hair like copper wire, bluedark eyes in a brittlewhite eggshaped face. Then the hair was brown down the hall above a slim back in a tangerine-colored slip, nonchalant pink heels standing up out of the bathslippers at every step.

"Ou-ou, Jimmee . . ." Ruth was yodling at him from behind her door. "But you mustn't look at me or at my room." A head in curlpapers stuck out like a turtle's.

"Hullo Ruth."

"You can come in if you promise not to look. . . . I'm a sight and my room's a pigeon. . . . I've just got to do my hair. Then I'll be ready." The little gray room was stuffed with clothes and photographs of stage people. Jimmy stood with his back to the door, some sort of silky stuff that dangled from the hook tickling his ears.

"Well how's the cub reporter?"

"I'm on Hell's Kitchen. . . . It's swell. Got a job yet Ruth?"

"Um-um. . . . A couple of things may materialize during the week. But they wont. Oh Jimmy I'm getting desperate." She shook her hair loose of the crimpers and combed out the new mousybrown waves. She had a pale startled face with a big mouth and blue underlids. "This morning I knew I ought to be up and ready, but I just couldn't. It's so discouraging to get up when you haven't got a job. . . . Sometimes I think I'll go to bed and just stay there till the end of the world."

"Poor old Ruth."

She threw a powderpuff at him that covered his necktie and the lapels of his blue serge suit with powder. "Dont you poor old me you little rat."

"That's a nice thing to do after all the trouble I took to make myself look respectable. . . . Darn your hide Ruth. And the smell of the carbona not off me yet."

Ruth threw back her head with a shrieking laugh. "Oh you're so comical Jimmy. Try the whisk-broom."

Blushing he blew down his chin at his tie. "Who's the funnylooking girl opened the halldoor?"

"Shush you can hear everything through the partition. . . . That's Cassie," she whispered giggling. "Cassah-ndrah Wilkins . . . used to be with the Morgan Dancers. But we oughtnt to laugh at her, she's very nice. I'm very fond of her." She let out a whoop of laughter. "You nut Jimmy." She got to her feet and punched him in the muscle of the arm. "You always make me act like I was crazy."

"God did that. . . . No but look, I'm awfully hungry. I walked up."

"What time is it?"

"It's after one."

"Oh Jimmy I dont know what to do about time. . . . Like this hat? . . . Oh I forgot to tell you. I went to see Al Harrison yesterday. It was simply dreadful. . . . If I hadnt got to the phone in time and threatened to call the police. . . ."

"Look at that funny woman opposite. She's got a face exactly like a llama."

"It's on account of her I have to keep my shades drawn all the time . . ."

"Why?"

"Oh you're much too young to know. You'd be shocked Jimmy." Ruth was leaning close to the mirror running a stick of rouge between her lips.

"So many things shock me, I dont see that it matters much. . . . But come along let's get out of here. The sun's shining outside and people are coming out of church and going home to overeat and read at their Sunday papers among the rubberplants . . ."

"Oh Jimmy you're a shriek . . . Just one minute. Look out you're hooked onto my best shimmy."

A girl with short black hair in a yellow jumper was folding the sheets off the cot in the hall. For a second under the ambercolored powder and the rouge Jimmy did not recognize the face he had seen through the crack in the door.

"Hello Cassie, this is . . . Beg pardon, Miss Wilkins this is Mr. Herf. You tell him about the lady across the airshaft, you know Sappo the Monk."

Cassandra Wilkins lisped and pouted. "Isn't she dweadful Mr. Herf. . . . She says the dweadfullest things."

"She merely does it to annoy."

"Oh Mr. Herf I'm so pleased to meet you at last, Ruth does nothing but talk about you. . . . Oh I'm afwaid I was indiscweet to say that. . . . I'm dweadfully indiscweet."

The door across the hall opened and Jimmy found himself looking in the white face of a crookednosed man whose red hair rode in two unequal mounds on either side of a straight part. He wore a green satin bathrobe and red morocco slippers.

"What heow Cassahndrah?" he said in a careful Oxford drawl. "What prophecies today?"

"Nothing except a wire from Mrs. Fitzsimmons Green. She wants me to go to see her at Scarsdale tomorrow to talk about the Gweenery Theater. . . . Excuse me this is Mr. Herf, Mr. Oglethorpe." The redhaired man raised one eyebrow and lowered the other and put a limp hand in Jimmy's.

"Herf, Herf. . . . Let me see, it's not a Georgiah Herf? In Atlahnta there's an old family of Herfs. . . ."

"No I dont think so."

"Too bad. Once upon a time Josiah Herf and I were boon companions. Today he is the president of the First National Bank and leading citizen of Scranton Pennsylvahnia and I . . . a mere mountebank, a thing of rags and patches." When he shrugged his shoulders the bathrobe fell away exposing a flat smooth hairless chest.

"You see Mr. Oglethorpe and I are going to do the Song of Songs. He weads it and I interpwet it in dancing. You must come up and see us wehearse sometime."

"Thy navel is like a round goblet which wanteth not liquor, thy belly is like a heap of wheat set about with lilies . . ."

"Oh dont begin now." She tittered and pressed her legs together.

"Jojo close that door," came a quiet deep girl's voice from inside the room.

"Oh poo-er deah Elaine, she wants to sleep. . . . So glahd to have met you, Mr. Herf."

"Jojo!"

"Yes my deah. . . ."

Through the leaden drowse that cramped him the girl's voice set Jimmy tingling. He stood beside Cassie constrainedly without speaking in the dingydark hall. A smell of coffee and singeing toast seeped in from somewhere. Ruth came up behind them.

"All right Jimmy I'm ready. . . . I wonder if I've forgotten anything."

"I dont care whether you have or not, I'm starving." Jimmy took hold of her shoulders and pushed her gently towards the door. "It's two o'clock."

"Well goodby Cassie dear, I'll call you up at about six."

"All wight Wuthy . . . So pleased to have met you Mr. Herf." The door closed on Cassie's tittering lisp.

"Wow, Ruth that place gives me the infernal jimjams."

"Now Jimmy dont get peevish because you need food."

"But tell me Ruth, what the hell is Mr. Oglethorpe? He beats anything I ever saw."

"Oh did the Ogle come out of his lair?" Ruth let out a whoop of laughter. They came out into grimy sunlight. "Did he tell you he was the main brawnch, dontcher know, of the Oglethorpes of Georgiah?"

"Is that lovely girl with copper hair his wife?"

"Elaine Oglethorpe has reddish hair. She's not so darn lovely either. . . . She's just a kid and she's upstage as the deuce already. All because she made a kind of a hit in Peach Blossoms. You know one of these tiny exquisite bits everybody makes such a fuss over. She can act all right."

"It's a shame she's got that for a husband."

"Ogle's done everything in the world for her. If it hadnt been for him she'd still be in the chorus . . ."

"Beauty and the beast."

"You'd better look out if he sets his lamps on you Jimmy."

"Why?"

"Strange fish, Jimmy, strange fish."

An Elevated train shattered the barred sunlight overhead. He could see Ruth's mouth forming words.

"Look," he shouted above the diminishing clatter. "Let's go have brunch at the Campus and then go for a walk on the Palisades."

"You nut Jimmy what's brunch?"

"You'll eat breakfast and I'll eat lunch."

"It'll be a scream." Whooping with laughter she put her arm in his. Her silvernet bag knocked against his elbow as they walked.

"And what about Cassie, the mysterious Cassandra?"

"You mustn't laugh at her, she's a peach. . . . If only she wouldn't keep that horrid little white poodle. She keeps it in her room and it never gets any exercise and it smells something terrible. She has that little room next to mine. . . . Then she's got a steady . . ." Ruth giggled. "He's worse than the poodle. They're engaged and he borrows all her money away from her. For Heaven's sake dont tell anybody."

"I dont know anybody to tell."

"Then there's Mrs. Sunderland . . ."

"Oh yes I got a glimpse of her going into the bathroom—an old lady in a wadded dressing gown with a pink boudoir cap on."

"Jimmy you shock me. . . . She keeps losing her false teeth," began Ruth; an L train drowned out the rest. The restaurant door closing behind them choked off the roar of wheels on rails.

An orchestra was playing *When It's Appleblossom Time in Normandee*. The place was full of smokewrithing slants of sunlight, paper festoons, signs announcing LOBSTERS ARRIVE DAILY, EAT CLAMS NOW, TRY OUR DELICIOUS FRENCH STYLE STEAMED MUSSLES (Recommended by the Department of Agriculture). They sat down under a redlettered placard BEEFSTEAK PARTIES UPSTAIRS and Ruth made a pass at him with a breadstick. "Jimmy do you think it'd be immoral to eat scallops for breakfast? But first I've got to have coffee coffee coffee . . ."

"I'm going to eat a small steak and onions."

"Not if you're intending to spend the afternoon with me, Mr. Herf."

"Oh all right. Ruth I lay my onions at your feet."

"That doesn't mean I'm going to let you kiss me."

"What . . . on the Palisades?" Ruth's giggle broke into a whoop of laughter. Jimmy blushed crimson. "I never axed you maam, he say-ed."

Sunlight dripped in her face through the little holes in the brim of her straw hat. She was walking with brisk steps too short on account of her narrow skirt; through the thin china silk the sunlight tingled like a hand stroking her back. In the heavy heat streets, stores, people in Sunday clothes, strawhats, sunshades, surfacecars, taxis, broke and crinkled brightly about her grazing her with sharp cutting glints as if she were walking through piles of metalshavings. She was groping continually through a tangle of gritty sawedged brittle noise.

At Lincoln Square a girl rode slowly through the traffic on a white horse; chestnut hair hung down in even faky waves over the horse's chalky rump and over the giltedged saddlecloth where in green letters pointed with crimson, read DANDERINE. She had on a green Dolly Varden hat with a crimson plume; one hand in a white gauntlet nonchalantly jiggled at the reins, in the other wabbled a goldknobbed riding crop.

Ellen watched her pass; then she followed a smudge of green through a cross-street to the Park. A smell of trampled sunsinged grass came from boys playing baseball. All the shady benches were full of people. When she crossed the curving automobile road her sharp French heels sank into the asphalt. Two sailors were sprawling on a bench in the sun; one of them popped his lips as she passed, she could feel their seagreedy eyes cling stickily to her neck, her thighs, her ankles. She tried to keep her hips from swaying so much as she walked. The leaves were shriveled on the saplings along the path. South and east sunnyfaced buildings hemmed in the Park, to the west they were violet with shadow. Everything was itching sweaty dusty constrained by policemen and Sunday clothes. Why hadn't she taken the L? She was looking in the black eyes of a young man in a straw hat who was drawing up a red Stutz roadster to the curb. His eyes twinkled in hers, he jerked back his head smiling an upsidedown smile, pursing his lips so that they seemed to brush her cheek. He pulled the lever of the brake and opened the door with the other hand. She snapped her eyes away and walked on with her chin up. Two pigeons with metalgreen necks and feet of coral waddled out of her way. An old man was coaxing a squirrel to fish for peanuts in a paper bag.

All in green on a white stallion rode the Lady of the Lost Battalion. . . . Green, green, danderine . . . Godiva in the haughty mantle of her hair. . . .

General Sherman in gold interrupted her. She stopped a second to look at the Plaza that gleamed white as motherofpearl. . . . Yes this is Elaine Oglethorpe's apartment. . . . She climbed up onto a Washington Square bus. Sunday afternoon Fifth Avenue filed by rosily dustily jerkily. On the shady side there was an occasional man in a top hat and frock coat. Sunshades, summer dresses, straw hats were bright in the sun that glinted in squares on the upper windows of houses, lay in bright slivers on the hard paint of limousines and taxicabs. It smelled of gasoline and asphalt, of spearmint and talcumpowder and perfume from the couples that jiggled closer and closer together on the seats of the bus. In an occasional storewindow, paintings, maroon draperies, varnished antique chairs behind plate glass. The St. Regis.

Sherry's. The man beside her wore spats and lemon gloves, a floorwalker probably. As they passed St. Patrick's she caught a whiff of incense through the tall doors open into gloom. Delmonico's. In front of her the young man's arm was stealing round the narrow gray flannel back of the girl beside him.

"Jez ole Joe had rotten luck, he had to marry her. He's only nineteen."

"I suppose you would think it was hard luck."

"Myrtle I didn't mean us."

"I bet you did. An anyways have you ever seen the girl?"

"I bet it aint his."

"What?"

"The kid."

"Billy how dreadfully you do talk."

Fortysecond Street. Union League Club. "It was a most amusing gathering . . . most amusing. . . . Everybody was there. For once the speeches were delightful, made me think of old times," croaked a cultivated voice behind her ear. The Waldorf. "Aint them flags swell Billy. . . . That funny one is cause the Siamese ambassador is staying there. I read about it in the paper this morning."

When thou and I my love shall come to part, Then shall I press an ineffable last kiss Upon your lips and go . . . heart, start, who art . . . Bliss, this, miss . . . When thou . . . When you and I my love . . .

Eighth Street. She got down from the bus and went into the basement of the Brevoort. George sat waiting with his back to the door snapping and unsnapping the lock of his briefcase. "Well Elaine it's about time you turned up. . . . There aren't many people I'd sit waiting three quarters of an hour for."

"George you mustn't scold me; I've been having the time of my life. I haven't had such a good time in years. I've had the whole day all to myself and I walked all the way down from 105th Street to Fiftyninth through the Park. It was full of the most comical people."

"You must be tired." His lean face where the bright eyes were caught in a web of fine wrinkles kept pressing forward into hers like the prow of a steamship.

"I suppose you've been at the office all day George."

"Yes I've been digging out some cases. I cant rely on anyone else to do even routine work thoroughly, so I have to do it myself."

"Do you know I had it all decided you'd say that."

"What?"

"About waiting three quarters of an hour."

"Oh you know altogether too much Elaine. . . . Have some pastries with your tea?"

"Oh but I dont know anything about anything, that's the trouble. . . . I think I'll take lemon please."

Glasses clinked about them; through blue cigarettesmoke faces hats beards wagged, repeated greenish in the mirrors.

"But my de-e-ar it's always the same old complex. It may be true of men but it says nothing in regard to women," droned a woman's voice from the next table. . . . "Your feminism rises into an insuperable barrier," trailed a man's husky meticulous tones. "What if I am an egoist? God knows I've suffered for it." "Fire that purifies, Charley. . . ." George was speaking, trying to catch her eye. "How's the famous Jojo?"

"Oh let's not talk about him."

"The less said about him the better eh?"

"Now George I wont have you sneer at Jojo, for better or worse he is my husband, till divorce do us part. . . . No I wont have you laugh. You're too crude and simple to understand him anyway. Jojo's a very complicated rather tragic person."

"For God's sake dont let's talk about husbands and wives. The important thing, little Elaine, is that you and I are sitting here together without anyone to bother us. . . . Look when are we going to see each other again, really see each other, really. . . ."

"We're not going to be too real about this, are we George?" She laughed softly into her cup.

"Oh but I have so many things to say to you. I want to ask you so many things."

She looked at him laughing, balancing a small cherry tartlet that had one bite out of it between a pink squaretipped finger and thumb. "Is that the way you act when you've got some miserable sinner on the witnessbox? I thought it was more like: Where were you on the night of February thirtyfirst?"

"But I'm dead serious, that's what you cant understand, or wont."

A young man stood at the table, swaying a little, looking down at them. "Hello Stan, where the dickens did you come from?" Baldwin looked up at him without smiling. "Look Mr. Baldwin I know it's awful rude, but may I sit down at your table a second. There's somebody looking for me who I just cant meet. O God that mirror! Still they'd never look for me if they saw you."

"Miss Oglethorpe this is Stanwood Emery, the son of the senior partner in our firm."

"Oh it's so wonderful to meet you Miss Oglethorpe. I saw you last night, but you didn't see me."

"Did you go to the show?"

"I almost jumped over the foots I thought you were so wonderful."

He had a ruddy brown skin, anxious eyes rather near the bridge of a sharp fragillycut nose, a big mouth never still, wavy brown hair that stood straight up. Ellen looked from one to the other inwardly giggling. They were all three stiffening in their chairs.

"I saw the danderine lady this afternoon," she said. "She impressed me enormously. Just my idea of a great lady on a white horse."

"With rings on her finger and bells on her toes, And she shall make mischief wherever she goes." Stan rattled it off quickly under his breath.

"Music, isn't it?" put in Ellen laughing. "I always say mischief."

"Well how's college?" asked Baldwin in a dry uncordial voice.

"I guess it's still there," said Stan blushing. "I wish they'd burn it down before I got back." He got to his feet. "You must excuse me Mr. Baldwin. . . . My intrusion was infernally rude." As he turned leaning towards Ellen she smelled his grainy whiskey breath. "Please forgive it, Miss Oglethorpe."

She found herself holding out her hand; a dry skinny hand squeezed it hard. He strode out with swinging steps bumping into a waiter as he went.

"I cant make out that infernal young puppy," burst out Baldwin. "Poor old Emery's heartbroken about it. He's darn clever and has a lot of personality and all that sort of thing, but all he does is drink and raise Cain. . . . I guess all he needs is to go to work and get a sense of values. Too much money's what's the matter with most of those collegeboys. . . . Oh but Elaine thank God we're alone again. I have worked continuously all my life ever since I was fourteen. The time has come when I want to lay aside all that for a while. I want to live and travel and think and be happy. I cant stand the pace of downtown the way I used to. I want to learn to play, to ease off the tension. . . . That's where you come in."

"But I dont want to be the nigger on anybody's safetyvalve."
She laughed and let the lashes fall over her eyes.

"Let's go out to the country somewhere this evening. I've been stifling in the office all day. I hate Sunday anyway."

"But my rehearsal."

"You could be sick. I'll phone for a car."

"Golly there's Jojo. . . . Hello Jojo"; she waved her gloves above her head.

John Oglethorpe, his face powdered, his mouth arranged in a careful smile above his standup collar, advanced between the crowded tables, holding out his hands tightly squeezed into buff gloves with black stripes. "Heow deo you deo, my deah, this is indeed a surprise and a pleajah."

"You know each other, don't you? This is Mr. Baldwin."

"Forgive me if I intrude . . . er . . . upon a tête à tête."

"Nothing of the sort, sit down and we'll all have a highball. . . . I was just dying to see you really Jojo. . . . By the way if you havent anything else to do this evening you might slip in down front for a few minutes. I want to know what you think about my reading of the part. . . ."

"Certainly my deah, nothing could give me more pleajah."

His whole body tense George Baldwin leaned back with his hand clasped behind the back of his chair. "Waiter . . ." He broke his words off sharp like metal breaking. "Three Scotch highballs at once please."

Oglethorpe rested his chin on the silver ball of his cane. "Confidence, Mr. Baldwin," he began, "confidence between husband and wife is a very beautiful thing. Space and time have no effect on it. Were one of us to go to China for a thousand years it would not change our affection one tittle."

"You see George, what's the matter with Jojo is that he read too much Shakespeare in his youth. . . . But I've got to go or Merton will be bawling me out again. . . . Talk about industrial slavery. Jojo tell him about Equity."

Baldwin got to his feet. There was a slight flush on his cheekbones. "Wont you let me take you up to the theater," he said through clenched teeth.

"I never let anyone take me anywhere . . . And Jojo you must stay sober to see me act."

Fifth Avenue was pink and white under pink and white clouds in a fluttering wind that was fresh after the cloying talk and choke of tobaccosmoke and cocktails. She waved the taxistarter off merrily and smiled at him. Then she found a pair of anxious eyes looking into hers seriously out of a higharched brown face.

"I waited round to see you come out. Cant I take you somewhere? I've got my Ford round the corner. . . . Please."

"But I'm just going up to the theater. I've got a rehearsal."

"All right do let me take you there."

She began putting a glove on thoughtfully. "All right, but it's an awful imposition on you."

"That's fine. It's right round here. . . . It was awfully rude of me to butt in that way, wasn't it? But that's another story. . . . Anyway I've met you. The Ford's name is Dingo, but that's another story too. . . ."

"Still it's nice to meet somebody humanly young. There's nobody humanly young round New York."

His face was scarlet when he leaned to crank the car. "Oh I'm too damn young."

The motor sputtered, started with a roar. He jumped round and cut off the gas with a long hand. "We'll probably get arrested; my muffler's loose and liable to drop off."

At Thirtyfourth Street they passed a girl riding slowly through the traffic on a white horse; chestnut hair hung down in even faky waves over the horse's chalky rump and over the giltedged saddlecloth where in green letters pointed with crimson read DANDERINE.

"Rings on her fingers," chanted Stan pressing his buzzer, "And bells on her toes, And she shall cure dandruff wherever it grows."

Stephen Vincent Benét
(1898–1943)

*Born in Pennsylvania, the son of an army officer, and edu-
cated at Yale, Benét had published two books of poetry before
his graduation; his first novel,* The Beginning of Wisdom, *was
published in 1921. Many volumes of poetry followed, most notably the long narrative poems,* John Brown's Body *(1928) and*
Western Star *(1943), the latter left unfinished at his death. He
wrote novels of no great distinction, several opera librettos, and
a number of fine collections of stories, including* Johnny Pye and
the Fool-Killer *(1938),* Twenty-Five Short Stories *(1943), and a
two-volume* Selected Works *(1942), from volume two of which
"The King of the Cats" is taken.*

THE KING OF THE CATS

"But, my *dear*," said Mrs. Culverin, with a tiny gasp, "you
can't actually mean—a *tail!*"

Mrs. Dingle nodded impressively. "Exactly. I've seen him.
Twice. Paris, of course, and then, a command appearance at
Rome—we were in the Royal box. He conducted—my dear,
you've never heard such effects from an orchestra—and, my
dear," she hesitated slightly, "he conducted *with it*."

"How perfectly, fascinatingly too horrid for words!" said
Mrs. Culverin in a dazed but greedy voice. "We *must* have him
to dinner as soon as he comes over—he is coming over, isn't
he?"

"The twelfth," said Mrs. Dingle with a gleam in her eyes.
"The New Symphony people have asked him to be guest-conductor

for three special concerts—I do hope you can dine with *us* some night while he's here—he'll be very busy, of course—but he's promised to give us what time he can spare—"

"Oh, thank you, dear," said Mrs. Culverin, abstractedly, her last raid upon Mrs. Dingle's pet British novelist still fresh in her mind. "You're always so delightfully hospitable—but you mustn't wear yourself out—the rest of us must do *our* part—I know Henry and myself would be only too glad to—"

"That's very sweet of you, darling." Mrs. Dingle also remembered the larceny of the British novelist. "But we're just going to give Monsieur Tibault—sweet name, isn't it! They say he's descended from the Tybalt in 'Romeo and Juliet' and that's why he doesn't like Shakespeare—we're just going to give Monsieur Tibault the simplest sort of time—a little reception after his first concert, perhaps. He hates," she looked around the table, "large, mixed parties. And then, of course, his—er—little idiosyncrasy—" she coughed delicately. "It makes him feel a trifle shy with strangers."

"But I don't understand yet, Aunt Emily," said Tommy Brooks, Mrs. Dingle's nephew. "Do you really mean this Tibault bozo has a tail? Like a monkey and everything?"

"Tommy dear," said Mrs. Culverin, crushingly, "in the first place Monsieur Tibault is not a bozo—he is a very distinguished musician—the finest conductor in Europe. And in the second place—"

"He has," Mrs. Dingle was firm. "He has a tail. He conducts with it."

"Oh, but honestly!" said Tommy, his ears pinkening. "I mean—of course, if you say so, Aunt Emily, I'm sure he has—but still, it sounds pretty steep, if you know what I mean! How about it, Professor Tatto?"

Professor Tatto cleared his throat. "Tck," he said, putting his fingertips together cautiously, "I shall be very anxious to see this Monsieur Tibault. For myself, I have never observed a genuine specimen of *homo caudatus*, so I should be inclined to doubt, and yet . . . In the Middle Ages, for instance, the belief in men—er—tailed or with caudal appendages of some sort, was both widespread and, as far as we can gather, well-founded. As late as the Eighteenth Century, a Dutch sea-captain with some character for veracity recounts the discovery of a pair of such creatures in the island of Formosa. They were in a low state of civilization, I believe, but the appendages in question were quite distinct. And in 1860, Dr. Grimbrook, the English surgeon, claims to have treated no less than three African natives with

short but evident tails—though his testimony rests upon his
unsupported word. After all, the thing is not impossible, though
doubtless unusual. Web feet—rudimentary gills—these occur
with some frequency. The appendix we have with us always.
The chain of our descent from the ape-like form is by no means
complete. For that matter," he beamed around the table, "what
can we call the last few vertebrae of the normal spine but the
beginnings of a concealed and rudimentary tail? Oh, yes—yes—
it's possible—quite—that in an extraordinary case—a reversion
to type—a survival—though, of course—"

"I told you so," said Mrs. Dingle triumphantly. "*Isn't* it
fascinating? Isn't it, Princess?"

The Princess Vivrakanarda's eyes, blue as a field of larkspur,
fathomless as the centre of heaven, rested lightly for a moment
on Mrs. Dingle's excited countenance.

"Ve-ry fascinating," she said, in a voice like stroked, golden
velvet. "I should like—I should like ve-ry much to meet this
Monsieur Tibault."

"Well, *I* hope he breaks his neck!" said Tommy Brooks,
under his breath—but nobody ever paid much attention to Tommy.

Nevertheless as the time for Mr. Tibault's arrival in these
States drew nearer and nearer, people in general began to wonder
whether the Princess had spoken quite truthfully—for there was
no doubt of the fact that, up till then, she had been the unique
sensation of the season—and you know what social lions and
lionesses are.

It was, if you remember, a Siamese season, and genuine
Siamese were at quite as much of a premium as Russian accents
had been in the quaint old days when the Chauve-Souris was a
novelty. The Siamese Art Theatre, imported at terrific expense,
was playing to packed houses. "Gushuptzgu," an epic novel of
Siamese farm life, in nineteen closely-printed volumes, had just
been awarded the Nobel prize. Prominent pet-and-newt dealers
reported no cessation in the appalling demand for Siamese cats.
And upon the crest of this wave of interest in things Siamese, the
Princess Vivrakanarda poised with the elegant nonchalance of a
Hawaiian water-baby upon its surfboard. She was indispensable.
She was incomparable. She was everywhere.

Youthful, enormously wealthy, allied on one hand to the
Royal Family of Siam and on the other to the Cabots (and yet
with the first eighteen of her twenty-one years shrouded from
speculation in a golden zone of mystery), the mingling of races
in her had produced an exotic beauty as distinguished as it was
strange. She moved with a feline, effortless grace, and her skin

was as if it had been gently powdered with tiny grains of the purest gold—yet the blueness of her eyes, set just a trifle slantingly, was as pure and startling as the sea on the rocks of Maine. Her brown hair fell to her knees—she had been offered extraordinary sums by the Master Barbers' Protective Association to have it shingled. Straight as a waterfall tumbling over brown rocks, it had a vague perfume of sandalwood and suave spices and held tints of rust and the sun. She did not talk very much—but then she did not have to—her voice had an odd, small, melodious huskiness that haunted the mind. She lived alone and was reputed to be very lazy—at least it was known that she slept during most of the day—but at night she bloomed like a moon-flower and a depth came into her eyes.

It was no wonder that Tommy Brooks fell in love with her. The wonder was that she let him. There was nothing exotic or distinguished about Tommy—he was just one of those pleasant, normal young men who seem created to carry on the bond business by reading the newspapers in the University Club during most of the day, and can always be relied upon at night to fill an unexpected hole in a dinner-party. It is true that the Princess could hardly be said to do more than tolerate any of her suitors—no one had ever seen those aloofly arrogant eyes enliven at the entrance of any male. But she seemed to be able to tolerate Tommy a little more than the rest—and that young man's infatuated day-dreams were beginning to be beset by smart solitaires and imaginary apartments on Park Avenue, when the famous M. Tibault conducted his first concert at Carnegie Hall.

Tommy Brooks sat beside the Princess. The eyes he turned upon her were eyes of longing and love, but her face was as impassive as a mask, and the only remark she made during the preliminary bustlings was that there seemed to be a number of people in the audience. But Tommy was relieved, if anything, to find her even a little more aloof than usual, for, ever since Mrs. Culverin's dinner-party, a vague disquiet as to the possible impression which this Tibault creature might make upon her had been growing in his mind. It shows his devotion that he was present at all. To a man whose simple Princetonian nature found in "Just a Little Love, a Little Kiss," the quintessence of musical art, the average symphony was a positive torture, and he looked forward to the evening's programme itself with a grim, brave smile.

"Ssh!" said Mrs. Dingle, breathlessly. "He's coming!" It seemed to the startled Tommy as if he were suddenly back in the trenches under a heavy barrage, as M. Tibault made his entrance to a perfect bombardment of applause.

Then the enthusiastic noise was sliced off in the middle and a gasp took its place—a vast, windy sigh, as if every person in that multitude had suddenly said, "Ah." For the papers had not lied about him. The tail was there.

They called him theatric—but how well he understood the uses of theatricalism! Dressed in unrelieved black from head to foot (the black dress-shirt had been a special token of Mussolini's esteem), he did not walk on, he strolled, leisurely, easily, aloofly, the famous tail curled nonchalantly about one wrist—a suave, black panther lounging through a summer garden with that little mysterious wave of the head that panthers have when they pad behind bars—the glittering darkness of his eyes unmoved by any surprise or elation. He nodded, twice, in regal acknowledgment, as the clapping reached an apogee of frenzy. To Tommy there was something dreadfully reminiscent of the Princess in the way he nodded. Then he turned to his orchestra.

A second and louder gasp went up from the audience at this point, for, as he turned, the tip of that incredible tail twined with dainty carelessness into some hidden pocket and produced a black baton. But Tommy did not even notice. He was looking at the Princess instead.

She had not even bothered to clap, at first, but now—He had never seen her moved like this, never. She was not applauding, her hands were clenched in her lap, but her whole body was rigid, rigid as a steel bar, and the blue flowers of her eyes were bent upon the figure of M. Tibault in a terrible concentration. The pose of her entire figure was so still and intense that for an instant Tommy had the lunatic idea that any moment she might leap from her seat beside him as lightly as a moth, and land, with no sound, at M. Tibault's side to—yes—to rub her proud head against his coat in worship. Even Mrs. Dingle would notice in a moment.

"Princess—" he said, in a horrified whisper, "Princess—"

Slowly the tenseness of her body relaxed, her eyes veiled again, she grew clam.

"Yes, Tommy?" she said, in her usual voice, but there was still something about her . . .

"Nothing, only—oh, hang—he's starting!" said Tommy, as M. Tibault, his hands loosely clasped before him, turned and *faced* the audience. His eyes dropped, his tail switched once impressively, then gave three little preliminary taps with his baton on the floor.

* * *

Seldom has Gluck's overture to "Iphigenie in Aulis" received such an ovation. But it was not until the Eighth Symphony that the hysteria of the audience reached its climax. Never before had the New Symphony played so superbly—and certainly never before had it been led with such genius. Three prominent conductors in the audience were sobbing with the despairing admiration of envious children toward the close, and one at least was heard to offer wildly ten thousand dollars to a well-known facial surgeon there present for a shred of evidence that tails of some variety could by any stretch of science be grafted upon a normally decaudate form. There was no doubt about it—no mortal hand and arm, be they ever so dexterous, could combine the delicate élan and powerful grace displayed in every gesture of M. Tibault's tail.

A sable staff, it dominated the brasses like a flicker of black lightning; an ebon, elusive whip, it drew the last exquisite breath of melody from the woodwinds and ruled the stormy strings like a magician's rod. M. Tibault bowed and bowed again—roar after roar of frenzied admiration shook the hall to its foundations—and when he finally staggered, exhausted, from the platform, the president of the Wednesday Sonata Club was only restrained by force from flinging her ninety-thousand-dollar string of pearls after him in an excess of aesthetic appreciation. New York had come and seen—and New York was conquered. Mrs. Dingle was immediately besieged by reporters, and Tommy Brooks looked forward to the "little party" at which he was to meet the new hero of the hour with feelings only a little less lugubrious than those that would have come to him just before taking his seat in the electric seat.

The meeting between his Princess and M. Tibault was worse and better than he expected. Better because, after all, they did not say much to each other—and worse because it seemed to him, somehow, that some curious kinship of mind between them made words unnecessary. They were certainly the most distinguished-looking couple in the room, as he bent over her hand. "So darlingly foreign, both of them, and yet so different," babbled Mrs. Dingle—but Tommy couldn't agree.

They were different, yes—the dark, lithe stranger with the bizarre appendage tucked carelessly in his pocket, and the blue-eyed, brown-haired girl. But that difference only accentuated what they had in common—something in the way they moved, in the suavity of their gestures, in the set of their eyes. Something deeper, even, than race. He tried to puzzle it out—then, looking around at the others, he had a flash of revelation. It was as if that couple were foreign, indeed—not only to New York but to all common humanity. As if they were polite guests from a different star.

Tommy did not have a very happy evening, on the whole. But his mind worked slowly, and it was not until much later that the mad suspicion came upon him in full force.

Perhaps he is not to be blamed for his lack of immediate comprehension. The next few weeks were weeks of bewildered misery for him. It was not that the Princess's attitude toward him had changed—she was just as tolerant of him as before, but M. Tibault was always there. He had a faculty of appearing as out of thin air—he walked, for all his height, as lightly as a butterfly—and Tommy grew to hate that faintest shuffle on the carpet that announced his presence.

And then, hang it all, the man was so smooth, so infernally, unrufflably smooth! He was never out of temper, never embarrassed. He treated Tommy with the extreme of urbanity, and yet his eyes mocked, deep-down, and Tommy could do nothing. And, gradually, the Princess became more and more drawn to this stranger, in a soundless communion that found little need for speech—and that, too, Tommy saw and hated, and that, too, he could not mend.

He began to be haunted not only by M. Tibault in the flesh, but by M. Tibault in the spirit. He slept badly, and when he slept, he dreamed—of M. Tibault a man no longer, but a shadow, a spectre, the limber ghost of an animal whose words came purringly between sharp little pointed teeth. There was certainly something odd about the whole shape of the fellow—his fluid ease, the mould of his head, even the cut of his fingernails—but just what it was escaped Tommy's intensest cogitation. And when he did put his finger on it at length, at first he refused to believe.

A pair of petty incidents decided him, finally, against all reason. He had gone to Mrs. Dingle's, one winter afternoon, hoping to find the Princess. She was out with his aunt, but was expected back for tea, and he wandered idly into the library to wait. He was just about to switch on the lights, for the library was always dark even in summer, when he heard a sound of light breathing that seemed to come from the leather couch in the corner. He approached it cautiously and dimly made out the form of M. Tibault, curled up on the couch, peacefully asleep.

The sight annoyed Tommy so that he swore under his breath

and was back near the door on his way out, when the feeling we all know and hate, the feeling that eyes we cannot see are watching us, arrested him. He turned back—M. Tibault had not moved a muscle of his body to all appearance—but his eyes were open now. And those eyes were black and human no longer. They were green—Tommy could have sworn it—and he could have sworn that they had no bottom and gleamed like little emeralds in the dark. It only lasted a moment, for Tommy pressed the light-button automatically—and there was M. Tibault, his normal self, yawning a little but urbanely apologetic, but it gave Tommy time to think. Nor did what happened a trifle later increase his peace of mind.

They had lit a fire and were talking in front of it—by now Tommy hated M. Tibault so thoroughly that he felt that odd yearning for his company that often occurs in such cases. M. Tibault was telling some anecdote and Tommy was hating him worse than ever for basking with such obvious enjoyment in the heat of the flames and the ripple of his own voice.

Then they heard the street-door open, and M. Tibault jumped up—and jumping, caught one sock on a sharp corner of the brass fire-rail and tore it open in a jagged flap. Tommy looked down mechanically at the tear—a second's glance, but enough—for M. Tibault, for the first time in Tommy's experience, lost his temper completely. He swore violently in some spitting, foreign tongue—his face distorted suddenly—he clapped his hand over his sock. Then, glaring furiously at Tommy, he fairly sprang from the room, and Tommy could hear him scaling the stairs in long, agile bounds.

Tommy sank into a chair, careless for once of the fact that he heard the Princess's light laugh in the hall. He didn't want to see the Princess. He didn't want to see anybody. There had been something revealed when M. Tibault had torn that hole in his sock—and it was not the skin of a man. Tommy had caught a glimpse of—black plush. Black velvet. And then had come M. Tibault's sudden explosion of fury. Good *Lord*—did the man wear black velvet stockings under his ordinary socks? Or could he—could he—but here Tommy held his fevered head in his hands.

He went to Professor Tatto that evening with a series of hypothetical questions, but as he did not dare confide his real suspicions to the Professor, the hypothetical answers he received served only to confuse him the more. Then he thought of Billy Strange. Billy was a good sort, and his mind had a turn for the bizarre. Billy might be able to help.

He couldn't get hold of Billy for three days and lived through the interval in a fever of impatience. But finally they had dinner together at Billy's apartment, where his queer books were, and Tommy was able to blurt out the whole disordered jumble of his suspicions.

Billy listened without interrupting until Tommy was quite through. Then he pulled at his pipe. "But, my dear *man*—" he said, protestingly.

"Oh, I know—I know—" said Tommy, and waved his hands, "I know I'm crazy—you needn't tell me that—but I tell you, the man's a cat all the same—no, I don't see how he could be, but he is—why, hang it, in the first place, everybody knows he's got a tail!"

"Even so," said Billy, puffing. "Oh, my dear Tommy, I don't doubt you saw, or think you saw, everything you say. But, even so—" He shook his head.

"But what about those other birds, werewolves and things?" said Tommy.

Billy looked dubious. "We-ll," he admitted, "you've got me there, of course. At least—a tailed man *is* possible. And the yarns about werwolves go back far enough, so that—well, I wouldn't say there aren't or haven't been werwolves—but then I'm willing to believe more things than most people. But a wer-cat—or a man that's a cat and a cat that's a man—honestly, Tommy——"

"If I don't get some real advice I'll go clean off my hinge. For Heaven's sake, tell me something to *do*!"

"Lemme think," said Billy. "First, you're pizen-sure this man is——"

"A cat. Yeah," and Tommy nodded violently.

"Check. And second—if it doesn't hurt your feelings, Tommy—you're afraid this girl you're in love with has—er—at least a streak of—felinity—in her—and so she's drawn to him?"

"Oh, Lord, Billy, if I only knew!"

"Well—er—suppose she really is, too, you know—would you still be keen on her?"

"I'd marry her if she turned into a dragon every Wednesday!" said Tommy, fervently.

Billy smiled. "H'm," he said, "then the obvious thing to do is to get rid of this M. Tibault. Lemme think."

He thought about two pipes full, while Tommy sat on pins and needles. Then, finally, he burst out laughing.

"What's so darn funny?" said Tommy, aggrievedly.

"Nothing, Tommy, only I've just thought of a stunt—something so blooming crazy—but if he is—h'm—what you think he is—it *might* work——'' And, going to the bookcase, he took down a book.

"If you think you're going to quiet my nerves by reading me a bedtime story——"

"Shut up, Tommy, and listen to this—if you really want to get rid of your feline friend.''

"What is it?''

"Book of Agnes Repplier's. About cats. Listen.

" 'There is also a Scandinavian version of the ever famous story which Sir Walter Scott told to Washingon Irving, which Monk Lewis told to Shelley and which, in one form or another, we find embodied in the folklore of every land'—now, Tommy, pay attention—'the story of the traveller who saw within a ruined abbey, a procession of cats, lowering into a grave a little coffin with a crown upon it. Filled with horror, he hastened from the spot; but when he had reached his destination, he could not forbear relating to a friend the wonder he had seen. Scarcely had the tale been told when his friend's cat, who lay curled up tranquilly by the fire, sprang to its feet, cried out, "Then I am the King of the Cats!" and disappeared in a flash up the chimney.'

"Well?'' said Billy, shutting the book.

"By gum!'' said Tommy, staring. "By gum! Do you think there's a chance?''

"*I* think we're both in the booby-hatch. But if you want to try it——"

"Try it! I'll spring it on him the next time I see him. But—listen—I can't make it a ruined abbey——"

"Oh, use your imagination! Make it Central Park—anywhere. Tell it as if it happened to you—seeing the funeral procession and all that. You can lead into it somehow—let's see—some general line—oh, yes—'Strange, isn't it, how fact so often copies fiction. Why, only yesterday——' See?''

"Strange, isn't it, how fact so often copies fiction,'' repeated Tommy dutifully. "Why, only yesterday——"

"I happened to be strolling through Central Park when I saw something very odd.''

"I happened to be strolling through—here, gimme that book!'' said Tommy, "I want to learn the rest of it by heart!''

Mrs. Dingle's farewell dinner to the famous Monsieur Tibault, on the occasion of his departure for his Western tour, was looked forward to with the greatest expectations. Not only would everybody be there, including the Princess Vivrakanarda, but Mrs.

Dingle, a hinter if there ever was one, had let it be known that at this dinner an announcement of very unusual interest to Society might be made. So everyone, for once, was almost on time, except for Tommy. He was at least fifteen minutes early, for he wanted to have speech with his aunt alone. Unfortunately, however, he had hardly taken off his overcoat when she was whispering some news in his ear so rapidly that he found it difficult to understand a word of it.

"And you mustn't breathe it to a soul!" she ended, beaming. "That is, not before the announcement—I think we'll have *that* with the salad—people never pay very much attention to salad——"

"Breathe what, Aunt Emily?" said Tommy, confused.

"The Princess, darling—the dear Princess and Monsieur Tibault—they just got engaged this afternoon, dear things! Isn't it *fascinating*?"

"Yeah," said Tommy, and started to walk blindly through the nearest door. His aunt restrained him.

"Not there, dear—not in the library. You can congratulate them later. They're just having a sweet little moment alone there now——" And she turned away to harry the butler, leaving Tommy stunned.

But his chin came up after a moment. He wasn't beaten yet.

"Strange, isn't it, how often fact copies fiction?" he repeated to himself in dull mnemonics, and, as he did so, he shook his fist at the library door.

Mrs. Dingle was wrong, as usual. The Princess and M. Tibault were not in the library—they were in the conservatory, as Tommy discovered when he wandered aimlessly past the glass doors.

He didn't mean to look, and after a second he turned away. But that second was enough.

Tibault was seated in a chair and she was crouched on a stool at his side, while his hand, softly, smoothly, stroked her brown hair. Black cat and Siamese kitten. Her face was hidden from Tommy, but he could see Tibault's face. And he could hear.

They were not talking, but there was a sound between them. A warm and contented sound like the murmur of giant bees in a hollow tree—a golden, musical rumble, deep-throated, that came from Tibault's lips and was answered by hers—a golden purr.

Tommy found himself back in the drawing-room, shaking hands with Mrs. Culverin, who said, frankly, that she had seldom seen him look so pale.

The first two courses of the dinner passed Tommy like dreams, but Mrs. Dingle's cellar was notable, and by the middle of the meat course, he began to come to himself. He had only one resolve now.

For the next few moments he tried desperately to break into the conversation, but Mrs. Dingle was talking, and even Gabriel will have a time interrupting Mrs. Dingle. At last, though, she paused for breath and Tommy saw his chance.

"Speaking of that," said Tommy, piercingly, without knowing in the least what he was referring to, "Speaking of that——"

"As I was saying," said Professor Tatto. But Tommy would not yield. The plates were being taken away. It was time for salad.

"Speaking of that," he said again, so loudly and strangely that Mrs. Culverin jumped and an awkward hush fell over the table. "Strange, isn't it, how often fact copies fiction?" There, he was started. His voice rose even higher. "Why, only today I was strolling through——" and, word for word, he repeated his lesson. He could see Tibault's eyes glowing at him, as he described the funeral. He could see the Princess, tense.

He could not have said what he had expected might happen when he came to the end; but it was not bored silence, everywhere, to be followed by Mrs. Dingle's acrid, "Well, Tommy, is that *quite* all?"

He slumped back in his chair, sick at heart. He was a fool and his last resource had failed. Dimly he heard his aunt's voice, saying, "Well, then——" and realized that she was about to make the fatal announcement.

But just then Monsieur Tibault spoke.

"One moment, Mrs. Dingle," he said, with extreme politeness, and she was silent. He turned to Tommy.

"You are—positive, I suppose, of what you saw this afternoon, Brooks?" he said, in tones of light mockery.

"Absolutely," said Tommy sullenly. "Do you think I'd——"

"Oh, no, no, no," Monsieur Tibault waved the implication aside, "but—such an interesting story—one likes to be sure of the details—and, of course, you *are* sure—*quite* sure—that the kind of crown you describe was on the coffin?"

"Of course," said Tommy, wondering, "but——"

"Then I'm the King of the Cats!" cried Monsieur Tibault in a voice of thunder, and, even as he cried it, the house-lights blinked—there was the soft thud of an explosion that seemed muffled in cotton-wool from the minstrel gallery—and the scene was lit for a second by an obliterating and painful burst of light that vanished in an instant and was succeeded by heavy, blinding clouds of white, pungent smoke.

"Oh, those *horrid* photographers," came Mrs. Dingle's voice in a melodious wail. "I *told* them not to take the flashlight picture till dinner was over, and now they've taken it *just* as I was nibbling lettuce!"

Someone tittered a little nervously. Someone coughed. Then, gradually the veils of smoke dislimned and the green-and-black spots in front of Tommy's eyes died away.

They were blinking at each other like people who have just come out of a cave into brilliant sun. Even yet their eyes stung with the fierceness of that abrupt illumination and Tommy found it hard to make out the faces across the table from him.

Mrs. Dingle took command of the half-blinded company with her accustomed poise. She rose, glass in hand. "And now, dear friends," she said in a clear voice, "I'm sure all of us are very happy to——" Then she stopped, open-mouthed, an expression of incredulous horror on her features. The lifted glass began to spill its contents on the tablecloth in a little stream of amber. As she spoke, she had turned directly to Monsieur Tibault's place at the table—and Monsieur Tibault was no longer there.

Some say there was a bursting flash of fire that disappeared up the chimney—some say it was a giant cat that leaped through the window at a bound, without breaking the glass. Professor Tatto puts it down to a mysterious chemical disturbance operating only over M. Tibault's chair. The butler, who is pious, believes the devil in person flew away with him, and Mrs. Dingle hesitates between witchcraft and a malicious ectoplasm dematerializing on the wrong cosmic plane. But be that as it may, one thing is certain—in the instant of fictive darkness which followed the glare of the flashlight, Monsieur Tibault, the great conductor, disappeared forever from mortal sight, tail and all.

Mrs. Culverin swears he was an international burglar and that she was just about to unmask him, when he slipped away under cover of the flashlight smoke, but no one else who sat at that historic dinner-table believes her. No, there are no sound explanations, but Tommy thinks he knows, and he will never be able to pass a cat again without wondering.

Mrs. Tommy is quite of her husband's mind regarding cats—she was Gretchen Woolwine, of Chicago—for Tommy told her his whole story, and while she doesn't believe a great deal of it, there is no doubt in her heart that one person concerned in the affair was a *perfect* cat. Doubtless it would have been more romantic to relate how Tommy's daring finally won him his Princess—but, unfortunately, it would not be veracious. For the Princess Vivrakananda, also, is with us no longer. Her nerves, shattered by the spectacular denouement of Mrs. Dingle's dinner, required a sea-voyage, and from that voyage she has never returned to America.

Of course, there are the usual stories—one hears of her, a nun in a Siamese convent, or a masked dancer at Le Jardin de ma Soeur—one hears that she has been murdered in Patagonia or married in Trebizond—but, as far as can be ascertained, not one of these gaudy fables has the slightest basis of fact. I believe that Tommy, in his heart of hearts, is quite convinced that the sea-voyage was only a pretext, and that by some unheard-of means, she has managed to rejoin the formidable Monsieur Tibault, wherever in the world of the visible or the invisible he may be—in fact, that in some ruined city or subterranean palace they reign together now, King and Queen of all the mysterious Kingdom of Cats. But that, of course, is quite impossible.

Willa Cather
(1873–1947)

Born in Virginia but raised in Nebraska, Cather graduated from the University of Nebraska in 1895 and began a career as a school teacher. Beginning as a sometime journalist, she became first a full-time editor (for McClure's, 1906-1912) and, after 1912, a full-time writer. Her first collection of stories, The Troll Garden, *appeared in 1905; her first novel,* Alexander's Bridge, *was published in 1912, followed by* O Pioneers! *(1913),* The Song of the Lark *(1915),* My Antonia *(1918), and thereafter by such books as* Death Comes for the Archbishop *(1927) and* Sapphira and the Slave Girl *(1940). Her collections of stories include* Obscure Destinies *(1932), from which "Neighbour Rosicky" is taken, and the posthumous* The Old Beauty and Others *(1948). She also published poetry and, in 1936,* Not Under Forty, *a volume of literary essays.*

NEIGHBOUR ROSICKY

I

When Doctor Burleigh told neighbour Rosicky he had a bad heart, Rosicky protested.

"So? No, I guess my heart was always pretty good. I got a little asthma, maybe. Just a awful short breath when I was pitchin' hay last summer, dat's all."

"Well now, Rosicky, if you know more about it than I do, what did you come to me for? It's your heart that makes you short of breath, I tell you. You're sixty-five years old, and you've always worked hard, and your heart's tired. You've got to be careful from now on, and you can't do heavy work any more. You've got five boys at home to do it for you.''

The old farmer looked up at the Doctor with a gleam of amusement in his queer triangular-shaped eyes. His eyes were large and lively, but the lids were caught up in the middle in a curious way, so that they formed a triangle. He did not look like a sick man. His brown face was creased but not wrinkled, he had a ruddy colour in his smooth-shaven cheeks and in his lips, under his long brown moustache. His hair was thin and ragged around his ears, but very little grey. His forehead, naturally high and crossed by deep parallel lines, now ran all the way up to his pointed crown. Rosicky's face had the habit of looking interested, —suggested a contented disposition and a reflective quality that was gay rather than grave. This gave him a certain detachment, the easy manner of an onlooker and observer.

''Well, I guess you ain't got no pills fur a bad heart, Doctor Ed. I guess the only thing is fur me to git me a new one.''

Doctor Burleigh swung round in his desk-chair and frowned at the old farmer. ''I think if I were you I'd take a little care of the old one, Rosicky.''

Rosicky shrugged. ''Maybe I don't know how. I expect you mean fur me not to drink my coffee no more.''

''I wouldn't, in your place. But you'll do as you choose about that. I've never yet been able to separate a Bohemian from his coffee or his pipe. I've quit trying. But the sure thing is you've got to cut out farm work. You can feed the stock and do chores about the barn, but you can't do anything in the fields that makes you short of breath.''

''How about shelling corn?''
''Of course not!''

Old tradition of Rosicky — phyiscal labor

Rosicky considered with puckered brows.

''I can't make my heart go no longer'n it wants to, can I, Doctor Ed?''

''I think it's good for five or six years yet, maybe more, if you'll take the strain off it. Sit around the house and help Mary. If I had a good wife like yours, I'd want to stay around the house.''

His patient chuckled. ''It ain't no place fur a man. I don't like no old man hanging round the kitchen too much. An' my wife, she's a awful hard worker her own self.''

''That's it; you can help her a little. My Lord, Rosicky, you are one of the few men I know who has a family he can get some comfort out of; happy dispositions, never quarrel among themselves, and they treat you right. I want to see you live a few years and enjoy them.''

"Oh, they're good kids, all right," Rosicky assented.

The Doctor wrote him a prescription and asked him how his oldest son, Rudolph, who had married in the spring, was getting on. Rudolph had struck out for himself, on rented land. "And how's Polly? I was afraid Mary mightn't like an American daughter-in-law, but it seems to be working out all right."

"Yes, she's a fine girl. Dat widder woman bring her daughters up very nice. Polly got lots of spunk, an' she got some style, too. Da's nice, for young folks to have some style." Rosicky inclined his head gallantly. His voice and his twinkly smile were an affectionate compliment to his daughter-in-law.

"It looks like a storm, and you'd better be getting home before it comes. In town in the car?" Doctor Burleigh rose.

"No, I'm in de wagon. When you got five boys, you ain't got much chance to ride round in de Ford. I ain't much for cars, noway."

"Well, it's a good road out to your place; but I don't want you bumping around in a wagon much. And never again on a hay-rake, remember!''

Rosicky placed the Doctor's fee delicately behind the desk-telephone, looking the other way, as if this were an absent-minded gesture. He put on his plush cap and his corduroy jacket with a sheepskin collar, and went out.

The Doctor picked up his stethoscope and frowned at it as if he were seriously annoyed with the instrument. He wished it had been telling tales about some other man's heart, some old man who didn't look the Doctor in the eye so knowingly, or hold out such a warm brown hand when he said good-bye. Doctor Burleigh had been a poor boy in the country before he went away to medical school; he had known Rosicky almost ever since he could remember, and he had a deep affection for Mrs. Rosicky.

Only last winter he had had such a good breakfast at Rosicky's, and that when he needed it. He had been out all night on a long, hard confinement case at Tom Marshall's,—a big rich farm where there was plenty of stock and plenty of feed and a great deal of expensive farm machinery of the newest model, and no comfort whatever. The woman had too many children and too much work, and she was no manager. When the baby was born at last, and handed over to the assisting neighbour woman, and the mother was properly attended to, Burleigh refused any breakfast in that slovenly house, and drove his buggy—the snow was too deep for a car—eight miles to Anton Rosicky's place. He

FLASHBACK

didn't know another farm-house where a man could get such a warm welcome, and such good strong coffee with rich cream. No wonder the old chap didn't want to give up his coffee!

He had driven in just when the boys had come back from the barn and were washing up for breakfast. The long table, covered with a bright oilcloth, was set out with dishes waiting for them, and the warm kitchen was full of the smell of coffee and hot biscuit and sausage. Five big handsome boys, running from twenty to twelve, all with what Burleigh called natural good manners,—they hadn't a bit of the painful self-consciousness he himself had to struggle with when he was a lad. One ran to put his horse away, another helped him off with his fur coat and hung it up, and Josephine, the youngest child and the only daughter, quickly set another place under her mother's direction.

With Mary, to feed creatures was the natural expression of affection,—her chickens, the calves, her big hungry boys. It was a rare pleasure to feed a young man whom she seldom saw and of whom she was as proud as if he belonged to her. Some country housekeepers would have stopped to spread a white cloth over the oilcloth, to change the thick cups and plates for their best china, and the wooden-handled knives for plated ones. But not Mary.

"You must take us as you find us, Doctor Ed. I'd be glad to put out my good things for you if you was expected, but I'm glad to get you any way at all."

He knew she was glad,—she threw back her head and spoke out as if she were announcing him to the whole prairie. Rosicky hadn't said anything at all; he merely smiled his twinkling smile, put some more coal on the fire, and went into his own room to pour the Doctor a little drink in a medicine glass. When they were all seated, he watched his wife's face from his end of the table and spoke to her in Czech. Then, with the instinct of politeness which seldom failed him, he turned to the Doctor and said shyly; "I was just tellin' her not to ask you no questions about Mrs. Marshall till you eat some breakfast. My wife, she's terrible fur to ask questions."

The boys laughed, and so did Mary. She watched the Doctor devour her biscuit and sausage, too much excited to eat anything herself. She drank her coffee and sat taking in everything about her visitor. She had known him when he was a poor country boy, and was boastfully proud of his success, always saying: "What do people go to Omaha for, to see a doctor, when we got the best one in the State right here?" If Mary liked people at all, she felt physical pleasure in the sight of them, personal exultation in any good fortune that came to them. Burleigh didn't know many women like that, but he knew she was like that.

When his hunger was satisfied, he did, of course, have to tell them about Mrs. Marshall and he noticed what a friendly interest the boys took in the matter.

Rudolph, the oldest one (he was still living at home then), said: "The last time I was over there, she was lifting them big heavy milkcans, and I knew she oughtn't to be doing it."

"Yes, Rudolph told me about that when he come home, and I said it wasn't right," Mary put in warmly. "It was all right for me to do them things up to the last, for I was terrible strong, but that woman's weakly. And do you think she'll be able to nurse it, Ed?" She sometimes forgot to give him the title she was so proud of. "And to think of your being up all night and then not able to get a decent breakfast! I don't know what's the matter with such people."

"Why, Mother," said one of the boys, "if Doctor Ed had got breakfast there, we wouldn't have him here. So you ought to be glad."

"He knows I'm glad to have him, John, any time. But I'm sorry for that poor woman, how bad she'll feel the Doctor had to go away in the cold without his breakfast."

"I wish I'd been in practice when these were getting born." The doctor looked down the row of close-clipped heads. "I missed some good breakfasts by not being."

The boys began to laugh at their mother because she flushed so red, but she stood her ground and threw up her head. "I don't care, you wouldn't have got away from this house without breakfast. No doctor ever did. I'd have had something ready fixed that Anton could warm up for you."

The boys laughed harder than ever, and exclaimed at her: "I'll bet you would!" "She would, that!"

"Father, did you get breakfast for the doctor when we were born?"

"Yes, and he used to bring me my breakfast, too, mighty nice. I was always awful hungry!" Mary admitted with a guilty laugh.

While the boys were getting the Doctor's horse, he went to the window to examine the house plants. "What do you do to your geraniums to keep them blooming all winter, Mary? I never pass this house that from the road I don't see your windows full of flowers."

She snapped off a dark red one, and a ruffled new green leaf, and put them in his buttonhole. "There, that looks better. You look too solemn for a young man, Ed. Why don't you git married? I'm worried about you. Settin' at breakfast, I looked at you real hard, and I seen you've got some grey hairs already."

"Oh, yes! They're coming. Maybe they'd come faster if I married."

"Don't talk so. You'll ruin your health eating at the hotel. I could send your wife a nice loaf of nut bread, if you only had one. I don't like to see a young man getting grey. I'll tell you something, Ed; you make some strong black tea and keep it handy in a bowl, and every morning just brush it into your hair, an' it'll keep the grey from showin' much. That's the way I do!"

FLASHBACK ENDS

Sometimes the Doctor heard the gossipers [*money*] in the drug-store wondering why Rosicky didn't get on faster. He was industrious, and so were his boys, but they were rather free and easy, weren't pushers, and they didn't always show good judgment. They were comfortable, they were out of debt, but they didn't get much ahead. Maybe, Doctor Burleigh reflected, people as generous and warmhearted and affectionate as the Rosickys never got ahead much; you couldn't enjoy your life and put it into the bank, too.

Rosicky's not concerned w/ money
Rosicky's enjoyment

II

When Rosicky left Doctor Burleigh's office he went into the farm-implement store to light his pipe and put on his glasses and read over the list Mary had given him. Then he went into the general merchandise place next door and stood about until the pretty girl with the plucked eyebrows, who always waited on him, was free. Those eyebrows, two thin India-ink strokes, amused him, because he remembered how they used to be. Rosicky always prolonged his shopping by a little joking; the girl knew the old fellow admired her, and she liked to chaff with him.

"Seems to me about every other week you buy ticking, Mr. Rosicky, and always the best quality," she remarked as she measured off the heavy bolt with red stripes.

"You see, my wife is always makin' goose-fedder pillows, an' de thin stuff don't hold in dem little down-fedders."

"You must have lots of pillows at your house."

"Sure. She makes quilts of dem, too. We sleeps easy. Now she's makin' a fedder quilt for my son's wife. You know Polly, that married my Rudolph. How much my bill, Miss Pearl?"

"Eight eighty-five."

"Chust make it nine, and put in some candy fur de women."

"As usual. I never did see a man buy so much candy for his wife. First thing you know, she'll be getting too fat."

"I'd like dat. I ain't much fur all dem slim women like what de style is now."

"That's one for me, I suppose, Mr. Bohunk!" Pearl sniffed and elevated her India-ink strokes.

When Rosicky went out to his wagon, it was beginning to snow,—the first snow of the season, and he was glad to see it. He rattled out of town and along the highway through a wonderfully rich stretch of country, the finest farms in the county. He admired this High Prairie, as it was called, and always liked to drive through it. His own place lay in a rougher territory, where there was some clay in the soil and it was not so productive. When he bought his land, he hadn't the money to buy on High Prairie; so he told his boys, when they grumbled, that if their land hadn't some clay in it, they wouldn't own it at all. All the same, he enjoyed looking at these fine farms, as he enjoyed looking at a prize bull.

After he had gone eight miles, he came to the graveyard, which lay just at the edge of his own hay-land. There he stopped his horses and sat still on his wagon seat, looking about at the snowfall. Over yonder on the hill he could see his own house, crouching low, with the clump of orchard behind and the windmill before, and all down the gentle hill-slope the rows of pale gold cornstalks stood out against the white field. The snow was falling over the cornfield and the pasture and the hay-land, steadily, with very little wind,—a nice dry snow. The graveyard had only a light wire fence about it and was all overgrown with long red grass. The fine snow, settling into this red grass and upon the few little evergreens and the headstones, looked very pretty.

It was a nice graveyard, Rosicky reflected, sort of snug and homelike, not cramped or mournful,—a big sweep all round it. A man could lie down in the long grass and see the complete arch of the sky over him, hear the wagons go by; in summer the mowing-machine rattled right up to the wire fence. And it was so near home. Over there across the cornstalks his own roof and windmill looked so good to him that he promised himself to mind the Doctor and take care of himself. He was awful fond of his place, he admitted. He wasn't anxious to leave it. And it was a comfort to think that he would never have to go farther than the edge of his own hayfield. The snow, falling over his barnyard and the graveyard, seemed to draw things together, like. And they were all old neighbours in the graveyard, most of them friends; there was nothing to feel awkward or embarrassed about. Embarrassment was the most disagreeable feeling Rosicky knew. He didn't often have it,—only with certain people whom he didn't understand at all.

Well, it was a nice snowstorm; a fine sight to see the snow falling so quietly and graciously over so much open country. On his cap and shoulders, on the horses' backs and manes, light, delicate, mysterious it fell; and with it a dry cool fragrance was released into the air. It meant rest for vegetation and men and beasts, for the ground itself; a season of long nights for sleep, leisurely breakfasts, peace by the fire. This and much more went through Rosicky's mind, but he merely told himself that winter was coming, clucked to his horses, and drove on.

When he reached home, John, the youngest boy, ran out to put away his team for him, and he met Mary coming up from the outside cellar with her apron full of carrots. They went into the house together. On the table, covered with oilcloth figured with clusters of blue grapes, a place was set, and he smelled hot coffeecake of some kind. Anton never lunched in town; he thought that extravagant, and anyhow he didn't like the food. So Mary always had something ready for him when he got home.

After he was settled in his chair, stirring his coffee in a big cup, Mary took out of the oven a pan of *kolache* stuffed with apricots, examined them anxiously to see whether they had got too dry, put them beside his plate, and then sat down opposite him.

Rosicky asked her in Czech if she wasn't going to have any coffee.

She replied in English, as being somehow the right language for transacting business: "Now what did Doctor Ed say, Anton? You tell me just what?"

"He said I was to tell you some compliments, but I forgot 'em." Rosicky's eyes twinkled.

"About you, I mean. What did he say about your asthma?"

"He says I ain't got no asthma." Rosicky took one of the little rolls in his broad brown fingers. The thickened nail of his right thumb told the story of his past.

"Well, what is the matter? And don't try to put me off."

"He don't say nothing much, only I'm a little older, and my heart ain't so good like it used to be."

Mary started and brushed her hair back from her temples with both hands as if she were a little out of her mind. From the way she glared, she might have been in a rage with him.

"He says there's something the matter with your heart? Doctor Ed says so?"

"Now don't yell at me like I was a hog in de garden, Mary. You know I always did like to hear a woman talk soft. He didn't say anything de matter wid my heart, only it ain't so young like it used to be, an' he tell me not to pitch hay or run de corn-sheller."

Mary wanted to jump up, but she sat still. She admired the way he never under any circumstances raised his voice or spoke roughly. He was city-bred, and she was country-bred; she often said she wanted her boys to have their papa's nice ways.

"You never have no pain there, do you? It's your breathing and your stomach that's been wrong. I wouldn't believe nobody but Doctor Ed about it. I guess I'll go see him myself. Didn't he give you no advice?"

"Chust to take it easy like, an' stay round de house dis winter. I guess you got some carpenter work for me to do. I kin make some new shelves for you, and I want dis long time to build a closet in de boys' room and make dem two little fellers keep dere clo'es hung up."

Rosicky drank his coffee from time to time, while he considered. His moustache was of the soft long variety and came down over his mouth like the teeth of a buggy-rake over a bundle of hay. Each time he put down his cup, he ran his blue handkerchief over his lips. When he took a drink of water, he managed very neatly with the back of his hand.

Mary sat watching him intently, trying to find any change in his face. It is hard to see anyone who has become like your own body to you. Yes, his hair had got thin, and his high forehead had deep lines running from left to right. But his neck, always clean shaved except in the busiest seasons, was not loose or baggy. It was burned a dark reddish brown, and there were deep creases in it, but it looked firm and full of blood. His cheeks had a good colour. On either side of his mouth there was a half-moon down the length of his cheek, not wrinkles, but two lines that had come there from his habitual expression. He was shorter and broader than when she married him; his back had grown broad and curved, a good deal like the shell of an old turtle, and his arms and legs were short.

He was fifteen years older than Mary, but she had hardly ever thought about it before. He was her man, and the kind of man she liked. She was rough, and he was gentle,—city-bred, as she always said. They had been shipmates on a rough voyage and had stood by each other in trying times. Life had gone well with

metaphor - believed in same
ideas

Want to enjoy life—not skimpy

them because, at bottom, they had the same ideas about life. They agreed, without discussion, as to what was most important and what was secondary. They didn't often exchange opinions, even in Czech,—it was as if they had thought the same thought together. A good deal had to be sacrificed and thrown overboard in a hard life like theirs, and they had never disagreed as to the things that could go. It had been a hard life, and a soft life, too. There wasn't anything brutal in the short, broad-backed man with the three-cornered eyes and the forehead that went on to the top of his skull. He was a city man, a gentle man, and though he had married a rough farm girl, he had never touched her without gentleness.

They had been at one accord not to hurry through life, not to be always skimping and saving. They saw their neighbours buy more land and feed more stock than they did, without discontent. Once when the creamery agent came to the Rosickys to persuade them to sell him their cream, he told them how much money the Fasslers, their nearest neighbours, had made on their cream last year.

"Yes," said Mary, "and look at them Fassler children! Pale, pinched little things, they look like skimmed milk. I'd rather put some colour into my children's faces than put money into the bank."

The agent shrugged and turned to Anton.

"I guess we'll do like she says," said Rosicky.

III

Mary very soon got into town to see Doctor Ed, and then she had a talk with her boys and set a guard over Rosicky. Even John, the youngest, had his father on his mind. If Rosicky went to throw hay down from the loft, one of the boys ran up the ladder and took the fork from him. He sometimes complained that though he was getting to be an old man, he wasn't an old woman yet.

That winter he stayed in the house in the afternoons and carpentered, or sat in the chair between the window full of plants and the wooden bench where the two pails of drinking-water stood. This spot was called "Father's corner," though it was not a corner at all. He had a shelf there, where he kept his Bohemian papers and his pipes and tobacco, and his shears and needles and thread and tailor's thimble. Having been a tailor in his youth, he couldn't bear to see a woman patching at his clothes, or at the boys'. He liked tailoring, and always patched all the overalls and jackets and work shirts. Occasionally he made over a pair of pants one of the older boys had outgrown, for the little fellow.

While he sewed, he let his mind run back over his life. He had a good deal to remember, really; life in three countries. The only part of his youth he didn't like to remember was the two years he had spent in London, in Cheapside, working for a German tailor who was wretchedly poor. Those days, when he was nearly always hungry, when his clothes were dropping off him for dirt, and the sound of a strange language kept him in continual bewilderment, had left a sore spot in his mind that wouldn't bear touching.

He was twenty when he landed at Castle Garden in New York, and he had a protector who got him work in a tailor shop in Vesey Street, down near the Washington Market. He looked upon that part of his life as very happy. He became a good workman, he was industrious, and his wages were increased from time to time. He minded his own business and envied nobody's good fortune. He went to night school and learned to read English. He often did overtime work and was well paid for it, but somehow he never saved anything. He couldn't refuse a loan to a friend, and he was self-indulgent. He liked a good dinner, and a little went for beer, a little for tobacco; a good deal went to the girls. He often stood through an opera on Saturday nights; he could get standing-room for a dollar. Those were the great days of opera in New York, and it gave a fellow something to think about for the rest of the week. Rosicky had a quick ear, and a childish love of all the stage splendour; the scenery, the costumes, the ballet. He usually went with a chum, and after the performance they had beer and maybe some oysters somewhere. It was a fine life; for the first five years or so it satisfied him completely. He was never hungry or cold or dirty, and everything amused him; a fire, a dog fight, a parade, a storm, a ferry ride. He thought New York the finest, richest, friendliest city in the world. Rosicky enjoys

Moreover, he had what he called a happy home life. Very near the tailor shop was a small furniture-factory, where an old Austrian, Loeffler, employed a few skilled men and made unusual furniture, most of it to order, for the rich German housewives up-town. The top floor of Loeffler's five-storey factory was a loft, where he kept his choice lumber and stored the odd pieces of furniture left on his hands. One of the young workmen he employed was a Czech, and he and Rosicky became fast friends. They persuaded Loeffler to let them have a sleeping-room in one corner of the loft. They bought good beds and bedding and had their pick of the furniture kept up there. The loft was low-pitched, but light and airy, full of windows, and good-smelling by reason of the fine lumber put up there to season. Old Loeffler used to go down to the docks and buy wood from South America and the East from the sea captains. The young men were as foolish about their house as a bridal pair. Zichec, the young cabinet-maker, devised every sort of convenience, and Rosicky kept their clothes in order. At night and on Sundays, when the quiver of machinery underneath was still, it was the quietest place in the world, and on summer nights all the sea winds blew in. Zichec often practised on his flute in the evening. They were both fond of music and went to the opera together. Rosicky thought he wanted to live like that for ever.

But as the years passed, all alike, he began to get a little restless. When spring came round, he would begin to feel fretted, and he got to drinking. He was likely to drink too much of a Saturday night. On Sunday he was languid and heavy, getting over his spree. On Monday he plunged into work again. So he never had time to figure out what ailed him, though he knew something did. When the grass turned green in Park Place, and the lilac hedge at the back of Trinity churchyard put out its blossoms, he was tormented by a longing to run away. That was why he drank too much; to get a temporary illusion of freedom and wide horizons.

Rosicky, the old Rosicky, could remember as if it were yesterday the day when the young Rosicky found out what was the matter with him. It was on a Fourth of July afternoon, and he was sitting in Park Place in the sun. The lower part of New York was empty. Wall Street, Liberty Street, Broadway, all empty. So much stone and asphalt with nothing going on, so many empty windows. The emptiness was intense, like the stillness in a great factory when the machinery stops and the belts and bands cease running. It was too great a change, it took all the strength out of one. Those blank buildings, without the stream of life pouring through them, were like empty jails. It struck young Rosicky that this was the trouble with big cities; they built you in from the earth itself, cemented you away from any contact with the ground. You lived in an unnatural world, like the fish in an aquarium, who were probably much more comfortable than they ever were in the sea.

On that very day he began to think seriously about the articles he had read in the Bohemian papers, describing prosperous Czech farming communities in the West. He believed he would like to go out there as a farm hand; it was hardly possible that he could ever have land of his own. His people had always been workmen; his father and grandfather had worked in shops. His mother's parents had lived in the country, but they rented their farm and had a hard time to get along. Nobody in his family had ever owned any land,—that belonged to a different station of life altogether. Anton's mother died when he was little, and he was sent into the country to her parents. He stayed with them until he was twelve, and formed those ties with the earth and the farm animals and growing things which are never made at all unless they are made early. After his grandfather died, he went back to live with his father and stepmother, but she was very hard on him, and his father helped him to get passage to London.

After that Fourth of July day in Park Place, the desire to return to the country never left him. To work on another man's farm would be all he asked; to see the sun rise and set and to plant things and watch them grow. He was a very simple man. He was like a tree that has not many roots, but one tap-root that goes down deep. He subscribed for a Bohemian paper printed in Chicago, then for one printed in Omaha. His mind got farther and farther west. He began to save a little money to buy his liberty. When he was thirty-five, there was a great meeting in New York of Bohemian athletic societies, and Rosicky left the tailor shop and went home with the Omaha delegates to try his fortune in another part of the world.

IV

Perhaps the fact that his own youth was well over before he began to have a family was one reason why Rosicky was so fond of his boys. He had almost a grandfather's indulgence for them. He had never had to worry about any of them—except, just now, a little about Rudolph.

On Saturday night the boys always piled into the Ford, took little Josephine, and went to town to the moving-picture show. One Saturday morning they were talking at the breakfast table about starting early that evening, so that they would have an hour or so to see the Christmas things in the stores before the show began. Rosicky looked down the table.

"I hope you boys ain't disappointed, but I want you to let me have de car tonight. Maybe some of you can go in with de neighbours."

Their faces fell. They worked hard all week, and they were still like children. A new jack-knife or a box of candy pleased the older ones as much as the little fellow.

"If you and Mother are going to town," Frank said, "maybe you could take a couple of us along with you, anyway."

"No, I want to take de car down to Rudolph's, and let him an' Polly go in to de show. She don't git into town enough, an' I'm afraid she's gettin' lonesome, an' he can't afford no car yet."

That settled it. The boys were a good deal dashed. Their father took another piece of apple-cake and went on: "Maybe next Saturday night de two little fellers can go along wid dem."

"Oh, is Rudolph going to have the car every Saturday night?" Rosicky did not reply at once; then he began to speak seriously:

"Listen, boys; Polly ain't lookin' so good. I don't like to see nobody lookin' sad. It comes hard fur a town girl to be a farmer's wife. I don't want no trouble to start in Rudolph's family. When it starts, it ain't so easy to stop. An American girl don't git used to our ways all at once. I like to tell Polly she and Rudolph can have the car every Saturday night till after New Year's, if it's all right with you boys."

"Sure it's all right, Papa," Mary cut in. "And it's good you thought about that. Town girls is used to more than country girls. I lay awake nights, scared she'll make Rudloph discontented with the farm."

The boys put as good a face on it as they could. They surely looked forward to their Saturday nights in town. That evening Rosicky drove the car the half-mile down to Rudloph's new, bare little house.

Polly was in a short-sleeved gingham dress, clearing away the supper dishes. She was a trim, slim little thing, with blue eyes and shingled yellow hair, and her eyebrows were reduced to a mere brush-stroke, like Miss Pearl's.

"Good evening, Mr. Rosicky. Rudolph's at the barn, I guess." She never called him father, or Mary mother. She was sensitive about having married a foreigner. She never in the world would have done it if Rudolph hadn't been such a handsome, persuasive fellow and such a gallant lover. He had graduated in her class in the high school in town, and their friendship began in the ninth grade.

Rosicky went in, though he wasn't exactly asked. "My boys ain't goin' to town tonight, an' I brought de car over fur you two to go in to de picture show."

Polly, carrying dishes to the sink, looked over her shoulder at him. "Thank you. But I'm late with my work tonight, and pretty tired. Maybe Rudolph would like to go in with you."

"Oh, I don't go to de shows! I'm too old-fashioned. You won't feel so tired after you ride in de air a ways. It's a nice clear night, an' it ain't cold. You go an' fix yourself up, Polly, an' I'll wash de dishes an' leave everything nice fur you.''

Polly blushed and tossed her bob. ''I couldn't let you do that, Mr. Rosicky. I wouldn't think of it.''

Rosicky said nothing. He found a bib apron on a nail behind the kitchen door. He slipped it over his head and then took Polly by her two elbows and pushed her gently toward the door of her own room. ''I washed up de kitchen many times for my wife, when de babies was sick or somethin'. You go an' make yourself look nice. I like you to look prettier'n any of dem town girls when you go in. De young folks must have some fun, an' I'm goin' to look out fur you, Polly.''

That kind, reassuring grip on her elbows, the old man's funny bright eyes, made Polly want to drop her head on his shoulder for a second. She restrained herself, but she lingered in his grasp at the door of her room, murmuring tearfully: ''You always lived in the city when you were young, didn't you? Don't you ever get lonesome out here?''

As she turned round to him, her hand fell naturally into his, and he stood holding it and smiling into her face with his peculiar, knowing, indulgent smile without a shadow of reproach in it. ''Dem big cities is all right fur de rich, but dey is terrible hard fur de poor.''

''I don't know. Sometimes I think I'd like to take a chance. You lived in New York, didn't you?''

''An' London. Da's bigger still. I learned my trade dere. Here's Rudolph comin', you better hurry.''

''Will you tell me about London some time?''

''Maybe. Only I ain't no talker, Polly. Run an' dress yourself up.''

The bedroom door closed behind her, and Rudolph came in from the outside, looking anxious. He had seen the car and was sorry any of his family should come just then. Supper hadn't been a very pleasant occasion. Halting in the doorway, he saw his father in a kitchen apron, carrying dishes to the sink. He flushed crimson and something flashed in his eye. Rosicky held up a warning finger.

''I brought de car over fur you an' Polly to go to de picture show, an' I made her let me finish here so you won't be late. You go put on a clean shirt, quick!''

''But don't the boys want the car, Father?''

''Not tonight dey don't.'' Rosicky fumbled under his apron and found his pants pocket. He took out a silver dollar and said in a hurried whisper: ''You go an' buy dat girl some ice cream an' candy tonight, like you was courtin'. She's awful good friends wid me.''

Rudolph was very short of cash, but he took the money as if it hurt him. There had been a crop failure all over the country. He had more than once been sorry he'd married this year.

In a few minutes the young people came out, looking clean and a little stiff. Rosicky hurried them off, and then he took his own time with the dishes. He scoured the pots and pans and put away the milk and swept the kitchen. He put some coal in the stove and shut off the draughts, so the place would be warm for them when they got home late at night. Then he sat down and had a pipe and listened to the clock tick.

Generally speaking, marrying an American girl was certainly a risk. A Czech should marry a Czech. It was lucky that Polly was the daughter of a poor widow woman; Rudolph was proud, and if she had a prosperous family to throw up at him, they could never make it go. Polly was one of four sisters, and they all worked; one was book-keeper in the bank, one taught music, and Polly and her younger sister had been clerks, like Miss Pearl. All four of them were musical, had pretty voices, and sang in the Methodist choir, which the eldest sister directed.

Polly missed the sociability of a store position. She missed the choir, and the company of her sisters. She didn't dislike housework, but she disliked so much of it. Rosicky was a little anxious about this pair. He was afraid Polly would grow so discontented that Rudy would quit the farm and take a factory job in Omaha. He had worked for a winter up there, two years ago, to get money to marry on. He had done very well, and they would always take him back at the stockyards. But to Rosicky that meant the end of everything for his son. To be a landless man was to be a wage-earner, a slave, all your life; to have nothing, to be nothing.

Rosicky thought he would come over and do a little carpentering for Polly after the New Year. He guessed she needed jollying. Rudolph was a serious sort of chap, serious in love and serious about his work.

Rosicky shook out his pipe and walked home across the fields. Ahead of him the lamplight shone from his kitchen windows. Suppose he were still in a tailor shop on Vesey Street, with a bunch of pale, narrow-chested sons working on machines, all coming home tired and sullen to eat supper in a kitchen that was a parlour also; with another crowded, angry family quarrelling just across the dumbwaiter shaft, and squeaking pulleys at the windows where dirty washings hung on dirty lines above a court full of old brooms and mops and ash-cans. . . .

He stopped by the windmill to look up at the frosty winter stars and draw a long breath before he went inside. That kitchen with the shining windows was dear to him; but the sleeping fields and bright stars and the noble darkness were dearer still.

V

On the day before Christmas the weather set in very cold; no snow, but a bitter, biting wind that whistled and sang over the flat land and lashed one's face like fine wires. There was baking going on in the Rosicky kitchen all day, and Rosicky sat inside, making over a coat that Albert had outgrown into an overcoat for John. Mary had a big red geranium in bloom for Christmas, and a row of Jerusalem cherry trees, full of berries. It was the first year she had ever grown these; Doctor Ed brought her the seeds from Omaha when he went to some medical convention. They reminded Rosicky of plants he had seen in England; and all afternoon, as he stitched, he sat thinking about those two years in London, which his mind usually shrank from even after all this while.

He was a lad of eighteen when he dropped down into London, with no money and no connexions except the address of a cousin who was supposed to be working at a confectioner's. When he went to the pastry shop, however, he found that the cousin had gone to America. Anton tramped the streets for several days, sleeping in doorways and on the Embankment, until he was in utter despair. He knew no English, and the sound of the strange language all about him confused him. By chance he met a poor German tailor who had learned his trade in Vienna, and could speak a little Czech. This tailor, Lifschnitz, kept a repair shop in a Cheapside basement, underneath a cobbler. He didn't much need an apprentice, but he was sorry for the boy and took him in for no wages but his keep and what he could pick up. The pickings were supposed to be coppers given you when you took work home to a customer. But most of the customers called for their clothes themselves, and the coppers that came Anton's way were very few. He had, however, a place to sleep. The tailor's family lived upstairs in three rooms; a kitchen, a bedroom, where Lifschnitz and his wife and five children slept, and a living-room. Two corners of this living-room were curtained off for lodgers; in one Rosicky slept on an old horsehair sofa, with a feather quilt to wrap himself in. The other corner was rented to a wretched, dirty boy, who was studying the violin. He actually practised there. Rosicky was dirty, too. There was no way to be anything else. Mrs. Lifschnitz got the water she cooked and washed with from a pump in a brick court, four flights down. There were bugs in the place, and multitudes of fleas, though the poor woman did the best she could. Rosicky knew she often went empty to give another potato or a spoonful of dripping to the two hungry, sad-eyed boys who lodged with her. He used to think he would never get out of there, never get a clean shirt on his back again. What would he do, he wondered, when his clothes actually dropped to pieces and the worn cloth wouldn't hold patches any longer?

It was still early when the old farmer put aside his sewing and his recollections. The sky had been a dark grey all day, with not a gleam of sun, and the light failed at four o'clock. He went to shave and change his shirt while the turkey was roasting. Rudolph and Polly were coming over for supper.

After supper they sat around in the kitchen, and the younger boys were saying how sorry they were it hadn't snowed. Everybody was sorry. They wanted a deep snow that would lie long and keep the wheat warm, and leave the ground soaked when it melted.

"Yes, sir!" Rudolph broke out fiercely; "if we have another dry year like last year, there's going to be hard times in this country."

Rosicky filled his pipe. "You boys don't know what hard times is. You don't owe nobody, you got plenty to eat an' keep warm, an' plenty water to keep clean. When you got them, you can't have it very hard."

Rudolph frowned, opened and shut his big right hand, and dropped it clenched upon his knee. "I've got to have a good deal more than that, Father, or I'll quit this farming gamble. I can always make good wages railroading, or at the packing house, and be sure of my money."

"Maybe so," his father answered dryly.

Mary, who had just come in from the pantry and was wiping her hands on the roller towel, thought Rudy and his father were getting too serious. She brought her darning-basket and sat down in the middle of the group.

"I ain't much afraid of hard times, Rudy," she said heartily. "We've had a plenty, but we've always come through. Your father wouldn't never take nothing very hard, not even hard times. I got a mind to tell you a story on him. Maybe you boys can't hardly remember the year we had that terrible hot wind, that burned everything up on the Fourth of July? All the corn an'

the gardens. An' that was in the days when we didn't have
alfalfa yet,—I guess it wasn't invented.

"Well, that very day your father was out cultivatin' corn, and
I was here in the kitchen makin' plum preserves. We had bushels
of plums that year. I noticed it was terrible hot, but it's always
hot in the kitchen when you're preservin', an' I was too busy
with my plums to mind. Anton come in from the field about
three o'clock, an' I asked him what was the matter.

" 'Nothin',' he says, 'but it's pretty hot, an' I think I won't
work no more today.' He stood round for a few minutes, an'
then he says: 'Ain't you near through? I want you should git up a
nice supper for us tonight. It's Fourth of July.'

"I told him to git along, that I was right in the middle of
preservin', but the plums would taste good on hot biscuit. 'I'm
goin' to have fried chicken, too,' he says, and he went off an'
killed a couple. You three oldest boys was little fellers, playin'
round outside, real hot an' sweaty, an' your father took you to
the horse tank down by the windmill an' took off your clothes
an' put you in. Them two box-elder trees was little then, but they
made shade over the tank. Then he took off all his own clothes,
an' got in with you. While he was playin' in the water with you,
the Methodist preacher drove into our place to say how all the
neighbours was goin' to meet at the schoolhouse that night, to
pray for rain. He drove right to the windmill, of course, and
there was your father and you three with no clothes on. I was in
the kitchen door, an' I had to laugh, for the preacher acted like
he ain't never seen a naked man before. He surely was
embarrassed, an' your father couldn't git to his clothes; they was
all hangin' up on the windmill to let the sweat dry out of 'em. So
he laid in the tank where he was, an' put one of you boys on top
of him to cover him up a little, an' talked to the preacher.

"When you got through playin' in the water, he put clean
clothes on you and a clean shirt on himself, an' by that time I'd
begun to get supper. He says: 'It's too hot in here to eat
comfortable. Let's have a picnic in the orchard. We'll eat our
supper behind the mulberry hedge, under them linden trees.'

"So he carried our supper down, an' a bottle of my wild-grape
wine, an' everything tasted good, I can tell you. The wind got
cooler as the sun was goin' down, and it turned out pleasant,
only I noticed how the leaves was curled up on the linden trees.
That made me think, an' I asked your father if that hot wind all
day hadn't been terrible hard on the gardens an' the corn.

" 'Corn,' he says, 'there ain't no corn.'

" 'What you talkin' about?' I said. 'Ain't we got forty acres?'

" 'We ain't got an ear,' he says, 'nor nobody else ain't got none. All the corn in this country was cooked by three o'clock today, like you'd roasted it in an oven.'

" 'You mean you won't get no crop at all?' I asked him. I couldn't believe it, after he'd worked so hard.

" 'No crop this year,' he says. 'That's why we're havin' a picnic. We might as well enjoy what we got.'

"An' that's how your father behaved, when all the neighbours was so discouraged they couldn't look you in the face. An' we enjoyed ourselves that year, poor as we was, an' our neighbours wasn't a bit better off for bein' miserable. Some of 'em grieved till they got poor digestions and couldn't relish what they did have."

The younger boys said they thought their father had the best of it. But Rudolph was thinking that, all the same, the neighbours had managed to get ahead more, in the fifteen years since that time. There must be something wrong about his father's way of doing things. He wished he knew what was going on in the back of Polly's mind. He knew she liked his father, but he knew, too, that she was afraid of something. When his mother sent over coffee-cake or prune tarts or a loaf of fresh bread, Polly seemed to regard them with a certain suspicion. When she observed to him that his brothers had nice manners, her tone implied that it was remarkable they should have. With his mother she was stiff and on her guard. Mary's hearty frankness and gusts of good humour irritated her. Polly was afraid of being unusual or conspicuous in any way, of being "ordinary," as she said!

When Mary had finished her story, Rosicky laid aside his pipe.

"You boys like me to tell you about some of dem hard times I been through in London?" Warmly encouraged, he sat rubbing his forehead along the deep creases. It was bothersome to tell a long story in English (he nearly always talked to the boys in Czech), but he wanted Polly to hear this one.

"Well, you know about dat tailor shop I worked in in London? I had one Christmas dere I ain't never forgot. Times was awful bad before Christmas; de boss ain't got much work, an' have it awful hard to pay his rent. It ain't so much fun, bein' poor in a big city like London, I'll say! All de windows is full of good t'ings to eat, an' all de pushcarts in de streets is full, an' you smell 'em all de time, an' you ain't got no money,—not a damn bit. I didn't mind de cold so much, though I didn't have no overcoat, chust a short jacket I'd outgrowed so it wouldn't meet on me, an' my hands was chapped raw. But I always had a good appetite, like you all know, an' de sight of dem pork pies in de windows was awful fur me!

"Day before Christmas was terrible foggy dat year, an' dat fog gits into your bones and makes you all damp like. Mrs. Lifschnitz didn't give us nothin' but a little bread an' drippin' for supper, because she was savin' to try for to give us a good dinner on Christmas Day. After supper de boss say I can go an' enjoy myself, so I went into de streets to listen to de Christmas singers. Dey sing old songs an' make very nice music, an' I run round after dem a good ways, till I got awful hungry. I t'ink maybe if I go home, I can sleep till morning an' forgit my belly.

"I went into my corner real quiet, and roll up in my fedder quilt. But I ain't got my head down, till I smell somet'ing good. Seem like it git stronger an' stronger, an' I can't git to sleep noway. I can't understand dat smell. Dere was a gas light in a hall across de court, dat always shine in at my window a little. I got up an' look round. I got a little wooden box in my corner fur a stool, 'cause I ain't got no chair. I picks up dat box, and under it dere is a roast goose on a platter! I can't believe my eyes. I carry it to de window where de light comes in, an' touch it and smell it to find out, an' den I taste it to be sure. I say, I will eat chust one little bite of dat goose, so I can go to sleep, and tomorrow I won't eat none at all. But I tell you, boys, when I stop, one half of dat goose was gone!"

The narrator bowed his head, and the boys shouted. But little Josephine slipped behind his chair and kissed him on the neck beneath his ear.

"Poor little Papa, I don't want him to be hungry!"

"Da's long ago, child. I ain't never been hungry since I had your mudder to cook fur me."

"Go on and tell us the rest, please," said Polly.

"Well, when I come to realize what I done, of course, I felt terrible. I felt better in de stomach, but very bad in de heart. I set on my bed wid dat platter on my knees, an' it all come to me; how hard dat poor woman save to buy dat goose, and how she get some neighbour to cook it dat got more fire, an' how she put it in my corner to keep it away from dem hungry children. Dey was a old carpet hung up to shut my corner off, an' de children wasn't allowed to go in dere. An' I know she put it in my corner because she trust me more'n she did de violin boy. I can't stand it to face her after I spoil de Christmas. So I put on my shoes and go out into de city. I tell myself I better throw myself in de river; but I guess I ain't dat kind of a boy.

"It was after twelve o'clock, an' terrible cold, an' I start out to walk about London all night. I walk along de river awhile, but dey was lots of drunks all along; men, and women too. I chust move along to keep away from de police. I git onto de Strand, an' den over to New Oxford Street, where dere was a big German restaurant on de ground floor, wid big windows all fixed up fine, an' I could see de people havin' parties inside. While I was lookin' in, two men and two ladies come out, laughin' and talkin' and feelin' happy about all dey been eatin' and drinkin', and dey was speakin' Czech,—not like de Austrians, but like de home folks talk it.

"I guess I went crazy, an' I done what I ain't never done before nor since. I went right up to dem gay people an' begun to beg dem: 'Fellow-countrymen, for God's sake give me money enough to buy a goose!'

"Dey laugh, of course, but de ladies speak awful kind to me, an' dey take me back into de restaurant and give me hot coffee and cakes, an' make me tell all about how I happened to come to London, an' what I was doin' dere. Dey take my name and where I work down on paper, an' both of dem ladies give me ten shillings.

"De big market at Covent Garden ain't very far away, an' by dat time it was open. I go dere an' buy a big goose an' some pork pies, an' potatoes and onions, an' cakes an' oranges fur de children,—all I could carry! When I git home, everybody is still asleep. I pile all I bought on de kitchen table, an' go in an' lay down on my bed, an' I ain't waken up till I hear dat woman scream when she come out into her kitchen. My goodness, but she was surprise! She laugh an' cry at de same time, an' hug me and waken all de children. She ain't stop fur no breakfast; she git de Christmas dinner ready dat morning, and we all sit down an' eat all we can hold. I ain't never seen dat violin boy have all he can hold before.

"Two three days after dat, de two men come to hunt me up, an' dey ask my boss, and he give me a good report an' tell dem I was a steady boy all right. One of dem Bohemians was very smart an' run a Bohemian newspaper in New York, an' de odder was a rich man, in de importing business, an' dey been travelling togedder. Dey told me how t'ings was easier in New York, an' offered to pay my passage when dey was goin' home soon on a boat. My boss say to me: 'You go. You ain't got no chance here, an' I like to see you git ahead, fur you always been a good boy to my woman, and fur dat fine Christmas dinner you give us all.' An' da's how I got to New York."

That night when Rudolph and Polly, arm in arm, were running home across the fields with the bitter wind at their backs, his heart leaped for joy when she said she thought they might have his family come over for supper on New Year's Eve. "Let's get up a nice supper, and not let your mother help at all; make her be company for once." *[handwritten: Polly's expression of gratitud]*

"That would be lovely of you, Polly," he said humbly. He was a very simple, modest boy, and he, too, felt vaguely that Polly and her sisters were more experienced and worldly than his people.

VI

The winter turned out badly for farmers. It was bitterly cold, and after the first light snows before Christmas there was no snow at all,—and no rain. March was as bitter as February. On those days when the wind fairly punished the country, Rosicky sat by his window. In the fall he and the boys had put in a big wheat planting, and now the seed had frozen in the ground. All that land would have to be ploughed up and planted over again, planted in corn. It had happened before, but he was younger then, and he never worried about what had to be. He was sure of himself and of Mary; he knew they could bear what they had to bear, that they would always pull through somehow. But he was not so sure about the young ones, and he felt troubled because Rudolph and Polly were having such a hard start.

Sitting beside his flowering window while the panes rattled and the wind blew in under the door, Rosicky gave himself to reflection as he had not done since those Sundays in the loft of the furniture-factory in New York, long ago. Then he was trying to find what he wanted in life for himself; now he was trying to find what he wanted for his boys, and why it was he so hungered to feel sure they would be here, working this very land, after he was gone.

They would have to work hard on the farm, and probably they would never do much more than make a living. But if he could think of them as staying here on the land, he wouldn't have to fear any great unkindness for them. Hardships, certainly; it was a hardship to have the wheat freeze in the ground when seed was so high; and to have to sell your stock because you had no feed. But there would be other years when everything came along right, and you caught up. And what you had was your own. You didn't have to choose between bosses and strikers, and go wrong either way. You didn't have to do with dishonest and cruel people. They were the only things in his experience he had found terrifying and horrible; the look in the eyes of a dishonest and crafty man, of a scheming and rapacious woman.

In the country, if you had a mean neighbour, you could keep off his land and make him keep off yours. But in the city, all the foulness and misery and brutality of your neighbours was part of your life. The worst things he had come upon in his journey through the world were human,—depraved and poisonous specimens of man. To this day he could recall certain terrible faces in the London streets. There were mean people everywhere, to be sure, even in their own country town here. But they weren't tempered, hardened, sharpened, like the treacherous people in cities who live by grinding or cheating or poisoning their fellowmen. He had helped to bury two of his fellow-workmen in the tailoring trade, and he was distrustful of the organized industries that see one out of the world in big cities. Here, if you were sick, you had Doctor Ed to look after you; and if you died, fat Mr. Haycock, the kindest man in the world, buried you.

It seemed to Rosicky that for good, honest boys like his, the worst they could do on the farm was better than the best they would be likely to do in the city. If he'd had a mean boy, now, one who was crooked and sharp and tried to put anything over on his brothers, then town would be the place for him. But he had no such boy. As for Rudolph, the discontented one, he would give the shirt off his back to anyone who touched his heart. What Rosicky really hoped for his boys was that they could get through the world without ever knowing much about the cruelty of human beings. "Their mother and me ain't prepared them for that," he sometimes said to himself.

These thoughts brought him back to a grateful consideration of his own case. What an escape he had had, to be sure! He, too, in his time, had had to take money for repair work from the hand of a hungry child who let it go so wistfully; because it was money due his boss. And now, in all these years, he had never had to take a cent from anyone in bitter need,—never had to look at the face of a woman become like a wolf's from struggle and famine. When he thought of these things, Rosicky would put on his cap and jacket and slip down to the barn and give his work-horses a little extra oats, letting them eat it out of his hand in their slobbery fashion. It was his way of expressing what he felt, and made him chuckle with pleasure.

The spring came warm, with blue skies,—but dry, dry as a bone. The boys began ploughing up the wheat-fields to plant them over in corn. Rosicky would stand at the fence corner and watch them, and the earth was so dry it blew up in clouds of brown dust that hid the horses and the sulky plough and the driver. It was a bad outlook.

The big alfalfa-field that lay between the home place and Rudolph's came up green, but Rosicky was worried because during that open windy winter a great many Russian thistle plants had blown in there and lodged. He kept asking the boys to rake them out; he was afraid their seed would root and "take the alfalfa." Rudolph said that was nonsense. The boys were working so hard planting corn, their father felt he couldn't insist about the thistles, but he set great store by that big alfalfa field. It was a feed you could depend on,—and there was some deeper reason, vague, but strong. The peculiar green of that clover woke early memories in old Rosicky, went back to something in his childhood in the old world. When he was a little boy, he had played in fields of that strong blue-green colour.

One morning, when Rudolph had gone to town in the car, leaving a workteam idle in his barn, Rosicky went over to his son's place, put the horses to the buggy-rake, and set about quietly raking up those thistles. He behaved with guilty caution, and rather enjoyed stealing a march on Doctor Ed, who was just then taking his first vacation in seven years of practice and was attending a clinic in Chicago. Rosicky got the thistles raked up, but did not stop to burn them. That would take some time, and his breath was pretty short, so he thought he had better get the horses back to the barn.

He got them into the barn and to their stalls, but the pain had come on so sharp in his chest that he didn't try to take the harness off. He started for the house, bending lower with every step. The cramp in his chest was shutting him up like a jack-knife. When he reached the windmill, he swayed and caught at the ladder. He saw Polly coming down the hill, running with the swiftness of a slim greyhound. In a flash she had her shoulder under his armpit.

"Lean on me, Father, hard! Don't be afraid. We can get to the house all right."

Somehow they did, though Rosicky became blind with pain; he could keep on his legs, but he couldn't steer his course. The next thing he was conscious of was lying on Polly's bed, and Polly bending over him wringing out bath towels in hot water and putting them on his chest. She stopped only to throw coal into the stove, and she kept the tea-kettle and the black pot going. She put these hot applications on him for nearly an hour, she told him afterwards, and all that time he was drawn up stiff and blue, with the sweat pouring off him.

As the pain gradually loosed its grip, the stiffness went out of his jaws, the black circles round his eyes disappeared, and a little of his natural colour came back. When his daughter-in-law buttoned his shirt over his chest at last, he sighed.

"Da's fine, de way I feel now, Polly. It was a awful bad spell, an' I was so sorry it all come on you like it did."

Polly was flushed and excited. "Is the pain really gone? Can I leave you long enough to telephone over to your place?"

Rosicky's eyelids fluttered. "Don't telephone, Polly. It ain't no use to scare my wife. It's nice and quiet here, an' if I ain't too much trouble to you, just let me lay still till I fell like myself. I ain't got no pain now. It's nice here."

Polly bent over him and wiped the moisture from his face. "Oh, I'm so glad it's over!" she broke out impulsively. "It just broke my heart to see you suffer so, Father."

Rosicky motioned her to sit down on the chair where the teakettle had been, and looked up at her with that lively affectionate gleam in his eyes. "You was awful good to me, I won't never forget dat. I hate it to be sick on you like dis. Down at de barn I say to myself, dat young girl ain't had much experience in sickness, I don't want to scare her, an' maybe she's got a baby comin' or somet'ing."

Polly took his hand. He was looking at her so intently and affectionately and confidingly; his eyes seemed to caress her face, to regard it with pleasure. She frowned with her funny streaks of eyebrows, and then smiled back at him.

"I guess maybe there is something of that kind going to happen. But I haven't told anyone yet, not my mother or Rudolph. You'll be the first to know."

His hands pressed hers. She noticed that it was warm again. The twinkle in his yellow-brown eyes seemed to come nearer.

"I like mighty well to see dat little child, Polly," was all he said. Then he closed his eyes and lay half-smiling. But Polly sat still, thinking hard. She had a sudden feeling that nobody in the world, not her mother, not Rudolph, or anyone, really loved her as much as old Rosicky did. It perplexed her. She sat frowning and trying to puzzle it out. It was as if Rosicky had a special gift for loving people, something that was like an ear for music or an eye for colour. It was quiet, unobtrusive; it was merely there. You saw it in his eyes,—perhaps that was why they were merry. You felt it in his hands, too. After he dropped off to sleep, she sat holding his warm, broad, flexible brown hand. She had never

514   *Willa Cather*

seen another in the least like it. She wondered if it wasn't a kind
of gypsy hand, it was so alive and quick and light in its
communications,—very strange in a farmer. Nearly all the farmers she knew had huge lumps of fists, like mauls, or they were
knotty and bony and uncomfortable-looking, with stiff fingers.
But Rosicky's was like quicksilver, flexible, muscular, about the
colour of a pale cigar, with deep, deep creases across the palm.
It wasn't nervous, it wasn't a stupid lump; it was a warm brown
human hand, with some cleverness in it, a great deal of generosity,
and something else which Polly could only call "gypsy-like,"
—something nimble and lively and sure, in the way that animals are.

Polly remembered that hour long afterwards; it had been like
an awakening to her. It seemed to her that she had never learned
so much about life from anything as from old Rosicky's hand. It
brought her to herself; it communicated some direct and untrans-
latable message.

When she heard Rudolph coming in the car, she ran out to
meet him.

"Oh, Rudy, your father's been awful sick! He raked up those
thistles he's been worrying about, and afterwards he could hardly
get to the house. He suffered so I was afraid he was going to
die."

Rudolph jumped to the ground. "Where is he now?"

"On the bed. He's asleep. I was terribly scared, because, you
know, I'm so fond of your father." She slipped her arm through
his and they went into the house. That afternoon they took
Rosicky home and put him to bed, though he protested that he
was quite well again.

The next morning he got up and dressed and sat down to
breakfast with his family. He told Mary that his coffee tasted
better than usual to him, and he warned the boys not to bear any
tales to Doctor Ed when he got home. After breakfast he sat
down by his window to do some patching and asked Mary to
thread several needles for him before she went to feed her
chickens,—her eyes were better than his, and her hands steadier.
He lit his pipe and took up John's overalls. Mary had been
watching him anxiously all morning, and as she went out of the
door with her bucket of scraps, she saw that he was smiling. He
was thinking, indeed, about Polly, and how he might never have
known what a tender heart she had if he hadn't got sick over
there. Girls nowadays didn't wear their heart on their sleeve. But
now he knew Polly would make a fine woman after the foolish-

ness wore off. Either a woman had that sweetness at her heart or she hadn't. You couldn't always tell by the look of them; but if they had that, everything came out right in the end.

After he had taken a few stitches, the cramp began in his chest, like yesterday. He put his pipe cautiously down on the window-sill and bent over to ease the pull. No use,—he had better try to get to his bed if he could. He rose and groped his way across the familiar floor, which was rising and falling like the deck of a ship. At the door he fell. When Mary came in, she found him lying there, and the moment she touched him she knew that he was gone.

Doctor Ed was away when Rosicky died, and for the first few weeks after he got home he was hard driven. Every day he said to himself that he must get out to see that family that had lost their father. One soft, warm moonlight night in early summer he started for the farm. His mind was on other things, and not until his road ran by the graveyard did he realize that Rosicky wasn't over there on the hill where the red lamplight shone, but here, in the moonlight. He stopped his car, shut off the engine, and sat there for a while.

A sudden hush had fallen on his soul. Everything here seemed strangely moving and significant, though signifying what, he did not know. Close by the wire fence stood Rosicky's mowing-machine, where one of the boys had been cutting hay that afternoon; his own work-horses had been going up and down there. The new-cut hay perfumed all the night air. The moonlight silvered the long, billowy grass that grew over the graves and hid the fence; the few little evergreens stood out black in it, like shadows in a pool. The sky was very blue and soft, the stars rather faint because the moon was full.

For the first time it struck Doctor Ed that this was really a beautiful graveyard. He thought of city cemeteries; acres of shrubbery and heavy stone, so arranged and lonely and unlike anything in the living world. Cities of the dead, indeed; cities of the forgotten, of the "put away." But this was open and free, this little square of long grass which the wind for ever stirred. Nothing but the sky overhead, and the many-coloured fields running on until they met that sky. The horses worked here in summer; the neighbours passed on their way to town; and over yonder, in the cornfield, Rosicky's own cattle would be eating fodder as winter came on. Nothing could be more undeathlike than this place; nothing could be more right for a man who had helped to do the work of great cities and had always longed for the open country and had got to it at last. Rosicky's life seemed to him complete and beautiful.

Appropriate graveyard
for Rosicky

William Faulkner

(1897–1962)

Born and raised in Mississippi, Faulkner left school to join the Royal Flying Corps in Canada; World War One ended before he could see service. After a brief stint at Oxford University and the University of Mississippi, and the publication of a volume of poems, The Marble Faun (1924), he spent some years as a journalist in New Orleans and began to write fiction. His first novel, Soldier's Pay, appeared in 1926, followed by, among others, Mosquitoes (1927), Sartoris (1929), The Sound and the Fury (1929), As I Lay Dying (1930), Sanctuary (1931), Light in August (1932), Absalom, Absalom! (1936), and Intruder in the Dust (1948). His Collected Stories appeared in 1958; ''Turnabout'' is taken from the third of these three volumes. Faulkner was awarded the Nobel Prize in 1950.

TURNABOUT

I

The American—the older one—wore no pink Bedfords. His breeches were of plain whipcord, like the tunic. And the tunic had no long London-cut skirts, so that below the Sam Browne the tail of it stuck straight out like the tunic of a military policeman beneath his holster belt. And he wore simple puttees and the easy shoes of a man of middle age, instead of Savile Row boots, and the shoes and the puttees did not match in shade, and the ordnance belt did not match either of them, and the pilot's wings on his breast were just wings. But the ribbon beneath them was a good ribbon, and the insigne on his shoulders were the twin bars of a captain. He was not tall. His face was thin, a little aquiline; the eyes intelligent and a little tired. He was past twenty-five; looking at him, one thought, not Phi Beta Kappa exactly, but Skull and Bones perhaps, or possibly a Rhodes scholarship.

One of the men who faced him probably could not see him at all. He was being held on his feet by an American military policeman. He was quite drunk, and in contrast with the heavy-jawed policeman who held him erect on his long, slim, boneless legs, he looked like a masquerading girl. He was possibly eighteen, tall, with a pink-and-white face and blue eyes, and a mouth like a girl's mouth. He wore a pea-coat, buttoned awry and stained with recent mud, and upon his blond head, at that unmistakable and rakish swagger which no other people can ever approach or imitate, the cap of a Royal Naval Officer.

"What's this, corporal?" the American captain said. "What's the trouble? He's an Englishman. You'd better let their M. P.'s take care of him."

"I know he is," the policeman said. He spoke heavily, breathing heavily, in the voice of a man under physical strain; for all his girlish delicacy of limb, the English boy was heavier—or more helpless—than he looked. "Stand up!" the policeman said. "They're officers!"

The English boy made an effort then. He pulled himself together, focusing his eyes. He swayed, throwing his arms about the policeman's neck, and with the other hand he saluted, his hand flicking, fingers curled a little, to his right ear, already swaying again and catching himself again. "Cheer-o, sir," he said. "Name's not Beatty, I hope."

"No," the captain said.

"Ah," the English boy said. "Hoped not. My mistake. No offense, what?"

"No offense," the captain said quietly. But he was looking at the policeman. The second American spoke. He was a lieutenant, also a pilot. But he was not twenty-five and he wore the pink breeches, the London boots, and his tunic might have been a British tunic save for the collar.

"It's one of those navy eggs," he said. "They pick them out of the gutters here all night long. You don't come to town often enough."

"Oh," the captain said. "I've heard about them. I remember now." He also remarked now that, though the street was a busy one—it was just outside a popular café—and there were many passers, soldier, civilian, women, yet none of them so much as paused, as though it were a familiar sight. He was looking at the policeman. "Can't you take him to his ship?"

"I thought of that before the captain did," the policeman said. "He says he can't go aboard his ship after dark because he puts the ship away at sundown."

"Puts it away?"

"Stand up, sailor!" the policeman said savagely, jerking at his lax burden. "Maybe the captain can make sense out of it. Damned if I can. He says they keep the boat under the wharf. Run it under the wharf at night, and that they can't get it out again until the tide goes out tomorrow."

"Under the wharf? A boat? What is this?" He was now speaking to the lieutenant. "Do they operate some kind of aquatic motorcycles?"

"Something like that," the lieutenant said. "You've seen them—the boats. Launches, camouflaged and all. Dashing up and down the harbor. You've seen them. They do that all day and sleep in the gutters here all night."

"Oh," the captain said. "I thought those boats were ship commanders' launches. You mean to tell me they use officers just to—"

"I don't know," the lieutenant said. "Maybe they use them to fetch hot water from one ship to another. Or buns. Or maybe to go back and forth fast when they forget napkins or something."

"Nonsense," the captain said. He looked at the English boy again.

"That's what they do," the lieutenant said. "Town's lousy with them all night long. Gutters full, and their M. P.'s carting them away in batches, like nursemaids in a park. Maybe the French give them the launches to get them out of the gutters during the day."

"Oh," the captain said, "I see." But it was clear that he didn't see, wasn't listening, didn't believe what he did hear. He looked at the English boy. "Well, you can't leave him here in that shape," he said.

Again the English boy tried to pull himself together. "Quite all right, 'sure you," he said glassily, his voice pleasant, cheerful almost, quite courteous. "Used to it. Confounded rough *pavé*, though. Should force French do something about it. Visiting lads jolly well deserve decent field to play on, what?"

"And he was jolly well using all of it too," the policeman said savagely. "He must think he's a one-man team, maybe."

At that moment a fifth man came up. He was a British military policeman. "Nah then," he said. "What's this? What's this?" Then he saw the Americans' shoulder bars. He saluted. At the sound of his voice the English boy turned, swaying, peering.

"Oh, hullo, Albert," he said.

"Nah then, Mr. Hope," the British policeman said. He said to the American policeman, over his shoulder: "What is it this time?"

"Likely nothing," the American said. "The way you guys run a war. But I'm a stranger here. Here. Take him."

"What is this, corporal?" the captain said. "What was he doing?"

"He won't call it nothing," the American policeman said, jerking his head at the British policeman. "He'll just call it a thrush or a robin or something. I turn into this street about three blocks back a while ago, and I find it blocked with a line of trucks going up from the docks, and the drivers all hollering ahead what the hell the trouble is. So I come on, and I find it is about three blocks of them, blocking the cross streets too; and I come on to the head of it where the trouble is, and I find about a dozen of the drivers out in front, holding a caucus or something in the middle of the street, and I come up and I say, 'What's going on here?' and they leave me through and I find this egg here laying—"

"Yer talking about one of His Majesty's officers, my man," the British policeman said.

"Watch yourself, corporal," the captain said. "And you found this officer—"

"He had done gone to bed in the middle of the street, with an empty basket for a pillow. Laying there with his hands under his head and his knees crossed, arguing with them about whether he ought to get up and move or not. He said that the trucks could turn back and go around by another street, but that he couldn't use any other street, because this street was his."

"His street?"

The English boy had listened, interested, pleasant. "Billet, you see," he said. "Must have order, even in war emergency. Billet by lot. This street mine; no poaching, eh? Next street Jamie Wutherspoon's. But trucks can go by that street because Jamie not using it yet. Not in bed yet. Insomnia. Knew so. Told them. Trucks go that way. See now?"

"Was that it, corporal?" the captain said.

"He told you. He wouldn't get up. He just laid there, arguing with them. He was telling one of them to go somewhere and bring back a copy of their articles of war—"

"King's Regulations; yes," the captain said.

"—and see if the book said whether he had the right of way, or the trucks. And then I got him up, and then the captain come along. And that's all. And with the captain's permission I'll now hand him over to His Majesty's wet nur—"

"That'll do, corporal," the captain said. "You can go. I'll see to this." The policeman saluted and went on. The British policeman was now supporting the English boy. "Can't you take him?" the captain said. "Where are their quarters?"

"I don't rightly know, sir, if they have quarters or not. We—I usually see them about the pubs until daylight. They don't see to use quarters."

"You mean, they really aren't off of ships?"

"Well, sir, they might be ships, in a manner of speaking. But a man would have to be a bit sleepier than him to sleep in one of them."

"I see," the captain said. He looked at the policeman. "What kind of boats are they?"

This time the policeman's voice was immediate, final and completely inflectionless. It was like a closed door. "I don't rightly know, sir."

"Oh," the captain said. "Quite. Well, he's in no shape to stay about pubs until daylight this time."

"Perhaps I can find him a bit of a pub with a back table, where he can sleep," the policeman said. But the captain was not listening. He was looking across the street, where the lights of another café fell across the pavement. The English boy yawned terrifically, like a child does, his mouth pink and frankly gaped as a child's.

The captain turned to the policeman:

"Would you mind stepping across there and asking for Captain Bogard's driver? I'll take care of Mr. Hope."

The policeman departed. The captain now supported the English boy, his hand beneath the other's arm. Again the boy yawned like a weary child. "Steady," the captain said. "The car will be here in a minute."

"Right," the English boy said through the yawn.

II

Once in the car, he went to sleep immediately with the peaceful suddenness of babies, sitting between the two Americans. But though the aerodrome was only thirty minutes away, he was awake when they arrived, apparently quite fresh, and asking for whisky. When they entered the mess he appeared quite sober, only blinking a little in the lighted room, in his raked cap and his awry-buttoned pea-jacket and a soiled silk muffler, embroidered with a club insignia which Bogard recognized to have come from a famous preparatory school, twisted about his throat.

"Ah," he said, his voice fresh, clear now, not blurred, quite cheerful, quite loud, so that the others in the room turned and looked at him. "Jolly. Whisky, what?" He went straight as a bird dog to the bar in the corner, the lieutenant following. Bogard had turned and gone on to the other end of the room, where five men sat about a card table.

"What's he admiral of?" one said.

"Of the whole Scotch navy, when I found him," Bogard said.

Another looked up. "Oh, I thought I'd seen him in town." He looked at the guest. "Maybe it's because he was on his feet that I didn't recognize him when he came in. You usually see them lying down in the gutter."

"Oh," the first said. He, too, looked around. "Is he one of those guys?"

"Sure. You've seen them. Sitting on the curb, you know, with a couple of limey M. P.'s hauling at their arms."

"Yes. I've seen them," the other said. They all looked at the English boy. He stood at the bar, talking, his voice loud, cheerful. "They all look like him too," the speaker said. "About seventeen or eighteen. They run those little boats that are always dashing in and out."

"Is that what they do?" a third said. "You mean, there's a male marine auxiliary to the Waacs? Good Lord, I sure made a mistake when I enlisted. But this war never was advertised right."

"I don't know," Bogard said. "I guess they do more than just ride around."

But they were not listening to him. They were looking at the guest. "They run by clock," the first said. "You can see the condition of one of them after sunset and almost tell what time it is. But what I don't see is, how a man that's in that shape at one o'clock every morning can even see a battleship the next day."

"Maybe when they have a message to send out to a ship," another said, "they just make duplicates and line the launches up and point them toward the ship and give each one a duplicate of the message and let them go. And the ones that miss the ship just cruise around the harbor until they hit a dock somewhere."

"It must be more than that," Bogard said.

He was about to say something else, but at that moment the

guest turned from the bar and approached, carrying a glass. He walked steadily enough, but his color was high and his eyes were bright, and he was talking, loud, cheerful, as he came up.

"I say. Won't you chaps join——" He ceased. He seemed to remark something; he was looking at their breasts. "Oh, I say. You fly. All of you. Oh, good gad! Find it jolly, eh?"

"Yes," somebody said. "Jolly."

"But dangerous, what?"

"A little faster than tennis," another said. The guest looked at him, bright, affable, intent.

Another said quickly, "Bogard says you command a vessel."

"Hardly a vessel. Thanks, though. And not command. Ronnie does that. Ranks me a bit. Age."

"Ronnie?"

"Yes. Nice. Good egg. Old, though. Stickler."

"Stickler?"

"Frightful. You'd not believe it. Whenever we sight smoke and I have the glass, he sheers away. Keeps the ship hull down all the while. No beaver then. Had me two down a fortnight yesterday."

The Americans glanced at one another. "No beaver?"

"We play it. With basket masts, you see. See a basket mast. Beaver! One up. The Ergenstrasse doesn't count any more, though."

The men about the table looked at one another. Bogard spoke. "I see. When you or Ronnie see a ship with basket masts, you get a beaver on the other. I see. What is the Ergenstrasse?"

"She's German. Interned. Tramp steamer. Foremast rigged so it looks something like a basket mast. Booms, cables, I dare say. I didn't think it looked very much like a basket mast, myself. But Ronnie said yes. Called it one day. Then one day they shifted her across the basin and I called her on Ronnie. So we decided to not count her any more. See now, eh?"

"Oh," the one who had made the tennis remark said, "I see. You and Ronnie run about in the launch, playing beaver. H'm'm. That's nice. Did you ever pl—"

"Jerry," Bogard said. The guest had not moved. He looked down at the speaker, still smiling, his eyes quite wide.

The speaker still looked at the guest. "Has yours and Ronnie's boat got a yellow stern?"

"A yellow stern?" the English boy said. He had quit smiling, but his face was still pleasant.

"I thought that maybe when the boats had two captains, they might paint the sterns yellow or something."

"Oh," the guest said. "Burt and Reeves aren't officers."

"Burt and Reeves," the other said, in a musing tone. "So they go, too. Do they play beaver too?"

"Jerry," Bogard said. The other looked at him. Bogard jerked his head a little. "Come over here." The other rose. They went aside. "Lay off of him," Bogard said. "I mean it, now. He's just a kid. When you were that age, how much sense did you have? Just about enough to get to chapel on time."

"My country hadn't been at war going on four years, though," Jerry said. "Here we are, spending our money and getting shot at by the clock, and it's not even our fight, and these limeys that would have been goose-stepping twelve months now if it hadn't been—"

"Shut it," Bogard said. "You sound like a Liberty Loan."

"—taking it like it was a fair or something. 'Jolly.' " His voice was now falsetto, lilting. " 'But dangerous, what?' "

"Sh-h-h-h," Bogard said.

"I'd like to catch him and his Ronnie out in the harbor, just once. Any harbor. London's. I wouldn't want anything but a Jenny, either. Jenny? Hell, I'd take a bicycle and a pair of water wings! I'll show him some war."

"Well, you lay off him now. He'll be gone soon."

"What are you going to do with him?"

"I'm going to take him along this morning. Let him have Harper's place out front. He says he can handle a Lewis. Says they have one on the boat. Something he was telling me—about how he once shot out a channel-marker light at seven hundred yards."

"Well, that's your business. Maybe he can beat you."

"Beat me?"

"Playing beaver. And then you can take on Ronnie."

"I'll show him some war, anyway," Bogard said. He looked at the guest. "His people have been in it three years now, and he seems to take it like a sophomore in town for the big game." He looked at Jerry again. "But you lay off him now."

As they approached the table, the guest's voice was loud and cheerful: ". . . if he got the glasses first, he would go in close and look, but when I got them first, he'd sheer off where I couldn't see anything but the smoke. Frightful stickler. Frightful. But Ergenstrasse not counting any more. And if you make a mistake and call her, you lose two beaver from your score. If Ronnie were only to forget and call her we'd be even."

III

At two o'clock the English boy was still talking, his voice bright, innocent and cheerful. He was telling them how Switzerland had been spoiled by 1914, and instead of the vacation which his father had promised him for his sixteenth birthday, when that birthday came he and his tutor had had to do with Wales. But that he and the tutor had got pretty high and that he dared to say—with all due respect to any present who might have had the advantage of Switzerland, of course—that one could see probably as far from Wales as from Switzerland. "Perspire as much and breathe as hard, anyway," he added. And about him the Americans sat, a little hard-bitten, a little sober, somewhat older, listening to him with a kind of cold astonishment. They had been getting up for some time now and going out and returning in flying clothes, carrying helmets and goggles. An orderly entered with a tray of coffee cups, and the guest realized that for some time now he had been hearing engines in the darkness outside.

At last Bogard rose. "Come along," he said. "We'll get your togs." When they emerged from the mess, the sound of the engines was quite loud—an idling thunder. In alignment along the invisible tarmac was a vague rank of short banks of flickering blue-green fire suspended apparently in mid-air. They crossed the aerodrome to Bogard's quarters, where the lieutenant, McGinnis, sat on a cot fastening his flying boots. Bogard reached down a Sidcott suit and threw it across the cot. "Put this on," he said.

"Will I need all this?" the guest said. "Shall we be gone that long?"

"Probably," Bogard said. "Better use it. Cold upstairs."

The guest picked up the suit. "I say," he said. "I say, Ronnie and I have a do ourselves, tomor—today. Do you think Ronnie won't mind if I am a bit late? Might not wait for me."

"We'll be back before teatime," McGinnis said. He seemed quite busy with his boot. "Promise you." The English boy looked at him.

"What time should you be back?" Bogard said.

"Oh, well," the English boy said, "I dare say it will be all right. They let Ronnie say when to go, anyway. He'll wait for me if I should be a bit late."

"He'll wait," Bogard said. "Get your suit on."

"Right," the other said. They helped him into the suit. "Never been up before," he said, chattily, pleasantly. "Dare say you can see farther than from mountains, eh?"

"See more, anyway," McGinnis said. "You'll like it."

"Oh, rather. If Ronnie only waits for me. Lark. But dangerous, isn't it?"

"Go on," McGinnis said. "You're kidding me."

"Shut your trap, Mac," Bogard said. "Come along. Want some more coffee?" He looked at the guest, but McGinnis answered:

"No. Got something better than coffee. Coffee makes such a confounded stain on the wings."

"On the wings?" the English boy said. "Why coffee on the wings."

"Stow it, I said, Mac," Bogard said. "Come along."

They recrossed the aerodrome, approaching the muttering banks of flame. When they drew near, the guest began to discern the shape, the outlines, of the Handley-Page. It looked like a Pullman coach run upslanted aground into the skeleton of the first floor of an incomplete skyscraper. The guest looked at it quietly.

"It's larger than a cruiser," he said in his bright, interested voice. "I say, you know. This doesn't fly in one lump. You can't pull my leg. Seen them before. It comes in two parts: Captain Bogard and me in one; Mac and 'nother chap in other. What?"

"No," McGinnis said. Bogard had vanished. "It all goes up in one lump. Big Lark, eh? Buzzard, what?"

"Buzzard?" the guest murmured. "Oh, I say. A cruiser. Flying. I say, now."

"And listen," McGinnis said. His hand came forth; something cold fumbled against the hand of the English boy—a bottle. "When you feel yourself getting sick, see? Take a pull at it."

"Oh, shall I get sick?"

"Sure. We all do. Part of flying. This will stop it. But if it doesn't. See?"

"What? Quite. What?"

"Not overside. Don't spew it overside."

"Not overside?"

"It'll blow back in Bogy's and my face. Can't see. Bingo. Finished. See?"

"Oh, quite. What shall I do with it?" Their voices were quiet, brief, grave as conspirators.

"Just duck your head and let her go."

"Oh, quite."

Bogard returned. "Show him how to get into the front pit, will you?" he said. McGinnis led the way through the trap.

Forward, rising to the slant of the fuselage, the passage narrowed; a man would need to crawl.

"Crawl in there and keep going," McGinnis said.

"It looks like a dog kennel," the guest said.

"Doesn't it, though?" McGinnis agreed cheerfully. "Cut along with you." Stooping, he could hear the other scuttling forward. "You'll find a Lewis gun up there, like as not," he said into the tunnel.

The voice of the guest came back: "Found it."

"The gunnery sergeant will be along in a minute and show you if it is loaded."

"It's loaded," the guest said; almost on the heels of his words the gun fired, a brief staccato burst. There were shouts, the loudest from the ground beneath the nose of the aeroplane. "It's quite all right," the English boy's voice said. "I pointed it west before I let it off. Nothing back there but Marine office and your brigade headquarters. Ronnie and I always do this before we go anywhere. Sorry if I was too soon. Oh, by the way," he added, "my name's Claude. Don't think I mentioned it."

On the ground, Bogard and two other officers stood. They had come up running. "Fired it west," one said. "How in hell does he know which way is west?"

"He's a sailor," the other said. "You forgot that."

"He seems to be a machine gunner too," Bogard said.

"Let's hope he doesn't forget that," the first said.

IV

Nevertheless, Bogard kept an eye on the silhouetted head rising from the round gunpit in the nose ten feet ahead of him. "He did work that gun, though," he said to McGinnis beside him. "He even put the drum on himself, didn't he?"

"Yes," McGinnis said. "If he just doesn't forget and think that that gun is him and his tutor looking around from a Welsh alp."

"Maybe I should not have brought him," Bogard said. McGinnis didn't answer. Bogard jockeyed the wheel a little. Ahead, in the gunner's pit, the guest's head moved this way and that continuously, looking. "We'll get there and unload and haul air for home," Bogard said. "Maybe in the dark— Confound it, it would be a shame for his country to be in this mess for four years and him not even to see a gun pointed in his direction."

"He'll see one tonight if he don't keep his head in," McGinnis said.

But the boy did not do that. Not even when they had reached the objective and McGinnis had crawled down to the bomb toggles. And even when the searchlights found them and Bogard signaled to the other machines and dived, the two engines snarling full speed into and through the bursting shells, he could see the boy's face in the searchlight's glare, leaned far overside, coming sharply out as a spotlighted face on a stage, with an expression upon it of child-like interest and delight. "But he's firing that Lewis," Bogard thought. "Straight too"; nosing the machine farther down, watching the pinpoint swing into the sights, his right hand lifted, waiting to drop into McGinnis' sight. He dropped his hand; above the noise of the engines he seemed to hear the click and whistle of the released bombs as the machine, freed of the weight, shot zooming in a long upward bounce that carried it for an instant out of the light. Then he was pretty busy for a time, coming into and through the shells again, shooting athwart another beam that caught and held long enough for him to see the English boy leaning far over the side, looking back and down past the right wing, the undercarriage. "Maybe he's read about it somewhere," Bogard thought, turning, looking back to pick up the rest of the flight.

Then it was all over, the darkness cool and empty and peaceful and almost quiet, with only the steady sound of the engines. McGinnis climbed back into the office, and standing up in his seat, he fired te colored pistol this time and stood for a moment longer, looking backward toward where the searchlights still probed and sabered. He sat down again.

"O.K.," he said. "I counted all four of them. Let's haul air." Then he looked forward. "What's become of the King's Own? You didn't hang him onto a bomb release, did you?" Bogard looked. The forward pit was empty. It was in dim silhouette again now, against the stars, but there was nothing there now save the gun. "No," McGinnis said: "there he is. See? Leaning overside. Dammit, I told him not to spew it! There he comes back." The guest's head came into view again. But again it sank out of sight.

"He's coming back," Bogard said. "Stop him. Tell him we're going to have every squadron in the Hun Channel group on top of us in thirty minutes."

McGinnis swung himself down and stooped at the entrance to the passage. "Get back!" he shouted. The other was almost out; they squatted so, face to face like two dogs, shouting at one another above the noise of the still-unthrottled engines on either side of the fabric walls. The English boy's voice was thin and high.

"Bomb!" he shrieked.

"Yes," McGinnis shouted, "they were bombs! We gave them hell! Get back, I tell you! Have every Hun in France on us in ten minutes! Get back to your gun!"

Again the boy's voice came, high, faint above the noise: "Bomb! All right?"

"Yes! Yes! All right. Back to your gun, damn you!"

McGinnis climbed back into the office. "He went back. Want me to take her awhile?"

"All right," Bogard said. He passed McGinnis the wheel. "Ease her back some. I'd just as soon it was daylight when they come down on us."

"Right," McGinnis said. He moved the wheel suddenly. "What's the matter with that right wing?" he said. "Watch it. . . . See? I'm flying on the right aileron and a little rudder. Feel it."

Bogard took the wheel a moment. "I didn't notice that. Wire somewhere, I guess. I didn't think any of those shells were that close. Watch her, though."

"Right," McGinnis said. "And so you are going with him on his boat tomorrow—today."

"Yes. I promised him. Confound it, you can't hurt a kid, you know."

"Why don't you take Collier along, with his mandolin? Then you could sail around and sing."

"I promised him," Bogard said. "Get that wing up a little."

"Right," McGinnis said.

Thirty minutes later it was beginning to be dawn; the sky was gray. Presently McGinnis said: "Well, here they come. Look at them! They look like mosquitoes in September. I hope he don't get worked up now and think he's playing beaver. If he does he'll just be one down to Ronnie, provided the devil has a beard. . . . Want the wheel?"

v

At eight o'clock the beach, the Channel, was beneath them. Throttled back, the machine drifted down as Bogard ruddered it gently into the Channel wind. His face was strained, a little tired.

McGinnis looked tired, too, and he needed a shave.

"What do you guess he is looking at now?" he said. For again the English boy was leaning over the right side of the cockpit, looking backward and downward past the right wing.

"I don't know," Bogard said. "Maybe bullet holes." He blasted the port engine. "Must have the riggers—"

"He could see some closer than that," McGinnis said. "I'll swear I saw tracer going into his back at one time. Or maybe it's the ocean he's looking at. But he must have seen that when he came over from England." Then Bogard leveled off; the nose rose sharply, the sand, the curling tide edge fled alongside. Yet still the English boy hung far overside, looking backward and downward at something beneath the right wing, his face rapt, with utter and childlike interest. Until the machine was completely stopped he continued to do so. Then he ducked down, and in the abrupt silence of the engines they could hear him crawling in the passage. He emerged just as the two pilots climbed stiffly down from the office, his face bright, eager; his voice high, excited.

"Oh, I say! Oh, good gad! What a chap. What a judge of distance! If Ronnie could only have seen! Oh, good gad! Or maybe they aren't like ours—don't load themselves as soon as the air strikes them."

The Americans looked at him. "What don't what?" McGinnis said. "The bomb. It was magnificent; I say, I shan't forget it. Oh, I say, you know! It was splendid!"

After a while McGinnis said, "The bomb?" in a fainting voice. Then the two pilots glared at each other; they said in unison: "That right wing!" Then as one they clawed down through the trap and, with the guest at their heels, they ran around the machine and looked beneath the right wing. The bomb, suspended by its tail, hung straight down like a plumb bob beside the right wheel, its tip just touching the sand. And parallel with the wheel track was the long delicate line in the sand where its ultimate tip had dragged. Behind them the English boy's voice was high, clear, childlike:

"Frightened, myself. Tried to tell you. But realized you knew your business better than I. Skill. Marvelous. Oh, I say, I shan't forget it."

VI

A marine with a bayoneted rifle passed Bogard onto the wharf and directed him to the boat. The wharf was empty, and he didn't even see the boat until he approached the edge of the wharf and looked directly down into it and upon the backs of two stooping men in greasy dungarees, who rose and glanced briefly at him and stooped again.

It was about thirty feet long and about three feet wide. It was painted with gray-green camouflage. It was quarter-decked forward, with two blunt, raked exhaust stacks. "Good Lord," Bogard thought, "if all that deck is engine—" Just aft the deck was the control seat; he saw a big wheel, an instrument panel. Rising to a height of about a foot above the free-board, and running from the stern forward to where the deck began, and continuing on across the after edge of the deck and thence back down the other gunwale to the stern, was a solid screen, also camouflaged, which inclosed the boat save for the width of the stern, which was open. Facing the steersman's seat like an eye was a hole in the screen about eight inches in diameter. And looking down into the long, narrow, still, vicious shape, he saw a machine gun swiveled at the stern, and he looked at the low screen—including which the whole vessel did not sit much more than a yard above water level—with its single empty forward-staring eye, and he thought quietly; "It's steel. It's made of steel." And his face was quite sober, quite thoughtful, and he drew his trench coat about him and buttoned it, as though he were getting cold.

He heard steps behind him and turned. But it was only an orderly from the aerodrome, accompanied by the marine with the rifle. The orderly was carrying a largish bundle wrapped in paper.

"From Lieutenant McGinnis to the captain," the orderly said.

Bogard took the bundle. The orderly and the marine retreated. He opened the bundle. It contained some objects and a scrawled note. The objects were a new yellow silk sofa cushion and a Japanese parasol, obviously borrowed, and a comb and a roll of toilet paper. The note said:

> Couldn't find a camera anywhere and Collier wouldn't let me have his mandolin. But maybe Ronnie can play on the comb.
>
> MAC.

Bogard looked at the objects. But his face was still quite thoughtful, quite grave. He rewrapped the things and carried the bundle on up the wharf and dropped it quietly into the water.

As he returned toward the invisible boat he saw two men approaching. He recognized the boy at once—tall, slender, already talking, voluble, his head bent a little toward his shorter companion, who plodded along beside him, hands in pockets, smoking a pipe. The boy still wore the pea-coat beneath a flapping oilskin, but in place of the rakish and casual cap he now wore an infantryman's soiled Balaclava helmet, with, floating behind him as though upon the sound of his voice, a curtainlike piece of cloth almost as long as a burnous.

"Hullo, there!" he cried, still a hundred yards away.

But it was the second man that Bogard was watching, thinking to himself that he had never in his life seen a more curious figure. There was something stolid about the very shape of his hunched shoulders, his slightly down-looking face. He was a head shorter than the other. His face was ruddy, too, but its mold was of a profound gravity that was almost dour. It was the face of a man of twenty who has been for a year trying, even while asleep, to look twenty-one. He wore a high-necked sweater and dungaree slacks; above this a leather jacket; and above this a soiled naval officer's warmer that reached almost to his heels and which had one shoulder strap missing and not one remaining button at all. On his head was a plaid fore-and-aft deer stalker's cap, tied on by a narrow scarf brought across and down, hiding his ears, and then wrapped once about his throat and knotted with a hangman's noose beneath his left ear. It was unbelievably soiled, and with his hands elbow-deep in his pockets and his hunched shoulders and his bent head, he looked like someone's grandmother hung, say, for a witch. Clamped upside down between his teeth was a short brier pipe.

"Here he is!" the boy cried. "This is Ronnie. Captain Bogard."

"How are you?" Bogard said. He extended his hand. The other said no word, but his hand came forth, limp. It was quite cold, but it was hard, calloused. But he said no word; he just glanced briefly at Bogard and then away. But in that instant Bogard caught something in the look, something strange—a flicker; a kind of covert and curious respect, something like a boy of fifteen looking at a circus trapezist.

But he said no word. He ducked on; Bogard watched him drop from sight over the wharf edge as though he had jumped feet first into the sea. He remarked now that the engines in the invisible boat were running.

"We might get aboard too," the boy said. He started toward the boat, then he stopped. He touched Bogard's arm. "Yonder!" he hissed. "See?" His voice was thin with excitement.

"What?" Bogard also whispered; automatically he looked backward and upward, after old habit. The other was gripping his arm and pointing across the harbor.

"There! Over there. The Ergenstrasse. They have shifted her again." Across the harbor lay an ancient, rusting, sway-backed hulk. It was small and nondescript, and, remembering, Bogard saw that the foremast was a strange mess of cables and booms, resembling—allowing for a great deal of license or looseness of imagery—a basket mast. Beside him the boy was almost chortling. "Do you think that Ronnie noticed?" he hissed. "Do you?"

"I don't know," Bogard said.

"Oh, good gad! If he should glance up and call her before he notices, we'll be even. Oh, good gad! But come along." He went on; he was still chortling. "Careful," he said. "Frightful ladder."

He descended first, the two men in the boat rising and saluting. Ronnie had disappeared, save for his backside, which now filled a small hatch leading forward beneath the deck. Bogard descended gingerly.

"Good Lord," he said. "Do you have to climb up and down this every day?"

"Frightful, isn't it?" the other said, in his happy voice. "But you know yourself. Try to run a war with makeshifts, then wonder why it takes so long." The narrow hull slid and surged, even with Bogard's added weight. "Sits right on top, you see," the boy said. "Would float on a lawn, in a heavy dew. Goes right over them like a bit of paper."

"It does?" Bogard said.

"Oh, absolutely. That's why, you see." Bogard didn't see, but he was too busy letting himself gingerly down to a sitting posture. There were no thwarts; no seats save a long, thick, cylindrical ridge which ran along the bottom of the boat from the driver's seat to the stern. Ronnie had backed into sight. He now sat behind the wheel, bent over the instrument panel. But when he glanced back over his shoulder he did not speak. His face was merely interrogatory. Across his face there was now a long smudge of grease. The boy's face was empty, too, now.

"Right," he said. He looked forward, where one of the seamen had gone. "Ready forward?" he said.

"Aye, sir," the seaman said.

The other seaman was at the stern line. "Ready aft?"

"Aye, sir."

"Cast off." The boat sheered away, purring, a boiling of water under the stern. The boy looked down at Bogard. "Silly business. Do it shipshape, though. Can't tell when silly four-striper—" His face changed again, immediate, solicitous. "I say. Will you be warm? I never thought to fetch—"

"I'll be all right," Bogard said. But the other was already taking off his oilskin. "No, no," Bogard said. "I won't take it."

"You'll tell me if you get cold?"

"Yes. Sure." He was looking down at the cylinder on which he sat. It was a half cylinder—that is, like the hotwater tank to some Gargantuan stove, sliced down the middle and bolted, open side down, to the floor plates. It was twenty feet long and more than two feet thick. Its top rose as high as the gunwales and between it and the hull on either side was just room enough for a man to place his feet to walk.

"That's Muriel," the boy said.

"Muriel?"

"Yes. The one before that was Agatha. After my aunt. The first one Ronnie and I had was Alice in Wonderland. Ronnie and I were the White Rabbit. Jolly, eh?"

"Oh, you and Ronnie have had three, have you?"

"Oh, yes," the boy said. He leaned down. "He didn't notice," he whispered. His face was again bright, gleeful. "When we come back," he said. "You watch."

"Oh," Bogard said. "The Ergenstrasse." He looked astern, and then he thought: "Good Lord! We must be going—traveling." He looked out now, broadside, and saw the harbor line fleeing past, and he thought to himself that the boat was well-nigh moving at the speed at which the Handley-Page flew, left the ground. They were beginning to bound now, even in the sheltered water, from one wave crest to the next with a distinct shock. His hand still rested on the cylinder on which he sat. He looked down at it again, following it from where it seemed to emerge beneath Ronnie's seat, to where it beveled into the stern. "It's the air in her, I suppose," he said.

"The what?" the boy said.

"The air. Stored up in her. That makes the boat ride high."

"Oh, yes. I dare say. Very likely. I hadn't thought about it." He came forward, his burnous whipping in the wind, and sat down beside Bogard. Their heads were below the top of the screen.

Astern the harbor fled, diminishing, sinking into the sea. The boat had begun to lift now, swooping forward and down, shocking almost stationary for a moment, then lifting and swooping again; a gout of spray came aboard over the bows like a flung shovelful of shot. "I wish you'd take this coat," the boy said.

Bogard didn't answer. He looked around at the bright face. "We're outside, aren't we?" he said quietly.

"Yes. . . . Do take it, won't you?"

"Thanks, no. I'll be all right. We won't be long, anyway, I guess."

"No. We'll turn soon. It won't be so bad then."

"Yes. I'll be all right when we turn." Then they did turn. The motion became easier. That is, the boat didn't bank head-on, shuddering, into the swells. They came up beneath now, and the boat fled with increased speed, with a long, sickening, yawing motion, first to one side and then the other. But it fled on, and Bogard looked astern with that same soberness with which he had first looked down into the boat. "We're going east now," he said.

"With just a spot of north," the boy said. "Makes her ride a bit better, what?"

"Yes," Bogard said. Astern there was nothing now save empty sea and the delicate needlelike cant of the machine gun against the boiling and slewing wake, and the two seamen crouching quietly in the stern. "Yes. It's easier." Then he said: "How far do we go?"

The boy leaned closer. He moved closer. His voice was happy, confidential, proud, though lowered a little: "It's Ronnie's show. He thought of it. Not that I wouldn't have, in time. Gratitude and all that. But he's the older, you see. Thinks fast. Courtesy, *noblesse oblige*—all that. Thought of it soon as I told him this morning. I said, 'Oh, I say. I've been there. I've seen it'; and he said, 'Not flying'; and I said, 'Strewth'; and he said 'How far? No lying now'; and I said, 'Oh, far. Tremendous. Gone all night'; and he said, 'Flying all night. That must have been to Berlin'; and I said, 'I don't know. I dare say'; and he thought. I could see him thinking. Because he is the older, you see. More experience in courtesy, right thing. And he said, 'Berlin. No fun to that chap, dashing out and back with us.' And he thought and I waited, and I said, 'But we can't take him to Berlin. Too far. Don't know the way, either'; and he said—fast, like a shot—said, 'But there's Kiel'; and I knew—"

"What?" Bogard said. Without moving, his whole body sprang. "Kiel? In this?"

"Absolutely. Ronnie thought of it. Smart, even if he is a stickler. Said at once, 'Zeebrugge no show at all for that chap. Must do best we can for him. Berlin,' Ronnie said. 'My Gad! Berlin.' "

"Listen," Bogard said. He had turned now, facing the other, his face quite grave. "What is this boat for?"

"For?"

"What does it do?" Then, knowing beforehand the answer to his own question, he said, putting his hand on the cylinder: "What is this in here? A torpedo, isn't it?"

"I thought you knew," the boy said.

"No," Bogard said. "I didn't know." His voice seemed to reach him from a distance, dry, cricketlike: "How do you fire it?"

"Fire it?"

"How do you get it out of the boat? When that hatch was open a while ago I could see the engines. They were right in front of the end of this tube."

"Oh," the boy said. "You pull a gadget there and the torpedo drops out astern. As soon as the screw touches the water it begins to turn, and then the torpedo is ready, loaded. Then all you have to do is turn the boat quickly and the torpedo goes on."

"You mean—" Bogard said. After a moment his voice obeyed him again. "You mean you aim the torpedo with the boat and release it and it starts moving, and you turn the boat out of the way and the torpedo passes through the same water that the boat just vacated?"

"Knew you'd catch on," the boy said. "Told Ronnie so. Airman. Tamer than yours, though. But can't be helped. Best we can do, just on water. But knew you'd catch on."

"Listen,' Bogard said. His voice sounded to him quite calm. The boat fled on, yawing over the swells. He sat quite motionless. It seemed to him that he could hear himself talking to himself: "Go on. Ask him. Ask him what? Ask him how close to the ship do you have to be before you fire. . . . Listen," he said, in that calm voice. "Now, you tell Ronnie, you see. You just tell him—just say—" He could feel his voice ratting off on him again, so he stopped it. He sat quite motionless, waiting for it to come back; the boy leaning now, looking at his face. Again the boy's voice was solicitous:

"I say. You're not feeling well. These confounded shallow boats."

"It's not that," Bogard said. "I just— Do your orders say Kiel?"

"Oh, no. They let Ronnie say. Just so we bring the boat back. This is for you. Gratitude. Ronnie's idea. Tame, after flying. But if you'd rather, eh?"

"Yes, some place closer. You see, I—"

"Quite. I see. No vacations in wartime. I'll tell Ronnie." He went forward. Bogard did not move. The boat fled in long, slewing swoops. Bogard looked quietly astern, at the scudding sea, the sky.

"My God!" he thought. "Can you beat it? Can you beat it?"

The boy came back; Bogard turned to him a face the color of dirty paper. "All right now," the boy said. "Not Kiel. Nearer place, hunting probably just as good. Ronnie says he knows you will understand." He was tugging at his pocket. He brought out a bottle. "Here. Haven't forgot last night. Do the same for you. Good for the stomach, eh?"

Bogard drank, gulping—a big one. He extended the bottle, but the boy refused. "Never touch it on duty," he said. "Not like you chaps. Tame here."

The boat fled on. The sun was already down the west. But Bogard had lost all count of time, of distance. Ahead he could see white seas through the round eye opposite Ronnie's face, and Ronnie's hand on the wheel and the granitelike jut of his profiled jaw and the dead upside-down pipe. The boat fled on.

Then the boy leaned and touched his shoulder. He half rose. The boy was pointing. The sun was reddish; against it, outside them and about two miles away, a vessel—a trawler, it looked like—at anchor swung a tall mast.

"Lightship!" the boy shouted. "Theirs." Ahead Bogard could see a low, flat mole—the entrance to a harbor. "Channel!" the boy shouted. He swept his arm in both directions. "Mines!" His voice swept back on the wind. "Place filthy with them. All sides. Beneath us too. Lark, eh?"

VII

Against the mole a fair surf was beating. Running before the seas now, the boat seemed to leap from one roller to the next; in the intervals while the screw was in the air the engine seemed to be trying to tear itself out by the roots. But it did not slow; when it passed the end of the mole the boat seemed to be standing almost erect on its rudder, like a sailfish. The mole was a mile away. From the end of it little faint lights began to flicker like fireflies. The boy leaned. "Down," he said. "Machine guns. Might stop a stray."

"What do I do?" Bogard shouted. "What can I do?"

"Stout fellow! Give them hell, what? Knew you'd like it!"

Crouching, Bogard looked up at the boy, his face wild. "I can handle the machine gun!"

"No need," the boy shouted back. "Give them first innings. Sporting. Visitors, eh?" He was looking forward. "There she is. See?" They were in the harbor now, the basin opening before them. Anchored in the channel was a big freighter. Painted midships of the hull was a huge Argentine flag. "Must get back to stations!'' the boy shouted down to him. Then at that moment Ronnie spoke for the first time. The boat was hurtling along now in smoother water. Its speed did not slacken and Ronnie did not turn his head when he spoke. He just swung his jutting jaw and the clamped cold pipe a little, and said from the side of his mouth a single word:

''Beaver.''

The boy, stooped over what he had called his gadget, jerked up, his expression astonished and outraged. Bogard also looked forward and saw Ronnie's arm pointing to starboard. It was a light cruiser at anchor a mile away. She had basket masts, and as he looked a gun flashed from her after turret. ''Oh, damn!'' the boy cried. ''Oh, you putt! Oh, confound you, Ronnie! Now I'm three down!'' But he had already stooped again over his gadget, his face bright and empty and alert again; not sober; just calm, waiting. Again Bogard looked forward and felt the boat pivot on its rudder and head directly for the freighter at terrific speed, Ronnie now with one hand on the wheel and the other lifted and extended at the height of his head.

But it seemed to Bogard that the hand would never drop. He crouched, not sitting, watching with a kind of quiet horror the painted flag increase like a moving picture of a locomotive taken from between the rails. Again the gun crashed from the cruiser behind them, and the freighter fired point-blank at them from its poop. Bogard heard neither shot.

''Man, man!'' he shouted. ''For God's sake!''

Ronnie's hand dropped. Again the boat spun on its rudder. Bogard saw the bow rise, pivoting; he expected the hull to slam broadside on into the ship. But it didn't. It shot off on a long tangent. He was waiting for it to make a wide sweep, heading seaward, putting the freighter astern, and he thought of the cruiser again. ''Get a broadside, this time, once we clear the freighter,'' he thought. Then he remembered the freighter, the torpedo, and he looked back toward the freighter to watch the torpedo strike, and saw to his horror that the boat was now bearing down on the freighter again, in a skidding turn. Like a man in a dream, he watched himself rush down upon the ship and shoot past under her counter, still skidding, close enough to see the faces on her decks. ''They missed and they are going to run down the torpedo and catch it and shoot it again,'' he thought idiotically.

So the boy had to touch his shoulder before he knew he was behind him. The boy's voice was quite calm: ''Under Ronnie's seat there. A bit of a crank handle. If you'll just hand it to me—''

He found the crank. He passed it back; he was thinking dreamily: "Mac would say they had a telephone on board." But he didn't look at once to see what the boy was doing with it, for in that still and peaceful horror he was watching Ronnie, the cold pipe rigid in his jaw, hurling the boat at top speed round and round the freighter, so near that he could see the rivets in the plates. Then he looked aft, his face wild, importunate, and he saw what the boy was doing with the crank. He had fitted it into what was obviously a small windlass low on one flank of the tube near the head. He glanced up and saw Bogard's face. "Didn't go that time!" he shouted cheerfully.

"Go?" Bogard shouted. "It didn't— The torpedo—"

The boy and one of the seamen were quite busy, stooping over the windlass and the tube. "No. Clumsy. Always happening. Should think clever chaps like engineers— Happens, though. Draw her in and try her again."

"But the nose, the cap!" Bogard shouted. "It's still in the tube, isn't it? It's all right, isn't it?"

"Absolutely. But it's working now. Loaded. Screw's started turning. Get it back and drop it clear. If we should stop or slow up it would overtake us. Drive back into the tube. Bingo! What?"

Bogard was on his feet now, turned, braced to the terrific merry-go-round of the boat. High above them the freighter seemed to be spinning on her heel like a trick picture in the movies. "Let me have that winch!" he cried.

"Steady!" the boy said. "Mustn't draw her back too fast. Jam her into the head of the tube ourselves. Same bingo! Best let us. Every cobbler to his last, what?"

"Oh, quite," Bogard said. "Oh, absolutely." It was like someone else was using his mouth. He leaned, braced, his hands on the cold tube, beside the others. He was hot inside, but his outside was cold. He could feel all his flesh jerking with cold as he watched the blunt, grained hand of the seaman turning the windlass in short, easy, inch-long arcs, while at the head of the tube the boy bent, tapping the cylinder with a spanner, lightly, his head turned with listening delicate and deliberate as a watchmaker. The boat rushed on in those furious, slewing turns. Bogard saw a long, drooping thread loop down from somebody's mouth, between his hands, and he found that the thread came from his own mouth.

He didn't hear the boy speak, nor notice when he stood up. He just felt the boat straighten out, flinging him to his knees beside the tube. The seaman had gone back to the stern and the boy

stooped again over his gadget. Bogard knelt now, quite sick. He
did not feel the boat when it swung again, nor hear the gun from
the cruiser which had not dared to fire and the freighter which
had not been able to fire, firing again. He did not feel anything
at all when he saw the huge, painted flag directly ahead and
increasing with locomotive speed, and Ronnie's lifted hand drop.
But this time he knew that the torpedo was gone; in pivoting and
spinning this time the whole boat seemed to leave the water; he
saw the bow of the boat shoot skyward like the nose of a pursuit
ship going into a wingover. Then his outraged stomach denied
him. He saw neither the geyser nor heard the detonation as he
sprawled over the tube. He felt only a hand grasp him by the
slack of his coat, and the voice of one of the seamen: "Steady
all, sir. I've got you."

VIII

A voice roused him, a hand. He was half sitting in the narrow
starboard runway, half lying across the tube. He had been there
for quite a while; quite a while ago he had felt someone spread a
garment over him. But he had not raised his head. "I'm all
right," he had said. "You keep it."

"Don't need it," the boy said. "Going home now."

"I'm sorry I—" Bogard said.

"Quite. Confounded shallow boats. Turn any stomach until
you get used to them. Ronnie and I both, at first. Each time.
You wouldn't believe it. Believe human stomach hold so much.
Here." It was the bottle. "Good drink. Take enormous one.
Good for stomach."

Bogard drank. Soon he did feel better, warmer. When the
hand touched him later, he found that he had been asleep.

It was the boy again. The pea-coat was too small for him;
shrunken, perhaps. Below the cuffs his long, slender, girl's
wrists were blue with cold. Then Bogard realized what the
garment was that had been laid over him. But before Bogard
could speak, the boy leaned down, whispering; his face was
gleeful: "He didn't notice!"

"What?"

"Ergenstrasse! He didn't notice that they had shifted her. Gad,
I'd be just one down, then." He watched Bogard's face with
bright, eager eyes. "Beaver, you know. I say. Feeling better,
eh?"

"Yes," Bogard said, "I am."

"He didn't notice at all. Oh, gad! Oh, Jove!"

Bogard rose and sat on the tube. The entrance to the harbor was just ahead; the boat had slowed a little. It was just dusk. He said quietly: "Does this often happen?" The boy looked at him. Bogard touched the tube. "This. Failing to go out."

"Oh, yes. Why they put the windlass on them. That was later. Made first boat; whole thing blew up one day. So put on windlass."

"But it happens sometimes, even now? I mean, sometimes they blow up, even with the windlass?"

"Well, can't say, of course. Boats go out. Not come back. Possible. Not ever know, of course. Not heard of one captured yet, though. Possible. Not to us, though. Not yet."

"Yes," Bogard said. "Yes." They entered the harbor, the boat moving still fast, but throttled now and smooth, across the dusk-filled basin. Again the boy leaned down, his voice gleeful.

"Not a word, now!" he hissed. "Steady all!" He stood up; he raised his voice: "I say, Ronnie." Ronnie did not turn his head, but Bogard could tell that he was listening. "That Argentine ship was amusing, eh? In there. How do you suppose it got past us here? Might have stopped here as well. French would buy the wheat." He paused, diabolical—Machiavelli with the face of a strayed angel. "I say. How long has it been since we had a strange ship in here? Been months, eh?" Again he leaned, hissing. "Watch, now!" But Bogard could not see Ronnie's head move at all. "He's looking, though!" the boy whispered, breathed. And Ronnie was looking, though his head had not moved at all. Then there came into view, in silhouette against the dusk-filled sky, the vague, basket-like shape of the interned vessel's foremast. At once Ronnie's arm rose, pointing; again he spoke without turning his head, out of the side of his mouth, past the cold, clamped pipe, a single word:

"Beaver."

The boy moved like a released spring, like a heeled dog freed. "Oh, damn you!" he cried. "Oh, you putt! It's the Ergenstrasse! Oh, confound you! I'm just one down now!" He had stepped in one stride completely over Bogard, and he now leaned down over Ronnie. "What?" The boat was slowing in toward the wharf, the engine idle. "Aren't I, Ronnie? Just one down now?"

The boat drifted in; the seaman had again crawled forward onto the deck. Ronnie spoke for the third and last time. "Right," he said.

IX

"I want," Bogard said, "a case of Scotch. The best we've got. And fix it up good. It's to go to town. And I want a responsible man to deliver it." The responsible man came. "This is for a child," Bogard said, indicating the package. "You'll find him in the Street of the Twelve Hours, somewhere near the Café Twelve Hours. He'll be in the gutter. You'll know him. A child about six feet long. Any English M. P. will show him to you. If he is asleep, don't wake him. Just sit there and wait until he wakes up. Then give him this. Tell him it is from Captain Bogard."

X

About a month later a copy of the English Gazette which had strayed onto an American aerodrome carried the following item in the casualty lists:

> MISSING: Torpedo Boat X00I. Midshipmen R. Boyce Smith and L. C. W. Hope, R. N. R., Boatswain's Mate Burt and Able Seaman Reeves. Channel Fleet, Light Torpedo Division. Failed to return from coast patrol duty.

Shortly after that the American Air Service headquarters also issued a bulletin:

For extraordinary valor over and beyond the routine of duty, Captain H. S. Bogard, with his crew, composed of Second Lieutenant Darrel McGinnis and Aviation Gunners Watts and Harper, on a daylight raid and without scout protection, destroyed with bombs an ammunition depot several miles behind the enemy's lines. From here, beset by enemy aircraft in superior numbers, these men proceeded with what bombs remained to the enemy's corps headquarters at Blank and partially demolished this château, and then returned safely without loss of a man.

And regarding which exploit, it might have added, had it failed and had Captain Bogard come out of it alive, he would have been immediately and thoroughly court-martialed.

Carrying his remaining two bombs, he had dived the Handley-Page at the château where the generals sat at lunch, until McGinnis, at the toggles below him, began to shout at him, before he ever signaled. He didn't signal until he could discern separately the slate tiles of the roof. Then his hand dropped and he zoomed, and he held the aeroplane so, in its wild snarl, his lips parted, his breath hissing, thinking: "God! God! If they were all there—all the generals, the admirals, the presidents and the kings—theirs, ours—all of them."

James Thurber
(1894–1961)

Born in Ohio, Thurber graduated from Ohio State University; from 1918 to 1920, he worked at the U. S. Embassy in Paris. Thereafter he became a journalist and in 1927 became associated with The New Yorker *magazine, in which virtually all of his work made its first appearance. Illustrator and superb cartoonist, as well as author of stories, sketches, parables, essays and parodies, he published* The Owl in the Attic and Other Perplexities *(1931),* The Seal in the Bedroom and Other Predicaments *(1932),* My Life and Hard Times *(1933),* The Middle-Aged Man on the Flying Trapeze *(1935),* Fables for Our Time . . . *(1940),* Men, Women, and Dogs *(1943), and* The Thurber Carnival *(1945), from which "The Evening's at Seven" has been taken.* Lanterns and Lances *(1961) is a collection of essays;* The Years with Ross *(1959) is an account of his years on the staff of* The New Yorker.

THE EVENING'S AT SEVEN

He hadn't lighted the upper light in his office all afternoon and now he turned out the desk lamp. It was a quarter of seven in the evening and it was dark and raining. He could hear the rattle of taxicabs and trucks and the sound of horns. Very far off a siren screamed its frenzied scream and he thought: it's a little like an anguish dying with the years. When it gets to Third Avenue, or Ninety-fifth Street, he thought, I won't hear it any more.

I'll be home, he said to himself, as he got up slowly and slowly put on his hat and overcoat (the overcoat was damp), by seven o'clock, if I take a taxicab, I'll say hello, my dear, and the two yellow lamps will be lighted and my papers will be on my desk, and I'll say I guess I'll lie down a few minutes before dinner, and she will say all right and ask two or three small questions about the day and I'll answer them.

When he got outside of his office, in the street, it was dark and raining and he lighted a cigarette. A young man went by whistling loudly. Two girls went by talking gaily, as if it were not raining, as if this were not a time for silence and for remembering. He called to a taxicab and it stopped and he got in, and sat there, on the edge of the seat, and the driver finally said where to? He gave a number he was thinking about.

She was surprised to see him and, he believed, pleased. It was very nice to be in her apartment again. He faced her, quickly, and it seemed to him as if he were facing somebody in a tennis game. She would want to know (but wouldn't ask) why he was, so suddenly, there, and he couldn't exactly say: I gave a number to a taxi-driver and it was your number. He couldn't say that; and besides, it wasn't that simple.

It was dark in the room and still raining outside. He lighted a cigarette (not wanting one) and looked at her. He watched her lovely gestures as of old and she said he looked tired and he said he wasn't tired and he asked her what she had been doing and she said oh, nothing much. He talked, sitting awkwardly on the edge of a chair, and she talked, lying gracefully on a chaise-longue, about people they had known and hadn't cared about. He was mainly conscious of the rain outside and of the soft darkness in the room and of other rains and other darknesses. He got up and walked around the room looking at pictures but not seeing what they were, and realizing that some old familiar things gleamed darkly, and he came abruptly face to face with something he had given her, a trivial and comic thing, and it didn't seem trivial or comic now, but very large and important and embarrassing, and he turned away from it and asked after somebody else he didn't care about. Oh, she said, and this and that and so and such (words he wasn't listening to). Yes, he said, absently, I suppose so. Very much, he said (in answer to something else), very much. Oh, she said, laughing at him, not *that* much! He didn't have any idea what they were talking about.

She asked him for a cigarette and he walked over and gave her one, not touching her fingers but very conscious of her fingers. He was remembering a twilight when it had been raining and dark, and he thought of April and kissing and laughter. He noticed a clock on the mantel and it was ten after seven. She said you never used to believe in clocks. He laughed and looked at her for a time and said I have to be at the hotel by seven-thirty, or I don't get anything to eat; it's that sort of hotel. Oh, she said.

He walked to a table and picked up a figurine and set it down again with extreme care, looking out of the corner of his eye at the trivial and comic and gigantic present he had given her. He wondered if he would kiss her and when he would kiss her and if she wanted to be kissed and if she were thinking of it, but she asked him what he would have to eat tonight at his hotel. He said clam chowder. Thursday, he said, they always have clam chowder. Is that the way you know it's Thursday, she said, or is that the way you know it's clam chowder?

He picked up the figurine and put it down again, so that he could look (without her seeing him look) at the clock. It was eighteen minutes after seven and he had the mingled thoughts clocks gave him. You mustn't, she said, miss your meal. (She remembered he hated the word meal.) He turned around quickly and went over quickly and sat beside her and took hold of one of her fingers and she looked at the finger and not at him and he looked at the finger and not at her, both of them as if it were a new and rather remarkable thing.

He got up suddenly and picked up his hat and coat and as suddenly put them down again and took two rapid determined steps towards her, and her eyes seemed a little wider. A bell rang. Oh that, she said, will be Clarice. And they relaxed. He looked a question and she said: my sister; and he said oh, of course. In a minute it was Clarice like a small explosion in the dark and rainy day talking rapidly of this and that: my dear he and this awful and then of all people so nothing loth and I said and he said, if you can imagine that! He picked up his hat and coat and Clarice said hello to him and he said hello and looked at the clock and it was almost twenty-five after seven.

She went to the door with him looking lovely, and it was lovely and dark and raining outside and he laughed and she laughed and she was going to say something but he went out into the rain and waved back at her (not wanting to wave back at her) and she closed the door and was gone. He lighted a cigarette and let his hand get wet in the rain and the cigarette get wet and rain dripped from his hat. A taxicab drove up and the driver spoke to him and he said: what? and: oh, sure. And now he was going home.

He was home by seven-thirty, almost exactly, and he said good evening to old Mrs. Spencer (who had the sick husband), and good evening to old Mrs. Holmes (who had the sick Pomeranian), and he nodded and smiled and presently he was sitting at his table and the waitress spoke to him. She said: the Mrs. will be down, won't she? and he said yes, she will. And the waitress said clam chowder tonight, and consommé: you always take the clam chowder, ain't I right? No, he said, I'll have the consommé.

Francis Scott Key Fitzgerald

(1896–1940)

Born in St. Paul, Minnesota, Fitzgerald grew up in the Midwest and attended Princeton University, from which he did not graduate. While briefly in the U. S. Army (1917-1918), he began his first novel, This Side of Paradise *(1920), which was an immediate success; his stories, which appeared in such journals as* The Saturday Evening Post *and* Scribner's, *were equally popular and earned him large sums. His second novel,* The Beautiful and the Damned *(1922), was followed by his major work,* The Great Gatsby *(1925) and in 1934 by* Tender Is the Night. *Collections of his stories include* Tales of the Jazz Age *(1922) and* All the Sad Young Men *(1926). Alcohol and dissipation, and also the mental breakdown of his wife, Zelda, led to the nervous collapse chronicled in the essays collected in* The Crack-Up *(1945, edited by his friend and college classmate, Edmund Wilson). Fitzgerald wrote plays and worked for many years as a Hollywood script writer; his unfinished last novel,* The Last Tycoon, *published posthumously in 1941, has a Hollywood setting. The* Stories of F. Scott Fitzgerald, *from which "The Long Way Out" is taken, appeared in 1965.*

THE LONG WAY OUT

We were talking about some of the older castles in Touraine and we touched upon the iron cage in which Louis XI imprisoned Cardinal Balue for six years, then upon oubliettes and such horrors. I had seen several of the latter, simply dry wells thirty or forty feet deep where a man was thrown to wait for nothing;

548

since I have such a tendency to claustrophobia that a Pullman berth is a certain nightmare, they had made a lasting impression. So it was rather a relief when a doctor told this story—that is, it was a relief when he began it, for it seemed to have nothing to do with the tortures long ago.

There was a young woman named Mrs. King who was very happy with her husband. They were well-to-do and deeply in love, but at the birth of her second child she went into a long coma and emerged with a clear case of schizophrenia or "split personality." Her delusion, which had something to do with the Declaration of Independence, had little bearing on the case and as she regained her health it began to disappear. At the end of ten months she was a convalescent patient scarcely marked by what had happened to her and very eager to go back into the world.

She was only twenty-one, rather girlish in an appealing way and a favorite with the staff of the sanitarium. When she became well enough so that she could take an experimental trip with her husband there was a general interest in the venture. One nurse had gone into Philadelphia with her to get a dress, another knew the story of her rather romantic courtship in Mexico and everyone had seen her two babies on visits to the hospital. The trip was to Virginia Beach for five days.

It was a joy to watch her make ready, dressing and packing meticulously and living in the gay trivialities of hair waves and such things. She was ready half an hour before the time of departure and she paid some visits on the floor in her powder-blue gown and her hat that looked like one minute after an April shower. Her frail lovely face, with just that touch of startled sadness that often lingers after an illness, was alight with anticipation.

"We'll just do nothing," she said. "That's my ambition. To get up when I want to for three straight mornings and stay up late for three straight nights. To buy a bathing suit by myself and order a meal."

When the time approached Mrs. King decided to wait downstairs instead of in her room and as she passed along the corridors, with an orderly carrying her suitcase, she waved to the other patients, sorry that they too were not going on a gorgeous holiday. The superintendent wished her well, two nurses found excuses to linger and share her infectious joy.

"What a beautiful tan you'll get, Mrs. King."

"Be sure and send a postcard."

About the time she left her room her husband's car was hit by a truck on his way from the city—he was hurt internally and was not expected to live more than a few hours. The information was received at the hospital in a glass-in office adjoining the hall where Mrs. King waited. The operator, seeing Mrs. King and knowing that the glass was not sound proof, asked the head nurse to come immediately. The head nurse hurried aghast to a doctor and he decided what to do. So long as the husband was still alive it was best to tell her nothing, but of course she must know that he was not coming today.

Mrs. King was greatly disappointed.

"I suppose it's silly to feel that way," she said. "After all these months what's one more day? He said he'd come tomorrow, didn't he?" The nurse was having a difficult time but she managed to pass it off until the patient was back in her room. Then they assigned a very experienced and phlegmatic nurse to keep Mrs. King away from other patients and from newspapers. By the next day the matter would be decided one way or another.

But her husband lingered on and they continued to prevaricate. A little before noon next day one of the nurses was passing along the corridor when she met Mrs. King, dressed as she had been the day before but this time carrying her own suitcase.

"I'm going to meet my husband," she explained. "He couldn't come yesterday but he's coming today at the same time."

The nurse walked along with her. Mrs. King had the freedom of the building and it was difficult to simply steer her back to her room, and the nurse did not want to tell a story that would contradict what the authorities were telling her. When they reached the front hall she signaled to the operator, who fortunately understood. Mrs. King gave herself a last inspection in the mirror and said:

"I'd like to have a dozen hats just like this to remind me to be this happy always."

When the head nurse came in frowning a minute later she demanded:

"Don't tell me George is delayed?"

"I'm afraid he is. There is nothing much to do but be patient."

Mrs. King laughed ruefully. "I wanted him to see my costume when it was absolutely new."

"Why, there isn't a wrinkle in it."

"I guess it'll last till tomorrow. I oughtn't to be blue about waiting one more day when I'm so utterly happy."

"Certainly not."

That night her husband died and at a conference of doctors next morning there was some discussion about what to do—it was a risk to tell her and a risk to keep it from her. It was decided finally to say that Mr. King had been called away and thus destroy her hope of an immediate meeting; when she was reconciled to this they could tell her the truth.

As the doctors came out of the conference one of them stopped and pointed. Down the corridor toward the outer hall walked Mrs. King carrying her suitcase.

Dr. Pirie, who had been in special charge of Mrs. King, caught his breath.

"This is awful," he said. "I think perhaps I'd better tell her now. There's no use saying he's away when she usually hears from him twice a week, and if we say he's sick she'll want to go to him. Anybody else like the job?"

II

One of the doctors in the conference went on a fortnight's vacation that afternoon. On the day of his return in the same corridor at the same hour, he stopped at the sight of a little procession coming toward him—an orderly carrying a suitcase, a nurse and Mrs. King dressed in the powder-blue suit and wearing the spring hat.

"Good morning, Doctor," she said. "I'm going to meet my husband and we're going to Virginia Beach. I'm going to the hall because I don't want to keep him waiting."

He looked into her face, clear and happy as a child's. The nurse signaled to him that it was as ordered, so he merely bowed and spoke of the pleasant weather.

"It's a beautiful day," said Mrs. King, "but of course even if it was raining it would be a beautiful day for me."

The doctor looked after her, puzzled and annoyed—why are they letting this go on, he thought. What possible good can it do?

Meeting Dr. Pirie, he put the question to him.

"We tried to tell her," Dr. Pirie said. "She laughed and said we were trying to see whether she's still sick. You could use the word unthinkable in an exact sense here—his death is unthinkable to her."

"But you can't just go on like this."

"Theoretically no," said Dr. Pirie. "A few days ago when she packed up as usual the nurse tried to keep her from going.

doubts begin

From out in the hall I could see her face, see her begin to go to pieces—for the first time, mind you. Her muscles were tense and her eyes glazed and her voice was thick and shrill when she very politely called the nurse a liar. It was touch and go there for a minute whether we had a tractable patient or a restraint case—and I stepped in and told the nurse to take her down to the reception room."

He broke off as the procession that had just passed appeared again, headed back to the ward. Mrs. King stopped and spoke to Dr. Pirie.

"My husband's been delayed," she said. "Of course I'm disappointed but they tell me he's coming tomorrow and after waiting so long one more day doesn't seem to matter. Don't you agree with me, Doctor?"

"I certainly do, Mrs. King."

She took off her hat.

"I've got to put aside these clothes—I want them to be as fresh tomorrow as they are today." She looked closely at the hat. "There's a speck of dust on it, but I think I can get it off. Perhaps he won't notice."

"I'm sure he won't."

"Really I don't mind waiting another day. It'll be this time tomorrow before I know it, won't it?"

When she had gone along the younger doctor said:

"There are still the two children."

"I don't think the children are going to matter. When she 'went under,' she tied up this trip with the idea of getting well. If we took it away she'd have to go to the bottom and start over."

"Could she?"

"There's no prognosis," said Dr. Pirie. "I was simply explaining why she was allowed to go to the hall this morning."

"But there's tomorrow morning and the next morning."

"There's always the chance," said Dr. Pirie, "that some day he will be there."

The doctor ended his story here, rather abruptly. When we pressed him to tell what happened he protested that the rest was anticlimax—that all sympathy eventually wears out and that finally the staff of the sanitarium had simply accepted the fact.

"But does she still go to meet her husband?"

"Oh yes, it's always the same—but the other patients, except new ones, hardly look up when she passes along the hall. The nurses manage to substitute a new hat every year or so but she still wears the same suit. She's always a little disappointed but she makes the best of it, very sweetly too. It's not an unhappy life as far as we know, and in some funny way it seems to set an example of tranquillity to the other patients. For God's sake let's talk about something else—let's go back to oubliettes.''

William Saroyan
(1908–1981)

California-born and bred, Saroyan spent his earliest years in an orphanage. After leaving school at age 12 to become a telegraph boy, he became manager of a San Francisco postal telegraph office. His first stories appeared in 1934, in which year he also published his first book, a collection of stories entitled The Daring Young Man on the Flying Trapeze, *which was both a critical and a commercial success. Other collections followed, notably* Three Times Three *(1936) and* Love, Here Is My Hat *(1938), from which "Ever Fall in Love with a Midget?" is taken. His novels include* The Human Comedy *(1943) and* Boys and Girls Together *(1963).* My Name Is Aram *(1940),* Here Comes There Goes You Know Who *(1962), After Thirty Years *(1962), and* One Day in the Afternoon of the World *(1964) are autobiographical volumes. Saroyan was also the author of many plays, the most important of which,* The Time of Your Life *(1939), won a Pulitzer Prize which he refused to accept, terming it "bourgeois patronization."*

EVER FALL IN LOVE WITH A MIDGET?

I don't suppose you ever fell in love with a midget weighing thirty-nine pounds, did you?

No, I said, but have another beer.

Down in Gallup, he said, twenty years ago. Fellow by the name of Rufus Jenkins came to town with six white horses and two black ones. Said he wanted a man to break the horses for him because his left leg was wood and he couldn't do it. Had a

554

meeting at Parker's Mercantile Store and finally came to blows, me and Henry Walpal. Bashed his head with a brass cuspidor and ran away to Mexico, but he didn't die.

Couldn't speak a word. Took up with a cattle-breeder named Diego, educated in California. Spoke the language better than you and me. Said, Your job, Murph, is to feed them prize bulls. I said, Fine; what'll I feed them? He said, Hay, lettuce, salt, and beer. I said, Fine; they're your bulls.

Came to blows two days later over an accordion he claimed I stole. I borrowed it and during the fight busted it over his head; ruined one of the finest accordions I ever saw. Grabbed a horse and rode back across the border. Texas. Got to talking with a fellow who looked honest. Turned out to be a Ranger who was looking for me.

Yeah, I said. You were saying, a thirty-nine pound midget.

Will I ever forget that lady? he said. Will I ever get over that amazon of small proportions?

Will you? I said.

If I live to be sixty, he said.

Sixty? I said. You look more than sixty now.

That's trouble showing in my face. Trouble and complications. I was fifty-six three months ago.

Oh.

Told the Texas Ranger my name was Rothstein, mining engineer from Pennsylvania, looking for something worth while. Mentioned two places in Houston. Nearly lost an eye early one morning, going down the stairs. Ran into a six-footer with an iron-claw where his right hand was supposed to be. Said, You broke up my home. Told him I was a stranger in Houston. The girls gathered at the top of the stairs to see a fight. Seven of them. Six feet and an iron claw. That's bad on the nerves. Kicked him in the mouth when he swung for my head with the claw. Would have lost an eye except for quick thinking. Rolled into the gutter and pulled a gun. Fired seven times, but I was back upstairs. Left the place an hour later, dressed in silk and feathers, with a hat swung around over my face. Saw him standing on the corner, waiting. Said, Care for a wiggle? Said he didn't. Went on down the street, left town.

I don't suppose you ever had to put on a dress to save your skin, did you?

No, I said, and I never fell in love with a midget weighing thirty-nine pounds. Have another beer.

Thanks. Ever try to herd cattle on a bicycle?

No, I said.

Left Houston with sixty cents in my pocket, gift of a girl named Lucinda. Walked fourteen miles in fourteen hours. Big house with barb-wire all around, and big dogs. One thing I never could get around. Walked past the gate, anyway, from hunger and thirst. Dogs jumped up and came for me. Walked right into them, growing older every second. Went up to the door and knocked. Big negress opened the door, closed it quick. Said, On your way, white trash.

Knocked again. Said, On your way. Again. On your way. Again. This time the old man himself opened the door, ninety if he was a day. Sawed-off shotgun too.

Said, I ain't looking for trouble, Father. I'm hungry and thirsty, name's Cavanaugh.

Took me in and made mint juleps for the two of us.

Said, Living here alone, Father?

Said, Drink and ask no questions; maybe I am and maybe I ain't. You saw the negress. Draw your own conclusions.

I'd heard of that, but didn't wink out of tact.

Called out, Elvira, bring this gentleman sandwiches.

Young enough for a man of seventy, probably no more than forty, and big.

Said, Any good at cards? Said, No.

Said, Fine, Cavanaugh, take a hand of poker.

Played all night.

If I told you that old Southern gentleman was my grandfather, you wouldn't believe me, would you?

No.

Well, it so happens he wasn't, although it would have been remarkable if he had been.

Where did you herd cattle on a bicycle?

Toledo, Ohio, 1918.

Toledo, Ohio? I said. They don't herd cattle up there.

They don't any more. They did in 1918. One fellow did, leastways. Bookkeeper named Sam Gold. Only Jewish cowboy I ever saw. Straight from the Eastside New York. Sombrero, lariats, Bull Durham, two head of cattle, and two bicycles. Called his place Gold Bar Ranch, two acres, just outside the city limits.

That was the year of the War, you'll remember.

Yeah, I said.

Remember a picture called *Shoulder Arms*?

Sure. Saw it five times.

Remember when Charlie Chaplin thought he was washing *his* foot, and the foot turned out to be another man's?

Sure.

You may not believe me, but I was the man whose foot was washed by Chaplin in that picture.

It's possible, I said, but how about herding them two cows on a bicycle? How'd you do it?

Easiest thing in the world. Rode no hands. Had to, otherwise couldn't lasso the cows. Worked for Sam Gold till the cows ran away. Bicycles scared them. They went into Toledo and we never saw hide or hair of them again. Advertised in every paper, but never got them back. Broke his heart. Sold both bikes and returned to New York.

Took four aces from a deck of red cards and walked to town. Poker. Fellow in the game named Chuck Collins, liked to gamble. Told him with a smile I didn't suppose he'd care to bet a hundred dollars I wouldn't hold four aces the next hand. Called it. My cards were red on the blank side. The other cards were blue. Plumb forgot all about it. Showed him four aces. Ace of spades, ace of clubs, ace of diamonds, ace of hearts. I'll remember them four cards if I live to be sixty. Would have been killed on the spot except for the hurricane that year.

Hurricane?

You haven't forgotten the Toldeo hurricane of 1918, have you?

No, I said. There was no hurricane in Toledo, in 1918, or any other year.

For the love of God, then, what do you suppose that commotion was? And how come I came to in Chicago? Dream-walking down State Street?

I guess they scared you.

No, that wasn't it. You go back to the papers of November, 1918, and I think you'll find there was a hurricane in Toledo. I remember sitting on the roof of a two-story house, floating northwest.

Northwest?

Sure.

Okay, have another beer.

Thaaaaanks. Thanks, he said.

I don't suppose *you* ever fell in love with a midget weighing thirty-nine pounds, did you? I said.

Who? he said.

You? I said.

No, he said, can't say I have.

Well, I said, let *me* tell *you* about it.

19th CENTURY AMERICAN AUTHORS

☐ **SELECTED WRITINGS OF RALPH WALDO EMERSON.** Foreword by William H. Gilman, University of Rochester. Fourteen essays and addresses including *The Oversoul, Politics, Thoreau,* and *Divinity School Address,* poetry including *Threnody* and *Uriel* and selections from his letters and journals. Chronology. Bibliography.   (520475—$4.50)*

☐ **EVANGELINE and Selected Tales and Poems by Henry Wadsworth Longfellow.** Edited by Horace Gregory, poet and translator. Also includes *The Witnesses, The Courtship of Miles Standish,* and selections from *Hiawatha.* Commentaries on Longfellow by Van Wyck Brooks, Norman Holmes Pearson, and Lewis Carroll. Includes Introduction, Bibliography and Chronology.   (520033—$3.95)*

☐ **LEAVES OF GRASS by Walt Whitman.** Introduction by Gay Wilson Allen, New York University. The text of this edition is that of the "Deathbed," or 9th edition, published in 1892. The content and grouping of the poems were authorized by the poet for this final and complete edition of his masterpiece. Index and Bibliography included.   (517024—$2.95)

☐ **WALDEN and ON THE DUTY OF CIVIL DISOBEDIENCE by Henry David Thoreau.** Afterword by Perry Miller, author of *The Puritan Mind.* Also includes a selection of poetry, *Sic Vita, Winter Memories, To The Maiden in the East, Smoke, Mist,* and *Inspiration.*   (521218—$2.25)*

☐ **RAMONA by Helen Hunt Jackson.** A powerful and romantic tale of true love triumphant, of exotic, passionate characters beset by tragedy, of pure-hearted nobility at odds with greed. Ramona, an illegitimate half-breed, has grown up the ward of overbearing Senora Morena. But her love for the Indian Alessandro plunges her into the poverty of the Indians. . . .   (522087—$3.50)

*Prices slightly higher in Canada